Resounding praise for
New York Times bestselling author
Anne Rivers Siddons

"One of the giants in contemporary Southern fiction."
Chattanooga Times

"Anne Rivers Siddons's novels are women's stories in the best sense, pulling you into the internal landscape of her characters' lives and holding you there."
People

"A gifted writer and a good storyteller."
Orlando Sentinel

"She has such a beautiful and commanding style of writing."
Sai

"In the front
Los An

"Siddons is a fine teller of tales."
Washington Post Book World

"Anne Rivers Siddons . . . will take you home again."
USA Today

Books by Anne Rivers Siddons

Fiction

SWEETWATER CREEK
ISLANDS
NORA, NORA
LOW COUNTRY
UP ISLAND
FAULT LINES
DOWNTOWN
HILL TOWNS
COLONY
OUTER BANKS
KING'S OAK
PEACHTREE ROAD
HOMEPLACE
FOX'S EARTH
THE HOUSE NEXT DOOR
HEARTBREAK HOTEL

Nonfiction

JOHN CHANCELLOR MAKES ME CRY

Up Island

ANNE RIVERS SIDDONS

Low Country

AVON BOOKS

An Imprint of HarperCollinsPublishers

Up Island was originally published in hardcover by HarperCollins in June 1997 and in paperback by HarperPaperbacks in June 1998.

Low Country was originally published in hardcover by HarperCollins in June 1998 and in paperback by HarperPaperbacks in June 1999.

FIRST EDITION

ISBN-13: 978-0-06-089468-9
ISBN-10: 0-06-089468-7

06 07 08 09 JTC/RRD 10 9 8 7 6 5 4 3 2 1

Up Island

This book is for Ginger Barber,
and high time

I went to the woods because I wished to live deliberately, to front only the essential facts of life, and see if I could not learn what it had to teach, and not, when I came to die, discover that I had not lived.

—HENRY DAVID THOREAU, *WALDEN*

ACKNOWLEDGMENTS

Ann Nelson of The Bunch of Grapes bookstore in Vineyard Haven has probably been thanked by so many authors that she could start her own literary society, but to all that gratitude I would like to add mine. She literally gave me "her" Martha's Vineyard, that up-island world of old families and secret places, and in addition, a great deal of her time and a great many of her own treasured personal books. This book is, in a unique way, hers; its errors of fact and interpretation are strictly mine.

CHAPTER ONE

YOU KNOW HOW PEOPLE ARE always saying "I knew it by the back of my neck" when they mean those occasional scalding slashes of intuition that later prove to be true? My mother was always saying it, though she was not always right. Nevertheless, in my half-Celt family, the back of one's neck is a hallowed harbinger of things to come.

I first knew my husband was being unfaithful to me, not by the back of my neck, but by the skin of my buttocks, which, given the ultimate sorry progress of things, was probably prophetic. I always thought it was grossly unfair that Tee got all the fun and I got dermatitis of the posterior, but there you are. According to my mother, again, it was a pattern we had laid down in stone in the early days of our marriage.

I had been having fierce itching and red welts off and on since Christmas, but at first I put it down to the five-pound box of candied ginger Tee's boss sent us and a savage new panty girdle that enabled me to get into my white beaded silk pantsuit. Later, when the itching and welts did not go away, I switched bath soap and body lotion, and still later had the furnace and air-conditioning unit cleaned and found some plain, unbleached cotton sheets for our bed. Still I felt as if I had been sitting in poison ivy, and often caught myself absently scratching in public as well as private. Teddy, my eighteen-year-old son, was mortified, and my best friend, Carrie Davies, asked me more than once, her elegant eyebrow raised, what was wrong. Tee would have teased me mercilessly, but he was not around much that winter and spring. Coca-Cola was bringing out two new youth-oriented soft drinks, and Tee and his team were involved in the test marketing, which meant near constant travel to the designated markets across the country. I could have scratched my behind and picked my nose at the same time on the steps of St. Philips and poor Tee, jet-lagged and teen-surfeited, would not have noticed.

When I woke myself in the middle of a hot May night, clawing my skin so that the blood ran, I made an appointment with Charlie Davies, and was distressed enough so that he worked me in at lunchtime the next day.

"Well, Moonbeam, drop your britches and lay down here and let's see what we got," he roared, and I did, not really caring that the paper gown Charlie's nurse had provided me with gapped significantly when I tied it around my waist. Charlie and Tee had been roommates at the University of Georgia, and I had known Tee only two weeks longer than I had Charlie. Charlie had married Carrie Carmichael, my Tri Delta sister, a week after Tee and I had married— we had all been in each other's weddings—and we had kept the friendship going all through med school and internship and then practice for Charlie and the early and middle years at the Coca-Cola company for

Tee. Charlie had probably seen my bare bottom more than once, given the house parties and vacations we four spent together.

He had called me Moonbeam after Al Capp's dark, statuesque, and gloriously messy backwoods siren, Moonbeam McSwine, since the first time we'd met. I allow no one else to do so, not even Tee.

I rolled over on to my stomach and Charlie pulled back the paper gown and gave a long, low whistle. "Shit, Molly, has Big Tee been floggin' you, or what? You look like you been diddlin' in the briar patch."

Despite his redneck patter, Charlie is a very good doctor, or he would not have any patients. Atlanta is full of crisp, no-nonsense out of towners who would draw the line, I thought, at being told to get nekkid and lay on down, unless the one saying it was supremely good at what he did. Charlie was. In time, the good-ole-boy gambit became a trademark, a trick, something people laughed indulgently about at parties. If it secretly annoyed more than amused me, I never thought to verbalize it.

"How bad does it look?" I said.

"Honey, how bad can your sweet ass look? The day Tee married you the entire Chi Phi house went into mournin' for that booty. Though now that you mention it, there seems to be a good bit more of it these days, huh?"

And he slapped me gently on the buttock. I felt it quiver like jellied consommé under his thick fingers. There was indeed more of me now than when I had married. Where once people had looked at me and seen a tall, sinewy, sun-bronzed Amazon with a shock of wild, blue-black hair and electric blue eyes, now they saw a big woman—a *really* big woman—with wild, gray-black hair, all teeth and leathery-tanned skin and swimming, myopic eyes behind outsized tortoiseshell glasses. Then, they had stared at the slapdash, coltish grace and vividness that had been mine. Now they simply stared at big.

"Christ, it's a goddamned Valkyrie," I had overheard someone say at last year's performance of *The Ring* when it came to Atlanta. Tee and I had both laughed. I seldom thought about the added pounds, since they did not for a moment inhibit my life, and Tee never seemed to notice.

"I mean the rash, or whatever it is, you horny hound," I said now to Charlie.

"Well, I've seen worse," he said. "Saw jungle rot once, when I was a resident at Grady."

"Come on, Charlie, what is it? What do I do about it? I never had anything like this before."

"I don't know yet," he said, poking and prodding. "I'd say some kind of contact dermatitis, only you don't have a history of allergies, that I remember. I'm going to give you a little cortisone by injection and some pills and ointment, and if it's not healed by the time you've finished them, I'm going to send you to Bud Allison. We need to clear this up. I don't imagine Tee is aesthetically thrilled by the state of your behind, is he?"

"I don't think he's even noticed," I said. "He's been out of town so much with these new Coke things that all we've had time to do is wave in passing. It's supposed to slack off in a couple of weeks, though, and I wish we could get rid of this by then. He'll think I *have* been rolling around in the alien corn patch."

"Gon' sting a little bit," Charlie said, and I felt the cool prick of a needle. Then Charlie said, "I thought he was back by now. I saw him the other day over at that new condominium thing in midtown, the one that looks like a cow's tit caught in a wringer, you know. I guess he was helping Caroline move in there; he was toting a palm tree so big only his beady eyes were peekin' out of it, and she was bent double laughing. She's a honey, isn't she? The image of you at that age, thank God. Y'all must be real proud of her. She working around midtown?"

He pricked me again.

"That must have been somebody else's beady eyes peeking out of that palm tree, Charlie," I said. "Ow. That does sting. Caroline is married and living in Memphis, with a brand-new baby. Honestly. You knew that; y'all sent the baby a silver cup from Tiffany's. Must have killed you to pay for it."

Charlie took his hand off my buttocks. He was silent for a space of time, then he said, "You get dressed and come on in the office, and I'll write you out those prescriptions."

I heard his heavy steps leaving the examining room. I heaved myself up off the table. It hit me as I swung my bare legs over the side. The skin of my face felt as if a silent explosion had gone off in the little room. I actually felt the wind and the percussion of it. The room brightened, as if flood lamps had been switched on, and when I took a breath there was only a stale hollowness in my lungs. A new hot, red welt sizzled across my left buttock.

"Tee has somebody else," I thought. "He has had, since Christmas, at least. That was Tee Charlie saw. He knows it was. And that was her Tee was moving into that condo."

I sat for a moment with my hands in my paper lap,

one cupped on top of the other, a gesture like you make in Communion, waiting to receive the Host. I could not seem to focus my eyes. My ears rang. Through it all, the skin of my behind raged and shrieked.

I stood up, dropped my paper gown, put on my clothes, and went out of the little room and down the hall and out through the reception area to the elevator. I thought of nothing at all.

When the elevator came, I got on with a handful of lunch-bound people, some in white coats, stared vacantly at the quilted bronze doors, and thought, the family. What is this going to mean for the family?

By the time I stepped out on to the hot sidewalk running along Peachtree Street, I felt as if I were on fire from the back of my waist to my knees. I had the absurd and terrible notion that the weeping redness was sliding down to my ankles and puddling in my shoes, the visible stigmata of betrayal and foolishness.

When I was small, my grandmother Bell lived with us for a time. She was a frail, sweet-faced little woman who was afraid of many things, including my mother, whose theatrical outbursts and exaggerations made her wince and shrink. Mother caught on to that in about one minute, of course, and often set about shocking and frightening Gran just for the sport of it. I suppose it was irresistible; even I, who adored Gran and often fled to her talcumy arms when Mother trained her silver arrows on me, wondered with the unforgiving contempt of the very young why Gran stood for it. But she always did. Her way of dealing with my mother and whatever else threatened her was simply to pretend that it did not exist. The sight of her chattering cheerfully about nothing and plying her small daily rituals while literally quivering all over like a terrified rabbit used to madden me, but I do it myself now. Like a savage who will not name or acknowledge a demon lest it draw the demon's attention, I deal with awfulness by becoming a caricature of middle-aged suburban normality.

I began doing it as soon as I stepped on to the sidewalk in front of Charlie's office. I swung my bag jauntily over my shoulder, pulled my chin up and tucked in the offending fanny, and turned left down the long hill toward Peachtree Battle, finding a long, loose, city stride and swinging along with a happy-to-be-in-the-world smile on my face. I nodded to pedestrians who passed me and looked with interest and approval at the beds of impatiens and begonias in front of the Shepherd Spinal Center. I noted with another silly nod of my head the electric sign in front of the Darlington Apartments that kept track of Atlanta's population: 3.7 MILLION. That sign was a source of annoyance to me most of the time; Atlanta's mushrooming population had long since made streets and sidewalks impassable. But on this day I beamed at it with the fatuous pride that I had felt when Tee and I had lived in our first small house, in Collier Hills, and the sign meant to me that my upstart town was becoming a real contender, an honest-to-God city. Take that, New York, Chicago, L.A., I said today under my breath. I looked down at my prancing feet in approval: just the right plain, low-heeled Ferragamo walking shoes a well-grounded Atlanta woman should wear on a hot spring day. The weight of my bag thumped against my side, and I was pleased: just the right, well-worn, lustrous

Coach handbag, nothing trendy or with initials on it that were not mine. All my totems were in order. But my heart was banging in slow, cold, breath-sucking beats.

My chastely Cliniqued mouth smiled wider.

I was nearly down to the entrance to Colonial Homes Drive, where for decades all the singles in my set lived until marriage and the move to Collier Hills on the way to Habersham Road or Ansley Park, when I heard a voice I knew shouting at me from the eddy of traffic.

Livvy Bowen was calling to me from her dirty old Saab, stopped beside me at a red light.

"Where on earth are you going?" she yelled in her not unpleasant New England honk. Livvy came south for the first time from a Boston suburb ten years before, when her husband, Caleb, was transferred to Coke headquarters to work on Tee's marketing team. Caleb was Harvard and Livvy was Radcliffe, and Atlanta was a thick stew of culture shock for both. Caleb had read the handwriting on the corporate walls and adjusted fast; Livvy never had. She hated the South in general, Atlanta in particular, liked Tee all right, and for some reason loved me. She had instantly, as I had her. Something in her raw bones and narrow, unmade-up face and acid tongue spoke to what my mother called the damnyankee in me. Mother spoke allegorically, of course; my parents were both Southern, back to their families' arrivals from England and Ireland, and that was more than two hundred years ago. I knew what my mother meant, though, and so, apparently, did Livvy. In her mouth, "damnyankee" was not a pejorative term.

"You're the only woman I know below the

Mason-Dixon line who doesn't run by Saks on her way to the grocery store," she said in the early days of our friendship, "and the only one who doesn't own a Judith Leiber bag. Do you even know what a Judith Leiber bag is?"

I didn't then, and can't remember now.

I said nothing on this morning, only smiled brilliantly at her. I couldn't think where to put her in this teetering new scheme of things.

"You've got on lipstick and panty hose," she said and grinned, gunning the hideous Saab's engine. "Who's died?"

I continued to smile. "Hi, Livvy," I ventured as the light changed. She did not move the Saab forward. Behind her, horns began to blow.

She stared at me for another moment and then said, "Get in the car."

"Livvy—"

"I'm not moving till you get in this car," she said, with the iron of old Massachusetts money in her voice. The chorus of horns swelled. I got into the car and slammed the door and she screeched away up Peachtree Street.

We did not speak again until she swerved into the fake fifties diner that newly occupied an old car wash and stopped.

"Where's your car?" she said. "Where have you been? What's the matter with you? You've got red blotches all over your neck and chest."

"I've been to the doctor," I said in my grandmother Bell's dreadful, sunny voice. "I've got some kind of allergy; it's nothing. Charlie Davies gave me some stuff for it. My car . . . my car . . ." I looked down at my blossoming chest; my backside was indeed colonizing new flesh. I smiled at Livvy. Even I knew it was what Tee calls a shit-eating grin; I could taste it on my mouth.

"I guess I left my car in the parking lot at Charlie's."

"Uh-huh. And you were going where?"

A little lick of annoyance managed to penetrate the smog of Bell denial.

"Who are you, Joseph Mengele? 'Vee haff ways to make you talk.' I was going home, of course; where do you think I was going?"

She just looked at me. My face flamed and my chest burst into a Flanders Field of red; I could feel it. I lived in Ansley Park, in the opposite direction of the way I had been walking, and had for nearly twenty years. I had been making for my parents' old home, the one I had grown up in, on Peachtree Hills Avenue. They had not lived there for the past five years, but in a condominium behind St. Philips Episcopal Cathedral in Buckhead.

I knew that Livvy knew that. I put my face in my hands and began to cry.

"Tee is having an affair," I sobbed. "I just found out. I don't know what to do about the family."

Livvy and Caleb live in a sprawling brick house in Brookwood Hills, a leafy old family enclave across from Piedmont Hospital and its attendant doctors' buildings. I have always loved that neighborhood. I wanted to look there when we were finally able to leave the Collier Hills starter house, but Tee felt Ansley Park had a more international feeling to it, and that was the direction Coke was going in. Many of the new transferees were buying and gentrifying the old town houses there, and besides, you could walk to the

Piedmont Driving Club. Tee's family had always belonged. Mine had never even been to a wedding reception there. So we found and remodeled our own tall town house with a tiny walled garden. I liked it, and had sunk a few roots and had raised my children there, but it never felt like Atlanta to me. "You can't just walk down the street on a spring evening in Ansley Park," I told Livvy once. "You have to have the right kind of suit. A jogging suit, or a cycling suit, or a Rollerblading suit, or a dog-walking suit . . . and the right kind of dog, of course. Lazarus definitely does not cut it in AP. I'm thinking of renting a dalmatian just to walk it."

"I'd be thinking of moving," Livvy snapped. "A dalmatian would be laughed out of Brookwood Hills."

We skidded through traffic and she hung a heart-stopping left across two lanes; we were in her sunny kitchen with cups of coffee before I could stop the treacherous sobs. I could not even remember the last time I had cried.

"Tell," she said, handing me a hot washcloth, and I mopped my face and told.

When I stopped talking, she snorted and said, "That's just shit, Molly. Tee's not having any affair. In the first place, you-all are joined at the hip. In the second place, when would he? Caleb's out with him when he's traveling; don't you think I'd know if Tee wasn't where . . . he said he was? Some doctor you've got. Some friend, too."

"Charlie *saw* him, Livvy—"

"Excuse me, pet, but how does Charlie know it was Tee? Every man in Atlanta in a certain class and age group looks just like Tee. Most of them work for Coke."

I had to smile, even through the thready galloping of my heart, because she was right, or partly. There is a type of wellborn Atlanta man who looks enough like Tee to be his kin, and may be: tall, lanky, blond-going-gray, hands jammed in pockets, with the shambling gait of the college athlete most of them were. Tee was the starting forward on UGA's basketball team the year we graduated and the team won the SEC championship; he still had the loose-jointed, pigeon-toed lope that went with the position. His hair was short now and gilded with gray, and fell over his forehead, and there were fine wrinkles at the corners of his blue eyes, but he was still snub-nosed and thin to the point of boniness, and his grin still charmed and warmed. We had been a stunning couple in college, a study in opposites but of nearly matched height, and we had known it then. I had long since forgotten. I wondered if Tee had.

"Charlie was Tee's roommate for four years," I said. "He'd know him if he saw him. He thought the girl—the woman—was Caroline. So she must be tall and dark and very young. And pretty, of course. Caroline is a very pretty girl."

"Crap. If the guy was hidden behind a palm tree, how could this wonderful Charlie be sure? It's not like you to jump to this kind of silly conclusion, Molly. You've never had any reason to doubt Tee's faithfulness . . . have you?"

"No," I said, and knew that it was true, knew it with the same baseless interior certainty with which I had known the truth of Charlie's words this morning. Tee had not strayed before this.

"If he was going to, don't you think he'd pick a better time?" Livvy said. "He's traveling with a team of nine people. He's almost never in the same city two nights in a row. He's in meetings from breakfast until midnight. Unless she's a stewardess with a key to the rest room, Tee's not banging anybody but you. And he's *sure* not doing it in those particular condos. Half of Coke lives there."

"But I've had this breaking out since Christmas, and that's when he started traveling . . . it's gotten really bad. It's like my body knew something that my head didn't, yet. I feel so damned sure, Livvy . . . and Charlie said stress could do that to you."

"So can poison ivy. So can whatever you wash your underwear in. I think you've slipped a cog. What could Tee possibly want that you don't give him?"

"I've gained a lot of weight," I said in a low voice. "I don't think about it much, but I know I have. I don't take the pains with myself that I used to. You should have seen me in college, Liv. I was homecoming queen my junior year. Tee and I . . . we were something to see together."

"You still are," she said. "Don't you know people turn around on the street to look at you? You look glorious. You look like an Amazon princess, or like . . . like . . ."

"If you say Moonbeam McSwine, I'll throttle you," I said, beginning to grin in spite of myself. Some of the cold weight had lifted off my chest. The fire in my fanny and neck was cooling.

"That, too," Livvy said, and reached over and put her hands over mine. Hers were warm. I realized only then that despite the day's sullen heat, I was as cold as ice, as death.

"Listen," she said. "I don't for a minute think you've got anything to worry about, and if you look at it rationally, you'll see that I'm right. But Moll . . . what if, just what *if*, there was somebody else? What would it mean to you, what would you do?"

I stared at her. What would it mean? Why . . . the end of everything. The end of the family. God, the family . . . why didn't she see?

"What do you think it would mean?" I said. "What would it mean to you? If it was Caleb, I mean?"

She shrugged. "Depends. On whether it was serious or a fling or some kind of silly midlife thing. Depends on how sorry he was."

She smiled. Her long Back Bay teeth were the color of rich old ivory. No anxious cosmetic bonding or bleaching for Olivia Carrington Bowen; even loving Carrie Davies, who knew how close I was to Livvy, had said once that Livvy looked like a horse.

"But the thoroughest of thoroughbreds," I'd rejoined shortly. Carrie had snorted, sounding herself like a horse. I knew that she did not approve of Livvy's and my friendship.

"She's not like us, Moll," Carrie had said. "She won't ever be. She doesn't even try."

"And that's why I like her," I snapped, hoping to put an end to the subject. And I had. My old crowd did not espouse Livvy Bowen, but in my presence they no longer denigrated her, either.

"And what would you do?"

"I'd snatch him baldheaded, and then her," Livvy said. "I'd give him two hours to wind it up quietly, and if he didn't, I'd tell Coke he couldn't keep it zipped, and tell her he had a penile implant. And if he still wouldn't, I'd throw his stuff out the door and change the locks and hire the meanest lawyer this side of the Mississippi River."

She looked at me with only a half smile. I thought that she was not altogether kidding.

"What about Dana and Elizabeth?" I said, thinking of Livvy and Caleb's two daughters, both in college in the East. "What about the family?"

"Dana and Elizabeth are neither one coming back home after school," she said matter-of-factly. "I've always known that. Much as I love them, they aren't going to be a big factor in my future. They'd have to make their own separate peaces with it. Molly, that's the third time you've said 'the family.' Not 'my family,' but '*the* family.' What is it with you and 'the family'? It's like you mean some kind of idea, instead of your own people . . ."

The family. The family . . .

When my mother married my father, she was twenty-one years old and an actress and dancer, or at least aspiring to be one. She was, he said once, as lovely as a silver minnow in a creek. Her name was Mary Belinda Fallon, but she called herself Belle Fallon professionally. She had had unpaid parts in a number of local theatrical productions and one badly paid part in the chorus of a touring company of *Lilli* at Chastain Amphitheatre in Buckhead, and was scheduled for a far better speaking and dancing role in the next year's touring production of *West Side Story*. Her blue-black hair and milky skin had caught the eye of more than one regional producer; she had reason to think she could go as far as her lithe legs and low, purring voice could take her. But then she met and married Timothy Bell, and since she could not be billed as Belle Bell, took the fatuous stage name Tinker Bell. It was Dad's nickname for her; he'd called her Tinker from the day he'd met her. She was as erratic and glinting and shining and ethereal as the frail, jealous sprite in *Peter Pan*, and she might well have gone on to make a name for herself on the stage, for she had, in addition to her looks and a middling talent, enormous presence. Even at home she had it, even at rest. I really think she was born with it.

But she was pregnant when she married Daddy, and by the time I was born, a giant of a baby according to her—a wrecker of pelvises and stomach muscles— her trajectory was broken, and she climbed into no more rarefied air than that of local theatrical productions and later, acting and dancing lessons. My poor mother: the heart of a gypsy, the soul of a prowling tiger, forever trapped in local productions of *Showboat* and *Auntie Mame*, and once, with notable success, *Hedda Gabler*. It was a bitter loss to her, and perhaps worse for the rest of us. It was catastrophic for me. She never ceased blaming me for it.

Oh, she never would admit that she did that, and in all fairness, probably did not know it. I certainly did not. I knew only that something about my size, my very person, was unseemly and worse: damaging. Dangerous. I can remember trying to fold myself into a smaller shape when I was no more than four, and slouching like a little old osteoporosis victim when my real spurt of growth started, at nine or ten. By twelve I was five feet eleven inches, within a hair of what I am now, and felt as unclean as a leper. Of us all in the smallish house on Peachtree Hills Avenue—my mother, my father, my granny Bell, my brother, Kevin, and me—only my father seemed to know what Tinker Bell was about with her little jeweled barbs flung gracefully at me, her fastidious little shudders and drawings aside when I blundered too close to her. At those times he would hold out his arms to me, or make a dry, small joke at my mother's expense, or sometimes simply say, in his quiet voice, "Tink . . ."

My mother would run at me then, and fold me into her arms and smother me with kisses that she had to stand on tiptoe to deliver, and say, in her lovely lilt, "As if it were your fault, my darling! As if you asked to be such a nice big armful!"

And, encircled in her warm, sweet, reaching flesh, I would feel the full, ponderous weight and height of my nice big armful, and her arms would feel as cold and alien to me as marble.

It would have been impossible not to see that Kevin, my younger brother and nearly the twin of my mother, fit with every slender, quicksilver inch of him into her arms. Flesh of her flesh might have been written for my mother and my brother.

Many years later, after a near killing loss, I found myself doubled over on my bed, arms folded across my stomach, rocking to and fro and weeping, in a kind of mindless mantra, "I want my mother! I want my mother!"

And knowing, in a terrible epiphany, that even though she was only ten or so blocks away, I had never had her, and could not now. There has never been anything in my life like that moment for sheer, monstrous aloneness. Never, not anything. I don't think there ever will be again.

It seems odd to me now that it was for her that I wept that day when, from the first moment of remembered awareness, it was to my father that I ran for comfort. But perhaps it is not so strange, after all. Any child knows, with a cell-deep certainty, when he has been given only half. Later, when that half has proved strong enough to sustain and propel, he may not miss the unproffered other half of sustenance so much, may not even remember a time when its absence starved and terrified. But the void, the abyss of its absence, is with the child always, and when great loss comes, as it so often does in the middle years, much of the attendant anguish is for that earliest loss. And so, on that hot day in a much later spring, I wailed for my mother and then got up and called my father. As he always had been, he was there, and as it always had, pain and fear shrank back. I have never been unaware as to whom I owed my life.

It used to make me wild when he would refuse to do battle with my mother, to avenge my hurt.

"I don't think ballet, darling," she said when I was six and wanted to join the magical classes she taught in our remodeled garage, where willowy little girls wore soft leather slippers and tied their hair high in severe buns and moved like wildflowers in the wind of her presence. A wall of scummed mirrors gave back their images, and a long bamboo bar was a trellis for them. It was the loveliest thing I had ever seen, and she was the mistress. If I were one of them, I would be one with her.

"Why?"

Even I could hear the whine in my voice.

"Because you are already far too big," she said coolly. She hated whining. I stopped doing it early. Now I hate it, too.

"I'll stop growing."

"You've only started growing. You'll reach the moon. You would look terribly out of place in a corps, and of course you could never hope to solo. You will be a giant, heroic woman; you must be the one who holds the ropes, not the acrobat. Whatever would the world do without its rope holders?"

"Swim," my father said when the tears over-flowed my bottom lashes. "You've got just the stream-lined build for it. You'll look like a mermaid in the water. I'll teach you."

And he did and signed me up for lessons at the Chastain Park pool, and cheered me on when the prowess he had predicted propelled me to victory after victory in the free stroke and relay. He took dou-ble shifts at the post office during my teenaged years to pay for my tuition at Westminster, and was always there to cheer me on when I brought home medals and cups for the school, even when Mother had a night class and could not attend. I was never popular at Westminster, not with the petite Buckhead girls whose cliques I aspired to, but I was known and applauded, and that gave me impetus enough to live with some equanimity until, in my last year of middle school, I suddenly began to come into my looks. It seemed to happen overnight; it almost drowned me at first. I was forever looking warily at the vivid image in mirrors and store windows. Who *was* that? Soon sidelong glances and a scattering of dates, usually with older (and taller) boys, followed. Miniskirts stopped look-ing, as my mother said, like tutus on a Clydesdale and started to showcase enough long, tanned, smooth-muscled leg to occasion whistles and calls from down-town construction crews. I began to stand to my height, and to stride instead of shuffle. I learned to smile openly and fully.

My father gave me all that.

And, when I wanted to try out for the varsity basketball team at the start of my junior year and my mother raised her silky black brows and said, "Do you really want to go lumbering around a gymnasium sweating like a draft horse with girls who have mustaches?," my father said, "You could model. There's a guy at the post office whose daughter is signed up with some model agency or something. She does fashion shows and even TV commercials. I'll find out about it."

And he did, and I signed with Peachtree Models and Talent that summer, and finished putting myself through Westminster and much of the University of Georgia on runways and in production studios. I learned to move and be comfortable with stillness, and to engage a camera with my eyes, even to lower my Amazonian bray to the clear, throaty voice I still have. Mother was proud of all that, though she could not resist giving me stilted instructions on moving and walking and stretching my neck, which had to be tossed out before the camera. And she began to shop for clothes with me, and even though she was wont to say things like, "Smocking and Twiggy baby dresses on someone your height are ludicrous, Molly. I don't even think they make them in your size," still, she steered me away from the kittenish excesses of mid-sixties dress that would have made me look ludicrous, indeed.

I could and did thank my father for all that, too.

But I could not make him defend me verbally to her, and that drove me early to rages of protest against the unfairness of her exquisite little sorties against me. Unfairness is the earliest and most irremedial of the world's wounds that a child encounters. It is never forgiven.

"Why don't you tell her to shut up?" I remember weeping once, when I had run to him yet again, this time over some obviously-to-me unflattering comparison to small Kevin. His natural grace and spilled-mercury vivacity, so like her own, were always being held up to me when I clumped or sulked.

"She doesn't mean to hurt you," my father said, holding me close enough to smell his familiar smell of Philip Morris cigarettes and sun-dried cotton undershirts. "She doesn't even realize she does it. It wouldn't be fair to her to yell at her."

"What about to me? What's fair to me? She's always liked Kevin more than me. He's her little boy."

"Well, you're my little girl, so we're even," he said.

And for the moment that would be enough.

It would invariably come up again, though, and I would rail at him once more: "Why won't you make her stop? I can't, but you could! You're always saying people can change if they really want to; if you told her to, she'd change."

"But I don't want her to change," he said. "If she changed, she wouldn't be her, and that would break my heart. She's the only magic I ever had in my life until you came along, Molly-o, and one day you'll see that she's the main magic in yours, too. You and I, we need magic. We're earth critters. She's our wings. Kevin has her wings, too. It balances out. All together, we make a family."

And we were at the heart of it, though I did not know it then.

Neither of my parents ever really had a family, so when they married, they simply made some rules for what they had and called it, if only in their minds, The

Family. They were not the first to make living, breathing individuals fit into the iron cage of an abstraction, not by any means. *Ozzie and Harriet* and *Leave It to Beaver* probably defined family for half the baby boomers born. But it is my own family—The Family—that is finally clearest to me, and I can trace easily the steps of its peculiar, tumorlike growth.

My mother, for instance, was abandoned by her feckless teenaged father when she was an infant and raised until age ten or so by her pretty, empty-headed, Irish mother in Savannah. When her mother, still only twenty-eight, took off with a hospital supply salesman to the Florida Panhandle, little Mary Belinda Fallon was taken in by her aunt Christy O'Neill in Atlanta, and raised with the O'Neills' quarrelsome, cloddish brood of children in a clannish, dilapidated part of the city near the old Fulton Bag and Cotton Mill. Belle Fallon was all grace and moonshine and cloud shadow, profoundly unlike the O'Neills and unwanted by them, and when she graduated from Fulton High she left the mill village and crossed town, to the northside. She got a receptionist's job at the Georgia Power Company during the day, and in the evenings, she took to the stage. There were few enough struggling local theatrical groups, and she was talented enough, and above all, attractive enough, so that she made her mark quickly. Belle Fallon at eighteen was the toast of Atlanta's minuscule theater-going public.

By the time she was nineteen, she was singing and dancing and emoting in almost every production mounted within the city limits, and in some in outlying Macon, Birmingham, and Tallahassee. By twenty she had snagged her first featured part in a national touring company. At twenty-one she met and married my father, and by the time she was barely twenty-two, I was born and her career was dying, and The Family had begun to emerge as if from developing fluid. My father, himself an orphan raised in the Methodist Children's Home in Forest Park, Georgia, had his own set of rules, his own blueprint for being a responsible adult, so he was content to let my mother draft the master plan for The Family. He knew no more of how to go about it than she did.

She began by assigning us all roles. Dad would be the provider, the supporter, the fixer, the protector. Beguiled by this creature of wood smoke and wild honey who had flown into his life and alit, he dutifully left his evening law studies at Oglethorpe University and went to work at the post office, where he stayed until his retirement forty years later. He made himself into a good household manager, a banker and accountant of some asperity, a fine handyman and fixer of things broken and faulty, and a steady and constant cheerer from the sidelines for the three lives he found himself in charge of. I think that my mother chose well: Dad seemed to me, all my life and his, to be content, indeed, happy, in his appointed role. In any event, he couldn't have helped but cheer her on in whatever she chose to do; I never saw a man so quietly and totally in love with a woman.

I could hardly resent that. The love spilled over on me in full measure, and to a lesser but equally constant extent, on Kevin. But Kevin, for most of his life until he left home, wanted only Mother. If that disappointed Dad, I never saw evidence of it. It was part of the dynamics of The Family, and therefore meet and right.

Mother was the flame on our hearth, the giver of light and dazzle, the lightning rod, the visible totem of The Family. She was who we were, in our collective souls and to the world. Almost every family has one of these, but they tend to be men, or certain children of the tribe. The role of nurturing, minding, enabling does not allow for much dazzle. I think my hapless mother tried to be and do it all until I arrived, hefty and draftlike from birth, and she recognized with relief the designated giver. From the time I could toddle I was taught to accommodate, smooth over, prop up, set right. I don't ever remember really minding. I did and do it well. My role gave me status and definition; there was never a time I did not know who I was to The Family. It was only when I aspired to anything outside the cage that I came to grief. Mother never unsheathed her arrows when I trod my road compliantly. That was when her whirling butterfly hugs and kisses were given; that was when her beautiful trained voice soothed and approved. As for those other times, I don't know what or who I might be now if it had not been for my father. As I said, his half flourished.

Kevin was our future, who we would be, how we would be known.

"Listen to him; he's already projecting," my mother gurgled with delight when Kevin howled in his ruffled bassinet. He was born graceful and pretty; he looked like her from the outset. His silky black hair was somehow hers as mine had never been, though to my eyes they were identical. His blue eyes were Fallon and not Bell, as mine were said to be. He had her delicate, porcelain features, and not the strong, carved ones I shared with my father. When he began to toddle, it was with her flat-footed, straight-spined dancer's gait. Even his tantrums were silvery and somehow theatrical. They made her laugh, as mine never did, and even my father smiled to see them. When Mother held him in her arms they seemed a Degas portrait: *Mother and Child*. Indeed, Dad once parted with a breathtaking amount of money to have a distinguished professor from the Atlanta School of Art paint them so, both of them bare-shouldered and bathed in dappled purple light from the blooming wisteria vine that sheltered our front porch. It is pure summer to look at; early summer, just before coarsening ripeness begins to swell. It hangs now in the living room of the condominium, as it did in the front room of the house on Peachtree Hills Avenue, where we sat when visitors came. Kevin and his wife wanted it when they first married, but Mother would not part with it. I knew of little else she had refused him.

So our paths were laid down from the beginning, and so we have continued since, in lockstep, four people destined and doomed to bear on our shoulders the living, holy ark of The Family. When I think of my mother's voice, it is this that I hear her say: "Family comes first, always. Blood is everything."

I told what I could of this to Livvy Bowen that morning.

"Your mother's obviously read too much William Faulkner and Tennessee Williams," Livvy said. "I can just see her in Williams. God. 'Blood is everything' my ass. Who does that make Tee and . . . what's Kevin's little wife's name again? I can't ever remember. Chopped liver? Official consorts? Does she include them in this family stuff? Do you?"

"Sally. Her name is Sally," I said, obscurely annoyed. My attempt to explain The Family to Livvy had obviously fallen short. "Of course she includes

them. Of course I do. Tee is family for me, just like
Sally is for Kevin. Tee and Caroline and Teddy for me;
Sally and Amanda for him. There was never any
question in Mother and Daddy's minds that we
would marry and have children. That's what makes
family."

But did it? Mother was drawn to Tee from the
beginning, I knew that; she teased and flirted with
him, charmed his conservative northside parents,
shone as if klieg-lit when we invited her to the driving
club, was the focus of all eyes at the parties we gave in
Collier Hills and later in Ansley Park. Tee gave my
mother the one thing her foreshortened career had not:
social status, a chance to show what she could have
been if not burdened early with a gigantic daughter
and dancing lessons in her garage.

But I don't think she ever approved of my marrying him. Tee should have been a woman. Then Kevin
could have had him, and so had the matched consort
that Mother had always envisioned for him. The only
time Kevin ever really defied her was when he married Dresden-exquisite, utterly conventional Sally
Hardy from below-the-salt Lakewood. Mother ceased
excoriating Sally—delicately, of course—only when
Kevin threatened to move with her to Nashville or
Charleston or somewhere out of firing range. I don't
think Mother ever saw that Kevin could not have lived
with a woman who was Tee's equivalent in money,
charm, and assurance. Where would he have drawn
his audience then?

No, I think Mother somehow thought he would
marry *her*. His mother, that oldest love. I don't think
she ever forgave Kevin Sally, any more than she did
me Tee Redwine. The order should have been

reversed. Both of us, in our choices, threatened the sleek skin of The Family.

"Well, the pattern has held, hasn't it?" Livvy said, nuking our cooling coffee in the microwave and producing pastries from Harry's in a Hurry, just up the street on Peachtree Road. "You're still the good girl, the dutiful one. Woman of the Year in Volunteerism, or whatever, last year, right? And Kevin's still the white hope. Top local anchor in D.C., with network written all over him. And your mother is still the family star, running those recitals all over town, still looking like a gazelle and wearing those incredible hats. And your dad's still wiring lamps and making bookcases in the basement, and going to all her recitals and all Teddy's tennis matches and all your awards banquets. Does any of you know who you are? Do you know who those people who live at your house are? Jesus, no wonder your butt itches at the thought of the act breaking up!"

I have always loved Livvy's blunt pragmatism, but she can be spectacularly wrong, too, in the manner of one who has always been so sure of her blood and money and place in the world that she has never had to question it. I knew that she was wrong now. But somehow her earth-rooted words soothed the sucking terror in my stomach and eased my shallow breathing. Something in my mind moved an imperceptible fraction of an inch forward, like a gear clicking into place, my self came flooding back, and the thin, acid, starving air around me thickened into nourishing normality.

"A fine one you are to pooh-pooh blood," I said, grinning around a mouthful of apple turnover. "Yours is bluer than ink and so is Caleb's. I don't notice any transfusions of rich, rude, peasant blood in your line, on either side."

"Blood is not a policy in either of our families," she said sulkily. Livvy hates being hoisted on the petard of her lineage.

"The hell it's not. That's just what it is."

We stared at each other over the antique cherry game table that the Bowens use for family meals—Liv had once told me that George Washington was supposed to have played cards on it on his way to the Battle of Mounmouth—and then we laughed.

Later we went to lunch. I offered the club, but Livvy dislikes it. She says the people who go there, even to play savage tennis, do not sweat, they mist. So we went instead to a funky little place on Peachtree Road called R. Thomas, overflowing with lovingly tended flowers and herbs and raffish, cheerful, talking birds in cages; the last bastion, Liv claims, of the Age of Aquarius. I like it, too; the vegetarian dishes are rich and wonderful, but no one I know frequents it. Carrie Davies isn't all that sure it's clean. So I go there only with Livvy. After lunch she dropped me back at Charlie's building to pick up my car.

"So when is Tee due back?" she said, sticking her head out the Saab's window.

"Day after tomorrow. But he goes right out again Monday."

"Do me a favor. Take the two days just for yourself. Cancel all your good works and let Teddy fend for himself. He's too old for you to hover over, anyway. Spend a day at Seydell and get the works—haircut, facial, massage, makeup, all of it. Then go to Neiman Marcus and buy yourself something fabulous to sleep in. Order in Friday night. Chill the wine, light the candles. Attack Tee the minute he walks in the door; take no prisoners. Whatever it was that was terrific about your first roll in the hay, do it again. *Then* ask him if he's having an affair."

"I couldn't ask that . . ."

"*Ask* him, Moll. Jesus, you Southern belles. How do you ever find out anything you want to know if you don't ask? I'll guarantee you'll like his answer."

"Well . . ."

"*Guarantee*. By the time you two get out of bed, your butt will be as smooth as a baby's. See if it's not."

I left her laughing. I was laughing, too. In the two hours I had spent with her, Livvy had given me back my old life, my old self, my old context. I drove back down Peachtree toward Ansley Park humming "Bye, Bye, Miss American Pie" under my breath. The sun was shining and the flower borders in the midtown office buildings looked festive and European. It was, at that moment, utterly absurd to me that I had ever thought Tee was anybody but my beautiful, comfortable old Tee; that I was a cuckolded wife instead of the cherished Molly I had always been; that the family was newly and sickeningly endangered. I could not even remember how the fear had felt. I stopped at a produce truck in a parking lot and bought huge red Florida tomatoes and cucumbers and the last of the Vidalia onions. I would make gazpacho for the weekend. Both Tee and Teddy loved it. Perhaps I would go by European Gourmet and pick up something wonderful for Friday night dinner. Maybe I *would* go to Neiman Marcus; it had been a long time since I had slept in anything but an old, extra-large Black Dog T-shirt that Livvy had brought me from Martha's Vineyard, where Caleb's family had had a summer place for generations. It was so old and washed that the shiny black dog stuff had half flaked off, and the Martha's Vineyard signature labrador was a dalmatian instead. Something pale and silky, maybe, to set off the swimming tan I hardly ever lost and make my light blue eyes flame in the dark, as Tee had sworn they did when we first went to bed together. And if there was time, perhaps a good blunt haircut to tame the wild black-and-silver tangle that I never could subdue. I drew the line at dye, or even a rinse. But the other things, maybe. No. Definitely.

When I got home, still humming, and tossed the tomatoes on to the kitchen table, Teddy called to me from the rump-sprung sofa in the library that was his television lair. I walked through my Eurotech kitchen and into the book-lined cave that Tee had made for himself and that the entire family had appropriated. I could see nothing of my son but enormous feet in new Nikes hanging over the sofa's arm, but I knew how he would look: a long sprawl of tanned, sinewy arms and legs furred with the soft gold of his thick hair, dark blue eyes half closed, long, mobile mouth chewing whatever he had fished out of the refrigerator. He is Tee from the top of his head to his soles, except that Tee would die before he wore an earring. Teddy has had his for two years. So far it has not sent him spiraling into delinquency or homosexuality.

Lazarus, so named because we got him from the pound only hours before his appointment in Samarra, would be lying on the floor beside the sofa with his big, hairy muzzle on Teddy's stomach, and Teddy would be lazily scratching the top of his head. Lazarus is huge and shaggy and looks put together from left-over dog parts. We have never been sure what breeds met in him to produce such a strange animal. All of us adore him, and he us, almost embarrassingly so, but none of us is under any illusions about Lazarus. He will learn no tricks, win no ribbons, save none of us from fire or attack. Lazarus's only talent is love.

I looked over the back of the couch. There they were, as I had pictured them. Lazarus thumped his tail, and Teddy raised a hand in languid salute.

"What are you doing home?" I said. "I thought you were taking Mindy to get her driver's license."

"We had a fight. She was acting like a shit. I told her so. I said I wasn't going to be responsible for her being a shit on wheels. I think her mom is taking her," my beautiful son said, not fully opening his eyes.

"Language, sport," I said automatically. "You're going to have to apologize to her, you know."

But I was not sorry they had had a fight. Mindy Terrell is a strident, possessive girl with spectacularly disquieting looks and an obsessive attachment to Teddy. She was, I had thought, older at barely sixteen than I had been at twenty-five.

"In a pig's ass," Teddy said. "Let her call me. And she will. Speaking of calling, Dad called a few minutes ago. He's coming in tonight. He said he'd be real late, so not to wait up."

"What's the matter?" I said, my heart beginning to suck and drag again. "Why is he coming in early?"

"I don't know. Nothing's wrong. He just said he wanted to see us, just wanted to talk to us. Said we'd have a long breakfast in the morning. He sounded homesick."

I smiled. Warmth spread through the middle of me. Tee used to cut his trips short sometimes just to come home and see us, and we'd always have a long

pancake and sausage and conversation breakfast the
next morning. The morning after the night of his
homecoming . . . my face colored at the thought of
those nights. He had not done it in a long time, though.
Did I have time for Neiman Marcus? No, but there was
that black chiffon thing he'd ordered for me, as a joke,
from Frederick's of Hollywood two Christmases back.
The one with the slit in the bikini panties. I wondered
if I could still get into it.

It makes no difference. I'll be out of it in no time, I
thought, running up the stairs toward our bedroom
with the idea of changing the sturdy, striped wash-
and-wear sheets for the ivory Porthault ones my
mother-in-law had given me for some unremembered
anniversary. She had them even on her beds in the
Redwine beach house on Sea Island. She also had
Isobel to wash and iron them. I had never taken mine
out of the ribbons they'd come in.

"Oh, by the way, Ma, how's your bee-hind?"
Teddy called up the stairs after me, and as if on cue,
the itching flame-stitched itself across my buttocks.

"Going to be fine," I called back, scratching hard.
"Charlie thinks it's an allergy."

"Jeez, I hope it's not to me or Lazarus, or to Dad."

"Don't flatter yourself," I yelled, and went into the
bedroom to peel off my panty hose and panties and
soak my affronted rear in a warm tub.

Tee was very late coming in. I have usually fallen early
into a light, waiting sleep since he has been traveling
for Coke on this assignment, but this time I was awake.
His step on the stairs was so familiar that I could feel it
in the beat of my blood; there was the place he always

broke stride, where the landing curved, and there was the next-to-top step that always creaked. I thought that there was something different about tonight, though, and then realized that his footsteps were slower, and heavier. Tired; he must be so tired. This insane traveling had gone on for far too long.

He came quietly into the bedroom, as he always did when I slept, and moved about with the ease of one who has undressed in this familiar dark many times before. I heard his shoes fall, and then the rustle that meant his pants were going down, and the little swish as he tossed them on the ottoman from the big blue easy chair under the window that looked out over the garden. The smaller swish of his shirt followed. He went into the bathroom and closed the door. I waited until I heard the toilet flush and the lavatory water stop running, and then reached for the switch on the bedside lamp. When I heard the door open again, I clicked it on.

"Hey, meester, you wan' a girl?" I called.

He froze in the flare of light, staring at me with near black, unfocused eyes. His face was emptied out and utterly still. For a moment my breath stopped. He looked mortally tired, bled white, old. His face was all angles and hollows in the shadows, and the stubble on his chin was so pronounced that I could see it from across the room. It is so fine and light a gold that you almost can never tell when he needs a shave.

"Honey?" I said tentatively, and sat up in bed in a great rustle of plastic. And then his face crumpled and he began to laugh.

Back in the silly seventies, a quintessentially silly woman named Marabelle Morgan had written a ludicrous antifeminist diatribe called *The Total Woman*. One of the husband-pleasing stratagems she had suggested was wrapping your naked self in Saran Wrap and meeting hubby at the door with a cold martini when he came home from work. Tee and I had hooted over it, and one night I had done just that, and we had ended up making love on the floor of the tiny vestibule that served the Collier Hills house as a foyer. I had had the striations of the diamond-shaped tiles on my back for days.

"Well, she's right, it works," Tee had said, panting.

Having tried and discarded the Frederick's of Hollywood ensemble as simply too sleazy to stretch over middle-aged flesh, I had remembered the Saran Wrap and done it again that night. For good measure, I had added a jumbo red velvet bow that had adorned our Christmas wreath, pulling it tautly over the worst of the weals and scratches on my bum. I was bathed, oiled, powdered, and shot all over with Sung, and my heart was galloping nearly as hard as it had on the first night Tee and I had ever gone to bed. When he began to laugh, I jumped, crackling and rattling, out of bed and ran to him and threw my arms around him. I pressed myself against him and rubbed as suggestively as I knew how; I kissed him all over his face and put my tongue in his ear. I felt his arms go around me, hard, and threw my head back and laughed aloud with joy. My clean hair swung into both our faces.

"You don' like me, I got a seester," I growled low in my throat.

Tee buried his head in my neck and scrubbed it back and forth, back and forth. He still did not speak, but I could hear his breathing thicken and deepen. I could feel him harden against my stomach, too, a ludicrous feeling muffled in plastic wrap.

"Wanna see if it still works?" I whispered into his hair.

I ripped the plastic wrap off and pulled him down on top of me on the bed. On the way down I reached over and clicked the light switch, sending the lamp rocking on its base. I gave him no quarter. I took him in my hand and guided him into me, clamping my legs around his waist and holding on as if I were in danger of falling off the rim of the world. He drove hard and deep, still not speaking, and I did not, either. Later for that. In the morning. Pancakes and sausage and Vivaldi and talk, sweet, slow hours of it. In the morning.

When we'd first made love, I was so nervous that my voice shot up an octave and I trembled all over, as if I were freezing. He was nervous, too, and half drunk; it was in our last year of school, after a Chi Phi party, in the apartment he shared with Charlie. Charlie was in Atlanta at Carrie's house; he was almost never in Athens on weekends that year. I remember that I closed my eyes and whimpered, and Tee, trying to soothe me, had whispered over and over, "It's gonna be good. It's gonna be so good, baby."

And to my immense surprise, it had been. It was so good that even before we found our rhythm, even before that first deepening and ripening, we both laughed aloud with surprise and pleasure. We were so exactly the same height and build that we fit as if we had been designed to illustrate one of the better sex manuals. There was not an inch of me, inside or out, that he did not cover exactly, fill perfectly. There was not an inch of him that I could not enclose. That had never changed, not in twenty-seven years.

And it didn't change this night. It was as good as

ever. If anything, it was deeper, warmer, faster, more urgent than ever before. When we finally lay gasping aloud and tangled together, coated with sweat even in the stale chill of the air-conditioning, we still had not spoken a word. I felt as if we had passed far beyond words, into a new place where, forever after, communion would be through our skin, through our mingled heartbeats, through the very blood that pulsed in our necks and wrists and throats. I lay steeped in moonlight, pinned to the bed with the sweet, sweaty weight of him, listening to his breath soften and slow in my ear. I felt his slack mouth on my neck. I felt invincible, boneless and weightless and young. I thought it would be fine simply never to move out from under him.

But finally my legs began to prickle and go numb, and I turned my face into his neck and said into his ear, a bubble of laughter catching in my throat, "And I was actually going to ask you if you were having an affair."

He began to quiver against me, as I have felt him do before a hundred times when he laughs silently after love, and I began to laugh, too. I stretched myself as far as I could, like a cat, laughing against the side of his face, rubbing his shaking shoulders, giddy and nerveless with completion and relief.

It was not until I felt the wetness on my neck, a small rivulet of it coursing slowly down the slope of my breast, that I realized he was crying.

CHAPTER TWO

HER NAME WAS SHERI SCROGGINS. She was an assistant attorney in Coca-Cola's legal department, thirty-two years old, estranged from her viciously Pentecostal family in the Florida Panhandle, divorced seven years from her citizens' militiaman husband, childless, possessed of a naturally acute legal mind and prodigious ambition, and definitely on Coca-Cola's inside fast track.

Tee wanted to marry her.

At dawn, through a ringing in my ears that sounded as if I'd stood too near a great explosion, I heard myself say in a tinny, puzzled voice, "How on earth can you marry her, Tee? Then she'd be Sheri Redwine."

Tee turned away from the window, where he'd been watching day break over Ansley Park (But how could dawn come? How could the sun rise on such a morning as this?), and said, "I might have known you'd make a joke of this, Molly."

If I could have felt pain through the stupid numbness that enveloped me, I would have flinched at his words. I had not been making a joke. I had meant just what I'd said: It seemed to me in my craziness that Tee simply could not marry a woman whose name ever afterward would be a bibulous joke. I had thought perhaps it had not yet occurred to him.

We had talked for hours. Or rather, Tee had talked. Talked, wept, talked, wept some more, talked and talked and talked. It was as if someone had pulled a stopper out of him. He sat on the side of our bed and babbled words that had, for a long time, no meaning to me, because they were about people I did not know. I said nothing, because nothing occurred to me. I sat half shrouded in crackling plastic wrap, sensing rather than feeling the small frown between my brows, leaning closer to him every now and then so that I could hear him better, so that perhaps some of this tidal wave of urgent, tear-borne words might make some sense. Grandma Bell could not have done it better. Every now and then I could feel my head shake from side to side, no, no, in a small gesture more of incomprehensibility than anguish. Anguish was not a part of that night. Anguish presupposes understanding. I did not know this man who wept on the side of my bed, and I did not know what he was saying.

Teddy had a biology project in his freshman year at Westminster in which he studied the effect of strong emotion on the human body. I remembered that one effect of great shock and fear was the widening of the pupil to admit all possible daylight, so that the ensuing brightness could better illuminate danger. I thought now that it was true. The bedroom where we sat was very bright, even though no daylight had paled the windows on to the garden yet. I seemed smothered, and floated in a buzzing, shifting cloud of radiant mist. Sometimes I could see so clearly through it that the stubble on Tee's chin stood out like cuttings in a hay field; sometimes he all but disappeared. Occasionally I could hear words and sentences with the clarity of gunshots in a silent forest, but mostly I sat and watched his mouth move and the tears run down his face, and could not hear what he was saying.

I sat and nodded and nodded, tilting my head to hear, my hands folded in my lap, as the stray words dived out of the mist at me, pecking like scavenger birds: "Sorry . . . sorry. Never meant it to happen . . . never meant to hurt you . . . doesn't mean I didn't love you, don't love you . . . I'm an asshole, an utter jerk; don't think I don't know it. . . . Don't think I haven't gone over this a thousand times in my mind, how to tell you . . . rather die than hurt you, but can't live without her, Moll . . . the lying and the sneaking around has almost killed both of us; she feels as bad for you as I do. . . . Needs me, Molly. Needs me in a way you never did . . . never had much of a family, never any security, never any cherishing . . . strong in a lot of ways but not in the ways you are . . . tell me what you want me to do now. Want me to move out? Want me to tell the kids? Want me to stay here with Teddy and let you go somewhere nice and think it out, Sea Island, maybe? Just tell me. . . . Not going to hurry you, not going to just leave you dangling; you'll always have what you need . . . tell me what you want me to do . . ."

Finally, after what seemed a very long time, the words stopped. The silence rang and the mist swirled. The room swam giddily. I said nothing, only sat looking at him, waiting for something else, I did not know what. But there must be something else. . . .

I blinked and the room came into focus. Tee got up and went and stood at the windows. Light was coming in now, pale, thin. That's when I said that about the name. About her being Sheri Redwine. After that, I could think of nothing else to say, so I waited some more.

Tee pulled up the slipper chair in the corner and sat facing me. I noticed that at some time he had put his clothes back on. When had he done that? All but his shoes and socks. He usually sat in the slipper chair to do that, but he did not move to do it now. He looked at me intently. I looked down at his bare feet, underwater white, and then at his face. He looked ghastly, burnt and then drowned.

"You must feel some way about this, Molly," he said finally, sounding fretful, querulous, his voice faint, like a child with fever. "There must be something you need to say. We can't not talk about it."

"It?"

"Molly . . . all of this I've been telling you. About . . . Sheri. The divorce. You've got to feel something about it. You've got to get it out . . ."

"Divorce? There's not going to be any divorce, Tee. I don't want a divorce, for heaven's sake; did you think I was going to punish you with that?"

He simply stared at me, then put his head into his hands. He laughed through his fingers, an exhausted, awful, little laugh.

"Molly, I may be a jerk and a cad and an asshole, but I am not a bigamist."

"You mean . . . you mean you want to *marry* her, Tee?"

He lifted his head and looked at me with dead, red-rimmed eyes.

"Jesus, what have I been saying to you for the past five hours?"

"Oh, Tee, why?" I whispered. There did not seem to be enough air in my lungs to speak aloud.

He closed his eyes. The endless tears began again, leaking from under his gold-tipped lashes. I had not seen Tee cry since his father's death six years before. Tears only for death, it seemed. But then, wasn't that what he was talking about? The death by murder of a marriage?

"She makes me alive again," he whispered.

"And I don't? We don't?"

"We . . . ?"

"Me. Caroline. Teddy. The family. You're talking about divorcing the *family*. How can you even think that, Tee? The family?"

"Molly . . . Caroline is gone. She has her own family now. And Teddy's going. He's going this fall. You know he isn't coming back, not to this house . . ."

"All right, then, me. What do I make you, dead? Tee, you know what we've had, what our life has been. You don't call that alive? All those years, Tee!"

He shook his head very slightly, as if the effort were almost too much. In the dim morning light he looked very young, as if he had just pulled an all-nighter at the fraternity house, studying with Charlie for finals. My heart swelled with love for him that was oddly maternal. Let him get it all out, this exhausted, fragmented boy that I loved, and then I could begin the business of soothing, sorting, mending.

"It's not the same thing," he said, his eyes still closed. "You know you and I don't have those kinds of feelings anymore. Not for a long, long time, not since . . . I don't know when. I'm not saying it's your fault, Moll. It's just . . . not like this. Not lightning, not light up the sky."

"Nobody has that forever," I said prissily, the schoolteacher I had been for a short time before Caroline was born. "That's for the beginning; you can't have it always."

"Yes," he said slowly, "I can."

"With this . . . Sheri, you mean," I said. "Does she put a little heart over the 'i', Tee?"

"Don't," he said. "Don't make fun of her name. She knows it's awful. It's her mother's idea of class, and she's too proud to change it. But she's come a very long way from that horrible family of hers. And she's done it all by herself. That's one reason . . . she's never really had a family. She doesn't even know what the word means."

"So now she wants mine."

"No," Tee said, smiling painfully. "Only me, I guess."

"Me, too," I said conversationally. "That's what I want, too. So I guess there's a little problem."

His face twisted and he stood up.

"I'll always take care of you," he said rapidly. "You'll never lack for money. You'll never have to go to work. The house will be yours for the rest of your life, if you want it. Or wherever you want to live. And school for Teddy. . . . You and Teddy will always be okay, Molly. I swear that to you. And anything Caroline wants or needs . . ."

"Tee, you don't make that kind of money," I said faintly. "Not for two . . . families. Or does she make an awful lot? Even then, it wouldn't be enough. . . . Don't you see how silly all this is?"

He looked at me for a long moment, then reached down for his shoes and put them on, standing balanced with his hand on the back of the slipper chair.

"I guess I should go on," he said, not looking at me anymore.

"Go on where?"

"Well . . . there. To her place. You can't want me to stay here."

"Your clothes . . ."

"I have some stuff there," he said, almost under his breath.

I knew that if he did, it was new. I knew all his clothes. There was nothing missing from his closet. Somehow this was dreadful beyond comprehension.

"It's that new condominium building in midtown, isn't it?" I said. "Charlie saw you moving her palm tree in. I thought he was mistaken. He thought she was Caroline. Does she look like Caroline?"

"She looks," Tee said, "a lot like you did when you were young, and don't think I don't know how that sounds. So just don't say it."

He picked up the briefcase he had put down beside the bureau the night before, a hundred years ago, but he did not move to go.

"So what about Caroline?" I said. "What about Teddy?"

"This weekend," he said. "We'll talk. I'll come over and the three of us will talk, and then we'll call Caroline. That will give you some time to digest everything, put it in perspective . . ."

I said nothing. Finally he moved to the bedroom door. He opened it and then looked back at me, over his shoulder.

"Molly. I'm sorry. I'm so sorry."

"Don't be," I said. "Nothing's changed. Nothing's going to. I'm not letting you leave the family."

He started to answer, but did not. The discarded plastic wrap clung for a moment to his feet, then he kicked it away angrily and went out the door.

The anguish came then.

*   *   *

I lay curled on our bed, knees drawn up to my chest,
arms crossed over it, until the pale square of light on
the scatter rug brightened into gold, and then the bled-
out yellow of another hot day. I thought of nothing in
particular, except that it was mortally important not to
move, lest the agony get loose from the pit in which I
had contained it, deep in my stomach, and flood over
and out, and kill me. I remembered that I had lain that
way twice before in my life, when severe menstrual
cramps had racked me in my early teenage years, and
again when I was pregnant with Caroline and Teddy.
Both instances had been about containment. And then
I thought, Well, of course, I lay this way before I was
born. In my mother's womb. Huddled as if against
cold. Even then, cold.

Sometime later in the morning I heard Teddy's TV
go on and his heavy footsteps, thudding down the
hall, followed by the click of Lazarus's toenails on the
polished hall boards and the jingle of his tags. Before I
could move, Teddy hammered on the bedroom door
and called, "Ma! Ma, you up? Where's Dad? Didn't he
come after all?"

I heard the knob begin to turn and found myself in
our bathroom, running water loudly, before I realized
I had moved. "I'm in the bathroom. Your dad's here,
but he had to go back to the office until late tonight.
He'll see us tomorrow for sure. He promised."

"Shit on youth brands," I heard Teddy grumble
outside the door.

"Youth brands make your car payments," I said,
wondering where in my shredded depths I found the
light, dry voice I habitually used with Teddy. He laughed.

"Well, then, if he's not going to be around till tomorrow, I'm going on to band practice after school, and then Eddie's. There's an Alabama concert at the Fox tonight. I thought I'd stay over at his place. That okay with you?"

"If Mrs. Cawthorne says it is."

"She does. See you in the morning sometime, huh?"

"Right."

There was a small silence and then he said, "Ma? You all right?"

"Fine," I sang out. "Just washing my hair. Listen, Teddy . . . are you taking Mindy tonight? Because if you are, you'll have to sleep at home. You know we said no all-nighters if there were girls along."

There. If that didn't sound like a normal Ansley Park mother, nothing did.

"Women, Ma. Not girls. Women. Nope. Mindy's history. Ol' Mindy's toast. Historical toast."

I felt a shocking wave of pure dislike for my son. The pain roiled and surged at its boundaries. Leaning over the washbasin, I clutched my stomach and stared blindly at the white-faced, wild-haired madwoman in the steamy mirror. Her blue eyes seemed to run like punctured egg yolks.

"It's so easy for you," I whispered to Teddy. "It's just so easy for all of you."

"Hasta la vista, baby," my unhearing son called, and thudded down the stairs and was gone.

Since I was already in the bathroom, I climbed into the shower and turned it on as hot as I could stand it, and sat down on the tile floor and turned my face up to it. The hot water was an absolute; while it pelted down on my blinded face I could not focus on anything else. I sat there until it began to go tepid, and then I climbed out and wrapped myself in Tee's white terry robe and slicked my hair back and went downstairs, leaving wet footprints on the thin, worn stair carpeting. It was stained with Teddy's teenaged years and scratched down to the matting with Lazarus's toenails; we had decided to replace it this fall, after Teddy went away to Georgia Tech. Lazarus, Tee said, was either going to have regular pedicures or get used to sleeping downstairs. Tee said . . .

The pain writhed and roared.

In the dim, silent kitchen I zapped a container of macaroni and cheese in the microwave and ate it, fed and watered Lazarus and let him out into the fenced-in backyard, got myself a diet Coke, and went into the library. Its cavelike gloom spoke to me of winter nights, with the fire snickering softly behind its screen and the television flickering. Only Teddy used it much in warm weather. I rolled the television set on its stand over to the end of the sofa, lay down full-length, covered myself with the plaid Ralph Lauren afghan Caroline and Alan had given us last Christmas, and clicked on the remote. On the screen a dark-haired, vulpine young woman coaxed hysterical tears from a black teenager and an older woman I thought might be the child's mother, and made a face of terrible, false sympathy as the tears escalated into screaming. The audience roared its approval. I turned the volume down as far as it would go, and for the rest of that day and into the evening I watched the screen as if the lives of the silent wraiths ·held captive within it were the only reality in the world. I found that I did not need their sound, only their movement.

At some point, in the middle of the afternoon, I

think, the phone began to ring. I let the answering machine take the calls until the bell threatened to break the skin of my fugue state, then I got up and tottered on numb legs over to the phone and turned the bell off. I did not play the calls back; I knew who they would be. My mother, wanting to know if I was going to take her shopping in the morning. The ladies of the Salvation Army auxiliary committee meeting I myself had called, and had missed. Livvy, to see why I had not been at our weekly doubles match with two other Coke wives at the club. I shuffled back to the sofa and watched television some more, watched and watched. Finally, I remembered Lazarus and let him back in, fed him, and scrunched over on the sofa as he settled in beside me, sighing happily, and fell into his familiar, twitching sleep on top of the afghan. Sometime later than that, long after dark, I slept, too.

The overhead light went on deep in the timeless, thick night—hot, because I had been shaking with chills all day and had not turned on the air—and Lazarus groaned and lifted his head. I sat bolt upright, eyes blinded, heart pounding.

"Why the hell didn't you tell me?" Teddy's furious, trembling voice cried, and I scrubbed at my eyes and squinted, then saw him, standing over the sofa, his fists clenched, his face red with rage and recent crying.

"Tell you?" I said stupidly. I could not think what he meant. What time was it? Why was I down here in the library, stiff and smothering from the afghan and the weight of the dog?

"Tell me Dad had a little piece on the side," he shouted. "Tell me old Dad was playing hide the wienie with Coke's pet legal eagle . . . or would that be eagless? Goddamn, Ma, *why didn't you tell me?* I'm not a fucking baby!"

"How do you know that?" I said thickly. "Who told you that?"

"You want to know who told me? *She* told me! Put her hand on my shoulder and stood there and told me like I was her goddamn little brother or something, smiling this shit-eating smile, saying she was sorry for my pain but after everything got straightened out she hoped I would one day be glad to have her in my life, like she was glad to have me in hers. Glad to have her in my life! Yeah, right, glad . . . Ma, she said you knew . . ."

"I don't understand what you're saying," I said. I did not.

"I saw them!" he shouted, beginning to cry again. "I saw them at the fucking concert! So did Eddie! So did everybody else I've ever known from school or anywhere else. And they saw me, and she gets up from her seat—they're in a box, of course, the Coke box—and comes down and puts her hand on me and says all that . . . *her*. Not Dad, her. Dad wouldn't even look at me. I had to go up there to the box . . . and even then, he wouldn't really look at me. He said he'd see us tomorrow and we'd talk it all out, and that he was sorry I found out this way; he'd really meant to tell me, but at least now we had it out in the open where we could deal with it. Deal with it! Deal with what? How long have you known about this? Why didn't you tell me?"

"Because it's not going to happen," I said, trying to push the words out on a wavering stream of breath. "This is just one of those things that happen to men your dad's age sometimes. It won't last, how could it? I didn't tell you because it's going to be okay. I didn't want you to worry. Nothing's going to happen to the family."

Teddy leaned close over me and closed his eyes and shouted, "He's going to marry her! You call that being okay? You call that nothing happening to the family? He's going to fucking marry her!"

"Teddy, language! Did he say that?"

"No. She did. She said she thought I should know, so there weren't any false hopes and stuff. She said it needed to be out, clean and honorable. Honorable! Jesus Christ!"

"What did your dad say?" I could barely form the words with lips that had gone stiff and numb.

"Nothing," my son said. "He didn't say anything. He had his eyes closed. Mom . . . he looked *stupid*! They both did. You know what they had on? They had on bike shorts, black bike shorts that matched, and Coke T-shirts. Jesus, Mom, Dad doesn't even *have* a bike . . ."

I almost laughed around the numbness, in sheer relief. It *was* some kind of madness, then. Some kind of male climacteric thing. We could work this out, ride this out. Tee in bike shorts? The image was simply ludicrous, nothing more. Where was the danger in this?

"Sweetie, it doesn't mean anything. I promise you. You wait and see. It's certainly not a good thing, but it's not fatal, either. In six months or a year we'll have forgotten all about it—"

"*She has a ring!*"

"What are you talking about?"

"She has a ring! He gave it to her! It's this big, ugly old green thing; she wears it on her right hand, but she showed it to me and told me that it was his covenant with her, and he didn't say it wasn't. He didn't say anything more. He looked like he was going to hurl right there in the Coke box. I hope he did. All over his bike shorts. All over hers."

I could not get my mouth to move. I tried to say something into the wreckage of my son's face, but I simply could not speak.

"Goddamn you all," Teddy said in a low, terrible voice and turned and ran from the library. I heard his footsteps pound up the stairs and heard Lazarus jingling behind him, heard his door slam, heard the inevitable music start. But I heard no more from Teddy.

I rolled myself slowly and in sections off the sofa and on to the floor.

"I want my mother," I heard myself sob. And I cried and cried for the woman only ten blocks away, who could not hear me.

And then I got up and called my father, called him out of sleep, and said, "Daddy, something's happened and I need to come home."

"Come on home, baby," my father said. "I'll put some coffee on."

When two become one, as people said of a conventional Atlanta marriage of my time, everyone knows the drill and swings happily into action. There are firm rules and rituals for the treatment of the newly wedded pair, for their fêting and giftings, for their duties and responsibilities. There are even prescribed ways of thinking about the couple that go back God knows how far, especially in the South. All of this saves a great deal of time and bother.

But when one becomes two, the opposite is true

and confusion reigns. More than confusion, I found. When Tee walked out, he left a kind of free-floating panic and an ensuing ostracism in his wake, only thinly veiled with sympathy. It was as if a sudden stench had settled over me, from which everyone was averting their nostrils while pretending it did not exist. Sometimes even I could smell it, lingering like body odor, and it made me feel slovenly and guilty, as if I should have bathed and so spared my friends, but had chosen not to. It was far worse because I felt in my very marrow that the same stench, if it touched Tee at all, lingered only momentarily. It was, I decided, the fatal fetor of vulnerability. No matter who was angry with him, Tee would not be perceived as vulnerable.

"It's fear, pure and simple," Livvy Bowen said, pouring a hefty slug of cognac into the coffee she had made. We were sitting in my kitchen on the third day after All That Stuff, as I thought of it, had happened. I had told no one but my parents and Caroline at the time, but in Atlanta the jungle drums are always out and poised, especially in what is fatuously called the Coca-Cola family, and I knew that almost everyone who mattered to me would know by then. Livvy, however, was the only one who had called, the only one who had come. She was ferociously angry at Tee, and smelled no stench on me. I knew she did not. I could have told if she had.

"Fear of what?" I said in my flat new voice that was as heavy as my body, my steps, my heart. Heavy and flaccid. I could not seem to shake off an endless, level white fatigue.

"Fear of it happening to them. Fear that if they get too close to you they'll catch some kind of virus and their husbands will walk out with some toots from the steno pool. Do they still have steno pools? Drink your coffee. You look like death."

"No, they have legal departments now," I said, sipping my coffee. The unstirred Hennessy puckered my mouth, but it did warm me a little, going down. In the middle of an unprecedented early heat wave, I could not seem to get warm.

"Listen, I want you to come over and stay with me for a while," Livvy said. "Caleb's going out again this weekend, and that way I'll be around if you want to start talking this out. I won't push you, I promise. But at least there'll be somebody around in your corner. You can spend the whole time sleeping if you want to. Just do it at my house, okay?"

"Oh, Livvy . . . Teddy's in my corner. Caroline is. My parents are . . ."

"Yeah, I can just hear your mother's tender words of sympathy and support now," she said and snorted. Livvy and my mother had disliked each other viscerally and instantly. "And I've already heard Teddy's. 'Goddamn you all'. . . It must have been a real Martha Stewart moment."

"He was devastated," I said defensively. "He's been a love ever since."

And so he had, my tall son, still white-faced and mute with misery and anger, but sticking to my side like a burr. Not literally . . . he did not dog me, or pressure me to talk. We did not talk much at all, in fact; had not, since he ran from the library the night of All That Stuff. But he was always in the house. School was out, and ordinarily Teddy would have vanished like a curl of smoke until September, but he did not go to the club to swim or play tennis, he did not go to band practice, and he spent little time on the telephone. The latter was the most alarming of all. Teddy's crowd, sprawling like puppies in the sun of approval and privilege since birth, checked in with one or another many times a day. The silent phone was ominous to me, and not only because Tee's call to say he was coming over to talk still had not happened. I hated the thought that my new contagion might spill out over Teddy. It seemed to me, drifting in my silent house, that nothing would or could happen until the telephone rang.

"Well, I'm sure he has, but you can hardly say what you think about Tee to him; it's the father-son thing," Livvy said. "You need to be with me. Whatever you want to say about the sonofabitch, I'll agree with you. Oh, shit, Molly, I'm just so *mad* at Tee Redwine! What a complete and utter asshole; I truly never thought it of him. And I'm just as mad at Caleb, and that whole little crowd of Coke princelings. They'll close ranks around him like the bunch of goats they are; see if they don't. Even while they're shaking their heads and doing the 'Aw, jeez' thing, they'll be covering his butt. I don't think anybody over there likes that bitch; did you know they call her the Eel Woman? Caleb says she's as slick and cold as a lamprey. But it ain't Tee who'll be cut out of the herd, oh no. Testosterone is thicker than blood or water."

I smiled at her passion, painfully but gratefully.

"You sound like you might have had a few words with Caleb about it."

"Only about five hours' worth," she said.

"Oh, Liv. I'm sorry . . ."

"Don't apologize! Don't you ever apologize for any of this," she said fiercely. "Don't you *dare* buy into that crap, that 'Somehow it must have been my fault, how did I fail him' shit. This is *Tee's* fault. This is Tee's shit. As it is, you'll end up paying the freight on it . . ."

"How? Why? Why should I pay for . . . whatever it is?"

"Oh, Molly," she said in exasperation. "You know as well as I do what happens in our crowd when a guy leaves his wife for a new toy. Haven't you seen it? For a little while it's all, 'Oh, poor thing, we must rally around her, what are friends for,' and then, after a while, after everybody gets used to him being part of a new couple, they'll begin to ask them back for dinner and little parties. You know, 'Well, of course she's awful, but after all, it's Tee!' And then it's like they don't remember who you are. Two or three times a year they'll maybe have you for the big Christmas open house—different hours from them, of course— maybe take you to the club with another of their divorced girlfriends . . . but for the big stuff, the fabric of their little lives, you're out of the loop. And she's in. They may never like her, and they'll probably despise the Eel Woman, but she'll be part of them because Tee is. This is his crowd, just like it's Caleb's now. This is guy stuff. This is the South. This is the Coke family. You think Coke is going to give a happy rat's ass about you? They're not even going to remember your name."

"They ought to fire her . . ."

"Fire her! Oh, right! What they did was promote her. Took her off Tee's team, of course; can't seem to outright condone the stuff, you know, but they trans-ferred her to community outreach and gave her a raise. And as for Tee, I hear he's in line for Paris or London in a year or two, if he wants it. Real hardship duty."

Paris or London . . . we had talked about it. How

many times? It had been something Tee was working toward, but we thought it would be much farther along, perhaps the last significant thing he did for Coke. I had loved the thought of the two of us in the blue hour, sitting on some gargoyled city terrace while the lights of Paris came on at our feet, or gardening in the long green twilight at a country house somewhere a few miles and hundreds of years out of London. Maybe, I thought, an insane giggle beginning to bubble up in my chest, they could bike in together every day in their matching latex shorts.

I snorted and Livvy looked at me.

"You don't think it's going to happen, do you?" she said slowly.

"Well, of course not," I said. "All that's if there should be a divorce, and there's not going to be any divorce. How can there be? He's . . . Livvy, we . . . Teddy and Caroline and I . . . we're what he *has*. We're what all those years have added up to for him. He can play around with having something else for a while; I mean, I hate it, of course, but in the end it's not going to matter because we're what he *has*. His whole life has been spent making what we add up to. And he's what *we* have. What would we have if . . . well, he's what we have, that's all. He's the sum of all those years and all that talk and all that laughter and all the trouble and the hard times and the . . . the . . . ordinary times, the thousands of times we brushed our teeth and . . . and rented a video, and talked on the phone to each other. All the things we've done together and planned and thought and worked for and seen happen, all the clothes that hang in our closets and the furniture we've always had . . . everything that we remember . . . who would all that belong to if we . . . didn't stay together?

There's just not going to be any divorce. Let him wear bike shorts and screw her in a midtown condo; it doesn't touch who he is or who we are together. He knows that as well as I do."

"Oh, honey," she said softly.

"Why, does Caleb think Tee's . . . going to be with her now?"

"Moll . . . Tee told him that he was. He told him that back in March or April. He just didn't get around to telling you."

"Because he knows it's not going to happen," I said, and got up. "I do think Caleb might have told you, though. It would have saved all of us a lot of pain."

"No it wouldn't, love. It just would have gotten it over sooner. But you're right, he should have told me. That's one reason I'm so goddamn mad at him. Okay, enough about it. You're not ready to deal with it yet, and that's okay. It's probably too early. But I still wish you'd come stay with me next week. Teddy's old enough to be on his own; you don't want to hang on to him. Who knows, you might even have fun with me. You know what we could do? We could do four or five days at a spa, Canyon Ranch, maybe, get a complete overhaul, do some serious shopping . . ."

"And get our hair bleached, and maybe even a little liposuction, a little nip and tuck? God, Livvy, I never thought I'd hear it from you. The classic woman-scorned, feel-good routine. Such a cliché."

"Maybe that's because it works," Livvy said matter-of-factly. "Well, then, we'll watch old movies and eat pizza for six days, or get drunk, or whatever you want to do. Will you come?"

"Not right now. But I love you for thinking of it,

and I may take you up on it later. Right now there's stuff that has to be settled, and it can't get done until I talk to Tee."

"Call him, then."

"It's his call to make. He'll have to do it sooner or later. He can't just pretend nothing's happened; he owes Teddy more than that, and Caroline. But it's his call."

"It's your call, of course, but I'm out of here for now," she said, getting up and hugging me. For a moment I stood loosely in her arms, feeling the strength and warmth of them, luxuriating in the simple human touch that meant love, and then I drew back and slapped her on the fanny and she turned to go. Then she looked back.

"How's your butt, by the way?" she said.

"Why . . . fine. Smooth as a baby's. Not a tingle for days," I said, realizing only then that it was true.

"Butt knows best," she said solemnly, and was out the door and gone.

CHAPTER THREE

TEE DID NOT, AFTER ALL, come and talk to Teddy and me.

He faxed us.

That one thing infuriated my father more than any of the sorry flotsam and jetsam cast up by the separation. Most of the proceedings he watched with a sort of grim, detached sorrow, but when he heard about the fax he exploded.

"What kind of sorry jackass faxes his family that he doesn't want to live with them anymore?" he shouted, throwing the *Atlanta Constitution* down on the floor of the screened-in porch.

"He may be a jackass, but he's our jackass," I said, hoping to divert him with humor. It usually worked, but not this time.

"No, he's not," my father said in a low, cold voice. "That's just what he's saying, only he's not man enough to say it to your faces. Well, by God, he'll say it to mine, or I'll know the reason why."

And he got up and strode toward the hall where the downstairs telephone sat. Cellular phones were not a part of my father's ethos.

"No, wait," I called. "In all fairness, Teddy told

him to fax. He wouldn't talk to Tee on the phone and he wouldn't see him."

"So what! Tee should have insisted; he should have just gone over there. This is his wife and son we're talking about. What's he going to do, E-mail Caroline?"

I said nothing. In the clear light of my father's rage, it did sound shabby and feckless. I don't know why I had not thought so earlier.

Tee had called on Sunday afternoon, late, and said that he'd like to come by and talk to both of us. I said, "Fine," as calmly and neutrally as I could, but my heart began the familiar galloping. If Tee didn't come to his senses soon, I thought, I'd simply go into cardiac arrest.

"So, okay, we'll be by in about an hour," Tee said, and I heard Teddy's voice on the upstairs extension. I had not realized he had picked up.

"What's this 'we' shit?" Teddy said coldly.

"I'm coming, too," a woman said. Her. It was her. I had imagined a silky, tongue-flickering purr, but the voice of my enemy was oddly flat and without resonance, with the nasal twang of the wire grass under it. It was, somehow, disarming.

Neither Teddy nor I said anything, and the voice went on: "It may be harder for all of us now, but it's not fair to let Tee carry this alone. I'm part of it, too. We need to know each other, you-all and I. We can build something honorable and lasting if we start out that way."

She sat beside my husband, perhaps touching him, and spoke of honor. I could not draw a breath deep enough to get a word out.

"Eat a shit sandwich," Teddy said. "If either of you's got anything to say to us, fax it."

"Teddy . . ." Tee began.

"You heard the kid," I said, and hung up. Teddy did, too. There was stillness, a silence from upstairs.

"You want to talk?" I yelled up into it.

"No," he called back.

We did not speak of the call again. I retreated into my white fugue. The fax came that evening.

It was a long one, addressed to both of us and signed by both of them. Teddy read it and crumpled it up and threw it into his wastebasket.

"I need to see it, too," I protested.

"No, you don't," he said, his back to me. "It's two pages of New Age shit that ends up saying, essentially, that he's leaving us and marrying her, and trying to make it sound like it's some kind of cosmic wonderfulness that's going to lift us all straight to heaven. He says he still loves us and will forever, and then she chimes in and says we can still be a family, a new kind of family. He says he'll wait to hear from either or both of us. He can wait for me till hell freezes over. You do what you want. I hate him. I hate that fucking bitch."

He began to cry, the coarse, ragged sobs of a young man no longer a boy, and ran into the library and slammed the door.

I stood outside it, my heart wrung with pain. I could not bear the sound of his grief. But I knew that this time I could do nothing to assuage it. Only Tee could do that. Finally I went up to our bedroom—my bedroom now—and sat down to call Tee back. Then I realized I did not know his new number. And I knew that if I could help it, I never would.

I did not reply to the fax, either.

Caroline called late that night from Memphis. He

had just talked to her, he and Sheri, and she was furious, wounded nearly mortally, inconsolable.

"How could he do this to me? How could you let him? My God, she's only a few years older than I am; what is he *thinking* of? Aren't you going to do something? Can't you fight a tacky little trailer park slut? If he thinks he's ever going to see his granddaughter again, he's out of his mind. Not while he's with her. My baby's not going within a hundred miles of that piece of trash. My God, she sounds like a washerwoman . . ."

Caroline was her daddy's girl, just as Teddy had always been my boy, my miniature Tee. It had always seemed natural, comfortable, an almost Wally and June Cleaver arrangement. Only then did I see what it might mean, how the crippling old patterns had repeated themselves. I stared at the phone in my hand in horror. Had I really done that to my children, perpetuated upon them the same vicious dance that I had been caught up in? If so, what else had I done, what other damage had I wrought, or let be wrought, without realizing?

"Can't you fight her? . . ."

Caroline's words stung my ears long after I had soothed her sobs with promises of a visit and hung up. Fight her? Fight who? How? I did not know how to fight anyone, certainly not this mythic creature, this arcane Sheri, without scruples or vulnerability, as intent as a young shark on the one thing she wanted: my husband. I had never known how to fight, only propitiate, only accommodate, only enable. It had always seemed enough. Poor Caroline. If anyone was going to march out and get her daddy back for her, it was not likely to be her mama.

Much later that year my father said to me, "I never could understand why you didn't get angry. If it had been me, or your mother, we'd have blown the bastard sky high. I thought for a while that you were protecting the kids, and maybe even us, but it seemed to me it went further than that. I admired you for it, but I wondered."

Anger? Dear God, of course there was anger. In those first awful days, when simply getting through one until it ended and became another was all I could seem to accomplish, I felt enough anger at Tee and Sheri Scroggins to blow the world apart. Oh, not always, by any means; there were long periods of pure, sheer pain that humbled and silenced me like a flailed ox, and there were intervals of crazy gaiety, of idiotic confidence that he would come back to us. These came mainly in the mornings when I woke, having forgotten for a few hours that catastrophe had struck, and when I first remembered it seemed simply so silly, so unimaginable, that I could only stretch and smile and think, "What have I been so worried about? Tee hasn't left us. How stupid."

And sometimes I just drifted in the soft cocoon of seductive listlessness that lay always just outside my consciousness, like a fog bank waiting to roll in. It became increasingly simple to let it.

But under it all lay the anger, red and bottomless, waiting to immolate the only world I had known. It licked at me mainly when the fact of Tee's betrayal collided with someone I loved— Teddy, Caroline, my parents. Then, I clenched and knotted everything inside me so that I could tamp it down, beat it back, chill its heat. Then is when I let the white fog come. Because I was afraid, I was terrified: I could not blow up the only world I had, the world of The Family. What would I do without it, who would I be, how would I live, who or what would provide the context for The Family?

"I guess I was afraid," I said that cold night to my father, and knew of course that I had been mortally, endlessly afraid. Naked and alone in space, no world around me? Anything was better, anything more bearable.

So in the best traditions of my grandmother Bell, I buried all of it deep. For me, that meant avoiding everyone but Teddy. I could not even see my parents after that first nighttime visit, could not run again to my father as I had then. Not yet. I gave Lilly the week off and canceled all my meetings and unplugged the phone. I stayed home and cleaned and polished silver and did endless laundry; I baked and mended and scrubbed patio furniture and cooked from-scratch meals for Teddy and me that neither of us ate. On one level it was infinitely comforting to get in touch with my house and my things again, handling them as I had not since the first days of our marriage, before we had help. I remembered how I had felt then, so full of joy that my blood prickled. Look at me, I did not think but might have, moving efficiently among the furniture of my life, what a good wife and mother I am. What a good woman. My price is above rubies. What could happen to me?

On another level, this caressing of my lares and penates put off the day when people came battering back into my life and it tumbled on again. I knew that. I figured I had about three days, four at the most, before the calls and visits began. At the end of the third day, I turned the phone back on.

The calls came, from my mother first: "Will you *please* call us? We're worried sick about you. If you don't call us today, we're coming over whether you want us or not. Do you need a doctor? Is Teddy all right? Have you talked to . . . you know, Tee, yet?"

From my father: "I trust you to let us know when you want to talk, baby. But don't shut us out much longer. There's nothing so bad we can't find an answer to it. Love you."

From Sally and Kevin in Washington, in tandem: "What's going on down there? Has Tee lost his mind? Do you need anything? Want to come up for a while? Want us to come down there and kill him? Call, Molly. We're worried."

From Caroline's husband, Alan: "When do you think you could come see us? We want to know you're okay, and I'm worried about Caroline. I've never seen her like this. You'd think her dad had died. She can hardly take care of Melissa. It would help if her father would call or come by himself; if you talk to him, will you tell him she's drowning? Or give me his number; I'll tell him myself. What a godawful thing to do . . ."

From my committees and boards and panels: "Don't worry about a thing. We're coping splendidly. Why don't you just take the summer for yourself and let us do some of the work now? Only, if you think you might want to take longer, do let us know; we'll need to make some plans for the fall."

Translation: "If you're going to be divorced by fall, maybe you'd better think about passing the torch. We love you, but you're not going to be who you were, and we need all the strength and bucks behind us we can get."

The luster and largesse of Coca-Cola rarely stands

behind ex-wives. A new divorcée would be a millstone indeed.

From Livvy: "Okay. I know. Burrow in. You have two and a half more days and then I'm coming over and get you."

From Sheri Scroggins every day, on the answering machine, since I hung up whenever I heard her voice: "This is not helping anything, you know, Molly. We feel for you, but it's only making things worse, you hiding like that. We really need to talk. Tee is in terrible shape."

From Tee, once, also on the answering machine for the same reason: "Molly, please call. Please answer. This can't go on. It's not fair to any of us. Sooner or later we have to sort things out. I'll come by myself. Or meet you someplace . . ."

From Ken Rawlings, our longtime lawyer and longer-time friend: "Molly, please understand I'm not calling in any official capacity. I'm sorry as hell about this whole thing. But it would be in your best interests to talk to Tee, and the sooner the better. You can afford to be generous, babe, you're holding all the cards. I love you both, and wish to hell this hadn't happened, but since it has, be the gal I know you are and call Tee. Or me. We're going to take care of you."

"Are you going to?" Livvy said on the morning of the fourth day. True to her word, she had been on my doorstep at nine. I knew she would be.

"What, call Ken? Hell, no. Or Tee, or the Eel Woman, either. I know what they want, but it's going to be harder than that for him to . . . you know."

"Get a divorce. Say it. D-I-V-O-R-C-E. Well, if you're not going to call Ken, you better call somebody. A lawyer, I mean. If you don't know any divorce guys,

I can recommend somebody who can eat Ken Rawlings for breakfast. And he doesn't have a thing in the world to do with Coke."

"Why? I'm not giving Tee a divorce. Not for that little nothing. Not for some little . . . piece of ass. He can beg until doomsday, they both can. There's not going to be any divorce, and I'm not talking to anybody."

She took a deep breath and blew it out again.

"Why would you want to hang on to somebody who's done this to you? How could a divorce be worse than this?" she said. "What are you afraid of? You're the smartest woman I know; there's nothing you can't do. You're going to have all the money you need, and the house; anything you want, if you're at all smart about it. That's where the good lawyer comes in. Tee doesn't have a leg to stand on. You must know that."

"But what if it's just a fling, what if he gets tired of her, or her of him? It's bound to happen, Liv; I can't think what on earth they could have in common but bike shorts . . ."

"It's not a fling. I've heard the talk from other people besides Caleb, Coke people. People who know them both. Tee may well indeed get sick of her, or her him, but the fool is bound and determined to marry her first. And even if they split up . . . Molly, could you live with him again after this? Could you really do that?"

I looked at her. I knew that I was never going to make her understand. And if not Livvy, certainly no one else. But, yes, I could live with Tee again after this. Because otherwise I wasn't anyone and it was too late to begin searching for another self, and what if I never did find one? You can't go through the world a spectre, so mutilated that more than half of you is gone, so lacking in substance that people can look right through you.

"You still love him that much?" she said softly.

"I have no idea if I love him at all," I said. "But there's not going to be any divorce."

She sighed, but said no more about it. We went to lunch at R. Thomas and talked to the cheerful, molting birds and drank wine and ate veggie pizzas. I felt almost normal, just a little fey and quivery, as if I were recuperating from a debilitating illness. Everything was eerily bright, and strange. But other than that, it was okay. I thought I could probably do the visits now.

As if on cue, they began that evening.

Mother and Dad rang my doorbell at six o'clock. I peered through the peephole, prepared to pretend I was not at home until whoever it was left, and saw one of my mother's flamboyant hats with my father's face looming over it, behind her. I could not see Mother's face, but Dad's was still and blank, as if he was having a passport photograph taken. My father was an essentially private and rather formal man who did not believe in dropping in on people, not even an abandoned and possibly suicidal daughter, and I felt a smile twitch at my lips. I opened the door.

Mother swooped in, carrying an armload of flowers wrapped in florists' waxed green paper. She laid the flowers on my console table and hugged me fiercely, standing on tiptoe and knocking her hat askew in the process.

"The mountains have come to Mohammed and are taking her out to dinner no matter what she says," she said into my shoulder blade. "How are you, darling? We just can't let you hide out in here any longer."

Over the waggling hat I looked at Dad. He

winked, and managed a grin, more a spasm, really. I could see the worry about me in his eyes, and in the deeper lines around his mouth.

"Hi, baby," he said, and at the sound of his voice something swelled and warmed behind my eyes, and I felt tears sting in them.

"Oh, now," Dad said, trying to find a place to hug me that wasn't engaged by my mother.

I backed out of her embrace and gave a great, rattling sniff and managed to smile at them both.

"Here come the marines," I said, and we all laughed more loudly than the words deserved.

"Oh, darling, you look like death warmed over," my mother said in her throaty tremolo. "When have you washed your hair? Or had anything to eat? You run right up and shampoo and shower and put on something pretty, and we'll have a decent dinner and some wine. Dad says he'll take us to the Ritz. We'll just sit out on the patio and wait for you."

"Mother, I—"

"Let me take my girls to dinner," Dad said. "It's been a long time since I had you both to myself."

There was such a look of helpless anguish in his eyes that I gulped the stupid tears back again and said, "I'd love that," even though I could think of nothing that I wanted less to do. I knew that it would make him feel better. Forward motion was my father's antidote for all crises; stasis was the ultimate anathema to him. And who knew? It might make me feel better, too. At least the Ritz-Carlton's dim, opulent dining room was apt to be safe. It was more a corporate haven than an Atlanta couples' watering hole. The only Coke faces I was apt to see were those of clients, and they were not likely to remember me.

I installed them with drinks on the little walled patio—shabby after several days' neglect—and went upstairs to bathe and change. I shampooed and blow-dried my tangle of hair and dragged a comb through it. My mother was right. It was weeks late for a trimming. Medusa hair. My eyes in the bathroom mirror looked huge and blanched of color, as if I had bobbed for a long time beneath the surface of water. Drowned eyes. The start of a tan I had gotten a few weeks back, swimming at the club in a spell of hot spring weather, had faded. I looked pale and sodden, as if I had just been pulled from water.

I plodded into the bedroom and put on a red silk shift and high-heeled sandals, added a slash of red lipstick that made me look as if I had been eating bloody flesh, and put on and then discarded the pearl choker and earrings Tee had given me for our twentieth anniversary. I did not, somehow, want jewelry, especially not this. It seemed almost obscene. When I went back downstairs my mother pursed her lips and stared at me for a long time, and said, "Well, it's a start. A haircut and some color and a little nip through Jenny Craig will make you feel a lot better, and then your old mother is going to take you shopping. You've only let yourself go a little; there's not a thing that can't be fixed. What we need now is an agenda."

"Belle . . ." my father began.

"It's a little late to start on the outside of me," I said to my mother. "What have you got for the inside?"

"It's never too late," she said briskly. "This is not the time to be negative. And don't knock the power of appearance. I've dealt with imagery all my life. It's the most powerful force on earth sometimes. If you put

your mind to it you can have that silly man back home
before—"

"Mother," I said, "I'm really looking forward to
having dinner with you. You're right, I've been stuck
in the house too long. But I'm not going to talk about
any bright little campaigns to make me over and win
back my wandering husband. If you can't drop it, I'm
not going."

She gave me one of her patented oblique looks
from under the brim of the hat, and then dropped her
feathery lashes.

"You're the boss, darling," she said, and on that
note the Bell family went out to dinner.

I walked behind her up the stairs and into the dining
room at the Ritz. She wore a sleeveless black linen
sheath of the sort Audrey Hepburn and Givenchy had
made popular in the early sixties. She had probably
bought it then; she could still wear the clothes she had
had as a young woman. Her arms were bare, very
white in the dusky light, and even at a distance you
could see the ridges of sinew and little wattled laps of
flesh that hung from underneath them. But there was
not an ounce of fat on them, nor on her legs, which
were knotted with muscle below the knee-length skirt,
and flexed sleekly as she glided through the room on
her high black heels. The black straw hat sat atop her
small head like a flower, but beneath it her neck was
corded, and ropy, too. When had she gotten so thin?
She was past leanness now, past the dancer's taut slim-
ness I was used to, thin to chicken bone and sinew, an
old woman's eggshell thinness. But she still held her
head high and her spine erect, and walked like a

woman who knew that every eye in the restaurant was fixed on her. And they were.

I felt the eyes slide off her and on to me, and thought how we must seem to the well-dressed, expense-accounted people at the tables around us: an exotic, somehow ossified Kabuki doll in an outrageous hat and her unwieldy offspring paddling along behind her like a gigantic duckling. Somehow I never doubted that everyone would know instantly that we were mother and daughter. Even strangers always knew that somehow. Something in my mother's pave-the-way stride, and my follow-along one, announced it. I was not unaware of that; sometimes I tried to outstride her and lead the way. My long legs should have bested hers every time. But her dancer's muscles and uncontainable presence always won. Mother led. The rest of us followed.

When we were seated, there was a solicitous business with menus and water glasses and the precise adjustment of chairs—something else that always ensued when my mother sat down to table, as she liked to say—and when she had rewarded the service with her brilliant smile and the waiters had gone away, she said, "Now. Before we have our drinks I just want to say one thing, and then we won't talk about it anymore."

I opened my mouth but she held up her fernlike claw of a hand and said, "No, let your mother have her say. I have a bit of a stake in this, too, you know."

And I was silent, because, of course, she did. She was as much a part of the corpus of The Family as any of us. I sat and waited.

"I just want to say that of course you aren't going to give that weak-witted husband of yours a divorce.

We know that. We back you up a hundred percent on that, and I imagine Charlotte Redwine does, too. It's unthinkable, having some South Georgia nobody in that old family; Charlotte isn't going to permit it. The trouble is that she's permitted Tee too much over the years; nobody ever said no to him. He doesn't know the meaning of the words 'responsibility' and 'hard choices.' He's always gotten just what he wanted, even before he knew he wanted it, because he's charming and smart and a Redwine. But he's not the one who controls the Redwine purse strings and he must know it. You just hang on. You've invested too many years in that boy, and you stand to lose too much if you let that little tramp have him without a fight. I meant what I said about the hair and the spa and all that, and that's just the beginning. When we all put our minds to it, you'd be amazed at what we can—"

"Your two minutes are up," I said, around a cold knot that felt perilously like the tiresome tears. "I hear you, but I'm not going to answer you now. I want a shot of single malt and then maybe another one, and then I want to order. And I'm going to have the most fattening thing on the menu, so you may as well save your breath."

I smiled to take the sting out of it, and she looked at me with an avian sharpness, but said no more. My mother's timing is perfect. It was my father who spoke next.

"Okay, here's your old man's two cents, and then the booze will flow and that will be the end of it. Molly, you don't have to stay married to that sorry boy if you don't want to. Maybe it would be better if you don't. Your mother's wrong when she says we all think you ought to hang on to him. I, for one, don't much think you should, though if you really want to, of course I'm behind you one hundred percent. But to my mind it's Tee Redwine who stands to lose, not you. And your dear mother, of course. She's gotten right addicted to the Driving Club over the years."

"Why, Tim Bell," my mother said tremulously, allowing her great eyes to widen. He smiled at her and covered her frail hand with his.

"I can still offer the Elks," he said, and she laughed reluctantly. I sat still and looked from one to the other. I had never known him to disagree with her before on matters pertaining to The Family.

"What does Teddy think of all this?" Mother said after a moment. "I'm sorry he didn't want to come with us."

"He's badly hurt, and he's furious, and he's way, way too protective of me," I said, only then really seeing that he had been, ever since he'd found out about his father's affair.

"He bolted out of the house to go over to Eddie's the instant you got there. He hasn't seen any of his friends for days. He's been hanging around the house with me. Oh, he stays in his room most of the time, or in the library, but he always knows where I am. I've got to insist that he get out more. He can't turn into a caretaker for me. He's got a life to live; he's got college to get ready for. And you know he and Eddie and Kip Hall were planning to drive Kip's car west on Route 66 and back again in August, before they start at Tech. Now he's talking about not wanting to go. I can't have that."

"No," Dad said thoughtfully. "He's got to go on with his life. I'll have a talk with him. After all, he really isn't losing his father, though I guess it must seem to him like he is right now."

"Not losing his father . . ." I said indignantly. "Of course he is . . ."

And then I fell silent. Of course he was not. Only I was losing. From the perfect skin of The Family, only I was being ejected. How could that be?

When I got home Teddy was in his room with the stereo booming. It was early, and I went up and knocked. It was a long time before he said, "Ma?"

"Yes."

"Come on in."

I went in. The room was in semidarkness; I could barely make out the lump under the sheet on Teddy's bed that would be Lazarus, who burrowed there habitually, as if returning to a cave. The lump stirred and a scruffy tail appeared, wagging, but Teddy lay still, on his back, staring at the ceiling.

"What's the matter? Did you-all decide not to go out after all?" I said.

"No, we went to the Hard Rock Cafe."

"It's awfully early . . ."

"I just didn't feel like hanging around there."

"What's the matter, Teddy? I know something is. Is it Dad?"

"They were laughing about it," he said in a tight, too young voice. "Oh, not at me, but about him and her. Chip Frederick and Tommy Milliken were there; both their dads are with Coke. They've both met her at some Christmas thing. Say she's hot stuff, a real babe. Said she was coming out of her dress at that party, and all the men were panting down it. Said they'd been taking bets on who finally got in her pants, but nobody ever thought it would be Dad. Eddie told Tommy he was going to knock the shit out of him if he opened his mouth one more time, and they left, but they were still laughing. I hate them. Him, too. I hope they all die."

His voice was matter-of-fact and too dry, as if the juice of life was gone from him. I would have preferred tears. Pain and anger tore through me. For that instant I wished Tee would die, too. Just die, before he could inflict any more pain on us.

"Your real friends aren't going to laugh," I said, walking over to put my hand on his head. But he flinched away from my touch, and I stood still.

"I know it," he said. "It's just that maybe I don't have as many of those as I thought."

"It will get better," I said thickly. "It really will. It's just that it's all new. People always talk about things when they're brand new. Give it all some time. I know how hard it must be—"

"I know you're hurting too, Ma, and I'm sorry, but I don't think you can possibly know how hard it is. You're not . . . you're not *kin* to him. I've got his . . . blood and his bones and his genes and stuff in me. How can he just walk away from that?"

"He isn't walking away from you, not really," I said, but he made a sharp little sound of dismissal.

"Bullshit. Listen, Ma, I just can't talk about it anymore now. I just can't. I need to get some sleep. You go on to bed and get some, too."

"Okay," I said softly, obscurely hurt, and turned to go.

"Ma?" he said after me.

"Yeah?"

"I love you."

"Me too you, Speedo," I said thickly, using for the first time in years the old nickname he had grown to hate. And I went to bed and, predictably, cried for a long time.

The next visit was from Carrie and Charlie Davies. They came by the following night about nine, in summer-dinner-at-the-club clothes: flowered sundress, blue blazer with khakis. Neither was smiling. Charlie sat in the oversized wing chair in the living room, where he always sat, his big hands dangling between his knees, looking around the room he knew as well as his own as if he had never seen it. Carrie sat next to me on the sofa and cried. She had started to speak when they first came in, and then had shaken her head and burst into tears, and I had sat beside her hugging her ever since. She could not seem to stop.

"Molly, I want you to know that I didn't know . . . that day," Charlie said heavily. "When you were at the office. I wouldn't have said anything for the world; I really didn't know . . . shit, I can't believe Tee was . . . and I didn't know it. I'd have blistered that old boy if I'd known . . ."

He fell silent. I noticed that he did not call me Moonbeam. I doubted somehow that he ever would again.

"I know," I said. "I know you didn't. Apparently not many people did, except Coke people. Tee was . . . they were . . . very discreet. Don't feel bad about it, Charlie. Nothing's settled yet. I think we can still work it out . . ."

Carrie's sobs escalated.

"I just can't believe it," she wailed. "I just can't . . . it's like it was happening to Charlie and me. It's like a death, almost. Everybody says the same thing, nobody can believe he would . . . Everybody's just heartbroken, Molly. We all just . . . cry when we meet. Oh, nothing is ever going to be the same again . . ."

I wondered if she had not heard what I'd said about working it out. And I remembered what Livvy Bowen had said, about couples feeling fearful and threatened when friends broke up, as if it were catching.

I hugged her harder and said into her hair, "You'll see. By Sea Island time, it'll all be behind us. Please stop crying, Carrie. You're going to look like a Cabbage Patch doll."

But the sobs strengthened, and I looked over at Charlie for help and read it in his miserable face.

"He's taking her to Sea Island, isn't he?" I whispered through stiff lips. Five of us couples who had been close at school had, for nearly twenty years, gone each summer to the Redwines' beach house at Sea Island for a four-day weekend. Tee and I, as hosts, had, of course, never missed it. I had only now thought of it.

"Molly," he mumbled, "there wasn't anything we could say to him. He called day before yesterday and said it was still on, and he'd rented the Drapers' house—I don't think his mama will let him use hers anymore—and he expected us all just the same as usual. Said if we still felt anything for him we'd come; he's having a bad time, too, you know. Nobody knows quite what to do; none of us want to go when she's there; it'll be just shitawful, but . . . well, this is Tee. He's my oldest friend, Molly. I can't just walk away from him. Of course, you know you'll always be our first love . . ."

I looked from his face down to Carrie's bent head.

"Carrie?" I said. "Are you really going?"

"Molly . . . I love Tee, too!" she wailed, and buried her head back into my shoulder.

I was still numb when they left, seeming to bolt from the house in sheer relief. I had wanted the comfort of my old friends' company, but now, I thought, I did not. What could I say to them? I could not again hold a sobbing friend so wrapped in her sorrow that mine could not penetrate. I could not again watch the new truths written in the averted faces of Tee's boyhood friends. I knew that I would not call any of them. I also thought that Charlie and Carrie's visit was sort of an official one, that they had served as emissaries for Tee's and my old crowd, and that I would not be hearing from many of them, either. At least until after the September house party. The thought of her, moving dark and eel-like on our wide, taupe beach, dancing with Tee to our old records, helping to boil the crabs at the traditional last-night beach bonfire—or could she even cook?—going into a cool, dark bedroom with Tee and closing the door at the end of the evening, laughing, a little drunk . . . I could not bear those images, and so I shut them away and went to bed early. This time I did not cry.

Ken Rawlings came next. He came two days later, at noon, on his way to a business meeting downtown. I was working in the patio garden and Lilly, thunderous and silent since she had come back to work and found her family in shards, directed him through the house and back to where I was attacking witch grass in the flower borders.

He was immaculate in summer-weight Coca-Cola navy blue; I was sweaty and dirt-smeared in torn shorts and the old Black Dog T-shirt. He sat gingerly on a wrought-iron lawn chair and I went on jerking weeds.

"I'm here to try again, baby," he said gravely. "I'm really worried about you. The company is, too. This . . . stonewalling is hurting everybody. I want to see you get the best possible deal out of this sorry mess, and so does Coke. You'd be surprised how many good friends you've got there. So I thought I'd see if you'd feel like talking some now. Believe me, it'll go better for you if you can manage it soon."

"Did the company send you, Ken?" I said, staring down into the tangle of dreadful, pale tendrils that were strangling my delphiniums. I could almost feel the airless gasping of throttled roots beneath the earth.

"No," he said. "They didn't. I came as the friend I am. But it's no secret that the company is worried about Tee as well as you. He's not in real good shape, won't be until things are settled between you."

"And . . . this Sheri person? Are they worried about her, too? Is she in bad shape? It would be a shame if two of your star players are out of the game," I said.

"They're worried about her, sure," he said neutrally. "She's a good lawyer, Molly, no matter what else you say about her."

I was silent, and then I said, my ears ringing with the words, "Ken, if I . . . if I should ever consent to a divorce or something . . . not to say that I will, but if I did . . . would you be my lawyer? I don't know any other lawyers, not as well as I do you . . ."

He was silent, too. Then he said, "I'll be handling things for Tee, Molly. I thought you realized that. I couldn't represent you, too, though I'd like to. But I can give you a very good referral—"

"So this is official, then, huh?" I said. I was beginning to get quite angry.

"I guess it is, yes," he said unwillingly. "But I'm
here because I love you, too. Believe me when I say
that you need to get on with this, for your sake even
more than for Tee's."

I stood up, dusting my hands on the rump of my
shorts. My knees cracked audibly.

"I appreciate your concern, Ken," I said. "But I
don't want any more solicitous little visits on my
behalf, and I don't want a referral. Divorce is not an
option."

He got up and turned to go, then looked back at
me. His face was grave with what looked to be real
worry, though with Ken you never knew.

"You don't want to underestimate this woman,
Molly," he said. "You really don't. I know I wouldn't."

"Well, I guess that's Tee's problem now, isn't it?"
I said, and he nodded and said good-bye and left. I
shoved the anger deep down where all the rest of it
simmered, and fell to battling witch grass again. By
late that afternoon I had gotten it all.

The next week, on a Wednesday, Charlotte
Redwine invited me to lunch at the Driving Club. She
had, she said, just gotten back from Italy the night
before, and she thought the first thing we should do
was sit down over a good lunch and talk this mess out.
I did not want to go; Charlotte and I have never had
much to say to each other, but I'd have to talk to her
sometime. Better to go on and get it over with.

I spent the night before trying to repair the gar-
dening damage to my nails and fiddling with my hair.
It was wild; there was nothing for it now but to call
Karl at the salon in the morning and see what he could

do with it. I hated the thought of that, too; all my friends went to Karl, and he would know as much as they did about Tee and me. Maybe I would try a new salon, a whole new look. But in the end I just telephoned the number that I could, now, dial in my sleep, and asked for an appointment.

"Come by at ten," Karl said. "I work you in. You going on to lunch? Good. We do something special for you."

I met Charlotte in the lobby of the club at twelve-thirty in a new linen shift from the Snappy Turtle—one of the few places left in Atlanta where you could get Old Atlanta clothes—and with an astonishing head of shining, jet black hair that swooped around my forehead and fell over one cheekbone, and felt silky and heavy as it swung against my neck and face. I didn't know yet if I liked the look of it, but I loved the feeling. I kept tossing my head just to feel that silken surge.

"Don't you look scrumptious?" Charlotte said, kissing my cheek and smiling her little cat's smile. She had colonized the choice umbrella table on the terrace by the pool, shaded by old trees and a wisteria vine. Her Tuscan tan made her teeth look very white, and her biscuit-colored shirtwaist fit her like her supple skin. Charlotte took exquisite care of herself. She always had. I must have been a sore trial to her at times.

It was very hot and still by the pool. Noon to one is reserved for adult swims only, and so no sleek, brown children splashed and shrieked their inevitable "Marco Polo." Only a lone swimmer cut the water lazily, swimming so skillfully that hardly a ripple broke the turquoise surface. I watched admiringly;

whoever it was had superb form. His dark head barely broke the water, nor did the pistonlike brown arms.

We ordered drinks from Carlton himself, the club's longtime maître d', as formal and beautiful as a carved ebony statue and as hallowed at the club as the old orientals and the original horse brasses in the men's grill. Carlton rarely served individual tables, but he hovered over us, nodding and smiling as if we were visiting royalty. I knew that he would have heard about Tee and me; Carlton knew everything. His attention, even though it was undoubtedly directed at Charlotte, warmed me. Our daiquiris—"Let's have something fun," Charlotte had said—were at our table in record time, and Carlton had added a single anemone to each, plucked from the huge summer bouquet in the foyer.

"For the Redwine ladies," he said and smiled, bowing himself away.

"Thank God for Carlton," Charlotte said, taking a deep swallow. "At least somebody still knows how to behave. Listen, darling, we're going to go over some things today that you need to hear, about the trust fund and a few of my little investments and this and that. I've made some changes, and I want you to know about them. But we're not going to talk about them until after lunch, and we're certainly not going to talk about Theron's behavior with that unspeakable little doxy until then. So drink your drink, and maybe we'll have another and I'll tell you about Italy, then we'll have something wonderful for lunch. I think we both deserve it, don't you?"

"We do indeed," I said, liking her more at that moment than I ever had. Charlotte had quite obviously never thought me suitable for her only son and heir, but the advent of the Eel Woman must have improved me considerably in her eyes.

We sat and sipped, chatting about her trip and looking about us at the flowered terrace. The tables were filling with the lunch crowd, most of whom she knew and some of whom I did, and for once I felt languid and lulled at the club, shaded by flowers and warmed in the sun of Charlotte Redwine's presence. They all had it, the Redwines, that almost palpable aura of rightness and immutability. Tee had his share, and his father had had his, but I thought it was Charlotte from whom the aura emanated. I waved and smiled at the people I knew, feeling as secure as a tender in the lee of a great ship.

Charlotte followed my eyes to the lone swimmer in the pool.

"He's very good, isn't he?" she said. "He swims like you used to. Or maybe you still do?"

"Some," I said. "I haven't much this summer. I need to get back to it."

And I realized then how much I had missed it, that rhythmic, dreamlike gliding, that suspension in an element as pure and simple as air. Missed the effortless pumping of the arms, the kick of the legs that started high in the hips, the slow, ritualized breathing when the head turned in the water . . .

The swimmer reached the end of the pool and pulled himself out with one smooth motion, and I saw that it was not a man after all, but a woman, long and slim and brown, with seal-dark wet hair plaited into a rope that was coiled around her small head. She wore a plain black tank suit cut high on her hips and to her waist in back, and for a moment, as she walked away from us toward an empty table at the edge of the patio,

I thought she was Caroline. And then I knew who she was. Charlotte saw my face and turned to look, and knew, too.

"That's her," she said in a small, brittle voice. "Isn't that her?"

"Yes," I said. The swimmer could, of course, have been anyone else at all, but I knew that she wasn't. I heard my breath whistling in my nostrils. It seemed very important not to look away from the woman in the black bathing suit, to take in that bright noon, the full and exact measure of her.

"How dare she come here?" Charlotte said in simple amazement. "Can she possibly not know this is a private club?"

I did not speak, because I could not. We watched as Sheri Scroggins held up a hand to Carlton, who was standing at the entrance to the patio, smiling benignly at his people taking their ease. He did not acknowledge her signal. No one had signaled to Carlton for service in decades.

Sheri's dark brows knit in annoyance. She snapped her fingers and called, "Waiter!" Heads turned all over the patio. Slowly and with immense dignity, Carlton moved to her table. She said something indistinguishable, studying a menu, not looking at him. He bowed slightly and turned and glided away; he might have been on wheels. Before the soft buzz of amazement and outrage could start, he was back with a frothy pink concoction thickly forested with fruit and flowers.

Sheri did look at him then.

"Did I say frozen? I did not. I said a plain daiquiri and that's what I meant. You can take this back right now and bring me another, and this time, get it right."

She did not raise her voice, but the flat twang reverberated around the quiet patio. I could hear indrawn breaths. Carlton's face went dead and still, and he turned and took the offending drink away. She went back to studying the menu, seemingly unaware of the hostility washing over her like surf.

"I will have her barred from this club," Charlotte said in a voice an octave higher than I had ever heard. "I will attend to it on the way out. This is outrageous. Carlton is one of us."

Despite my shock, I almost laughed. By now, I supposed, he almost was, and I wondered what that might mean to Carlton in his life outside the club, providing, of course, that he had one. Then the laughter died. Tee came on to the patio and walked over to Sheri's table, kissed her on the cheek, and sat down opposite her. His back was to us. I was glad, at least, for that.

His mother drew in her breath to speak, then let it out in a long, ragged sigh. I did not look around the patio, but I knew that a good fifty pairs of eyes were fixed, first on Tee and Sheri Scroggins, and then on Charlotte and me. Out of the corner of my eye I saw two figures, women, get up and drift languidly toward the ladies' lounge. The club phones, I figured, would be tied up until two o'clock.

The two of them leaned their heads together, one dark and one fair, over the menu, and all of a sudden I was looking at Tee and myself. Tee and me, when we were young and first in love and all things seemed possible. He looked, in the dappled shade, hardly older than he had then, his snub face lit by his slow smile. And she . . . she was, in her tallness, the width of her shoulders, the sleek, wet, dark hair, the flash of blue across the pool that was her eyes, the way she tipped her head to his . . . she was me. A much younger me, so full of vitality and the nearness of him that I hummed with it. Oh, her features were different . . . there was, somehow, a sort of Toltec cast to her face, a remote, sensuous, faintly cruel bluntness. But the surface resemblance was astonishing. No wonder Charlie had thought she was Caroline. Caroline looked remarkably like I had at that age. Now, of course, few people remarked on the similarity.

"She looks like me. Like I used to, I mean," I said stupidly, as if I were remarking on the weather.

"She looks nothing at all like you," Charlotte said. There were two hectic red spots on her cheeks, and she was breathing audibly. "She looks just like what she is, a South Georgia shantytown whore. Theron is out of his mind. I can put a stop to this, and I will. I imagine she thinks she's hooked herself a rich man; I can disabuse her of that, and him, too, with one phone call to our attorney. Which I shall make the instant I get home. Whatever happens, my dear, you and Teddy will never lack for anything. I promise you that. Are you finished? I think we've both had enough of this spectacle."

She rose, gathered up her little Chanel bag, and walked with her long, graceful, athlete's stride across the patio ahead of me, not looking to see if I followed. I did, of course. Followed blindly along in her wake with my chin held as high as I could manage, looking neither to the right or the left, conscious on every inch of me of eyes fastened on both of us like leeches. My heart was pounding so hard I could hear it. We had to pass their table to leave the patio. I thought I would die rather than do it.

I did not see him notice us, but I felt it.

"Mother," he said in a voice I did not know, a silly voice, high-pitched. "Molly . . ."

Sheri Scroggins was in front of us suddenly, barring our way. She looked like a panther who had just come out of a dark jungle river. The black suit was still damp, as was the lightless black hair, which was unplaited now and flowed over her shoulders like a cape. She smiled. She seemed to have too many teeth, all bone white in the tawny gold of her face. The eyes burned as blue as methane.

"We haven't met, but we should," she said, including Charlotte and me both in the smile. She held out her hand. I noticed that the fingers were blunt, spatulate, and the nails were bitten to the quick. I did not speak.

"You're right," Charlotte said in a voice like iced steel. "We haven't."

She walked unhurriedly around Sheri Scroggins, then paused and looked down at her son. He sat with his mouth open, simply looking at us. We might have been apparitions.

"I never thought I raised a fool, Theron," she said to Tee, and walked off the terrace and was swallowed by the huge old rose bushes, drooping with their fragrant cargo, that shielded the entrance. I could not move.

"Molly . . ." Sheri Scroggins said.

I looked at her, straight into her eyes.

"Mrs. Redwine," I said, and walked away after Charlotte.

Behind me I heard Tee call, "Molly. Mom . . ."

I shook my head without looking back. The myriad eyes seemed to leave smoking pits in the flesh of my back. I could still feel them when the attendant brought our cars around to where we waited, silent now, under the stone porte cochere.

"This will never happen to either one of us again," Charlotte said grimly as she got into her big blue Mercedes. The Redwines had a driver, but she hardly ever used him.

I smiled at her, surprised that I could make my mouth move, and got into my little Toyota wagon and drove home through the silent, snaking streets of Ansley Park, grateful for once that we lived there instead of Brookwood Hills or Buckhead. This trip took only minutes. I don't remember thinking anything at all during it.

Teddy was out when I got home, but Lazarus was there, thumping his tail from under the wrought-iron table on the patio, where he retreated in hot weather.

"Have you been out? Want to go for a walk?" I said to him, but he only thumped his tail harder and grinned at me, his tongue lolling out of his mouth and dripping. Lazarus was a sensible dog. He could not be lured out in midafternoon during a heat wave.

"Later," I said, and went up the stairs to the bedroom. My bedroom now. I closed the shutters against the hot, gray whiteness outside, took off my dress and shoes, and lay down on the bed.

I had thought perhaps that I might need to cry, or at least wrestle with feelings too powerful to permit yet. I waited. But I did not cry and I did not feel anything except the familiar sleepiness. Sleep tugged at me like an undertow, and finally I turned on my side and let myself slide down into it. It was thick and black and deep, and I don't know how long it would have held me under if the telephone had not waked me two hours later. By then the white heat was seeping out of the afternoon behind the shutters, and the idiot throbbing of the television from the downstairs library said that Teddy was home.

I fumbled with the receiver, dropped it, retrieved it, and finally put it to my ear.

"Hello," I said thickly. I sounded to my own ears as if I were drunk.

It was my mother's voice, round and full and carrying, trained. For some reason the sheer perfection of it irritated me almost beyond reason.

"Oh, I woke you, didn't I?" she said, and I thought I could hear the creamy smugness of one who never, under any circumstances, slept in the daytime.

"That's okay. What's up?" I sought to exorcize the treacly stupidity with briskness.

"I have a lovely plan," she caroled. It was the voice she had used when I was small and she wanted to motivate me to make some change in my imperfect self, to amend somehow the sheer unsuitableness that this large, square child was for a dancer, a feather, a curl of flame. The irritation mounted.

"And that is?" I said.

"That is a day of pampering just for us. Like I told you the other night at dinner. I have us an appointment at Noelle in the morning—hair, makeup, massage, nails, a salt scrub, whirlpool—and then you can take me to the club for lunch and we'll show off our fabulous new selves. And then I'm taking you shopping. To Neiman Marcus. No more of those little wrap skirt thingies. Real glamour clothes. Something you've never worn in your life. New shoes, too, with four-inch heels. And after that a little workout at Jeanne's. Don't worry. I'll do the beginner's with you this time.

Once you see how good you feel, you'll want to go on with it, I know . . ."

"Mother," I said. "Just once, do you think you could take me just like I am? Could you bear to have lunch with me without the makeover and the four-inch heels? Plain old me in a little wrap skirt thingy? Just once?"

"Well, you needn't get snippy with me," she said, injured or projecting injury, I was never sure which. "Of course I'll take you like you are. You're my daughter. Only . . . well, just like you are doesn't seem to have gotten you very far, does it? Oh, darling, I didn't mean it that way . . ."

"That's just what you meant," I said, irritation suddenly flaring into rage and past that into something else entirely, a kind of wildfire that swept everything inside me away and left only surging, boiling red.

"That's just what you meant and it's what you've always meant. I've never been good enough for you; too big, too awkward, too . . . too plodding, too *earthbound* . . ."

"Darling, not at all! Forget the spa stuff and the shopping, then; we'll just go sit on the patio at the club and talk, like we haven't done in ages. Wouldn't that be fun?"

"No!" I shouted. "It would not be fun! It would not be fun at all! I did that today, Mother, with Charlotte, and you'll never guess who else was there. Tee and his new lay. Tee and the famous other woman. Tee and his little brown whore, dripping wet and falling out of her bathing suit, playing kissy-face with my husband for all of Atlanta to see. No, it was not fun and it never will be again, because I am never setting foot there again as long as I live. So if you want to go to lunch with me, you're going to have to go somewhere where you don't know the waiters and they bring you a check. Like practically everybody else in the world does. I hate to tell you this, Mother, but you can kiss the Driving Club good-bye."

My mother's voice dropped into that low, thrilling timbre that she used when she played dark, tragic heroines or did serious public service television spots.

"You mean you're going to give up your own club, give up Teddy's very birthright, just for some little tramp who isn't going to last another six months? I thought better of you. I truly did, Molly."

"No you didn't," I said, my voice shaking with fury. Where did this endless boiling redness come from? I was afraid I could not stop it, and I did not really want to.

"No you didn't. You never thought better of me in my life. You aren't even thinking of me now, you're thinking of you, and how it's you who're going to have to give up hanging around the goddamned Driving Club. Do you have any idea how it felt today? To sit there and see a woman kissing your husband, a woman who could have been you, thirty years before? To sit there and feel like a damned Clydesdale and watch a . . . a fucking water nymph sitting where you should be sitting? No. I don't think you do."

I paused for a breath, and my mother was silent. Then she said, thoughtfully, as if she were giving the matter judicious consideration, "I really should have let you study dance when you were little. I see now that it was a mistake not to let you. Dancers don't go soft and thick and puddingy when they get older. They turn into greyhounds, not oxen."

Only someone who had known her intimately for all the scalding years that I had could have heard the cold, silvery desire to wound under her sorrowful words. The red rage exploded.

Through ringing ears I heard myself say, "No. Not greyhounds. They don't turn into greyhounds. Have you looked at yourself lately, Mother? Old dancers turn into hyenas. And you know what hyenas do, don't you? They eat their young."

There was a long silence, a kind of hollow rushing, over the wire, and then she hung up. She did not slam the phone down, but replaced it with infinite gentleness. I remember thinking very clearly, sometime soon I'm going to be terribly sorry I said that. But at that moment I felt only the need, urgent and smothering, to go back to sleep. The blinding redness had faded as if it had never been, and I felt emptied out and aching to be filled with simple oblivion.

I slept until nearly midnight, when the phone rang again, and when I answered it, it was my father, telling me that my mother had had a stroke or a seizure of some sort while she was working out at her makeshift barre in the spare bedroom, and had died in the ambulance on the way to Piedmont Hospital.

CHAPTER FOUR

IN THE DAYS AFTER MY MOTHER DIED, I had the same dream over and over: I was walking down a crowded city sidewalk washed in graying late-afternoon light, and I passed one of those sets of steps leading down to basement doors that you see so often in New York and London, though not, in my experience, in any other cities. But instead of a door leading to a shop or apartment, there was a kind of grating that gave way to a subterranean tunnel, like a subway tunnel, and there, looking out through the grating along with several other people, was my mother. In the dream I stopped, though no one else around me did. It was as if I alone saw the grated window and the tunnel.

My mother looked straight ahead, not sad, not happy, not angry, not alive, not dead. She had on one of her hats, I think the black one that she had worn the last time we had had dinner, at the Ritz-Carlton. She and the others looked as if they were waiting for something, perhaps a train to somewhere.

I bent down and said to her, "What are you doing down there?" She looked at me then, and though she did not smile, I thought that she regarded me with favor, or at least not with anger.

"We come here every afternoon at four to wait," she said.

I always woke up after that, my hair soaked with sweat, my heart pounding. It was a terrible dream, though I could not have told why. And indeed I did not, for I found that there was simply no one now to tell my dreams to.

Lying there in the damp, tangled bedclothes I would realize over and over again the first and realest loss that divorce brings with it. There is no longer anybody to tell your dreams to, not on the pulse of the moment, when they are most vivid and need most to be told. There is nobody to talk to about the most intimate and secret tendrils that curl through your mind, at least not at the time of their flowering. No one to laugh with, to show things to, to wish casual wishes with—not when those impulses are first born.

So the first great loss is immediacy, spontaneity. You can tell the dreams, voice the fears and longings, laugh the laughter, wish the wishes, of course, but it will be later, to someone deliberately chosen, at a remove, a considered sharing. There is no longer anyone there to be a mirror for you, so that you lose first a primal sense of yourself that has been a part of you for so long. Or, at least, I found that was so for me. Perhaps this is true of death, too, and long separations; I cannot speak to those yet. My mother had not been a mirror for me in many years. It was Tee who had listened in the nights, laughed, argued, received, given back. It was Tee who had been as there to me as I was to myself, and now he no longer was. For a long time I really hated him for that simple removal of his presence when I had something I needed to say.

I could not tell my dream to my father, who was

dumb and still and leaden with loss; I could not have added my anguish to the weight he bore. I could not tell Kevin, who came immediately with Sally, nearly wild with grief for his mother. He was furious with me and would not speak to me at all; I had blurted out to him the details of my last conversation with Mother, and for months, indeed almost a year after, he was adamant in his belief that I had killed her. My father flared at him when he first voiced that sentiment, the first and last sign of animation I saw in Daddy during the whole terrible time of mother's death and funeral, and after that Kevin blamed me only with his cold silence. Telling him of the dream or anything else was out of the question. I did not know pretty, one-surfaced Sally well enough, and never would, and I could not burden Teddy with the weight of the dream. He had not been especially close to his grandmother, but loss is loss, and Teddy had had enough of that recently. Caroline, still wounded, did not come home. So finally I told Livvy.

"What do you think it means?" I said on the afternoon before Mother's funeral, while she lay in her closed coffin in the dim, tribal splendor of Patterson's and received her last homage from her students and admirers. Livvy had come with sandwiches and a bottle of cold white wine, and we sat in her car in the parking lot while we ate and drank. Kevin was doing noon chatelain duty, and would not have welcomed my presence. I knew I had an hour or so free, and the dream was a burden I desperately needed to share.

"I think it means you've got a lot of unfinished business with your mother," Livvy said. "I think *you* think your mother can't go on to her rest or whatever until you've atoned in some way for, quote, killing her, unquote, or paid some kind of stupid penance. And I think you're nuts. Your mother said something really shitty to you and when you got mad and talked back to her, she went home like a spoiled little girl and danced herself to death. I think it's just like her, and I'm pissed off at her because she's left you drowning in guilt and gone off where you can't possibly follow and make it right. And I also think that your father knows that in his heart of hearts, and who the hell cares what Kevin thinks? He'd have found a way to blame you if you'd been on Uranus when she died."

As always, Livvy was a powerful anodyne, but I had the feeling that the relief was temporary. I knew that my mother wasn't going to let me walk away that easily.

"I think I see her all the time, too," I said. "In crowds. I was walking through Saks yesterday trying to find something black for the service and I saw her so clearly in the handbag department that I started toward her before I remembered. And I thought she was on the phone this morning. I mean, I know it was Carrie Davies, but it still sounded like Mother. I'm scared to death I'm going to see her with Daddy and react, and that would just about finish him off. He's said several times that he can't see her; that it would be so much better if he could just see her. I think he means in his mind, though. Not like I'm seeing her. I almost told her in Saks to go materialize to the one who needs her."

"I think all that's probably normal," Livvy said, licking mayonnaise off her fingers. "She's always been the most powerful person in your world, and all of a sudden she's not in it anymore. How can you not see her, and dream about her? What I wish you could do is dump the guilt. Maybe the Catholics have something; you can just go to confession and get some novenas to say, or whatever they do, and be done with it. What's it going to take for you?"

"I don't really feel guilty," I said. "How come you're so much smarter than me? Why, if we're such soul mates, do you know all this stuff and I don't?"

"Because you're the one in the middle of it," she said. "If it was me stewing in all this crap and you outside it, you'd see it, too. You know it as well as I do, you just can't get to it right now."

I laughed, a ragged, thin little laugh but a laugh nevertheless, and reached over and hugged her across the waxed paper and potato chips package.

"If I were a lesbian, I'd marry you," I said.

"If you were a lesbian, you'd be a lot better off right now," she said. "Now what can we do about this Oedipal guilt of yours? Wasn't it Oedipus who killed his mother or something?"

"He killed his father and married his mother," I said. "I guess matricide by daughter is so bad they don't even have a myth for it. You think I'm just talking, but I really don't feel guilty. Maybe I will later, but right now I don't. I feel terrible for Daddy, and I think I'm going to miss Mother an awful lot when I really take it in, but right now all I feel is tired to death and kind of stunned. And I can't stop thinking about Tee. I keep waiting for him to come make all this all right. Maybe it's that I can take in either infidelity or the death of my mother, but I can't handle both at one time. Nobody was meant to get it all at once like this."

"Are you kidding? That's what middle age is," Livvy said. "One loss after another. It's hell. Didn't anybody ever tell you? And by the way, speaking of the devil, have you heard from Tee since your mama died?"

"I called him that morning," I said. "I did it totally without thinking; I just dialed his office, and when Patty answered, I said, 'Sweetie, I need to talk to Tee right now,' as if nothing had happened. I didn't even identify myself. But she knows my voice, of course; I bet she nearly dropped her teeth."

"I bet she did," Livvy agreed. "So what did he say?"

"He wasn't there. He'd gone on some kind of department retreat or something down at Callaway Gardens. From the way Patty hemmed and hawed, I'd say the Eel Woman went with him, but I didn't ask."

Livvy started to laugh.

"Shit," she said. "Do you know where they've gone? They've gone to spend a weekend with that idiot on television who walks on fire, you know the one who's supposed to motivate people to tap their hidden powers and reach their impossible dreams? The department's got him down there teaching all the little Chi Phis to walk on fire. I told Caleb I'd build a fire of another kind entirely under him if he went. He wouldn't have, anyway. But you can bet Her Eeliness did. She's probably slithering over hot coals on her belly as we speak. Hope it fries her abs."

"Oh, God," I said, and began to laugh, helplessly, along with her. It struck me that for a woman who'd lost a husband and a mother in a matter of days, I was laughing entirely too much. But the alternative was crying, and I simply did not think I could do any more of that.

I was right. Whatever font the tears had flowed from dried up. I cried no more for my mother, or indeed for anyone or anything else, for a very long time. I sat through my mother's funeral between my father and my son, as dry-eyed as a wooden puppet, and probably resembled one. I found it hard to move my arms and legs and head, and stared at the rector of the little Episcopal church where my parents had gone for years, and where Tee and I had married, as if he alone could sustain life and breath in me. When the service was over, my muscles were sore.

I had not been in the church in a long time; Tee and I had always attended the larger and grander cathedral of St. Philip, in Buckhead, where his family had been communicants and benefactors for generations. I liked this little stone church. Its low, beamed ceilings felt enclosing and comforting, and its simple stained-glass windows, with reds and amethysts prevailing, made the interior seem awash in rosy light. Often, in the cathedral, I had the urge to look over my shoulder, to press myself into the ends of pews and the recesses of walls, to feel ridiculously as if I had come to church in my underwear, or forgotten my shoes. I often thought of *Murder in the Cathedral* when I entered. But on the day of my mother's funeral, I felt again the sense of protection and enclosure that little St. Margaret's had always given me, and was grateful to slide into it as if into sleep.

It was very crowded. My mother was, by that time, a local legend, often referred to as "a civic treasure." Three generations of Atlantans had seen her perform, or had studied with her, and it seemed to me that most of them were in the congregation that day. The story that she had died dancing had gotten out, and both the television and news media had picked up on it, closing their brief, sound-bitten eulogies with inanities such as, "True to form, she died dancing" and "Like the trouper she was, she died with her dancing shoes on." None, of course, mentioned that it could be termed a case of death by daughter. Only Kevin had done that, and he only once.

He sat on the other side of my father in the first row of pews and cried soundlessly for his mother, Sally sniffling beside him. Because he was a rising anchor in Washington and considered one of their own, the local media all ran at least one shot of Kevin, his clever, handsome face blurred with grief and his head bowed, coming out of the church. Behind him in one or two of the shots, I looked severe and forbidding in my new Saks black, almost Medea-like. The new haircut made me someone even I hardly recognized; it was like looking at an actress impersonating me. I had my head tipped forward so that the smooth wings of hair obscured my face, but you could still tell that it was immobile, frozen. In contrast, Kevin looked vulnerable and very human, infinitely appealing. The brief television clips looked subtly wrong, skewed; it should have been I who wept for my mother, Kevin who was stalwart. Atlanta was still the Deep South, however far in spirit we believed we had left it behind. In the traditional South, women wept and men forbore.

It was a morning funeral, for the day was very hot, and Arlington Cemetery, where Mother and Daddy had their plots, broiled gently under the punishing fist of the sun. There were few family members, for the Bells did not have much family, but many others came: old friends from Peachtree Hills, friends of mine and Tee's, Daddy's lodge members, many fans of my mother. At the edge of the circle, aloof and regal in white linen that somehow looked more correct than the surrounding sea of black, Charlotte Redwine stood. I had not seen her at the church, nor at Patterson's in the days before, but she had sent a basket of delicacies and wine from her favored caterer, and an armful of flowers from her garden, to the house via Marcus, her driver, and had enclosed a note to me pledging her continuing support.

"Your darling mother, I always so admired her style and spirit," she wrote. "You must, if you can, think of me as your mother now."

She did not mention Tee. He was not at the church, nor at the cemetery. It would have been appalling taste if he had been, I suppose, but the only loss I truly felt on that hot, numbed day was that of Tee's tall body by my side. That side felt naked.

Everyone told me later what a lovely funeral and a somehow joyous graveside ceremony it was, and almost everyone mentioned the ducks. Arlington is full of little lakes and ponds, and over the years people have relocated their Easter ducklings there, so that nowadays the background accompaniment to any interment is a raucous, peevish honking. Canadian geese on their way north or south stop off to join the remittance ducks, too, and sometimes the minister or whoever is handling the interment is forced to stop and wait until a particular gaggle of ducks and geese works out a honking dispute. Everyone always smiles and looks at each other, as if to say, "Life goes on, after all. Wouldn't he/she have loved it?" The ducks added a rowdy carnival note to the going out of my mother, and it seemed to please everyone but Kevin. He glared, as if he would like to wring sixty-odd necks. For my part, I struggled so hard with the illicit, unseemly laughter that my face was red and sweating when finally we left the undertakers to their task and walked with my father back up the hill to the car. Even Daddy smiled.

"Gave her a real five-star sendoff, didn't they?" he whispered to me.

I came as close to weeping then as I ever would for my mother, except in a time and place still far distant.

We went back to my house, where Lilly and the caterers were putting the finishing touches on the tasteful little buffet lunch for family and friends that custom here dictates. Daddy had asked me to host it; he said that he could no more imagine having my mother's final festivities in the cramped condo than he could have downtown in Centennial Park. The right place would have been the old house in Peachtree Hills, where what he calls our real life was largely conducted, but that was impossible, of course. A computer salesman and his family lived there now. So I agreed, and bestirred myself with Lilly to put the house to rights and polish silver and order flowers and drag the old ivory damask that had been Tee's grandmother's out of the cedar chest. It was not lost on me that if my mother had not died, my house very well might soon have slept indefinitely beneath a coverlet of dust and lightlessness.

"It looks real pretty, baby," Daddy said when we came in from the searing brightness of the day. "Your mother would like this very much."

And it did look pretty, but I somehow doubted that my mother would have liked it at all. All told, I thought she might well have preferred Centennial Park, thronged with the thousands of people who had admired and applauded her over the years.

I am always surprised by how much I enjoy after-funeral affairs. There is sorrow, of course, the degree depending on how large a displacement the deceased will leave in the air of the various worlds represented at the feast, but it is seemly sorrow, and serves to leaven the yeasts of both hilarity and malice. There will be laughter, but it will be the laughter of loving recollection. There may be tears, but they will be the gentle tears of nostalgia and fondness. No one will vilify the absent honoree or any of the present mourners. Maybe later, after the guests have gone on to wherever they go after consuming the funeral meats, but not in the very house of mourning itself. Everyone knows everyone else almost by definition, and they are all on their best behavior, which is seldom the case when the group gathers elsewhere. There are hugs, cheek and lip kisses, comradely back claps and biceps punches, compliments and confidences.

Carrie Davies once said wistfully, at the funeral of the first of our group to die, that none of us had behaved this sweetly toward each other since the Chi Phi formal our senior year. She was right. I enjoyed my mother's funeral so much that I forgot for long stretches of time why we were gathered, and when I remembered, it seemed simply absurd that the gathering was about her death.

Her life, though, that was another matter. She was fully as present as any one of us: The talk was all of her, and her place in each of our firmaments. She might have been out in the kitchen. Surely in a moment she would sweep into the room in one of her absurd hats and kiss cheeks and pat sleeves, and her laugh would tinkle into the waiting air, and life would swirl on around her as it always had. I have

never felt, before or since, quite the perfect, uncompli-
cated tenderness that I felt for my mother on the day
that we buried her.

No one spoke of Tee, or the affair, or what I would
be doing next, or what he would. They would the
minute they were out the door, I believe, but not here,
not on this day. Tee was, for the first time in his life,
not a part of one of our gatherings. Wine and Bloody
Marys flowed without his making them, shrimp salad
and cheese biscuits and strawberries were eaten without his sharing them, toasts were made to which he
did not raise his glass. It was, I suppose, my first party
on my own in this house, and thanks to my mother, it
was a roaring success. Tee should have been by my
side; of course he should have. But his absence left no
bruises. I was surprised at the grace of my solo effort.

Even my father felt its benison. He had a rare-for-
him Bloody Mary, and smiled often and genuinely at
his and Mother's last mutual guests, and once or twice
I heard him laugh aloud. It did not seem strange. This
final postgame party was a time and place unto itself.
Only later does the real world resume itself. Then was
when I would worry about my father. Then was the
time in his life that would, if anything could, simply
defeat him. I smiled at him and laughed with him and
resolutely refused to think of what might happen to
him when we closed the door on our last guests. It did
not even occur to me to wonder what might happen
to me.

In the end, though, Tee did come to Mother's bon
voyage party. Just as the afternoon shadows were
falling across the patio and the first guests were making
noises about leaving, the doorbell rang and Kevin went
to answer it. He came back into the living room holding

an arrangement of blood-red roses so massive that only the top of his head showed over them, only the blue of his eyes glinted through them. Kevin was all pigeon-blood velvet from his waist to his crown. His arms could hardly contain the roses. There must, I thought, have been a hundred of them. All of them were perfect, breath-stopping, rococo. My first thought was that they must have cost almost as much as the party had. My second was that they were the most ostentatious things I had ever seen. I could tell by the little gasping rush of breath that swept around the room that everyone else thought so, too. Everyone present at my mother's funeral reception would talk for years about this most stunningly inappropriate of floral offerings.

My mother, I thought, would have adored them.

"Well, my goodness, who on earth?" Sally chirped, breaking the silence.

"Good lord," my father said.

"Florist's delivery," Kevin muttered from behind the juggernaut of roses. "One I didn't know."

I walked over and took the envelope that trembled, like a butterfly, on the topmost petal. It was creamy, heavy stock, and addressed to Daddy, Kevin, and me. I opened it.

"Our deepest sympathy and love," the card read.

It was signed, "Tee and Sheri." The handwriting was strong and black and slashing, not Tee's.

"Another emerging nation heard from," I said, and handed the roses to Sally and walked into the kitchen, my cheeks and chest flaming. Behind me the silence spun out. It was a full minute before the low rush of talk started.

I was in the kitchen splashing water on my face when Livvy came in.

"Christ, I thought she was the one raised in a barn," she said incredulously. "What, did somebody punch a hole in him and all his taste and manners ran out? I never saw such a vulgar bunch of flowers in my life, and I never, ever in my life heard of a guy and his mistress sending flowers to his not-even-ex-wife. They'll be lucky if Coke doesn't send them both to Edie Summers."

Edie Summers was a fiftyish, perennial debutante who taught manners and social graces to the spawn of the big houses of Buckhead. Tee had once, he had said, had an aching adolescent crush on her when he was a freshman at Westminster and she was a senior. She had since been transmogrified into such a porcelain paragon of seemliness and perfection that there seemed nothing left for her, after her banker husband died appropriately on the tennis court at the Driving Club fifteen years before, but to open a small, perfect academy dedicated to varnishing the children of her classmates with her patina. Their parents paid dearly for it, and Edie prospered, and there were few Buckhead teens who left for college who did not know how to comport themselves.

The comporting itself was another matter entirely. Tee and Charlie used to say that the wildest kids who went through Chi Phi rush all over the South were Edie's kids. I spluttered into my cupped hands at the thought of Tee and the Eel Woman in Edie's implacable clutches, and bent at the waist, laughing. Livvy laughed with me.

When we had stopped, I said, "Poor Daddy. What a stupid, awful thing for him to have to cope with. Tee ought to be shot; he ought to know better. What did Dad do with them? I ought to be ashamed of myself for running out like that."

"He didn't have to cope with them," she said. "I took them away from Sally and stuffed them in the downstairs john and locked the door. You can throw them out or send them to Piedmont or whatever after the party. I personally would take them over to Coke marketing and insert them, thorns and all, up Tee's ass, one by one, but that's up to you. Caleb got your dad another Bloody Mary and he and Charlie Davies took him out on the patio and asked him about wiring lamps. Everybody's stopped buzzing and is gearing up to leave. The great flower hoo-ha *est fini*. Crisis management is my specialty. You may kiss my ring."

And sure enough, by the time the last guest had gone and Daddy and Kevin and Sally and Teddy and I had plopped ourselves down in exhaustion on the cooling patio, Tee and his terrible roses and his awful paramour had been tucked away somewhere in our collective tribal subconscious, to be given their indignant due when we could get to them. This was it now, the time I had been dreading for days, the hour when, for all of us, but most especially for my father, the real world rocketed back into motion and the real anguish must begin.

We did not speak at first, only looked around at each other, and I had a swift, panicky moment of thinking that I honestly could not bear the pain Dad must feel. I knew by then that for myself, I could bear it with an ease that was rather appalling. I had, somehow, during the funeral and the gathering that followed, buried my mother as deeply in my own center as we had in the earth of Arlington Cemetery. Later, I thought; later, when the time is right and I can do it properly, I can think about her. There's plenty of time. This time right now is for Daddy.

Finally Dad said, "I thought it went real well, didn't you-all? I'm always surprised at how many people have seen her plays and concerts. The church was SRO. And this was nice, Molly, this little to-do this afternoon. Good food. And all those young people . . . your friends, I guess, and Kevin's. It was nice of them to come . . ."

His voice trailed off and he looked vacantly into space, his hands folded over the small melon of his stomach as if he were waiting to be called for dinner, or for the rest of his life. I thought of the awful subway dream and closed my eyes for a moment. When I opened them, he was still looking patiently into nowhere.

"It was a really pretty party, Molly," Sally said, and then winced. "Or reception, I guess. Very easy and elegant, nothing too stiff or formal. Mama Bell would have liked it."

Mama Bell wouldn't have liked it a bit more than she liked the plain little church or the loudmouthed ducks who had stolen her thunder, I thought in my new, becalmed clarity. She'd have held out for the Driving Club or nothing.

Aloud I said, "Thank you, Sally. I couldn't have done it without you. And you too, Kev. Of course."

"Of course," Kevin said. His voice was a husky rasp. Of us all, Kevin seemed the only one whose emotions were properly anchored to reality. He had lost the love of his life and he was bereft and angry. Angry mostly at me.

Another little silence spun out, and into it Teddy said, "I think I'll go make myself a sandwich, Ma. Can I fix one for anybody else?"

"There's a ton of stuff left," I said. "Didn't you get any?"

"I had peanut butter and jelly in mind," he said, and Dad and I smiled at each other. It was an instinctive smile, our old one.

"I'll see you before you go, Grampa," Teddy said, and dropped a kiss on top of my father's head as naturally as if he had done it every day for years. But Teddy had not kissed anyone in his own family since he'd turned ten. My heart squeezed with love for him.

We were drifting toward silence again. Into it I heard my own voice saying, in the tone I am told I use in my various committee meetings, "Well, I guess we need to make a few plans. Kevin, I know you and Sally will be going on back in the morning, and Teddy's getting ready for his trip west. What about you, Dad? Have you thought what you might like to do in the next few days?"

My father did not answer, only studied middle air, and Kevin and Sally looked at me in disbelief, as if I had farted loudly in some solemn, sacred ceremony. I blushed furiously. I sounded officious and insensitive and horrible even to my own ears, and could not imagine where the fluting words had come from, except that I felt a need, as strong as anything I have ever experienced, to get everyone and everything in some sort of order.

"Sorry," I whispered miserably to my father, but the need remained, pulsing like an abscessed tooth.

"Don't be, baby," he said presently, heavily and without inflection. "You're right. We do need to make some plans. Life isn't going to stop for us."

Except that, of course, for him it had.

"Come to us," Kevin said. He said it firmly and strongly, in his anchor voice. He did not often use it off the air. It always surprised me when he did, that this authority lived in Kevin.

Dad looked at him, one eyebrow raised.

"I mean it," Kevin said. "Come stay with us for a while. We'd love that, wouldn't we, Sal? You never have, not for any length of time. Mother never liked Washington. Come stay for a few weeks and get to know my world, my town. I'll take some time off, and we'll go to the National Press Club, and the White House press room, and I'll introduce you to some of the big enchiladas—Brokaw, Jennings—and we'll go down to the Eastern Shore and do some fishing, and go to the galleries and restaurants—"

"Oh, come, Daddy Bell," Sally cried. "I redecorated the guest room just for you and . . . for you. The drapes have ducks on them. Mandy would be so excited . . ."

Mandy was Kevin and Sally's eleven-year-old daughter. I did not think she had ever been excited about anything except horses.

"Just like Molly at that age," Mother used to say. "All arms and legs and feet and shoulders. Except, of course, with Molly it was swimming, not horses."

Poor Mandy. Damned by her dominant genes.

"It would be nice to spend some time with Mandy," Daddy said dutifully, but I did not think he was even aware of what he said. He seemed to me much as he always had, loose-jointed and laconic and sweet-tempered, except that there did not, now, seem to be any core to him. I thought that if the rest of us got up and left the patio, he would simply sit there until someone came to fetch him and tell him what to do. I was right, I was not going to be able to bear this . . .

"Then you'll come?" Kevin said.

"It's something to think about," Daddy said.

"No!" I cried. Again, Kevin and Sally looked at me in disapproving alarm. Daddy continued to study air.

"I mean, not right now; he needs to be here. There are all these things to be done, and then he needs time to take it in. He needs to be where he's always been; he needs quiet and familiarity to sort it all out. I'm going to help. We can be at the condo in the daytime, and at night he can come to me . . ."

I ran out of steam. The words had been a near frantic tumble. My father did look at me then.

"You've got too much on you right now, baby," he said. "I appreciate it, but I'm not going to drape myself all over you like a sack of salt. I'll holler if I think I need any help."

"No, it's only logical," I persisted. "You don't even like that stuffy little condo and I've got this whole big house, and besides, it's my job. It's what we do, us women . . ."

I smiled to let him know I was half-joking, but I could tell he saw through it.

"What's what you do?" he said mildly. I knew that he really saw me now, perhaps for the first time that day.

"Look after people," I said lamely.

Daddy sighed and looked at us, Kevin and me, before he spoke.

"What I need now is to be by myself," he said mildly. "To be alone with your mother. We haven't said good-bye, and I need to do that. She just looked at me in the ambulance; she never did say anything. I didn't either, that I can remember. We just . . . looked. She had this intent, sort of preoccupied look on her face, in her eyes, and then her face changed . . . and she died. But we never said anything to one another. That's what I've got to do next."

I felt my eyes fill, but it was Kevin who spoke. "When . . . when her face changed . . . did she look afraid?" he asked. I could scarcely hear him.

"No," Daddy said. "She looked surprised. I appreciate your asking, both of you, but I need to stick around the house until I can see her clearly again, till I can see her like she was and not like at the last . . ."

"But then you'll come," I said stubbornly. "Won't you? And we can start doing all the stuff you'll need to do. Or I could come to your house . . ."

He drew a deep breath and let it out slowly. He smiled a little.

"No. Then I'm going fishing. I'm going with Harry Florian. We've been talking about spending a couple of weeks at Homosassa for years. Now I reckon we'll do it. And then I'm going to sell that cussed condo and find another place. That's the first thing I'm going to do when I get back."

"Well, I can help there, at least," I said. "There are all kinds of nice little places around midtown, full of charm and individuality, most of them not too pricey, and they're all close to us . . ."

"Close to who?" my father said cautiously.

"Well, you know . . . to us."

"There's not any you," Kevin drawled. "Were you perhaps forgetting? What 'us' were you referring to?"

Abruptly the killing, red fury surged back, crashing down over me like a great wave. I felt myself lifted on it; I surfed on its curl. I rode it higher and higher. And, abruptly, then I pushed it down. That red wave had already taken my mother.

"I don't want to hear any more of that kind of talk," my father said to Kevin. It was nearly his old voice, out of my childhood. He looked at me with love and, I thought, a kind of weary pity.

"I'm tired of the city, Molly," he said. "I think my time in the city is just about over. The city was your mother's place. The country's mine. I thought I might look for a little place up around Jasper, or maybe even down in Lowndes County. Around home. I've still got some good friends there. I could have a garden, and a real workshop. And I wouldn't be more than a few hours away from here . . ."

His voice cracked, and I knew he meant away from the raw new mound on the shady, duck-haunted hill at Arlington.

"What would I do then?" I said desolately. "Who would I have then who's left of my family?"

"Honey, you have to start now making a life for yourself," Daddy said, as if Kevin and Sally were not on the patio with us. "And you have to make it by yourself. It can't be built around Teddy or me. Neither one of us is going to be with you that much longer. Besides that, I just can't . . . take the weight right now. And Teddy shouldn't have to."

"Then what can I do for you?"

It was a cry out of the innermost part of me, where the child he had loved and lifted up still lived.

"Well, you can come take care of her clothes, if you want to do something for me," he said, smiling a little. "I thought I could do that, but it turns out I can't seem to."

"I will," I said. "I'll start on it in the morning."

*   *   *

But I couldn't, either. I got up the next morning so freighted with heaviness and darkness that I could scarcely breathe; I thought I was actually sickening with some sort of virus. After breakfast I threw up, something I do so rarely that the very throat and stomach muscles involved felt alien, and I realized that I could not sort through my mother's clothes, could not touch and finger and fold away her spare little dresses and sweaters, could not handle her hats. They would smell of her and her smell would cling to me; they would swarm with memories, like bacteria. The bacilli of love and rage and hurt that they harbored would paralyze me. I rinsed out my mouth and called Carrie Davies, who had said she would do anything, anything at all that I needed. I got her answering machine.

I called Livvy.

We met at my parents' condominium. My father was not there. He had, he'd said on the phone that morning, some things he needed to pick up around town, and then he was going to lunch with Harry and a couple of his other fishing and football cronies. I knew he would be collecting things of Mother's that she had left in the various dressing rooms or offices of the theaters and auditoriums where she had acted and danced.

"If it's too hard, I can do that," I said. "But I'm glad you're going to see people. It's the way, isn't it? Just start right in? I hope it helps, Daddy."

"No, I want to do it," he said. "And I don't know if it's the way or not. Is there a way? I don't think it's going to help much, baby, but you can't sit down and die, too, can you?"

Why not? I thought suddenly.

"Of course not," I said.

So Livvy and I went into the orderly, banal rooms

where my parents had lived the latter part of their lives together, and into the bedroom that my mother had used, and into her closet, and I watched as Livvy methodically folded away her things into the plastic leaf bags I had brought. Afterward we would take them to the Salvation Army. It was not so hard after all, not if I did not have to touch her clothing. I could watch. I could do that.

"Isn't there anything you want?" Livvy said as we got ready to carry the bags to my car. "Some of her things are lovely, and they're in perfect condition. You'll be sorry later if you don't keep something."

"No. Nothing would fit me. And her handbags and accessories would just look silly. They're for little people. They'd look like toys on me."

"Keep this," Livvy said. "You'll regret it terribly if you don't keep something, so keep this. It would make a terrific sun hat if you took the flower off."

She tossed the black hat my mother had worn to our last dinner, at the Ritz-Carlton, on to the bed, and I smiled in spite of myself. Livvy was right. I found that I did want it, after all. My mother would indeed follow into the rest of my life in the warp and weave of her big black hat.

"You know," she said as we trudged out with our bags, "you and that hat should just get on a plane and come up to the Vineyard in a month or so. I'm going up by myself then; Caleb isn't coming till much later. We'd have all that time together, with no obligation and no pressures, just you and me and the beach and the ocean."

"I can't be social now, Livvy," I said. I knew that she and Caleb knew half the summer population of Martha's Vineyard.

"We won't be," she said. "I don't want to, either.

You'd be a great excuse. You know, you've never really been anywhere on your own, without Tee and or the children along. You ought to see how it feels. You might end up liking it very much."

"Next year, maybe . . ."

"Why 'next'?" I saw that she was going to push it. "Why, exactly?"

"Well, Teddy and school and all . . ."

She just shook her head impatiently, but she did not say anything else.

My father left two days later for Lake Homosassa with Harry and Martin Short and Philip Hines. I had been spending a good part of each day with Daddy, though he had not asked me to, and I got up very early and went over to say good-bye on the morning that they left. In the hot, colorless dawn he looked much thinner and older, and so ill and bruised that I had the sudden, panicky feeling that he would not be coming back to me. I hugged him fiercely.

"Please call me every day," I said into the shoulder that, as it always had, smelled of starch and laundry powder, clean and acid.

"I'm going to be out on the lake most days," he said. "How about once every two or three days?"

"Daddy . . . what if I need you?"

"What if you don't?" he said, and hugged me hard. I didn't say any more, and they drove away, and I stood staring in the driveway until Harry's old wagon vanished around a long curve of Peachtree Road. Then I went home and sat down on the patio and drank a cup of coffee. Teddy was spending the night at T. J. Campbell's house.

"I don't know where my folks are," I said aloud into the brightening day. Nothing in the still air responded.

In the following weeks I fussed over Teddy until he became distant and sullen with me, and after we had an out-and-out fight, ugly and flaming with accrued pain, I realized what I was doing and called Caroline and Alan and arranged for the visit that they had said they wanted. Caroline sounded distracted and dull; of course I must come immediately, she said, they'd been waiting for me to decide when. But she did not sound glad. She did not sound any way at all. The pretty lilt that had always lived in Caroline's voice, that always seemed to me so essentially Southern, was gone. Anger at Tee flared afresh, for the dying of his daughter's lilting voice.

From Tee, back from his fire-walking, I heard nothing. There were no more calls from Sheri Scroggins, either. The whole world seemed caught in a bubble of hot, stale timelessness. I was glad, finally, to board the plane that took me out of my own summer miasma and into that of Memphis.

But it was not a good visit, and I cut it short by two days. Caroline was so faded and snappish that she seemed someone I hardly knew; there was literally nothing left of the flush of easy vivacity about her that had always reminded me so of Tee. Alan was distracted and silent; he often stayed late at his office, apologizing and talking of a landmark case being readied for court. The baby slept, cried, and slept. Caroline had a cleaning woman and an afternoon sitter for the baby, and we did indeed go to lunch and shopping and around to see the sights of Memphis, but the heat and humidity were stupendous, and we did not talk much about anything of substance. Every time I ventured into her life, or spoke of mine without her father, her eyes filled with tears and she cut me off sharply and shrilly. She did not say so but I knew that she was still angry with me for not, somehow, preventing Tee from leaving her, and I knew that if I stayed much longer, the childish hurt I felt at her accusatory pain would turn to anger, and I would widen and harden the gulf between us that was, I hoped, still temporary. So on the third day of my visit, when the baby developed one of the indistinguishable thin, mewling, summer colics that the children of the South are heir to, I simply went home. Caroline wept and hugged me and promised a long Christmas visit and did not protest my leaving. I felt nothing on the trip home but fatigue and relief.

When I got out of the cab and went into the house in Ansley Park, the front door was unlocked and I heard voices on the patio. I had not expected Teddy home from Eddie's parents' summer place in Highlands until the weekend, and my heart lifted. I was finding that among the myriad small deaths surrounding this separation, one of the worst was coming home at twilight to an empty house. The thought of hugging my son and Lazarus made me as giddy as a sudden whiff of pure oxygen.

"Guess who's coming to dinner?" I called out, and ran through the dark library and out on to the sunny patio.

Instead of Teddy and Lazarus, it was Tee, who looked blankly up at me from the chaise. Sheri Scroggins, in shorts and a tank top, sat at his feet. Both were frozen in place, sweating tall glasses in hand. Both stared at me as if I were trailing tattered grave accouterments.

I felt that patio wheel around me. It was like walking into the wrong house. Tee's long body owned this patio. I had seen it stretched out there on the chaise countless times. I almost expected to see my own face on the body of the woman who sat at his feet.

"Molly—" Tee began. My heart lurched at the sound of his slow, deep voice saying my name.

"I want you to go now," I said. I sounded in my own ears like a prissy little girl mouthing words her mother had taught her.

Sheri stood up. Her body was splendid; it did not look real in the slanting afternoon light. It simply had no imperfections. She made a smile, which did not reach her eyes, of her long red mouth. After the first glance, I did not look at her.

"You had no right to come into my house when I was gone," I said to Tee. "I want you to leave, and I don't want you to come back again . . ."

But my heart shook with my wanting him to stay. It was Sheri who answered me.

"It's his house, too, Molly," she said in the grating twang that I had come to loathe. "In fact, it's solely his house, I believe. Your name is not on the deed."

I still did not look at her.

"Why are you here?" I asked my husband.

"I wanted to see it," Sheri said again. "I wanted to see Tee's house. There was no reason for me not to. We'd have called before we came, of course, but we didn't know you'd be here. Tee's been having some ideas about it, haven't you, Teeter?"

She smiled down at him around the dreadful nickname.

Tee still did not speak. He just looked at me.

"Cat got your tongue?" I said. I knew I sounded bitchy. I could think of no right way to talk to this man who was and yet was not my husband. I wished that they would just vanish, and I could go upstairs and go to sleep.

"I've been thinking that it might be a good idea if I bought the house from you, Molly," he said finally. He looked at Sheri, not at me, and I knew whose good idea it was. This woman had come with my husband into our home, and seen it, and wanted it for herself.

"The house is not for sale," I said.

"That's really not your decision to make, is it?" Sheri Scroggins said.

"Shut up," I said to her, and to Tee, "You want my house, too?"

He looked at me then. There was something new in his eyes, a kind of edge, a thin hardness like lacquer.

"I'm prepared to make you an extremely generous offer for it," he said.

My throat thickened until I could scarcely push words past it.

"You said . . . you said it would be mine always," I said. "You *said* that. You said it the first night, when you told me about all this. You said anything I wanted or needed. I assumed you meant the place we live, the place the family lives . . ."

He looked away, and I could no longer see the new hardness.

"You assume a lot, Molly," he said in a low voice.

"When did I get to be the enemy, Tee?" I said.

He looked down at the bricks of the patio. I did, too. I thought of the autumn weekend we had laid them, he and I, an October long ago, with Teddy helping resignedly and Lazarus tracking wet grouting in and out on his big paws.

"Don't, Molly . . ." Tee said.

"You don't need this big house, Molly," Sheri

Scroggins said. She spoke soothingly, as you would to a child or a demented person. "Why would you want it? A big old white elephant . . . with what we're prepared to give you, you could get yourself the most fabulous condo in Atlanta, or another, smaller house . . . anything you wanted. But we all need to be sensible now, and get down to talking about specifics. We've let this go on too long as it is. Can't you see the sense in letting Tee have it?"

"No, I cannot see the sense in it, because this is my fucking home, you idiot," I shouted at her. Her face went still and narrow.

"My life is here," I said into the fox-sharp face. "My memories are here. My history is not disposable, and if it was, it would not be to you. Do you understand me?"

She was silent, then she shrugged.

"I wouldn't be so sure of that if I were you," she said.

"Sheri," Tee said.

"No!" Her nasal voice cracked like a lash in the still, thick air. "I'm tired of placating her! I'm sick of soothing, and indulging, and waiting for her to be reasonable about all this! *I'm running out of time, Tee!*"

She turned and stormed off the patio. Her butt did not jiggle in the short, tight pants, I noticed. At the door she turned.

"You make her understand that," she said, and vanished.

I just stared at Tee. He looked back. Presently he shrugged, a tiny movement.

"You look pretty, Molly," he said. "I like your hair that way."

I turned away and stood looking over the ivy-carpeted wall at the skyscrapers of midtown. We had often stood here just so, he and I, looking at them; we were suburban enough so that their proximity still charmed and thrilled us.

"Get out of here, Tee," I said.

He went without saying anything else. In a few moments I heard the front door shut.

Teddy and Lazarus came home around dusk. I was still sitting on the patio. With his newly developed antennae for trouble, Teddy knew at once that something was wrong. I told him about finding his father and Sheri Scroggins on the patio when I got home from Memphis.

I thought that he would be outraged, but he was not surprised. My mind made one of those in-the-air connections it seems to make when pain and crisis have sharpened it.

"They've been here before, haven't they? When I've been away? Did you tell them when the coast was clear?"

It wasn't fair, but I was past that.

"They've only been here once," he said, sitting on his spine and regarding his long legs stretched out before him. Tee sat that way often. "That I know of, anyway. I didn't tell them anything. It was the afternoon you left for Caroline's. I don't know how they knew you were gone."

"And you just let them in."

He lifted his head and stared at me. There was a too-old weariness on his face.

"He holds the deed, Ma. He can come in whenever he wants to, and bring whoever he wants to," he said.

"And you were here the whole time?"

"Yep."

"With her."

"I don't even think about her."

"This is *our* house, Teddy," I said, foolish tears starting in my eyes. I struggled to keep my voice steady. "This is *our* home. This is the family place."

Suddenly he was on his feet, shouting.

"I miss him, Ma, okay? I love him and I miss him. I can't . . . just because you . . . Ma, *listen*—"

"Teddy—"

"No. Listen. Go on and do it, Ma. Just go on and do it. This way . . . it's just . . . it's not going to change anything, and I can't stand it any longer! Give him the goddamned divorce and let's get us some lives! I can't look after you anymore, Ma!"

I could not get a deep breath.

"Of course you can't," I whispered finally. "I wouldn't want you to. I've never wanted you to do that. I mean, your trip, school . . . I *want* you to do those things. You know I do, don't you?"

He scrubbed his fists angrily in his eyes.

"Ma, how can I do those things until I know you're able to . . . get on with things? That you're looking at some kind of life ahead of you? Dad isn't coming home, you know that. Don't you know that? I've tried to be around as much as I could, until maybe you do know it, but, Ma . . . I can't take his place."

"Oh, God, baby, I *never* wanted you to do that," I said in pain.

He just looked at me.

The next morning I called Livvy and got the name of the lawyer from her, the one she had said could make mincemeat of Ken Rawlings. I called and made an appointment. And then I called her back.

"Were you serious about having a guest at the beach?"

"Is the pope a Catholic?"

One month later, almost to the hour, I huddled in a bucketing seat behind a seemingly teenaged pilot on a seemingly toy Cape Air commuter plane out of Boston, peering through the open curtain over his shoulder into a wall of solid, swirling, white fog. In my cold hands I clutched my mother's big black hat. Behind me a dozen or so other passengers read or napped or fussed over children; no one but I seemed convinced that death was imminent. Just behind me two whining children accompanied by a grim-faced man unwrapped a ribbon-tied box of Godiva chocolates and began to demolish them.

"Fine," the man said. "I'll just tell Mrs. Michaels that you ate up her hostess gift."

Divorced daddy, I thought through my terror, glad to be distracted from it. "Got the kids for a week's vacation and wishes he didn't. I don't know who I pity the most."

The plane gave a great, wallowing lurch, and I stifled a small scream, and shut my eyes, and when I opened them the fog was parting and I could see, far below, the lights of a tiny runway winking steadily. The plane banked sharply and plunged toward them.

"Spencer Tracy and Van Johnson and I thank you," I said to the baby pilot, voluble with relief.

"Yeah?" he said. "Well, you're welcome. Glad to oblige."

I knew he had no idea at all who I was talking about. When he had bumped the plane down on to the tarmac and brought it to a jack-rabbiting stop, he opened the door and held his arm out to me so that I could step out on to the flimsy metal steps. Down here the fog still swirled.

"You have a nice time on the Vineyard, now," he said, and I thanked him and ducked my head and stepped out of the little plane into nothing at all.

CHAPTER FIVE

LIVVY PICKED ME UP at the stark little airport that serves the Vineyard, and drove me through the stunted, fog-shrouded state forest in the middle of the island, over to Edgartown and Chappaquiddick. She drove a battered, old green Jeep Cherokee that lurched and bucketed over the pitted tarmac, and all the way to Edgartown and then to the Chappaquiddick ferry she chattered. Livvy did not chatter at home; indeed, she denigrated, in her dry, honking, rich-Yankee voice, all our friends who did. Since that included most of the women we knew jointly, Livvy honked about it quite a lot. I might have pointed this out to her in other circumstances, but on this fog-haunted drive I was so overwhelmed by the pervasive strangeness of everything that I could only sit and watch the sliding, shifting landscape lurching past outside, and listen to her tumbling spate of words.

"It's pretty, isn't it, in the fog? Well, it's pretty all the time, but I like it especially when it's foggy. It might be a hundred or two hundred years ago, any time at all, really. I miss these fogs in Atlanta. I've never seen one on a Southern beach, not in summer. The water's too warm. They're caused by warm, wet air meeting cold water, you know. Our water's pretty cold out there, especially on the Atlantic side. Look how the trees press right up to the road; what does that remind you of? Almost every part of the Vineyard reminds people of different places . . ."

"Transylvania?" I ventured. The gnarled tree trunks and dark chiaroscuro of leaves outside, seen through scarves and skeins of drifting fog, did look eerie. Anything at all might appear out of that mist; you might hear the breaths and cries of anything . . .

She grinned.

"A lot of people think it looks like the Black Forest, or the Vienna woods. I always think of Sweden when I drive through here. I spent two interminable days on a train going through Sweden, right out of college, and I swear it looked just like this. Scrub oaks and pines, with some taller pines thrown in. Endless trees, as flat as a flounder. I thought I'd die of boredom till we got to Stockholm. We played bridge all the way."

"Of course, Sweden," I said acidly. "What was I thinking of?"

I had never seen the Black Forest or the Vienna woods, nor the monotonous forests of Sweden. The traditional postgraduation European tour I might have taken was preempted by my June wedding to Tee and our Ocho Rios honeymoon. Caroline came along the summer after that, and in due time, Teddy, and then our traveling was limited to places toddlers would be tolerated. Later we traveled to Mexico and Canada and several places in the Caribbean, but these, too, were family sorties; we had been saving Europe because we knew that there was a very good possibility that Tee would be posted there. I had thought we would have ample time then to see Europe's magical places from a base in London or Paris or Rome. Now they would shed their magic on Tee and the Eel Woman. I wished, suddenly and fiercely, that I had insisted on the graduation trip my parents had offered before I rushed to the altar, and took only a modicum of comfort from the fact that the one who might most have savored saying "I told you so" was past saying anything at all.

Livvy took no notice.

"There's a part of the Vineyard that looks almost Caribbean; that's our part, with the blue, blue water and all the white sails and the flowers and the white sand. And there's a part that looks for all the world like Bermuda, right around Edgartown, and a part that looks like the English Lake District. And there are parts that could easily be the Scottish moors, up island . . ."

"Up island?" I said. Somehow the word wrapped itself around my chilly heart like warm, cupped hands. It sounded remote and unreachable, safe above the swarming countryside, kissed by sun and air.

"Up island . . ." I repeated it.

"The west part of the island, back that way," Livvy said, gesturing. "I forget why it's called up island and the east part down island. It's mainly where the year-rounders and the old families live. There are some awfully grand summer houses up there, but mostly the summer people congregate around Edgartown and Oak Bluffs and Vineyard Haven, down island. I guess it's because there are so many good places to keep a boat. A lot of up island is wild coast and rocks. Summer people tend to be boat people."

"Are you and Caleb boat people?"

I had never heard Livvy talk much about sailing,

or anything else that she and Caleb did in this chameleonlike place. It seemed a destination so apart from her life in Atlanta that I thought she simply saw no point in speaking of it. Now I wondered how we could have become so close without my knowing whether or not, in her summers, Livvy sailed a boat.

"Yep," she said. "I have a little catboat that's really the kids', but I sail it more than they do. And Caleb has a Shields. He'll take us out when he gets up here, but you'll like sailing with me in the catboat better. It won't scare the piss out of you like the Shields when he puts it on its lee rail. The cat's a nice, fat, wallowy little boat just perfect for gunk-holing."

"Gunk-holing . . ."

"I think it means just messing around. I don't hear it anywhere but up here."

"You've even got your own private language."

"Oh, you bet. For example, I'll show you some beetlebungs in a little while. And if you were here in the spring, you could hear the pinkletinks."

"I'm not going to ask. It all sounds insufferable," I said, meaning it.

"Well, I'm not going to tell you, so there," Livvy said happily, and turned right; suddenly we were out of the misty countryside and in the heart of the barely controlled chaos that is Edgartown in high summer.

"I don't think I ever saw so many people in such a small space," I said, turning my head this way and that to take in the tangle of crowded, cobbled streets and lanes that converge downtown in that primmest and prettiest of little New England towns.

"It's the rain," Livvy said. "Brings them into town in droves. Merchants love rain."

Scrimmed with mist and occasional rain showers,

the cobbles gleaming wetly, the street lamps, lit against the dark day and haloed with iridescent collars, the town center might have been a slice out of another time, a preservationist's fondest dream. But the blatting, honking, barely creeping tide of automobiles jockeying for nonexistent parking spaces belied the dream, as did the well-lit shop windows displaying antiques, upscale casual clothing, fancy foodstuffs and wine, and an astronomical number of realtors' signs given the size of the town. The people hurrying through the slanting rain, their heads ducked or shielded by golf umbrellas, might have belonged to another time, though, shrouded as they were with billowing raincoats or slickers and hats—except for their feet. Surely no former citizens of Edgartown, corporeal or otherwise, ever wore deck shoes without socks. Almost every foot I saw that morning, however, was Top-Sidered and sockless. I glanced down at Livvy's feet; she, too, wore weathered brown deck shoes that left her tanned ankles bare. My sturdy navy Ferragamos almost itched with wrongness on my sodden feet.

"I don't have any deck shoes," I said. "Will I have to go home?"

"No, but you can't go out anywhere," Livvy said. "You'll embarrass your hostess beyond belief. I think there are some around the house that will fit you. They get left behind in droves."

"I could buy some."

"Oh, God, no. They can't look new. You really *couldn't* go anywhere then."

"I thought you said we weren't going anywhere anyway," I said. "That was the whole point, just to kick back with you. No social stuff."

"Well, there won't be any strictly social stuff," Livvy said, not looking at me. "Just drinks now and then with some people you'll like, and maybe some sailing, and sunning at the beach club. Real laid-back. It's just us, Molly."

I was silent. Livvy's "just us" was no one I knew. I felt a faint stirring of anxiety, down deep where the numbed rage slept. I had never considered that there was a whole other Livvy Bowen who was old-shoe familiar to people I did not and probably never would know. The anxiety stretched and flexed. What if she was another Livvy altogether? What if my Livvy, the one to whom I had fled for refuge and peace on this strange, misted island, no longer existed?

"You don't have to put your head out the door if you don't feel like it," Livvy said, waving at a couple who huddled on a street corner, laughing. "But I think it would be good for you if you did. Nobody up here knows you as the other half of Tee; they'll take you at face value, and they'll love you, and that will do more for your spirits than six months of therapy. You'll go home ready to lick your weight in tigers, not to mention the loathsome Eel Woman."

The anxiety gave a savage lunge and made it into my upper chest, almost bursting out of my mouth. Before I had come to the Vineyard I had, at Carrie and Charlie Davies's urging, had a couple of sessions with a psychiatrist who was a med school buddy of Charlie's. The doctor pointed out that the sudden wildfires of anxiety that had begun to overtake me at unpredictable moments, ever since I had called my new lawyer, were almost surely manifestations of the rage and sorrow that I could not seem to express, and that until I had worked through the original emotions,

I could expect more of the outbursts of near panic. He had suggested a course of therapy beginning immediately, but I wanted, all of a sudden, nothing but to get out of Atlanta and on to Martha's Vineyard, and said that maybe I would consider it when I got back.

He did not like the idea of my running away, but did not push the therapy, and wrote me a prescription for Xanax and one for Prozac. I still had them, unfilled, in the bottom of my bag. Watching the boiling crowd of wet people on the narrow streets, some of whom I would probably have to meet and spend time with, I wished that I could swallow several of each. The anxiety was really quite uncomfortable. It rarely lasted very long, but it left my hair soaked with perspiration and my hands trembling.

"If it gets too bad, try to face it and examine it," my shrink had said. "Sometimes it will go away if you look at it and see what it really is. Of course, the best thing would be to tell your husband and your brother and your mother just what you think of them, but you're obviously not ready to do that. So look the fear in the face and see what's there."

So I did. In the middle of teeming Edgartown, stalled in traffic by a seemingly endless line of creeping four-wheel-drive vehicles, I looked inside myself to see what it was I was so afraid of. And I saw only emptiness.

I had never been afraid of strange places before, had loved them, in fact; had been hungry to taste and explore and experience the very differences of each new place that we went. But the operative word was "we." I had never traveled without Tee. Wherever in the world I went, I went as part of a unit, part of the family of Theron Redwine, and was therefore safe because I knew precisely who and what I was. My basic self could not be changed, could not be lost.

But travel does change you. We know that instinctively; it is for that, I think, that we leave our homes and go looking for the rest of the world. Not just to see it and know it, but to be changed by it. Or, at least, the strong and healthy and safe among us do. The others—those of us who have suddenly lost ourselves or never really had them—are instinctively afraid of strange places. If the shards of self we take to them are themselves changed, what will we have left? Who, then, will we be? Will we be anyone at all?

Will we look inside and see emptiness?

I sat in Livvy's Jeep that morning and literally shook all over with the terror that I would lose the last remnants of myself on this island, and never be able to get me back. And hated myself for the fear.

"Are you okay?" Livvy said. "Your hands are shaking."

"I haven't had any breakfast or lunch," I said, forcing normalcy out between dry lips. "Are you going to feed me?"

"Chowder," Livvy said. "Made from clams I dug myself this morning, before you even thought about getting up. It's the only thing for a day like this. And first a Bloody Mary. How does that sound?"

"Like I've died and gone to heaven," I said, and it did. The anxiety went sulking back to its pit. The people on the streets looked benign and agreeable again, even their feet. Maybe I really was only hungry.

We finally inched our way on to the wallowing little On Time Ferry—"because any time it runs is on time"—and were decanted into the equally dense fog of Chappaquiddick Island, where the Bowens' summer house was. All I knew of Chappaquiddick was the painful incident of the young Massachusetts senator and the drowned secretary, and that seemed so antiquated now as to be merely quaint, an anecdote out of another time. I looked about curiously, but could make out only swirling mist and rain and the blurred shapes of low trees and scrub.

"The beach club is over there, but you can't see it," Livvy said, pointing, and I looked, and indeed could not. "We'll go swim and have lunch tomorrow. It's supposed to fair off."

Just past a phantom gas station and a community center, she swung the Jeep hard right. The fog thickened, until the yellow fog lights seemed to bounce off its solidity. I could see nothing at all. Then she turned right down a smaller lane and bumped slowly past the great masses of what I supposed to be summer homes, and pulled into a gravel and sand drive at the very end of the lane. A vast grayness loomed up before us, seeming to reach high into the sky, supposing that you could have seen the sky, and she cut the Jeep's engine and said, "We're here."

We sat silently for a moment, and by some trick of the wind off the water the fog parted for a moment, like a curtain being swished aside, and I saw a tall Victorian house dead ahead of us, shingled in dark gray-brown and girdled around with stone-pillared porches. Even here, at what was obviously its rear entrance, it looked imposing and formidable, bearing its bulbous curves and mansards and turrets upright, like an old corseted dowager. A few dark pines leaned over it, old trees by the gnarled look of them, and the latticework around the back door dripped tangled vines of old white roses. A severely clipped privet hedge ran beside it on both sides, around to the front, turning a faint sepia and russet-red with the looming autumn, and there seemed an infinity of white-shuttered windows, all blank like sightless eyes, and many chimney pots, scrabbling fingerlike at the thick sky. No lights burned.

"My lord," I breathed involuntarily, and Livvy laughed and said, "Welcome to Harbor House," then the fog swept in again and left me looking only at whiteness, though beyond the house I could sense, if not see, the immense presence of water.

"You said it was a cottage," I said, reaching into the back of the Jeep for my suitcase.

"Well, we call everything on the Vineyard a cottage if it's seasonal," she said. "It's the Old Yankee ethos, you know. Plain living and high thinking."

"You couldn't live plainly in that if you tried," I said.

She snorted. "Wait till you've seen the inside. It's falling apart, but Caleb won't let me change anything from the way it was when he was a boy unless it's rotted and fallen in under you, and then it has to be as much like the original as possible. What I wouldn't give to fill the damned thing up with Ralph Lauren and microchips."

"You do have electricity, don't you?" I said. Under my feet the porch boards creaked and yawed.

"Barely. Caleb only lets me light one room at a time, the one we're in, and even then it has to be an old forty-watt bulb like his sainted grandmother used. Sometimes he even gets out the goddamned oil lamps."

"And you with every computerized gizmo in the world in your house at home," I said, grinning. "And

Caleb with Windows 95. Why don't you light it up like the Atlanta stadium when he's not here?"

"He reads the electric bill with a magnifying glass. I've long since gotten used to the idea that my husband goes a little mad when he gets up here. It's the Bowen family curse. But now that you're here, I'm going to burn every light in the house all day long, and tell him you've got seasonal affective disorder and it's doctor's orders."

She opened an ornately scrolled screened door, reached in and flicked a switch, and the living room of Harbor House bloomed into dim, yellow light. I followed her in. Even cowed by the fog and the darkness of the big house and shaken with the dregs of the anxiety, I had to laugh. It looked like a stage set for *The Addams Family*. Age-darkened vertical planking covered the walls, wainscotted halfway up with a plate rail full of mauve, floral-painted china. The dark floors were covered with thin, worn, old orientals and islands of dismal straw matting. The walls held portraits that had either faded badly or needed their glass washed; I could make out no faces. What light there was came from antiquated old wall-mounted or hanging fixtures grudgingly wired for electricity, and from a few table and bridge lamps set about. The light they gave out was the color of pale urine. The furniture was dark, ornate, antimacassared or shawled, and looked militantly unsittable. Curved and balustered stairs in a corner led up to an open upper gallery from which a series of closed doors led into what I assumed were bedrooms. In the immense, murky space above the first-floor living room hung a great, grotesque chandelier made exclusively of antlers. Looking farther, I could see that mounted heads of who knew what were hung around the room, just under the gallery. I thought you might well find a griffin up there in the gloom, or a unicorn.

"So where's the staff?" I said. "Hanging upside down from the ceiling waiting for dark?"

"Don't I wish," Livvy said, striding through the dark room toward the front of the house. I followed her.

"I'd gladly take a staff of vampires over none at all," she said over her shoulder, "but I've only got a lady who comes to clean once a week. Caleb thinks servants are ostentatious on the island. Of course his family's got about a hundred in Boston. But Mamadear, his virulent old grandmother, never had them here; said she came to rusticate, not to live like she did at home. So of course I can't have them either. Old bat. I guess it doesn't really matter. Nobody ever goes into the back drawing room unless there's a big party. We live in the front of the house and upstairs, and even Caleb is smart enough to shut up about preserving that."

We went through another dark old door and I saw what she meant. Here at the front of the house, overlooking the invisible water, were low-ceilinged, bright rooms full of shabby rugs and comfortable rump-sprung furniture, with beamed ceilings that bounced back the light. Even on this close, dark day, they glowed with warmth and use and life. A cluttered kitchen full of scarred 1950s fixtures and potted geraniums gave on to a long, window-walled room where the family obviously ate and lived: gut-spilling wicker easy chairs, cockeyed ottomans, shelves disgorging dog-eared books and games and puzzles, islands of soft faded rag rugs and one or two dingy sheepskin ones, a big trestle table surrounded with unmatched chairs, racks of sailing and tide charts, and small tables holding models of sailing vessels of every sort. Half models hung about the walls, rubber boots and sneakers and Top-Siders were scattered everywhere about the floor, and above the doors and a great, smoke-stained fireplace laid with a waiting fire hung paddles and oars and transom plates and quarter boards from vessels gone but obviously not forgotten. Beyond this room was a small paneled library so jammed with books and newspapers and magazines that only a couple of spavined morris chairs were free for sitting, and beyond all of it, outside the small-paned casement windows, the big porch held more old wicker and a hammock and a swing, and looked out into the white blankness that Livvy said was Katama Bay. I loved all of it, instantly. The knot of anxiety loosened and the cold sweat on my brow dried. I could find a lair here.

"It's perfect," I said. "I'm so relieved. I thought the whole Bowen family was richer than God, and I'd have to tiptoe around Palladian windows and gold-plated fixtures."

"Oh, they're richer than God, all right," Livvy said, touching a match to the fire. It sprang to life and began to lick at the chill with hungry little tongues. "Or we are, I guess. This is Vineyard rich. Not like Newport at all. Not even like Nantucket. No ostentation allowed. God forbid anybody add any comfort to the old places, much less luxury. The only thing that's permissible to spend money on is a fund to save the piping marsh doohickey, or one of the land trusts. And even then, you do it anonymously."

"Where's the fun in that?"

"Precisely. Oh, well. Snuggle down in that throw in front of the fire and I'll bring the Bloodies. There's lots of fun in that."

There was. We had our Bloody Marys in front of the fire, and then had seconds, and we talked and talked and talked. Or Livvy talked, of her summers here, and of the men and women and children who peopled them, and of the places on the Vineyard that were dear to her, and of the gradual rhythms that one slipped into here, if one spent a long enough time: rhythms laid down, not by a clock, but by the comings and goings of the light and the sea. I lay on the old chintz couch wrapped in damp mohair, watching the flames and listening to her spin out her fabric of summer and sky and ocean, a fabric that did not include me in its warp and woof, and so was as detachedly fascinating to watch as a movie unfolding: What would happen next? I felt mindlessly content, slung hammocklike between worlds, rocked in the rhythm of her words, lulled with fire and vodka.

We ate our chowder before the fire, too, when the pearly light went out of solid white nothingness outside and the fog was lost to larger dark. Just before we went up to bed, Livvy opened the door on to the porch and leaned her head out and sniffed.

"Wind's changed," she said. "I can smell the open ocean. It'll be fair by morning."

I got up and went and stood behind her, and took a long, deep breath, smelling it for the first time, that salt-sweet, kelp-heavy, infinitely fresh breath of the sea that I have since come to need as my own breath: the breath of Martha's Vineyard. It was like plunging your hot face into a wet, cool spray of spume. There were other notes in it, flowers, I thought. But I did not know what they were. I exhaled and drew in another breath.

"It smells heavenly, doesn't it? I've never smelled anything like it."

"There's not anything like it," Livvy said.

My room upstairs was a small, low-ceilinged cave up under the eaves, with rough, white-plaster walls and pine beams weathered the color of smoke-dark honey. A narrow iron bed was piled high with down pillows and covered with an old white pelisse spread. A mottled, ivory feather pouf lay folded at its foot. There was not much furniture, just a curly rattan writing desk and chair, a wardrobe with an organdy scarf and white china jars and bottles on it, and a ridiculous and wonderful chaise lounge made of wicker, facing the casement windows and piled with pillows and a blue plaid throw. Beside it a table held magazines and books and a rowdy bouquet of zinnias in a blue vase.

"It's a tiny little room, but it has the best view of the bay in the entire house, and I've always loved it," Livvy said. "I hide up here for hours sometimes, when the house is too full of people. And even when it's hot, it's high enough to catch any breeze that comes off the water. Open your casements tonight and pull up the pouf; it's the best sleeping in the world."

After we had hugged good night and she had gone, closing the door behind her, I did just that: I peeled out of my clothes, scrubbed my teeth in the tiny, minimal, adjoining bathroom, skinned into a long-sleeved nightgown, and opened the windows. A river of fresh sea wind flowed in. I ran across the floor and jumped into the bed, pulling up the camphor-smelling pouf and snuggling down until only my eyes peered out, gave a great sigh, and relaxed. When I was a child, I had never felt quite safe until my ears were covered with bedclothes, even if it was only a sheet on hot nights. Now I lay, covered to the ears in freshly aired old sheets and goose down smelling of sun and salt air, having only to lift my head a bit to plunge it into the great, wet-salt stream that was the living breath of the Vineyard. I lay very still, smelling it and waiting to see what would come to me, which of the old pains and sorrows I had lain with for the past weeks, which of the guilts and regrets and what-ifs. My mother: Would my mother come, in her hats and her glinting ambiguity and her disapproval? Tee, in the fresh redness of his betrayal? My father, in his quiet, inexorable grief? My needing, hurting children? Which? Who?

But no one came. I had brought none of them with me to this tall room on this fogbound island. I had landed here alone, and if I felt naked and lost to myself, I also felt lighter than I had in years. Almost— though I did not dare even think the word—free. Maybe I did not know, quite, who I was yet, and maybe no one out of my world lay beside me, but neither, so far, did pain and fear and sadness.

I can do this, I thought, and shut my eyes; when I woke, it was to the sun.

Livvy was right; there are several distinct small countries on Martha's Vineyard. From that first morning, when the sun and sea wind turned the surface of Katama Bay to blue metallic chop and Katama and Bluefish Points across it looked like a New England primitive sea scene, I could smell the separate breaths of all of them. It has been the strongest and longest held conviction of mine about the island, that when I am in one part of it I can smell the exhalations of the others.

On Chappy I can smell the peat-brown wetness of the moors of Chilmark; in Vineyard Haven I catch the loamy hot-pine-needle breath of West Tisbury. On a wild Squibnocket Beach I smell the rich, fishy exhalations of the clam flats of the Great Ponds. The rowdy scent of summer wildflowers follows me all over. The hot, dusty, tobacco-colored smell of autumn scrub oak creeps into even still, foggy spring nights in Menemsha. People talk about the great light of the Vineyard and the huge weight of the living past, but I think both are born of its disparate smells. To me, all its essential otherness is.

All this gave me, from that first day, the sense that I was in a very foreign place, separated not by seven miles but many thousand times that from the mainland. It is not for nothing that the Vineyarders say they are going to America when they mean the Cape, or perhaps to Boston beyond it.

On that first morning, I stood looking at white sails on blue water as clear and shadowless as childhood, and smelled the secret, far-dark breath of a brook that had its genesis in the high glacial moraine up island, laid down in the Pleistocene by the Buzzard's Bay lobe of the Wisconsin glacier. I did not, of course, know the facts of this, but in that smell was the dark old truth of it. Old, old . . . from the very beginning, the sheer and sentient age of the Vineyard called out to me.

"I think I'm in love," I said to Livvy, standing in my nightgown on her front porch and stretching my arms up to meet the brightening day.

"Told you," Livvy said. "So what do you want to do first? Walk? Swim? Sail?"

"Eat?"

We ate breakfast on the porch, at a small table set with a blue cloth and old Quimperware, with a mason jar full of beach roses in the center. We ate melon and sweet Portuguese bread from the farmers' market in West Tisbury, Livvy said, and beach plum jelly that she'd made herself.

"*You* made jelly? Livvy, you can't even turn the microwave on."

"Well, this is my specialty. Everybody on the Vineyard brags about their goddamned beach plum jelly; you have to learn to make it or they don't let you off the ferry. I picked the plums, too. Do you like it?"

"It's heaven. Will you give me the recipe?"

"Not on your life. Find your own beach plums. Make your own jelly. It's the law of the Vineyard."

After breakfast we took the Cherokee and went over to the ocean side of Chappy and walked on the great wind-scoured beach that stretches from Wasque Point to Cape Pogue. The glitter off the surf was relentless, and beyond it the deep blue swells of the Atlantic rolled and heaved. The wind was strong and cool, picking up the fine golden sand in little whorls here and there and tossing it high in mini-cyclones. Low dunes topped the beach, crowned with undulating green sea grass. The sand was the color of golden tea with cream, and it shone in glistening smears where the surf met its packed surface. Because of the reflections in the shining slicks, and the radiant spume that the wind blew off the tops of the breakers, nothing seemed corporeal or solid; everything was in motion, restless, breathing, murmuring, shifting. Fishermen in rubber boots stood at the edge of the surf, casting, but their reflections in the wet sand seemed at times realer than they did. It was a glorious beach, but not a soothing one, not a place where three separate great elements met in a magical stasis, as they did on our beach at Sea Island. Here everything surged and shifted, was too big, too open, too lonely. There seemed to me no human scale here.

It was beautiful though. After we had walked almost an hour we shucked off our sweatshirts and ran into the surf. After the first shock of cold, I felt as if I were swimming in champagne, or liquid diamonds. Lying in the sun afterward, feeling its red weight on my closed eyelids and shoulders and thighs, I laughed aloud in sheer well-being.

"I haven't felt this good since camp," I said to Livvy, lying beside me. I remembered it suddenly: the wonderful, weightless, washed feeling of lying under hot sun with cold water drying off your body. A young feeling, before it seemed necessary to think ahead.

"I never felt this good at camp," Livvy said. "I went to camp in northern Maine. There were maybe two days at the very end of August when human beings could swim. We swam every day from July to September. I was cold for two months."

"Did you good, didn't it? Stiffened up your spine."

"I'd rather have been spineless and warm."

We went home and showered and changed and went to the beach club for lunch. I did not want to go, but Livvy was adamant.

"You have to see somebody sometime," she said. "And if we don't go, I'll have to cook, and that means going into Edgartown for groceries, and I hadn't planned to leave Chappy for days and days. We'll just eat lunch and then go sailing. Or not, whatever you want to do."

So, because I could not gracefully refuse, I went, grumpily and defensively, in white pants and a red T-shirt and borrowed boat shoes and, as an after-thought against the sun, my mother's great floppy hat, and I had a very good time. At noon on a week-day the club was full of women and children; the few men I saw were in pairs and obviously on their way somewhere else: sailing, or golfing, or arranging hos-tile takeovers. The women were, on the surface, much like me and Livvy: not sleek, not coiffed, not "done." Some were young and slim and some were older and not, but none seemed unduly aware of the state of their bodies. I did not get the old Atlanta sense of body anxiety. All were tanned and many were freck-led; all had well-worn, serviceably cut bathing suits or shorts or pants soft from many washings; all smiled with their unlipsticked mouths and unmascaraed eyes, displaying the sound, unbleached teeth and stubby, pale lashes of New England. All spoke in the genial honk that Livvy had. All drew me as comfort-ably into their ranks and their afternoon as if I had just gotten on to the island for the summer from Wellesley. Their children were like well-raised chil-dren everywhere, busy and loud and only marginally whiny. Their teenagers were remote and cool but unfailingly polite. None of either sex wore an ear or nose ring.

No one asked me what I was doing on the Vineyard. No one asked me what my husband did, or where he was. No one called my mother's hat darling or adorable, though one or two did ask me where they could get one like it.

"She inherited it from her mother," Livvy said, grinning wickedly. "It's an heirloom." I had the wit to say, "Well, she left the silver and the stock portfolio to my brother, but she knew I'd rather have something personal," and everybody laughed. It was as if I had known them a long time, these plain, solid women from the big, square houses we passed on the island, with their slightly frayed bathing suits and their open, angular smiles and their cool old family millions. I had been right the night before. I could indeed do this.

After a Bloody Mary and a wonderful baked bluefish, we went back to Livvy's house and I slept, deeply and sweatily, on the piled white bed under the rafters, and woke when the first blue of the evening was coming into the air, feeling detached and temporary, like an astral traveler accidentally parted too far from her body. The sense of being fervently alive in every cell and atom, but not having a corporeal receptacle for all this pulsing selfhood, was very strong. But it was not unpleasant. I fairly floated down the stairs to find Livvy.

We took a sunset sail in her little catboat, ghosting on the pink-mirror surface of Katama Bay as far up as the mouth of Edgartown Harbor. The harbor was full of activity: big white yachts slipping silently in past Edgartown Light, fishermen coming in with the day's bounty, launches plying to and fro, taking people to and from docks and dinner, small sailboats like ours crossing and recrossing the soft breeze. Edgartown, its lights just blooming, looked like a pointillist's painting. The afterglow from the west stained the water dappled peach. Over on Chappy the beach roses glowed on the darkening dunes, and beyond them the lights in the big houses were coming on. Smells of picnic smoke and grilling meat and fish mixed with the hundred breaths of the Vineyard. I never forgot that twilight sail. Even though we repeated it practically every night for almost two weeks, it is that first night that I remember when I look back now.

Day followed golden day, in a run of clarion-clear weather that had everyone saying, "It just doesn't seem possible that fall is right around the corner, does it? Not possible that pretty soon we'll be back home and school will have started . . ."

I shut my ears to those wistful, end-of-summer eulogies. I did not want to hear them, and somehow managed not to. Time was, for me, suspended in the amber of those perfect days, each one as same and whole and simple and seamless as an egg. Fall was not coming for me. School was not starting for me. On the top level of my mind I knew that summer was slipping by, that in a matter of days Caleb would be joining us for his annual holiday, and then he and Livvy would begin closing the house and getting the boats hauled and stored, and I would pack and take an ephemeral, jackrabbiting little airplane back to Logan and then a lumbering Delta jet on to Atlanta. But the other levels of my mind did not know this, and for long stretches at a time I forgot that I was a woman contemplating divorcing her husband for his adultery with a younger woman; a woman who had run away to an island to hide; a woman with, suddenly, a dead mother and a grieving father and an angry, heartbroken son and daughter and a puzzled, anxious dog and a medium-sized house in a silly little enclave of a big city, all to which I owed allegiance and service. I don't think any essential wounds began to heal, precisely; it was far too soon for that. But I do think that, in those long summer days, the bleeding began to stop.

"See?" Livvy said over and over. "I told you. Didn't I tell you?"

"You did," I said. "I'm sorry I ever doubted you. I'll never argue with you again."

We walked, late one night, along South Beach, with Edgartown Great Pond on our right and the star-silvered Atlantic on our left. It was the time of the Pleiades, that great, late-summer meteor shower, when the very sky above you arcs and blooms with huge, hot flowers. We had been to dinner at L'étoile, in the Charlotte Inn in Edgartown; my treat, because I wanted in some measure to repay Livvy for what her island was giving me. We wore silky, unaccustomed dresses, but no panty hose, and carried our high heels in our hands. Livvy had said we ought to see the meteor shower from the beach, away from most of the lights. It was spectacular, magical, and we oohed and ahhed with the rest of the shadowy people who were out in the soft, warm, black night to see the stars fall out of the sky.

Abruptly, my eyes pricked with tears, the first I had felt in a long time. But they were not, now, tears of hurt.

"I want to thank you," I whispered to Livvy. "I mean it. Before I came up here I didn't know if I could . . . do all this. But now I know I can. As long as you're here, I can do it."

She was silent for a time, and then she said, "This is just like school, isn't it? You and your best friend out on an adventure that doesn't have anything to do with anybody else, certainly not with any man. Or no, not school, but right after, when you're out and working and you've made your first adult best friend, and you're off doing something totally perfect that's important just because it's the two of you who want to do it, not to please any man, but just to please yourselves. I remember it from my first year working in Boston, before I met Caleb. It was very heady. Very grown-up, if that's not too silly a way of putting it. Somehow it defines you for yourself."

"Grown-up indeed," I said, and hugged her shoulders lightly. But the euphoria was gone. I really did not know what she meant. I had never done that, never had a grown-up best friend and gone off with her on an adventure designed simply to please ourselves. This was my first sense of it, that taste of liberating, solitary wine. All before had been shared with Tee.

The essential gulf between Livvy and me yawned palpably. I had not thought of it since we met. The stars seemed to dim a little in their arcs and soon stopped. We walked back to the Jeep in silence.

After that, as if the paling stars had foretold it, things changed.

CHAPTER SIX

THE NEXT MORNING I WOKE with my head buried under my pillow, a pounding sinus headache, and a dull sense that it was very late. I burrowed out from under the pouf that I had pulled up in the night and saw that though the room was filled with grayish light, as if I had waked before sunrise, the bedside clock read 9:30 A.M. I plodded heavily to the window and pulled aside the curtains. The air was opaque with slanting rain and the stunted trees along the shore were lashing in the wind.

"Shit," I said aloud to the headache and the day, and crawled back under the covers. I slept again, until Livvy's voice called me to the telephone.

I took the phone in the kitchen, where Livvy, wearing a tatty old blue sweater that looked to be Caleb's, jeans, and thick wool socks, was seated at the round oak table making lists.

"Who is it?" I said, my voice dense with sinus and sleep.

"I don't know. Some woman. Good morning to you, too," she said grumpily.

"Sorry," I muttered, feeling fussy and offended, and picked up the phone. Only then did a little knot of

anxiety form in my stomach. Who could be calling me?
My father was still fishing at Homosassa, Teddy was
somewhere near Santa Fe with Eddie, and I knew viscerally that Tee would not call. Carrie Davies, with
bad news about Lazarus, whom they were keeping?
The Eel Woman? My stomach heaved. I had all but forgotten about her; how could I have?

"Hey, sugar, how you doin'?" a sweet voice trilled.
Missy Carmichael, my new lawyer. She of the Laura
Ashleys, velvet headbands, and the collection of trophy
testicles in formaldehyde she allegedly kept on a shelf
in her office. By now I was firmly persuaded of her
prowess in divorce court, but the molasses voice gave
me the same shock of involuntary dismay it had when
I'd first spoken with her. How could that little-girl
drawl stand up against the relentless hammering of a
ruthless male divorce attorney? How could it stand up
to even a headstrong client, which I certainly, so far,
was not?

"And those great big brown eyes and corkscrew
curls," I had wailed to Livvy after she had summoned
me to lunch to meet Missy. The sharklike attorney
Livvy had promised had a full caseload, but recom-
mended his young associate, Missy Carmichael, in
such glowing terms that even Livvy was impressed.
She met Missy before I did, on the pretext of picking
something up at her shark friend's office, and had
promptly arranged the luncheon. She told me, with a
wicked grin, that Missy had brown doe eyes and a
headful of Shirley Temple curls and stood five two in
her Maud Frizons. I had called Missy, doubtfully, and
the little cricket voice had done nothing to dispel my
fears.

"You just wait till you see those big brown eyes

narrow and hear that sugary little voice drop to a growl," Livvy said. "Carl told me she's never yet lost a case that went to court. The whole Suit Rack quails when they see her name on the docket opposite them."

"The Suit Rack" was Missy's appellation for Atlanta's corps of trial attorneys. Their name for her, Livvy said, was unspeakable. Fortunately for me, she added, she had earned it fair and square.

But the disembodied voice still sounded fey and kittenish, and my heart, already heavy with rain and a sort of premonitory dread, sank. Had Missy been the wrong choice after all?

"Reason I called is that I need a check," Missy said. She rarely minced words, I had found. "I've authorized a whole bunch of depositions and put a good private investigator on retainer, and I need to pay them up front. Stick one in priority mail to me and then I can go do my thing and you can go do yours. You wearin' your sunblock? I had a sorority sister used to go up there every summer, and she got skin cancer before she was thirty."

She named a figure that made my mouth go dry, but I promised her I'd mail the check and wear my sunblock and we hung up. It had been our agreement, the only one I thought I could live with: that she would do whatever she thought was necessary to get me the best terms possible in the divorce, and would not report to me or even contact me unless and until it was absolutely vital. The terms were mine, not hers; she disliked them intensely and, I could tell, felt contempt for me for insisting on them. She even told me that in other circumstances she would not touch a case in which she had so little contact with her client. But the partner-shark had insisted, and she was coming up for full partnership, and besides, she knew the Eel Woman from bar meetings and by reputation.

"Time somebody sank her little ship," she had said. "I'd purely love to be the one to do it. She's givin' all us girls in the bidness a bad name. And I don't have much doubt that we can mop up the floor with your honeybaby. For a big Co'Cola doowah he sho ain't playin' with a full deck. Brain has descended into his dick; I see a lot of it in guys 'bout his age. I love these cases, I really do. I might've taken this one pro bono, except you ain't poor and I ain't stupid. The one rule we got to have is when I say 'Money,' you say 'Comin' right up.'"

And I had agreed to her terms, because she had agreed to mine. I knew she would be expensive, but Tee had said anything I wanted, anything I needed, and if he were truly serious about the divorce, he would not object to the checks I wrote. I had never, in all the years of our marriage, been extravagant. The large balances he kept in our joint checking and savings accounts remained comfortable. To me, any amount seemed a fair price to pay for getting the thing done with a minimal amount of knowledge, not to mention participation. I had even left Missy a key to the house and garage, because she had wanted to get its contents catalogued and cost-estimated and I had not had the heart for that.

"Was that Missy? I thought I recognized the lisp," Livvy said when I did not speak.

"Everything okay?"

"I guess so. She needs another check. She's hiring a private investigator. God, it sounds so—squalid."

"Well, this *is* getting interesting," Livvy said. "Is

she on Tee's trail, or the E.W.'s? I'd have said the latter, but you never know."

"I have no idea," I snapped, suddenly fiercely annoyed. My head hurt, and the matter-of-fact talk about the divorce made my heart flutter sickly, as it always did, and I did not like the curiosity in Livvy's voice. It sounded avaricious and mean.

"You must have some," she persisted. "Maybe Tee's got a whole string of E.W.s, everywhere there's a youth brands market. *That* ought to get you the gold watch and everything."

"Of course he doesn't!" I said. "That's not terribly funny, Livvy."

"Feeling a little snappish this morning, are we?"

"I guess we are, aren't we?"

We looked at each other, and grinned unwillingly.

"Sorry," we said together.

"It's the damned weather," Livvy said. "It looks like it might turn into a nor'easter, and that means three or four days of this shit. I hate to lose these last days to that, with Caleb coming and all."

"I don't know," I said. "It sounds okay to me. We could have fires and eat soup and read books and listen to music and drink and talk and laugh at everybody we know. You said way back that you'd like to do that."

"I didn't mean during the only time Caleb has up here," she said. "And I've hardly seen anybody yet. None of the really good parties start until the last couple of weeks."

"Who haven't you seen that you wanted to?" I said. The implication seemed clear and hurtful to me. "I certainly haven't meant to keep you from seeing your friends."

"I didn't say you had," she said, staring out at the rain. "It just sort of hasn't come up. Usually you see everybody at the end-of-summer parties, but people tend to forego those if the weather is really stinking."

"Parties . . . I didn't think there were going to be any parties."

"Well, there hardly *are* any till late summer. Oh, there are parties all over, every night if you want to go to them, but not anybody's that Chappy people usually go to. Ours are just us. You know. You've already met almost everybody."

"Not the men," I said, feeling somehow troubled and threatened by the talk of parties.

"Well, Jesus, I thought you didn't want to see any men."

"I wasn't criticizing you, Livvy," I said. "You go on to your parties; I want you to do that. I want both of you to. I'm perfectly happy staying here and reading and stuff. In fact, I'd like that."

"Well, that's going to make all these women you claim you like so much very happy. All of them have said how much they look forward to seeing you at their parties. I mean, it's just what we do up here, Molly, take ourselves to each other's parties. It's not like they're these huge social things."

"I know. It's just us. Just you," I said mulishly.

She was silent, and then turned away and gathered up her lists.

"I have to go into Edgartown," she said. "We're out of just about everything. I ought to be back before lunch, but just in case I'm not, there's some of that bluefish pâté and some crackers left, and I think some of the Greek salad. That's what I was going to fix, anyway."

"Wait a minute and let me get dressed and I'll come with you," I said, feeling contrite. I had been distinctly unpleasant to Livvy this morning. I got up and went over and put my arm around her.

"I'm sorry again," I said. "I'm being a jerk. I have the mother of all sinus headaches, and I guess I'm still not used to talking casually about all this business. Let me take you to lunch somewhere bright and warm and funky. I'd like to see the Black Dog."

She hugged me back, briefly.

"No, you wouldn't," she said. "Not in Vineyard Haven on a rainy day in August, you wouldn't. As it is I'll have to wait an hour to get on the ferry. I can promise you don't want to go out in this with sinus. Why don't you stay and make us some lunch and maybe a hot rum something or other? I do better at the A&P if I can hit it alone and work fast."

"I just thought I might find something new to read . . ."

"I'll bring you something. Really. If you get a sinus infection, I'll never forgive myself. I won't be long."

And she grabbed a yellow slicker from a peg beside the back door and was out and gone in a swirl of rain and a whoop of wind off the bay. The door slammed shut and I stood staring at it.

"Same to you, bubba," I said under my breath. But the wind really did seem fierce, and the bay water heaved and rolled sickeningly. And the old house did indeed seem to wrap its arms around you . . .

I took a shower and washed my hair, and put on jeans and a heavy sweatshirt, then went back down to poke in the refrigerator and pantry. Livvy had, of course, only been thinking of my welfare. I felt guilty and graceless, and decided to make something hot for lunch, from scratch. The cold pâté and salad did not tempt me at all on this pelting, wind-shrieking day. And Livvy would be drenched and exhausted.

The larder really was bare, but I found some evaporated milk and two cans of clams and three ears of the native corn we had had for supper a couple of nights before. I made a kind of chowder from them, and added butter and a generous dollop of sherry. It was wonderful, hot and thick. I found cornmeal and the not-yet-washed bacon skillet, and made corn bread with the drippings. By noon I had them steaming on the countertop under cloths, and had fashioned a buttered rum thing that was so good I had one while I waited.

By one o'clock Livvy still had not come, and I had another rum. At two I put the chowder and corn bread away, and then put them back out on the kitchen table, coldly ostentatious, so that she could not miss them. Then I went upstairs and climbed into bed to sleep off the rum. For the first time since I had arrived, the house felt cold and damp.

She came in at three-thirty. When she did not come upstairs, I got out of bed and went down. She was sitting at the kitchen table, cheeks wind-flushed, drinking coffee and regarding the accusing chowder and corn bread without expression.

"I wish you hadn't bothered," she said when I came into the kitchen. "I feel like a heel. I ran into a couple of the girls in Edgartown and we decided to get some lunch. I'd have come on home if I'd known you were going to do this—"

"It's no problem," I said, magnanimous now that I had her on the defensive. "We can have it for supper."

She sighed.

"I told Gerry Edmondson we'd come for drinks and supper tonight," she said. "Peter's just gotten here, and I thought since you didn't go out today you might like a change of scene. But we surely don't have to—"

"Oh, no. I'd like to, really. I just thought, with the rain and all . . ."

For the rest of the afternoon we were unusually silent, for us, and somehow I could never seem to heave things between us back into the old, easy groove.

The evening with the Edmondsons, in a cottage half a block away and roughly the size and age of Livvy's, was not a success. I knew that this was not because of the chemistry between Livvy and Gerry and Peter Edmondson, both of whom she had gone to country day school with. So it had, by a process of elimination, to be me. I did not know what was wrong. I had laughed heartily and long with Gerry Edmondson at many of the beach club lunches and I knew that she liked me as much as I did her. You can always tell about that. And I liked chubby, sweet-faced Peter Edmondson immediately, and treated him, or tried to, with the same light badinage that I used with Caleb, or Charlie Davies. But things never jelled; Gerry's laughter was a trifle loud, and she did not often look at me but did often look at Livvy, and clung to Peter as if it had been years since she had seen him, and gradually more and more of their talk centered on people I did not know. After exclaiming and smiling until my cheeks hurt at the antics of people whose names I knew I would not remember, I gave up and went into the little library and read old copies of *Yachting* and *Audubon*. The tone of the sharp-edged, constricted talk that drifted from the kitchen softened considerably after that.

"I guess there's no sense asking you if you had a good time," Livvy said as we were getting out of the Jeep back at her house. We had not spoken until then.

"Not much," I said. I was foolishly near tears, and could not have said quite why. And then, suddenly, I did know.

"It was really true what you said to me back home, when I first told you about Tee, wasn't it?" I said thickly. "Once you're a solo act you automatically become a threat to every other woman you know. I felt about as welcome as a bastard at a family reunion! Did she think I was going to snatch Peter up to bed right before her eyes?"

"That's simply not true," Livvy said tiredly. "You're being paranoid. Gerry and Peter have one of the best marriages I know. How could they make you feel at home? You never said anything, not a word. It's kind of hard to draw somebody out who just isn't going to be drawn."

"Be fair, Livvy," I said. "You know all you-all talked about was people I'd never heard of. What was there for me to say to that?"

She rubbed her eyes with her fists.

"We've been yanging at each other all day," she said. "Let's go to bed and when we get up, let's start over. I don't want to fight with you. I love you."

"Me, too," I said. "Let's do that."

But when I got up the next morning, to a day of wild wind and tossing gray seas but no rain, there was a note in the kitchen that said, "Gone sailing with Trish Phipps. You'd hate it in this wind. Heat up the chowder and let's have it for lunch."

And I did, and we did . . . but we shared it with Trish, who came back with Livvy. They laughed and babbled about the wildness of the wind and water, and about their ineptness, which I knew was gratuitous talk; Livvy was a good sailor and she had told me that Trish was the first woman commodore of their yacht club back home. I was silent once more. Resentment burned deep inside me like a gas flame on low.

That evening the phone rang twice, and twice Livvy said, briefly, "No, I don't think so, but thanks anyway. Maybe later."

After the second call I said, "If you're refusing things because of me, *please* don't. I'll feel awful if you do. I don't have to be with you all the time, Livvy. We're not joined at the hip."

"It's not anything I much want to do, anyway," she said. "If I really want to go somewhere and you don't, I'll go, I promise. Both of those were great, huge things for the Clintons. You knew they were on the Vineyard again this year, didn't you? They'd be terrible mob scenes, and besides, I met them last summer at the Styrons'. It's not like I'm one of his groupies."

But she was, or almost; of all my friends, Livvy was the one who, with me, not only thought Bill Clinton the better of many evils, but really liked him. I knew that she probably did want to go to his parties.

For the rest of the night I felt vaguely guilty, and could not seem to think of anything to say.

Just before bedtime, she said that she thought she might run into Boston on the early ferry with Gerry and see if her hairdresser could cut her hair.

"You're welcome to come, but you'd be bored silly," she said. "Gerry's got the dentist, and I can't think of anybody left in town who could show you around. And Gerry got the last two reservations on the ferry, though you could always try standby . . ."

"I don't think so, no," I said, knowing that she did not want me to come, or she would have insisted. "I think I might like to go and see what up island is like, though, if you don't need the car."

"By all means," she said. "But I warn you, you're probably not even going to be able to get through Edgartown. There's secret service everywhere, and Gerry says lots of the main routes are just plain blocked off."

"I think I'll try it, anyway. I love the way it sounds: up island . . ."

"Good luck," she said, smiling.

The next morning she was gone before I even stirred. Feeling like a child left behind by the adults, I got into the Jeep and clashed its gears off toward the On Time Ferry, headed up island, bound for that part of the island where, she had said, the old island people lived.

"The real people," I said aloud, not without spite.

But after all, I never got there. The harbor was so thick with boats that it looked like a field of drying laundry, and the On Time Ferry seemed permanently lodged on the Edgartown shore. After waiting in a honking, steaming line for nearly half an hour, I got out of the Jeep and walked up to the head, where a tall man in the official Vineyard men's uniform—khakis, polo shirt with an alligator on it, sunglasses—seemed to be in charge. I did not recognize him, but that meant nothing; he had the unmistakable air of one who would tell you what you could do when.

"Is there a problem with the ferry?" I said.

"It's been delayed indefinitely," he said pleasantly and neutrally. I could not see his eyes behind the black-mirror sunglasses.

"Why?" I asked, I thought reasonably enough.

Izod, or maybe Lacoste, smiled and shrugged. Neither the smile nor the shrug was large.

"Because the President is out sailing with one of the Kennedys and there's a million-to-one chance he might come into the harbor, and everybody in Massachusetts with a boat has come over to gawk," an exasperated woman behind me said. I thought I recognized her from the beach club, but if she knew me she gave no sign.

I looked back at the alligator man, who simply shrugged again. All of a sudden the whole thing made me very angry. The thought of getting out of Edgartown, of finally reaching up island, shimmered with glamour and charm.

"So we're stuck over here until he gets done with his little sail? What if there's an emergency?" I snapped.

He looked at me steadily.

"Is there?"

"No, but what if there was? There are children on this island—"

"If there's a real emergency, we can have a helicopter over here in five minutes," he said. "The ferry should be operating again in time for people to finish their errands and whatever before nightfall."

"Oh, perfect," I said, and stomped back to the Jeep and maneuvered it out of the line and turned around. I went back to Livvy's house, clashing the gears petulantly.

It was very hot and still after the two days of rain and wind, and the water looked like rippled blue silk. I thought how good it would feel, cool and tingling on hot skin, and decided that perhaps I would swim. But then I stretched out in the porch hammock and watched the boats bobbing, a solid mass stretching from shore to shore, until their motion, and that of the hammock, lulled me into a deep, thick sleep. It was not the kind that refreshes you, but the sort that imprisons and exhausts. Sometime during it I dreamed again of my mother and the barred window under the city sidewalk.

This time it was I who stared down at her silently, and she who addressed me. She still wore the black hat, the same one, I saw, that I had up in my bedroom, and I could not see her eyes under its brim, but I could see her mouth clearly, red with shiny lipstick and talking, talking. Her teeth looked bone white, perfect. Her lips moved and moved.

"You have to get up," she said. "It's very late. Why do you always do this on a school morning? You know I don't have time to keep calling you. It's the third time this week. Get up, Molly. You're sleeping your life away. Get up, get up, get up . . ."

Since I was not sleeping at all in the dream, but standing there looking down at her, I was puzzled and agitated, and tried to bend down to tell her it was not early morning back in the Peachtree Hills house and I was not in bed, but in the manner of such dreams, I could not move. The sensation of straining to do so was so strong that I could feel the ache in my arms and legs, and thought, This is no dream. But still I could not move or speak.

"Molly!" she said, loudly and sternly. "You get up this minute! I'm not going to tell you again! Getupgetup getupgetup . . ."

She accompanied this litany by running the metal

clasp of her clutch purse along the bars of the grating, making a loud burring sound. For some reason I found it nearly intolerable. I made a superhuman effort to move my muscles, and finally did, and was in the hammock again, sweat running down my neck and back, heart pounding. The burring noise turned into Livvy's kitchen phone.

I reached it on what must have been the eighth or ninth ring, stumbling and thick-tongued. It was my father. I was so stupid with sleep and the residue of the dream, so drugged with the almost palpable sense of my mother, that at first I could not think.

"Daddy, where are you? Are you here?" I said.

He laughed. "Woke you up, didn't I? No, I'm at Kevin's. That's one reason I called. I wanted to let you know I'll be here for a while."

"At Kevin's . . . what for? Are they okay?"

"They're fine. I just thought it was time I came to visit. I never really have, you know, not for any length of time. And Kevin had a little vacation time left, and we thought we might take Mandy to Jamestown and Williamsburg and maybe do a little fishing in the tidewater. Sally's doing the decorations for some kind of charity thing and this is a good time to get out from under her feet . . ."

He fell silent. For a moment I could not think of anything to say. Certainly there was no reason why my father should not visit his son and his family; but still I felt uneasy about it, as if he were play-acting his enthusiasm, talking too volubly about it. I also felt a small, unmistakable curl of what could only be jealousy, and under all of it was the formless but nevertheless firm certainty that there was something wrong with his voice. For the first time I could ever remember, even in the days just after Mother's death, my father sounded tentative, almost frail.

"Are you all right?" I asked.

"Sure I am. Can't I go visit your brother for a couple of weeks without you thinking something's wrong?"

"Of course. But . . . two weeks? You've never stayed away from home that long . . ."

After a pause he said, "Well, baby, your mother never could seem to get away for very long. Now I've got the time and nothing to keep me here. You'll be up there for another two weeks or so, won't you? And Teddy's not going to be around. I'm finding . . . I'm finding that I don't think I can stay in the condo, Molly. It didn't bother me when she was . . . you know, alive, but somehow I just can't stay there now. I'm going to stay up here awhile, I think, and Ralph's going to look for a little apartment for me—he knows what I want—until I decide where to light. Don't you worry about me. This is just what I want to do."

"Oh, Daddy, you know you can stay with us! With me—you know we've got all that room, and you'd be near everything; you could walk wherever you wanted to—"

"We've been over that, baby. I'm not going to live with you and Teddy. It's not right, and neither of us would enjoy it. I'm not at all sure you ought to stay in that house, come to that—maybe you're the one who ought to be looking for a smaller place, that you can handle alone—but at any rate, it's done. I've put the condo on the market. Ralph's doing that, too. It ought to move pretty fast. With any luck I'll have a new place before I wear out my welcome here."

"Daddy . . . oh, Daddy . . ." I said, tears near the surface, though I couldn't have said why. It was only that always before, I'd known where to find him, had a place where he was to run to, if I should need it. But I could not run to him in Kevin's house.

"Well, will you stay with us some this fall? Maybe on weekends, when Teddy's home? Will you do that?"

"Well . . . another reason I called, Molly, is about Teddy. He called last night, and asked me to talk to you about this before he called you. I didn't want to at first; he needs to fight his own battles, but after I heard, I think it makes some sense. So I said I'd put my stamp of approval on it, for what it's worth, and then he'll call you. He'll probably do that tonight . . ."

"My God, what is it?"

"Relax, it's nothing dire. Pretty good plan, in fact, I think. Molly, you know they stopped in Phoenix? Spent a couple of days there with that friend of Eddie's? Well, while they were there they went to a party given by some friend of the friend who's studying architecture at the University of Arizona, and he and Teddy clicked, and the next couple of days Teddy went around with the friend of the friend, seeing the department and the work they were doing, and some of the new stuff going up in the Southwest, and the countryside, and the upshot is that Teddy is on fire to stay out there and study architecture. I never heard him this excited about anything, Molly. I've always sort of worried because he's been so cool about everything, but he's just eaten up with this. Not just the field, but the country, the Southwest . . . he wants to design for the high desert, as he calls it; I think he really does want to do that. In fact, I think he'll find a way to do it whether or not any of us approve. So I thought I'd see if I could smooth the way a little with you, because I know you were counting on having him around the next few years . . ."

I took a deep breath while I tried to assimilate this. Teddy? Studying in Arizona? In love with the high fawn and purple cliffs of a place utterly alien to the country of his home? Building houses for that strange, inhospitable land; perhaps staying to live among its people? What on earth was he thinking; what was my father thinking, to give his approbation?

I let the breath out in a low, controlled stream, and said, "Well, he can think again. I never heard of such a thing. He's all set at Tech; I've paid the tuition, he's got a room and a roommate, he's signed up for rush . . . if he has to study architecture, and this is the first I've heard of it, he can do it just as well or better at Tech. They've got a world-class department. And besides, it would cost at least twice as much to go to school out of state, and I think architecture's a five-year course . . . I don't think his father would ever agree to that."

"He has agreed to it," my father said. "Teddy called him first. Tee thinks it's a great idea. He's already said he'd be glad to handle the cost—"

"Well, goddamn him!" I cried, rage swamping me. "Of course he said that! Anything to get back on Teddy's good side after what he's done! And besides, it'll get Teddy off his back, won't it? He won't have Teddy's accusing eyes on him everywhere he turns with that snaky bitch . . ."

"Another reason I said I'd tell you first was so that you could get this out of your system before you talk to him," my father said. "I know how hurt and angry you are at Tee. So am I. But I hope you're not going to let that interfere with Teddy's welfare. Molly, he sounded so happy. Happy like a man is happy, not like a teenager being giddy. I hope you'll think about that before tonight, when he calls. He needs to make a separate life with his father, no matter how you and Tee resolve it. And frankly, if it's going to be a long, messy process, I'd think he might be better a little apart from it. I know how you'll miss him, but this way you can plan what's right for you, without having to factor in Teddy's immediate welfare—"

"Teddy is my family! You are my family! Both of you are . . . and both of you want to leave me! What have I *done*?"

I could hardly see for the fog of red that danced in front of my eyes.

"Honey, you think about it, and you talk to Teddy, and then you call me back here in the morning. Nobody's leaving you, not really. I think of it more as maybe freeing you to look after yourself. You've never really been able to do that before. Here's your chance—"

"I don't want to be free!"

I shouted so loudly that I could hear my own voice reverberating in the still, hot kitchen. I wondered, in the ringing silence that followed my outburst, precisely where my father was calling from. I realized that I could not remember all the nooks and crannies of Kevin and Sally's elegant Georgetown row house, the one that so suited a going-places TV anchor and his perfect wife and child. Wherever he was, I knew Daddy would be alone, that he would not risk anyone else overhearing what he had to say to me. Alone in a strange house, by himself in an overdecorated corner of his son's home, reaching out in his solitude to smooth things over for me . . .

"I'm sorry I shouted," I said in a low voice. "I must sound like a spoiled brat. I think it's an awful idea, but of course I'll listen to Teddy when he calls. It's just that . . . I feel so alone, Daddy. From . . . being connected to everybody to all by myself in one summer . . ."

"I know."

I winced. He did know.

We said our good-byes and I went back out on the porch and sat down in a wicker rocking chair to think about it. I knew I would not get back into the hammock.

Daddy must have called Teddy in Phoenix immediately, because I had not sat there for more than half an hour before my son called.

"You having a good time?" he said. He sounded as if he were in the next room, and suddenly I missed him with a pull I could feel in my very womb.

"Yeah, but I miss you," I said, determined not to whine, weep, or lay any other burden on him.

"Miss you, too. Listen, I know you've talked to Granddaddy, and I know you're not too red hot on my staying out here. I just wanted to try to tell you how it is, what it means to me. It was so sudden, Ma, and I guess it sounds hasty and un-thought-out to you. But it's . . . I can't explain it right. It's like all of a sudden I literally saw the thing I was supposed to do with my life. Everything from here on out fits. It's like I was just born, somehow . . ."

My father was right. Somehow Teddy did sound, not like a boy, but a man, a man newly confronted with a passion that he knows is going to change his life. His voice made the fine hairs on the back of my neck stand up. I remembered his anguish the night I came home to find Tee and Sheri Scroggins in my house, the night I had accused him of letting them in; I remembered the cry that had seemed literally torn out of him: "Let's get us some lives! I can't look after you anymore!"

"Teddy," I said, "if that's really what you want to do, then you must do it. I only . . . I just don't know about the expenses, for one thing. Your dad says he'll be glad to handle them, I know, but he could change his mind and then where would you be? I don't know what I'm going to have in the way of money, exactly; and it might be that . . . Sheri . . . won't want him to spend the extra money, and then you'd be out there and have to come back, and that would be *so* hard . . ."

"No, Ma, she's all for it. She got on the phone when I called Dad—I guess she was listening in—and she said by all means, I should follow my bliss. She's talking about this TV thing she saw, about this guy Joseph Campbell—"

"I watch PBS, too, Teddy," I said, hating Sheri Scroggins even more for making New Age twaddle out of something that had moved me deeply. "Well, I'm not surprised. That's one less of us for her to have to contend with . . ."

He was silent, and then he said, "Ma, the only reason I called Dad first was because I didn't know who would be, you know, handling the money and stuff, and I figured he probably would, and I wanted to get it all arranged without having you worry about it. I didn't want to talk to her, and I wouldn't have if she hadn't gotten on the phone. But she was decent about it, Ma. I still think she's a bitch, and I always will, but she was . . . not bad about this."

"Well, then, so be it," I said, my head literally spinning, as if with vertigo. I put out my hand to the kitchen table, to steady myself. "I guess I'm going to have another Philip Johnson on my hands. You are coming back before you start out there, aren't you? To get your clothes and things?"

"Well, I'm coming back, sure, but probably not for a while," he said. "School starts sooner out here. I'm already registered, and I'm staying with this guy I met, Grady McPherson, until Dad's check comes and I can get a place and some stuff for it. I had enough to cover registration. I've got a lot of work to make up. So it'll probably be nearer Thanksgiving. Listen, Ma . . . I can't tell you . . . I mean, I need for you to know what this means, this country and all. Ma, I want you to be okay, too. I'll probably see almost as much of you as I would have at Tech. And if you really need for me to, I can always come home . . ."

"I'm perfectly okay, baby," I said. "I'll miss you, but I'd miss you at Tech, too. We'll do fine, me and Lazarus. And Granddaddy will be around . . ."

But where will he be? And who?

"I love you, Mom. You know that, don't you?"

"I love you, too, Teddy."

I was still sitting at the kitchen table, staring at nothing at all, when Livvy and Gerry Edmondson came in from Boston, laughing and griping good-naturedly about the traffic in Edgartown and on the ferry.

"My God, what happened to you?" I said, looking at Gerry. Her left wrist was in a cast.

"I've been swanned," she said and grimaced, laughing a little.

"Swanned?"

"Yeah, and I know better, so I got what I deserved. There's a pair of swans on the Mill Pond, they've been

there forever, and everybody feeds them, including
me, so they're not really wild. I was up there yesterday
to get some stuff at one of the roadside vegetable
stands and stopped for lunch at Alley's and after lunch
I took my leftover sandwich down to the pond for the
swans, and there were some of the babies right up on
the bank, and they came running and I started to feed
them, and all of a sudden the old cob was on me like a
duck on a june bug, flapping his wings and hissing. He
literally broke a little bone in my wrist before I could
get out of there. I forgot how fierce they are about their
families. You think swans are so graceful and serene
and noble, but they're meaner than hell when somebody threatens the nest or one of the babies. They mate
for life, you know. You'd think I was going to swan-
nap those babies . . ."

"God, that's just wonderful," I breathed. "About
the way they feel about their families, not about your
wrist. Lord, that must have hurt. I had no idea they
were so strong. I'd love to see them sometime. Where
did you say they were?"

"They're all over the Vineyard, but this particular
pair are in West Tisbury, up island, and I wouldn't recommend it unless you know judo."

Up island again. Up island, where the roots of the
old families went three hundred years and more deep,
where the last glacier had left a near impregnable
fortress, where stone walls and old forests gave order
and shelter.

Where even the swans fought savagely to keep
their families intact.

The tears that I could not seem to shed prickled in
my eyes and nose, and I turned away so that Gerry
and Livvy would not see them.

"I'd love to see those swans," I said again. "I tried to get up island today, but Clinton was out sailing and the ferry wasn't running. Nobody could get off Chappy. How long is he going to be here, anyway?"

"Through the weekend," Livvy said. "He leaves the day Caleb gets here. Listen, if you really want to see swans, I can show you those and twenty more besides. And the prettiest part of up island, to boot. It'll mean going to a party, though."

"It might be worth it to see the swans," I said. "What kind of party?"

"Well, a pretty big one, I'm afraid. But nice people. Really interesting. It's for the Clintons, as a matter of fact, the night before they leave. A thing at the Hartnells' in Chilmark. You know, he's the historian and she's the one with the fabulous gardens that've been in every magazine in the world? I think he was a Rhodes scholar too, though it would have been before Clinton. Their house is supposed to be incredible and, of course, her gardens. I've never seen them. We got invited because I was on a committee with her last summer for a literacy action thing to benefit the Tisbury Senior Center. The invitation is for me and Caleb, and since he won't be here, you've just got to come with me. That's one house I'm not about to walk into by myself. Will you, Moll? I promise we won't stay long, and I won't leave your side, and we'll stop and see the Tisbury swans and then I'll take you down to see hers. Their house is right on Chilmark Pond, and there are lots of them down there. Come on. You don't have to speak to another soul but me if you don't want to."

"Please come, Molly," Gerry said. "You'll be the one other person there Peter and I know besides Livvy."

I doubted that, but I thought suddenly how ridiculous I must seem to them, hiding in Gerry and Peter's den because they were talking of people I did not know, having to be coaxed with swans and gardens and the promise that I would have to speak to no one at a party for the President of the United States.

"I'd love to go," I said. "I don't suppose there's a chance in the world I've got the right thing to wear, but I'd love to go anyway."

"Wonderful," they cried together, and we all laughed. Soon after that Gerry left, and Livvy and I spent the best night we'd had together since the one on South Beach, drinking Merlot and eating linguica and pasta and talking of everything in the world except the fact that come autumn, Teddy as well as Tee would be gone. Somehow I never got around to telling Livvy that.

So far as the swan situation went, the trip up island was a disappointment. The fabled pair that inhabited the pond in West Tisbury was nowhere to be seen, though Livvy did point out to me the big mound of dried grass and straw on the far shore that was their nest.

"Probably out maiming small children," Gerry said sourly. She looked wonderful in a white linen sundress, her brown shoulders shining in the last of the light over the pond. She wore high-heeled sandals and had a rich paisley shawl thrown over her arm. She was, suddenly, a different woman from the one in the faded bathing suit I had laughed with at the beach club for many days. I did not know this woman. Livvy, in black silk palazzo pants and a silk halter, was more familiar; I had seen her dressed for a party many times before. But somehow, standing here on the verge of this old village pond, with a scattering of tall white houses and village buildings behind her, she was different, too. There were shadows about her that were of otherness as well as twilight and old trees.

Even without the swans, I loved up island. It was exactly right, just as I had imagined, had somehow known it would be. Traffic here was sparse. It was still and silent in the sunset light from Vineyard Sound to the west; the land gave away none of its old secrets, but it reached out for you, too, took you in. Something inside me that had been clenched and anxious, though I had not known it, relaxed. I took a deep breath and smelled rich earth and wood smoke from somewhere, and flowers drying in the sun, and somehow the earthy musk of animals. The sense of the sea was far away here. West Tisbury might be a small New England village hundreds of miles inland.

We had come across the island on the same road I had come in on, past the airport, through the state forest. Even in the fading light, the scrub oak and pines seemed dark, dwarfed, exaggerated, an operetta forest. Breaking out into the village, I seemed to breathe easier. The orderly old white farmhouses, the Congregational church and the post office and police station and town hall all spoke of a real and ongoing life, of work done and rest taken, of families who lived on the land as well as played on it.

"It's charming," I said. "It looks like everybody's dream village, the way you imagine perfect, old-fashioned life to be. Is it mostly farms around here, or what?"

"It was once, I think," Livvy said. "Not so many people farm or raise sheep anymore; to own a lot of land up here now is to be taxed to death. Lots of the old families have sold off most of their land to off-islanders and summer people. People do carpentry and plumbing and building and whatever, or have regular jobs in Vineyard Haven or maybe Edgartown and Oak Bluffs. It's not exactly idyllic. There's a lot of outright poverty on the Vineyard. Winters up here are killers. There's some money, of course; some of the old families are land rich still, if nothing else, and some of them have a lot of summer rental property. The Ponders—they're the island's oldest family, came here on a Crown grant in the middle 1600s—have about fifteen houses they rent out, I've heard, and about nine more in the family compound. You'll see and hear Ponder all over the Vineyard. The first ten generations of them were preachers, I think, and every one of them seems to have been a selectman at one time or another."

"Will any of them be at the party?" I asked.

"I doubt it," Livvy said. "I don't think they're very interested in the goings-on of the new people, even though the Hartnells have been here since the mid-fifties. I've never met one of them in all the summers we've been coming here."

Which meant, I knew, that the old families had never been asked to the parties on Chappy and most probably vice versa. That knowledge made me obscurely happy.

"What about the Portuguese? Do they mingle?"

"No. Not with us and not with the old Vineyarders. Not much, anyway, that I know of. It really is a pretty striated little island, when you come right down to it."

"Awfully small not to know your neighbors," I agreed.

"Well, that's true anywhere, don't you think?" Gerry said, rather sharply, and I realized she must have thought I was criticizing the Vineyard as a place where prejudice ruled.

"Of course," Livvy said. "You know it is at home, Molly. How many times do you go to parties in Vine City, or vice versa?"

I was annoyed, even though I knew they were both right.

"I don't think they have many parties in Vine City," I said.

There was a crisp little silence, and I retreated under the shade of my mother's hat brim. The hat was, after all, a mistake; perhaps the entire evening was. Somehow I could not seem to put a foot right these last few days. I did not know if the fault lay with me or them, but assumed, as I always had, that it was mine. In strange country, I always seemed to defer to those who were not strangers.

Like the hat.

"Oh, wear the hat," Livvy had caroled when I had come downstairs in the only fairly dressy thing I had brought, a black-silk knit pants suit in which I traveled, that showed no wrinkles even if I slept in it. It was serviceable and respectable, but not much else. The only dress I had brought was denim. The black did need something to give it panache.

"Do, it's wonderful," Gerry had agreed. "So go to hell. You'll be a sensation."

So I had put the hat on, and unbuttoned the jacket a couple of buttons to show off the chunky gold necklace I had borrowed from Livvy, and did indeed look, at least in the watery old mirror upstairs, like a carefree woman going to a big party on a summer night. I had gotten my tan back during the long beach club mornings, and it and the shadow of the hat made my eyes burn blue and my teeth flash white.

"Not bad, for an abandoned wife," I said to myself, leaning over to see if the cleavage the neckline revealed was too . . . cleaved. It looked pretty good to me, for a party. I had never lacked ample cleavage.

But now, in the silence and shadows of up island, I felt that the swooping hat was silly and theatrical, and the unbuttoned suit jacket just plain tacky. I hitched at the jacket to pull it higher, and started to button it up again, then stopped. I had meant no criticism, and I wasn't going to let Gerry Edmondson's touchiness intimidate me. She had been dour from the beginning of the evening; Peter, she said, had gotten tied up in Boston and couldn't make the party. We were, this night, three women without men. I knew that Livvy and Gerry felt the absence, but I liked it. It rather leveled the playing field.

"Let's go find some more swans," I said.

Out of West Tisbury the countryside changed again. It became wild and craggy and sweeping, a place of salt meadows and stone walls and great glacial boulders, bare and wind scoured and beautiful. Like Scotland must be, I thought. Here along South Road you could see the old houses, crowning the moors or nestled into the folds of the cliffs to the east that gentled themselves down to the ponds and overlooked the wild beaches and the sea. In the center of the island, around West Tisbury, you could see only the little overgrown lanes that led to the houses. I liked this land of gnarled openness, but it was the little hidden forest roads that seemed to call out to me. If I lived here, I knew that I would make for the forest like a captive wild creature finally released.

Just before we reached the turnoff for the Hartnells' house on Chilmark Pond, just past the cemetery where, Gerry said, John Belushi was buried, there was a long driveway on the right, leading up to a tall, gray-shingled house near the top of the glacial ridge. It sat alone in a cluster of leaning outbuildings, and you could tell, even from the road, that it was very old. At the roadside, beside the driveway, a hand-lettered sign read, "Furnished camp available, free in exchange for caretaking and light swan-tending duties. Winterized. Call," and it finished with a telephone number.

I was enchanted. "Swan-tending! What a magical come-on; who wouldn't want to spend a winter tending swans? How do you tend swans, anyway? What's a camp?"

"You tend them with a lot of respect and an AK–47," Gerry said, but she was smiling, good humor restored. "Camps, I think, are these really rustic little shacks or something that some of the year-rounders have, mostly around Menemsha, where they go to rough it beside the water and fish and stuff. I think a lot of them live in their camps when they rent out their houses in the summer. That's a Ponder house, so it must be a Ponder camp. I've never heard of one being winterized. And I don't think I've ever seen one. Peter says they're neat, like a boy's playhouse or tree house or something, but I don't think I'd want to spend a Vineyard winter in one. And I don't know why you'd be tending swans; they usually spend the winters in the saltwater ponds along the shores, where they're

protected from the wind and the water doesn't freeze.
If they don't migrate. I think a lot of them do."

"A man could do worse than be a tender of
swans," I said, paraphrasing Robert Frost.

"Not much," Gerry said.

A cluster of balloons fastened to an inconspicuous
mailbox on our left marked the entrance to the
Hartnells' road, and we turned in and followed the
bumping dirt lane down toward a thick fringe of trees.
Beyond them I caught the glitter of water, and beyond
that the dark blue line that was the Atlantic. Unlike
most of the other up-island houses, I could not see this
one, and realized that it must be a low house, built to
nestle in the trees.

"Have we got the right night?" I said. There was
no sign of life from the twisting lane.

Then we turned the last sharp curve and there was
a meadow with perhaps a hundred or more cars
parked in it, being guided in by young men in dark
pants and white shirts, carrying walkie-talkies.
Beyond the meadow, out of a nest of old shrubbery
and stunted waterside trees, the tiled roof of a long,
low house raised its peaked head. Even from here I
could hear the soft boom of percussion, and a low hum
that must be conversation, spiked every now and then
with laughter. Without any warning at all my mouth
went dry, and my heart began to pound.

"I think I'd do better with swans," I said faintly.

"Don't be silly. It's the party of the year. Come on,
you'll know all the Chappy people," Livvy said, and
took my arm and marched me across the meadow
toward the house. On my head my mother's hat
flopped uncomfortably, as if a large black bird were
perched there, deciding whether or not to take off.

We walked through a hedge of dark old rhodo-
dendrons and the house came in sight. It was a replica
of an English stone cottage, I saw, or what might pass
for one: mossy gray walls, tiled roof with more moss
growing from it, mullioned and leaded windows,
small cottage gardens rioting with perennials. I saw
that the gardens sloped down to the shore of the pond
in a series of small, roomlike spaces enclosed by stone
walls and arbors thick with vines and tall hollyhock
and sunflower fences. There must have been half a
dozen of them. The last few were out of sight below
the trees that fringed the pond. Benches and garden
lights and bits of old statuary and birdbaths sat about,
looking not at all like the miniature golf courses Livvy
had said she bet they did.

"Trolls," she had said. "I hear she has garden
trolls beside her koi pond. Too twee for words."

But there was nothing twee about these gardens,
or the house they surrounded. Both were absolutely
charming in the light off the twilit sea, looking more
like a painting or a dream than a place where people
lived and worked and spread manure and swatted
mosquitoes.

In and about the gardens and on the wide terrace
that fringed the house on all sides there must have
been three hundred people. At one end a small
orchestra played. Old-fashioned Japanese lanterns
glowed in the arbors and trees that hung over the terrace. I could see another knot of people gathered
around what must be the bar, at the other end of the
terrace. White-coated waiters floated through the
crowd like butterflies, bearing trays of drinks and
hors d'oeuvres.

"I think I'll walk down to the water and see if the

swans are around first," I said through the cotton in my mouth. "Anybody want to come with me?"

"Molly, what on earth has gotten into you this summer? At least come and meet your hostess . . . oh, all right," Livvy said and sighed. "Come on. I'll walk down with you. Then you're going to have to mingle. I said I wouldn't leave you, didn't I?"

But she did leave me. The words weren't out of her mouth before a swarm of women in bright silks and cottons detached themselves from the crowd and bore down on us, chattering and peeping like birds. Before I could blink my eyes they had surrounded Livvy and were bearing her away.

"Where have you *been* all summer?" they trilled. "We've been looking all over for you! Do you realize it's almost time to go home and we haven't even had lunch? I heard you had a guest; has she been ill, or what? Has she gone? Come talk to Dink. Toby . . . Stuart . . . Potter . . . they've been asking all summer where you and Caleb were . . ."

Over their heads I saw Livvy looking back at me, her mouth making sounds.

"Come on, keep up with us," I thought she said, but could not be sure. I turned to Gerry, but she was no longer there. I started after them like a clumsy duckling trying to keep up with a flock of—yes, swans—but a waiter with a tray backed into me, and by the time he had apologized and brushed the white wine off my black lapels, the swan pack had disappeared into the general maw of the crowd. Pure terror pinned me suddenly to the terrace, where I stood. I took a glass of wine from the waiter and drank it down and looked about me, smiling broadly, like a woman who will soon be joined by a hundred incomparably chic and interesting friends, and waited. Surely when the tide cast Livvy up, she would come back for me.

When she hadn't, perhaps half an hour later, I found a waiter and swiped another glass of wine and slipped off the terrace and down the path into the darkening garden. To the west, the sky over Menemsha was vermilion and purple and pink and gold, but down here on the opposite shore, the soft, thick night was falling fast. By the time I had stumbled through three or four garden "rooms" it was completely dark, and all the little ground lights had come on. Stars chipped the sky, but there was no moon yet. I remembered that it had risen late these past few nights. As soon as I reached the fourth garden room, the crowd of strollers had thinned, until I was alone. Only then did I slow down and take a deep breath. The path made a sharp turn and went down a flight of shallow stone steps, and I was in the last space, a trellised square with vines hanging low over a small pond, and an incredible smell of earth and dampness and flowers. Something like jasmine scented the night, but I did not think jasmine grew this far north. Whatever it was, it soothed my pounding heart and hot face like cool water. There were stone benches encircling the trees nearest the pond, and I sat down on one that girdled a huge old oak, so thick that I could not have put my two arms around it. Letting my breath out in a long sigh, I drained my glass and put it down on the bench, and stared at the dark water. Dark shapes and flashes of gold and orange wheeled and darted in its depths: the famous koi. Where were the trolls?

"Hey, you stupid fish," I said aloud. "I don't like your party. I want to go home."

And I did, wanted it with the simple, consuming,

one-pointed misery that I had felt as a child the first time I was sent to Camp Greystone, homesick and too big and knowing no one among the flock of girls my mother had decreed I share my summer with. I purely and simply wanted to go home. To whom was not, at that moment, important. I did not think that far ahead. Later I loved camp, but not that first time.

As clearly and grotesquely as if the koi had answered, I heard my mother's voice. It was not the impatient one, but the lazy, indulgently amused one that stung infinitely worse.

"You're hiding again, aren't you, Molly? How many times have we talked about that? *Never* run. *Never* hide. It looks so craven, darling. You are just plain too big to shrink away from things. Even small women should never do it. I would not dream of it. Now get up and go back up there and show those tacky women what your mama taught you."

I sat still for a moment, pinned to the bench with shock and anger. And then I got up and tossed my glass into the lush plantings around the pond. The koi roiled and splashed.

"You shut up," I whispered, and then said aloud, "you just shut the shit up."

By the time I reached the terrace again, I was trotting smartly.

I was almost back to the first garden room when I heard Livvy's voice. It was sharp with annoyance and, I thought, worry.

"I can't imagine where she's gotten to. I never saw her after you-all shanghaied me. Are you sure none of you did?"

I opened my mouth to call out to them in the darkness. But then Gerry Edmondson's voice said, "Are

you kidding? In that hat? If we'd seen her, we'd know.
So would everybody else. They'd still be laughing."

Once again I froze. I felt as if I'd been struck in the
stomach. It had been Gerry who had urged me, along
with Livvy, to wear my mother's hat. It suddenly
burned my forehead as if it had been set alight. I
shrank back into the shadows of a group of slender
poplars. I stood in the Italian garden room, screened
from their view by poplars and tall urns.

"I wouldn't know her if I saw her," said a voice I
did not recognize. "What does she look like?"

"Like Jane Russell in *The Outlaw* from the neck
down. From the neck up she looks like Auntie Mame."

Trish Phipps. Livvy's sailing partner. My face flamed.

"Not *the* hat!"

Corky Fredericks, Livvy's first Radcliffe roommate. I knew her from the beach club, too.

"Yep. The famous hat. Mawmaw's hat, as y'all
undoubtedly know. I think it's an old Southren custom, to wear your dead mama's hat."

Gerry again, aping my accent expertly.

"Shut up, all of you," Livvy said. "She's my best
friend, and she's going through an awful time. You
know that."

Oh, bless you, Livvy!

"Well, what the hell am I, chopped liver?" Gerry.
"I've known you since we were six years old."

Jealous, then. I felt obscurely better.

"My best Atlanta friend, idiot," Livvy said. "And
I'll admit she's been acting a little odd. She's not normally like this. But then she's not normally being
divorced for a thirty-year-old Coca-Cola lawyer who
looks like Angelica Huston, either."

"Ah jus' knew Co'Cola would be involved in it

somehow," Trish Phipps said, picking up Gerry's thick accent. "When is honeychile goin' home, then? Or is she gon' stay with you and Caleb forever? I hear those unattached Southern belles are real big on livin' with other folks. Shoot, I don't reckon it would be so bad. She could take in y'all's washin'. Look after ol' Caleb, don-cha know. Wonder if she wears the hat to bed?"

There was a soft explosion of laughter. Most of it I recognized from the beach club mornings.

Livvy's rose over it, reluctant but clear.

"Shut up, everybody. Help me look. She might be sick."

I slipped through the line of poplars and hurried down through the floodlit meadow until I found one of the parking attendants. I asked for Livvy's Chero-kee. When he had consulted a list on a clipboard, he walked me there, shining his flashlight on the flat-tened grass.

I got into the backseat and curled up in as small a ball as I could make of myself, and closed my eyes, but not before I had torn off the hat and flung it to the floor. I should have been angry, but I was not. I felt nothing but a terrible mortification, and a profound desire not to talk, to Livvy or anyone else.

When they finally found me, I kept my eyes closed and muttered, "I'm sick. Leave me alone," and they did. We made the long, dark ride down island and across to Chappy in silence. Once Gerry started to say something, but Livvy cut her off.

"Save it," she said shortly.

When we had dropped Gerry off and parked out-side Livvy's cottage, I sat up and said, "I'm going to run on in. I must have eaten something that disagreed with me. I feel awful."

"I'm sorry," she said in a distant voice, and I knew that she did not believe me. I could not even imagine what she thought I had been doing during the party. Crouching and shivering in the Jeep, probably.

I got out in silence and hurried upstairs to my room and closed the door.

"In the morning," I thought. "In the morning I'm going to call and change my reservation and go home as soon as I can. I don't have to see any of those women again. I don't even have to see much of Livvy."

But she defended you, the rational part of my mind pointed out.

But she laughed, said the other part, the larger and older part.

I thought I would not sleep, but I was asleep before I could turn over. I had the subway dream again; in it my mother said, in the strange, hollow, mechanical drone, "Hold your shoulders up. It just makes you look bigger when you slump. Hold your shoulders upupupupupupupupup . . ."

I woke very early and went downstairs and called Missy Carmichael at home, to tell her to have the house opened for me.

"Hey, I was gon' call you when I got to work," she said. "Something's come up. Two somethings, in fact. Bad news short-term, real good news long-term."

"Why am I not surprised? Shoot," I said tiredly.

"Well, the worst of it, but maybe the best in the long run, is that Tee's closed your joint checking and savings accounts and opened another one in your name. It's got five thousand dollars in it. There'll be another five thousand deposited every month. I called that Lorna woman you said you'd told about me, because our private eye needed another little shot of moola, and she told me. She didn't have your number up there or she'd have let you know directly."

When I didn't reply, she said, "I know. It's a shitty thing to do, but it's not illegal. You'll have enough money to cover your and Teddy's living expenses fairly comfortably, but you won't ever have any reserves unless you've got some stashed I don't know about. I assume you don't."

"No."

"Well, don't worry about my fees for the time being. This is going to look so godawful to a jury that we'll probably get every red cent he's got, so if you can tough it out for a while, it'll be a real bonus. Of course it's her, but it's going to look like he's the heartless jackass instead of just being pussy-whipped."

I took a deep breath. "What's the second thing?"

She fairly crowed. "This is going to be the kicker. This is going to set you up for life. Now he wants the house, or rather, she wants to live in it, so he's saying, or his lawyer is, that since it's legally his, he's just going to keep it and move you somewhere else, or, and I quote, 'Provide adequate housing for you.' Adequate, my ass. He is flat-out teetotally stupid, thank God for our side. Cuts off your money and then tries to throw you out of the home you've lived in for twenty years? I don't think so."

My heart began the familiar dragging thunder again.

"When will that happen? Surely not for a long time? I was going to ask you to get the house opened for me. I'm coming home as soon as I can . . ."

"Oh. That could be a problem," she said slowly. "Of course you've got the right to live in it until he gets a court order for you to vacate, or you settle it privately, and that could take some time. But the thing is, it would look *much* better to a jury if it looked as though you were being super-cooperative, that you moved out the minute you heard he wanted it. I was hoping you wouldn't come back to the house. I was thinking you might rent something short-term; I could have found something for you, but of course you couldn't manage a decent deposit now. . . . Shit. Isn't there somebody you could get a short-term loan from? You said Mrs. Redwine was solidly in your corner . . ."

"I won't do that. I'll never do that," I said.

"Well, could you stay up there for a while, another month or two, maybe?"

"Absolutely not. It's out of the question."

"Molly . . . this is not the time to hang tough about this. This is the time to be so cooperative your shit don't stink. Later, *then* you can play hardball . . ."

The strength ran out of my legs abruptly. I sat down on the edge of the kitchen table.

"I'll call you back, Missy," I said. "I just can't talk any more right now."

"Okay," she said reluctantly. "I know this is tough. I told you it would be, with that trailer trash involved. But try to think of something soon. I've got to get back to Tee's asshole lawyer before long."

I hung up and rose and went out on the porch that overlooked Katama Bay. It was so early that the water was still and flat and pink-stained, a mirror for sunrise. Only a few white sails ghosted slowly over the surface. For the first time, the high white light of summer seemed to have given way to the lower, golden slant of coming autumn. It was warm, nearly hot, but I could almost feel the still white chill of the first frosted mornings here. I sat down on the chaise and put my face in my hands and closed my eyes.

"Feeling better, I trust?" Livvy said behind me. Her voice was high and sharp. She wasn't going to let last night go.

"Yes, thank you," I said formally, not turning.

"You want to tell me the nature of your sudden malady?" she said. "Just so I can explain to all the people who wanted to meet you, of course."

"I'd have thought they were too busy laughing at my hat to worry about it," I said. My voice sounded prissy in my own ears, snippy and aggrieved.

She sighed, a long sigh. "I'm sorry you heard that. They were acting like shits. Women in groups like that are bad about ganging up on other women, especially outsiders. I guess we do it at home, too. It isn't that they don't like you . . ."

"Oh, of course not. I could tell that."

"Look, I'm sorry I snapped at you," she said. "There was a call on the machine from Caleb last night. He can't come. Youth brands has got some new crisis in Chicago or somewhere, and he's having to go there for at least two weeks. I'm devastated; it's the first time he's ever missed the Vineyard. But I shouldn't take it out on you."

Two weeks. Her husband is going to be away from her for two weeks and she's devastated. Try two months, or two years, or forever, toots, and then tell me about devastation, I thought.

"You better make real sure he hasn't got a little action going in Chicago," I said meanly, out of my pain and humiliation from last night. "There's a lot of that going around Coke, you know."

There was a silence, and then she said, "That was

the rottenest thing you've ever said to me. Just because you can't hold on to your husband, doesn't mean I can't mine . . ."

I wheeled around to face her.

"Livvy . . . I'm sorry," I said. "It's just that . . . last night . . . I heard you laughing, too."

"Well, Jesus Christ, excuse me for being human," she cried. "You know, Molly, it hasn't been the easiest thing for me, trying to cuddle and cajole you along, trying to read your moods and find things to take your mind off Tee. I'm sorry I laughed, but if you heard that, you heard me defending you, too. It seems like that's all I've done for the last two weeks."

"Well, don't worry about it, because I'm going home as soon as I can," I said, and then I remembered.

She read my face.

"What is it?" she whispered, the quarrel forgotten. Livvy could always tell when things were really dire with me.

I told her, trying to keep my voice matter-of-fact and level, trying not to cry.

"Oh, baby," she said, hurrying toward me. "That complete and utter turd. That bitch. What are you going to do?"

"I guess . . . call Mrs. Redwine," I said. "See what she's willing to do."

"No, God!" she cried, involuntarily, and I smiled at her in spite of the pain in my chest. "You can't do that! You must never do that! You'll never be free of her. Listen—stay here. Stay here as long as you want to. You can close off the upstairs and keep the house reasonably warm with the fireplace and space heaters till almost December. Take all the time you need; surely Missy will have it worked out by then. You said you loved the Vineyard, and I'm going back home as soon as I can get a plane. You'll be able to spread out and relax and think."

"Oh, Livvy . . ." Pain twisted my heart. My spiteful words about Caleb were driving her home; how could I have planted that poison seed in her heart? Sickened by my own bacilli, I was spreading them now to Livvy, the person, besides my father and children, and, once, Tee, I loved most. Had loved . . .

She shook her head impatiently.

"No. It wasn't you. I decided that last night. I don't know why, but I just can't stay up here any longer without him. I need to at least see him before he goes off to Chicago or wherever. Stay, Molly. At least let me make up a little bit for last night, and for the other times. I love you, and I certainly haven't acted much like it."

"I love you, too," I said, choked, and we hugged for a long time.

She left two days later. When I got back from the airport, in the Cherokee, I came into the empty cottage and sat down, waiting for the warmth and peace I had felt when I had first come here to flood over me. Instead, what came was anxiety so strong it was almost real fear. I got up and walked out on to the deck and looked at Katama Bay, and all of a sudden I knew that I could not stay here, in this house, on this beach, on this little island, alone in this huge, wide, shelterless, shadowless seascape. I knew that I would die here, alone, of fear and loneliness and loss and pure exposure.

I got into the Jeep and drove through the teeming mess that was Edgartown in late August, up Edgartown–West Tisbury Road through the stage-set forest to South

Road, up island. Up island. . . . The trip felt as inevitable and right as my own heartbeat.

When I reached the big shingled house on the crown of the glacial ridge, I looked to see if the sign was still there, on the road beside the mailbox. It was. "Furnished camp available . . . light swan-tending . . ."

I turned in so quickly that the Jeep bucked like a wild thing, and I did not slow down as I climbed the long hill.

CHAPTER SEVEN

T HE HOUSE STOOD IN FULL SUN on the slope of a ridge
that seemed to sweep directly up into the steel-blue
sky. Below it, the lane I had just driven on wound
through low, dense woodlands, where the Jeep had
plunged in and out of dark shade. But up here there was
nothing around the house except a sparse stand of wind-
stunted oaks, several near-to-collapsing outbuildings,
and two or three huge, freestanding boulders left, I
knew, by the receding glacier that had formed this
island. Above the house, the ridge beetled like a furrowed brow, matted with low-growing blueberry and
huckleberry bushes. At the very top, no trees grew at all.
I looked back and down and caught my breath at the
panorama of Chilmark Pond and the Atlantic Ocean. It
was a day of strange, erratic winds and running cloud
shadow, and the patchwork vista below me seemed
alive, pulsing with shadow and sun, trees and ocean
moving restlessly in the wind. Somehow it disquieted
me so that I had to turn and face the closed door of the
big, old house. I had come here seeking the shelter of the
up-island woods, but this tall, blind house, alone in its
ocean of space and dazzle of hard, shifting light, offered
me no place to hide.

I was about to turn away, my raised fist not, after all, having knocked, when a voice from inside called, "Who's there? I know somebody's there."

I sighed. After that I could not simply drive away.

"I've come about the sign down on the road," I called. My voice sounded huge and hollow in the vast, windy silence.

"Oh, how lovely," the voice called back, and I smiled in spite of myself. It was a sweet, high voice, like a child's, but there was something unchildlike in it, too, a kind of timorous fragility that you hear only in the voices of the very old or the ill.

"Push the door open, it sticks. I can't come to you," the voice said, and I did, and stood in the cave-like darkness of a room that seemed enormous and smelled of camphor and dust and trapped summer heat. After the dazzle of the hillside, I could see nothing, and stood blinking for a moment.

"Are you in? I can't see you for the glare. Come over here where I can see you," the voice said, and I walked slowly toward it, feeling my way and bumping into looming, clifflike pieces of furniture. In the middle of the room I stopped, as blind as if I were an eyeless cave creature, and then a dim yellow light came on in the far corner, and I could see again.

I stood in the middle of what must have been a living or drawing room once, but now was a sickroom, or at least the corner I could see was. A hospital bed stood there, beside a round table spilling over with books and magazines and glasses and saucers and spoons, and in the bed a tiny woman lay, propped up on piled pillows of linen so old they were ivory yellow, like old teeth. On the other side of the bed, a tall window looked out on to what must be the backyard, but an old-fashioned roller shade was pulled down so that no one could see in or out. On a table, a small lamp was lit. There were vases and glasses and jars full of flowers everywhere, some fresh, some drooping, some completely brown and dry. Among them, under the yellow covers and against the yellow pillows, the little woman looked as tiny and sere as the mummy of a child, and as yellow, almost, as the bedclothes.

Her tiny face was crosshatched with delicate, fine lines and wrinkles, the skin a polished ocher against which wisps of silvery white hair stood out like dandelion fuzz. Lord, she was old; she looked too old to be alive, almost, in her high-buttoned white nightgown and the sparse nimbus of hair. But her black-dark eyes burned with joy, and her smile was as white and delighted as a young child's. I smiled back; it was impossible not to.

"The swans? You've come about the swans?" she said.

"Well, I saw the sign and I was curious . . ."

"Would you come a little closer? I can't find my glasses and I don't see well anymore . . ."

I walked forward, into the circle of light from the painted china lamp. She drew in a breath, and her face seemed to flame with a kind of rapture.

"*Portugués?*" she whispered. "You are *Portugués?*"

Before I could answer, another voice called from the back of the house, "*Ingles, Luzia, se faz favor.* Speak English."

It was such a deep voice that I thought at first it was a man's, but there was something feminine in it, something fruitful and dark in its depths.

"But, Bella, she is *Portugués* and she has come for the *cisnes.* The swans, I mean . . ."

"I'm afraid I'm not Portuguese," I said hesitantly, for it seemed of enormous import to her that I was. "But I did want to know more about the swans, and the camp . . ."

She peered up at me and then shook her head.

"I see now that you aren't. Your eyes are blue, of course . . . it's just that you are so big and so dark, and your teeth are so white. There are a lot of Portuguese women who look like you. But never mind, you're here about the swans and that's all that matters."

There was the sound of heavy feet and an enormous woman came into the room from somewhere back in the house. I gaped; at first she seemed to me simply a mountainous black shape looming over me, a creature as much of the dark as the other little woman was, somehow, of the light. But at second glance I could see that she was simply a painfully obese, very tall old woman dressed in black stretch pants and a black overshirt, with her dark hair wound in braids around her head and black, soft shoes on her feet. She leaned on a cane and smiled at the little woman and at me, and the impression of menace faded, though her smile was chilly and formal.

"I am Isabel Ponder, and this is my cousin, Luzia Ferreira. I'm sorry I didn't hear you knock. Luzia must have given you a turn, crouching in here in the dark like a little old toad."

The smile widened and sweetened for a moment, then melted back into its polite chilliness.

"No, it's all right. I really hadn't knocked yet. I saw . . . I saw your sign a few nights ago, and I thought I'd come and see about the camp. I think I might be staying on the Vineyard for a while, and it sounded . . .

it sounded charming. I mean, the bit about tending the swans . . ."

I knew I was babbling, and fell silent under the weight of that fixed smile and the still, dark eyes.

"I thought that up! That's my line! I said it and Bella wrote it down," the little woman bubbled, and this time we both smiled at her.

"It's a nice line. It's the reason I stopped," I said, as you would to a child, and she clapped her hands. What was it, I thought, early Alzheimer's? Illness and weakness? Just the onset of extreme old age?

"Yes. It is," Isabel Ponder said. "Well. So you're interested in the camp? Please sit down and tell me why you are. It's terribly isolated and the winters can be very hard here, and I can tell you aren't an islander. You're not even a Northerner, are you?"

We sat down on a sagging sofa in front of the hospital bed. I clasped my hands together in my lap and faced her as you would a headmistress, or one to whom you were applying for a job. She was panting for breath by the time she had settled herself, drawing great, hoarse, laboring breaths that whistled in her chest, but she was still formidable.

"I'm not a Northerner, no," I said with as much composure as I could muster. "I'm a Southerner. From Atlanta. I came up to visit friends and I . . . I thought I might stay for a while, and I didn't want to impose on them; they're over on Chappaquiddick, and they need to close the house . . . and when I saw your sign it just seemed to be . . . I thought . . . I liked the look of it."

What was the matter with me? This woman needed to know nothing except that I was interested in looking at her camp. I owed her nothing else but my name and my interest. But I found myself anxious to please her.

"My mother's name is Belle, too. Was, rather," I said.

"Ah. She is not alive, then?"

"No. She died . . . not long ago. . . ."

How can that be? Mother, where are you?

"Oh. And you are alone now."

"No. I have a son and a daughter and a husband . . . well, not exactly a husband, not for long . . . and my father is still alive, and I have a brother in Washington . . ."

"But you still want to spend the winter in a camp on Martha's Vineyard," Isabel Ponder said. Her words seemed to mock me, if not her tone, which was perfectly neutral.

"I . . . yes. I think I do," I said crisply. "Depending on its suitability, of course."

"It is quite suitable," she said, unsmiling. "You said you don't exactly have a husband, or won't have for long. You're separated, then? You're being divorced?"

"I'm doing the divorcing, actually," I said lightly and desperately. Why could I not just stand up and go? This inquisition was unthinkable.

"Ah. Was he cheating on you?"

This time I did stand up.

"I'm sorry to have taken your time—"

"Bella! You say you're sorry right now!" the little old woman in the bed cried out in such anguish that I turned to her instinctively. "It's all right," I said softly.

"Luzia is right. I'm being terribly nosy and impolite," Bella Ponder said, but she said it heavily and roughly, as one would who was not used to apologizing.

"It's just that . . . I sympathize, you see," she went on. "My husband left me, too, when my son was only a baby. That's when Luzia came to help us out. I know how hard it is. I didn't mean to offend you."

"No, she didn't. She really, really didn't," Luzia Ferreira said from her bed. She was actually wringing her hands together. It was for her that I sat back down and said to Bella Ponder, "It's very recent. I'm still having a hard time getting used to it. But it's the main reason I might like to stay on here for a while. My father is with my brother in Washington, and my daughter lives in Memphis with her husband and baby, and my son is at school out West. I just didn't feel like going home yet, somehow."

She nodded, studying me.

"So . . . no family at home. You thought you might have a little adventure in a different place, get your head straight, all that. Tell me, are you tough? Can you take bitter cold weather? Can you take isolation? Can you cope with being snowed in, and power failures, and weeks and weeks without the sun, and mud up to your knees, and spring looking like it will never come?"

"I'm tough," I said, a pallid anger stirring at last, deep down inside me. "I can't think of anything this island can hand me that I can't take. But I don't see any point in talking about it anymore. You've obviously got serious doubts about me. I think you'd be much happier with someone from the island. Surely there's someone, a member of your family, who could tend your swans. My friend says yours is the oldest family on the island, and that there are lots of you around—"

"We can't have anybody from the island," Luzia wailed, and I turned to look at her. Great tears were

sliding slowly down her little brown walnut of a face.
I stared in surprise and pity.

"I am not close to my husband's family," Bella
Ponder said. "I will not ask them for help. Whoever
takes the camp is going to have to do some things for
Luzia and me, too, and there are other caretaking
duties that will be involved. I need to know that whoever is in the camp is strong and capable, and will stay
for . . . as long as I need them. Several months, at least.
How do I know that you won't get homesick for your
family, or that you won't go back to your husband in a
month or two? It's not going to do me any good if you
are going to do that."

"I can't promise that," I said. "I don't have any
idea how long I want to stay. I'd thought I'd try it a
month at a time, and just go from there. Of course, if I
did agree to take it and I'd promised to do specific
things for you, I wouldn't just go off and leave you in
the lurch. I'd wait until you got someone else, if I
decided to go back home . . ."

"We can't do that," Luzia cried. "Don't you understand?"

"Hush," Bella Ponder said to her cousin without
looking at her. "I guess that's fair enough. There
wouldn't be much work involved in helping us out, just
a few groceries gotten in once or twice a week, and
driving us to the doctor when we have to go. Luz has
been in bed since she broke her hip three years ago; got
osteoporosis, too. And my heart doesn't seem to want
to go like it once did. Too damned fat, that's for sure. I
can't walk much. Can't do stairs, can't carry things. But
we never did go out much. You wouldn't be burdened
by us. And those sorry swans; well, mainly they have to
be fed, and the water in the pond has to be broken up

twice a day so it doesn't freeze up on them. Spoiled old fools won't leave that pond, not even in winter when all the others are down on the deep salt ponds where it doesn't freeze. Won't even go back to wherever it is that they belong in the summer like they're supposed to. Luzia has spoiled them to death, and now she can't take care of them, and I can't either . . ."

"Please look after Charles and Di," Luzia said in her sick child's voice. "It isn't their fault I spoiled them so. I never thought about making them dependent on me; I just thought it was so nice that they wanted to spend their time on the pond with us . . . well, you're a mother. You understand how it is to worry about what happens to your children when you can't take care of them any longer . . ."

I looked over at Bella Ponder, a quick, alarmed glance. Surely this crippled old woman did not think of the swans as her children?

I caught a fleeting expression of what, amazingly, looked to be anguish in Bella's dark eyes before she sensed me looking at her and rolled them indulgently.

"Luz never had children of her own, and that's hard for a good Portuguese girl," she said, smiling her wintry smile. "She loved my little son, and when he went off island to school she missed him terribly, so when these two took up with us down at the camp, she just adopted them. Miserable, overgrown turkeys, it was like having two devil-possessed toddlers around the house, only these never grew up. They're still as cantankerous today as the day they flew in. But they'll come running for Luz like lost children; I try to take her down to the camp a few times during the summers. It's been three years since we spent much time down there, but they don't forget."

"Well, of course they don't," Luzia Ferreira said. "Have you forgotten *your* mama?"

"Charles and Di," I said. "Are they royalty?"

In the yellow bed, the tiny woman beamed. "They are, sort of. They came the summer of the royal wedding, and since they were still youngsters then, and a new couple—you could tell that—I named them Charles and Diana. They're devoted to one another. You should see the way he hovers over her, and brings her the best food, and hisses and beats his wings when he thinks anybody is too close to her. Still in love after all these years . . ."

"Not like their namesakes," I said, smiling. "You aren't afraid they'll have a scandalous breakup one day?"

"No," she said seriously. "Swans mate for life. They're not like us about that. Loyalty and faithfulness mean everything to them."

"Not to mention biology," snorted Bella Ponder, but she was still smiling.

"Are there others?" I said. "Do they have children? What do you call them . . . cygnets, isn't it?"

"They had babies the first spring," Luzia said. "But something got them . . . a fox, or snapping turtles, or maybe a dog. After that they never did again, that we knew of. I think . . . I think they just decided that each other was enough for them. It's quite unusual, I understand. You'll see for yourself, when you get down there. You're going to like them, and I do believe you're the one they're going to choose to take my place. I can just tell. I don't think foolishness bothers you, does it?"

Somehow that touched me to the core. I felt tears prickle in my eyes.

"I guess it doesn't," I said. "I've lived with it a long time."

"Well, then." She slumped back against the pillows, obviously exhausted. "You go with Bella and see for yourself. It's just the right thing; I could tell when you rang the doorbell. But then, you didn't ring, did you? I just knew you were there; that's even better. I am so grateful."

And she closed her eyes. The lids were blue and papery and veined, but the lashes lay sweetly on the old cheek. I looked at Bella.

"Can we see the house?"

"Of course. Just let me get my things," she said.

Her things were a huge canvas boat tote crammed with paper bags and a beautiful old silver-headed cane. Even with the cane, it took me a very long time to get her out to the Cherokee and into it. When we finally achieved it, she was white and sweating and gasping alarmingly for breath, and I was soaked with nervous perspiration. What would I do if this old woman had a serious, or even fatal, heart attack in the Jeep? I did not know where the nearest hospital was, nor the nearest fire station. Was there even a phone in the big house? Yes, wires were stark against the blue sky. But I couldn't possibly lift her . . .

She soon got control of her breath, though.

"Damned flabby heart," she said calmly. "You can see why we need a little help. It's funny, isn't it? You never think it's going to happen to you. When I first came to this island I was as strong as any man, and for more years than I can remember I took care of myself and my boy and Luzia, and that big old house, and the camps . . . and Luzia, well, you should have seen her when she came. You'd never have known she's older than me. She was like a little lick of flame, or a piece of the wind, always moving, always running and singing and laughing. We used to run all over those woods, and swam in the pond . . . No, you never really do think it's going to happen to you."

I looked over at the wrecked old gargoyle under my lashes. I could no more imagine her and the frail little old mummy in the big yellow bed running like puppies through the woods and in and out of the bright, cold water than I could imagine elephants, or monuments, dancing. Pity tore at my heart.

"Where did Luzia come here from?" I said.

"From West Bedford, just outside Boston," she said. "A lot of my people and hers lived there when she and I were young. There was a regular colony of Portuguese for a while; some of the men were at the Hanscomb Air Force Base, and others worked in Cambridge and Boston. Luzia and I were both born there, and we went to high school there. I was working in a restaurant in Cambridge when I met my husband; he was at Harvard then. When he . . . left us, my son and I, I needed help, and Luzia's parents were about to move back to Portugal, so I asked her to come here, and she's been here ever since. She's all I have of family now . . ."

"Your son . . . is he . . . not alive?" I said hesitantly. I had not gotten the sense of tragedy from her, only bitterness, a formless anger.

"Oh, yes. I meant family here. My son just . . . doesn't come here anymore. He has no more use for his father's people than I do, and apparently they have none for him. None of them have ever made a move to contact him. None of them made a move to see him when he was here, when he was just a little boy. That's why I sent him off island, so he could grow up and go to school among his own people, in West Bedford. He's come back very few times since."

"How old was he when he went away?" I said.

"Eight. He was eight."

Eight years old. My God, poor little boy. To lose his father at two, and then his mother and his aunt and his very world at eight . . . no wonder he did not come back to this island.

"Where is he now?" I asked. "What does he do?"

"He's a schoolteacher. He teaches in a private school in Washington State," she said. Her voice was flat. "He teaches English literature, I believe, somewhere just outside Seattle."

The "I believe" spoke of distance and pain, and I did not pursue it, except to say, mildly, "That's a long way away."

"Yes," she said. "That's a pretty hat."

I saw that she was looking at my mother's hat in the backseat, and I accepted the change of subject.

"It was my mother's."

"She had good taste. I'll bet she was a pretty woman."

"Yes, she was," I said.

She directed me back to the right, where we bumped in silence along the deserted, close-grown road, and then left on to Middle Road, which bisects the up island landscape, between South Road and North Road. We were driving along the glacial spine of the island now, and I did not try to converse with her; the sweeping vistas of meadows and boulders and moors and ponds and the great silver sea beyond claimed my eyes. Up island, in that moment, seemed as remote and empty of humanity to me as the Scottish

moors it resembled. It was crisscrossed with beautiful
old piled-stone walls that, now, seemed to define
nothing at all, and here and there a great piled old
house, or an obviously new and opulent one, dotted
the green and gray, or broke the racing cloud scud
from the tops of the ridges. And then, abruptly, we
were in the little town of Chilmark, with its community center and firehouse and huddle of stores and
church and schoolhouse. I drew a breath of relief; here
were life and the living. Men and women ambled
about the crossroads or proceeded in trucks and Jeeps
through the intersection where the famous beetlebung
trees loomed, beginning now to be tinged with
promissory scarlet. It was near noon, and children ran
in and out of the old shingled two-room school. It was
such a classic, pastoral village scene that I grinned to
myself, thinking what Tee would have said about it,
and then, remembering, amended the thought to what
Livvy would have. I did not mind the Disneyesque
quality of it, though; this was real, and powerfully
endearing, somehow touching a chord deep within
me. Wasn't it, after all, like this that people were meant
to live? In villages, as neighbors, wrapped in water
and hills? I smiled at Bella Ponder.

"So pretty," I said.

"Pretty is as pretty does," she said, and pointed
right, and I turned on to Menemsha Cross Road.

The two old Ponder camps lay across North Road,
at the end of one of a nameless warren of small, wild
lanes that eventually led down to the waters of
Vineyard Sound, near Menemsha Bight. It seemed to
me that we bumped through the low-growing, close-
pressing forest interminably, seeing nothing but overhanging branches and undergrowth—ferns and vines

and the stunted trunks of trees—only occasionally catching a glimpse ahead of silver-gray, which spoke of open water and the sky. At the head of each tiny lane a ramshackle mailbox leaned, or sometimes a weathered, falling-down wooden gate that could have deterred no one. I asked Bella if any of the lanes had names, and she said that a few did: She could remember Prospect Hill Road, and Cranberry Road, and Beetlebung and Kapigan Roads, and, of course, Pinkletink.

"But," she added, "I don't think our road ever had a name. People just call it Ponder Camp Road. That's as good as any, I guess."

She pointed again, and I swung the Jeep on to an even tinier, more green-choked road, and slowed to a snail's pace as I felt my way through the ruts and vegetation. There was no glimpse of sea or sky now, only the relentless, scratching, pressing green. The roadbed was appalling.

"This must be impossible in winter," I said.

"Not if you've got four-wheel drive," she said. "I can't remember ever being stuck in here."

Of course not, I said to myself, chastened.

I followed a sharp turn to the left, then stopped the Jeep abruptly with a soft gasp. In a clearing just ahead sat a small, shingled, two-story cottage, gone dark brown now with age and weather. To one side of it, and a bit in front, a larger cottage stood, this one all on one level and shrouded with some sort of creeper going scarlet. Like the first, its trim and shutters were white, this one's seeming new-painted and glistening in the unaccustomed sunlight of the clearing. From its mossy stone chimney a wisp of ghostlike smoke curled. Flowers in window boxes rioted red and yellow and peach and pink against the old shingles:

tuberous begonias, I saw. We could not grow them in this vivid perfection at home, though I had tried. The windowpanes shone. Behind and above it, the little two-story cottage looked dim and shabby and un-loved, its chimney cold, its windows scummed and opaque with spiderwebs. Beyond both the still, dark water of a little pond gleamed, ringed with emerald water weeds and rushes and small, wind-shaped trees. One end of it was thick with leathery-green water lilies. At its near edge, beside a listing little gray dock, a half-beached skiff lay, its faded red paint obscured in patches by the relentless vines. Beyond all of it, the sil-ver of the sea tossed and flashed.

It was so utterly, picturesquely lovely, so some-how ridiculously operettalike, that I simply laughed. My heart squeezed with enchantment.

"Where are Hansel and Gretel?" I said. "Surely no self-respecting witch would eat them up in this place."

"It's right nice, isn't it?" she said complacently, knowing of course how it looked; hadn't she said she and Luzia had spent most of their summers here? I could see, suddenly, what a bitter loss this place must be to both of them. The old farmhouse on its wind-scoured hill was beautiful, in a stark and lordly way, but this secret glade, with its sunlit pond and the promise of the sea always before it, was sustenance and shelter. I could literally see it frilled in the first ten-der pink and green of spring; see it wrapped in silent, succoring snow; see it, as I would soon, licked by the fire of autumn. I had been right in what I sensed: This is what had waited for me up island. I knew before I got out of the car that I would take the camp.

"May I go in?" I said eagerly, turning to her.

"Why don't you go see the swans first?" she said.

"Take them a little bite and get acquainted, give me time to get myself up for walking some more. Then I'll show it to you."

"I can go in by myself; I don't want you to make yourself ill," I said.

"No. There are things I want to tell you about the house. Take that top paper bag and go scatter some of that barley on the edge of the water and some right in it. They'll be along; they don't go far from the water."

I dug the first paper bag out of her tote and got out of the Jeep and walked across the glade to the pond's edge. The air smelled of pine and sun-sweetened grass, of the clean, fishy smell I associated with childhood lakes and creeks. There was, under the deep silence, a kind of hum that might be insects or just the living heart of the wood itself. I stretched and smiled, and walked carefully out on to the old dock, feeling it sway and hold, and tossed handfuls of the cracked barley she had given me into the water, and more behind me on to the grassy fringe of the pond. For a moment there was only the silence and then there was a kind of liquid rustle, and the sound of moving water, and a great white bird came gliding through the rushes toward me.

It was a mottled gray-white, as though years of wear and winters had dimmed the luster of its feathers, and its bill was bright red-orange, with a black mask above it and a black knob jutting over the bill from its forehead. Its neck was curved in the beautiful, tender S curve that I associated with fairy-tale books and old engravings. It was enormous; I was shocked at its size. It must have weighed a good sixteen or seventeen pounds. I don't know why I was surprised; I had seen swans before, in zoos and botanical gardens. But somehow, here in this wild place, with nothing but quiet water between me and it, it looked large indeed, and formidable.

It stopped in the water and looked at me, tilting its head to one side. Then it raised its wings over its back so that it was one huge, ruffled puff of white: lovely. I was captivated. I knelt and reached my hand out to it, offering barley.

"Hello, you pretty thing," I said. "Are you Charles, or Di? Want a little nibble of brunch?"

From around a clump of reeds a white tornado erupted, rushing awkwardly at me, hissing and grunting. I had heard grunts like that from alligators on television nature shows: I jumped back reflexively, but not before the wind of great, flailing wings brushed my bare arms and face. It seemed that the whole glade, and the air over the pond, were filled with whirling, whistling wings.

I cowered on the dock, covering my head and face with my arms; the wings slowed and stopped, and I risked a look. A second swan, much larger than the one who still lingered in the water, was waddling angrily back and forth along the bank under the dock, looking up at me and darting its big head, on the end of its serpentine neck, like a snake. Charles, no doubt of that. I had, I supposed, threatened Diana.

I stood frozen, effectively treed on the dock by the absurd swan, remembering the cast on Gerry Edmondson's wrist, put there by a swan in a West Tisbury pond. Staying here was out of the question, I thought: I couldn't go through this twice a day indefinitely. What if one of them broke *my* wrist; I wouldn't even be able to drive. I felt a deep, childish sorrow start in my stomach: This place had spoken so clearly to me of something I had not even known I needed.

The Jeep horn began to blare, and I looked back. Bella Ponder's black head was thrust out the window.

"Stand your ground!" she rasped. "Don't run. He'll stop in a minute. It's all show."

I stood still, and soon the marauding cob stopped his furious lunging and hissing, and settled his great wings to his side again. With a final, baleful glare at me, he turned and waddled awkwardly back to the water and glided silently across it to where the barley lay on the bank. The pen followed him, serene in her settling white feathers. When she began to peck at the grain, he did, too, and soon both were feeding greedily, backs to me. I tiptoed off the dock and back to the Jeep, feeling sheepish and cowardly. In my head I could hear Livvy: "You didn't take it because a *swan* chased you?"

"I didn't realize they were so big," I said aloud in a small voice.

Bella was panting from the effort of shouting.

"I should have brought the swan stick. It's an old walking cane of my husband's grandfather's, made of black oak, as hard as iron. I never feed those savages that I don't bring it along. Luzia hates it, but it works like a charm."

"You don't hit them?" I said, horrified.

"Of course not. Luzia would leave on the next ferry. I just shake it at them. At him, really. They may be mean, but they're not stupid. They'll back off every time. Like I said, it's all show. They know where their meals come from. Lord, but I'll be glad when somebody can take over for me. I don't know if I can keep up the room service much longer."

"Is that what they eat, grain?"

"No. They eat submerged water plants and sometimes the gleanings left in the fields. Barley is what the royal Europeans used to feed them to fatten them for the table. If one of them ever gets too far out of line, at least he won't taste like old shoe leather."

I laughed, and she grinned fleetingly. I found myself liking this rude old woman without quite knowing why.

"So shall we do the cottage now?" I said.

"I think I'll send you ahead after all," she said, "and tell you what you need to know after you've seen it. My heart's still fluttering a little."

She did look white and tired, and so I nodded. "Will I need a key?"

"No. They're never locked," she said, and I started off toward the larger cabin.

"No," she said. "That's not for let. It's the other one, the smaller one."

"I'm sorry," I said. "I just thought, with the fire lit and the windows and the flowers and all . . ."

"I'll tell you about that one when you get back. The little one is cozier in the winter, and it needs a lot less care. It's a little out of shape right now, but I can get it ready for you at a moment's notice, if you like it. It's where Luz and I always stayed."

So I walked past the Hansel and Gretel cottage and went up the stone steps of the little two-story cottage and across the sagging porch and pushed the ancient white-painted door open.

The little house was indeed little; it was tiny. The downstairs consisted of one large room with tiny, diamond-paned windows so scrimmed with dirt and overgrown with outside vines that it was nearly impossible to see; when I flicked on a lone brass lamp on a rickety table, nothing happened. I made out a

huge, age-and-smoke-blackened fireplace that domi-
nated one wall, and a spavined old sofa covered with
a filthy quilt facing it, and a couple of what looked like
wooden kitchen chairs circa 1900. The ceiling was low
and beamed and black with the smoke of years, and at
one end a faded cretonne curtain was drawn back to
expose a kitchen so rudimentary that I literally shuddered at the thought of trying to put a meal together in
it. There was an iron stove with the flue leading out a
tiny, high window; a pitted, old, white gas range; a
sink on pipe legs; and a refrigerator that had its motor
sitting sadly atop it. There was one linoleum-covered
counter, and open shelves above it held a few tins so
weary and dim that it was impossible to tell what they
contained.

At the other end of the room, a cramped staircase
rose into the gloom of the second floor. I climbed it, my
heart sinking steadily toward my stomach. The risers
were so narrow that I had to go up sideways, and the
pitch was so steep that I clung to the rough pine wall
as I climbed. I did not think I would spend a week here
before I tumbled down it and broke something vital to
my well-being. Up here were two cubicles obviously
used as bedrooms, one slightly larger than the other,
with tiny closets closed off by curtains and narrow
iron bedsteads in each. Thin, stained mattresses sat
atop them. Both had dirty old footlockers, chests of
drawers that might have housed a Barbie doll's
wardrobe, and a straight chair apiece. Both had long,
floor-to-ceiling windows scummed with grime and
cobwebs, but when I went to one and rubbed a space
in the dirt, I saw that they overlooked the whole sweep
of glade and pond and the sea beyond, and that from
up here you had a panoramic view of Vineyard Sound.

It was blue now instead of the morning's restless pewter, and dotted with white sails. It was lovely: This vast seascape would be the first thing you saw when you raised your head from your pillow, providing you kept the windows clean. I thought of the dancing stipple of sea light on the ceiling in the summer, and the flickering white snow light of winter. I thought of curtains and deep comforters and plaids and copper lamps and banked fires, and piles of books on bedside tables, and pottery bowls of apples, and maybe a little radio spilling out Brahms. . . .

You would not be cold here. Each bedroom had an iron stove like the kitchen's, with a solid wooden box to hold wood or whatever they burned, and I had noticed that in a corner of the dim kitchen a big, if ancient, hot-water heater held court. There was a tiny bathroom opposite the bedrooms, but I had not yet had the heart to look in it. When I did, I winced at the dirt, but saw that it had a big, old-fashioned clawfoot bathtub with a shower curtain, so there must be a shower, and a bulbous toilet and washbasin that spoke of 1920s Sears Roebuck. The floor was wide-planked wood, and I pictured rag rugs and copper pots of chrysanthemums, even though it was now an inch deep in grime and had the leprous remnants of old linoleum in peeling patches across it.

I thought, also, of my huge sea-green bathroom at home, of the shining glass blocks and hanging plants and the Jacuzzi we had put in two years before, and the soft, incandescent lighting, and the double sinks and view of the park, of the bentwood rocker where I sometimes sat with a glass of wine while Tee bathed. . . .

I shook my head briskly and felt my way back

downstairs and across the dark living room and porch, back to the Jeep. She sat looking at me stolidly, and said nothing.

"I'm afraid it's out of the question," I said rapidly. "It's just too . . . primitive. I mean, I've never even tried to start a woodstove before, and if one of the appliances broke down I wouldn't know what to do, and then if anyone should want to visit me, I have no idea where I'd put them, and it's just so far away from everything . . . and I do have to take the Jeep back to my friend's house; I'd have to buy a car, and I didn't see a phone . . ."

She took a deep breath.

"I apologize for the shape it's in. I don't blame you for worrying about that. I thought it would be the bigger one that I'd be offering, but . . . it didn't turn out that I could, and I didn't have enough notice to get this one cleaned up. But I promise you that I can have it shining for you whenever you'd like me to, and as for the phone, I'll be glad to have one put in; there's a line in here anyway, for the other one. And there's an old four-wheel-drive truck in my shed you could use; I'll never drive it again, nor will Luzia. You know, when it's all clean, and the sheets and curtains are fresh and up, and there's a fire in the fireplace and something cooking on the stove and music playing—I've got an old radio you can have, too, and a little TV set we've never even watched—it's one of the coziest places you'll ever see. And the sunsets . . . well, the Menemsha sunsets are famous all over the world, and from the porch of this one you have the best view of the sunsets on the entire island. On a fall or winter night it's really something special. We used to stay down here until the snow literally ran us out, Luz and I; I put in the stoves so we could stay on in the winters, and we did that until she fell. Those were good nights, I can tell you. Once or twice we saw the northern lights out over the water . . ."

Her voice was hypnotic. I saw them, too.

"Why don't you try it and see, oh, until April, maybe?" she said. "If you really wanted to go home for a little while over Christmas or something, I could always find somebody to do for us for a few days, I guess. Of course, you'd be surprised how nice Christmas is out here in the woods. We spent several here before Luz fell, once with company, and it was like an old-fashioned Christmas out of a picture book. There was fresh snow, and the deer came right up to be fed, and the birds all came for the suet, and there's all kinds of wild holly around, and we put us up a little spruce from the woods, and cooked a turkey . . . we both still talk about that Christmas. I'll bet your boy would get a kick out of an old-fashioned New England Christmas like that, and your dad and your daughter and her family, too. I've got several single beds in the barn I could move in, and there's a sleeping alcove under the stairs that'll hold a double. If you could see your way to stay through the winter and help us out, I can get this place fixed up so you won't know it in no time at all."

Snow, holly, deer, a fire, a little tree beside the fireplace—the scene unrolled in my head like a home movie, a happy one. And the money . . . Until April. Eight months. Forty thousand dollars saved . . . I could live a very good while indeed on that, back in Atlanta. I could plan a life in that amount of time.

I turned to her. "Why aren't you talking to your family?" I said. "I don't want to pry, but I don't understand why you want me so badly. There must be so many of you . . ."

"Like I said. I won't ask them for help," she said. "I don't need to bore and burden you with the reasons. If you really can't see your way clear to do it, I can find somebody else. I don't mean to distress you by appearing to beg."

She looked defeated. Simply that. Proud, old, sour—and defeated. Her life in this enchanted wood was already over, and soon it would be over entirely. I, on the other hand, was seeking a place to plan the rest of mine. I felt a powerful turn of empathy and remorse. It could so easily be me in a few years, trying in the midst of the wreckage of a failing body to secure a future for myself and perhaps some faithful, ailing companion. What, to me, were a few months? What waited at home for me, anyway?

"If you can really get it livable, I'll stay until April," I heard myself say. My voice rang in my own ears.

"Thank you," she said, and dropped her eyelashes, but not before I saw the wash of tears there. They were gone when she raised her head, though.

"When would you like to come?"

"Well . . . when could you get it ready?"

"Day after tomorrow?" she said.

"Really? So soon?"

"There'll be no problem. You'll see," she said strongly.

"Would you want me to sign anything? A letter of agreement, or something?"

"No. I think you honor your word," she said.

"Well, then . . . it's a deal," I said, and gave her my hand, wondering if I had truly lost my mind. Probably.

But, on the other hand, if I had signed nothing and it turned out that she could not, after all, get the camp livable, there was surely nothing to prevent me from going elsewhere. What could I lose?

She took my hand in her large old one. It felt cold and dry and rough, like the skin of a long-dead animal. I knew that hand; I had held others like it in my days as a volunteer at Grady Hospital, Atlanta's huge charity medical facility. It was the feeling of failing life systems: heart, lungs, circulation. I knew that I was holding mortality in my hand.

"Deal," she said.

I got into the Jeep and put the key in the ignition, and she said, "There's something else."

I turned to look at her. She was looking over at the other house. I don't know why, but the hair on the back of my neck stood up.

"What?"

She spoke without looking at me.

"It's my son. He's had to come home for a little while; he had an operation on his leg, and he needed somewhere to convalesce, and he asked if he could come here. It used to be his favorite place in the world, these old camps. I couldn't say no. It happened after I'd put the notice up on the road, and I just didn't get around to taking it down. I'd have put him in the smaller one, but he can't manage the stairs yet, and somehow I just didn't think anybody would really ask about the camps. We can't have him at the big house; I can't even take good care of Luz. Of course she'd want him; she'd cry and tease for him to come up there until she drove me crazy, so I just haven't told her he's here yet. He only came a couple of days ago; a friend from his school brought him, and he won't be here long, I don't think. Just maybe till late winter. It shouldn't take a lot of time. But he's going to need just a little bit of looking after . . ."

"And you want me to do a little bit of caretaking for him, too," I said, my heart sinking again. "Mrs. Ponder, I'm not a nurse. I can't take care of an invalid . . ."

"He doesn't need a nurse," she said. "He wouldn't have a nurse. He insists on doing for himself, and he's such a contrary loner, he wouldn't want anybody around helping him even if he needed it. All he needs is for somebody to get him in some groceries a couple of times a week, and maybe take him over to the hospital in Oak Bluffs once a month or so for the doctor to see how he's coming along. I don't think you'd be seeing enough of him to even know he was over there. He's got trunks and trunks full of books, and he had his big old stereo shipped over, and he's working on some kind of book of his own. You wouldn't have to go in, even, just leave the groceries on the porch. He could put you out a list . . ."

"It's just that I didn't count on having anybody so near . . ."

"Well, he's a nice boy. He wouldn't be a bad neighbor to have, even if you had to see him every now and then; he really minds his own business, always has. Real polite, though. Listen, I've brought him a few things to tide him over; I've got them in the tote. Why don't you just take them in to him, and meet him, and tell him who you are? See for yourself how easy it would be. He knows somebody will likely be coming . . ."

I wondered how he could possibly know that unless she had called him from the big house before we had left. But I said nothing, only looked at her helplessly. It did not, in fact, seem like a great deal to ask; I could get his groceries on the same days that I did Bella and Luzia's, and maybe even take him to his doctor's appointments at the same time they had theirs. And it might, after all, be rather nice to look out into the winter nights and see the warm yellow of a lit lamp, smell the smoke of a fire nearby.

"Well ... all right," I said. "If you're sure he knows I'm coming."

"He knows," she said.

I started toward the larger camp and then stopped and looked back. She had her head in her hands, but she lifted it and looked at me, perhaps feeling my eyes on her.

"What's his name?" I called.

"Dennis," she called back. "I call him Denny."

I went on up the path and the steps, gray stone like the smaller one's, but scrubbed and lined with late geraniums in pots. The porch floor had been scrubbed, too, and big earthenware jugs of chrysanthemums sat on either side of the door. In spite of the smoke coming from the chimney the day was warm, and the white front door was ajar so that only a screened door separated the inside from the out. I peered in, but could see nothing for the dazzle of sunlight behind me. There was no sound. I rapped my knuckles lightly and waited.

No one answered, so I rapped again, and then called out, "Hello? Is anyone here? I've brought some things from Mrs. Ponder ..."

There was still no response, and so, tentatively, I pushed the screen open and went in. Like the living room in the big farmhouse, this one was all murk and shadows, but it smelled of lemon polish and freshly ironed linen. I stood, waiting for my eyes to adjust. When they did, I saw first that a large chair was over-turned and lay in the middle of the wooden floor, and then that beside it a little table was upended, and had spilled books and a pitcher holding wildflowers down beside the chair. Wrongness flooded the room and lifted the hairs at my nape again, and I began to back out on to the porch. And then I saw the man who lay behind the chair, and my heart and breath stopped.

I had no doubt in that instant that he was dead. His face had the silvery-yellow sheen of the few dead I had seen, and he lay utterly, totally still, on his back, with his arms flung out to his sides. His eyes were closed and looked as if they had been closed for hours; their lids were dark and bruised-looking, and in the pallor of his face the circles under them stood out like paint smudges. His hair was a dusty, lightless black streaked with iron gray and fell over his forehead, and he had that pinched and shrunken look at the base of his nostrils that I had noticed during my duties in the oncology ward at Grady: the look of a tool that is no longer needed. His mouth was bloodless and a little open. Even in my shock and fright I could have told that he was Bella Ponder's son. The carved, attenuated features were the same, except that his were no longer informed by life.

I made a small, strangled sound and took as deep a breath as I could manage, and my heart lurched for-ward. How could I go out and tell that old woman that her son was dead? Perhaps I should call someone else, a hospital, the rescue squad; hadn't she said there was a phone in this cottage? I took a tentative step farther and looked around for it.

"And who the fuck might you be?" a voice said,

with no force behind it, but clear nevertheless, and deep.

I gave a small scream and looked again: His eyes were open and his head was turned toward me. His eyes were a strange light gray, the color of clear winter ice, and I saw that his face was so thin that the ridges of his brow and cheekbones stood out like rock under depleted soil. He still had no color but the dreadful, translucent ivory.

"Lie still," I whispered. "I'm going to call someone to help you, and then I'll get your mother . . ."

"You'll call nobody and you will not get my mother," he said, and his voice grew a bit stronger. He was struggling to sit up. I started toward him to help and he made a violent gesture at me: Get back. I stopped. It was only then that I noticed that he had only one leg. He was wearing khaki knee-length shorts, and one long, spidery leg was stretched out before him. The other shorts leg was empty. Whatever had happened to him had taken it at least at midthigh.

"I guess you're the handmaiden my mother has hired or bribed or otherwise charmed to look after me," he said, and his voice was cold and level, though still weak. "Who are you? Another royal Coimbran cousin-in-exile? Or is your name maybe Rakestraw or Fowler or Phipps? Or even Ponder? If so, how much did she pay you? If not, are you a bona-fide, official sister of charity come to fill your quota of one-legged gimps? Do tell, pray do, and end my poor befuddlement."

There was such venom in his voice that I could not think of anything to say. He was obviously not in immediate extremis and even more obviously did not want me in his house, but on the other hand, his pallor was truly appalling and I *had* found him lying on the floor, looking quite dead. And he did indeed have, as he himself said, only one leg. Conditioned by years of volunteer work and even more years of my mother's maxims about my place in the world, I went over to him and held out my hand.

"My name is Molly Redwine," I said. "I'm not anybody's handmaiden. I came about the camp your mother advertised, and she just now told me about you, and asked me if I'd consider doing a few errands for you until you recuperated, and if I'd come bring you some things she has for you. She can't walk far herself; I'm sure you know that. She said nothing at all about your having . . . about the seriousness of your illness or your operation or whatever it is, and she has offered me no money at all, nor would I take any if she had. I'm sorry if I startled you. You scared me to death. I thought you were dead. I have no intention of bothering you and I will leave the instant I can get you on your feet again, or whatever it is that you need, but I'm not going to leave until then because your mother can't help you and it doesn't look to me as if you can help yourself."

He looked away, lying still, and then said, "I'd appreciate it if you'd help me up. I was trying to get situated in the chair and I missed it and fell. I still can't get up very well when I fall. I've been taking . . . treatments that make me weak. I shouldn't have talked to you like that. But I don't need any help, and she knows that I don't want any, and still she . . . Well. If you'll give me a hand you can be on your way, and I hope you'll tell her for me to stay the fuck out of my business and my house. No offense, of course."

I tightened my mouth and went over and held my

hand down to him. Leaning on me heavily, and with me pulling, he eventually made it to his feet—or, rather, his foot—and I pulled the chair up behind him and he sank into it, whiter than ever and breathing shallowly.

When he did not speak, I said, "You've been taking chemo, haven't you? I've done a lot of work with oncology patients. I know the look. It's none of my business, but it doesn't look to me as if you're nearly ready to be out of the hospital, to say nothing of way out here, without anyone with you full-time. I don't want it to be me any more than you do, but you really do need somebody. I'm going back and tell your mother that, and tell her to go on back home and call you and work it out with you if she can't get up here herself. It's suicidal for you to be here like this by yourself."

I turned to go, and he said after me, "You're right. It's none of your business. Tell her whatever you like; I'm not talking to her and I'm not having anybody gawking and groping around here every day, helping me pee and wash myself and eat. You can tell her that, as long as you're telling her things. Oh, and thank you very much for your concern, Molly . . . ah, Redwine, was it? You're not from around here, are you, Molly? I have to hand it to her; I never thought she'd try it with somebody from America."

He closed his eyes and turned his head away, looking dead once more. I stood still, my heart hammering with the malice and sheer sickness of him, and then I turned and strode toward the Jeep to tell Bella Ponder that I would not, after all, be taking her up on her offer.

CHAPTER EIGHT

IT COULDN'T HAVE BEEN more than a minute's walk
back to the smaller camp and the Cherokee, but it
felt as if it took a very long time. I seemed to be walking in slow motion, as against a heavy current. There
was a clarity to the air that snapped details into sharp
focus, as if every leaf, blade of grass, stone, glimpse of
water had been edged in light. I could see a ladybug on
a leaf, a scaldingly red miniature, and make out the
whorls and slivers, the velvety green algae beard, of
the pilings of the old dock. I felt dully sad and terribly
tired. I had been up and down with this place so often
in this short morning, so suffused with hope and rightness one moment and doubt and regret the next. But
now there was only the sense of possibilities lost to me.

For this situation was impossible. I could not care
for the sick and virulent man in the larger cabin and I
could not accommodate the sly old colossus who
sought to bring us together. I was repelled by the one
and mortally weary of the other. I could, I knew, look
for a house somewhere else up island, but I knew also
that none would ever suit me after this one. Anything
else would have holes in its magic, belong to a duller
and more dangerous world.

I thought that I would simply go home. There would, surely, be apartments that did not require enormous deposits. I might not like them, but I could manage. Nothing, as my mother used to say, is cast in stone.

But anger at the old woman and her son lay deep under grief for the haven that had been dangled and then snatched back.

I did not look at Bella Ponder until I reached the Jeep. When I did, she was smiling at me, a smile that exposed her pale gums and was somehow unpleasantly false and slyly propitiatory. I would have bet a lot that this old woman did not often propitiate. I knew that she knew I was angry with her; how could she not?

"I hung your mother's pretty hat on your door," she said, pointing, and I looked; it was there. I looked back, saying nothing, waiting.

"People seem to be doing that all over the place these days," she said chattily. "Down island, I mean. Only hats you see much up here are Landry's Fish Camp hats and a few Red Sox things. Look kind of silly on your front door, wouldn't they? But I thought it might be sort of nice for you, to have your mama's hat hanging on your own new door. It looks pretty against that white, don't you think?"

I did not look at the hat on the door again. I took a deep breath.

"Mrs. Ponder," I said, "you have not been straight with me from the very beginning. Everything, all the stuff about fixing up the camp and putting in a phone and giving me a car and a TV . . . it was all for that, wasn't it? That back there?"

I gestured toward the larger camp. She did not

speak. She dropped the brilliant black eyes and looked at her lap.

"You knew your son had more wrong with him than just a little operation on his leg; you knew he was an amputee, and that he had . . . a malignancy. I've done volunteer work with cancer patients for half my life; I know what it looks like. I know what it *is* like. I know what it requires in the way of caretaking. Your son was lying on the floor stock-still and as white as a sheet; I thought he was dead. He'd been trying to sit in a chair, and fell and couldn't get up. Just trying to sit in a chair. When I tried to get help for him, he said . . . well, you wouldn't believe what he said. Or maybe you would. I can't and won't take care of a man in the shape he's in, and I can't and won't have anyone talking to me like that. He should be in a hospital or a rehabilitation facility, or maybe even a hospice; at the very least he needs a full-time nurse with him. If he won't see you, surely you should be looking for somebody who could live in and take proper professional care of him. It's absolutely suicidal for him to stay alone, and it's absolutely out of the question for me to look after him."

I had been looking at the ground while I delivered myself of the speech; I have always had a hard time with confrontation and ultimatums. When there was no answer, I looked into the Jeep at Bella Ponder.

She was crying. Incredibly, her eyes closed and her mouth struggling with itself not to distort, Bella Ponder sat in Livvy's Cherokee and wept. I knew that they were not crocodile tears; they were as grudging and painful to her as if she wept blood. It was like watching a monolith, a great statue, suddenly begin to cry. I knew that it would be nearly unbearable to her;

she might inveigle and cajole and lie and even, ponderously, flirt, but to weep in front of a stranger would be more than her awful dignity would permit her.

Under my righteous little spurt of anger I felt embarrassment and a sympathy that was entirely unwanted and nearly excruciating. I turned away so that she could compose herself, my heart pounding, tears stinging my own eyes, hating both the heartbeat and the easy wetness.

Behind me, Bella Ponder's heavy, defeated voice said, "He won't let me help him. He hasn't spoken to me since he left this island, practically. He said he'd shoot at the visiting nurse if I sent her. He won't have his Ponder kin, not that they'd come if I asked them, which I wouldn't. He'd only agree to have somebody who didn't know any of us, somebody from off island, and then only if he could pay them. I couldn't find anybody like that; there's not anybody like that up island in the winter. And then you came along and it was like somebody sent you to us; you were all those things he said, and you even looked like . . . you seemed kind of like one of us in the bargain. Luz was right; you have the look of a Portuguese about you, somehow. She thought it was a sign, and I didn't know but what it was, too. I knew you wouldn't take any money to look after Denny, so I offered you everything else I had, that I could think of. I was going to let him think I was giving you his money, not that he's got much. His wife and his girl get most of it, I hear, and he'll have had to quit his job. He couldn't have anything to speak of or he wouldn't have come out here. I didn't . . . I haven't seen him in over forty years. I knew it was cancer, but I guess I didn't know it was so bad. He said . . . the only thing he said on the phone was that he thought he wouldn't need anybody past March or April. I thought he meant he'd be well by then, and he'd leave, but I guess maybe that wasn't what he meant . . ."

Her voice, suddenly frail and old, trailed off, but when I looked at her I saw that the tears had not stopped. They slid silently down the big, seamed, brown face, leaving trails like a snail's on earth.

I looked over at the door of the smaller camp. My mother's lacy black hat stood out against the pocked white like a spider on old snow. It looked fixed, inexorable. This is my outpost in this place, it said. Here I live. Get in here and start doing what you know you should be doing.

I took another deep breath, feeling it shake in my lungs.

"Mrs. Ponder," I said again, "I'm never going to ask you what's wrong between you and your son. I don't even want to know. But if I should stay and try to do some things for him—and I said *if*—he'll have to stop talking to me like he just did. I really can't have that. And you'll have to stop trying to manipulate me. *And* I insist on at least having the visiting nurse; why couldn't he just pay her if he wants to pay somebody?"

"She doesn't take pay. She's a county service," Bella said. Her voice was still soft and even deferential, but it was two decades younger. "Denny wouldn't take county help, and I wouldn't ask for it. My God, our people come from royalty back in Portugal, ours and his; he's named for King Dinis, who was a direct forebear. Everybody who knows anything at all about the Portuguese knows about King Dinis. He was called the troubadour king, the poet king. He built more than a hundred castles in

Portugal in the twelfth century. I think Denny gets his talent from him; he writes beautiful poetry. Some of it's been published. You think a Miara from Coimbra is going to take charity?"

Oh, God, I thought, nearly overcome with a great, helpless, white fatigue. This poor, awful, grotesque, proud, silly old woman. She would have recognized my mother in a nanosecond. They're the same person. Who on earth would bother with her and her awful, dying son?

But I knew who was probably going to bother.

I reached across her into the glove compartment of the Cherokee and pulled out the pad and ballpoint pen that Livvy kept there. I wrote on it; I scribbled for quite a long time. Then I jerked the sheet from the pad and gave it to her. She read it carefully, her face impassive but still tear-stained, and gave it back to me and nodded. I folded the sheet small and took it up on the front porch of the larger camp and pushed it under the closed door and came back to the Jeep.

"Get somebody to come get his answer in the morning, and call me and tell me what it is," I said. "I want him to sign it, too. If he agrees to it—*all* of it, everything—I'll take the camp. I'll try to keep it and look after him a little, with some outside help when I think I need it, if and until he gets so he needs hospitalizing. I'm out of it then, no questions asked. I may stay on after that, or I may not. I'll try to let you know as far ahead as possible if I don't. And I'll only do this if you agree not to put me in the middle of whatever this mess between you is, and if you both agree that I can call the visiting nurse or somebody whenever I think it's necessary. That's it. No more talking."

Bella smiled. It tried its best to be a humble smile,

but triumph oozed from it like sap from a maple tree. For some reason, that came near to amusing me. I would have been somehow disappointed if I could so easily bring this elemental force to her knees, I knew. Disappointed and perhaps just a bit frightened of my own power. I had never been able to do that with my own mother. It would have been disconcerting, to say the least, to be able to do it with anyone else's.

We did not speak again until I had reached the farmhouse and opened the door on her side to help her get out and make her way up the steps. After I had hauled her to her feet, she put her hand on my arm and looked down into my face. Few people are able to do that. It was an odd sensation.

"I want to thank you for what you're doing," she said, and shook her head impatiently as I started to speak. "I don't mean about Denny; there's no way I can thank you for that. I mean what you're doing for Luz. I was about one day from having to call somebody about those swans. The last two times I've gone down to feed them, I thought I wouldn't get back. And I couldn't let them starve. And I sure couldn't ask anybody else to feed them and bust up that ice all winter. They'd laugh in my face. Not that folks around here are mean to animals, I'll give you that, but they've got other things on their minds, and they sure aren't sentimental about swans. There's too many of them pecking around up here, and they do too much damage. Somebody would have just shot them and that would have been that. It would have killed Luz. So I thank you."

Then she took my arm and, leaning heavily on it, made her way back up the steps and into the old house, stopping every few seconds so she could gulp in air. When we finally got inside, her face was nearly

purple, and sweat ran down it like rain. I put her into
a chair beside Luz's bed and got a glass of water from
the dark old kitchen. It smelled of spices and tomatoes
and illness.

She sipped the water, and Luz smiled at us, an
irresistible smile, full of joy and gaiety. It moved me
even more than Bella's tears had.

"I knew you were going to save the swans," she
said. "I said so before you left for the camp. Didn't I,
Bella? I said, 'Bella, this is our *Santa Cisna*, who's going
to take care of Charles and Di for us. I've prayed every
night to the Virgin to send her. And here she is.' I said
that."

As soon as I satisfied myself that Bella Ponder
could breathe again, I left and went out to the
Cherokee. I drove back to Chappaquiddick with the
radio tuned to a Boston FM station playing Baroque
music. Halfway between West Tisbury and Edgartown *The Water Music* began, spilling its liquid notes
out into the car, and I grinned at the radio.

"Okay," I said aloud. "I know a conspiracy when I
hear one."

I knew that Dennis Ponder would agree to my
terms. I could not have said how, but I knew it as certainly as I knew that it was the On Time Ferry whose
deck wallowed beneath my tires, and not the *QE2*.
Everything about this strange, freighted morning was
bright with portent. And though I had no wish at all to
be anyone's *santa*, of the swans or anything else, I was
glad of the knowledge. The song of the little camp and
the glade and the pond was loud in my ears; it swam
in and out among Handel's silvery notes, playing with
them, vaulting over them. I knew I had been right
about up island.

I felt almost manic with anticipation, as gleeful as a child with a daring, secret plan, when I went into the old house on Katama Bay. But I had no sooner sat down at the kitchen desk and pulled the telephone to me to begin the series of calls I had to make than the great, glittering brightness outside curled into the kitchen like smoke and wrapped around me, and the elation left. In its place was the crawling unease I had felt here for the last two days. I got up and went to the porch door and looked out, looking both ways and up into the sky to see whose prowling shape I seemed to almost catch from the corner of my eye. But there was nothing, only the fractured diamond surface of the dancing bay, and the late summer light playing in the trees and grasses that bent in the wind, and the shadows of the small clouds that rocketed across the afternoon sky. The wind was hard; I could hear it making a crooning sound that had little to do with summer and soft, golden light; it prowled in my blood and bones. The vista from the porch was too big by far, too exposed. I pulled the curtains and sat back down. The restlessness in me that wind and space called up came very near to fear. But with the curtains drawn and the lamps lit, I felt better.

I did not think I could stay much longer in the house on the water, though. Not this house. Not this water.

First I called Teddy at school and, miraculously, reached him at his apartment. He was home for lunch, he said, and I smiled, seeing in my mind as well as hearing the sandwich that bulged in his cheek as he spoke. It struck me that I would love little more right then than to make a sandwich for my son, and I played the scene out in my mind, and found to my

amazement I could not picture my own kitchen. Instead, I saw myself slicing bread and spreading mayonnaise in the cramped kitchen of the camp in the
glade, scrubbed now and bright with fall flowers and
noon light.

I told him what I was going to do, and he nearly
choked on the sandwich and then laughed aloud.

"Way to go, Ma," he crowed. "My Robinson Crusoe
mom! What brought this on, as if I didn't know?"

Suddenly I did not want to tell him that my house
was, in effect, not mine anymore. It sounded impossibly theatrical, nauseatingly poor me. It was, after all,
Teddy's house, too; why had I not considered where
he would go if he wanted to come home? This separation was, after all, about other people as well as me. It
had been that that had outraged me from the beginning, and yet in all the time I was falling in love with
the camp, I had not thought of Teddy.

"It's not a sure thing yet," I said, feeling my grand
adventure deflate like a circus balloon. "I wasn't going
to do it without consulting you . . ."

"Well, I think it's cool," he said. "How long do
you think you'll stay? A month? Two?"

"Well . . . actually, I thought longer than that.
Through the winter, at least. Teddy . . . there are some
reasons I don't feel I can come back to Atlanta for a
while. Missy thinks it's best, too. I can't . . . it's probably not a good idea for me to live in the house for a
while, and money's going to be a little tight, not that
that's anything for you to worry about. It won't affect
you . . ."

"Is he cutting off your money?" my son said, and
there was ice and pain in his voice.

"No," I said. "It's my own decision. As I said, it's

not going to affect you. But listen, I thought you might like to come spend Thanksgiving with me up here. We can have a real, old-fashioned New England Thanksgiving. Maybe Grandpop can come, too. It's really very beautiful up here. I'd love to show it to you . . ."

There was a silence, and then he said, "Ma, since you aren't going to be home anyway—in Atlanta, I mean—would you care if I went camping with some of the guys? There's a guy in my structures class who lives near the Anasazi ruins in Arizona, and a bunch are going. I'd give my eyeteeth to see that. But listen, if you're going to be up there by yourself—"

"I'm not going to be by myself," I said hastily. "The Anasazi, wow! I'd kill you if you *didn't* go. I'll call Grandpop. I bet he'd love to rough it in the woods . . ."

"Mom, he's going to Aunt Sally's folks' with them. I talked to him the other night. Listen, why don't you call Caroline? What better company for Thanksgiving than a new baby? In Tennessee, if not up there . . ."

"Well, that's just what I'll do," I said heartily, knowing that I would not. Caroline had not yet mustered the nerve to take the baby to the park by herself. She would faint at the very thought of up island. My throat closed up; I had had no idea how much I missed Teddy until I heard his voice. Missed and loved him; loved him enough to insist that he try his new wings.

"If they can't come or you can't go there, just call me. I'll be there with bells on," he said.

"No need, I've met a lot of people up here who're looking out for me," I said lightly. "I'm the belle of the bay."

"I'll bet. Any interesting guys? Any action?"

"Only one," I said. "And he's as mean as a snake and one-legged besides."

Forgive me, Dennis, I said to myself. But right now you're more use to me as fodder to amuse my son than anything else. And besides, you owe me.

"Just your speed," Teddy said, and we laughed together. Even over the telephone, even with the disappointment and the missing, it felt good.

I meant to call my father next, but instead I stretched out on the sofa, and slid instantly into a long and vivid dream about my mother. It was not the usual dream about the grated subterranean window, or at least not just that. It began in the same way, but it went farther into the country of nightmare and panic than I had ever been in my dreams before, and I know that I will remember the precise, sweating texture of that dream until the day that I die.

It started out the same: with me on the city street looking down to see the barred subterranean window where my mother always sat in the black hat, waiting. But this time the window was empty, and I turned to my father, who stood beside me in the crowd, and said, "She's not there."

"Maybe she's found what she was waiting for," my father said, looking around. I looked around, too, and saw my mother standing ahead of us on the sidewalk, facing backward in the crowd so that she looked at us. She wore the hat, and she was smiling with pleasure and sweetness. In my dream my heart gave a great fish leap of joy. I knew that she was dead, but nevertheless, there she was, smiling her approval at me. I did not point her out to my father, who was still looking about eagerly, or any of the crowd going past, lest they become aware of her suddenly, and somehow frighten her away. It seemed, with the senseless sense of dreams, entirely possible for my dead mother to be with me as long as I did not call attention to her. I did not understand why my father could not see her, though.

I went close to her and whispered, "I'm so glad to see you. You look so pretty in that hat."

I did not point out to her that I knew she was dead. It was as if she herself did not know, that for her to know would be to lose her.

"I've always liked this hat," she said. It was her voice, no doubt of that, low and full and with that hint of husky theatricality that I had always so envied. "I don't think there's anything like a big hat to play up a woman's eyes. I'd give it to you, but it's meant for somebody else."

I could not say, No, it's not, I have it, so I just nodded and said, politely, "Oh? Who?"

"Your father," she said. "This hat is for your father. Can you find him for me?"

"I don't know where he is," I said in the dream, but my eyes flicked to my father of their own volition, and I saw her see him, and start toward him in a little rush of joy. She took the hat off and her hair flew free around her pretty head, and she held it out and called, "Darling! Come and get your hat!"

I turned, and behind me my father had seen her, and was starting toward her, his whole heart and soul in his eyes. He reached out for her hand and the black hat.

In that instant I knew that if he touched the hat he would be dead, too, and gone with her, and after that I would see them both in the terrible window, waiting for whatever it is the dead wait for.

"NOOOO!" I screamed, and woke myself up.

It was a full five minutes before I could stop shaking, stop the cold sweat that ran down my face and neck. My heart pounded for long after that. I looked at my watch and saw that I had slept for nearly two hours. Outside the drawn curtains, the sun would be setting. Blackness would be coming across the water from Nantucket.

I went to the phone and called Kevin's house in Washington. Kevin answered; he sounded as he did on the air. I wondered if he put his coat and tie on when he answered his telephone; he sounded as if he did.

"How is Daddy?" I said without preamble.

"Daddy's awful," Kevin said, and my galloping heart raced faster.

"What?"

"Depression," Kevin said. "Full-blown clinical depression. No doubt about it. We did a special on it a couple of months ago. It's all there, the lethargy, the sleeping, the lack of interest in everything, the loss of appetite, even the sloppy personal habits. It's a delayed reaction to Mother, I know. He's been in denial ever since she died, and now it's caught up with him."

"Have you had him to a doctor?" I said, pain for my father all but drowning me.

"He won't go, but I've talked with a shrink friend of ours, and he says there's no doubt of the diagnosis. He gave us a prescription for Prozac, but I don't think Dad's taking it. Sally doesn't want to monitor him, and I can't stay home and see that he does. Listen, Molly, I'm glad you called. I've been meaning to call you. You're just going to have to take over now. He's making no plans to go back to the condo, and we've decided that he ought to move in with you. It's the obvious solution, and it could be a help to you, too. But I know he'd take it better if the suggestion came from you."

I told him then about Tee and Sheri and the house in Ansley Park, and why Missy thought I should not live in it, and about the money, and then about the camp on the pond and the plans I had made.

"Well, if that's not the most harebrained, selfish thing I've ever heard in my life," Kevin exploded. "And the most typical. Get it all worked out for little Molly and let everybody else go hang. I guess it doesn't matter to you that Sally cries herself to sleep at night, and Mandy can't have any of her friends over anymore. Dad just sits there. He just sits there in the living room with the TV set on, not watching, not talking, just sitting there . . ."

I took a deep breath. It shook as I exhaled.

"Kevin, you know that never once in my life have I worked things out for myself and let everybody else go hang. You know that. That was unfair and untrue. If anybody in this family works things out for themselves and lets everybody else . . ."

I let it trail off. I did not want to fight with him. I never won.

"Okay, okay, I know," my brother said, and let his breath out on a long sigh. "That was below the belt. But we're all near to cracking. Look, if you can't go back to your house, and I think your lawyer is wrong, by the way, maybe you could go live with Dad, in the condo. He's not even trying to sell it anymore. It would solve all your problems, and he'd have somebody with him. I think he has to have that. Maybe you could get him to go for some help; we sure can't. I don't know but what he's not suicidal."

"Kevin! *Daddy?*"

"You haven't seen him, Molly."

"Let me talk to him."

After a bit my father came on the line. I listened very carefully, but to me he sounded just as he always had; the slow, mild voice was the father's that I knew and none other.

"Hey, baby, they lynched you yet?" he asked, and I laughed. It was an old joke of ours, that I tanned as darkly as an African-American in the sun.

I told him about the camp, and about the old ladies and Dennis Ponder, though I softened that considerably, saying only that Dennis was recuperating from leg surgery, and I tried to make the plight of the old ladies merely funny and crochety. I said nothing about my reasons for not coming home or about my severely curtailed financial circumstances; no reason to burden him with that. But I dwelt at length on Charles and Diana, and was rewarded with his old, rich chuckle.

"That must be a sight to see," he said. "I'm going to read up on swans. Maybe I can find some arcane tidbit of swan psychology that will help you with the old man. Well, babe, good for you and all your plans. Sounds to me that you've gone from the frying pan into the fire, though; from looking after one family to looking after another, with an ornery feathered family thrown in."

I had not thought of it that way, and was not sure I liked the implications.

"Well, they're not my family," I said lightly. "That's why I can do it, I think. There's really not much to it, and I'm not emotionally involved with anybody. That's the killer. That's not going to happen again."

He laughed again, but comfortably.

"So you say."

I asked about Thanksgiving and he said yes, he had indeed committed to Sally's parents.

"Would you come for Christmas?" I said hesitantly. All of a sudden it was very important to me that he say yes.

"Well, that would be fun, wouldn't it? Snow and swans and all that? Sure, if you're still up there," my father said.

I got Kevin back on the line.

"He sounds okay to me," I said.

"He's trying to spare you," Kevin said. I could tell by his voice that he was angry again.

"I don't think so . . ."

"Shit, Molly, it's what he's always done. You were always his baby."

And you were always Mother's, and now you're not anybody's, and that's what all this is about, I did not say. I waited. There was a silence. Then he said, "Molly, you go on home and take care of him. Enough is enough. You're the only one who can do anything with him."

"I can't do that," I said.

"What is it, you want to kill him, too?" Kevin said, and I hung up on him, shaking. But I was not surprised. I knew that he would always feel that I had killed our mother. Whether or not he was right, he had the power of his cherished conviction about that. It would always be his best weapon against me.

I got up from the desk and poured myself a small glass of the lovely, thick, tawny port that Livvy had brought over from Boston; Portuguese port from the Duoro River region, she had told me. It tasted like smoke and honey going down. I brought the glass back to the desk and sipped at it as I dialed Missy Carmichael.

Missy hooted at the idea of me in the cabin on the pond all winter, with my ill and eccentric entourage, but she favored the idea all the same.

"It'll sound divine to a jury," she purred. "You living in a freezing hovel far away because you can't afford to come home, especially at Christmas. I can make hell's own amount of hay with that."

The trial. How could I have forgotten about the trial? It did not seem real at all.

"Any idea when that will be?" I said. The whole notion made me more tired than I thought possible. I slumped in my chair.

"Well, it's funny," Missy said. "Tee's beating around the bush about the trial. He's missed the last two meetings with us; she's always there, breathing fire and brimstone, but he just . . . hasn't shown. I don't know why, and I don't think she does, either. It sounds to me as if she doesn't know where he is a good bit of the time. He sure ain't taking my calls. I finally called the Eel Woman at the office to try to get some answers. She blew me right out of the water. Meaner than fresh cat shit these days, no doubt about that. But it doesn't look like she can do anything with him any more than we can. I can't help but wonder if he's having second thoughts. If I were him, I'd be afraid to tell that woman I had any doubts, either; hand you your balls back, she would. So the answer to your question is, I don't know. You'll eventually have to come home, but not for a while at this rate.

You'll stay with me when you do, of course. Oh, and that little geisha at your bank called and Tee's first payment to your new account has come in. She didn't know how to call you, so she asked me to let you know. You can draw on it whenever you want to. You probably ought to open yourself an account up there, if you're serious about staying. It would show good intent if you did."

I did not know how I felt about Tee's wishy-washiness. I found that I could not fit any possible change of heart on his part into any scenario for the future I could imagine, so I dealt with it by simply not thinking about it. I buried it deep, along with all the other flotsam and jetsam of this awful summer. I would take it out and look at it later, when it might make more sense. I asked Missy to send some of my winter clothes, and hung up, feeling more rootless and suspended than ever. I took an apple and went over and walked on South Beach, thinking the sunset and the fresh wind might dispel some of the murk in my head. But the sun had slipped behind a great bank of silver-shot gray clouds in the southwest to die, and the sea had turned a terrible, beautiful, flashing pewter, all motion and coldness. When the lone family left on the beach packed up their things and disappeared over the dunes to their car, I fairly flew to the Jeep and drove back to Livvy's. Aloneness had turned into a great, personal thing that stalked me like a panther.

The phone was ringing as I came into the kitchen, and I grabbed it up as if it were a lifeline thrown into black water. Any voice, any voice at all . . .

It was Livvy. Caleb was working late and she wanted to talk. I could tell that she had had one and perhaps more of her sundown glasses of wine. I poured myself more of her port and settled in to listen. Her voice warmed me, like the liquor going down. In all the strangeness around me, Livvy seemed as palpable as if she sat in the room. She told me the news of our set, which made no more sense to me than if she spoke of a group of aborigines she had read about, and then said that Caleb had told her that the gossip around the office was that Sheri Scroggins was living in my house in Ansley Park. Tee, she said, was almost never in town anymore, but she supposed that he had installed her there.

"Even she wouldn't dare, unless he had," Livvy said. "You'll probably have to pry her off your rug like a tick. I wonder if they plan on just letting you find her there when you come home? Speaking of which, have you made any plans yet? I don't care how long you stay up there, but the pipes will freeze eventually, and people are asking me. Carrie Davies, that chalice of all that is fine and fair in Southern womanhood—oh, all right, I know she was your sainted roommate—called me last night wanting to know. She hemmed and hawed and finally let drop that poor old Lazarus is driving her crazy. Says he has a certain doggy odor, and I gather he licks his balls—not that Carrie would say so, of course. I'd take him but I'm going with Caleb to Chicago for a youth brands conference, and then we thought we might go up to Mackinac Island for a week or ten days. Kind of a second honeymoon."

She giggled, and I smiled into the empty room. I was glad things were still good with Livvy and Caleb. My poison hadn't found its mark, then.

It was only after I hung up that I realized I had not told her of my decision to stay here. I could not think why I had not.

I called Carrie Davies. Listening to her piping treble chiming through its scale, I wondered why I had never noticed what a shrill voice she had. Livvy had once said Carrie sounded like a hedgehog looked like it ought to sound, "all tiggywinklish." I had defended Carrie, but now I saw what Livvy had meant. Carrie and Atlanta seemed as far away as the dark side of Uranus.

"It might be a while before I can get back," I said to her finally, when she had run down. I had no intention of telling her my plans yet. "I know Lazarus can be a little much. Could you or Charlie take him to the Ansley Animal Clinic until Dad or I get home? Dr. Newman knows him. He's boarded him before."

"Well, of course," Carrie said, the alacrity of deliverance clear in her voice. "Maybe that would be better. He's really pining for you, I think. He howls a lot. Oh, here he comes; listen, Lazarus, here's your mommy. Say something, Molly . . ."

"Hey, big dog," I said into the telephone, feeling foolish, and was rewarded with a long, mournful howl.

My heart literally cramped with pain and homesickness for him. Here at last was reality.

"Carrie, do you think Charlie could possibly put him on a plane up here for me?" I said, wondering why I had not thought of it until now. Of course, that was what the camp and the glade called out for: Lazarus. Big, goofy, clumsy, loving Lazarus. The swans would just have to work it out.

"I guess so," she said doubtfully, seeing her imminent deliverance seeping away. "Ah . . . when would you want him?"

"Can you give me a week?"

There was a silence, and then she said, warmly, "Sure. What's a week between me and this old guy? You know, it's Tee who really ought to be taking care of him, but the way he's acting, I wouldn't let him take care of an iguana. Did anybody tell you that he's moved that little hussy into your house? I guess I shouldn't tell you, but I think you've got the right to know . . ."

"I heard," I said. "It's okay. Little does she know that there's colorless, odorless, death-dealing radon seeping from the basement as we speak. Asbestos, too. She'll be toast in a month."

"Really?" gasped Carrie.

"Why do you think I'm not coming home yet?" I said, knowing that she would take it literally, and that it would be all over Buckhead by this time tomorrow.

I thanked her again for sitting Lazarus and hung up. My good humor was restored enough so that the rising wind outside did not really bother me, and when I finally crept upstairs to sleep, I dreamed, not of my mother in her haunted subway, but of the quiet woods outside Menemsha.

The next morning Bella Ponder called to say that Dennis had accepted my terms, and the day after that I moved up island.

CHAPTER NINE

THE DAY I MOVED WAS THICK and gray; last night's wind had blown in a canopy of low clouds that promised rain. The drive up island was dun-colored, but the beginning colors of autumn were oddly enhanced by the dullness. The stand of beetlebung trees at the crossroads in Chilmark was beginning to redden a leaf here and there. Livvy had said that in the autumn they were one of the Vineyard's glories. My first New England autumn: I felt as excited as a child going on a vacation in new territory. It was how I would live, I thought; how I would create a new life up here: I would taste as fully as I could each new experience, new sight, new sound. I would leave my baggage at home. I did not want to waste any time on regret and pain. The great stew of unresolved emotion over my mother and my marriage would just have to simmer on the back burner until I got around to it.

Moreover, if I were going to make a fresh life in this place, I had better get on with it right away. For the first time I felt, on that drive, an urgent sense that my time of being was no longer limitless. The sense left a residue of sucking blackness, as if a curtain had parted briefly and let me look into an abyss. "Mortality," my mother used to exclaim. "You can't live until you confront your own mortality." But somehow she had never confronted her own, probably not even when it happened. I dumped the mortal blackness into the stew pot with the rest of my ghosts and slammed the lid down.

The first thing I did when I drove into the glade was to stop by and look in on Dennis Ponder. Get it over with; set up a routine; lay a firm foundation of quick, impersonal, no-nonsense contact. I would, I thought, try checking on him first thing in the mornings and late in the afternoons. That way, if he needed anything, I could get it during the daytime and deliver it to him before dinnertime. Like feeding the swans, I intended that the care and feeding of Dennis Ponder be as efficient and nominal as I could make it. I did not imagine he wanted me hovering over him any more than Charles and Diana obviously did.

No smoke curled from the chimney of the larger camp this morning, though it was considerably cooler than the day before. I walked up the steps and across the porch, and lifted my hand to knock, then saw that the door was ajar. I was instantly uneasy.

"Mr. Ponder?" I called, halfway expecting to hear nothing, as I had before. But a voice called out, "Come in. Back in the bedroom."

I walked through the big living space, seeing that a fire was laid but not lit, and that the stove in the kitchen was unlit, too. There was a wood box beside it like the one in my kitchen, this one filled with neatly hewn logs, and the stove's black-iron door stood open, but no fire burned inside. There was no coffee or tea on the counter, no sign of breakfast. Either he could manage easily after all, and had already eaten and cleaned up after himself, or he was unable to manage at all and

I would have to do it. I prayed it was the former. I could not imagine feeding that cold, white man.

I went to the doorway of the big downstairs bedroom behind the living room and looked in. A floor lamp burned there, and he was sitting in an upright chair beside it, dressed and combed. His plaid shirt was buttoned up to the neck and the collar was far too big for his throat. It was the look of the old, or the sick. There were piles of books all over the room: on the unmade double bed; on the floor beside it; spilling off the desk and the one easy chair; still occupying moving boxes stacked against the wall. He had one open on his knee, and was making notes on a legal pad. At first he did not look up, and I stood there, waiting. I was determined not to speak first. Then he finished writing and did look at me.

He looked marginally better. His face was not so waxen yellow, though it was still pale, and the bones still made ridges through the translucent skin. He had not shaved, and there was a dark shadow of beard around his mouth and on his cheeks and chin. His eyes were dark and sunken under level black brows, and his mouth was long and mobile, the pale lips full in contrast to the rest of the desiccated face. If he had been well, it would have been a sensuous mouth. His black hair had damp comb tracks in it, and fell in a shock over his forehead. Forehead and cheeks were cut with deep lines of pain and weakness; I knew those lines from my hospital work. They furrowed what I could see of his brow, too, and bracketed his mouth. I was reminded of someone, and could not think who until I remembered seeing, late one evening the summer before, an old movie with Gregory Peck and Jennifer Jones called *Duel in the Sun*. Dennis Ponder

reminded me of the indolent outlaw played by
Gregory Peck in that movie, if Peck had been much
older and wasted with cancer. Even with the stigmata
of the disease on him, Dennis Ponder was a handsome
man. Or, at least, had been. The resemblance to his
mother was less today, but still apparent, though how
that might be I could not have said; Bella was near to
being grotesque. But still, in her son's face, you could
see what she once might have been . . .

"How are you this morning?" I said when he still
did not speak. He stared at me a while longer, then
smiled. It was not a warm smile. I thought that his
mouth pulled tight in pain would look the same way.

"I'm sorry, I don't mean to stare," he said, and his
voice was as colorless as his face. "You really look
remarkably like what I remember of my mother. I
thought for a minute yesterday you were one of our
endless kin; the Miara ones, of course. My mother is
very good at importing relatives. But you're not one of
us, of course; she wrote me a remarkably thorough
dossier on you: outlander through and through, you
are, aren't you? No ties at all to this sacred sod. Why
you want any is one of God's great mysteries, I suppose, but that's your affair, as is everything else about
you, and I assure you it will remain so. I'm sorry I
snapped at you yesterday. I'm told I'm not to do it
again."

It was not a pleasant little speech.

"That's right," I said. "You're not. So. How are
you today? You look a good deal better than you did
the last time I saw you."

"How am I?" he said, and smiled, the skeletal
teeth flashing white. "I expect you know how I am. My
mother's note also said that you work with cancer

patients back home in . . . Atlanta, is it? She is quite excited about that; thinks it's a sign that *Santa Maria* sent you to us. As you can see, when it comes to *Santa Maria*, no stone has been left unturned."

He gestured and for the first time I noticed that there was a carved black-and-gold crucifix, obviously old, over his bed, and two or three painted statuettes of the Virgin Mary, and a heavy old mahogany reredos against one wall, flowers and candles set out on it.

"I know something about malignancies," I said evenly.

"Then perhaps you'll know what I mean when I say that I have had a stage-four adult soft-tissue sarcoma that made shit out of my knee, found a home in some lymph glands, and headed uptown. By the time we found it there was no way to save the bottom leg and knee, and there's no way now to know if any more of it will have to go. I'm among the elite; it's very rare, especially in adults. It has been treated with radiation and chemotherapy, and I had the last treatment just before I came here. There is not any pain except in the part of the leg that is gone, which I understand is called phantom pain and is quite common. The itching is worse than the pain. The real pain comes next if the chemo doesn't work, which I will not know for a while. Nor will I know where; this baby travels. Mainly I am weak and still nauseated, but I understand this should pass. I still sleep quite a lot. As you see, I have not lost the hair on my head or face, though for some reason I lost all my body hair. I'm as slick as a boiled frog all over; I hope the notion does not appall you, or even worse, turn you on. What I will need from you is for you simply to check on groceries and things like that, and to take me to my doctors' appointments.

Those should be minimal, and the first is not for almost a month. I need no help with meals or bathing or household duties."

"Have you had your breakfast?" I said. "I didn't see any dishes, and your stove isn't lit."

His face colored faintly.

"I left my crutches in the bathroom," he said. "I just haven't gotten them yet. I'm still learning my way around this place . . ."

His voice trailed off and he looked down at his legal pad. I knew that he had not yet been able to retrieve the crutches, and was trying to put the best possible face on it for me. I knew, too, that he would rather fumble for the crutches, crawl on his knees, do without food and warmth than ask me to help him. For some reason, it made me angry.

I went into the bathroom, got the crutches, and stood them up against his chair. Then I went back into the living room, touched a match to the fire, lit the kitchen stove, and made coffee. I turned on the gas oven, put a couple of slices of bread on a baking sheet, and left it on the counter. I got butter and the ubiquitous beach plum jelly out of the refrigerator and set them beside the sheet. Then I went back into his bedroom.

"I got some things started for you," I said. "For God's sake, tell me when you need help. It takes about five seconds to do what needs doing, and it's one of the agreed-on conditions."

"Ah, yes, the conditions," he said. "Well, thank you, Molly whatever your last name is. From now on I'll remember the crutches, and I'll stay in the bedroom while you minister; you'll find a list of things I need on the table in the living room. That's where it will always be. I won't get in your way; I'll be working in here most of the time."

"Your mother says you're working on a book," I said, I hoped pleasantly.

"My mother is full of shit," he said, "but yes, I am. Do you know anything about publishing, Molly By Golly?"

"I've had a little experience," I said stiffly.

"Wait, don't tell me . . . you edited the Junior League cookbook. Am I right?"

He was, or nearly. It had been the Grady Hospital Auxiliary cookbook. My face burned.

"I'll leave you alone," I said. "If you should need me, just call . . . or no, I guess my phone's not in yet. Maybe you could—"

He gestured at the bedside table, and I saw then that an old-fashioned bronze dinner bell with a carved handle sat on it. Charlotte Redwine had one on her dining-room sideboard, only in silver.

"My mother has provided for all my needs, physical as well as spiritual," Dennis Ponder said. There was color on both cheekbones now, like hectic flags against the pallor. Somehow it did not make him look healthier. "There's even a crucifix in the kitchen, right over the portable toilet, in case I feel in need of a bit of blessing while taking a shit."

"Poor baby," I said meanly, and turned and left the room. This man was odious, dying or no, and I felt neither sympathy for nor curiosity about him. I picked up the grocery list that sat on the split log table in front of the scarred leather sofa, and went out into the gray morning. Down on the pond I caught a whisk of white. The swans were no doubt waiting for their breakfast, too.

"Tough patootie, you stupid turkeys," I said to them. "You can just wait till I have some coffee. Go glom some underwater plants. Eat some algae. Live a little."

It did not help my mood at all that the second man in one summer had compared me to a woman who loomed large in his life. I hated the first comparison and didn't at all care for the second.

"Maybe I'll get my head shaved and my nose pierced. What would you think of that?" I called to the swans as I got out of the Jeep. They had left the pond and were waddling up the bank toward me and, I supposed, their breakfast, lifting their great wings ominously. The larger, Charles I was sure now, began the snaky hissing.

"Terrific way to get your breakfast," I said, moving quickly up on to the porch of my camp. "Really makes the cook feel appreciated. For that you'll wait until I go out for groceries."

I stopped on the porch and looked around. Bella Ponder had been as good as her word. Someone had done some serious work on the smaller camp. From the bronze chrysanthemums in iron pots beside the front door to the swept and scrubbed porch floor and the shining windows, the outside of the little house had been transformed. Two rickety but clean twig armchairs and an old hammock on a freshly painted white iron stand stood on the porch, and there was a sheaf of early autumn foliage in a tin bucket on a twig table. I smiled. I could always spend my time on the porch if the interior was too grim. The real cold would not begin for a month yet.

But when I went inside I saw that there would be no need to do that. It might have been a different room. It, too, was swept and scrubbed; the fireplace was cleaned and laid with logs, ready to light; the two straight chairs had been joined by an old leather morris chair that looked as though someone had polished it; a round table laid with white crockery and a jar of wildflowers sat under the window at the end of the room. Old-fashioned white priscilla curtains, limp from years of wear but clean and ironed, framed the windows. A couple of thick plaid blankets smelling of camphor were draped over the sofa back. In the kitchen, which had been scrubbed, too, the wood box beside the iron stove was filled, and the stove itself looked newly blacked. Cooking stove and refrigerator had been scoured. There were a couple of place settings of age-bleached Fiesta ware, yellow and blue, on the open shelves, and a coffeepot and a tea kettle on the stove, and a new tin of coffee stood ready with a can opener beside it. I opened the refrigerator; it was tiny and stained, but it smelled sweetly of baking soda, and inside it sat a carton of cream and a paper plate with four sweet rolls on it. Crocks on the counter held some odds and ends of table and cooking ware, and there was a big iron cooking pot, an old iron skillet, and a battered baking sheet on an ancient but sturdy little butcher-block table that I had not seen before. A bottle of dish-washing liquid and a tin of scouring powder stood beside them. Even before I went upstairs to reconnoiter, I made coffee in the pot, old but serviceable and electric, and plugged it in. Then I saw, on a top shelf, the little plastic radio, and turned it on. It was set to a classical station, and Pachelbel's *Canon* spilled out into the sunny room. I smiled again.

"Thank you, Bella," I said aloud.

Upstairs was transformed, too. It was largely a matter of cleaning, I saw, but the difference soap and water and wax made was enormous. The long windows were framed in the same white priscillas, and gleamed from a scrubbing with, I thought, ammonia; the sharp, clean smell lingered. Beyond them the pond lay quiet and the sea beyond it glittered like still, silver satin. I could not see the swans from here. Pale, watery light lay in patches on the old pine boards of the floor, which had also been scoured and polished, and a faded rag rug stood in the middle of the room. The narrow iron bed had been replaced by an elaborate maple one, like something out of a turn-of-the-century bedroom, and it was made up with fresh old linen and piled high with quilts. Another bureau had been moved in, this one painted white, and on it stood another jar of the wildflowers that I had seen downstairs. There was now a small, white wicker desk under one of the windows, with a chair, and the two straight-backed chairs had been joined by an old-fashioned slipper chair covered in faded cretonne. The closet curtain was clean and ironed, and the footlocker had been replaced by a big old trunk with a cornucopia of grapes carved on it. It stood at the foot of the bed with a bulbous old black-and-white RCA television set on it. I grinned. There had been one like it in my grandmother Bell's house, before she had come to live with us. I had watched rudimentary cartoons on it for hours.

The other, smaller bedroom was similarly refurbished, and the bath gleamed as much as was possible, given the condition of the enamel. The remnants of old linoleum had been pried up and the floor scrubbed and left bare, and another faded rag rug was laid down

beside the shiplike old bathtub. The disreputable
shower curtain had been replaced with a new one, a
stiff, shining sheet of virulent aqua that smelled of new
plastic. Clean blue towels were piled on a table beside
the washbasin. A little potted geranium sat on the win-
dowsill, and there was new Ivory soap in the soap dish
and an aerosol can of room deodorizer. I squirted
experimentally and coughed. Country Lilac exploded
violently into the little room. No natural smell could
survive here.

I looked out the little window that overlooked a
small backyard cleared out of the forest. Beside a
tarpaulin-covered woodpile an old blue pickup truck
stood, high and bulbous like the bathtub. The
promised vehicle. Grinning, I went downstairs to have
my coffee. I would stop on my way to take the Jeep
back, I thought, and thank Bella Ponder. She had done
far more than had been called for. Even the old pickup
shone. She must have hired a small army; there was no
way she could have done any of this herself.

"I'm going to do just fine here," I told Mozart,
who had replaced Pachelbel on the radio. "This is definitely a doable thing."

I drank my coffee and ate a sweet roll; it was but-
tery and tender and obviously homemade. Then I
started out the door to the Jeep. An explosion of hissing white met me on the porch steps. Charles and
Diana, obviously not accustomed to waiting, had
decided to march on the house and demand their
breakfast. I ran back inside and slammed the door in
their black-knobbed faces. Exasperation joined the
alarm that jolted my heart. I had not taken this enormous step, left all that I knew and come to this wild
place, to let a couple of spoiled old birds confine me to

quarters every day. Even if they were the size of ostriches and had been known to break forearms.

I stumped into the kitchen and looked around for something to feed them; perhaps they would settle for the rest of the sweet rolls. And then, in a tiny cubicle of a pantry beside the water heater that I had not noticed before, I found two big sacks of the cracked barley that Bella fed them, and a stout stick that must have begun life as a broom handle. I poured the barley into the old tin pail that sat beside the sacks, picked up the stick, and went out to discharge my primary duty. Slowly, like a native bearer beating my way through a dense jungle, I advanced toward the pond, the swans surging and flapping and hissing and grunting around me, keeping always just a step beyond my swishing stick. When I had reached the pond and dumped the barley, and they had snaked their heads out to attack it and abandoned me for the moment, I went back to the camp, my steps measured, my spine very straight, the stick at the ready, refusing to look back. I was both amazed and horrified at myself. The temptation to whack the elegant necks had been almost overpowering.

When I got into the Jeep and started out of the glade, they were both gliding on the pond, looking like an enchanted woodcut out of Sir Thomas Malory.

"Shitheads," I muttered. "Maybe you can beat me up, but I can starve you. You do not have a level playing field here. The sooner you get that through your mean little heads the better."

Bella and Luzia were obviously waiting for me. When I got to the big house, the front door was open and they both called to me to come in. When I did, I found them dressed in fresh, flowery cotton and sitting erect, Luz in the little yellow bed and Bella in a chair beside her, their hands folded in their laps, smiling hugely. A tray with a steaming teapot and more of the sweet rolls stood on Luz's bedside table. The flowers in the room were fresh. The piles of books had been neatened. They stared at me, wordless, waiting, barely able to contain their glee. Even Bella's dark face looked like a huge, expectant child's.

"Well? What do you think? Isn't it pretty? Aren't you pleased?" Luz piped, unable to contain herself.

"I am utterly dumbfounded, and totally pleased," I said, laughing at them. "I never would have thought it was possible. It must have taken some powerful magic."

"No, but it took almost all the money we had for the month. Bella hired six men and a lady," Luz said happily, and I winced and Bella frowned.

"Luz," she said quietly, and the little old woman fell silent, looking from Bella to me in shamed confusion.

"Then I thank you from the bottom of my heart, and I hope that one day I can find a way to do something just as splendid for you," I said, and the little brown face lightened again.

"What will it be?" she cried.

"It'll be a surprise," I said, and she clapped her hands.

Bella poured tea and urged another sweet roll on me.

"They're the only thing I could do for you myself," she said. "The cleaning crew took them down when they went. Is everything all right? Did they forget anything?"

"Absolutely nothing," I said honestly. "I can't

imagine wanting or needing anything else. It's miraculous. I love it."

"We knew you would," Luz said. "Bella said it was a good investment. And," she smiled slyly, "I know about Denny."

Bella Ponder rolled her black eyes, and I smiled at Luz.

"I hope we all still feel that way when the winter's over," I said.

"What happens then?" Luz said, and Bella said quickly, "I know I said I wouldn't pry, but can you tell me just a little about Denny? I thought maybe he'd give you a note for me, but I guess not . . ."

I was torn between pity and irritation. Pity won.

"He seems a good bit better this morning," I said. "He was up and dressed and working, and he gave me a list of things he'd like to have when I go shopping. I'll take your list, too, if you have one. Oh, and thank you so much for the truck; I'll be able to take my friend's Jeep back to her house now. And the radio and the TV . . ."

"Phone will be in by the end of the week," Bella said, waving a large, impatient hand. "What about the cancer? Did he tell you about that? Is he hurting? What do the doctors say about it? What do you know about the kind that he has?"

"Not much," I said honestly. "I usually worked with the incurables. He doesn't know . . . no one has apparently said that his was incurable by any means. He goes back for a checkup in a month, but he's through with his chemo. And he says there isn't any pain. Just some phantom discomfort where the missing leg was. On the whole, I think he's doing as well as he could. He seems eager to go on with his work. I'm to pick up his lists from the living room; he's working in the bedroom for now. I don't want to disturb him, but I will insist on seeing him with my own eyes at least once a day. I don't think he's terribly pleased about that."

I did not tell them any more about the carcinoma, or what I knew about it. I saw no reason to alarm these old women yet, even though I knew that eventually they would have to know the worst. As it was, Luz's little chin was quivering.

"You didn't say it was cancer, Bella," she said, her voice thin and trembling. "You didn't say Denny just had one leg now."

"Well, now you know everything, and it's not so bad, is it? Molly says he's doing just fine, and she should know."

Luzia set her mouth.

"So when will we see him?"

"Well," his mother said, looking away, "he can't get around much yet. He's still learning how to use the crutches. And he takes some medicine that makes him real tired. So I expect it will be a while."

"Can he come for Christmas?"

"We'll see. Hush now."

Bella looked at me.

"Did he say anything about his wife and daughter? Are they still out West, does he see them . . ."

"You know we agreed that I wasn't going to get into that," I said as gently as I could, but firmly. "Really, Bella, I just can't. I have a lot of things I've got to work through myself."

I thought of the shining camp, and the old car, and the appliances. She had done so much, even if it was in the nature of a bribe.

"I tell you what, though," I said. "If he tells me anything on his own, and I don't think it's confidential, I'll tell you."

I knew I was safe. Dennis Ponder was not going to surrender one more iota of himself to me than was necessary to sustain life.

"Well, I'll appreciate that," she said, apparently giving up. I rose to go, but she said, "Stay just a minute. Luz has been looking forward to company for days. Luz, do you remember that you said you were going to tell Molly how it was when we were growing up back home, in West Bedford? About the music and the songs, and the wonderful things we had to eat, and the old stories?"

And the little old woman in the bed sat up straighter and, like a good child and with joy in her dark eyes, spun me a glittering story of a life lived, as nearly as was possible, as a Portuguese king's kin among the alien corn of a blue-collar American neighborhood. It was full of exotic color and smells and odd, dark music, and old chants and gilded pageantry, and heroes and saints and bittersweet, perfumed things to eat and drink, and of a provenance so enchanted that even a child could have told it was fantasy; I knew that I would never know what Luz's childhood had really been like, or Bella's, for that matter. I wondered if either of them knew, really. It did not matter. The stories were enthralling. When Luz's head began to droop toward the pillows and I got up to leave, I realized from Bella Ponder's sly smile that I had been as deliberately and skillfully mesmerized as the listeners to Scheherazade's wonderful stories, and for much the same reason: so that Bella's only link to her son would stay alive.

I smiled back at her. My smile said that it was all right, she and Luz might spin their web at will, so long as they knew that I knew. She nodded.

As I went out the door, she called after me.

"Was he more polite this time? Did he treat you better?"

"He was fine," I said over my shoulder. I wasn't going to get into that, either. "And I did fine with the swans, too, although I thought I was going to have to whack them."

"Wish you had," she said, closing the door. "Save somebody the trouble."

I drove Livvy's Cherokee back to Chappaquiddick under the low, gray sky, left it in the garage, and called the Edgartown taxi. Waiting for it, I walked down to the edge of Katama Bay and looked over at the little town, shining like a child's toy village in the shafts of iridescent light that shot occasionally down from the clouds. It looked no more real than a doll's village, either, and I was not sorry, when the taxi finally came, to leave it behind and start back on the Edgartown–West Tisbury Road, up island. I did not look back toward the town or the sea.

The Ford sputtered obediently into life when I started it, and I drove it gingerly down the rutted, overgrown little lane toward Middle Road. It was tall and ponderous and had, apparently, no springs left; it was like wrestling a tank through the undergrowth. I did not care. This shiplike old truck could, I thought, get me through any kind of weather the Vineyard could throw at me. I felt tough and competent; I whistled experimentally through my teeth, to see if I could still do it. I could.

I went all the way to Vineyard Haven for sup-

plies, hoping not to have to go out again for a week
or so. The first of Tee's checks had been duly waiting
at Livvy's Edgartown bank, and the first thing I did
was to open an account at the Compass Bank on
Main Street. I withdrew a reckless amount of cash
and bought more pots and pans, cleaning supplies,
propane for the lanterns I had found in the pantry, a
pin-up reading lamp and a floor lamp, and a score of
lightbulbs. All of a sudden it seemed imperative that
I not lose the light. At the A&P, crowded even off-
season, I bought food and sundries. I would, I
thought, look in the want ad pages of the Vineyard
Gazette for a used freezer; the old refrigerator in the
camp had none.

After that I went over to the Black Dog and bought
bread and sweet rolls and had a bowl of Quahog
chowder for lunch, then treated myself to a couple of
sturdy Black Dog sweatshirts. The air, even at noon,
had a pinch to it. They would feel good on chilly mornings. Walking back to the Ford I passed the Bunch of
Grapes bookstore and, on impulse, went in. I had
planned to find a library for my reading material;
books were one expense I thought I could forego. But I
came out laden with both paperbacks and hardbacks,
thinking with delight of the moment when I slipped
between my silky old sheets and turned on my new
reading lamp and opened a new novel. Home:
leisurely reading in bed would always be, for me, one
of its cornerstones. Promising myself a modest shopping spree later for lamps and pottery and throw rugs
and such, I loaded up the old car and wrestled it out of
its parking space, turning it out on to the state road
toward home.

I stopped in front of the larger camp and took

Dennis Ponder's groceries in. He was nowhere in sight, but music drifted softly from the closed door of the bedroom. I recognized "Vissi d'Arte" and smiled; unless I missed my guess, it was Renata Tebaldi singing. I loved opera, and Tebaldi's *Tosca* had been my first recording. I had seldom listened to it at home, though. Tee and Teddy snorted at it. This would give me something else neutral to talk to Dennis Ponder about at the times when contact could not be avoided. He could hardly snarl at me for loving "Vissi d'Arte."

I put the groceries on the table in the kitchen. A note there said he was sleeping and did not wish to be wakened. He had forgotten to put Scotch and wine on his list; if I had some, he would appreciate the loan. If not, I was to get him some single malt and four bottles of a good Merlot tomorrow. He did not specify brands. Here's where I mess up royally, I thought. This could well be a trap. Looking around, I saw that a bowl and spoon and glass stood draining on the sideboard, and a small saucepan sat in the sink. So he had managed some sort of meal for himself. I put away the perishables and tiptoed out, only then realizing that I had been holding my breath. One curmudgeon down, I thought, only two more to go.

The swans behaved no better when I took them their barley. This time they were out on the water, and I thought I might scatter it unmolested, but they were there in full flapping, hissing battle mode before I got the first handful cast on the verge of the pond. I picked up the stick and struck the ground with it so hard that dirt and grass flew. Diana shrank back for all the world like a vaporous Victorian virgin, and Charles advanced, hissing and grunting, almost to my ankles, so I thumped the ground again and he drew back. But one of the great wings connected with my shin, and almost knocked me to my knees. I knew that I would have a monumental bruise there. I whacked once more, and he stopped his posturing and glared at me malevolently with his flat jet eyes.

"You and what army?" I hissed at him. He hissed back, but then turned away and began grandly to peck barley. When I went back to the camp, neither of them followed me. I refused to limp, though my shin hurt smartly, and felt only slightly ridiculous trying to save face in front of a pair of neurotic swans.

"Molly the Swan Killer," I said aloud, and laughed. It struck me then that I was doing quite a lot of talking to myself. Well, so what? Who was there out here to hear me?

That night the low sky began to weep rain. It started as I was heating mushroom soup and Black Dog bread in the gas stove, a soft pattering on the old cedar shake roof. It sounded wonderful, like a magic circle of protection being drawn around the little house. I poured a stiff shot of sherry into my soup and took my tray into the living room. I lit the fire and turned on the little radio, now engaged with something sinuous and symphonic, and ate my supper on the sofa by firelight. I could not imagine ever in my life being lonely again. Contentment almost smothered me.

The spell of the night lasted when I climbed the perilous stairs to my bedroom and slipped into the high maple bed. I had brought a cup of cocoa and a new Anne Tyler, and I sipped and read until my eyes grew heavy and I turned off my lamp and slid into my first sleep in this place. The last thing I remember before the soft dark closed over me was the gentle tattoo of rain overhead.

Two hours or so later, I woke drenched with sweat and choking on my own cry. I had dreamed of my mother, not in her subterranean grotto this time, but sitting on the slipper chair across the bedroom from me. She wore her faded and darned leotard and tights, and she was so knobbed and corded she might have been carved from pale wood. Her arms were outstretched to me, hands curled into imploring claws, and her face was contorted with rage and terror. She was saying something to me, but I could not hear what it was; it was as if all my senses but sight were dead, for I could not move. The dream was in slow motion; my mother formed her poor, monstrous words as if under fathoms of deadening water. She cried, silently and awfully. I only knew that I was crying, too, when I realized I was seeing her through the silvery blur of my tears. What? I tried to say to her over and over, What? What do you want from me? What can I give you?

Then she was up and gliding toward me, slowly, slowly, her hands reaching, her mouth making the silent scream of need, her tears flowing, flowing. I tried so hard to shrink away from her touch that, just before she reached me, I woke myself with an enormous, sickening wrench. My cry of horror and pity still echoed in the room. There was no other sound. Sometime during the dream the rain had stopped.

It was long minutes before I could get up and go into the bathroom and wash my face. My hair was matted with sweat. My T-shirt was soaked. I changed it and drank a glass of water, and then, reluctantly, crept back into my bed and pulled the covers over my ears, leaving only my nose exposed. I did not dare look across the room where my mother had sat. I lay still, feeling so alone in the alien bed that my very skin cried out for touch, for the warmth of living flesh against it.

"Tee," I whimpered silently, but then realized that it was not his touch that I wanted. That warmth flickered and died.

"Lazarus," I whispered aloud, and felt peace and comfort steal over me like warm water. Less than a week now. In less than a week he would lie there as he used to when Tee was out of town, his big, slack, sweet, smelly body giving to me unstintingly its full measure of sustaining warmth. I felt the nightmare recede like a train going away.

I sat up and looked where my mother had sat, and saw now the trail of a white quarter moon on the water of Vineyard Sound, beyond Menemsha Bight. It looked as though you could walk across it, a bridge to somewhere magical, somewhere as remote and safe as the moon that cast it.

I lay back again, put my arms out to embrace the place where Lazarus would soon lie, and went back to sleep.

Thus ended the first day.

Grandma Bell was forever telling us grandchildren that the Bible said not to put old wine into new wineskins. But I found that I was unable to get myself through those first days in the little camp without establishing a routine, making a trellis of sorts for them, and that the routine was nearly identical to the one I had followed all of my adult life. I slept in only on weekends. I woke with the light. I washed and dressed and had my breakfast, then I did my fixed chores: checking on Dennis Ponder, feeding the swans, checking to see if the old women in the big house needed anything, consulting my own lists. Then I would go out in the stately, bucketing old Ford on the business of procuring things: to the general stores at Menemsha, Chilmark, or West Tisbury if the various lists were minimal, to Vineyard Haven if they were longer or at all esoteric. I would come back then and deliver my groceries, usually stopping for tea or coffee with the old women, almost always putting groceries away in Dennis Ponder's empty kitchen, with the strains of Puccini or Verdi drifting from the bedroom.

I would turn my attention to my own nest then. I painted, rearranged furniture, laid down scatter rugs, hung curtains and set out new towels, arranged flowers bought from roadside stands, hung the winter clothes that arrived from Missy in the scanty closet, organized shelves and kitchen cabinets, made lists of things I wanted to add as the little structure came gradually alive. The camp was like a child's playhouse, my very own: no one's needs to be met but mine, no one's taste reflected but mine. I grew as fussy and particular about where to put what, which books should lie where, what cushion should grace what corner as a little old maiden lady. I think that it was partly because there was so little space and I had so few things to mess about with; at home, where the flotsam and jetsam of all our lives and years was as abundant as dust, it was possible only to try and contain it all, never mind arranging it. Here, in this sparsity of space and objects, I found that I cared inordinately what trinket or pillow or vase went where, what color book jacket sat next to another. Toward the end of the day I would find myself adjusting for the fourth time in an hour a new pottery pitcher I had bought at an antique shop, and would snort with disgust and stop and make coffee. Then I would check on Dennis again, determinedly waiting until he showed himself if I had not seen him that day, feed the swans again, and come home to what I had begun to think of as the "real" time of the day, the time when I stopped doing errands and fiddling about and sat down to feel my way into my new life.

I usually lit a fire, for early autumn evenings chilled fast on the pond, and even the great sunset fires burned cold. I put an opera on the little cassette recorder that had been my first purely self-indulgent purchase besides books, and sank on to my sofa and put my feet up. I had it in mind, in these still blue hours, to savor the very particular tastes that made this place itself and none other; to truly and fully bear witness to the slow turn of the season; to try and bring the snarled yarn of the previous summer into some sort of order. I even thought, on those very first evenings, that if I sat very still and summoned my mother from the vault deep inside me where she was stashed in my waking hours, I might begin to come to grips with her death, if not, yet, her life. I might even, I thought once, early on, begin to make some peace with the Tee that had been and the Tee that would, from now on, be.

But I suspect it was too early for those things, and maybe even too early for any sort of interior journeying whatsoever, for I invariably fell asleep on the sofa and woke with a dying fire, a darkening room, a silent tape recorder, and a crick in my neck. In those first days up island, I seemed drowned in an uncharted sea of sleep. The daytime kind refreshed. The nighttime haunted.

My mother came to me for the first four nights that I slept in the camp. It was the same dream, with only minor variations of circumstance: Sometimes I knew she was dead but she did not, sometimes it was the other way around. Wakening from those latter dreams, I would wonder if it was simply what she wanted so desperately from me: simply my knowledge that she was dead. But then I would have the dream again, and her need seemed so consuming, so anguished and ravenous, that I thought it must be life after all that she sought, some sort of life that I could neither understand nor grant her. All the dreams ended in cold sweat and hammering heart and the hopeless black residue that such dreams leave. I grew tired and listless. On the fifth night I slept on the sofa downstairs before the fire, and I did not have the dream. I experimented after that, and found that for some reason I slept relatively dream-free in a nest of blankets in the tiny sleeping nook under the ground-floor stairs, so I dismantled the iron twin bed in the smaller upstairs bedroom and set it up there. The cubbyhole was neither as comfortable as my original bedroom nor nearly as pretty, and I saw no vista of light on sea when I awoke, only old, smoke-honeyed pine walls pressing over and around me. But I stayed, for my mother did not visit me there. Perhaps, I thought on the first morning, she still came nightly to the room upstairs with her silent screams and her weeping, to beckon and implore to emptiness. For some reason it was an awful thought. I found myself reluctant to go into that room at night, for fear that I might see her there.

But my strength and spirits lifted. It seemed a fair trade-off.

Shortly before I was to go to Boston and pick up Lazarus, I stopped in to check on Dennis Ponder. The front door was unlocked, so I went in, as we had agreed, and found him seated on the living-room floor surrounded by open boxes of books and household clutter. He was pale that morning, paler than usual, and there were streaks of dust on his face and in his hair. He was looking down at something in his lap. His legs—or leg—was covered with a thick plaid blanket such as I had in my cabin, and a fire sputtered on the hearth, threatening to go out. There was an empty coffee cup overturned on the sisal rug beside him, and a drying stain on the matting. His eyes were closed and he sat very still. I thought he might be meditating or doing some sort of self-hypnosis, he was so still and seemed so far away. But I did not like the look of his face, and so I spoke, though reluctantly.

"Are you all right?" I said.

He did not lift his head, but he opened his eyes, still staring down into his lap. I saw that there was a framed photograph there; though I could not see what it was, and felt a stab of pity. His wife and daughter?

"Yes," he said.

There was more silence, and then I took a deep breath and said, "The fire is dying and your coffee has spilled. You're paler than death. I know we said I wouldn't hover unless it was necessary, but it seems to me that it is, unless you're willing to tell me why it isn't. So I'm going to stand here until you do that. Then I'm out of here."

Finally he looked up at me. I saw, with shock, that

his eyes were reddened, as if he had been crying. But the dying fire was rolling its smoke out into the room, so it could have been that. I went over and piled more logs on it and poked it up, and the chimney did its work and sucked the smoke away.

"Thanks," he said from the floor. "I was about to do that. Sometimes it just seems simpler to choke on the smoke."

It was the first time he had mentioned anything at all about the difficulty of his situation.

"That's why I look in twice a day," I said. "I wish you'd let me tend to things like that."

He made a dismissive gesture with one hand and the long mouth twisted slightly.

"The prostheses they make these days are hardly short of miraculous," I ventured, trying to sound neutral and professional. "I'm sure your doctor has told you that. It would make getting around a thousand times easier. Have you considered it?"

"Is that so, Mollycoddle?" he said and smiled. I would just as soon he hadn't. "Do you just happen to have one out in the car? Want to run and get 'er and let's strap 'er on and have a trial run? Care to dance?"

I was silent. My face flamed.

"I used to be a runner," he said, and handed the photograph up to me. I looked: He knelt there, captured forever on a track in the sun of what looked to be the Northwest, misted mountains and evergreens dark behind the track and a huddle of corrugated iron outbuildings. He was crouched in the classic runner's starting position, one hand ahead of him touching the cinders delicately. His head was up, facing the camera, and his hair hung in his eyes. He was smiling and squinting into the sun, and he looked thin and young and so handsome it hurt your heart to look at him.

"Was this in college?" I said.

"No. That was Harvard. This is after that, when I was first in Seattle. I ran relay then, and I still ran until . . . recently. I was an Olympian, in fact. We didn't medal, but we were there. Mexico City. I remember that high, thin air and the sun . . ."

"I'm sorry," I said softly.

"Me, too, I didn't mean to yell at you. Are you going to report me?"

"To whom? The paraplegic police? No. I'm not going to tell your mother on you, if that's what you mean."

The "Mollycoddle" had stung me.

"But you are going up there."

"Yes. They need some things from the grocery store."

"Listen, Molly . . . would you get something from there for me?"

"If it's okay with your mother," I said prissily.

"She's got . . . I think she's got my running stuff. Some shoes, and shorts and things, and the medals and stuff. Loretta . . . my wife sent them to her sometime after we separated. If she's kept them, I'd like to have them back. Will you get them?"

"Dennis . . . why don't you just pick up the phone and call her and ask her for them? This is ridiculous. You don't have to see her if you don't want to. She can't get down here and you can't get up there. I don't like being a go-between."

His face closed. "It's okay. I really don't need any more stuff lying around here. I don't know what I'm going to do with all this."

I sighed. "All right. I'll ask."

"Thanks," he said gruffly, and went back to his sorting.

"Do you need a hand with that?" I said from the doorway.

"No."

Bella Ponder thought she had the running things in the attic, but she didn't think she could get up the stairs to get them. I offered to go, but she said hastily that I'd never find anything in the jumble up there, and she'd get her cleaning lady to go when she came next.

"Why does he want those old things? Did he say? He sure isn't going to use them," she said, looking avidly at me. She was pale and perspiring today, even though the air outside was brisk. The sitting room was heated to near tropical stuffiness. Her eyes looked like currants sunk in rising dough.

"He didn't say," I said. "I guess he's just trying to get his things all together. He must have been really good, to be an Olympian. It must be hard to be that good and know you can't run again."

She swung her big, dark head away.

"There's worse things," she said.

I got up to go, but she went on talking, looking out the lace-scrimmed window across the meadow and down toward the water. I stopped. She sounded as if she didn't know she was speaking.

"He could always run like the wind," she said. "A lot of Portuguese can do it. I was as fast as lightning when I was little, though you'd never know it now. It was one of the things they never forgave him for, just another sign of his being half-Portuguese. That was the sin, you know. Up here, that's the worst sin there is. Oh, we can do their work, all right, but mix our blood with theirs? They wouldn't have anything to do with me and my cousin and my boy from the beginning, those almighty Ponders and Rakestraws, and so ons. Come from a long line of little old bowlegged, spavined farmers and sheep grubbers, most of them do, and we come from a thousand years of kings, but they didn't know that, or care. I don't reckon Ethan ever told them, either. I'm not sure he ever believed it himself. They weren't talking to him much, not after he brought a Portagee over here to live in their middle and have their grandson. After a year or two there wasn't any contact between us. I can snub, too, and with a lot more justification.

"So they don't know my son, none of them, and he doesn't know them. Doesn't know his father, either, I don't guess, unless he remembers from when he was two years old. Ethan just . . . left us. For a long time he sent money every month, until Dennis went over to the mainland, I guess, but I never heard directly from him again. I don't know if Denny did or not. So far as I know, I'm still married to him, unless he's dead. He probably is."

"Bella . . ." I spoke, to stem the spate, but it was as if she did not hear me.

"We moved to a little old rented house up on Pilot Hill, Luz and I and Denny, and Denny started to the West Tisbury School, and Luz and I did whatever we could find to do to keep food on the table. I baked for the stores around here. When I feel like it, I'm as good a cook as there is on this island. Luz was a seamstress for a long time. Nobody had hands like those little ones of hers. We did fine, the three of us. The Miaras and Ferreiras can do honest work even if the blood in our veins is blue. But then, when Dennis was about eight, it seemed to me like he was losing his feeling for his Miara people and wanting to be a Vineyarder, and I wanted him to keep his heritage above anything else, so I sent him to my family in West Bedford. I wrote him every day, and they sent letters and photographs, and I sent what money I had, and my father and mother did what they could for him, and the rest of the family—there were lots of us there then—just doted on him. He was smart, and handsome, and such a funny, sweet-tempered little boy. He made all A's in school, and got real big scholarships to Harvard, and worked in the library to help put himself through. But in all that time, he never came back over here. Somehow I wasn't all that sorry. It would have killed me if they'd gotten him, those Ponders. I always meant to go over there to see him, but somehow we just didn't . . . and then he graduated and went out West and started teaching school out there, and later on he married some California woman, and they had a daughter—they call her Claire, I think; I don't imagine his fancy wife cared to have a Portuguese name in her family. Rich, I think they were. Not that I care. I've never met her, nor my . . . granddaughter. I've never even had a letter from them. Not even a picture."

"All that time, and you never saw your son?" I breathed, in pain for her and Dennis Ponder, too. I could not understand. Family; they were family. . . . "All that time, and you were so near each other? It can't be more than . . . what? A hundred miles? Two hundred?"

"A long way longer than that," she almost whispered.

"Does he remember this house?" I said.

"I don't see how he could. I don't think he was ever up here. This was Ethan's mother's and father's house. When the old lady died, a letter came from an attorney in Chicago saying my husband wanted it to come to me and then go on to Denny. The deed was in it. I called his office, but all he would say about Ethan was that the instructions about the house were given to him years before, by letter, and that he didn't know where Ethan was now. So we moved up here, Luz and I, but most of the time we still stayed down in the littlest camp. Well, I told you. Later on we stayed there all the time, till Luz fell. I expect Denny does remember the camps. He stayed with us there until we left, in the littler one. Yours. The bigger one, where he is now, was his father's private property. Ethan used to go down there and stay for days and weeks at a time sometimes. I've never been in it. I didn't know what he did there. I don't think Denny's been in it, either, until now. But he knows the place. He knows the pond and the Bight. He always did love it. Always."

She stopped talking then, and got up and went ponderously into the kitchen. I waited for a bit, but she did not return, so I kissed the dozing Luz on the forehead and left. I felt endlessly, wearily sad for them, and vaguely annoyed, and baffled by the enmity that had led to the estrangement. But I was really not curious. I did not want to know any of this. What a sere, minimal way to live; what a huge, ongoing fee this angry, ridiculous old woman insisted on paying for her life. What a huge fee she exacted from others.

On the appointed day I went to Boston to get Lazarus. He was so ecstatic to see me that he wet the floor of the baggage section, and capered in circles, and howled and barked and panted, and knocked over baggage and me and a dour little man in a bowler hat, who started to protest, then looked more closely at this huge, hairy, grinning maniac of a dog and stalked away.

I hugged Lazarus and rubbed my face into his grizzled coat and inhaled his doggy, disreputable smell that no disinfectant soap could ever completely banish, and cried and cried.

"Old goofy," I sobbed over and over. "You big, stinky, old goofy. What took you so long? Did you walk all the way? Oh, come here, goofball, and let me smell you; you smell like J. Walter Puppybreath, and I've missed you so much . . ."

It was after dark when we got home, and I had to drag him by his straining leash up the steps of the little camp. He was wild to dash off in all directions at once, to search out the genesis of each new smell and sound, who knew, maybe to slay swans with a joyous vengeance. I would have to be careful with Lazarus and the swans. I fed him and ate my own dinner, and we settled down on the sofa, where he promptly went to sleep on my legs, as he had a thousand times before, making disgusting little snicking, snoring noises, waking every now and then to discharge the duty that had so distressed Carrie Davies: the loving licking of his balls. Home. I was home. Or, rather, home had come to me. I fell asleep, too.

Eventually we stumbled off to bed, Lazarus and I, in the nook under the eaves, but he refused to sleep on the folded blanket I had put down for him beside my bed, and there was obviously no room for both of us in the little bed. So finally, reluctantly, I led him upstairs and we settled into the big maple bed. No sooner had I drifted into a dog-soothed sleep than my mother came.

This time I woke before the dream played itself out, and had no clear image of her in my mind. Only the sweat and the fear lingered. Lazarus's big head was lifted, and he was staring into the corner where the slipper chair sat. Of course it was empty; what had I expected? But his grizzled upper lip was lifted ever so slightly, and the ruff of his neck stood up in little stiff spikes. My own hair stood up.

"I'm not going to put up with this shit anymore," I said to Lazarus, and got out of bed, stomped downstairs, got the black straw hat off the hat rack and brought it up and hung it on the wall over the chair. I hung it with thumbtacks, and impaled the brim every two inches so that it would not fall.

"Come get it if you want it," I said to the corner of the room, and went back to bed. Lazarus waited for me, looking sleep-drugged and put upon. He curled into the curve of my waist, an inert behemoth, and did not wake again until the dazzle of the morning sun lit the long windows. I didn't, either.

CHAPTER TEN

WHEN I WOKE THE NEXT MORNING, I knew before I opened my eyes to the dazzle of water light that something profound had changed about this place. Then I felt Lazarus stir against my hip, and heard the groan that meant he was waking up. I smiled, eyes still closed, and waited. There it was: the sibilant fart that meant the waking-up process was completed. I leaped out of bed before the smell could smite me and ran around it and hugged him.

"Morning, stink-dog," I said into his neck. "Your first fart in your new home. How was it? Did the earth move? Oh, I am so glad you're here! I have so much to show you!"

It is Lazarus's special gift not to be dismayed by changes of scenery. He is amazed, delighted, or puzzled, depending on the circumstances, but he is never afraid when he finds himself in a place new to him. This morning he took off in circles around the room, sniffing everything and thumping his scrofulous tail. Then he worked his way through the upstairs, skidded down the perilous steps, and circled the first floor, his nose and tail working overtime, his tongue lolling out goofily. During the entire tour he grinned his doggy grin, making little busy, cataloguing sounds in his throat. Apparently the cottage was going to be an endless source of enchantment to him. I followed him, as ridiculously pleased as if he were a favored human approving my new nest.

Like most animals, I knew that he would also find his own special place, the one that would become, if he was not repeatedly ousted from it, the nest he retreated to for sleep, meditation, and the occasional sulk. It was where he would be when he was not doing anything else. After three or four sweeping explorations of the downstairs, he trotted into the little niche under the stairs, sniffed it mightily, and curled up on the single bed there, sighing in contentment. I sighed, but I knew that if I wanted the comfort of his company in my bed, it would have to be down here in this dark-golden cave. I wondered if I could fit a double bed here, and thought perhaps if I gave up a bedside table I might, just. I would ask Bella Ponder if she had another in her resourceful attic. If not, perhaps I could find a used one in the Vineyard *Gazette* want ads. They seemed to harbor everything else.

I fed Lazarus and ate a bagel, then took the bucket of barley and the swan stick and started for the pond to feed Charles and Di. Get it done early, I thought, so they would not storm the porch and start an ongoing territorial war with Lazarus. Somehow I did not think he would win it. I thought I had shut the screen door firmly behind me, but before I was halfway to the water a brindle bullet passed me, nose to the earth, at the speed of a heat-seeking missile. I broke into a run, calling him, but before I reached the reeds that sheltered the verge of the pond I heard contact being made and slowed my steps. What transpired next was in the lap of the beast gods.

The grunting, hissing, barking, and thrashing reached fever pitch, and then I heard a great splashing and thought, Well, what do you know? He's driven them back into the pond. From now on I can leave the stick at home and just take Lazarus. And then I reached the spot where I could see past the reeds and saw, on the bank, the patrolling swans, their great wings spread over their backs in the classic busking display of outrage and choler I had become used to, their serpents' necks darting back and forward, their black-knobbed, orange bills open and hissing like monstrous teakettles.

Lazarus stood, knee deep in the water, head down, growling at them.

"Oh, shit," I said tiredly, and hoisted the stick and went to rescue my dog.

He disappeared into the reeds while I beat the enraged Charles and Di back and scattered their barley, and I thought perhaps he had retreated to the house. I did not see him anywhere, in fact, and so I went on up to the larger camp to check on Dennis Ponder and get his grocery list. I would, I thought, have to warn him about Lazarus, otherwise the barking might alarm him.

I had reached the porch steps when I heard a hoarse shout and a thud from inside, and then a sharp yelp, and a kind of shuddering moaning that chilled my heart. Then I saw that the unlocked door had been pushed open, and I lunged up the steps and into the living room. I saw no one, but I could still hear the odd moaning, and a kind of viscid slurping that could only mean Lazarus, eating or drinking something. Dear

God, what had he done to Dennis Ponder? I was so terrified that I could not even speak when I gained the doorway to the kitchen.

Dennis Ponder lay on his back, his hands up to his face, my dog crouched over him, snuffling nose to his exposed throat. Dry cereal was scattered everywhere, and a kettle had shrieked itself dry on the stove. Dennis Ponder was weeping and pushing feebly at Lazarus. I stood still for an awful moment, unsure whether to run for the phone and dial 911 or grab my dog by his collar. I had never seen him go for anyone's throat before, and the thought flashed through my roiling mind that he had gone mad, or berserk.

"Lazarus!" I screamed, and lunged for his collar. "Don't move," I yelled to Dennis Ponder in the same breath. "I'll call for help in a second."

I had the whining, protesting dog dragged out of the kitchen and into the living room and was reaching to shut the kitchen door when I heard Dennis Ponder take a great, gulping breath of air, and say, "No, don't, wait, he's not hurting me," and realized that he was not weeping at all. He was laughing. The wet shine on his face was Lazarus's endorsing slobber; he had been licking Dennis's face with the love-at-first-sight fervor I had seen him display only once before, when he was a puppy and we first brought him home and introduced him to Teddy. I let go of his collar and he skidded back into the kitchen and resumed his licking.

"Jesus Christ, dog, if you don't stop, you'll have to marry me," Dennis Ponder said, choking on his laughter, and I dropped my arms to my side and began to laugh, too, shakily.

"I thought he'd knocked you down and half-killed you," I said weakly. "I thought he'd gone crazy,

or something. I'm so sorry, Dennis. I've never seen
him behave so badly with a stranger before. Are you
okay? Let me help you up . . ."

He sat up, shaking his head. Lazarus sat, too, close
beside him, grinning his weak-witted grin and lolling
his tongue.

"I can do it," he said to me, and to Lazarus, "Since
you knocked me down, you can just help me up,
buddy. Sit!"

Lazarus sat, while I goggled. We had been gently
asked to leave obedience school, he and I, before he
mastered "sit" or much of anything else. Dennis put
one arm around the dog and used the other to push
himself up. Slowly, with sweat beading his white forehead, he inched his way to a kneeling position, using
Lazarus for leverage. Finally he stood erect. Lazarus
had not moved. When Dennis Ponder transferred his
weight to the kitchen counter, Laz gave a great sigh
and lay down on the floor beside him. "There," you
could almost hear him say. I simply stared.

"I meant to warn you about him," I said to Dennis.
"He just got here yesterday. I was going to keep him at
home until he got used to things. He's not a bad dog,
but he's as big as an ox, and he never did have any
manners. He got away from me while I was feeding
the swans, and I never even saw him start up here. I'll
make sure he's locked in from now on . . ."

"Don't lock him up on my account," Dennis said.
"Just ask him to knock or something before he busts in
here. I thought a werewolf had me. Lazarus; is that his
name?"

"Yes. He was one step away from the tomb when
we got him. He's been grateful ever since," I said.
"Look, I can't have him knocking you down every

time he gets in here; we'll have to think of another way for me to get in so you can lock your door. Is there a spare key? Never mind, I'll ask your mother if she has one . . ."

"I can't imagine that she doesn't have an extra key to any structure on the island by now," he said neutrally. "No, I'm not going to lock this guy out. He's welcome any time. I had a big dog like him back home. Commander, his name was. I think he was part wolf. I've missed him a lot."

I did not ask what had happened to Commander. Either he was dead or the vanished wife and child had taken him. Either way, it was not anything I wanted to get into.

I pulled Lazarus's leash out of my pocket, snapped it to his collar, and pulled him away from Dennis. He backed up, rolling his eyes at me.

"Where are you going with him?" Dennis said.

"I was going to take him with me while I did the shopping," I said.

"Why don't you leave him with me?" Dennis said. "If he gets loose he's bound to make somebody mad at him, and that's no way to start out on this island. It doesn't take much."

"I see dogs out with their owners all the time," I said. "There's one in every truck I pass."

"Yeah, well, wait a day or two. He doesn't even have his bandanna yet."

I laughed. He did, too.

"I sort of wanted to introduce him to your mother and Luzia. I don't even think I told them about him, and I should have," I said.

His face closed. The laugh was gone.

"You'd do better leaving him here, then," he said. "If

I recall correctly, Cousin Luzia is deathly afraid of dogs. I know I could never have one when I was little . . ."

The way he said "Cousin" was neither familiar nor gentle. It spoke of contempt, almost of animosity. Whatever the estrangement between him and his mother, then, it included Luz Ferreira. For the first time, a faint tendril of curiosity prickled at me.

"I will, then, this one time," I said, reaching for the grocery list that lay on the counter. "But from now on he stays with me or at home. I can't have him creating havoc in this heavenly place."

He smiled grimly.

"We certainly can't have that," he said. Then, almost casually: "What do you talk about, you and the Virgin Queen and her consort?"

I looked sharply at him, but he was not looking at me. His fingers were curled in Lazarus's ruff.

I was certainly not going to say, "You," so I said, "Oh, I don't know. Everything and nothing. Mostly they talk and I listen. Luz has been telling me about your family, and about the old days in Portugal, and about growing up in West Bedford, only she calls it 'in America.' What a wonderful heritage you have, all full of kings and knights and soldiers and crusades. King Dinis the Troubadour, he of the thousands of castles . . ."

He snorted.

"My family is no more descended from King Dinis the Troubadour than we are from Vlad the Impaler," he said. "That old charlatan; she's been blathering about King Dinis since I can remember. Our people were probably fishermen, and on other people's boats, at that. Most Portuguese came over here as hired hands on the whalers out of the Vineyard and

Nantucket that stopped in the Azores, and we've been hired hands ever since. But my mother can't handle that notion. Her family—and mine—ran a hole-in-the-wall restaurant in Cambridge or worked at the air force base in West Bedford; my mother met my father while she was slinging linguica in Cambridge and he was at Harvard. She's a fake, but at least she knows she is. I don't know if Luz has the sense to know it or not. You ought to call them on it."

I felt a wash of sadness. I hoped old Luzia Ferreira did not know that she was not the spawn of kings; I hoped that she never knew it. Bella, either, for that matter. I thought that they had very little else. I, for one, was not going to take their blue blood away from them.

I unsnapped Lazarus and he loped back to Dennis Ponder and began to lick his hand.

"You must smell like his daddy," I said.

"Your departed husband? That could be a problem," he said nastily, and I looked at him sharply. His face was pinched and shuttered, a kind of fastidious distaste in his eyes. It was as if he were already regretting the moment of shared laughter. The poison in his mother's name ran deep.

"My son," I said briefly, and turned to go.

"I'm sorry," he said, but he did not sound as if he was. He sounded so sarcastic that I said, "Maybe *I* should lick your face."

He only looked at me, cold and distant and untouchable in the fortress of his illness.

"Or maybe I should just kick your gimpy behind," I muttered under my breath as I walked out to the truck. I was suddenly very tired of the Ponders and all their complicated, shape-shifting kin. I regretted leaving Lazarus behind. I did not want to have to go back into Dennis Ponder's house for him.

When I did go back, letting myself as quietly into the front door as I could, Dennis Ponder was asleep on the sofa in front of his dying fire, and Lazarus lay on the floor beside him. I stood for a moment, looking down at man and dog. Dennis looked so white and depleted that I thought I might have imagined the morning's brief moment of rallying laughter. With sentience gone from his long, carved face he looked very near to death, and I wondered once more if he was. I did not know anything about his kind of sarcoma, and did not want to know. But perhaps I should learn more. How awful it would be to come and find him dead, or to have to attend that dying . . .

Fear and anguish stabbed at me and I bid it be gone, down to the place where my other wounds and terrors lay. It went, but slowly. I stood, breathing shallowly, until it was gone.

"Come on, Laz," I whispered, and Lazarus thumped the floor with his tail and got up. He looked for a long time down at Dennis Ponder, sniffing him, and then trotted over to me and sat still for his leash. But when I got him to the door, he looked back at the sleeping man and whined slightly.

"No," I said. "You've got your own walking wounded to look after. This guy doesn't need us."

That night, after dinner, Lazarus and I sat for a while in front of our own fire. I listened to a cassette of *Turandot* I had treated myself to, and he dozed and twitched and sighed and trembled with dreams, and woke and stretched and dozed again. I lay suspended between sleep and waking, swung in a hammock of music and firelight, my hand lying loosely in my dog's rough coat.

"So far so good," I thought drowsily. "I can do this. This really is a doable thing."

With the coming of Lazarus, up island became a different place to me in more ways than one. Without being at all conscious of it, I began to reach out, to venture farther and farther from the camp and the glade, to extend my path past the two small cabins, the big house on the ridge in Chilmark, and my shopping trajectory. My trade route, I had laughingly called it to Teddy during one of our rare phone conversations. Only after Lazarus arrived did I see how constricted was the path I had allowed myself. With his hairy, grinning presence in the truck, I felt empowered to go almost anywhere up island I wanted. It was as if, in some very real way, Lazarus was my permission to roam.

That I needed one was a disturbing notion, when it finally occurred to me. I had spent two or three days forging with him into places I had only wondered about before: wild, boulder-strewn Lucy Vincent Beach, where the wind straight out of Spain nearly knocked us both off our feet; the slick, odorous, time-stopped docks of Menemsha, where Lazarus's busy nose cast him straight up into dog heaven; the breath-stopping cliffs of Gay Head, striped in the sun like a child's cross section of an enchanted earth; the little chapel at Christiantown, deep in the thinning, burning forest, where Thomas Mayhew, bearer of another of the oldest family names, had his early mission to the Wampanoag Indians; the wonderful field of great, cavorting white statues in West Tisbury;

Beetlebung Corners, afire now with the thousand scarlets of autumn; down the tiny lanes of West Tisbury, named for what they were in the beginning: Music Street, Old Court House Road, New Lane; down tracks so small and rutted that they seemed impassable, only to find weathered gates barring the way before I could reach the ends.

For those few days I explored in a cocoon of delight and anticipation, never once feeling tentative or unwelcome. Even after Lazarus and I had blundered into one or two private driveways and had to turn around under the level eyes of householders; even after he had scattered the cranky swans on the Mill Pond in West Tisbury and a roving flock of guineas on the lawn of the Chilmark Congregational Church, I did not feel timid or constrained to flee, as I would have before. A woman alone in the places we went would be an unspeakable intrusion; a woman with a great, gamboling dog on a leash was somehow natural and acceptable.

"You're my ticket to ride," I said to Lazarus at the end of one of our days of sightseeing. But that evening, before the fire, in the time when introspection came, I thought that it was not a terribly admirable thing, to have lived my way almost to my midcentury mark, and still need a reason, some sort of permission, to go and see what was around a corner or over a hill.

"Well, at least it's getting better," I said to the dog. I said quite a lot to him in those first days. "Before it was my mother's permission, and Dad's, and then Tee's and Caroline's and Teddy's and the entire boards of directors of half a dozen worthy organizations. Now it's just one dumb dog. Maybe I can do it by myself when I grow up; what do you think?"

It was an autumn of unearthly loveliness, at least to me, accustomed as I was to the humid, muted autumns of the Southeast. Every morning was born scarlet and silver over the pond and the Bight, and the sun was soft and cool on bare forearms and heads in the noons. Blue dusks came quickly and died in incredible conflagrations of rose, purple, orange, and silver over the Sound. Nights were so clear and cold that the stars looked like chips of diamonds, like Scott Fitzgerald's silver pepper. I went often and sat on the little dock with Lazarus, wrapped in one of the hefty blankets, and stared up at the sky, seeing the crystal constellations appear as if out of developing fluid. I kept Laz on his leash, for the swans, bedded down somewhere in the forest of reeds, would often wake and grumble and flap in the darkness, but they never came storming over to see why their tormentor and their serving wench were abroad in the night. Once there was a meteor shower so vivid and close that Lazarus barked and rushed at each luminous, streaking trajectory, and I simply sat still and let them fill me with their cold fire. Everything up here on this New England island was sharp and clear and light-limned, I thought; there was none of the sense I often had back home of slogging waist deep through some allegorical, as well as physical, swamp. Up here, I lived and walked up on the very surface of the earth, almost able, if I stood on tiptoe, to touch the great, open skies.

"The most wonderful thing is," I said to my father sometime that autumn, on his weekly phone call from Kevin's house in Washington, "that the only things you smell are earth and water and sky things. Salt and pine and spruce and smoke and that cold, dark smell that I think is the way the very earth up here smells. You know how, in the winter at home, you start to smell stale air and automobile exhaust and piled-up, rained-on garbage? Up here it's just natural things."

"Sounds okay by me," he said, and I could hear the smile in his voice. "You get some pretty natural smells down here, too, though. I went with Sally to dish up lunch at a soup kitchen the other day; she does it once a week. Not a deodorant user in the bunch. Couldn't get much more natural than that."

I laughed heartily at this little joke. Kevin kept telling me how depressed our father was, how low he had sunk. But I heard none of it in his voice. On some level I knew he would not allow me to hear it if he could help it, but on another, higher one, I simply put it all down to Kevin's continuing campaign for first place in our mother's heart. Her death did not seem to have stopped that war in the least. I might have seen, had I been more clearly attuned to such things, what message my determined chirpiness was sending my father: Do not disturb this fragile thing I'm building. Do not dare to tell me that you hurt. But I was not attuned, and I did not see it. Anything outside the small, careful circle of my days did not seem real, and I was determined that that would continue.

I kept Atlanta at bay by simply refusing to think about it.

"Later," I would say to myself or perhaps aloud, for I was talking as freely to Lazarus now as I ever did to Tee or Teddy or Caroline. Dear Lazarus; he talked back only with his endorsing tail.

"Later. I know I have to think about it; I know there's a lot I have to deal with. But I don't have to do it now. I've damn well earned the right to heal in my own way, and right now what I need is just to . . . forget it. All of it. Right now is for here and for me."

Eventually, I said it often enough that I actually believed it. I was quite able to keep my stubborn other life at arms' length. I was blithe and flip with Livvy and Missy when they called; I literally never called them. I talked little to Caroline; her litany of pain and outrage at her father never varied and never abated. I listened, I said "mmm-hmmm" and "of course." Often, I thought with irritation, Get a life, my child. Or go and look after the one you've got. A husband and a new daughter and a new house ain't chopped liver. It wasn't you, after all, who got left, literally, without a roof over your head.

That it had not been me, either, not literally, did not occur to me.

I talked even less to Teddy. He was in love with his courses and his life in the Southwest; the few times I did catch him, the burning joy in his voice made me both joyous for him and cold with loss. I told him about the camp and Lazarus and our days in the wild, as it were, but I do not think he heard me. Teddy had gone to live in the arid fire of the sun; the secret forest place I had found for myself could not exist in his burning world. I knew that he would hear me when he could. Until then I would not insist. With Teddy I merely listened and rejoiced.

Tee did not call. Missy could not find him. I did not care.

"But it's getting better and better for our side," Missy said in one of our conversations, at the start of November. "I have it on the word of somebody who was there that the Eel Woman threw a party at your place a night or two ago for her merry band of Cokies.

Threw it all by herself, I mean; she was the sole host. The word is that Tee was in Santa Barbara or someplace *way* away. How do you like them apples?"

"Was it trick or treat?" I said, leaning over to pick a burr out of Lazarus's ruff. We had been out on the beach at Squibnocket Point that afternoon, as far east as you could go until you set foot on Madagascar 3,000 miles away. It had been transcendent. My head still roared with it.

She laughed, but she said, "Molly, it's your house. Don't you care?"

"I must," I said. "How can I not? It just doesn't seem real. It's like you're telling me about a movie you saw."

"You're trying to make it go away, I know, and I don't blame you. Whatever it takes is fine, until we can get this thing to trial and you can come home again. But don't drift too far away. You do have to come back, eventually, you know."

No, I don't, I mouthed silently to Lazarus. To her I said, "I'm not trying to make it go away so much as I'm trying to make this stay. This hasn't been easy, Missy. If I've got to be here, then the only way I can do it is to be all the way here. I don't have the focus or the energy to live in two places at once."

"Well, just don't get too comfortable," Missy said.

But in those early days, with the splendid autumn, as exotic as old Persia, unfolding around me, I was as lulled and dreamish as if spellbound. Even Dennis Ponder's overhanging illness and unchanged remoteness did not shatter the dome of contentment around me. Even Bella Ponder's unsated hunger for her son, even Luzia Ferreira's mothlike retreat into childhood, did not penetrate it.

Even my mother could not come in. I had found a serviceable iron double bedstead posted on the bulletin board at Alley's and had paid the son of the seller to bring it over and install it in the niche under the stairs, and there I slept now, with Lazarus by my side, arched over with the listing angles of the old stairs, wrapped around with the darkness of old boards and the lingering, piney dust of decades. Not much light of any kind, sun or moon or fire, made its way into my cave, and apparently my mother could not, either. She appeared at the edge of it many times in the lengthening nights, pale and frantic in the cold, but she did not come into my space, and I could no longer make out her expression, or see what her outstretched hands reached for. I hardly marked her coming before drifting into deeper sleep, and Lazarus did not seem to mark her at all. It was as if, like the light, dreams got left at the lip of the cave. I sensed more than I saw her, and the immediacy of anguish and horror she had brought with her were dimmed. I slept without tossing and without waking, and woke without weariness for the first time in many weeks.

But gradually a sense of something missing crept into the days, bringing with it a skulking restlessness, a sly anxiety that sometimes felt almost like guilt, and it was not long until I caught the sense of it. I needed someone or something to take care of. I had done what I could do by myself to the little house, my daughter and son were out of my reach, and my charities at home were, according to Livvy, purring along without me like great, contented cats with open-handed new owners. It was, I supposed, too much to ask that my essential nature would change radically along with my lifestyle; my mother's legacy was too enduring, her conditioning too powerful, for that. The swans took merely minutes of my time, and I wanted no deeper connection to Dennis Ponder or to Bella and Luz; I realized that I knew literally no one else on the island. I was beginning to toy unenthusiastically with the notion of finding some volunteer work to do in Vineyard Haven or Oak Bluffs—surely Edgartown, blessed as it was among villages, did not need volunteers—when Dennis Ponder solved the problem for me. Or rather, Lazarus and Dennis did.

On a gray afternoon in early November, when I was curling up for a nap in front of the fire simply because I could not think of anything else at the moment to do, Lazarus came bounding into the cottage barking as if he had treed all the raccoons in Massachusetts. I had left him off at Dennis's that morning, at Dennis's request, and I thought immediately that Dennis must have tired of his tongue-lolling presence and sent him home. But Lazarus would not stop barking, and finally he put his nose into my ear and gave such a yelp of anxious annoyance that I sat up, then got to my feet. Immediately he turned and ran for the larger camp, and I ran behind him, sure in my thumping heart that something was amiss with Dennis.

Nothing seemed to be at first glance; he sat on the floor in the living room, covered from the waist down with a blanket and dressed in a red-and-black jacquard turtleneck sweater that stained his high cheekbones with color, surrounded by a literal sea of books. All the boxes that had been crammed with volumes and piled against the walls were empty and overturned, and I saw that a few had been placed in the bottom of the bookshelves that flanked the fireplace. The fireplace itself was cold; the fire I had lit that morning had gone out and there was an obstacle course of boxes and books between Dennis and the hearth. The room was cold, and only one lamp burned. Even in midafternoon, it was as dim as dusk. I could see that Dennis Ponder's eyes were closed, and that he was massaging the stump of his leg through the blanket. It was somehow such an intimate moment, a man alone with naked pain, that I closed my own eyes, then I said, "Can I give you a hand? Lazarus came and got me, and I was afraid something was wrong."

He did not open his eyes for a moment, or speak, and I thought that he would dismiss me as brusquely as he usually did, but finally he looked at me, the black eyes dull, and said, "I guess you could make a fire, if you would. I can't get to the fireplace for these fucking books, and I can't seem to get moving until I get warm. I guess you'd call it a conundrum."

I threaded my way through the books and threw logs on the fire and lit them, and waited until a yellow blaze flared up. Then I went into the kitchen and put on the kettle for tea, turning on lamps as I went. The light seemed to banish some of the cold. Then I came back and sat down on Dennis's sofa.

"You're hurting some, aren't you? What have you been doing, heaving these books around? It's too much for you right now . . ."

It was a stupid thing to say; of course he had. How else would they have gotten all over the floor? I flushed and waited for the inevitable sarcastic reply, but he said only, "I couldn't stand them a minute longer. I've been thinking I really ought to get them catalogued and on the shelves before I start my own work; otherwise I'm not going to be able to find things when I need them. I didn't realize I had so many. It would take weeks even with two legs. It's going to take me a year. I fall on the floor twice for every three books I get on the shelf."

It was such a flat, unemotional statement that I looked more closely at him in surprise. Instead of his usual white venom, I saw now simply defeat. The frail energy of anger was gone.

"I could do this," I said, surprising myself profoundly.

"If you couldn't find anybody else you'd rather have do it, I mean," I said when he did not speak.

"I've done it before, for the public library's literacy action program in Atlanta," I went on, aware that I was babbling. He still did not speak. "It was more than just a little charity project; we catalogued and shelved thirty thousand books that were donated for the program. And I had two years of library science in college. I never made under a B plus . . ."

He began to laugh and pushed the gray-shot black hair off his face; the firelight and the laughter deepened the flush of color that the sweater gave him. He looked almost as young as the photograph he had shown me when we'd first met. He did not, for that moment, look ill at all.

"I wasn't doubting your credentials," he said. "I have no doubt at all that you can do a very creditable job at whatever you turn your hand to. I was just thinking that you keep on offering to save my ass even when I'm being as bad a dickhead as I can to you. Are you a Quaker, by any chance? A Jehovah's Witness? An angel of the Lord?"

"I didn't mean to pry," I said stiffly, getting up. My eyes stung and my face burned.

"Oh for God's sake, sit down, Molly," he said. "I wasn't being snotty. I meant it admiringly. I just don't do admiration well. Fix us some tea, or better yet, a slug of Scotch, and let's talk about this cataloguing thing. You're right. It *is* too much for me right now, but it needs doing in the worst way. I can't live with my books in a mess."

I saw his color deepen and then recede, and knew without knowing how I did that he had thought, very clearly, that perhaps he would not live at all, and if not, what difference did orderly books make?

I said quickly, "I'd love to help. I could work out here and you could work in your bedroom. A couple of hours a day for a month or two would probably do it. I'd be very quiet, and I wouldn't have to be under your feet at all. Your foot, I mean. Oh, Lord, Dennis, I'm sorry."

He laughed again. "Don't apologize. It's uncontrollable. We don't even do it with the thinking part of the brain; it's something older and deeper. Maybe the cerebral cortex. I met Betty Rollin right after she had those two mastectomies and wrote that book, and promptly told her how much I admired her on the boob tube."

All of a sudden it was all right. We laughed. I brought a tray with tea and Scotch and we drank some of both, and listened to a tape of Don Shirley's *Orpheus in the Underworld*, and talked a little about the book project. The fire snickered sturdily behind its screen, and Lazarus snored softly on the rug before it, and by the time the twilight came down and I stood up to go we had decided that I would work a couple of hours three or four mornings a week, and that, as I had suggested, he would begin sorting the notes for his book

in his bedroom, and unless he called out to me or left
me a note, I need not check on him.

"I wouldn't mind, but I'm not very good company
when I'm working," he said. "I've been told that I snap
and snarl. That shouldn't come as too much of a surprise to you."

"What's your book about?" I said, and then
flinched. I did not think it was the sort of thing one
asked a writer.

But he said, equably, "It's about a lot of years
spent in the company of kids. About what they really
think, as opposed to what we think they do, or wish
they could. At least, it's about what I know about that.
It's called 'In the Company of Tigers.'"

"And are they? Tigers, I mean?" I said, smiling.

"You bet they are. Don't you know that? You have
a son, you said . . ."

"A daughter, too. Yes. I can see what you mean.
Often they are, just that. As pure and beautiful and
ruthless as that . . ."

"Precisely."

Before I reached the door he called, "Did Lazarus
really come and get you?"

"He really did," I said. "Did you send him?"

"No. I guess, after the third or fourth time I fell on
my ass, he thought it was time to take matters in his
own hands."

"Nosy bastard, isn't he?"

He was still laughing when I closed his door. I
walked down the hill in the fresh, cold darkness,
Lazarus larruping at my heels, feeling as sated with
leftover glee as if I were a child coming home from the
circus.

The leftover gaiety held until I stopped at the

farmhouse later that evening with groceries for Bella and Luz. I felt, running up the front steps and letting myself in, almost as if I were a daughter of the house, bringing youth and air and sustenance into it. But the room was dark, the lamps unlit, and Bella lay on the sofa, covered with an afghan, breathing windily like a ponderous, beached sea creature, and Luz was crying.

"Don't pay any attention to her; she's just acting up," Bella whispered. Her voice was so weak that I could hardly hear her, and she was white and filmed with sweat. Alarmed, I went over and switched on the lamp and looked down at her. Her lips were blue.

"Bella, I'm calling the nurse," I said, but she shook her head violently.

"It's already going away," she said. "She just provoked me till I yelled at her. Sometimes I think she does it on purpose. But the nurse scares her to death. Maybe you could make us some tea; that's one of the things she's crying for. I've just been too tired to make it."

I made the tea and brought it in. Bella was sitting up by then and did look a little better, though she was still sweating. In her rumpled bed Luz sniffled and cut her eyes at us.

"What's the trouble?" I said, wishing with all my heart I did not have to ask. But the fact that there was trouble hung in the air like rotting grapes.

"Oh, I always tell her a story this time of day, or read to her, and I didn't today," Bella wheezed. "She used to read to Denny this time of day, and we just kept on reading aloud when he left. Then, when she started to fail, I read to her. Or sometimes she told me stories she made up, but she doesn't do that much anymore. Anyway, it just seemed like my voice was too weak to do it this afternoon. I told her that over and over, but she'd forget and beg me again, and after a while I just lost my temper. I'm sorry for that, but she does try you sometimes."

I averted my eyes from her big, white, miserable face. Poor old women, yoked together by decay and failed expectations like two old oxen who had always toiled in tandem, and could no longer do so.

"Maybe I could read to her sometimes," I said, knowing as I said it that I was going to be sorry. But what, after all, was a half hour or so of reading?

"Oh, yes!" Luzia cried, her sulk forgotten. But Bella shook her head stubbornly.

"We don't have any books she hasn't read a million times. And anyway, I don't want to bother you. We agreed that I wouldn't."

But she was looking at me slyly from under her lashes.

"Oh, Bella, please," Luzia whispered, the tears beginning to flow again.

"I'd like to," I said. "I used to read aloud to Caroline and Teddy. I've sort of missed it. I'll get some from the library; what sort do you like, Luz?"

"Oh . . . stories. You know. Adventures and things. About places way off that I've never been to. And I like stories about animals . . ."

"Maybe I can find some about swans," I said, and left her clapping her hands, and Bella smiling faintly. The morning's benevolence flickered again as I drove home. It felt good to be needed, as long as I could control the precise degree of the need.

The next morning, when I took Lazarus and went to begin the book job, Dennis Ponder was his old self again, remote and chilly and impatient. After I had called into the bedroom a couple of times to ask questions that needed answering before I could continue, I heard him sigh and scramble laboriously to his feet, and heard the thump of the crutches for what seemed a very long time before he stood in the doorway scowling at me.

"I thought you said you knew how to do this," he said. "If you're going to be yelling in there every five minutes about this and that, I'm not going to get a fucking thing done. I should have known there wasn't a woman alive who could resist the urge to chatter."

It was such a consciously, crankily malicious thing to say that I smiled at him. He sounded like Teddy in an adolescent funk. But his words stung, all the same.

"Okay," I said calmly. "I'm just going to sort the books into piles by types today and save the questions for when that's done. Or maybe we could agree to have one small question and answer session at the end of every work day. I could write them down on a piece of paper and slide them under the door to you. Or throw them in with a chunk of raw meat. And I don't chatter. And I asked you exactly two questions."

"Yeah, sorry," he muttered, and shuffled back into the bedroom and closed the door with a small slam.

"Shithead," I mouthed at him. From inside I heard him mutter something to Lazarus, who lay on the rug beside the bed, and heard Lazarus's tail thump in answer.

"Shithead and Benedict Dog," I said, and set about my sorting.

At the end of the morning I had most of the books

separated into huge, spilling pyramids, by subject, around the room. I was sitting on the floor, lost in a volume of Isak Dinesen, when I heard him come thumping into the room.

"I got hooked and forgot what time it was," I said. "I'm done for the day. You ought to be able to get through the piles to the kitchen okay . . ."

"Isak Dinesen," he said, looking down at the book in my hands. "Some say the best natural storyteller in the world."

His voice was not so cold now, but tired, a little weak. I realized that it would be a pattern with him, the letting down of his guard to let me in a millimeter, then the hasty withdrawal and the coldness, and then another microscopic thawing. Well, fine. If I scared him that badly, so be it. I wanted no more closeness than that, either. I just did not want any more of the glacial sarcasm. If I was only going to have four living beings to talk to—two ill old women and a dog and Dennis Ponder—I did not want that talk to be constrained and unpleasant.

I had a sudden thought.

"I wonder if I might borrow this book for a day or two?" I said. "I promise I'd take good care of it. I'm short of books and I don't have a library card yet."

"Take it, by all means," he said aloofly. "I only read science books now."

"What a pity. Why is that?"

"I don't have time for speculation," he said stiffly. "And I'm short on patience with what-ifs."

"I want to read it to Luzia," I said defensively, feeling as though he had condemned me for my frivolity. "She's past the stage where she can read for herself, and your mother is getting too weak to do it."

He said nothing, and then he said, briefly and coldly, "What's the matter with my mother?"

"I think it must be congestive heart trouble," I said. "I don't know any more about it than that. I'm not carrying tales from her, if that's what you're worried about."

"I didn't say you were."

I got to my feet, then remembered.

"Oh, I didn't know what to do with these. I can shelve them along with the others, but some of them seem pretty old and valuable to me. I thought you might want to keep them separate somehow. The damp up here isn't going to be good for them, and they're awfully fragile already."

I gestured to a box I had found at the end of the morning, full of beautiful, crumbling old leather volumes that seemed to be mainly concerned with ships and the sea. After a page had disintegrated into silky dust in my fingers I had not handled them further.

He limped over and looked, then looked away.

"Just leave them there for now," he said. "They're my father's. They came from some lawyer's office after he died last year. I haven't looked at them yet."

"He's dead, then," I said.

"As a doornail."

"Do you remember him at all?"

"No."

I paused, then said, "Do you know that your mother doesn't know he's dead?"

He shrugged.

"Should I tell her?"

"Why?" he said, his mouth curled around the word. "She's done just fine all these years as an abandoned wife. On second thought, though, why not? She could get even more mileage out of being the Widow Ponder. Open up a whole new world for her."

I took the Dinesen book and went home without saying anything else. This was as far as I went with the Ponders, *mère et fils*. If Bella needed to know that her husband was dead, I assumed that the anonymous lawyer would tell her. Or maybe he already had. With her penchant for drama and manipulation, who knew?

That afternoon I opened the Dinesen book and prepared to read to Bella and Luz. It was a happier scene today; the fire burned bright, Bella had managed a tray of tea, and Luz looked as expectant as a child waiting for story time.

"That's a pretty old book," she said, reaching out to touch it. "Where did you get it?"

I hesitated, and then said, "I found it in a box."

I did not want to introduce Dennis Ponder into the day.

"Like lost treasure," Luz said.

"Like that."

I opened the book, cleared my throat, and began to read: "I had a farm in Africa, at the foot of the Ngong Hills . . ."

Thanksgiving Day was wild and windy, with curtains of rain spattering the windows and the last of the leaves whirling wetly to earth. Lazarus and I spent it alone. I had gotten a ready-roasted chicken and some packaged stuffing for Bella and Luz, but had suggested no getting together to share the meal. Luz had a virulent, nose-running cold, and Bella looked strange when I delivered the food on Thanksgiving Eve, as remote as a monolithic statue, gone away somewhere inside herself. Dennis had persuaded me not to look in on him. He was going well on his notes, he said, and did not want to be disturbed. He would call me if he needed me. He did not ask me if I had plans for the holiday, beyond saying that he was willing to do without Lazarus for the day, seeing as it was a family day.

"I'll call you around six, anyway," I said.

"Suit yourself," he said.

I had dreaded the day alone, but it turned out to be a good one. I built a big fire and kept it roaring, and I lay on the sofa before it with Lazarus, reading Oliver Sacks, from Dennis's library, until about four, when I made myself an omelet and fed Laz and the swans. Then I fell asleep on the sofa and dreamed of my mother.

In this dream she was, for the first time in many weeks, back in her subterranean barred room, only this time she did not importune me silently. This time her eyes were fixed on the back of my father's head. He sat in the seat in front of her, staring straight ahead. I knew that he had not seen her yet, but I also knew that he soon would, and would turn to her . . .

I woke myself up sobbing with fear, and got up and called Kevin's house in Washington. I knew that they had all gone to Sally's parents for the day, but thought perhaps they had already gotten back. I needed to hear my father's voice more than anything I ever remembered needing.

When he answered, I was a little surprised. He literally never answered Kevin's phone. I remembered that he would not answer ours, either, when he was at our house in Ansley Park. It was part of his old-fashioned gentleman's code, not to intrude his voice on to another's telephone.

His voice sounded as thick and weak as if I had wakened him from a long sleep, and I asked if I had.

"Caught me in the act," he said. "I was trying to slip in some zees before everybody gets back and the ball games start."

"I thought you were going with them," I said.

He was silent for a moment, then he said, "I really didn't want to, baby. I had some paperwork I needed to catch up on. And I got it done, so I'm that much ahead."

I knew then that they had not wanted him, and he had caught the scent of that as surely as if it were painted on the air. I made some loving, senseless chatter and called Kevin back late that night.

"You didn't take him with you for Thanksgiving," I said without preamble. "What's next, a boarding-house on Christmas Day?"

"Hell, no, we didn't," Kevin snapped. "And have him sit in Sally's folks' house crying all day? He cries now, you know, Molly. He just sits there with tears running down his face, looking at nothing. Happy Thanksgiving, huh? Sally and Mandy cry all the time, too. You think you can do any better with him, you come do it."

"I damned well can do better than that," I said, my voice shaking with fury. "Put him on."

He sounded his old self, but then he always did, to me.

"Daddy, could you possibly come and stay with me for a while up here?" I said. "There's so much to do to this place that I just can't do; I need somebody who knows something about building, and wiring and things. And Lazarus misses you awfully, and so do I, and there's this pair of outlaw swans I'm stuck with feeding twice a day, and they almost beat me to death with their wings when I try, and they run Lazarus right into the water, and I just don't know what I'm going to do when winter comes..."

My father chuckled. It was his old chuckle—wasn't it?

"Swans, huh? I heard they could be mean. Run old Lazarus right into the water, have they? I reckon I'll have to see that."

"You mean you'll come?"

"I reckon I will. For a little while, anyway. If you're sure—"

"Oh, Daddy, I'm sure!"

I began to plan our Christmas the instant I put down the phone, ours and my father's. We would cut a tree from the surrounding forest, gather branches of holly and fir, and string cranberries for the birds; I would show him all of up island, and we would sit before the fire, drink his favorite Scotch and eat popcorn, and listen to the old carols, and we would, finally, talk.... And it would snow. Of course it would snow.

By the time I went to pick him up at Logan, my fantasy of Christmas had reached towering, tottering Dickensian proportions. It even did, indeed, on the night before he came, begin, ever so gently, to snow.

But it was not my father who got off the plane in Boston and stood, blinking in confusion, looking around for me. Not a father I had ever known, not one I could even imagine. This man wore my father's face, but it was a sagging mask, pale and slack and decades older. And he was thin, so thin, and he shuffled, and his smile when he saw me never did reach his eyes. And though he listened attentively as I prattled of this and that, and showed him the landmarks on Cape Cod and on the road from the ferry in Vineyard Haven toward up island, he did not often speak, and I was not sure he heard me. And when he saw the glade and the pond and the house, with the electric candles in the windows, glowing in the early blue dusk, and the fat, ribbon-tied wreath on the door, and Lazarus leaping with joy at the door, he could manage to say only, "Well, now, this looks homey."

And when I took him upstairs to the big bedroom where he was to stay and he saw my mother's hat on the hat rack, he began to cry.

CHAPTER ELEVEN

I HAVE ALWAYS BEEN INFAMOUS in our family for delayed reactions. Tee always used to tell Caroline and Teddy to call him, not me, when the grease fire spattered up, the fuse blew, the pipe broke.

"Otherwise we'll be treading water by the time your mom realizes there's a problem," he'd said.

He would have simply shaken his head at me in that awful moment when I stood in my upstairs bedroom and held my sobbing father in my arms. For it was only then that I realized that my mother was truly and finally dead.

I realized on the pulse of the instant that he was gone, though. The man I knew as my father died to me at the instant my mother did, and became, incredibly and grotesquely, my child. I became, in an eye blink, both an old orphan and a new mother. It was as bad a moment as I have ever had. A terrible white, roaring noise filled my head. When it faded, I realized that I was patting my father's back as I had Caroline's and Teddy's, when they were small and in distress. It was pure instinct, and I dropped my hand as if his poor back were burning.

He lifted his head presently and looked at me, and

his face was melted and ruined with grief and hopeless-
ness.

"I can't be of any more use to you, baby," he whispered. It was not his voice, not even his whisper.
"Something's broken. I can't stop this goddamned crying. It's absurd and obscene and it scares the people I
love most and me, too, and I can no more stop it than I
can fly. I wish with all my heart that it had been me."

"No!" I cried, knowing what he meant. Terror and
desperation took me over. "I couldn't stand that! Don't
you ever, ever say that again! I need you any way I can
get you! If you never lift another finger, if you cry for the
next hundred years, I still need you! Don't you know
that? If you say that again, I'll run away; I'll just . . . leave!
I promise I will!"

We both stopped, he crying and me shouting, and
looked at each other, then began to laugh. Run away?

"As long as you don't hold your breath till you turn
blue," he said, and we laughed again, far longer and
louder than was warranted. I didn't care. It got us past
the moment.

Presently he went over and sat down on the freshly
made bed and looked around the room. I had lit the fire
in the iron stove, and had brought in armfuls of bitter-
sweet berries and a little pot of blooming paperwhites;
the last of the sun stained the long windows vermilion
and gold, and struck silver and pewter off the pond's
surface and the Bight beyond it. The room looked both
lovely and loving, I thought. My house would wrap its
arms around my wounded father.

"It's a pretty room," he said. "You've made a real
pretty place up here. But I know it's your room; isn't
there anywhere else I could sleep? I can't turn you out of
your bedroom."

I shook my head.

"There's another bedroom up here if I wanted to sleep in it, but Laz picked us out a little nook under the stairs, and I really love it now. It's like hibernating for the winter. I never could sleep up here, somehow, and Laz won't. You're not putting us out."

He looked around some more, then back at me.

"Do you dream about her? Does she come to you up here? Is that it?"

I stared at him. He smiled faintly.

"Yes," I said finally. "It's not a good dream. I don't seem to have it so much downstairs."

His smile was as sweet and wistful as a child's. Tears dried on his cheeks.

"Maybe she will to me, up here. She hasn't, yet. She hasn't to Kevin either, he says." He chuckled. "He'd be furious if he knew she'd picked you over him."

"He's going to be furious anyway, just as general policy," I said, taking him by the arm. "Come on downstairs. Sun's over the yardarm. I got you the Macallan."

He followed me down the precipitous steps, pausing to rap his knuckles against a joining or inspect a load-bearing beam here and there, nodding as if satisfied.

"You don't want to be too hard on your brother," he said. "He's mad because it's her he wants and me he got. I don't imagine he even knows why."

"He's a jerk, and I can be as hard on him as I want to," I said.

We had reached the bottom of the stairs, and he turned to me to say something else, but a great battering, hissing, flapping uproar started on the porch. Blows rattled the door. Lazarus sprang at it, snarling and barking angrily.

"Godalmighty," my father exclaimed.

"It's the damned swans," I said, running for the barley bucket and stick in the pantry. "I completely forgot to feed them this afternoon."

As if to illustrate my words, two beautiful, furious heads appeared at the long window beside the door, darting back and forth, pecking at the rippled old glass. Great wings battered and battered. My father sat down on the bottom step and began to laugh.

"Does Walt Disney know about this?" he said.

I opened the door an inch or two and the space was filled with a snowstorm of feathers and stabbing orange beaks. I slammed it again.

"They've never done this before," I said. "Just marched on the house like this. But I've never been this late feeding them, either. What on earth are we going to do? They can break bones . . ."

"Give me the stick and hold the dog," my father said. "And get over there behind that chair."

"Daddy, they really can hurt you; I know a woman who got her wrist broken . . ."

He opened the door and walked out on to the porch, into the sea of whirling white. He slammed the door behind him, and I watched, breath held, through the glass of the window, holding the hysterical Lazarus firmly by the collar.

My father raised the stick and struck the porch a mighty blow.

"Shut up," he said mildly.

Charles and Di did. Not only that, but they stopped the vicious, bullying attack and stood looking at him, tilting their V-shaped heads this way and that. Their wings were still lifted over their backs in the classic busking position that I had learned meant trouble, but they did not flap and hiss and grunt anymore. Very gradually, they lowered their wings and stared. My father gestured for the bucket, and I handed it to him out the door and shut it again.

"Where do you feed them?" he called to me, not taking his eyes off Charles and Di.

"Down on the edge of the pond, right down that path beyond the reeds," I called back.

"Okay," he said to the swans. "Now. If you want to eat, you're going to have to act like ladies and gentlemen. No fighting, no pushing, no hissing, no flapping. Got it? Let's go."

And he turned his back on them and marched down the steps and along the path, into the gathering dusk around the pond. Charles and Di waddled ponderously along behind him like imprinted ducklings. Lazarus stopped lunging and barking and sat down. I simply stared.

"How did you do that?" I said when he got back to the house. "I thought the next step was an AK–47."

He sat down on the sofa in front of the fire, rubbing his hands and grinning. It was the phantom of his old grin.

"Swan psychology."

"No, really."

"I went to the Library of Congress and read up on swans when you first told me about them," he said. "Interesting birds, swans. These are mutes, you know. They don't have caws or cries. They are not, however, your typical swans."

"So I gathered. What *is* typical?"

"Well, sometime when you've got a day or so I'll tell you what I know now about mute swans. Meanwhile, you better let me do KP."

"Why do you think I inveigled you up here?"

We sat sipping Macallan until the sun was long gone and the moon rose, cold and high. I had made a pot of chili, but neither of us was very hungry. It was enough, for me, to sit in my warm little house, wrapped in firelight and the comfort of my father's presence, and hear his voice answer mine. Presently he said, "So tell me about all this," and I did. I told him about the uneasy August on Chappaquiddick, where I could find no shelter, and about the pure solace of finding up island and this small, lost world, and about the colors and tastes and smells of autumn here, and about the deep, clean, pure solitude that so nourished me. I told him about Bella Ponder and Luzia Ferreira, and about Dennis Ponder, and about their place in my new world and mine in theirs. I talked of moonlight on the water off Menemsha, and stars that fell flaming from a crystal sky into my pond, and about the fires that burned in the beetlebung trees and the magic in the old gray stone walls of Chilmark, and about guinea fowl and geese and swans and gargantuan dancing statues, and the clean silver smell of newly caught fish on Dutcher's Dock, and about the rich, silent past that still lived and breathed in the old houses and little gated lanes up island. He listened and nodded, and occasionally he smiled or said, "Mmm-hmmm."

When I wound down and stopped to take a long swallow of my Scotch, he stretched mightily and rubbed Lazarus's head and said, "Now tell me about back home. About where it stands with Tee and all that. I gather from Kevin that you don't feel like you can go back and live in your house, but that's all I do know. Teddy's too full of the desert country to be much good as a source of unbiased information, and Caroline's too full of hurt and spite. You got enough money? Made any plans beyond this winter?"

I closed my eyes and looked south in my mind. Atlanta and all that it held for me seemed to pulse and fester there like a red carbuncle. I recoiled from it. I looked over at my father and shook my head, smiling.

"There's nothing that won't keep, Daddy. To tell you the truth, I don't think much about it, and talking about it seems like just plain more than I've got the strength for right now. We have plenty of time. Don't let's spoil this lovely night. You don't know how I've looked forward to having you up here with me."

He nodded agreeably and finished his Scotch and leaned back, his long legs stretched out in front of him toward the fire.

"You've got yourself a real magic kingdom up here, haven't you, baby?" he said slowly. "Complete with a couple of maidens in distress and a fallen knight in need of nursing. Even a pair of swans on the moat."

I looked at him to see if he was being sarcastic, but his face was still and his eyes were comfortably closed.

"It's not like that," I said. "I certainly don't think there's anything magical about it. But what's wrong with feeling happy here? Or at least, peaceful . . ."

He sat up and clasped his hands and rested them between his knees, staring into the fire.

"I worry about you, Molly," he said. "I haven't been so sunk in my own misery that I don't know things are bad for you at home. I don't blame you for not wanting to fool with it. Tee and that little hussy of his haven't cut you enough slack to even stay in town. But, baby, this up here, as pretty and picturesque as it is . . . this is not real. This won't carry you, either. If I'm hearing you right, that's Alzheimer's and heart failure up there in that

farmhouse. That's cancer over next door. That's suffering and dying; it's mess and pain and fear . . ."

"Not to me," I said emphatically. "We agreed,
Daddy. We agreed that past a certain very particular
point, I would not get involved in things here. I made
that perfectly clear from the outset."

He shook his head, smiling a little.

"You can't be a little bit involved with pain and
death, Molly. It's like being a little bit pregnant. Besides,
you're your mother's daughter, no matter how hard
you're trying not to be. That's what you're really running from, you know, why you're hiding out up here.
You're hiding from her. What she still is, what she's
made of you."

"That's just not true. I don't even think much about
her, Daddy. I mean to, but somehow I just don't."

"You dream about her," he said. "The deepest,
realest part of you is thinking about her."

I felt a wave of cold unease break over me. Could he
be right? Could it be that I had buried my mother deep,
only to find that she grew more vividly real here in my
own soil, more hungrily alive than ever, like Madeline
Usher?

Sweat broke out at my hairline. I looked at my
father. He was still staring at the fire, and all of a sudden
his face was so slack and gray and empty that I was
stricken with remorse. He had come a very long way
this day.

"It's bedtime," I said. "Why don't you go on up? I'll
bring you up some chili."

"Thanks, but I think I'll pass on the chili," my father
said. "I could do with another slosh of the Macallan,
though."

"Then take the bottle with you," I said, rising and

kissing him on the cheek. "Tomorrow I'll start showing you everything, but we've got lots of time. Sleep till you wake up."

"Good night, baby," he said, kissing me on the forehead. I watched him as he climbed the treacherous stairs. Slowly, so slowly . . .

"Good night, Daddy," I said softly into the firelight. "Sweet dreams."

I spent a good half hour the next morning tiptoeing around trying not to wake him before I realized he wasn't upstairs at all, was not, in fact, in the house. When it dawned on me, I felt a cold, still shock somewhere in my chest, and threw my coat over my robe and went out on to the porch. I found Lazarus there, his leash fastened to the leg of the heavy iron hammock stand. He was sitting, but he was as far toward the porch door as he could get, and the leash was straining, and he was whining softly. I ran across the porch and down the path toward the pond, icy dew stinging my feet in my flimsy scuffs, heart in my mouth. I did not even know, on any conscious level, why I was so frightened, or why I was so sure my father had gone down to the water. I did not call out to him, more from fear of what I would not hear than what I would.

I found him sitting on the end of the dock, his legs dangling over the water, regarding Charles and Di. They stood on the bank in their accustomed dining place, heads together, looking back at my father. From the scattering of husks around them I could see that he had already fed them. They seemed at ease, and except for a half-hearted hiss in my direction, they did not flap or fuss or threaten. If I had been at all sentimental about

swans, or at least about these two, I might have said that
they had been communing with my father. And then I
thought, Well, the mere fact that they haven't tried to kill
him could be construed as communication.

"What are you guys talking about?" I called softly
from midway down the path, where I had stopped.

My father looked around at me, smiling. He was
pale and drawn, but some of the lax, heartbreaking
weakness had gone out of his face.

"All sorts of things. The high price of barley. The
shoddy work they're doing on nests now. The scandalous way people let dogs just go anywhere these days.
You know, Molly, I think the female has something
wrong with her wing. I don't think she can fly. I'll bet
that's why they've hung around here all these years. She
can't go, and he won't leave her."

"Why do you think that? Her wings seem to flap
just fine to me."

"Well, look, while she's still like that. See how one of
them just droops, so that the tips drag in the grass? The
other one doesn't. His don't."

I looked closer, and saw that he was right. Diana's
left wing did seem to hang lower; the snowy tips drab-
bled on the wet, front-whitened verge of the pond. I realized then that I had never seen them before when their
wings weren't drawn back in the horrendously familiar
busking position.

"Come to think of it, I've never seen them flying," I
said.

"They don't, unless they're moving on. Too much
trouble. Next to the trumpeters, these mutes are the
biggest swans there are, almost the biggest bird. It takes
them more distance to get airborne than any other bird
alive. It would take the whole length of this pond, I

expect, and even that might not be enough. They'd have to want to go somewhere a lot more than they do now for them to try to get launched."

"Sorry, guys," I said to Charles and Di. "I misjudged you. I thought it was pure sloth and greed that kept you here. I've been telling everybody you were spoiled brats."

"Well, that's not to say they're not," said my father. "Maybe just not entirely. See there, Molly? Nobody is ever as simple as you think they are."

"I guess not. You want to come with me to check on Dennis and the old ladies? I told them you were coming, but I guess I should introduce you. You won't have to fool with them after this."

"Sure," he said. "I'd like to."

I unleashed Lazarus while my father and I ate breakfast, and when we reached Dennis Ponder's camp Lazarus was waiting for us, as I knew he would be, sitting in the doorway to Dennis's bedroom and thumping his tail. Dennis stood behind him, dressed and balanced on his crutches. I tried to look at him with my father's eyes and almost gasped aloud; why had I ever thought he looked better these days? He looked like a half-melted snowman propped up with sticks. His shirt collar and cuffs stood out a good two inches from his neck and wrists, and it seemed to me that there was much more steel gray now in the black hair that hung over his forehead. It was far too long, too, I saw: It badly needed cutting. Not your problem, a voice in my head said, but my hands itched to get at his hair with scissors. I wondered how it would feel under my fingers.

All my life I have been surprised at the ease and naturalness with which my father meets people. I don't know why I should be, still; I have seen it happen over and over again. I suppose we get used to thinking of people close to us in a certain way: my father, the sweet but not too sophisticated old Irishman from the South Georgia wire-grass country, none too wise in the ways of the world. I was wrong, of course. My father has an innate courtesy, a delicate consideration for others that is almost Navajo in its depth. He is also keenly interested in literally everything and everybody he encounters, or at least he had been, before this awful summer. I watched these qualities reach out to Dennis Ponder now, and watched Dennis respond to them like a half-wild horse under firm, gentle hands.

They spoke in slow, exploratory half sentences to each other, as men will when they first meet, but there was nothing tentative about my father's interest in Dennis, none of the quickly averted eyes that the very ill must come to despise, none of the false heartiness. And there was nothing supercilious or cold in Dennis's response to him, as there had been, and often still was, in his dealings with me. The two men sat on the sofa in front of the fire and drank the coffee that I brought in, and talked peacefully of nothing, even the long silences between their words comfortable. Lazarus slept the sleep of the just on the hearth rug, his nose and toes twitching in his doggy dreams, his two, for now, main men content to be with each other. I fidgeted and sulked. Dennis's behavior toward my father was patently an insult to me, I thought. It was as if he were trying to show me the kind of person he could be when his patience was not being tried by fools.

I roused out of my huff to hear my father laughing quietly, and saying, "Tigers is right. My granddaughter has two earrings in one ear and a white stripe like a skunk's down the back of her head, and looks at you out of those yellow eyes as if she'd like to take a bite out of you. How on earth do you handle the girls? The boys are bad enough."

I knew that they were talking of Dennis's work, and of the book he was writing, and put an interested smile on my face.

"Actually, I didn't handle girls," Dennis said. "Castleberry is all male. It's probably one of the last all-male, private prep schools left in the country, and that can't last. It's just that nobody's filed a class-action suit against it yet. Too busy with the Citadel and VMI."

"Did you like that? Working with just boys?" my father asked.

"Very much. I find them far less distractible. And I've never been good with girls. Somehow we don't connect."

There was a silence, and then he turned to me and said, "And it's not that I have the old Jesuit thing about little boys, either."

"Well, I should think not," I said stiffly. "Why would you think I thought you did?"

"Some people have," he said briefly. I did not reply. I was seething inside. It had been an unwarranted thing to say.

"I do have a daughter," he said to my father, who nodded agreeably. "I don't see her. Her mother thinks I don't care much about her; she says I was always distant from her, and am much worse since the divorce, so she doesn't let me see her at all now. Maybe she's right. I never could think of much to say to Claire. Girls are not the snap to raise that boys are."

My dad winked at me.

"Takes some doing," he said. "Sometimes they turn out okay, though."

"I hope mine did. I hope she does," Dennis said. "I keep thinking I ought to try to see her again . . ."

He did not say, "now that I'm sick," but I heard it in my head.

"How old is she?" my father said.

"Ten."

I was surprised; I had thought his child must be much older. He was at least my age, and probably more; it was not possible, with the illness, to say. It had been either a late marriage or a late fatherhood. Either way, the separation must be recent. That must still hurt. I wondered how I would feel, separated from Teddy and Caroline and knowing that I was desperately, perhaps mortally, ill. Unwanted pity swept me.

"We need to get on," I said to my father. "Dennis is working, and I've got to get groceries for the ladies. I'll get back to the books next week, Dennis, and I'll stop in with your stuff later today . . ."

"No hurry. Spend some time with your dad," Dennis said pleasantly, and then to my father, gruffly, "I'm sorry for your loss."

My father looked at me, and Dennis caught the look.

"My mother wrote me," he said. "Molly is as close-mouthed as a flounder about personal things."

"Well, thank you," my father said.

"A nice man," he said to me as we got in the truck and headed for the farmhouse. "Pity about his sickness. He does well with it."

"I guess so," I said, wishing perversely that he could see Dennis Ponder in the midst of one of his arctic spells. "Of course, he's never once told me he was sorry for *my* loss. I can certainly see why he says he doesn't connect with women. Do you realize he told you more about himself in half an hour than he has me in two months?"

"Well, you said you had an agreement," my father said. "I don't have any agreement. Maybe he just needs to talk. It's usually easier for a man to talk to another man about personal things."

"Oh. It's a guy thing, huh?"

He chuckled. "I guess so. Do you care?"

"No."

But oddly enough, I found that I did, just a little.

I had not told Bella and Luzia that I would bring my father up to meet them that morning, but they were ready to receive distinguished company nonetheless. The fire burned brightly, the teapot steamed on the tea table, there was a bunch of fresh-cut, berry-laden holly in a beautiful old brass urn I had not seen before, and the old women wore what must have been their best, and makeup. Bella's dull black rayon was draped with a magnificent old red paisley shawl shot with gold threads, and her hair was piled on top of her head so tightly that her black eyes slanted like a Chinese empress's. Indeed, she looked for all the world like a slyly serene Buddha, huge and richly adorned. Luz wore an ivory linen nightgown that buttoned up to her wattled throat, and another shawl, this one in shades of soft rose and green, wrapped her small shoulders. Bella had brushed the thistledown hair until it stood out around her tiny yellow face like a silver nimbus, and put a dab of pink lipstick on her little mouth. She looked like a mummified child, dressed forever in her grandmother's clothes.

"Well, you both look absolutely beautiful," I said, smiling at them. "Is all this for my old pa?"

"Is there a law against a body putting on something

decent for a change?" Bella said archly in her deep voice. Her face was flushed crimson, whether from rouge or illness I could not have said.

"Bella said a mysterious stranger was coming to see us," Luzia said and giggled. "Don't I look pretty? I feel like a princess in this shawl. It was my great-grandmother's. She really was a princess. Tell them, Bella . . ."

"Hush, Luz, you promised you wouldn't babble," Bella growled, but she smiled fondly at the tiny woman in the bed.

"I can well believe it of both of you," my father said, smiling and bowing slightly to the old women. He had taken off the tweed hat he always wore outside, and held it in his hands. Bella took it from him and laid it tenderly on the tea table.

"Nice to see a man's hat in this hen's roost," she said. "I always did like the look of that."

She cut her black eyes at him and smiled so archly that I had to stifle a giggle myself. Bella Ponder was flirting with my father! I wondered if he knew. If he did, he did not betray it by so much as the lift of an eyebrow. As I said, Daddy is nothing if not a gentleman.

"Bella, can I tell him about King Dinis?" Luz pleaded. "I'm sure he doesn't know, and I don't want him to think we're just ordinary, normal people."

"Later, maybe," Bella said, glaring at her. "I don't imagine he thinks we're normal, by any stretch."

Again the sly cut of the eyes, and the arch smile.

"Anyone would say extraordinary," my father said and smiled, and went and sat down by Luz. "I'd like to hear all about it sometime when we have more time. I think I have to go shopping with my daughter in a little while. Could I come one day especially to hear about King Dinis?"

"Oh, yes! When? Today? Bella, can he come today . . ."

"Let the poor man have a little time with his daughter before you start rattling in his ear," Bella Ponder said. "Nobody much wants to hear those old tales these days, anyway."

"I do," my father said, and I knew that he did. Luz knew, too. She settled contentedly and watched and listened while my father worked his quiet magic on Bella Ponder. It was no more, really, than his extreme interest, and the mild but total focus of his eyes, but before long Bella was babbling like a teakettle herself. I went in to replenish the coffee and found a fresh loaf of bread on a tray, still warm from the oven. I sniffed; it smelled wonderfully of vanilla and something vaguely foreign. Sweet bread, then. I wondered what it had cost Bella to bake it. She had said she didn't bake much anymore. There was a cake of firm white cream cheese on a saucer beside it, and a jar of homemade beach plum jelly. I put them all on a tray and brought them out.

". . . But he doesn't even speak to me anymore," Bella was telling my father, and I sighed. The saga of Dennis's defection again. "I've always wondered what they did to turn him against me, over there in America. I sent him so he could learn about his true heritage, but so far as I know he hates even the mention of the Portuguese. He wrote me right before he came that he wanted absolutely nothing Portuguese put in his house. I managed to sneak in a little touch here and there, though. It's a proud heritage. He mustn't forget it."

"I don't imagine he will," I said, thinking of the *santos*, and the reredos in Dennis Ponder's bedroom. So far he had not objected violently to them, at least not in my presence. Or maybe it was just that he knew he was stuck with them; he certainly could not move them out.

"You must be wondering why we don't speak," Bella said to my father.

"It's a hard thing when families break up," he said mildly.

"Oh, it is! You don't know the pain that I live with in my heart," she said eagerly. "And I don't mean this silly weakness of mine. My son has been a knife in my heart since the day he left me. I wish I knew why he hates me so, but my family has long since gone back to Portugal, what's left of it, and I will never know unless he decides to tell me. But it had to be something they said or did . . ."

"Denny was the cutest little boy," Luz piped from her bed. I had thought she was sleeping; she had been nodding, her eyes closed.

"He was like my own; we played together all the time. He loved the old stories, and the games. When he gets better, he's going to come and see me. Bella promised. We can't go down there, you know."

Bella Ponder rolled her eyes at us.

"You never know what she hears and what she doesn't," she said. "I never told her that; it would be cruel. He doesn't want to see either of us. Luz is . . . childish, you know. She was always like this. No wonder Denny liked to play with her; it was like playing with another child. She's gotten worse since she fell, but not all that much."

"Does Denny remember me?" Luz said wistfully to my father.

"He hasn't said. I just met him, you know. But I'll bet he does," Daddy said. "He remembers about when he was a little boy here."

Bella Ponder's head whipped around to my father.

"What? What does he remember?" she said. "What did he tell you about that?"

"As I said, very little. He said he remembers his grandmother, and his cousins. He used to go to school with them, and play with them at recess. Not much more than that."

I looked at Bella Ponder. I thought she had said her son never knew his Ponder relations. She did not look at me, but her color deepened.

"What else does he remember about that time? Did he say?" she muttered. Her breath had begun to rasp in her chest.

My father smiled at her, a gentle smile, but I saw something in his face close, and knew that Bella had crossed a line with him.

"He didn't say much else about anything," he said. "We didn't talk very long. He's busy, and I didn't want to tire him. It hasn't been all that long since his operation, and it's not an easy one to get over."

"He's very sick, isn't he?" Bella said.

"I don't know, Mrs. Ponder, but I suspect he is," my father said quietly.

Bella stared into his face for a long time. The black eyes shone with tears abruptly, and she turned her head away. But then she said, very softly, "Thank you. You could have lied to me. Most people would have."

"I'm not going to do that," my father said.

"Will you come again?"

"Of course, if you like."

"Will you . . . tell me about my son? I promised your daughter I wouldn't ask, but if he's so sick, I want to know about him . . ."

"I don't think I can promise you that," my father said. "Not unless he agrees to it. But I'll see if he will."

She nodded. Presently we got up to leave. I collected the grocery list and walked out behind my father, with Bella.

"You bring your daddy back," she said. "He's a nice man. A good man. You're a lucky girl to have a father like that, to come all the way up here to be with you. Mine wouldn't have done that, no more than Dennis's would. You take care of that man."

"I will," I said, and surprised us both by kissing her on the cheek. My father had done it again; I knew more about Bella and Luz Ferreira from this brief meeting than I had learned in all my days with them before.

"Sad ladies," my father said, getting into the truck. "Nice, but real sad. They both miss that boy something awful; it's too bad. It doesn't seem like any of them have a lot of time left . . ."

"You know, it just doesn't ring right when Bella says she never got around to going over to the mainland to see him," I said. "All those years, and she never got around to it? If it were Teddy or Caroline over there and me over here, I'd have swum over there. There's got to be something else . . ."

"Oh, yes. Something really tragic is buried in there somewhere, I suspect. But it's her affair, hers and his. We mustn't pick at it, or pry. I tell you one thing, though, whenever I next feel down in the dumps and sorry for myself, I'm going to remember those three people."

"They seem to be doing all right, though, don't you think?" I said, anxious for him to agree with me. "I mean, considering everything."

But he just shook his head.

"It's hard enough, losing to death. It must be nearly unbearable, losing to life. Well, I guess you know about that, don't you, baby?"

"I guess so," I said. But it did not feel like the same

thing at all. Somewhere deep down in the middle of me, I knew that my loss of Tee was not on the same scale of pain. Why that was true was a thing that would nag at me, I knew, for weeks to come. I had thought it was the worst pain I could know.

The three weeks before that Christmas were exquisite. Whenever I think "winter," it is not the Southern winters I have always known—landscapes of sepia and gray and fields the color of an old lion's coat, and soft, sulky, wet days—but those short weeks before the turning of the light toward spring up island. Days were cold and dry and clear, and the sun hung low in the south, so that the light, instead of pouring down from overhead, seemed to flow over the fields and the sea like thin silver wine from an overturned cask. The sea glittered in its shallows and the pond was crumpled foil, but it was a dulled glitter, nothing like the glass shards that the sun struck off the sea in August. That up island winter light . . . it still glows in the best of my dreams.

"Another magic light day," I would say to my father as we headed out in the truck with Lazarus to explore Menemsha or Lucy Vincent or Gay Head or one of my little secret up island trails.

"Seems like it," he would say mildly, and smile at me. But I knew that he felt a deep, harrowing stab of pure pain whenever something particularly lovely or remarkable took his breath, because his first impulse was to show it to my mother. I still felt that, too, sometimes, the need to tell Tee about things, even though I almost never wished him with me anymore. Then one morning, after a brief, pristine little snow that was gone by afternoon but left the glade and the pond such perfect silver miniatures that I cried aloud with joy at the first sight of it, I saw the brief slash of pure, burning orange that was the swans' beaks in all that photographic negative black-and-white, and I turned and ran back up the hill and pulled Dennis Ponder out on to the porch of his cottage to see. He did not laugh at me this time, but nodded and limped back into his house and brought his camera and took a few shots, and before he went back to work he said, "Thanks. I'm letting the leg make me miss too much."

I was as proud of myself as if he had given me a good-conduct commendation and it was only much later that I realized that it had been him, and not Tee, that I'd first thought of when I'd seen the swans.

"What does that mean, then?" I asked myself, but there seemed to be no answer except "nothing at all."

We were busy enough those first days so that I do not think my father felt the terrible, bone-sucking depression that he had at Kevin's, though I know that the sadness was still heavy and constant on him. When we stopped, as we finally had to do in the late afternoons, he would fall silent and sit very still, his face blank and empty, looking bleakly at nothing. I knew, though, that for him those nothings were filled with my mother, and I often wondered what he saw. Her presence was as palpable in the little house as if she had just left the room; I felt her everywhere, perhaps brought near by the sheer power of his wanting, and she still came in my dreams, even if she did not enter the niche under the stairs anymore. I wondered if she came to him upstairs. I did not think so. I thought that he would have been happier if she had.

But on the whole he did well. He admired the places I took him with unfeigned interest, and he asked me a thousand questions that I realized I probably should have known by now about up island, and he busied himself around the house with tools borrowed from Bella Ponder or Dennis, so that soon there was not a squeaking board or a drafty knothole or a thumping pipe or a faltering stove in evidence. He made a small split-log parson's table for the living room, found and rewired and hung a reading lamp for me so that I could read in my cave, installed a swinging dog door, and made a splendid insulated doghouse for Lazarus in the backyard so that he could indulge himself in swan-scanning or raccoon-barking far into the nights if he chose. Laz loved it, but he always came in before dawn. I never woke up in that place without his solid, odorous weight snugged softly into the curve of my hip or knee.

My father began gradually to take over some of my chores for Dennis Ponder, too. He let me do my morning's cataloguing and shelving alone, content to stay behind and putter in the cabin or take the truck and go into Chilmark or West Tisbury. He loved the truck. But he was soon going in the afternoons to take Dennis's groceries to him and do the afternoon check, and then the visits became daily affairs, purely because each man wanted it so. I was vaguely annoyed. I felt proprietary about my father to a degree I would not have thought possible, and did not want him co-opted by the cold, pale man across the glade. We had an agreement, after all. There would be no intimate contact. And I resented that my father needed more than me.

"What do you talk about all the time?" I fumed one afternoon when he came home late, and the hot cheese rounds I had made to go with our Scotch had cooled into little rubbery circles.

"Well, just the things that people talk about," my

father said. "Books. Music. The weather. How it used to be up here. The old families; that's interesting to me. Being one of them, there's not much Dennis doesn't know about their history, even if he doesn't know the current crop. It's a pity he won't reach out to his kin now. Seems to me he'd want his people around him. But I don't think that's going to happen. Lot of bitterness there, though I declare I can't quite see why, if he doesn't even know them. Like we said, there's something bad there. And we talk about the other folks up here, the ones who've only been here for a generation or so, or less than that. There's a lot of them, way more than the old-timers. A real mixed bag. Storekeepers and fishermen and artists and writers and lawyers and real-estate people—seems to me half the island is trying to sell the other half some land, or buy it from them. Lot of building going on up here; Dennis says there's a lot of anger about that, too. There are more really poor people here than you'd realize, he says, and a lot more folks just making it, and I can see why the temptation to sell any little piece of land you've got is so strong if your family is hungry. On the other hand, nobody, especially not the old families who've still got a lot of land, wants to see happen up here what's happening down island. But the taxes are killing them. It's got a lot of people at their neighbors' throats."

"How does Dennis know all that if he hasn't been back to the Vineyard since he was eight years old?"

"He keeps up," my father said briefly. "He's always taken the *Gazette*. Anyway, we talk about a lot of things. You ought to come join us sometime. You know a lot more about books and music than I do. Seems to me that's what he's mostly hungry to talk about."

"Well, let him ask me himself, then."

He chuckled.

"Would you go?"

"No. That's not part of the deal."

"Well, then."

Perhaps, I thought, going into the kitchen to heat up supper, I resented it just a bit that Dennis Ponder needed more than me, too. I had found my carefully structured caretaking routine extremely satisfying; an uninvolved angel of mercy suited me perfectly. Dennis had never once indicated that he wanted more. I guess he really doesn't, I thought. Not from me, at least.

I went by the farmhouse twice a day now, but now my father went with me two or three times a week, and on those days we stayed longer, and Bella put out a tea tray and some of the sweet bread she had baked that first time. *Massa Sovada*, she said it was called: Portuguese sweet bread. The spice I had wondered about was saffron.

"It's Easter bread," Luz said. "We always had it after early Mass on Easter morning. And Holy Ghost soup; Bella, remember how Denny used to love that? He called it HoGo soup when he was tiny, because he couldn't say the whole thing. Remember, Bella?"

"I remember."

On those afternoons my father would tell a story out of his Southern boyhood to Luz, and then she would tell him one of her dark, splendid tales of royalty and battles and gold. Sometimes even Bella would chime in with a story, usually about King Dinis and his times. It seemed to me that the old ladies knew no stories but those that had happened in a distant, magical past. And occasionally, when I came alone, I would read the women something short, a poem or a part of a chapter from a longer book I was reading. That

Christmas we were reading T. H. White's *The Once and Future King*, my own college favorite and still, I think, Teddy's, and even old Bella was charmed with the rich, lyrical tapestry of kings and knights and animals who talked, and swords that stuck fast in stones except for orphan toys. I had given a little glad cry when I came upon it in Dennis's library, and had asked if I could borrow it.

He had only nodded.

"It's an odd book for you to have, if you don't mind my saying so," I said. "It's the only piece of out-and-out fantasy I've seen among all your books."

"It's not mine," he said.

Later that evening I had looked at the flyleaf: "To Claire from Daddy, love at Christmas" was written there in Dennis's backward-sloping hand. I wondered why he still had the book, but I was glad. It was soon Luz's favorite of all the things I read to her, and I read it to her over and over far into the spring.

They did not ask again about Dennis, though sometimes when my father was with me he would offer some small tidbit like, "Dennis walked as far as the pond with me yesterday. When he leans on Lazarus or me, there's almost no place around the glade he can't go by himself."

Or, "Dennis and I put up a bird feeder at his camp. We counted seven redbirds there last evening."

And Bella would be content with that. It was as if they had a tacit agreement. She did not wheedle, tease, or hint for more news of her son. But she always said, "Thank you, Mr. Bell," when he offered news of Dennis, and my father always nodded gravely. He never became Tim to her in all the time he knew her, and she never became other than Mrs. Ponder to him. Child of the

Deep South, I did not think it strange. Nearing fifty, I still called the parents of my friends Mr. and Mrs.

But he spent the most time with the swans. In the early mornings, and again at sunset, when he took the bucket and went to feed them, he often squatted down on the bank or the dock and spent an hour or so just being with them. Hanging out, he said. He never took the stick now, and he still did not permit Lazarus to go with him, though Laz fairly danced up and down in his eagerness to promise that he would not chase Charles and Di.

"Later, maybe, after you've proved you can hold it in the road," Daddy would say to him.

I would see my father there, hunkered down with his arms wrapped around his long legs as he had done ever since I could remember, his tweed hat pushed back on his head, staring at Charles and Di. Sometimes he spoke; I could see his lips move. Sometimes they made noises back. But they never flapped or hissed at him, and they lifted not a wing at my father. I never knew what passed between them. I knew only that when I crept out to join them, fascinated by his taming of the two big, belligerent birds, they would immediately pull their beautiful, dingy-tipped wings back into the busking position and the grunts and hisses and snaky neck dartings would start.

"They act like I throw rocks at them," I said bitterly to him one night when I had been ousted once again. "I might as well do it. What do you and Luz have that the rest of us don't?"

"Pure hearts and simple minds," he said. "*Real* simple minds. You know I told you I thought Di had something wrong with her wing? She does. There's a break in the bone right where it goes into her chest, or shoulder, or whatever. The edges don't quite come together. She could never fly with that."

"How do you know?"

"She let me feel it. She didn't like it, but she let me."

"Shit," I said in frustration, and then, "I'm sorry, Daddy. It's just that I feel like a washout up here. I'm supposed to be taking care of two old ladies and a sick man and two old swans, and all four of them like you better than they do me."

"They know I'm not going to stir up their lives, make them change," he said. "I'm no threat to anybody. It's not fair, I know. I'm reaping all your good work."

"Well, I certainly am not going to stir them up or change them," I cried indignantly. "I've never done a single thing that would make any of them think that. We have an agreement . . ."

"I know, your famous agreement," my father said and smiled. "I don't care what kind of agreement you've got with who, Molly. There's just something about you—an energy, an impact, a kind of presence—that makes people know instinctively that it's not possible to stay unchanged by you. It's the one part of your mother that's clearest in you, and I think it's the thing about you she just couldn't leave alone. You don't even know you have it, I don't think. But it's there. None of these folks is ready to let go of what's eating them, and so they stay a little shy of you. I think they're afraid you're going to heal them in spite of themselves."

"Why . . . you never said anything like that to me before," I said wonderingly. "I didn't know I had . . . that. I thought Mother had all that in the family, she and Kevin. I thought I was the . . . you know, the one who made things work. The plain one."

"Oh, baby," he said. "That's her doing, too. I could

always see when she did it, but she couldn't help doing it and I couldn't stop her. Plain one? Do you ever look in mirrors anymore? When you walk into a room, it's not possible for people to look away. That's not very comfortable for some people. I suspect it's not to Bella or Dennis. They're too busy staring inward at their pains and their hates. As for the swans, who knows? Maybe I smell like Luz and you don't. Maybe you smell like Lazarus."

I laughed and went away cheered. He could always do that. On the way into the kitchen, I sneaked a look at myself in the wavy, speckled old mirror on the hat rack. I looked the same as I always did to myself: tall, filling the entire mirror, having to stoop a little to see the top of my head, tousled by the wind and flame-cheeked from the cold. There *was* a vividness there, though: a pure blue glint from my eyes, the steel-and-silver streaks in my hair, the wash of summer tan that still lay over the bridge of my nose.

". . . an energy, an impact, a kind of presence . . . ," I whispered to the woman in the mirror. She flushed and dropped her eyes.

But all that night I was pleased, and felt pretty.

In the next few days, my father and Dennis Ponder started work on a nest for the swans under the porch of my camp.

"You'll never in the world get them under here," I said, watching as Dennis coiled and formed the dried reeds and grasses that my father cut from the pond bank with an old scythe he had found and restored to brightness in Dennis's toolshed. Dennis sat cross-legged, or what would have been cross-legged, on the cold earth, with a rubber poncho over his lap, and the low winter sun on his head. His black-and-gray hair shone in the slanted light, and the sun was laying faint streaks of color on his cheekbones and forehead. He looked almost well, almost young.

"I'm betting on Tim," he said to me. "If he thinks they need a winter home, then they need a winter home. He might be right. I hear it's supposed to be one of the worst winters we've had in years and years. The pond's apt to freeze right down to the bottom."

"Worst winters? It's been gorgeous so far," I said, looking up at the low, serene blue sky. The winter glitter lay far out on Vineyard Sound this morning; I was getting accustomed to it now, but it still beguiled me. Only small, puffy white clouds like those of the summer sailed slowly up from the south.

"I remember a winter or two that started out like this," Dennis said, "and ended up with us being snowed in for days and weeks at a time. It seems to me we just plain had worse winters then. Maybe we're starting into another cycle of that. It doesn't usually get too bad until after Christmas, anyway. The water coming up from the Gulf is too warm until midwinter. But the Vineyard *Gazette* had a piece about it, and the weather idiot on Boston TV has been hollering about it. And your dad says the skinny at Alley's is that there's a bad one coming. Lots of talk about caterpillars and acorns and lichens."

"Far be it from me to contradict a caterpillar," I said. "You want anything before I head out? I just made some coffee."

"Got any sweet rolls? Lazarus and I have worked up an appetite."

"Coming up."

I was so delighted to have him hungry that I

brought two big slices of the Portuguese sweet bread Bella had sent us home with, as well as the sweet rolls. Lazarus swallowed his in one gulp. Dennis looked at his and set it ostentatiously aside.

"Did she send you some Holy Ghost soup along with it?" he said neutrally.

"No," I said. "If you don't want that, give it to Daddy when he comes up. He loves it. Nobody's trying to force you to eat Portuguese. God forbid."

I took off for Vineyard Haven at rather too high a speed, rattling fiercely down the path through the tangled skeletons of the low scrub and the bare winter woods. There was no way I was going to please Dennis Ponder, I knew. There was always going to be at least one small thing amiss with everything I did for him. I thought that if it had been my father who offered the *Massa Sovada*, Dennis would have eaten the whole loaf and asked for more. I was still fuming when I got back. It was not yet noon, and I thought that they would still be working on the nest, but the yard was empty and piles of rushes and grass still waited to be woven into it, drying in the sun.

My father was not in the house, but came in while I was putting the groceries away.

"Are you done already?" I said.

"Nope. Dennis had a kind of bad turn, so I took him back up. I'm afraid this was too much for him, but he was doing so well . . ."

I put down the groceries and moved toward the coatrack for my coat. "I'm going up and have a look . . ."

"No. He said to tell you he'll be all right. He just wants to lie down. Let him be, baby. He's promised to call if he needs help, and I think he will."

"But I'm responsible—"

"No. Ultimately, he's responsible for himself. Leave him that at least."

"What kind of bad turn?"

"Some pain. A dizzy spell. A little nausea. I don't know. He knows what to do for himself. Let's let it be for now."

"He goes back soon for a checkup," I said. "I think it's next week. I've got it on my calendar."

"I know. Next Wednesday. I'm going to take him. He says he'll go in sooner, if this keeps up. I gather it's the first pain he's had in a while."

I let it go. My father would take care of it. I laughed at myself as I ladled soup into our bowls; how many times in my life had I thought just that: My father will take care of it.

"I'm so glad you're here," I called out to him

"I am, too," he called back. "You're terrific company for an old man, Miss Molly. Young one, too, come to that. Tee is the dumbest ass in six states."

Tee . . . for just a moment I simply could not think who he meant.

The day that he took Dennis to the doctor in Oak Bluffs was the day that the weather turned and my Dickensian Christmas died. The morning had been white and still, with a thick felting of gray-white clouds piling in from the northeast over the Sound. The air felt wet and sharp. By the time my father returned home in the truck with Dennis, the first flinty little flakes of snow were skirling down, and the temperature had dropped twenty degrees.

My father's face was grim. He was quiet for the balance of the morning and spent the early afternoon hours hunkered on the dock in silent communication with Charles and Di. Neither, yet, would follow him up to the

nest under the porch, though they trailed him everywhere else. When he came in for our pre-dinner drink,
he was still abstracted and closed.

"How bad is it?" I said finally. I had shrunk away
from asking before. With the start of the snow my dream
of my perfect woodland Christmas had bloomed like a
flower; I did not want anything dark or sharp to intrude
on it. But eventually I had to ask.

"He's not doing very well, I don't think," he said.

"Has it come back? Is he going to lose more of his
leg? Is he dying?" I prodded.

"I don't think they know yet," my father said. "He's
due for some more chemo right before Christmas. I
know he was hoping to avoid that, so I guess they've
found something else. Or maybe it's just precautionary.
He doesn't say much about it. And he doesn't want
either of us to come by tonight. He has enough food, and
he wants to sleep. Today tired him a lot. The effort to
walk with those crutches is exhausting."

"I don't know why in the world he won't consider a
prosthesis," I said. "He's in good shape; he's an athlete.
It would give him back a lot of mobility."

He looked at me.

"There's no sense doing it yet if they're going to
have to take more of the leg. And it could well be that he
just doesn't have enough time left to justify it."

We had a silent dinner that night, and he went to
bed early. I lay before the fire with Lazarus, too lethargic
to stir myself to get up and do the dishes. I hadn't gotten
around to it yet, but it was in my mind to ask Dennis
Ponder to share Christmas dinner with us and Teddy
and Caroline and her family. All of them had agreed to
come. But now I did not want to mention Christmas to
him. It might sound trivial, or at worst, heartless. Some

of the enchanted glitter flaked off my dream holiday and drifted to the ground.

At nine-thirty Teddy called. He chattered and beat around the bush until I said, "You aren't coming, are you?"

"Oh, Ma . . . I can still come if you really, really want me to. But here's the thing, see. Dad is spending Christmas in Aspen, and he wants me and Barry to come have Christmas there, and then he's going to treat us to a week of skiing. Everybody out here skis, Ma. I need to learn. And I haven't seen him since . . . well, I haven't seen him. And you've got Granddad there with you, and Caroline and them are coming . . ."

He fell silent. My heart twisted with pain.

"Teddy, I can see why you'd want to go skiing. Aspen sounds wonderful. But the idea of you spending Christmas with them . . . this Christmas, especially . . ."

"I don't think there's any 'them' to it, Ma," Teddy said. "She's not coming. It's just Dad. I think she's going to spend the holidays with her family, or something."

I was silent. Not bloody likely, I thought, not the Eel Woman. Not in that trailer in the Georgia wire grass with those cold, whining people. What should I make of this, then?

"I know she's not in our house any longer," Teddy said, surprising me. I hadn't known that he knew about that.

"Well . . . that's a relief. I'll have to get the fumigators in. So . . . yes, of course, sweetie. I think that sounds like something you'd enjoy. And you're right, Caroline's family is coming, and Daddy's here. We'll miss you, but this will be something really special for you."

If I sounded like I was playing Mildred Pierce he did not notice.

"You're the best, Ma," he said. "How about if I spend part of the summer with you? If you're still there, I mean. And how about if we call you Christmas Day?"

"Summer would be fine," I said heartily. "And sure. We'll look forward to hearing from you on Christmas Day."

I was halfway expecting the next call, and it came an hour later.

Caroline's voice came over the wire, sharp and anxious. I thought for one startled moment that it was my mother.

"Are you snowed in? The weather said New England was having a terrible blizzard," she said.

"Nope. It's beautiful," I said gamely, but I had not looked outside since dinner. Now I could hear that the wind had risen, and was moaning around the chimney. All of a sudden I was cold.

"Well, listen. We're going to have to cancel. The baby has had a fever that will not come down, and I just can't drag her out to some remote island with no medical facilities. Not in a blizzard. I mean, what if you lost power? Didn't you say you only had woodstoves? I just can't take the chance, Mother."

"You're probably right," I said, my heart sinking slowly like a stone in viscid mud. "But the Vineyard has fine medical facilities. There are a lot of quite wealthy people here, Caro. They insist on the best and they get it. If she gets better, she'd be quite safe here. It's not the Yukon, you know."

"I just can't, Mom. Would you have taken me or Teddy there when you were a young mother?"

"I guess not," I said, feeling as though I had never been a young mother.

"We'll call, of course. On Christmas Eve and

Christmas Day and everything. Lord, I wish you'd come on home and live like a human being, especially now that Dad's little doxy is out of the house. That's where we all really ought to be having Christmas."

I did not even ask her how she knew Sheri Scroggins had left our house. If Teddy knew, in far-off Arizona, surely the jungle drums had reached Memphis. I hung up and lay for a while thinking how much my ideas of comfort, even of luxury, had changed since I had come up island. To me this place felt more soothing and secure than the Ansley Park house ever had, more totally mine.

Before I went to bed, I opened the front door and put my head out. The bone-chilling wind almost knocked me backward. I saw, in the yellow glow of the security light my father had put up, that the ground was deep with drifted snow, and the branches of the nearest trees were weighted with it. The wind's voice was huge and old and wild, and I slammed the door against it. As I got into bed in the under-stairs cave, my bed lamp flickered, then went out. I got up again, built up the fire, pulled more blankets out of the cupboard and laid them over my sleeping father, and piled more over me and Lazarus. My Christmas dream sank without a bubble.

It took until late afternoon the next day for the power company to get the lights back on up island, though I heard on the transistor radio that Edgartown never lost power. Well, of course not, I thought sourly, dragging more wood. And if they had, they could just burn money for heat and light. When I said as much to my father, he smiled faintly and said that I sounded like a proper up islander.

Dennis Ponder had his first chemo treatment three

days before Christmas. By late that afternoon he was vomiting. By nightfall my father and I were taking turns holding his head and wiping his face. I came home when he finally fell into an exhausted sleep, looking waxen white and already dead, but my father stayed the night, dozing on the sofa and listening for Dennis's call. He was better in the morning, but only a little. I stayed in his camp until after lunch, making soup and putting it in the freezer for him, listening to see if he needed me. He did not. He only wanted, he said weakly, to be left alone. Finally I did just that.

I had planned to take Christmas dinner up to the farmhouse and share it with the old ladies, but on Christmas Eve they called to say that they were both down with something that entailed nausea and diarrhea and coughing, and so I went out again, in the teeth of still another nor'easter, with groceries and aspirin and cough medicine, and spent the night making chicken soup and Jell-O and the things that I remembered from Teddy and Caroline's childhood sicknesses, and dozing in the cold guest room. Daddy spent the night on Dennis's sofa once again, with Lazarus on the rug beside him. On Christmas Day we met at our camp about two in the afternoon, red-eyed and scratchy-throated ourselves, looked at each other, rasped "Merry Christmas," and went to bed. I never cooked the turkey I had bought and stuffed, and we never even opened our presents.

"I tell you what," I croaked as cheerfully to my father as I could, "let's open them on New Year's Eve. New Year's Eve is always awful, no matter where you are or how you feel. That'll cheer us up. Maybe Dennis will feel better and he can join us. Let's just call this Christmas a wash and sleep through the rest of it."

"Done," my father said. "You don't know how I've

been dreading this day. Now it's almost over. Thank God for small blessings."

"I love you, Pa," I said, tears welling in my eyes, not for my mother but for the maimed man she'd left behind her.

"Love you too, baby. You're my best Christmas present," he said. "You always were."

I crept into bed, intending to think about the Christmases at home with my mother, and of the ones in Ansley Park with Tee and the children, to begin to probe those deep, dark wounds, but instead I fell asleep and slept hard and dreamlessly, and when I woke it was to near darkness and swirling snow and a kind of hard joy that we had, indeed, gotten through.

We did, indeed, get colds, my father and I, and the week between Christmas and New Year's passed in a kind of snow-felted fever dream. Dennis was better, though weak; he did not want us, and we did not dare take our colds into his house. The old ladies had the visiting nurse, complaining bitterly about the intrusion, but insisting that we not bestir ourselves on their account. I could literally hear Bella's lungs filling with fluid as we spoke on the phone, but for once did not rush to check on her. Whatever we had might well kill her, and surely a registered nurse would serve them better than either my father or me. We slept, we read, we sipped soup and tea, my father and I, and we watched endless daytime television. Except for feeding Charles and Di, who still stubbornly refused to come to the nest under the porch and circled mulishly in a smaller and smaller circle of unfrozen pond, neither of us went out for several days. Even though the house was chilly, and I could never seem to build the fire high enough or get the

stoves hot enough, I was not cold, and I don't think
my father was. We lay about cocooned in camphor-
smelling wool, surrendering gratefully and even happily to what could not be helped. I remember being,
in those few days, quite content. I think my father
was, too.

On New Year's Eve we got drunk. There isn't
any other way to put it. Perhaps it was that all three
of us were weak and hollowed out by illness, and
deliriously grateful to be up and about again.
Whatever it was, I, who had not been drunk since
college, before I married Tee, got so sodden with
bourbon and flown with joy that I did a bump and
grind in the middle of the hearth rug to the habañera
from *Carmen*. My father, whom I had literally never
even seen tipsy before, told stories that, he said, he
had heard forever around the fires at night in the
fishing camps he loved; they were so childishly and
good-humoredly obscene that Dennis and I laughed
until tears rolled down our helpless, foolish faces.
And Dennis Ponder, whose drinking habits I had no
ideas at all about one way or another, sang. He stood
propped on his crutch before the fireplace in the little
house he remembered from his childhood, his head
thrown back to show his corded white neck, and sang
opera. He sang "Nessun Dorma" and "E Lucevan le
Stelle" and most of the tenor arias from the Puccini
operas, and he even sang snatches of Wagner, from
The Flying Dutchman and *Tannhäuser*. He had a
startlingly beautiful voice, and he spilled it effort-
lessly out over us. For perhaps the hour that he sang,
he looked and sounded as well and young and
vibrantly alive as any man I have ever seen, and I
realized, when he stopped and looked at us almost

shyly, that more than anything in the world, I wanted
to go over and kiss him. So I did.

"Thank you," I said weepily into his hair, which by
now nearly brushed his shoulders. It smelled of shampoo and wood smoke. "It was a great gift you just gave
us. The gift of self . . ." only I said "shelf," and he
laughed, and so did my father, and then so did I. After
that, we laughed at everything.

"Being drunk is the only way," I remember pro-
nouncing. "The only way. We should have done this
ages ago."

"We'll do it from now on," my father said owlishly.
"There's not enough bourbon on the Vineyard to hold us."

"We don't have to sober up at all," Dennis said.
"Not until . . . not until we want to. Maybe never."

This was brushing too close to things under our glee
that hurt, so I cried, "I know! Let's tell secrets!
Everybody has to tell one thing that he's never told anybody else before. It can be anything, as long as nobody
else has heard it."

They laughed and cheered. Encouraged, I poured
myself another glass of bourbon and said, "I'll go first.
Nobody on earth knows this, now. It's a complete secret.
But you know, the night Tee told me about ol' Sheri
Scroggins? The very night the Eel Woman entered my
life? Well, that night, when Tee came in from out of
town, I met him wearing nothing but three rolls of Saran
Wrap. Isn't that incredible? Three whole rolls it took to
wrap me up. Can you blame ol' Tee for running off with
a lawyer?"

I laughed uproariously. No one else did.

"Don't you think that's funny?" I demanded, leaning over to peer into first my father's eyes, then Dennis's.
I had to lean quite close; their eyes kept blurring.

"Oh, baby," my father said, softly and soberly, and I saw that there were tears in his eyes. I squinted; was I seeing correctly?

"I think he was a goddamned fool," Dennis Ponder said. He was not laughing, either.

"Yeah, but see, here's this really, really *big* lady with this wild black hair and a psycho-something rash on her butt, wrapped up in three rolls of Saran Wrap, like a big old Christmas present . . ."

"I think I'd like to kill Theron Redwine," my father said tightly.

"I think you're beautiful," Dennis said. "I'd love to see you wrapped up in Saran Wrap."

"Now I know you're drunk," I chortled, pointing a finger at him and almost falling over on the rug.

"Guilty as charged," Dennis said, and we all laughed some more.

"Okay, now you," I said to him, and he closed his eyes as if in thought and finally said, "I stole all my cousin Luzia's underwear once, when I was about seven, and buried it in the Peaks' sheep corral under a pile of dung. Their ram dug it up. Mr. Peak took a photo of him with her brassiere on his horns."

We roared.

"Why did you do that?" my father said.

Dennis looked startled. "I forget," he said. "I think it was something I saw . . ." He stopped laughing and his voice trailed off. Then he shook his head. "I don't know. Something . . ."

"It'll come," I said. "Now, Daddy. What about you?"

"Well, once when you kids were little I took you down to Tenth Street to see an adult movie," he said. "I didn't know it was when we went in, but I caught on pretty soon, and I didn't take you out. Your mother washed your mouths out with soap for weeks, the questions you were asking. I should have confessed, but I never did."

We laughed again, and then I said, "It's all such tame stuff. Now we have to tell something really big. Something that changed things. Dennis, you start; Daddy doesn't have any secrets. I'll tell you what I want to know. I want to know why you don't speak to your mother and Luz."

I paused and grinned around the room slyly, pleased with my daring. I did not see my father's frown, or the cold stillness that ran like a shadow over Dennis Ponder's face.

"I don't remember," he said levelly. I should have dropped it, but I did not.

"Come on, it's New Year's Eve. Of course you remember. You have to tell. No secrets allowed between us."

He looked up at me; I was capering around the living room, too full of bourbon and my own cleverness to sit still.

"It was something I saw. That's all that's your business, Molly. I owe you a lot, but I don't owe you that."

It penetrated even my drunken fog then: I had gone too far. I was not so drunk that I could not feel my cheeks flame.

"I'm sorry. That was really out of line. I apologize. Look, I've got some champagne on ice; let's uncork it. By the time midnight comes there'll still be enough for a toast."

I could tell that he did not want to stay, but my father's face was so stricken by my gaffe that apparently Dennis could not bring himself to leave. He nodded. My father nodded. I raced off to get the champagne, my cheeks and chest and forehead still burning. I knew that I would loathe myself in the morning.

But the champagne did the trick. By the time the little ormolu clock I had found at a flea market chimed twelve, we were laughing again, and we toasted the New Year and hugged each other and threw our hardware-store glasses into the fireplace. Outside the circle of firelight and liquor and hilarity, the world howled, and dark shapes slunk through it. But inside it, just for this one night, we were safe and warm. I would have done anything to keep that circle unbroken, but eventually sleep took me.

I remember that my father helped me to bed, and Dennis Ponder kissed me on the forehead and said, "Good night, Cinderella. I'm going to remind you in the morning of every dance you danced and every song you sang."

I woke sometime later, and heard them still talking before the fire, still laughing, but quietly, now. Sometime even later, I heard a kind of fussing, scurrying noise under the porch and sat up, blinking, and then realized fuzzily that the swans had made their way up from the pond and settled themselves into the nest my father and Dennis had made them. I was trying to rouse myself to get up and tell them about it when sleep took me down for good.

In the morning Dennis was gone, and my father was bustling around the kitchen cleaning up. He grinned at me when I crept into the room, my head pounding, my mouth and throat furry with thirst.

"If you feel like you look, you should go back to bed," he said.

"Was I just unbearably awful? Never mind. I know I was. I've never done that before," I said. And then, remembering, "Oh, God, I've got to go up and apologize to Dennis. That was just a shitawful . . . sorry, Daddy . . . thing to ask him."

"No. Let him be," my father said. "I put him to bed on the sofa and he woke up awfully sick. I had to literally carry him over to his place. We should never have let him drink. I fault myself on that."

The pain and alarm I felt was quite different from the cringing guilt over my insensitive question the night before. The depth of it surprised me. I was suddenly terrified for Dennis Ponder.

Sometime in the night before, everything had changed. I could not remember much of what we had said to each other, but I thought of him differently now, in a new way. He was not simply the sick man across the way for whom I had contracted to care. He was someone who had poured out a liter of his very essence to me, as I had to him. He was real now. He was a living, funny, gifted, difficult, suffering, perhaps dying person who for one moment had reached out to me. I could have pulled away, as I had done all the weeks before, but I had not, and so I could never again think of him as I had before. For a moment I wanted that back desperately, more than anything. I did not want this whole, real, wounded new Dennis Ponder in my life. But there he was, and there, I knew, he would remain.

I wonder how I seem to him now? I thought. I wonder if I'm different to him? What's happening to us? Are we changing into other people up here, or just into whoever we were meant to be to begin with?

Maybe that's the magic of this place, I thought, going upstairs to take my shower. I stood under the hot water, eyes closed, surrendered to it, until it began to run cool, and then cold, but the strange new reality of Dennis Ponder and me would not wash away.

CHAPTER TWELVE

THE CATERPILLARS AND THE old men at Alley's General Store were right about that winter. Conceived, the delighted weatherpeople said, of El Niño and the lingering ash clouds from Mount Pinatubo, great storms rolled east week after week, borne along on the jet stream, which clung to New England like a lover. Snowstorm followed snowstorm or, if conditions were just right, ice blanketed the Vineyard. The snows soon lost the luster of novelty and began to be hardships, but they never lost their power to enchant. A hushed white, perfectly still morning in the glade was still the stuff of held breath. Daily the blue-white yard was crisscrossed with the delicate traceries of whatever hungry animals had come foraging during the nights: skunk, raccoon, deer, an occasional opossum, the lacy evidence of a hundred birds around the bird feeder. Often, at the edge of the front porch overhang, there would be the furious, swooping snow angels made by the swans' wings as they protested the intrusion of their hungry neighbors. We saw, too, the wide, deep spraddle of their webbed feet as they waddled flat-footedly back to the pond. In those bitter early days of January, my father went down almost hourly to break up the ice on the pond so that the indignant Charles and Di could paddle.

"You'd think they'd be glad to give it up till spring," I said, fretting about my father's habit of going out in the bitterest weather in only his flannel jacket and tweed hat. "They don't need to drink it; they've got the water you put out under the porch. I think they just insist on it to jerk you around. Why don't you try leaving it frozen for one night, and see what happens?"

"It's their job," he said mildly. "It's what they do. I don't mind whacking ice. It could get old if this doesn't let up for a while, though."

It didn't. As I said, the snows were tolerable because of their beauty. But the ice was different. Oh, it was beautiful, all right; the rare glitter of sun off the crystal branches along the lanes, the incredible sight of entire forests of curly scrub oak blazing and clicking under an iron-blue sky; the bone-chilling morning when we skidded down to the docks in Menemsha to buy scallops and found the Bight a solid sheet of steel-gray ice—I will never forget those sights.

But the ice brought cold and danger along with the extravagant chandeliers it hung up island. Branches and wires came down and it was often days before crews could get to them. Cold darkness prevailed. People could not flee to the little towns for light and warmth because the roads were treacherous; each storm brought news of an accident that harmed, and once or twice, killed. More than once the governor declared the Vineyard a disaster area, and National Guard trucks rolled ponderously off the ferries with supplies for farm animals and people in the worst-hit areas, only to skid helplessly off the roads and end up, turtlelike, on their sides. In the end, it was neighbor slogging and sliding across fields and down lanes to neighbor with food and firewood or propane that saw up island through. On one of my rare, perilous, crawling trips to the store I heard an old man telling a child, "Maybe the folks up here ain't so kissy-kissy most of the time, but by God they make good neighbors in hard times."

I had not thought that many people knew I was there, in the little camp at the end of the lane, or that Dennis Ponder had come back. But twice, when I went out in the morning to stock the bird feeder, I found that someone had been down the lane with a small plow mounted on the front of a vehicle, and once there was a paper sack full of scallop chowder, crackers and bread, milk, and a bag of apples. There was no note on the bag, and no name. I came very close to tears that morning. My father smiled.

That same morning, because of the plowed lane, I was able to get to Middle Road and down to the lane that led to the farmhouse. I had thought I would have to leave the truck and walk up, but the lane, too, had been plowed. I carried my bag of provisions into the kitchen and found that a paper sack similar to the one left at my door sat on the kitchen table.

"Who's the Good Samaritan who brought your food?" I said to Luz, who was nodding by the smoldering fire. Bella, she said, was still upstairs.

"I don't know. We knew it wasn't you because you'd come in. Bella says we're not going to eat it. We don't take charity. I wish we did. I can smell scallop soup. I don't think I had any breakfast."

I was appalled, and furious with Bella.

"Luz, how often do you miss your breakfast?" I

said gently. "Does Bella always stay upstairs this late in the morning?"

"Yes, but I don't mind. I always save my bread from supper. She comes down by lunchtime. It's just that she needs to sleep; I don't think she sleeps much at night. I hear her coughing almost all night long."

I went into the kitchen and heated the scallop chowder and brought it in with a chunk of bread I found under a white dishcloth; there was little else in the kitchen. I had not been able to get there with food for several days. The anonymous offering of soup and crackers would have seen them through two more days if I could not have made it today. I was very angry. I wanted to shake Bella Ponder until her fat jowls quivered. Her arrogant pride was going to kill them both.

At first Luz hesitated over the soup.

"Eat the damned soup," I snapped. "You can always pretend that the peasants brought it as an act of homage."

I was immediately sorry for the sarcasm, but Luz's little face brightened and she tucked into the soup hungrily. She did not speak until the bowl was empty.

"I'm glad you thought of that. The soup was wonderful," she said. "I'm glad you thought of that about the peasants. I'm going to tell Bella, I'll bet she never thought of it."

"You do that," I said grimly. "And you tell her I'll stop by this afternoon if I can still get up the hill. I'll bring some more soup, and part of an apple pie I made."

I kissed her cheek, put another blanket on her bed, and built up the fire.

"Can you believe it?" I fumed to my father when I

got home. "She can't even get down the steps to feed Luz; they're cold and they're hungry, and they won't eat hot chowder somebody brings them because they don't take charity! I swear, it's getting to be time to do something about them. Get them into a home, or get a full-time nurse in, or something. I can't let them starve and freeze, and I can't count on getting over there until this weather lets up."

"It doesn't look like their neighbors are going to let them starve or freeze," he said.

"Well, but they won't eat the food. I told you what Luz said Bella said about that. Who should I call? The visiting nurse? It's the only number I've got. Isn't there some kind of organization for the elderly on the island? It seems like I've seen something on a sign in West Tisbury . . ."

"There are a couple of organizations for us old farts, I think," he said. "It seems to me I've heard they deliver hot meals and health care and all kinds of stuff to shut-ins, and I know they've got people who'll take you to the doctor or to the senior center for a meal. The senior center's a nice place; I've dropped by there a few times and played some Scrabble and shot a little pool. Got the pants beat off me the first few times, but I'm getting my game back. I don't think there's much for Bella and Luz if they won't ask, though. As for getting them into some kind of residential place, you're probably right, but that's not your job to do. Only someone connected to the family could do it legally. That's Dennis, I guess. I wouldn't imagine he's up to it right now, and probably not inclined to tackle the old ladies if he was. I think the best and only thing we can do is what we're already doing. The weather can't last forever; I hear from the old-timers around Alley's and the senior center that the Vineyard winters aren't usually much worse than Atlanta's."

I knew he was right. I looked at him with interest. I could no more imagine my father playing Scrabble and pool with the elderly men of Chilmark and West Tisbury than I could imagine doing it myself, but there was no good reason for my surprise. He had always had two or three close friends with whom he had done things; it stood to reason that he must miss that. On reflection, the fact that he had quietly moved to find companionship for himself, instead of clinging to Dennis Ponder, said much about his adjustment, and the lifting of the terrible depression.

"I'm proud of you," I said, giving him a quick hug. "You've done what I should have been doing all along: getting to know some of the other people up island. I think I've just assumed that they were what Bella and Luz and Dennis said they were: tight-knit old families who don't want any truck with anybody else. That doesn't make any sense, does it?"

"No," he said. "But you needed some time to heal and some space to do it on your own terms. I always thought when it was time, you'd stick your nose out and get to know a few folks. If you're ready for that, I could take you with me to the senior center next time I go. Having you around would probably jump-start a lot of pacemakers."

I grinned.

"You got a deal. I've forgotten what it feels like to rattle a chain."

"Pity," my father said. "You need to remember how that feels. And some folks I know need to remember how it feels to get 'em rattled."

"If you're referring to Dennis, that's ridiculous. That's almost obscene."

"Hell, Molly, the man's a long way from dead," he said irritably. "If you hadn't been so squiffed New Year's Eve you'd have seen that Dennis was acting like a rooster in the henhouse around you. You've got to stop burying your men folks before their time. Makes them cranky."

I just rolled my eyes at him. But the conversation lingered. Before I went up to check on Dennis that afternoon, I put on some lipstick and brushed my skunk-striped hair until it shone. I had not done either for a long time. It felt good. By the time I gained the porch of the larger camp, there was a spring in my step that had not been there since the siege of bitter cold had started.

He was lying on the sofa in front of the fire, Lazarus sighing and twitching on the rug beside him. I had only seen him once or twice since New Year's Eve. While he was so desperately ill from the chemo he had seemed to want only my father, and with my new, skin-prickling awareness of him, I was willing to give him that. But by now I found that I wanted to see him; needed to see for myself that he was still there, still alive. Simply that. I knew that he had only two more chemo sessions, and I found that I had been thinking of the time beyond them as a time when I would have back the man who had laughed and sung on New Year's Eve. But now, looking at him, I thought, with a surge of desolation, that I might have seen the last of that man in that first glimpse.

He looked terrible. He was white and still and the thick hair was lusterless and dry now, hanging messily around his collar. His face was sunken and yellow.

During the long spells of nausea, he had lost a lot of the weight he had regained, and even his hands, lying still on the blanket that covered him, were thin to bone and white to transparency. I stood staring intently until I saw the blanket rise and fall shallowly over his chest, then I tiptoed into the room.

"You don't have to do that," he said, his eyes still closed. They were ringed in gray-blue, and his beard was thick and blue on his jaw.

"I'm not asleep. Just listening to the tick of ice on the roof. Doesn't sound a damned bit cozy, does it?"

"I brought you some scallop chowder," I said. "I'm going to heat it up and we're both going to have some. It's colder than a well-digger's butt in Arkansas out there, as my dad says, although I could never understand why a well digger would have a cold butt in Arkansas. And then I think I'm going to cut your hair. You'll feel a lot better without it straggling down your neck. I might even shave you."

He opened his eyes and rolled his head on his neck until he could see me. It was a weak gesture, sick and resigned.

"I'll let you cut my hair and shave me if you'll make that Scotch instead of chowder," he said. "I'd just throw it up. For some reason, booze stays down. Maybe we could get drunk again. What do you say? Sing a little? Dance a bit?"

The rictus on his white lips frightened me until I realized he was smiling, or trying to. It was dreadful to see, heart-wrenching. I found myself wishing that he would snap at me as he would have before.

I went and got the Scotch and poured us both some, and handed his to him. When he raised the glass to his lips, his hand was trembling so that some of the amber liquid spilled down his chin. I took the glass and held it while he sipped, and presently his hand was steadier, and he took the glass back.

"Where's Tim?" he said, struggling to sit up. I started to help him, then sat still.

"He's down cracking the ice for those damned swans for the thousandth time," I said. "Then he's going to take some soup over to the farmhouse. He needed to go now, before it starts to ice up too badly. He'll stop by on his way back, he said."

He was silent for a while, sipping Scotch. I watched the fire and the sleet ticking on the windows, and, when I thought I was unobserved, his face. It looked, in the firelight, a bit like Roualt's head of Christ, stark and tortured and finished. My fingers itched to get at the hair and beard.

"So what's going on at the farmhouse?" he said finally. There was reluctance in his voice, but something else, too. A kind of slackening, a loosening of something that had held tight, like a vise. I knew he was not simply making conversation. He was too sick and weak for that. I wondered whether to put a bright face on the two old women's plight or to tell him the truth.

"It's not very good," I said. "They've gotten to the point where they can't really take care of each other. Your mother doesn't come downstairs until midday; I think she's coughing so badly at night that she simply has to sleep in the mornings. It leaves Luz on her own, with no food and no heat. I'm going to start going first thing, and Daddy's going to take the afternoon trip. That is, if the weather ever lets up. It's getting almost impossible to get up that hill to the farmhouse. I know this isn't what you wanted to hear, but I'm afraid the time is coming when they need more care than Daddy and I can give them, and you're the one who would have to make the arrangements about a nursing home, or something. Or, at least, okay, whatever we can arrange. I'd spare you this if I could, but I'm afraid for them. They won't take help."

And I told him about the food that was left but uneaten.

He shut his eyes again, and let his head roll to the side. His face was pinched and colorless.

"Goddamn that stupid Portuguese pride," he said. "She never would take what people offered her. She never would. People tried to help when Daddy left; I remember the pies and cakes and covered dishes that came into the house, even if I don't remember him. She dumped them all out and washed out the dishes they came in and made Luz take them back. God knows that bigoted old Gorgon, my Ponder grandmother, made her life miserable enough over being Portuguese, but she did reach out to her after he left. Mother did everything but spit in her face. I don't know if I blame her, but it would have been a start toward some healing. It could have meant a different life for her, and for me, too. But she had King Dinis. What else did she need? Now they're up there freezing and choking on their precious pride. Well, let King Dinis come save them. I don't give a shit. I'm only sorry you and Tim have gotten stuck with them. Let them go. Call the county and dump them."

"I haven't minded until now," I said. "I like your mother. I'm truly fond of Luz. And they gave me the start of a life back when they let me have the camp. I'm not going to just abandon them. But I promise I won't mention them to you again."

He shook his head weakly, and sighed.

"I'm sorry," he said. "You've got enough problems of your own. I'll try not to add my natural sweetness and generosity to them. Keep me posted on the old babes. If it comes right down to it, I'll figure out what to do about them. Provided, of course, I'm still around by then."

My heart flopped in my chest like a fish. He had never come so close to the subject that hovered always in the air over our heads.

"Dennis," I said, "if I can hold your head while you barf, I think I deserve to know what's going on with you and the leg. I'm not going to run on about it, and I'm not going to tell anybody—who would I tell? *People* magazine? I don't talk about you to your mother, if that's what bothers you. But I want to know. I . . . we care about you and the way you feel, Daddy and I. It's hard to think about you over here going through God knows what when we're right over there not doing anything to help . . ."

He turned his head to look at me again. He did that for quite a long time. Finally he said, "I don't know myself. They found some more . . . involvement with the bone in my thigh, that's why the chemo. It was hurting a good bit. It hasn't done that until now, not really. They're going to check after this course of chemo is over, and then they may want to take some more of the leg. I've already told them that's out. I've got some painkillers. I don't use them much, but they're here if I need them. And I've got some stuff to help me sleep. I don't use that, either. But it's here . . . if I need it. So far, scotch is better. I'm not going back after the last chemo treatment. I'm not going to give them any more of my leg. If it gets too bad, I'll decide then what to do. Who knows, this round may do the trick. Either way, I should know before spring. It's not going to prolong your tour of duty. I'm not asking you to re-up."

My eyes stung and I shook my head mutely. He saw it, and said, "I'm sorry again. I didn't mean that the way it sounded. I'm not used to nice women."

It was such a matter-of-fact pronouncement that I laughed, startled. He smiled, too.

"'Thus spake Zarathustra.' It's true, though. I seem drawn to your basic Grendel's mother type. The nice ones I manage to run off before they can apply for sainthood."

"You sound like the hero in a bad romance novel," I said. "A wild, bad boy until he's redeemed by a good woman's love. What decent long-suffering women have you managed to run off?"

"Two wives," he said. "One daughter." He was not smiling now.

"Why is that, Dennis?" I said quietly. It seemed to me that I was very close to seeing past the wall of illness and rudeness now.

"I grew up knowing only one thing about women, and that was that they will leave you," he said. "I made up my mind early on to be the one who did the leaving. I don't think I ever knew that consciously, until I got sick and had to stop and look inside. By that time, it seemed too much trouble to try and change things. I don't think there's that much time left, even if this leg turns out to be okay. I don't have the staying gene in me. I couldn't have. Neither of my parents had it . . ."

"Your father may have left you. But your mother didn't," I said. "She's still here. Right up there where she's always been, still waiting. All it would take is one word from you . . ."

He laughed, shortly and bitterly. "Is that what she told you? That she's waited for me all these years? That old bitch. She doesn't even know what's true and what isn't anymore."

I said nothing. I wanted, suddenly, no more of this. I was tired of the stubborn, senseless little drama of mother and son that had played around my head since the first day I had come up island. I stood up to go, snapping my fingers for Lazarus.

"Wait a minute," he said, and I stopped.

"Could you do one thing for me?"

"Of course."

"There used to be a sled in the woodshed out there. A blue Flexible Flyer. I wondered if it was still there. Would you mind looking?"

"Of course not."

I went out into the deepening blue of the January night. An early moon was rising, huge and white and low. It looked like a disk cut from bone, and polished. It would light the night almost like daylight, I knew. The Wolf Moon, my father said the old men at Alley's called it.

The sled was at the back of the woodshed, covered with a filthy old tarpaulin.

"Still there," I reported. Dennis smiled.

"I got that sled for Christmas the year before I went to America," he said. "It was a winter like this one, cold, with lots of snow. I don't remember any ice, though. We had our Christmas at the little camp, where you and Tim are. After dinner we went out on that hill that goes down to the water on the other side of the dock, and tried it out. I still remember my mother running like a deer, pushing that sled and belly-flopping down on it, shooting down the hill yelling like a Wampanoag. If they yell. I've never heard one. Her hair was in braids down to her waist, and they stood straight out behind her . . ."

I saw it in my mind, a tall, slim woman and a dark little boy, lifted off the earth on a snowy Christmas Day, literally, for a moment, hung between heaven and earth.

"Is she dying?" he said.

"I think so."

"How long?"

"I have no idea. It's congestive heart failure. I don't know much about that. I think the danger would be pneumonia, or something like it. I can find out . . ."

He shook his head.

"No."

And then, "She's very fat now, I know. Tim told me. I wish you could have seen her when she was young. She was . . . very beautiful."

"I wish I could have, too."

"There's something of her in you. Something of her like she was then, I mean. I told you that the first day, didn't I? Physically, I mean. There's no similarity in any other way."

"How do you know?" I said.

"I know."

His eyes drifted shut again, and I took Lazarus and went back to the little camp. I felt heavy and thick, freighted with a hopeless sadness, but under it was the beginning of elation. He had let me come close tonight. For just a moment, he had opened a door. . . .

"Looks like it's going to be a pretty night," my father said when I came into the kitchen. "Why don't we go out for dinner? There's a spot I keep hearing about. We ought to try it out before another blizzard hits."

The Red Cat Restaurant sat in the brilliant snow beside the state road in West Tisbury. After the empty, moon-washed snowscape we had traveled through, it looked like the confluence of all the lights and warmth and human companionship in the world. Cars and trucks and all-terrain vehicles were parked around it, and I could hear a little surf of rock music, thumping and cheerful, when I opened the door of the truck. All of a sudden I could hardly wait to get inside, to be part of a community again, even one unknown to me. I felt like a child going to a party, shy and awkward, but with a small fountain of secret glee in my stomach.

"I had no idea I'd missed this so much," I said to my father.

"Missed what?"

"Lights. People. Just going out to dinner."

"It ain't Buckhead."

I laughed.

"Right now it looks better to me than the Ritz."

We went in to the low, rambling, warm-lit building and were ushered to a table in a corner. On the way to it my father nodded to a couple of tables where men and women sat, and they smiled and nodded back. One of the men was pouring something from a paper sack, and he lifted the sack and said, "Evening, Tim."

"Ready for a game sometime soon?" another said.

"Any time," my father said.

It struck me that the men and women looked much as we did, or vice versa: ranging from young middle age to the sturdy elderly, bundled into parkas and scarves and caps or dressed in sweaters and turtlenecks and wool pants. Most wore boots. All looked healthy and weathered and simply glad, like us, to be out at the Red Cat on a snowy night.

"We could almost pass, couldn't we?" I said to my father as we sat down.

"Wouldn't miss it far," he said. He pulled a paper sack from the pocket of his jacket and put it on the table.

"Would madame like a cocktail before dinner?"

We sat and sipped the Macallan and I took a long, fussily elaborate time choosing from the menu. I loved this place and this night. I wanted to prolong it as much as possible. I finally decided on lamb shanks in red wine and sat back and drank some more of the Macallan.

"You could get drunk just from the sheer excitement of being with people, couldn't you?" I said.

"You could get drunk quicker on that stuff," he said mildly. "Don't you go getting cabin fever on me, and turning into a deep-woods lush. I can't have you dancing on tables here."

We talked lightly of things that did not seem to matter much, just for the sensation of doing such a wonderfully ordinary thing as making small talk in a restaurant. But finally we fell silent.

"I think Dennis may be thinking about killing himself," I heard myself say and gasped aloud. I had not known I thought that.

"Why do you say that?" my father asked. He did not seem shocked.

"I don't know, exactly. He's not going back to the hospital for any more surgery, you know. And he won't know for a while if this chemo is working. I don't know what the chances are of that, and he isn't about to tell me. I know a recurrence isn't good. But he said he had painkillers and sleeping pills, and that he would make up his mind how to use them if he needed them. Those were almost his words. It just now struck me that that's what he might have been talking about."

"Does it shock you? Scare you?" my father asked.

I thought about that.

"It doesn't shock me, I don't guess. But I hate the idea. I just hate it, Daddy. A man as young as he is, with such gifts, with so much to live for . . ."

"Maybe he doesn't think he's got so much to live for," my father said. "He's lost his wife and his daughter and his job and his leg. He's estranged from all his people. He's had a good bit of pain and there may be more coming. You can sort of see his point—"

"Daddy! I can't believe you're saying this about Dennis! He's your friend; you act almost like he's a son sometimes . . ."

"I won't wish bad pain on any man, Molly," he said. "I know about that. I wouldn't wish it on my worst enemy, and I certainly am not going to wish it on Dennis. You're right; he is my friend. Only he knows what his limit is. If he reaches it, I hope I can be there with him, but I'm not going to stop him."

"You knew he had this in his mind . . ."

"I knew it was an option with him, yes. There are others, some that I don't think he can see yet. I hope I can help him do that. If I can't . . ."

"If you can't, then you'll help him die. Is that it?"

He looked away and shook his head.

"Molly, there are just some things you don't know about. You haven't lived long enough to get to them yet. Not enough has happened to you. Let's drop this. It's Dennis's business."

"Oh, Daddy . . . hasn't there been enough death?" I said.

"When you get to be my age, it seems like there's never enough death," he said bleakly. "There's always more in the trough, just waiting. You can't stop it. The best you can do is try to deal with it decently."

"And helping a man commit suicide is decent? Oh, Lord, I'm sorry, Daddy. I'm spoiling this night for you," I said guiltily. "I promise to shut up about things I can't change. I love being here with you. I'd rather be here right now than anywhere in the world I can think of."

"You're some kind of daughter, Molly," he said. "Some kind of woman, come to that. Don't ever stop talking to me about what's on your mind."

"Sometimes I think we ought to just go on and jump in and talk about Mother," I said. "And I start to bring it up, and then I just can't. Are you waiting for me to do it?"

"No. I thought I'd be able to do it up here, in a place she wasn't part of, but so far I can't. It's like she's *too* far away. I can't feel her. Maybe I'll have to go back home to do that. I've been thinking that maybe it's time for that . . ."

"No, don't. Not yet," I said. "Please stay. Stay until spring. Until we know about Dennis. I don't think I could go through . . . and what about the swans? You can't leave the swans . . ."

He smiled at me, an amused smile like the ones he had sometimes given me when I was a child.

"Molly, I have to go home sometime. You do, too, as far as that goes."

"Why? I can't see one reason on earth why either one of us should go back to Atlanta right now. Not one."

"Because it's home," he said. "Because it's what we have. Because it's what we are as well as where. It's where all our context is. It's where everything we have left is."

"There's nothing left there for me," I said. "Tee's gone. Caroline is gone. Teddy's as good as gone. You're talking about finding a place out in the country. What's left there for me?"

"Oh, Molly," he sighed, and put his hand over mine. It was weather-chapped from his ice-breaking, and callused from the carpentry jobs around the camp. It felt as warm as a hot-water bottle. I squeezed it.

"Don't you know you're more than the sum of other people?" he said. "If you don't know that by now, what's it going to take?"

"All my life that's what I've been," I said. "I can't just change now."

"I think you can and you'd better," my father said.

We were finishing our dinner—the lamb shanks were rich and melting, cooked with tomatoes and wine and caramelized onions—when a woman came over to our table and stopped. She had fair hair and was small and stocky, dressed in a Fair Isle pullover and gray stretch pants, and her face was tanned and pleasant. Her eyes were clear and pale; there was something about them . . .

"Excuse me, but aren't you Mrs. Redwine?" she said.

I nodded.

"I'm Patricia Norton," she said. "I'm Dennis Ponder's second cousin once removed, or something, and Bella is my some kind of aunt. I just wanted to say that we all appreciate so much what you're doing for Denny and Aunt Bella and Luzia. We've been terribly concerned about them, but we haven't been able to do much for them. I guess you know by now that we don't see them, or vice versa. It makes it hard to know what to do."

"Please sit down," my father said. "I'm Tim Bell, Molly's father. I could have told you were some kin to Dennis. You've got the eyes."

I saw that she did, those ice-gray eyes that startled.

She laughed. "The Ponder eyes. We all look like we can see through solid rock. Straight through the dirt down to hell, my grandmother Ponder used to say. That was Dennis's grandmother, too, his father's mother. A grim old Gorgon if ever there was one born. She hated seeing those eyes in that wild little Portuguese face of Denny's, when he was little. They were the only thing about him that said Ponder, but they said it loud and clear. She couldn't pretend he wasn't at least half hers."

"Please sit," I said. "It's such a relief to meet some of Dennis and Bella's people. We've been wondering who to contact about them. Things aren't very good with any of them. So far we can handle it, but I don't know how long we'll be able to, and we don't have the authority to get any sort of official help for them . . ."

She sat, and ran her hands through her short hair in a gesture of annoyance and frustration; I think women everywhere on the planet do it. My own thatch often stood up in spikes from a similar gesture.

"You shouldn't have to. We're all embarrassed that two nice strangers are having to deal with our own. I was going to come down and talk to you about them when the weather cleared, but it doesn't look like that's going to happen. I should have done it before.

Tell me about them. I can tell the others. We'll think of something."

I told her what I knew of Dennis Ponder's plight, and of Bella and Luzia's. Her face softened with real grief. She was, I thought, a pretty woman, though you didn't see that at first. There was something about her of Livvy, something strong, something that would endure. I thought I would like to have her for a friend. If I had been going to stay up island, that is.

"Oh, it's such a mess," she said. "It all started with Grandma Serena. I don't know where all that spite and bile and hate came from, but it corroded the whole family. There wasn't anybody in it that she didn't spill it over. Grandpa Ethan just plain went to sea and never came back because of it; she didn't know for a year or two whether he was dead, or just gone. When she found out he was dead, she didn't miss a step. She had little Ethan, after all. Denny's father. By the time he got away from her and over to America, to Harvard, he was just like her, colder than a dead mackerel and meaner than cat manure. I think he married Bella just to spite his mother. If there was anything Grandma Serena hated worse than the Portuguese, I don't know what it was. And none of us ever knew why; she would just say that they were shiftless and sly and lazy and low class, and would steal you blind if you didn't watch it. Most of us think the only stealing any Portuguese ever did to Grandma was Grandpa Ethan. He spent an awful lot of time around the Azores. Well, anyway, at the end of his junior year here comes Ethan home with this tall, beautiful creature with Portuguese written all over her, and a waitress in a restaurant at that. Grandma started in on Bella the day she got off the ferry. It didn't take Ethan but two or three years to get tired of his little joke and cut out for who knows where, but by that time there was Denny, and I guess Bella just couldn't think how to get him out from under Grandma's hate any other way than to send him off island to her people. That finished him with Grandma. She wrote him out of her will the day Bella shipped him off. None of the famous Ponder land was going to end up with any Portuguese, no sir. Of course, it did anyway, in the end. But it went to Bella, not Denny. I think Grandma's probably still spinning over that. By that time Bella had turned into . . . what she is now. She wanted none of us and nothing from us. I can't say I really blame her, considering how Grandma and Big Ethan treated her and Denny. But the rest of us would have liked to make amends, only she wouldn't let any of us near her. I can't imagine why she's stayed all these years, just her and poor little old Luzia. I was hoping to get to know Denny a little, though, only from what you say there may not be time . . . oh, what a mess it all is! Nobody can hurt each other like family, can they?"

"No," I said past the knot in my throat. Poor old woman, ossified into her bitterness like a corroding statue. Poor Dennis, dying of a coldness next to the bone . . .

"It was you who plowed us out, wasn't it? And left the soup and the apples?" my father said, smiling at Patricia Norton. "And plowed out Bella and Luz?"

She grinned back, and nodded.

"I've got a little plow on my Cherokee. I've been plowing the ladies out every winter since I married Tom Norton and his Jeep. She thinks the county does it, or I think she'd pile the snow back over the road. I know she doesn't eat the food I leave, but I keep hoping Luz sneaks some of it. Now that I've met you, though, maybe we can figure out some way to get them all some help, and get some of the burden off you. I'll call a war council of the others over the weekend."

"Let's wait a while," my father said. "All of them are pretty weak, and it's just so damned cold. I don't want to stir things up just yet. Let's try to go on like we are until early spring. It's not a burden so far; we'll tell you if it gets to be. And we'll give you bulletins along the way. Molly's got a reasonable and decent agreement with Bella and Dennis. It's working fine for now."

After she had gone and we had paid our bill and left for home, I looked over at my father. His profile was calm in the thin silver light of the Wolf Moon, but he was chewing on his bottom lip, and I knew that that meant he was puzzling about something.

"They're not what Bella said," I said to him. "The up islanders. The old families. They're not cold and distant at all. They'd have taken all of them in; they'd have done that years ago. Do you think she knows that? How could she not?"

"Bella thinks what she needs to think," he said. "Don't take that away from her. It's hard, and it's wrong, but it's what's kept her going all these years. She'd have nothing if she lost that."

"Oh, God, it's just so stupid," I said. "So wrong and so useless. They don't think that way about the Portuguese; you can tell that. Only that awful old grandmother thought that. But all these years . . ."

"They were her years, Molly. Dennis is wrong about the up islanders and about his mother, too, I think, but the hate is what's driving his engine now.

When he's done with the chemo, though, I think I'm going to set them both straight. Oh, they won't thank me. But neither one of them needs to die thinking what they think now."

The cold, old sadness came back up into my throat, like bile.

"Maybe they won't die," I said. "That's always a possibility."

"Yes, it is," he said, and reached over and put his hand over mine. Neither of us said any more until we reached home.

In the days that followed things got a little better. Dennis finished the chemo, and if he did not regain the weight and color, at least the terrible, enervating nausea stopped. He began to come out once in a while during the mornings when I was working on his library, and he sat on the sofa and talked while I sorted and shelved. Most of the talk was about the books themselves, and the manuscript that was growing infinitesimally slowly in his bedroom. But once in a while he would let something personal drop, as lightly and quietly as a leaf falling from a branch. And always, when that happened, I would offer him a little chip of myself, another leaf from my tree. When February came roaring in on the shoulders of yet another winter storm, we both had a small, neat pile of each other's leaves.

Once he asked me, out of the blue, if I had ever slept with anybody besides Tee.

"Why do you ask?" I said, my face flaming.

"Because I wanted to know," he said reasonably. "You don't have to tell me, of course. I was just thinking what a waste it would be if you hadn't. What a waste for you and for some guy."

My cheeks burned hotter.

"No, I haven't," I said. "We got married awfully young. You just didn't do that back then, not in my crowd. Now I wish I had. I may never know what I missed."

I spoke lightly, but he said, "I wish I could have shown you. I really wish that. It would have been quite something, I think. From my standpoint, at least."

"Dennis," I said. "Are you making a pass at me?"

"No," he said. "What, a one-legged man making a pass at a woman?"

"I wasn't aware that it was the leg that was necessary," I said, and then blushed so deeply that I could feel it on my chest and arms and forehead.

He laughed.

"You almost make me wish I didn't have cancer," he said, and we both laughed, and the moment passed. I did not know if I was sorry or not.

Things were not good with the old women, though. Luzia caught a cold on one of the nights when her fire went out, and I spent almost all day for a week at her bedside. She needed a great deal of nursing care, and when she got better, Bella caught the cold and it went straight to her laboring lungs. The coughing and gasping were so bad that I finally called an ambulance, but she flatly refused to go to the hospital, and the attendants could not move her huge bulk. So I set up my contagious ward in her bedroom and settled in for another spell of nursing.

My father took over the library for Dennis, and he came every night to read to the old ladies while I got their supper. We both grew pale and worn and more tired than I can ever remember being for any length of time. I would fall asleep on the sofa after dinner; he would fall asleep sitting up in his chair at breakfast. He did that for the second day in a row one bitterly cold, ice-sheathed day in the middle of February, and I roused him and sent him up to bed.

"You sleep all day, and I mean it," I said. "I'll get you up when it's time to go up to the farm tonight. You can take over then, and I'll sleep."

He was too tired to protest, and so it was I who took the truck and went up the hill to the farmhouse in the dusk, to read to the old ladies. The ice was so bad that day that I had to leave the truck halfway up the lane and walk the rest of the distance, slipping and sliding and muttering weary curses. It was, I suppose, the reason that they did not hear me coming. The truck always made a lot of noise.

The door was unlocked, as it always was, so that whoever was expected could enter. But the house was dark. Almost always by this time Bella was downstairs, and had lit the lamps and the fire. I felt a prickle of unease on my forearms and scalp. For some reason, I felt that I should whisper, tiptoe. Do not stir up trouble, my grandmother Bell would have said, and maybe it will go away.

I saw them before I got even partway into the living room. I stopped dead and tried to breathe, but could not; when breath finally came it was so shallow and high in my throat that I almost felt it whistle. My head felt light and my face stung as though I had been slapped, hard. Afterward I knew that it was shock, but I also knew that it was not the sort of shock that I might have expected to feel. There was nothing grotesque about them, nothing obscene. Rather, they simply seemed totally exotic, totally out of any context I had. The first thought that penetrated the still white dome of the shock was that they looked Indian, something from a frieze on an ancient temple in a lost garden somewhere, one of the exquisite little erotic Indian miniatures that the Victorians so prized. They lay together on the bed at the far end of the room, intertwined so that it was hard to tell where Luz's delicate, withered arms and legs left off and Bella's colossus's limbs began. They were naked, and the firelight played over them: ivory, white, black, gilt, gold. They were kissing. It was a kiss of great and complex tenderness and old love, and of simple hunger. I averted my eyes and tiptoed out of the room and shut the door softly. All the way back down the icy driveway I tried as best I could to tiptoe.

By the time I reached home I had begun to shake all over, a very fine, silvery trembling. Everything I did, I did with great, precise care: parked the truck, got out and made my way over the spoiled old snow to the porch, opened the door, laid down my bag of groceries and the book I was reading to them. It was still *The Once and Future King*; Luz had asked again for the scene where the Wart pulls the sword out of the stone. Poor Luz. So in need of empowerment. Or perhaps not. Perhaps that was one of the things she found in Bella Ponder's great white arms. I found myself beginning to cry, silently.

I told my father, of course. I could not keep my tears from him, and I needed the ballast of his mind and voice. He listened while I poured it out, nodding. When I had finished he reached over and took my hand in both of his.

"Molly, baby. What is it that upsets you so about it? Is it because they're women, or they're old, or sick and maybe dying? What?"

"I guess it's that . . . that . . . I just didn't *think* about them that way. I mean, it must be like walking in on your parents when you're little and seeing them . . ."

". . . and you have to change the way you think about them forever after. Is that it?"

"I guess so. Oh, Daddy, I don't care if they're women, or old . . . I guess I care because of Dennis. Don't you see? That's what he saw. When he was just a little boy; that's what he saw them doing, and right after that they . . . she sent him away. I don't think he would have been shocked, providing he understood what they were doing, which I doubt. Small children don't shock easily. It's that she chose Luz instead of him. That's what he's lived with all the time. His mother loved her cousin more than she did him, and she sent him away when he found out about it. After his father, it must have seemed the ultimate betrayal. I'm not angry at Bella for loving Luzia, for God's sake; I'm happy she *has* someone to love. It's obviously a very real and very old love. I'm angry at her for sacrificing her son to it! That's monstrous!"

Somewhere during my outburst the shock had turned to rage; I had felt it happening. Even as the fire of it scorched at me, I wondered at it. What business was it of mine? Why should I care about these three people I had known such a short time and would not, could not, know for much longer? Danger flared with the anger. Beneath all of it I was frightened.

My father sat back and stretched his legs out to the fire. He sighed. He looked impossibly weary.

"I know that's the way Dennis feels about it," he said. "He thinks she was afraid that he would tell somebody, and it would get back to her mother-in-law and the other Ponders, and all the other old families, and they would simply drive Luzia off the island. That she—Bella—couldn't protect her, and that they would hurt her beyond repair. I have an idea it had gone on a long time by the time she married Denny's father and came over here with him; she must have been frantic to get away from that Portuguese Catholic enclave they lived in. What kind of future could she and Luz have had there? Maybe she did use Ethan Ponder, but no worse than he used her. He must have found out when Denny was very small. It was his excuse to leave, even if it wasn't his reason. And by that time they were stuck. They couldn't go back to the mainland. And Bella couldn't take a chance on his telling . . . or that's what Dennis thinks anyway. I don't think that's all there is to it, but he's not ready to listen to any other ideas yet. He may never be."

"If you don't think that, what do you think?"

"I'm not sure. I do know that she loved that little boy, though. And I know that she loves him now, as much as any mother ever loved a son, even if it's in her own grotesque way, and she's torn up about him. Ah, Lord. What a mess of unhappiness. What a swamp of pain and lies."

"Dennis told you, then."

He nodded. I was not surprised at that, but I felt a flicker of resentment that he had told my father and not me. But then I remembered our agreement.

"Do Bella and Luz know you know?"

"No. And they must never know either of us do, unless they decide to tell us. You're not to go telling Dennis what you saw, either."

"Oh, Daddy . . . as if I would!"

"This is a hell of a conversation for a father to be

having with his daughter," he said, and I managed a watery smile.

He went to bed then, practically dragging himself up the stairs hand over hand, and I lay down on the sofa and watched the flames. Sadness and bitterness lay in my stomach like a sickness. A terrible pity underlay it all. It seemed to me then that the worst suffering in the world was inevitably born of love.

I am still not sure how I would have handled what I knew, or if I could have made some kind of peace with it, because before the week was out everything changed again, and in the face of the change the love of two sad old women in a farmhouse on a Chilmark hill simply did not seem out of the ordinary to me anymore.

We had an abrupt softening of winter the morning after I saw Luz and Bella together, and when I awoke, head aching dully, bones as sore and troubled as if I had been in an accident, the snow was turning to slush and the icicles that had hung from the trees and porch eaves were dripping, and a weak, repentant sun had come sidling out to bathe the glade in milky light. Even before I opened the front door I could sense the change, and when I did I felt the softness of the air on my face, and smelled, not spring, but a cold, fresh, sweet, faraway *promise* of spring. I stretched, feeling better. I would have a shower and wash my hair and maybe go into Vineyard Haven and buy something unnecessary for the cottage. Perhaps my father and I would have lunch there. Maybe I would go into the Bunch of Grapes and treat myself to a new book, or a pile of them. Later I might, finally, cut Dennis's hair. I looked at my watch. It was very late. I went upstairs to wake my father. How on earth could both of us have slept so late? Except that we were both so very tired . . .

He was not there. His bed had been slept in, but he was not in the room and not in the cottage. Well, of course, the swans. He'd gone to feed the swans. How on earth it was that they had not waked us with their hissing, battering cacophony I could not imagine; they never failed to go into their indignant act of swanly starvation when we were late with their breakfast.

I threw on a coat over my pajamas and went down the path toward the pond. Out over the Sound the sky was a clear, pale, washed blue, and the water was still and streaked in darker shades of blue. The white smoke of spume that the cold wind blew off the tops of the whitecaps on the hard, iron mornings was gone. The Irish had a word for this sort of weather: a soft day.

My father was sitting on the end of the dock. His head was bowed and he was very still; at first I thought he had drifted into one of the little neck-crippling naps that he sometimes took sitting up. But then I saw that he was looking into the water, watching a swan circling in the cleared patch. Circling, circling. And as I came nearer I heard the sound that the swan was making, and I never want to hear it again, awake or in my dreams. The swan's head was thrown up to the sky, the long neck in a fierce, beautiful arch, and it made a great, rusty, desolate cry that sounded as if it were being torn out of the elegant throat. I never heard a mute swan make such a sound again.

I did not see the other swan. I did not know which one this was. I do know that my blood ran cold and thick, an icy sludge in my veins.

"Daddy . . ." I whispered.

He did not turn.

"It's Charles," he said. His voice was small and dry. "Diana is . . . gone. I found some feathers and a few splashes of blood in the reeds, but she's gone. I looked everywhere. Something got her in the night, fox or something. I don't know what their predators are. She couldn't have flown away with that wing. He's been doing this since I got here. It's been almost two hours."

Grief and pity for the two bereaved old creatures at the pond nearly brought me to my knees.

"Daddy, come up to the house now," I said, forcing my voice not to break. "How can it help him if you freeze to death? Let me fix you some breakfast. Maybe she's just hurt somewhere, and she'll come out when you're gone; don't animals hide when they're hurt? Later we'll look for her. Laz has a great finding nose . . ."

"No. She's not here. He would know. Don't you see? He knows she's gone; he doesn't know where she is; he's calling her. I didn't know they could do that."

"Daddy, come on."

He turned and looked at me. His face was absolutely gray and still. There was nothing in his eyes.

"Don't natter at me, Molly," he said, and I heard, incredibly, irritation in his voice. I could not ever remember hearing it before. It was a weak, peeved, *old* kind of irritation.

"But you're going to get sick . . ."

"Then I get sick! Can't you stop hovering for once in your life?"

Hurt flooded me. My eyes filled. I turned and stumbled back up the path. But by the time I had

gained the porch, the hurt had receded and pain and
dread had taken its place. He had simply had too
much; this last hurt was past enduring. He loved those
swans; this was too much; this was not right; this had
gone over into the realm of pure cosmic malice.
Besides, maybe he was wrong. Maybe Diana would
come back. Maybe in a little while he would come up
and tell me she was back and did not seem too badly
hurt . . .

But he did not come back. I went up and got
Dennis Ponder and we went back to the pond, he
limping and holding on to my arm and Lazarus's
head. My father was still sitting there. Charles had
stopped the circling and crying, and was riding flac-
cidly on the water, his head down as if he were about
to plunge it under the surface in search of food. He
was drifting in idle circles, one black foot sheltered in
the sweep of his wing, as I had often seen them both
do. He looked like a ship with its rudder broken.

"Will you come up to the house with us now,
Tim?" Dennis said quietly. "You need some food and
something to drink. After we've had both, I'll come
back down here with you and we'll build a fire and
wait with him."

My father looked at him.

"Do you know how it feels?" he said. "I do. I know
how it feels. I don't know how else I can help him, but
I can be here with him."

"Tim . . . just for half an hour. That's all. Just for
that."

In the end my father went with him. Somehow I
knew that I must not join them. It might have hurt my
feelings once, but it did not now. I made coffee and put
it into a thermos, and made sandwiches and wrapped

them in foil, so that when they went back to their vigil they would at least have some sustenance.

But they did not need the coffee or the sand- wiches, and I found them days later, cold and begin- ning to mold, in the pantry where I had left them. When they went back to the pond, scarcely half an hour later, Charles was gone, and he did not come back.

CHAPTER THIRTEEN

$\mathbf{F}$OR A WHILE AFTER THAT, my father went to the pond
several times a day to look for Charles. He did not
say that was why he went, but of course it was—in the
hope of seeing, yet knowing he would not see, that
frigate of white sailing mulishly in the tiny circle left of
clear black water.

I went, too, in between trips to Dennis's camp and
down to the farmhouse and into town for supplies. I
went, as my father did, hoping, but knowing it was a
futile hope. Somehow I knew that the silent whiteness
that had swallowed Diana could not sustain Charles's
life.

Dennis went, too; every now and then when I
went, I saw the tracks of his one good foot and the holes
made by the crutch, and the paw prints of Lazarus
beside them, deeper from taking Dennis's weight.

None of us spoke to the other about going to the
pond. It was as if to speak of it would open a gate to
more pain than we could bear, any of us.

When my father went, he stayed a while. I know
he kept the ice broken up, because when he came back
the stick was always black and wet. But I do not know
what else he did there. At the very beginning he was

obsessed with how Charles had managed to get himself airborne.

"He wouldn't have had enough open water," he said over and over. "He'd have needed the whole pond to get his momentum up, and there was almost no clear water. But I know he did, somehow, because I'd have found him if something had happened to him around the pond. I've been everywhere. I'd have found him."

Each time he came back, my father was duller and sadder and quieter. I would have given anything I had to take some of the pain, but I knew that I could not. It was not only Diana that he mourned.

"Let him be," Dennis said when I voiced my worry to him. "He's coming to terms with your mother being gone now. I don't think he's really stopped to do that before."

"Do you think Charles flew away?"

"I don't know. No. I think whatever got her, got him. But I'm not going to tell Tim that. This godforsaken place is going to leave him something, anyway."

After a week or so my father went less and less often. One evening toward the end of February, another great storm came down on us on its battering crystal wings, and I watched as he looked up from his newspaper toward the rack where his coat and hat always hung by the front door, hard by the black hat of my mother's that I had moved there. He always put them on before he went down to the pond. I saw him decide, saw his eyes drop to his paper and then lift to the fire, watched as he sat still. He did not seem to see the fire or the room around him; soon he got up and went upstairs to his bedroom. He did not go to the pond again.

I knew that he was not sleeping much in those days. I would wake in the night in my cave under the stairs and hear his footsteps over my head as he wandered around his room. I heard him go into the bathroom, heard the bed creak as he got back into it and creak as he got up again. Sometimes, not very often, I heard him come downstairs to the kitchen and go back up again, and once or twice I found a coffee cup on his bedside table, but more often I found the bottle of Scotch. Lazarus heard him, too, and would lift his head and look at me and whine softly, and I would pat his head and say, "Go back to sleep. He wouldn't want to think he'd waked us."

I asked him about it, finally.

"I'm okay," he said. "I'm fine. I guess I've just slept myself out. You know how good the sleeping is up here; it's almost all I've done since I came. And I'm getting some reading done that I've been wanting to do for years. You ever read Thoreau? 'I went to the woods because I wished to live deliberately.' Now that's a fine thing. Maybe I can do that up here. I never could at home."

He began to sleep later and later in the mornings, and I let him. Often I would hear no sound from his room by the time I was ready to go up and work on Dennis's library, and would tiptoe up the stairs and look in on him, and he would still be sleeping, a motionless mound in a cool, dark room, only the soft rise and fall of the quilt over him speaking of life. In those moments, I did not feel as if it were my father I stood looking at, but Caroline or Teddy, a child loved but strange and somehow imperiled in sleep. The uneasiness of that would stay with me through my day.

He would be up when I came back in the early afternoon, of course, and would have done this or that around the cottage; we would talk desultorily of his day's occupation. More and more often he fell asleep in the late afternoons before the fire, and I could not bear to waken him to go and read to the old ladies, so I began to take that task back over, too. Perhaps it was just as well that I did. Bella and Luzia seemed to me terribly diminished, possessed by winter and illness and fretfulness, steeped in old age and darkness. The acute stage of Bella's flu, or whatever it was, had passed, but the horrific cough lingered, and she was unable to get up and down the stairs, so she had made a bed for herself on the sofa across from Luz's bed, and there she stayed most of the time, a great, bad-tempered, musty black crow in a slatternly nest. In addition to the reading, I now began to air and straighten the bedding and the room when I went in the afternoons, and wash the stale dishes piled in the sink in the cold kitchen, and put on pots of soup and stew for their dinner, and bring wood and build up the fire, and clean out and light the stove against the coming night. The feral winter still held the island in its talons; I would think, as I watched the sleet or snow beginning yet once more to spill from the soiled, stretched gut of the sky overhead, of the first flush of lemon-icing forsythia and the red flowering quince at home, of the frail shoots of daffodils green against the wet, black earth. Bella and Luzia both had told me how transcendentally lovely the Vineyard's spring was, and Patricia Norton had spoken of it, but in those evenings in the dark farmhouse on the lush moor, with only firelight and the dim-watted bulbs in the old lamps for light, spring seemed simply unreal, a fever dream, a madman's sad hallucination. We would, I felt, be stricken into this tableau of cold and lightlessness forever.

Dennis had drawn back inside himself. As if the death of Diana and the disappearance of Charles had severed some tender new cord connecting him to the world, he retreated into his room, working silently and feverishly on his book. I heard the sounds of industry as I worked at the shelves in the living room: the riffling of pages and occasionally the furious tearing as he jerked a page from his legal pad and crumpled it; the slide and splash of pages as one of his tottering piles of reference books fell over; his under-the-breath exclamations of impatience; the constant accompaniment of Mozart or Verdi thrumming away under the muted bustle. But he no longer came out and sat and talked as I worked, or called out to me from his bedroom, and even Lazarus often gave up on him and came clicking out to where I worked, sighing greatly and collapsing against my legs in boredom and abandonment.

"Any old port in the storm, huh?" I would say to him, and he would sigh again, and slide into his disjointed, doggy sleep. But presently he would jerk awake, and look accusingly at me as if I had kidnapped him, and get up and pad back into Dennis's bedroom. Aside from leaving groceries, I did not bother Dennis. It was as if he were engaged in some fierce contest, a race against some immutable deadline, to finish his book. I could not dwell on that. I did not think he felt worse, or any differently than he had for a while; I got no sense of that. It was just that for a little while he had been present to me, and now he was not. I did not know if he saw my father during the times I was in Chilmark or West Tisbury or

Vineyard Haven, if Dad came across the snowy glade and sat with him as he once had. If they met, neither spoke of it. It was as if winter had stopped time in its last days, and our life and community had stopped with it.

Tired, my God, I was tired in those bleak, low-ceilinged days. I was so tired that I did not even recognize the feeling as such, just that I seemed mired in a lethargy born of this strange, dingy, gray stasis that held us fast. It did not even occur to me that I needed surcease and could probably have it by calling Patricia Norton or someone for help with the old ladies. Looking back, it seems incredible that I did not realize that our situations were uncomfortable and rapidly growing untenable, but at that time I didn't. It simply seemed that the one important thing was to keep going forward as I had been. Just to keep the minimal routine of our days spinning slowly without their sagging and toppling. Just that. I still do not quite know what malign alchemy held the glade in its grip in those days. I only know that it came with the soft-footed thing that took away Diana, and there seemed at the time to be nothing that could lift it.

Trouble boiled like hot water in the lengthening days. Luz developed bedsores of such ferocious suppuration that I finally had to call the visiting nurse. I had not even known she had them; she had turned as coy and fussy as a two-year-old about letting me help her change her clothing and take her sponge baths, and Bella had backed her up, saying belligerently that of course she could still bathe Luz; she did so every morning. What did I think she was? I only found the sores when I lifted Luz to put clean cases on the pillow

behind her and smelled the sick, sweet odor of putre-
faction under her clothing.

When I pulled away her nightgown she shrieked
and I nearly vomited, and went that instant and called
the nurse. When I got back Bella was sheltering Luz in
her great arms, glaring at me for making her cry, and
when the nurse arrived, Luz's shrieks reached such a
crescendo of noise and hysteria, and Bella's shouts of
protective rage were so terrible, that the poor, weary
woman simply put out some medical supplies on the
porch and told me how to clean the wounds, saying
that Luz should be seen by a doctor. And she left. Bella
finally let me clean Luz's sores as best I could, holding
the tiny woman in her arms and crooning to her as I
worked, trying not to gag, and watched me as I
applied the antibiotic salve and bandaged the wounds.

"But you're going to have to let me get a doctor up
here to look at them," I said. "And let the nurse come
and change these bandages every day. Otherwise she'll
have to go to the hospital."

"No," Bella said, not looking at me. "You do it.
You can do it; you did a good job tonight."

"Don't you understand? The infection could get
into her bloodstream. She could get very sick. She
could die. She's awfully frail, Bella. These sores should
have been seen to a long time ago. I can't help either of
you when I don't know anything's wrong. You'll have
to tell me when you aren't feeling well."

"Oh, I will," Bella said, smiling radiantly at me
with her blue lips. I knew she would not.

The sores did soon begin to heal, but one morning
Bella fell in the kitchen and could not get up, and I
found her there that afternoon when I came, almost
unconscious and soiled with her own urine. Luz was

wailing thinly and monotonously from the living room. This time I did not try to reason with either of them. I went to the telephone and called Patricia Norton. She was there in fifteen minutes, her strong, pleasant face red with cold. I met her on the steps.

"I'm sorry. I hate to bother you. But they ran the nurse off last week, and I think that if she starts screaming that hard in the state she's in, it will just stop her heart. My father isn't well, or I'd ask him . . . I just need someone to help me lift her back on to the sofa in the living room. I don't think she's hurt or has had an attack. She just can't get up. I'll take it from there if you can help me . . ."

Patricia looked around the dingy living room and her brows drew together. I saw her take a deep breath, mouth closed, nostrils flaring, as if stifling shock.

"I had no idea it was this bad," she said in a low voice. "I don't see how you've managed by yourself this long. Let's get her on the sofa, and then I'm going to call the others and we're going to make a plan and go talk to Dennis whether or not he wants to listen, and get them both into a hospital or a home as soon as possible. This is . . . not acceptable.

"You'd better not tell her who I am," she added under her breath as we went into the kitchen where Bella lay. I had covered her with a quilt, and she looked, in the dimness, like a vast, helpless amphibian cast up on a dark beach.

"Won't she know?" I whispered back. "You look an awful lot like a Ponder."

"I don't think so. I haven't been in this house since I was nine or ten. None of us has."

But Bella did know. She knew, and she began to scream like a banshee for Patricia Ponder Norton to get out of her house. She did not stop screaming all the while we pushed and pulled and hauled and swatted at her, not while we frog-walked her across the kitchen and living room and dumped her on to the sofa, and when she reached that haven she threw a vase and the heavy brass lamp at Patricia. Her lips turned navy blue and her face deep magenta, and she began to choke and gargle and rasp.

"I'll call for an ambulance on the car phone," Patricia said, and ran out into the frigid darkness. The wind was high that night, and crooned around the corners of the house; I almost lost her words in the swell of it.

By the time the tri-town ambulance came hooting and fish-tailing up the glassy driveway, I had cleaned Bella Ponder and she lay, pale but calm and smiling, under a cocoon of clean blankets, sipping cocoa. It was obvious to the EMTs that, as she said, she did not need emergency ambulance service.

"My young friend gets terribly excited," she said, smiling her great white shark's smile at the two exasperated young men. "I didn't know she'd called you until you came up the hill. I'd never have let her if I'd known. I have these little spells all the time. My doctor knows about them. It's Dr. Cardin, over in Oak Grove; he's got his offices in the hospital. You can ask him. I'm awfully sorry about this. Can we offer you some cocoa?"

We could not. The men went away, carefully blank-faced, no doubt cursing hysterical off islanders who called for help when help was not needed on icy, dangerous nights.

I looked at Bella. She did not look back.

"If you do that to me again, our agreement is off

and I'm leaving," I said, my voice shaking with anger. "And don't think I won't. You have people of your own who can and want to help you. One of them came tonight. Next time I'll let them."

"I promise I won't," she muttered, dropping her eyes. Her eyelashes lay on her waxen cheeks like black silk fans. I had seen Dennis's lashes like that, in the exhausted sleeps that followed his chemo. Dennis . . . She would do it again, of course, if it happened again. But at the moment I was too tired to think ahead. I built up the fire and the stove, heated some stew for them, and went home and fell into bed. I did not wake until past nine the next morning.

All the next day the white blanket of my fatigue dragged behind me wherever I went, and by the time I was to go up and read to Bella and Luz, I did not think I could take another step.

I got up slowly from the sofa, where I had dropped after coming in with groceries for all three houses, and the room took a slow, majestic spin around me. I shook my head and held on to the arm of the sofa and the spinning ceased, but my knees were still watery. I listened for any sound of my father upstairs, and when I heard none, climbed the stairs hesitantly. I hated to disturb any sleep he might find for himself, but perhaps, just this once, he would take the groceries to the farmhouse and read to the old women. If I did not sleep, I thought I would die.

He was sitting on the edge of his bed, staring out at the pond and the Sound beyond it. The evening was very cold, but the sky was clear, a tender, soft lavender that gave back a watercolor wash to the quiet water. The moon was full, or nearly so; later, I knew, there would be a silver-white path down the water to the horizon, and the lingering snow would be flooded with blue-white light. I did not think my father saw any of it. His eyes were fastened on another, different distance.

I went and sat down beside him, and put my arm around him.

"Can't you sleep, Daddy? Want me to make you some cocoa?"

He shook his head, not looking at me. He was still staring at the hat.

"Well, then, maybe a Scotch. I'll fix you one and you can have it up here while I run over to the farmhouse, and then we'll have dinner. I got some clam chowder from the Black Dog."

He did not answer, and I was beginning to feel real alarm when he turned his face to me. It was naked with yearning, terrible to see. I tightened my grip on his shoulders.

"She almost came, baby," he said, and his voice was a rasp. "I fell asleep when the sun was going down, and for a minute she was there. Just for a minute . . . and then I woke up. And I can't go back to sleep now; I don't sleep in the nights, and she won't come in the daytime. I brought that hat up here, thinking she might know, somehow, but she still doesn't come . . . if I could just sleep in the nights. Just one night . . . I know she'd come. I know she would."

I put my head down on his shoulder silently, thinking for a moment how wonderful it would be to just give up, let go, opt out, let someone else take over. But there was no one else. I could not ask this wrecked old man to care for anyone else. He could not even minister to himself.

I remembered something.

"I have some sleeping pills," I said. "Charlie Davies gave them to me before I left Atlanta. I haven't taken all of them. Why don't you try one? I don't think they're very strong, but they worked for me. You're right, you do need to sleep at night."

He nodded slowly.

"Maybe that would do it. Maybe it would," he said, and the frail hope in his voice was more than I could bear. I jumped up and ran downstairs and got the pills, for the moment the fatigue forgotten.

When I got back upstairs he was already lying flat in bed, covered with the quilts, and his bedside light was off. I gave him the vial of pills and he shook one out and took it with the water I had brought.

"You want it now?" I said doubtfully. "What about dinner?"

"I'll get some later," he said back. There was almost a merriment in his voice, like a child who knows a secret. I turned away from him.

"Sleep tight, Daddy," I said.

"Thank you, baby," he said back. "Would you pull the door to when you go?"

I did so, leaving him there, waiting to go and meet my mother in the country of his sleep.

I went downstairs in such a fever of anger that I almost forgot the old ladies' groceries as I stumped out to the truck. I knew why she did not come to him in his sleep. It was because, for the last two weeks or so, she was spending her nights with me, and the dreams she brought with her murdered sleep as effectively as Macbeth. Every night she came, usually about three A.M., so that I had only had a couple hours' sleep and would get little more after I woke from the dreams. She came and she raged like a wild beast, a madwoman, from behind her bars. She thrust her hands and arms out through the bars of her subterranean lair and clawed the air with them, and she raged and shrieked and howled out her impotent fury. In my dreams I was no longer afraid of her, but I felt a profound, all-enveloping despair. Whatever it was she so wanted, I could not give it to her. I did not understand her furious pleas. The despair would last long after I woke, until dawn broke, earlier now, and I slid back into the thin sleep of exhaustion. I thought that if my mother did not stop howling at me in my sleep I would go mad.

I stood still, beside the truck, the bag of groceries in my arms.

"I hate you," I said clearly and dispassionately to her, in the cold, silken air. "If that's what you want, then that's what you've got. I hate you for what you're doing to both of us. You're killing me with your furies and your fits, and you're killing him with your absence. Why the hell can't you just go to him one time? God knows you've got enough presence to spread over six states. Put some where it's needed."

I drove carefully up the still frozen hill toward the farmhouse. I was still bone-tired, but I felt a bit better. Perhaps my father would sleep this night. Perhaps I would, too.

But it was not a better night, after all. Bella and Luz had obviously been quarreling all afternoon, and were still at each other when I came in. The house was cold and stale and malodorous with whatever food Bella had not put away in the kitchen, and the fire in the living room was out, and papers and magazines and used tissues were scattered all over Luz's bed and the floor, and all of a sudden I could hardly bear the fusty mess of sickness and age. My temper flared again.

"Whatever it is you're fighting about, just stop it right now," I snapped. "I'm tired to death, and I've got to rake out this place and get you some supper, and I don't feel like listening to you snipe at each other while I'm doing it."

"It's her fault," Bella said stubbornly, sounding like a gargantuan sulking child. "She insists that you're reading *Once and Future* to us, and I can't tell her you've read that twice already and that we're in the middle of *Penrod and Sam*. I'm not going to listen to *Once and Future* again. I'm sick of it. It was my time to choose, and *Penrod* is what I chose, and *Penrod* is what I want to hear. You tell her so."

Luz began to wail. "That's not so! We were reading *Once and Future*. I know we were! She's just mad because I spilled stupid soup on her stupid crossword puzzle. I know we're reading *Once and Future*, and I want to hear about the Wart and the sword!"

"Shut up!" Bella shouted. "You little old baby, you just shut up! You get your way all the time because you're a little old crybaby! I spend all my time doing for you, and you keep wanting everything . . . !"

"Big old bully!" shrieked Luz. "You're the one who gets her way all the time! You get your way because you're the biggest and you can walk and I can't—"

"HUSH!" I shouted, and they both stopped and looked at me, the whites of their eyes showing.

"Just be quiet. I will not listen to this. I'm not going to read either one tonight. I'm going to straighten this place up and heat your supper, and then I'm going home and get some sleep. You can watch television or scream at each other, I don't care, but I'm not reading to you."

And I didn't. I stalked into the kitchen and washed their dishes and emptied the garbage and heated their clam chowder and brought it to them, and I picked up the room and built up the fire, all in a stony silence. They pleaded and promised, and Luz began to sniffle again, but I held firm. I could not wait to be out of that spoiled-smelling farmhouse and into the clear, cold air.

"Now," I said to myself when I was under way, skidding down the long lane to Middle Road. The rising moon hung low over the Atlantic, and I could see that it left its luminous paths on sea and Sound alike. The whole world was light and shadow: snow drifted on stone walls, woods, moors, beaches, and boulders, the occasional blue bulk of a house, windows lit yellow. Over it all, great clouds of stars swarmed. I took a deep breath and waited to feel better. But I did not. Bullying two sick old ladies had not helped at all. I felt craven and cowardly and ashamed of myself, and I felt a deep, despairing fear for my father, and the fatigue was back in all its sucking power, and under it all there trembled something so akin to red, killing rage that it frightened me. I thought that if it surfaced, something would happen that would change the world forever. Something would die. Something else, perhaps, would be born.

I took a deep breath and pushed the anger back down. I drove on carefully, thinking determinedly of nothing but supper and bed. I remembered that Lazarus was still at Dennis Ponder's cabin, and if Dennis should happen to fall asleep, he would be there all night. Somehow I could not bear the thought of that. I skewed the wheel and the truck slid into

Dennis's yard. I got out and went softly up the steps; he would undoubtedly still be working in his bedroom, and I did not want to talk to him this night. I would just open the front door and whistle for Lazarus.

But Dennis was sitting on his sofa before a leaping fire, sipping Scotch and listening to *Nabucco*, and Lazarus was lying on the sofa beside him with his head in Dennis's lap. I stared at them, suddenly wanting to strangle both my traitorous dog and the man who had lured him away from me. Dennis and Lazarus stared back at me.

Dennis had recently shaved, something he seldom did in the evenings. His thin face had a shine to it, of fresh-shaven skin, and just the tiniest wash of color— or perhaps it was only stained by the fire. Whatever it was, he looked better than I had seen him for a long while. He wore the red jacquard sweater that I liked, and khaki corduroy pants which, if they were too large, did not look it because of the enveloping sweater.

"You look like you're going out on the town," I said, purely for something to say. "What's the occasion?"

"I don't know," he said, still looking hard at me. "All of a sudden I realized I hadn't shaved in two days, and hadn't bathed in more than that. It struck me that cabin fever had set in. I don't think I've looked up from that manuscript for a week."

"Is it going well?"

He jerked his head impatiently.

"I really don't know, or care much, right now. It hit me suddenly that what the world really needs now is a pompous treatise on boys from a man who only knows about them because he's afraid of girls. I guess it's been my night for epiphanies."

"How you know about them doesn't matter, only that you do," I said. "I thought it was a wonderful idea. You can't mean you're going to stop—"

He held up his hand and I fell silent. One unwritten rule we had was that I did not ask him about his work.

"Right now I'm more interested in you. It's like I haven't really seen you for weeks. What in hell is the matter with you? You look like you've been whupped through hell with a buzzard gut, to quote a housekeeper from Mississippi my wife once hired."

My eyes flooded with tears, and a great, cold salt lump came into my throat. I turned away, afraid I was going to cry in front of Dennis Ponder and loathing the idea.

"Molly, turn around here," he said, and I did.

"How long has it been since you've had any sleep?" he said slowly. "What's going on over there? What's happening to you?"

I shook my head mutely, and he reached over and got the Scotch bottle and poured some into his empty glass and handed it to me. He gestured for me to sit down. I sat as if I had been a child bidden to do so. Laz lifted his head, thumped his tail, and went back to sleep.

I took a gulp of the Scotch.

"I didn't mean to just walk in on you," I said. "I was on my way back from the farmhouse and I remembered Laz was still here. I was just going to whistle for him. I can't have him just living over here."

"You didn't disturb me. I thought you might come by. I was ready for some conversation, I guess. But it looks more like you're ready for some sleep. Is it Tim? Are you worried about Tim? I knew he hadn't been by, but I thought he was letting me work, like you've been doing."

The Scotch burned in my stomach. It felt wonderful. Something loosened just a hitch.

"I am worried about him," I said. "He's not sleeping . . ." And I went on to tell him about my father's deepening depression since Charles and Di were no longer on the pond, and about his terrible nighttime sleeplessness and his days spent in exhausted slumber, and the conviction he had that my mother would come to him in his dreams if only he could sleep at night.

"He's even moved her hat upstairs to his room. He sits and stares at it," I said. "He's nobody I know, Dennis. And the old ladies . . ."

I fell silent. We weren't to talk about his mother and Luz, either, unless he initiated the conversation. That was another rule.

"Tell me," he said, and so I did. I finished with the quarrel and my stalking out of the house without reading to them, and how ashamed I felt about that, and how worried I was about both of them. He said nothing, only stared at me.

"There's more, isn't there? You're not sleeping. Why not?"

So I told him about the nightly dreams in which my mother raged and stormed at me from her subterranean barred cave, and about the terrible feeling I had that she wanted something from me, but I could not understand what it was.

"The dreams happen in the very middle of the night, so that when I do get back to sleep, it's dawn and I have to get right up again," I said. The warmth of the Scotch was loosening my limbs pleasantly, and my head felt sinuously furry. "And by the time I go up to read to the old women and get their suppers and clean up, I can hardly move."

He frowned.

"Tim was doing that, wasn't he?"

"He hasn't been, for two or three weeks. Almost since Di was killed and Charles left. He sleeps in the daytime, Dennis. I can't bear to bother him about the old ladies."

"So you just go ahead and do it. Christ, Molly. How long do you think you can keep that shit up?"

"I don't know. I guess until something changes, one way or the other."

I flushed. I did not want him to think I meant until he took a turn for the worse, or died, or until one of the old women did. He grinned briefly.

"Well, we've got to get you some help. What would help most?"

"I think . . . being able to sleep through the night. Just that. Oh, Dennis . . . *What on earth does she want from me?*"

It was literally a cry, torn out of a part of me that I did not know was so close to the surface. I was shocked at my own vehemence.

Dennis considered for a long time. And then he said, "Maybe she just wants her hat back."

We looked at each other for a long moment, and then I spit a mouthful of Scotch into the fire-warm air and began to laugh. In a moment he did, too. In the blink of an eye we were laughing so hard that neither of us could get our breaths, and long, wheezing gasps punctuated the insane laughter in the living room. And still we laughed.

Just as suddenly something inside me burst and I began to cry. I cried and cried. I sobbed and strangled and howled aloud like a woman at the Wailing Wall; sounds came out of me that I did not know a woman could make. I gagged and retched and wept some more, and struggled for breath, only to begin to cry again. He sat watching me for a moment, then he moved over on the sofa and put his arms around me and held me while I cried. He did not pat me, or whisper that it would be all right, or offer me a handkerchief. He just held me.

It was a long time before the awful, primitive sounds stopped long enough for me to gasp out, "I hate her! I hate her with all my heart! And I hate him! First she left me—she did that a long time ago, before she finally did it for good, and I hate her for all those times—and then he left me, too! I knew she would do it eventually, and I finally got used to the fact that Tee did it, but Daddy . . . he was never supposed to leave me! He was never supposed to do that!"

"Oh, Molly," he said finally. "He hasn't left you. He's just . . . out of touch right now."

"You haven't seen him," I wept. "You don't know . . ."

"I know what depression is like. I know that. I went that route right after the first surgery, when I knew that I would have to leave the school and come home to my mama because I didn't have a penny left to my name. No family, no job, no money, no leg, and no future . . . I was a mess. I slept all day and stared at the television all night. I was afraid to live and afraid that I was going to die. I was afraid to go to sleep. I was paralyzed in more ways than one. I literally couldn't move. It's a terrible thing. There isn't anything worse. I know that. I'll look in on Tim tomorrow. See what I can do."

"You don't feel that way now, though," I said, heaving myself up out of his arms and mopping my face. I felt as hollowed out and as light as a balloon, a dummy of a woman.

"No. It's funny. Now I seem to be able to function only right in the moment, like a small child. Just in the day I'm in. I guess it's the not knowing . . . what's going to happen. If I knew one way or the other, I think I'd be depressed, or terrified, or angry, or whatever. It's why I've refused to go back to the doctor, I think. But lately I've just been sort of . . . focused inside myself. Time to come out now though, I think. Past time."

He reached over and pushed the damp hair off my hot face. I could not even imagine how terrible I must look. But he smiled.

"Nobody's being good to you, are they?" he said. "Not for a long time, if they ever were. Nobody's taking care of you. It's all the other way around."

"It's okay. I don't usually mind—"

"I mind. We're going to do something now just for you. Something absolutely wacko and off-the-wall. Oh, hell, it's for me, too, of course. You up to an adventure?"

"What?"

"I'm not going to tell you. I'm going to show you. You'll have to do some of it. First, I want you to go out to the shed and get the sled. You remember? Will you do that?"

"Dennis . . . we aren't going sledding in the middle of the night!"

"Go get the sled. Are you a total wimp?"

"No," I said, suddenly filled with gaiety that bordered on giddiness. The iron fatigue had lifted. I was floating on Scotch and release.

"I'm no more wimp than you are! I'll show you who's a wimp!"

I raced out of the cottage and around back to the shed where the sled still lay, silent and grimy beneath the tarpaulin. Overhead the moon rode high like a white schooner, and the earth leaped and blazed with light from it, and the stars, and the reflection off the deep-creamed snow. My boots scrunched as I hauled the sled around the side of the cottage, and snow flew in little silvery puffs from the laden branches of the evergreens when I knocked against them. The air was cold and so dry that it felt like ginger ale in my lungs. It smelled of cold salt and pine and the peculiar, wet-blue smell of snow at night. I drew in great gulps of it, as if I could never get enough. By the time I reached the porch, I was giggling.

He was dressed and waiting for me. He wore his parka and a scarf and gloves and a dark watch cap like the scallop fishermen who went out of Menemsha wore, and his teeth and the whites of his eyes flashed in the shadow of the porch. He had one crutch and he was leaning on Lazarus with his other hand. I moved up to help him, but he motioned me away.

"I can do it," he said. "We've been practicing."

And he put his hand on Lazarus's back, then together they inched down the steps, Dennis holding on and hopping, Laz carefully taking his weight, waiting until he felt it full before going down another step. They managed the steps and stood beside me in quite a short time. I felt tears prickle again.

"He's a good dog," Dennis said. "I'd forgotten what it was like to have a good dog."

I don't remember precisely how we made it down the path to the dock and up the hill beyond it, but we did, slipping and sliding and laughing. Sometimes Dennis leaned on me and sometimes on Laz, and sometimes he was able to manage with just the crutch. By the time we gained the crest of the long, smooth, snowy hill, we were both panting. I felt my cheeks flaming with exertion and laughter, and I saw the flags of color in his. We stood together silently for a time, looking down the long swoop of white gleaming under the moon, out over the blue and white and black pond and the glittering Sound beyond it, wrapped in the quilted silence that a snowfall gives to the world. I don't think I have ever seen anything lovelier than that night of late snow and moonlight up island. It still burns silver and black sometimes, when I close my eyes.

"Okay," he said presently. "This is how we'll have to do it. I don't think it'll be too hard on you. We'll get the sled right there on the very edge of the slope, and I'll lie down on it, and you run along behind, pushing, and then, when it takes the crest, you just belly-flop down on top of me."

"Dennis, I'll mash you to a pulp! I must outweigh you by twenty pounds."

"Not anymore," he said. "Come on, Molly. That's the way everybody does it when they want to go two on a sled. You won't hurt me. I've got a ton of clothes on."

And that's what we did. We maneuvered the sled to the lip of the hill that ran steeply down to the verge of the pond, and he lay down on it on his stomach, with Lazarus dancing and barking beside him in the snow. I took a deep breath, and reached down and put my hands on the back of the sled and gave a tentative push. Nothing happened.

"Give it everything you've got," he shouted, and I pushed with all my might, and the sled shot forward, creaking on the snow, and I bounded after it, and half-leaped, half-fell on top of him as it shot off down the hill.

Somewhere halfway down, in the cold rush of the wind and the flying, stinging spume of snow, I became aware that I was laughing and crying at the same time. My ears were full of the *whushhh* of the sled's runners and Dennis's laughter and Lazarus's manic barking as he capered and floundered and slid after us. As soon as the tears left my lower lids, they froze on my cheeks and hot, new ones took their place. I did not care. I was not crying for grief, but for joy. This was what it was, then, to be airborne. This was what it was to be free.

The sled flew down the last sharp segment of the hill and shot out on to level ground and down to the edge of the pond, and hit the ruff of reeds where Charles and Di used to lurk, snow-mounded now, and turned over, toppling us both off into deep, soft snow. I fetched up, lying directly atop him, struggling for breath, hair in my eyes, laughing, laughing. His face was directly beneath mine, but I did not realize it until I felt his breath warm on it and realized that he was laughing, too. He reached around me and pushed the hair out of my eyes, and I lay looking down at him.

For what seemed a very long time we simply lay there. I could feel our hearts beating together through the heavy clothes, and feel his warm breath. His eyes were very close, and wide open, and dark. Unreadable eyes. His mouth was soft and slightly open, like a child's nearing sleep. I felt my laughter slow and die, and his did, too.

He pulled my head down to his, then, and kissed

me. It was a very long kiss, complex and searching, seeking hard, and seeming to find what it sought in my own mouth. I felt myself slacken into the kiss, going more deeply into it, more deeply into his arms. It felt strange, to be held by arms that were not Tee's, to be kissed by a mouth that did not taste of Tee's. But not that strange. Soon it no longer felt strange at all. The kiss went on and on.

In a little while I felt the hard, muffled surging of him against me, and laughed in pure delight.

"Hello," I whispered into his mouth. "What's this?"

He pulled his head away and looked up at me. His face in the moon and snow light was beautiful. He was grinning.

"Good God. I can't believe it," he said, beginning to laugh. "Do you think it's possible for a one-legged man to fuck in a snowbank?"

As it turned out, it was.

CHAPTER FOURTEEN

I STAYED AT DENNIS'S ALL THAT night and for much of
the next day. I slept and slept. It was the sort of sleep
you think you remember from childhood or adoles-
cence but really don't: silent, sweet, voluptuous, bottomless. It seemed a separate element to me: I would
dive and glide and turn and roll in it as a seal might, in
beneficent water; I would sink deep and soar up to the
very sunlit surface of it, stretch and dive down again. I
was conscious of no need at all to surface except sati-
ety. When I had had enough, far past noon the next
day, I woke up.

Sunlight was pouring into the bedroom, but it did
not fall where I was accustomed to seeing it, and for a
moment I simply lay, slack-limbed and rested in all my
parts, looking at the pale rays with dust motes dancing
in them, falling on a quilt and a rug and an armchair I
did not know. I started to smile out of sheer well-being,
and then I remembered where I was, and why, and sat
up with my breath huffing out of my throat.

"Oh, God," I whispered to myself, eyes squeezed
shut. "I made love to Dennis Ponder in a snowdrift
and spent the entire night in his bed. Oh, shit! What
does this mean? I don't know what this means!"

And then I looked at my watch and vaulted out of bed as if catapulted, tangling myself in the bedclothes and falling to my knees on the rug. I scrambled up again, searching for my clothes. It was nearly two-thirty in the afternoon, and nobody but Dennis knew where I was. My father would be frantic, the old ladies would be cold and hungry and possibly worse. I found my clothes, still damp from last night's snow, on the floor beyond the chair and skinned into them, grimacing slightly at the unaccustomed but not unpleasant soreness in parts of me where no soreness had been for a very long time. I glanced in Dennis's filmy old bureau mirror and saw a madwoman with tousled hair and a flushed face, raked my fingers through my hair, and ran into the living room barefoot, looking for my shoes.

Dennis Ponder had not been in the bedroom, but he was in the living room. He stood with his back to the room, looking out the window at the sun striking light off the snow, holding a cup of coffee. He wore a black turtleneck and chinos and a work boot, and he balanced on the back of the sofa as he stared out. Lazarus lay beside him, and he turned and thumped his tail at me when I came in the room, but Dennis did not turn. I stood stock-still, feeling my face beginning to flame, unable to think of a single thing to say to him. So far as morning-after etiquette went, I had had need of it only once, long ago, and in that instance I had married the partner. I had no casual postcoital talk.

I cleared my throat to speak, and he said, "If you want to forget it ever happened, we'll say no more about it. If, on the other hand, you enjoyed it as much as you said you did, let's go back in there and do it again. It's your call."

"I . . . oh, Lord, Dennis, I have to go! My father doesn't know where I am . . ."

"He knows. I called him last night after you'd gone to sleep," he said. He still did not turn his face to me.

"But Bella and Luz . . ."

"I went," he said.

"You what?"

"I didn't want to wake you, so I went over there and built up a fire and heated up some soup. Don't make a big deal out of it, Molly. You were half dead and it's past time I stopped letting you carry the whole load. The truck's got the oldest automatic transmission in the Commonwealth of Massachusetts, but it has one. The county's gotten to the road and somebody's plowed out the driveway. It was no problem."

"Dennis . . . my God . . ."

He turned then, and I could see that his eyes were rimmed with red and his nose was pink. There was no doubt that he had been crying. I felt shock and hope and dread collide in my chest.

"Can you tell me about it?"

"No. Not now. Maybe in a little while. The thing is there's nowhere you have to rush off to, so let's have some lunch and a glass of wine and see where things go. Last night was . . . more than I thought I was going to have again in my life."

I felt the flush on my cheeks flood down over my chest. I saw my shoes beside the door and went and got them and sat down on the sofa, busying myself with them. My whole body felt on fire. Every place he had touched me last night seemed limned with light and flame.

"I . . ." I began, and choked, and cleared my throat. "I enjoyed it, too," I said, stupidly and primly.

He laughed.

"Can you look at me? Okay, that's better. Now. Tell me what's on your mind. Did my magnificent hairless body turn you on? Did my one-legged state repulse you? Did the earth move? Should I have lit two cigarettes and handed you one? What?"

"I . . . you know, Dennis, I've never done that with anybody but my husband before. This wasn't anything like that, and thank God for it, but I don't quite know yet how to act. Did I like it? You must know I did. But I don't know, I just don't know . . . if I can jump right in bed and do it again. I mean . . . I hardly . . ."

"You hardly know me?"

He laughed again but there was not so much warmth in it this time.

I nodded. That really had been what I meant and even in my addled state I realized how utterly ridiculous a notion it was. I might never know Dennis Ponder any better than I did now.

"I guess I mean maybe we should talk about what sort of relationship we're going to have," I said miserably. I could not seem to make myself sound any way but absurd.

"What relationship?" he said. "What relationship could we have but the one we do?"

"I sort of thought we needed to let things develop, see what common interests we have, get to know one another in . . . other ways, too. We already have a lot in common . . ."

"Molly . . ."

He sighed, and came and sat down beside me on the sofa.

"Listen. We made love. We screwed, to put it another way. It doesn't mean we're engaged. It doesn't mean I won't respect you tomorrow. You don't want any other kind of relationship, I can promise you. What would be in it for you?"

"I don't just screw, Dennis."

"I know you don't. I didn't think of it as just screwing. It was . . . something else entirely for me. But I'm not exactly a prime candidate for a long-term relationship, to use a New Age term I loathe only slightly more than 'special.'"

"You mean you think you're dying?"

"I mean I don't know. But I know I'm not dying this afternoon, and all I'm proposing to you is a suitable occupation for the rest of this afternoon."

"Dennis, I just don't know if that's enough," I said softly.

"It's all I have," he said.

We sat looking at each other, seeing no quarter in each other's eyes. And then he said, "I won't hassle you about this. If you feel like it, you let me know. The offer stands."

I laughed in spite of myself.

"What do you want me to do, just tap on your shoulder in the middle of some afternoon and say, 'Please, sir, can I have some more?'"

"That, or 'Let's fuck,'" he said mildly, and I laughed again. The awkwardness went out of the air. I felt absurdly good, young and lighthearted and sensuous and admired. I could remember that feeling from the very earliest days of Tee's and my courtship, that delicate, flirtatious, breath-held time when all things seemed wonderful and possible but there was no hurry about anything. The sense of delectation was high. I wish I had had a lot more of that feeling before I had what came next. I wanted, suddenly, to tell it to

Teddy: Don't rush into anything, take that long, delicious, teasing time that's your due before you settle on someone. I wished I could have told it to Caroline, too. I wondered if Dennis Ponder had ever had it. Somehow, I did not think so. It presupposed too much self-delight, too much sheer playfulness. I thought Bella might well have murdered any capacity he had had for those things.

Bella . . .

"Dennis, your mother . . . how is she? Physically, I mean. It must have been an enormous shock for her, not to mention old Luz. Do I need to see about them? Or . . . do you want to go again? I don't intend to pry, but I have to know how to play this now."

"I don't think I'm going to be able to tell you much about my mother, Molly," he said. "I went, she was surprised, she cried, she carried on, she prayed, she got to coughing and gasping. I gave her a shot of Scotch and calmed her down and stayed until they'd eaten and were about to drop off to sleep, and then I came home. You probably ought to check on them in a little while, but I think they're fine. She's too old and sick to make much of a fuss, and Luz is too out of it. Luz didn't turn a hair, by the way; she just looked up and said, 'You may be tall, but I know you're Denny. Where's your other leg?' And I told her I left it in Seattle, and she just nodded. Luz is exactly the same as she was when I left, except wrinkled. But my mother . . . my God, she's grotesque, isn't she? And a real wreck physically. Well, I guess neither one of us is much of a prize. And that's it. That's all I know about it right now. If there's any more, maybe I'll tell you about it. Or maybe not."

"All right," I said faintly, and as it happened, that

was all I ever did learn about that first meeting of Dennis Ponder with the terrible, sad old woman who had thought she could only have one love.

But after that, he went frequently to the farmhouse on the Chilmark moor. He went a couple of times in the mornings so I could do other errands, but mainly he went in the evenings, because that was when Bella was strongest and most alert, and when Luz was most focused, and when his own carefully husbanded energy burned highest. Once or twice he went alone in the truck, but usually I drove him so I could have the use of it, and picked him up again when I was done with whatever I had to do. We did not specifically agree on it, but gradually he took over the late-afternoon reading.

"It's not that we don't like the way you read," Luz told me sweetly on one of the first days Dennis read, "but this is our Denny, and when he reads about kings it's nice because he's descended from one, just like we are. It's the same king, you know, King Dinis. It's like hearing about family."

And Bella nodded, her black eyes flaming with joy.

I did not look at Dennis when she said that. From the very beginning, we all pretended that there was nothing in the least unusual about the fact that Dennis Ponder, son of this house and this huge old woman, sat reading to her in the dusk of a place from which he had been banished more than forty years before. I don't think to Luzia there was anything extraordinary about it; in the tapestry of her shadowy mind it was little Denny, to whom she had read only a heartbeat ago, who sat with her in the lamplight now. But it must have been an unimaginable effort for Bella to conceal her radiant pride. Yet she merely sat quietly, looking interested and appreciative, like a lady to whom a well-bred youngster is tendering a special, small social favor. I don't know how she managed it. Her florid mind must have been roiling with the sort of baroque maternal passion she had not been able to indulge for many decades. I wondered if Dennis had laid down any ground rules about how they would all behave, and decided not. Whatever there was in his heart for his mother and Luzia Ferreira now, I knew it could not be simple love, not in any ordinary filial sense of the word. Perhaps the pretense that all was as usual was necessary for him to go into that house at all. Perhaps Bella's facade of mere pleasantry was in the nature of a child's pretending not to see a wild little animal so as not to frighten it away. It was an infinitely delicate and careful balancing act that the three of them conceived. I would not have asked about it for words. Bella never told me how she felt, and Dennis did not until much later.

On the first evening that I dropped him off to read to the old women, I said, "The books they like to hear are on the table by Luz's bed. We're in the middle of *Penrod and Sam*, but Luz is going to beg for *The Once and Future King*. It's Bella's turn to choose. Don't let them start fighting about it; it makes Bella sick, and it takes forever to calm Luz down."

"I brought my own book," he said. "They'll get it or nothing."

"What? The Marquis de Sade?" I teased.

"*Mother Courage*," he said dryly. But he did not show me the book.

When I came back, in the clear green light that you get on the twilight moors of Chilmark every now and then in the earliest spring, the house was quiet, and I let myself into the living room softly so as not to disturb the old women if they had fallen asleep. But they had not; they sat in their familiar little tableau, Bella sprawled back in the big recliner that by now bore the indelible shape of her great buttocks, Luz snuggled into her tattered linens. Dennis sat opposite them in a spavined old morris chair, his leg outstretched on a hassock. The fire whispered, and Palestrina trickled from Dennis's cassette recorder. A single old milk-glass lamp shone down on the book he was reading from, and in its light I saw that Luz wore a smile more of the air than the earth, and the nacreous tracks of tears traced Bella's blank moon of a face.

"'I went to the woods because I wished to live deliberately,'" Dennis read in his deep voice. Or perhaps he was reciting; I could not see his face in the shadows. "'. . . to front only the essential facts of life, and see if I could not learn what it had to teach, and not, when I came to die, discover that I had not lived.'"

He let his voice trail off, and sat for a moment with the book in his hands.

"That's enough for now," he said. "A little Thoreau goes a long way."

The old women did not beg for more, but sat quietly, turned inside themselves. I turned away and moved softly into the kitchen so that none of them would see that I, too, like Bella, was crying.

On the way home we were silent, and finally I said, "My father was reading that, too. He quoted just that passage to me not long ago. I wish . . . I wish he would go with you sometime when you go up there to read. He used to do it all the time. They loved hearing him. Oh, I wish . . . I wish." I fell silent. There was no use talking about it.

"Do you know the rest of the quotation?" Dennis said after a moment. "'I did not wish to live what was not life, nor did I wish to practice resignation unless it was quite necessary.' Maybe for Tim it's quite necessary right now. I know from experience that you have to get down to the resignation, to get done with everything that isn't life, before you can begin to see what is. I think that's where he is right now. You can't go there with him. Nobody can. He's the one who decides when to go on from there."

"*If* he decides to go on from there."

I had hoped that Dennis would rush to allay my worst fear, but he did not.

"If he does," he agreed.

We did not speak again until he got out of the truck at his camp, and held the door open so that Lazarus could come bounding into it. I did not go in with him; I had not done so since that first day. He was as good as his word. He had not pressed me to stay, or for anything else. Often, like that evening, I wished he would. I needed his warmth and his touch, but I could not bring myself to ask. In my mind I could hear my mother on a long-ago Saturday when I had been thirteen and called my friend Dickie Hembree up the street to come over and go to the movies with me: "You never, *never* ask a young man to take you anywhere, Molly. It's cheap. It sounds desperate. It sounds like you can't get a date any other way. With your height and those big breasts, you're always going to have to be careful not to look desperate. A real beauty can get away with it, maybe, but the rest of us ordinary girls have to be very, very careful not to look desperate."

And she had given me her brilliant, quicksilver smile to show that she included herself in the pantheon of ordinary girls. But I had long known that she lived in that other world, and felt even larger and more graceless than usual. I called Dickie back and said never mind, and never asked a boy or a man for attention again. I could no more have asked Dennis Ponder to make love to me than I could have asked him to grow a new leg, no matter how badly I wanted to. Somehow, I realized that night, I had expected him to know that. I was obscurely angry with him because he apparently did not. I was irritated with his homilies about my folks, too. I wanted him to feel my fear, not quote Thoreau at it.

The day after that, everything changed.

In an odd way, my father was better. He was sleeping well, he said, and suddenly felt like an outing for the first time in months. After that, he was out and about once more, as he had been before the awful deadness sucked him down. On the first day or two he took the truck when I wasn't using it, but a day came when both old ladies had doctors' appointments and I had to drive them into Oak Bluffs, and the truck was not available to him for a full day; that evening he came home from Menemsha with a disreputable old blue Toyota that he had bought from a sign posted in Poole's Fish Market.

"You need the truck, and I thought I might do some exploring down island, go check on some of the old farts at Alley's and the senior center," he said. "See how they wintered over."

I simply stared at him. It was an enormous change

from the terribly diminished man he had been, of course, but somehow he seemed even stranger to me now: abstracted, oddly exalted, with a kind of luminosity about his face that had never been there before. He seemed to be constantly listening to something just out of my hearing range, and often he smiled at it.

"It's a fine car," I said heartily when he brought it home. "And you'll never know how glad I am to see you feeling better. Why don't you take it up and show it to Bella and Luz? They've been asking about you. And take Dennis with you, why don't you? Do you remember that I told you he was seeing his mother again? You go and tell me what you think about that; I can't tell what's going on with them, and he sure isn't talking about it. He misses you, too . . ."

"I'll look in on them in a day or two," he said. "And Dennis needs to get on with his work. Later on I'll spend some time with him. Yes, I recall that you did tell me about him getting back together with Bella. That's fine, isn't it? You tell him I'm happy for him."

And he would kiss me on the cheek and go out to his old car and lurch away down the lane, hideously rutted now from the deep freezes and melting snows of the hard-dying winter, and I would not see him again until after dinner.

"What did you do today?" I would ask, heating up the food I had saved for him.

"Oh, sat in on a game of pool at the center," he would say. "Took three dollars off of Martin Golightly. Went over to the big hardware store in Vineyard Haven and looked at some roof tiles. We're going to have to do something about this roof when the weather warms up a little. Cost about twice what they do back home; maybe I'll do a little comparison shopping. No thanks, baby, I had something to eat at Back Alley's. You wrap that up in foil and I'll have it tomorrow."

And he would climb the stairs to his bedroom and prepare for bed. Oh, perhaps he would sit for a half hour or so and watch some television with me, but never more than that, and though he smiled and replied to my chatter with his old banter, I could tell that he was tired and wanted only to go to bed. And because he had so very much sleep to make up for, I did not object when, in a very short time, he kissed me on the cheek and climbed the narrow stairs. I should have been reassured with the change, and on one level I was, but underneath the relief something did not seem right, and I pushed the strangeness as deep as I could simply because I did not think I could stand any more worry.

One noon I ducked into Alley's to pick up a jar of mayonnaise and turned when I heard someone say, "Molly? Molly Redwine?"

It was Martin Golightly, the man to whom my father was closest up island, the one whose snooker expertise was legendary at the senior center and around the stove at Alley's.

"Well, hello," I said, smiling at him. "I hear my father finally beat you. He must have drugged your root beer."

He looked at me oddly.

"How is Tim?" he said. "We've missed him. We all thought you must have been so wintered in down there on the pond that you couldn't get out, but it's not like him to let a little weather keep him away from the snooker table. Is he okay? You tell him there are at least three guys waiting to whip his tail."

My face felt stiff.

"I'll tell him," I said. "The roads have been pretty bad down our way, but they're softening up now. He'll probably see you in a day or two."

"Glad to hear it," Martin Golightly said, and turned back to the stove and his coffee. I went home and waited for my father. When he came in, long after dinnertime, I called him on it. My heart was beating violently. I was terrified without quite knowing why.

He sighed and sat down beside me on the sofa.

"She comes every night now, Molly," he said, his face translucent with the strange joy that had played over it for the past week or so. I stared at him. When had he gotten so thin? He looked as if he were being consumed by something inside him as fiery as a nebula.

"Oh, Daddy," I said, my voice trembling.

"Every night. At first I thought it was just a fluke, but she comes closer and closer every night. I knew it was just a matter of being able to sleep at night. And now that I can . . . now that I can . . . Molly, she looks beautiful. And she's happy. I can tell that. She stays longer and longer; it's like she's playing, teasing me like she used to do when I first met her. I know I shouldn't have lied to you, but I was afraid that it wouldn't last, and it would have been worse if she didn't come back and I'd told you about it . . ."

"But where do you go if you don't go to Alley's or the center? What do you do all that time?" I said, my voice quivering.

"I drive around. I walk. I walk for miles. I've been places I never knew were on the island; this afternoon I spent hours and hours on Lucy Vincent, and yesterday I went up on the Gay Head cliffs. It's all so beautiful. It's

like I'm seeing it through her eyes, showing her the
Vineyard for the first time . . ."

"Daddy . . ."

"Don't start on me about this, Molly," he said
fiercely. "I have her back. I never thought I would. I
love you like the light in my heart, but I'm not going to
let you meddle with this."

And he turned and went upstairs. I sat looking
after him, drowning in his strangeness.

After that I left him alone, and he slept through his
nights in the company of my mother and wandered
alone in the soft gray days, and a morning came when
it was finally spring.

It was a time of glittering white frosts in the morning, and clear, pale, earlier dawns, and the silvery clat-
ter of the cardinals and redwings in the scrub forests.
The lyrical pinkletinks called and called, in the brushy
swamps. There was no green yet on the tracery of the
wet black branches, but you could feel it was down
there, deep, pushing slowly upward like blood toward
a beating heart.

On one of those first soft evenings, Tee called.

I was alone. My father was out on God knows
what wild hill, and Dennis and Lazarus had gone
down to the pond, Dennis to throw sticks and Laz to
retrieve them. I had seen little of Dennis since I had
learned where my father went in the daytime and how
he spent his nights; somehow I simply could not tell
Dennis about that. To voice it would have made it too
real. Like my father earlier, I found myself increasingly consumed by a need to sleep, and now that I had
more free time on my hands, that is what I did. I slept
in the afternoon while my father roamed and Dennis
worked or went up in the truck to read to the old

women, and I slept longer in the mornings. Whenever I think of the coming of that spring, I think of it through a haze of sleep as tender as the first flush of pale green on the lilac bushes up island.

I was dozing when Tee's call came, and for a moment I could not think how to respond to the voice on the telephone that was at once strange and as familiar as my own heartbeat. It seemed to come out of a time and place as far away as my childhood. For weeks now I had heard no voice from Atlanta. Missy and Livvy both had finally told me, in annoyance, to call when I had some idea of what I was going to do; they were tired of calling and getting the same hedging answers from me.

"How you doing?" Tee said, his voice warm with his old, intimate interest, and I said, stupidly, politely, "I'm just fine. How are you?"

"Well . . . you know," Tee said. "Not so fine. Stewing in my own juice, having fucked up yet again."

He laughed, the deep, lazy laugh that had been the first thing I had loved about him. Suddenly I had a flash: Tee at twenty-four, sitting in the sun on the beach at Sea Island, his hair bleached gilt, laughing at me and lighting the world up with it. It had been the first time after our marriage that we'd gone there. In the background Charlie and Carrie Davies laughed about something.

I blinked, and the vision went away.

"What have you fucked up, Tee?" I said. For a preposterous moment I could not think what he might mean. It was an expression he used a lot, capable both of charming and disarming.

"What haven't I?" he said. "Listen, I just wanted to see how you were doing. Nobody has heard from you. I got your number from Missy, who, incidentally, is about as pissed at me as it is possible for one human to be at another, closely followed by my mother. I've been thinking about you. I missed the family at Christmas."

I said nothing, thinking that he had been with Teddy then and wondering if he didn't count his son as family.

"So when do you think you might come home?" my husband asked.

"Why on earth do you care?" I said, almost amused at him. "Is this about the house? You-all can have the house. I told Missy to tell you that. Did she not?"

"Yeah, she told me. Moll . . . there's not any more us-all, I don't think."

He waited for an answer, and when I did not, he said, "She isn't here anymore. Sheri. I'm not seeing her anymore. She's transferred to marketing in New York and asked for Europe and will probably get it. It's with my total blessing. I'm the one who, I guess, broke it off."

"Hmmm," I said. "And just what is it she'll be marketing in New York and Europe?"

There was a silence, and then he said, "I deserve that, of course," but I could tell that he did not think he did.

"What I mean is, I'm not going to marry her," Tee said. "It . . . turned out to be just what my mother called it, a bad itch in the pants. You probably called it worse than that, and I don't blame you. I think that I was just plain and simply afraid of getting old, and she came along just at the time I was most vulnerable."

"Poor baby," I said.

"Okay, okay. There's a lot more you need to say to me, and that I need to hear. I don't blame you for that, either. I called to see if we could start to talk now. I'd hoped you'd come on home now that the house is empty again . . . that was a stupid damned thing, I know . . . but I could come up there one weekend. I've already checked about planes and ferries. We could talk face-to-face . . ."

"No, we couldn't," I said, my ears ringing with what really was, now, suppressed laughter, and put the telephone down.

It rang again and again and finally stopped. By that time my laughter had exploded and waned and stopped, and I sat in the dusk feeling that all the sleep in the world would not be enough, and knowing that I would never drop off. I got up and went into my bathroom and opened the medicine cabinet to take one of the sleeping pills that Charlie Davies had given me. This was one night I did not intend to toss and turn like a hagridden mare.

The pills were not there. I knew suddenly where they were. I ran up the steps to my father's bathroom so fast that I stumbled twice and almost went headfirst down into the living room. The vial of pills was there, but it was empty except for two. There was another bottle, full, beside it, with my father's name and the name on the label of a doctor I did not know in Oak Bluffs. I knew now where my father's sleep came from, knew on what wings my mother came to him in the nights when he went down deep.

I was at Dennis's camp pounding on his door before I even realized what I was doing.

I spilled it all out, with him sitting on the sofa before the fire watching me but not moving to touch me as I jabbered frantically in my fear and anger, or when the tears of despair started down my face.

Finally, when I stopped simply because I was too drained to talk or weep any more, he said, "Leave him alone, Molly."

"Dennis! Leave him alone? What if he . . . you know . . ."

"Leave him alone. It's his business. If pain gets too bad, there ought to be an out. Everybody deserves that much. Even an animal deserves that much."

Rage flared deep in my chest where the awful fear had been.

"Oh, good, Dennis. Very good," I cried. "That's just what he said about you when I told him about the pills you had, and what you said about them. He said for me to let you alone, that I didn't know enough about pain yet to know what I was talking about. Well, fuck him and you both, because I do. I know as much about pain as either of you ever will, and I'm god-damned sick of both of you, with your contingencies and your neat little plans for getting out when your famous pain gets too bad. What about the ones of us you leave behind? What are we supposed to do for our pain?"

"Who do *I* leave?" Dennis said coldly.

"Oh, God, I am so *sick* of hearing that! Your daughter! Your family! Don't you know what that *means*?"

He got up and limped to the window and pulled the curtain aside and looked out into the night. The window was raised just a little, and I caught the smell of fresh, wet earth and soft, sweet salt from the Bight, smells to break the heart. Eliot had said it: "April is the cruelest month . . ."

"How many times do I have to tell you what I am?" he said in a lifeless voice. "I'm stone-broke. I'm probably flat out of time. I have one leg and a dick that works part-time and seventy-five pages nobody wants to read by a man scared pissless of women, who only knows the little boys he's paid to know. Some book. Some expert. Some legacy for my so-called family."

"You have your mother," I said. He turned and looked at me, but said nothing. His eyes were as dead as his voice.

"I knew about it, Dennis," I said. "I saw them one night. I saw what I guess you saw. I know that I can't even imagine how awful it was for you for a long, long time, but you have her back now . . ."

"For how long, assuming that I did have her back or even wanted her? She's probably going to kick off before I do."

I was very angry, but under it there was pain as fresh and red as new blood.

"You have me, goddamn you."

"They hired you," he said.

For a while I simply said nothing, and then I said, my voice shaking, "You are behaving just horribly. Just horribly. What is the matter with you?"

"I have the exquisite, unassailable excuse of probably being about to die," he said. "The question is, what is the matter with you?"

"My husband called me tonight," I said, beginning to sob. "He isn't getting married after all. I don't know how I ought to think about it . . ."

He laughed and walked away toward the kitchen, hopping on his one good foot, balancing on furniture.

"Congratulations," he flung at me over his shoulder. "But I really must refer you to Ann Landers. She is, I think, more your style."

I blundered out of the camp, treacherous tears beginning. When I got home, my father was already upstairs asleep. In the light from the slightly opened door I could see that he had a small, secret smile on his face.

I was still crying, softly and hopelessly, when I got into bed, but the two Halcions I had taken kicked in quickly, and I was asleep in my cave under the stairs even before Laz got up off the hearth rug and came wagging and padding to bed.

When the telephone rang, deep in the night, I woke swiftly and cleanly and reached for it, so sure that it was Dennis apologizing for his behavior that I was already framing my reply: "I quite understand. Let's say no more about it."

Restrained, noncommittal, dignified. Altogether better than he deserved.

But instead of Dennis's contrite voice, I heard a breathy, small gulp, as if a child were sucking in air, and then a soft, bubbling, frantic spill of sound that I listened to in consternation for about half a minute before I realized it was Luz, and that she was speaking Portuguese.

"Luz! It's Molly. English. Speak English, please," I said, and she stopped and drew a long, sobbing breath, and said, all at once, "Bella is making funny noises. Like a duck, quack, quack! Molly, come! I don't like this! She won't get up!"

I bolted upright, already reaching for my blue jeans.

"Listen, Luz. Call 911. Can you do that? Hang up the phone and then dial 911, and when somebody answers, tell them you need help at the Ponder farm off Middle Road. They'll come right away. I'm right behind. Do you understand? Hang up and dial 911."

"She looks funny," Luz whimpered, and put the telephone down. I could hear her rustling around in her bedcovers, making small, mumbling sounds, but she did not pick up the phone again and she did not hang up.

I called 911 myself and ran out of the house and across the glade to Dennis's. A light in the living room still burned, and when I hit the porch, running hard, he was at the door, looking out. He still wore the clothes he had had on, and he was pale and red-eyed.

"Come on," I said before he could speak. "It's your mother. Luz called and I can't be sure what's wrong, but something is. I've called 911."

"Shit," he said softly. And we did not speak again until I had helped him into the truck and was jerking it around to make the hard left into the lane. Then he said, "I've been expecting this for a while. I guess you have, too."

"For some reason I really haven't," I said. "I don't know why. I've always known she was very ill. But it could be nothing; you can't depend on Luz, and I've had some false alarms with Bella before. Let's don't jump to conclusions."

"Good old Molly," he said between clenched teeth. "Ever the voice of reason. By all means, let us not jump to conclusions."

I whipped my head around at him.

"Don't you dare start on me again, Dennis," I said. "I don't know what's wrong with you tonight, and

right now I don't care. Just don't you speak to me
again that way."

He was quiet for so long that I looked over at
him. He sat with his head down, his hair falling partly
over his eyes, and his hands on the dashboard were
clenched and white-knuckled.

"You're hurting, aren't you?" I said, my chest contracting with fear. Were any of us going to be spared
on this horrible night?

"Not so much. A little. It's not the bad stuff, I don't
think. I banged my stump the night we went sledding,
and it's gotten sort of inflamed. I was going to call the
doctor in the morning and see if he could give me a
shot, or something."

"Why didn't you tell me? I could have put something on it for you. I've got stuff at my house . . ."

"I really don't think our relationship has pro-
gressed to the point that I'd feel comfortable showing
you my stump," he said prissily, and I blinked incredulously before I realized that he was teasing me.
Before I could even smile, he said, "I'm sorry, Molly.
I've been a prick tonight. I guess . . . I really didn't want
to hear that about your dad or your husband. My
mother, either. The world is just shit-full of things I
don't want to deal with tonight, but there's no reason
for me to take it out on you. I'd start this day over if I
could."

"I don't mind," I said. "It's okay. It really is."

So much for dignity and restraint. If I had not been
so frightened for Bella, I might have grinned like a
Cheshire cat at Dennis Ponder. But I was frightened,
and so was he. I could feel his fear in the soft darkness,
smell it, like acrid smoke.

There were no lights in the farmhouse but the

struggling fire, but it was enough to see that Luz was crouched on the floor beside the overturned recliner with Bella Ponder's big head in her lap. Forever after I wondered how Luz had gotten herself out of bed and across the floor. She herself did not remember. In the fire-flicker her little yellow face was as serene as that of a seraph high on a cathedral, eyes closed, and she rocked Bella's head back and forth and sang to her a little Portuguese song in a minor key that sounded like a child's song, a nursery air. I ran to them and knelt down, leaving Dennis to make his way into the house with his crutch. I wanted to be the first to see Bella Ponder. If it was too bad, perhaps I could make her look a bit better before her son saw her.

It was bad, I could see that at once. Bella lay on her back where she had fallen from the recliner, her great arms crossed and her fists pressing into her chest, her face absolutely colorless, the white of dead narcissus. Huge, pearled drops of sweat stood on her forehead and at her hairline. Her eyes were closed. Her lips were slate blue, working silently.

"*Ajudar-me,*" she whispered. "*Ajudar-me. Papa, ajudar-me . . .*"

"Bella," I said, and she opened her eyes. They were flat and black and focused on something beyond me. The pupils were pinpoints.

"Mama?" she said, and I knew she had gone into a far country where I could not follow.

"It's Molly," I said, dabbing at the sweat on her forehead with the tail of my shirt. Luz smiled and rocked, smiled and rocked, sang and sang.

Behind me I heard Dennis's voice slip into the little nursery song along with Luz. I was surprised somehow that he knew Portuguese, but it stood to reason.

He had heard it for the first seventeen years of his life.

Dennis came then, flopping awkwardly down on the floor beside his mother.

"Bella," he said tentatively, and then, "Mother. Mama. Can you hear me?"

Bella's eyes came back from the far country and saw him. They widened, and a small smile curved the terrible blue lips up. *"Papa,"* she whispered. *"Magoar. Papa . . ."*

"It's Dennis, Mama," he said. His voice was hardly stronger than hers.

"Dennis! Ah, Dennis, obrigado . . ."

I closed my eyes briefly. I did not know if she thought she was addressing king or son. I did know that she would not stay long in the farmhouse, one way or another.

Dennis Ponder looked at me, wildness in his gray eyes.

"An ambulance . . ."

"I called from home. Let me get a blanket. We shouldn't move her . . ."

The tri-town ambulance came howling into the yard then, and I ran to the door to let the crew in, switching on lights as I went. Just before I jerked the front door open, I heard Dennis, whispering, "Don't you dare die on me. Don't you fucking dare leave me again, old woman . . ."

He went with them in the ambulance to the hospital in Oak Bluffs. I stayed behind with Luzia, wondering what to do next, wondering what on earth, now, my role was in the farmhouse and on the pond, what the right thing to do was. It seemed to me that there would certainly be an immutable up island ritual for this, but I did not know it.

One of the young EMTs, a square, sandy-haired youngster who looked vaguely familiar, had helped me get Luz back in bed. He did it tenderly and respectfully, saying, "Let's get you back where you belong, Miss Luzia," and I thought that he must somehow know Luz, but could not think how that could be. Bella had not let medical help come into this house for years. Luz, mumbling and vague, let us tuck her in, and lay there smiling expectantly, as if waiting for a treat.

"Thank you," I said to the boy. "I don't quite know what to do next . . ."

"Somebody's coming," he said. "Just hang on. We'll take care of them."

And he was out the door and into his vehicle before I could ask who. When it had screamed away toward Middle Road, I drew my chair up to Luz's bed and took her hands.

"You mustn't worry. Dennis is going to take good care of her, and we aren't going to leave you alone."

"I know," she said sleepily. "She told me. Would you read to me, please? I haven't heard *The Once and Future King* in ages and ages." And I picked up the flaccid book, which fell open to a point near the middle, and began to read as the sky over the sea to the east began to lighten infinitesimally: "'A white-front said, "Now, Wart, if you were once able to fly the great North Sea, surely you can co-ordinate a few little wing-muscles here and there? Fold your powers together, with the spirit of your mind, and it will come out like butter. Come along, Homo sapiens, for all we humble friends of yours are waiting here to cheer."'"

I had not gotten far before there was a quiet knock at the door and Patricia Norton let herself into the room.

"I'm so glad to see you," I said simply, not wondering, at that moment, how she had known to come.

"My oldest son is one of the EMTs who took the call," she said, laying her coat on a chair and coming over to sit down beside me. "He called me just after they got your call. I've been sort of waiting for this; Jeremy knew to call if he was on duty if and when it happened. Do you know anything yet? Does Dennis know?"

"I don't know what it is; Luz called, and when we got here Bella was almost unconscious, but I'm nearly sure it's a heart attack. Dennis went with her to the hospital. I stayed with Luz, of course . . ."

"Well, I've come to sit with her if you want to go on to the hospital. I expect you do. You've been the closest thing to family Bella has had for a while, and Dennis won't know anybody over there. He'll need some backup. How is he doing about it, by the way?"

"It's hard to say. You probably know they've been sort of reunited for a little while, but it's hard for me to tell how he feels about her. It's been wonderful for her, of course. I know that he was . . . singing to her in Portuguese just before the ambulance came . . ."

Patricia's gray Ponder eyes filled with tears and she smiled. "Then she'll be okay whatever happens. But he may not be. You go over there, now. I've called some of the others and there'll be somebody along to spell me directly. Come on back here when you can; we'll be here. If there are . . . plans to make, we can help you do that. We'd go on over to the hospital, but none of us knows if Dennis would want us or not. I'll let you be the judge of that. But we'll be here."

"I don't know why," I said, my own eyes at last

beginning to fill with tears. "She's frozen you out her entire adult life. And Dennis has simply . . . written you off."

"I remember him so well," she said softly. "He was my best friend for a year or two; I never had another quite like him. He was all laughter and mischief, the best of the Ponders, before his grandmother's cold spite could kick in. We all remember him, and some of us remember Bella, too, when she first came to the Vineyard. I barely remember, but I know I never saw anybody so beautiful, or so vivid and full of life. It was a Ponder who brought her here and a Ponder who made her what she is. Seems to me Ponders ought to hop to now and see if we can help fix things for Denny. There aren't enough of us left that we can afford to lose one."

I pressed her hand with mine; it was warm and rough and felt somehow like my father's, though she could not have been much older than I.

"I'll let you know the minute I know anything," I said, and went out into the just-born morning. Behind me, I heard Patricia Norton begin to read, taking up where I'd left off: "'The Wart walked up to the great sword for the third time. He put out his right hand softly and drew it out as gently as from a scabbard . . .'"

Isabel Miara Ponder died in the hospital at Oak Bluffs at 6:14 that morning. She was dead when I got there. When I came hurrying down the corridor, Dennis Ponder was sitting in the dim, scruffy waiting area off the elevator lobby, his hands folded in his lap, looking down at his lone foot in a boot to which the rich black mud of spring still clung. When he heard my footsteps, he looked up, and I saw in his face, white and still and oddly formal, that she had gone. But still I formed the words with my lips, though no sound came: "How is she?"

"Gone," he said in a neutral voice. "About fifteen minutes ago. The doctor's in there now doing . . . whatever you do. Then I have to do . . . whatever you do. Thing is, I don't know what you do. Do you? I guess you do; you just went through this with your mother, didn't you?"

I nodded slowly. I felt numb and so tired that I did not think I could stand up any longer. I sat down on the cracked Naugahyde sofa beside him.

"Bad year for mothers," he said.

"Dennis, I'm so very sorry."

He reached over to my hand and patted it absently. I don't think that he knew he held it.

"I know you are, Molly. She was a lucky old woman, to have you to be sorry for her. She just as well could have had nobody."

"She had you. You'd have been here whether or not I was."

"No," he said slowly. "I really don't think I would have. Listen, are you hungry? I'm starving. Do you think there's somewhere around here to get a bagel or something? I guess it's okay to leave. She's sure not going anywhere."

"Let's go back to the farmhouse," I said. "There's somebody waiting for us there you're going to remember, and she'll make us some breakfast. Just tell the nurse at the desk. Bella . . . your mother . . . I think she's supposed to stay here until the, you know, funeral home people come and get her. The nurse will know that."

"I don't know any funeral home people, not here

and not anywhere," Dennis said, hopping beside me down the hall. His crutch made a rubbery, squelching noise on the dirty white tiles.

"Your people know. They'll take care of it. They already know about your mother."

"I'll bet they do," he said. "Ding dong, the witch is dead."

"They're not like you think, Dennis," I said. "They never were. They're nothing like your mother taught you they were. If you don't know anything else about this island, you need to know that."

He was silent until we got into the truck and headed out of Oak Bluffs. I cut through the fabled camp meeting grounds, silent like a Victorian Brigadoon in the still, chilly morning, and drove along the beach road through Hart Haven into Edgartown and onto the Edgartown–West Tisbury Road, heading up island. The morning sea was like a silver-pink mirror except for an early ferry wallowing west toward Woods Hole. The main street of Vineyard Haven was just coming to life. Over everything the sharp, cold air of early spring breathed quietly.

"Do you know what she told me in the ambulance?" Dennis said.

"What?"

"She told me that after that time—that I saw them together, you know about that—that after that, I was over at the Peaks' sheep farm playing with the little Peaks like I did sometimes, and we were playing around the corral with some of the grown-ups watching us, and Mr. Peak's old ram mounted one of the ewes, and I laughed and pointed and yelled, 'My mama and Aunt Luz do that!' And old Mrs. Peak asked me, 'What do you mean, Dennis?' and I told everybody what I had seen them doing. Mrs. Peak must have gone straight to my grandmother, because Mother said that that night Grandmother came to the house on Music Street and told her that she knew about her and Luz, and that she was going to take me away from her and raise me herself, as a proper Ponder, and see that Mama never set eyes on me again. Mama said Grandmother threatened to run her and Luzia right off the Vineyard. I was sent off island less than a week later."

He fell silent, and I simply drove, numbed and stupid with pain. Then he said, "She said she sent me because she knew they'd take me away, that they could do that, and so that at least, if I was with her family, I'd stay part of her. But it was the wrong thing to do if that's what she wanted, Molly, because if I'd stayed on the Vineyard, at least I'd have seen her now and then. I'd have *had* to at least run into her . . ."

"She did the only thing she knew to do to keep you," I said around the aching lump in my throat. "Maybe it was wrong, but she didn't know any other way. You have to remember that in spite of being a married woman, she was still very much a girl, and a pretty simple one at that."

"She could have sent Luz away and kept me with her."

"No. She'd have lost you to her mother-in-law anyway, and then she'd have been totally alone. And if she'd gone back to her people, what sort of life could she have had? Having to pretend Luz was nothing to her but a nice, accommodating cousin . . . and you'd have grown up and gone out into the world anyway, and there she would have been, growing old without you *or* Luz, with only those fanatic old Catholic royalists around her. By then she'd gone too far beyond that, don't you see? You can't ever go back to what you were before you've loved somebody . . ."

"That time at the sheep farm," he said, as if he had not heard me. "That was when I buried Luz's underwear in the sheep manure and the ram dug it up. You remember, I told you about that New Year's Eve? I don't mind so much that they told her what I said about seeing her and Luz, but I hope before God they didn't tell her that I made a joke of it . . ."

"I hope so, too," I whispered. It was all I could think to say.

Back at the farmhouse, Patricia Norton met us at the door, looked at our faces, and held her arms out. After a long moment, it was Dennis who walked into them, not I. They looked at each other, he and Pat, out of the same rain-gray eyes, and after we had eaten Pat's pancakes and drunk her coffee and looked in on Luzia, who slept peacefully in a clean gown under clean sheets by a newly built fire, he reached out and tweaked the back of Pat's sandy hair, where it straggled over her collar.

"It used to hang down almost to your waist," he said. "You wore it in two pigtails."

"And you dipped the ends of them into the inkwells at school," she said. "My mother had to cut five inches off it. She was furious, but I was delighted. I hated those damned braids."

"It's been a long time, Pat," he said. "I wonder if it's just plain been too long."

"No," she said. "Not to us. We've all wondered if we'd ever get to know you. Whether or not we do now, we'll at least get a look at you. The eyes are all

Ponder, of course, but the rest of you is her. It'll be nice to have that of her still."

"I'm not real sure what happens next," he said.

She laughed. "That's one thing we Ponders do know, how to bury other Ponders. Unless you want to take her back to America and bury her where her people are, we'll take it from here. With your approval, of course. There's a whole tribe of us in the Chilmark cemetery. We outnumber John Belushi about three hundred to one, but of course he gets all the press."

He smiled then.

"I've missed you, Pat. I wonder why I didn't know that," he said.

"About Luz . . ." I began.

"My sister Hannah is coming in to sit with her in a little while," Pat Norton said. "And some of the others will spell her. Luz seems okay, considering. I don't think she comprehends, do you?"

"I don't know. It doesn't seem that way so far," I said. "Thanks, Pat. When I've looked in on my father and cleaned up, I'll be back to take over."

"Molly," she said, putting an arm around my shoulders, "let us do it. God knows we did little enough for them while Bella was alive. Maybe they wouldn't have let us, anyway, but we could have tried harder. This is ours to do now."

Then what is mine to do? I thought desolately, but did not say it aloud. It seemed an almost unimaginably selfish thought.

On the way back to the pond, Dennis laid his head against the back of the seat and, despite the truck's drunken lurching, slept. Or I thought that he did. But just as we reached the cutoff down to the Ponder camps, he said, eyes still closed, "They weren't what she told me. I don't think they ever were. Just my grandmother, and I guess my father. In the long run they could have accepted her and Luz; maybe they knew anyway. They've accepted more than that in all the hundreds of years they've been in this place. She could have had some kind of life here. I could have . . ."

"You still can," I said softly, but he did not answer.

Though it was nearly nine-thirty when I got home, there was no sound from my father's room upstairs. Lazarus lay quietly on the rug in front of the dead fire, waiting for me. He thumped his tail and rose to meet me, and went with me up the stairs to wake my father and tell him about Bella Ponder. But the curtains were still drawn, and he was still asleep. I shook him gently.

"Let me sleep," he murmured, not opening his eyes. "She's here. Let me sleep."

I went back downstairs and shucked off my clothes and slept, too.

They buried her in the old cemetery on a day so warm and still and tender that you could almost feel the leaves pushing out of their woody prisons, the first flowers stirring and fretting to be born. The sky over the Sound was a fresh-washed blue, and small, puffed, silver-limned clouds sailed slowly in from the south. From all the moist places up island the pinkletinks chimed. Every now and then the querulous honk of a returning goose broke the late-morning silence, and up at the edge of the cemetery one of the small roving herds of guineas darted and gabbled and dipped their ridiculous pinheads into the grass.

There were perhaps twenty assorted Ponders, plus their spouses and progeny, on hand, standing quietly around the newly-dug grave as the young minister from the Congregational church in Chilmark read the simple old service for the burial of the dead. I stood alone at the back of the small crowd; Dennis stood in the middle, obviously uncomfortable in a dark, rumpled suit that hung on him like a scarecrow's. I had helped him pin the left trouser leg up that morning, so that it did not flap. There were no hymns sung, and no one said the elegiac words over the dead that I had dreaded. It would have seemed a sacrilege. No one seemed to expect Dennis to say anything, either, and he did not. When the short service was over and the concluding prayer done, the Ponders who remained up island shook his hand gravely, and some of them patted him awkwardly on the back, and Pat Norton, who stood beside him, said, "We didn't think a get-together back at the farmhouse would be a good idea, with Luz there and all, but all of us will call you in a day or two. You'll have more dinner invitations than you ever had in your life. And there are people lined up to sit with Luz in eight-hour shifts for two or three days, until you can decide what should be . . . you know, done about her. I guess you don't know any more than we do about any family she might have left in America. If you want to see about nursing homes on the island, or some other kind of facility, I think we can help you there. There are one or two state-supported places. You just let us know. I'd bet that there's enough cash in Bella's account to see you through the first few weeks and get Luz settled somewhere. Molly, you know where she banks, don't you? Banked, I mean? They'll know. Nobody will hassle you about getting into her account, I don't think, Denny. After probate, you'll have the farm, of course, but we can certainly help out some . . ."

"Go home, Pat," Dennis said, kissing her on the cheek. "You're going to drop in your tracks. If you've left anything undone, I can't imagine what it is. I'll think about Luz and let you know. I don't have to say thank you, do I?"

"No. But 'I'm sorry about the pigtails' would be a good start."

Back at the farmhouse, after the Ponder cousin who was sitting with Luz had made us coffee and cut one of six or seven cakes that had come tiptoed out, we sat down in the living room and looked at Luz Ferreira. She looked back, alert and sweet-faced, smiling her joy at seeing Dennis again. The Ponder cousin had combed her hair into a silver halo and put a dab of lipstick on her little mouth, and there was a cloud of something that smelled like old-fashioned rosewater in the stale air. Dennis and I looked at each other. She could not have weighed ninety pounds, but she loomed as large in the dim old room as Bella ever had, as massive as an anchor. What on earth was going to become of her now?

"We need to talk a little now, Luz," Dennis said finally. "We need to talk some about Bella, and then about . . . what we're all going to do later. We need to make some plans."

The sweet smile deepened. It was obvious to me that she did not comprehend that Bella was gone. I wondered if she ever would, and when she did, who would be there to help her bear it.

"All right, Denny," she said, like a good child. "And then you can help me pack. I have a suitcase all my own; it's blue. Bella gave it to me for Christmas . . . sometime."

My heart contracted with pity.

"Where are you going, sweetie?" I said softly, pushing the spindrift hair off her face.

"Why . . . home with Denny. I know I can't stay here. I can't climb the stairs. Bella said I was to go with Denny now. I guess I'll stay until she comes for me. I don't remember what she said about that."

I could feel pure pain twist my face; I buried it in her hair so that she would not see it.

"Oh, honey," I began.

"Who wants some ice cream?" Dennis said loudly. "I saw some Chunky Monkey in the freezer. It seems a shame to let it go to waste."

"Oh, I do," cried Luz, clapping her hands.

I just looked at him.

"Come on in the kitchen and help me, Molly," he said. "You can carry the bowls."

He was halfway across the floor before I got up and followed him.

"We can't put this off forever," I whispered. "We were halfway there. Why didn't you just go on with it? There's not going to be a better time to tell her . . ."

He was fumbling in the freezer.

"Can you get her ready? Pack up some things, and all?" he said over his shoulder.

"Ready for what?"

"Ready to come back to my place with me."

"You have got to be kidding," I said, slowly and fervently.

He turned to look at me.

"No. It makes sense. You wouldn't have to be running up here every five minutes, and no one else would either. No one would have to stay. You'd have both of us right down there at your doorstep. And there's a lot I can do for her, more than you think . . ."

"Dennis, she just needs so much . . ."

"It would kill her to put her in some kind of home, Molly," he said.

I was quiet for a long time, trying to think it out, trying to feel how it would be. The dwindling old woman, the very sick man, there in the glade with me. With me and the father I was, ever so slowly, losing. With only me and a dog and a place of straw under the steps where two swans had been but no longer were . . . could I feel that?

Could I do that?

Yes, I could.

"You know you'll probably have to do it eventually," I said slowly.

"But not now. Not today. By God, Molly, not yet."

"Denny?" Luz called from the living room.

"Coming. Just getting your stuff together, toots," he called back.

I went upstairs to find Luzia's blue Christmas suitcase and pack her things.

It took a long time to get her moved into Dennis's camp. Patricia Norton and her son and a friend carried Luz's tiny body and her few possessions—scuffed, old-fashioned children's things—to the friend's Explorer, where the backseat had been removed. I went ahead with Dennis and together we moved his things out of the downstairs bedroom and I put fresh linen on the bed that would, now, be Luz's.

"Where will you sleep?" I said, shaking out quilts

and fluffing pillows. I had brought them from the farmhouse, new ones that Bella had obviously put away for a rainy day. Oh, God, Bella . . . they smelled of camphor and lavender, but they still bore their tags, and the creases of newness. Somehow, they turned the rough, masculine room into the bower of a young girl.

"On the sofa in front of the fire," he said. "You have no idea how often I fall asleep there anyway. Don't frown, Molly, it'll be much better. My books will already be where I am and I won't have to get up and stump around in the dark looking for them, and I can get at the Scotch a lot easier, and if you should just happen, one fine day, to come around saying, 'Please, sir, can I have some more?' I won't have to throw old Luz out of her room, and nobody will have to worry about corrupting the morals of an old lady."

I looked at him, startled. Was he teasing me? He had been quiet and withdrawn all day, gone inside himself, I thought, against the weight of whatever it was he felt as he watched his mother lowered into the earth of up island. I realized that I was not likely ever to know what that was. I realized, too, that I was probably not ever going to be able to tell when he was teasing me.

How long, for Dennis Ponder and for me, was "ever" going to be?

He was not smiling, but something in his eyes was more alive, more present, than I had seen all day.

"We couldn't have that," I said, and bent to pick up the pile of used bedding.

"Molly."

"What?"

"Are you? Going to ask?"

I straightened up and looked at him.

"Am I going to be around *to* ask, Dennis?" I said.
He frowned.

"Why wouldn't you be?"

"My contract was with your mother. I have to assume it's void now."

"Your contract, if you want to call it that, was with me. She was just an agent. I don't see any reason to void it unless you want to. Luz and I still need some looking after. I've gotten better about what I can do, but I don't know . . . how long that will last. I'd have to get someone for Luz whatever happens. Why can't it be you? Do you . . . are you thinking of going home?"

I shook my head impatiently. I had not been thinking of anything. Too much had happened too fast. Now, though, I saw just how profoundly our situation had changed. He *was* better, or at least had learned the parameters of his small world so well that he could operate in it almost unaided. Whether it was healing or mere adaptation, I did not know, but it was real. There were resources, now, to help with Luz; his Ponder kin stood ready, if he should ask. And the powerful chord that held me to the glade had always been, I knew now, Bella Ponder. Without her presence looming from the farmhouse on the moor, my hold on this small world felt flaccid and tenuous. I hung in the air of the glade, unable to touch earth, unable to fly away.

And, of course, there was my father. I could see it so clearly, all of a sudden. What had I been thinking of? I needed to get help for him and I needed to do it quickly. Why had I not seen it before?

On the other hand . . . Atlanta. I saw it clearly, in a split-second crack of clarity: the anonymous tiled clinic for my father, with the daily visits and the drugs and the steps forward and the slides back, and the needless, endless "family therapy." And then the "long-term facility . . ." I had volunteered at enough mental health facilities to know where clinical depression in the elderly generally led.

And the sessions with Missy and Tee and some smooth-visaged, feral lawyer, in Missy's ridiculous Laura Ashley office. Endless, endless . . . Or else, the talks with Tee alone, in the Ansley Park house he had wanted to give to Sheri Scroggins and now wanted back; the dull rehashing of hurt and anger and guilt where before there had been laughter and easiness and old, warm love. Could I do that? Could I sit in my own library or on my own terrace with Tee Redwine and try to reconstruct a life he had blown to smithereens? Did I want to?

And if I didn't, what did I *want*? And who? Was there anything at all available to me that could possibly last?

"Dennis," I said, "I don't even know where home is."

"Then stick around until you figure it out," he said, and turned away to finish pushing a box of books out of the room with his crutch.

From my own camp the silent pull of my receding father was as strong as that of the moon on the tide.

"There's the little matter of Daddy," I said. "It seems to me neither of us has given that much thought. I don't think it can wait, now."

He did not speak. When finally he started to, we heard the crunch of the Explorer's tires coming into the glade, and it was time to bring Luzia Ferreira home.

It was late, after dark, when I finished at Dennis's and walked home across the glade. The moon path lay thick and satiny on the Sound, and though there was still no green on the branches of the hardwoods, there was the foreshadowing of it in the pervasive wet, cold greenness that shimmered from the earth and water. I was very tired. Luz had been as giddy and over-wrought as a child in a new place, and had had to be soothed and read to and fed by hand. She remembered the swans when she saw the glade, and cried out so frantically to go and see them that Dennis had finally said, rather sharply, "Hush. It's past the swans' bed-time. Tomorrow will be soon enough for the swans," and she had subsided, and soon forgotten them in the shower of words from *Anne of Green Gables* that he was reading to her. It must, I thought, have been his daughter's book. I did not know what he would tell her about the swans, but I was determined not to be there when he did it.

I called out to my father, but got no reply, and went up the dark stairs to look in on him. It was barely eight o'clock, but he was already deep in sleep. Whether or not the pills had taken him no longer mat-tered; night and sleep were his world now. I saw, with my new clarity, that he was already more than half gone from me, half down there with'her.

I knew then that I would have to take him home. The weight of the knowing almost bent me double.

My mother came to the edge of my cave that night. Free of her subterranean bars, she fluttered there for a long time, and for some reason I could not see her clearly, but the sense of her was terribly strong. In my dream I literally willed my eyes to see her and finally they did; she was smiling. It was a small, curved, kit-ten's smile; I had seen it many times before, when she had made her point, won her game. As I stared, she turned away and then she faded.

"No, you won't," I said to her in my dream, between clenched teeth, and I struggled so hard to reach her that I could feel, in sleep, the sweat start on my face. But I could not reach her, and I could not wake.

Beside me, on the floor, I could hear Lazarus begin to growl, softly and eerily, and then I heard him spring up and scrabble across the floor and out the dog door, and heard his great, booming barking begin. Still I struggled in sleep, caught in the tendrils of the dream. When the barking did not stop, I woke abruptly.

He was still barking. There was a purposeful note in it: It was not the barking that meant he was bored and simply wished to start a commotion. I sat up in the damp, tangled sheets, aching all over from the force of my struggle to wake, feeling thick and heavy and mindless. The barking went on and on. Outside, the morning light was pale and new.

I knew Lazarus would not stop until I stopped him, so I got up and pulled on the clothes I had left in a pile beside my bed—my funeral clothes; what a long time ago that seemed—and started heavily for the door. I heard Dennis then.

He was shouting hoarsely from down by the pond, over and over. I could not make out what he was saying. My heart literally stopped. Daddy . . .

But then I heard that he was saying, "Get Tim! Get Tim! Molly, bring Tim!," and I turned and scrambled up the stairs and into my father's bedroom and shook him hard. I knew without seeing why Dennis wanted my father. I will never know how, but I did.

He did not want to wake, and he did not want to come with me when he did, and was petulant and then quite sharp with me; I simply grabbed him by his shoulders and pulled him out of bed and jerked him to his feet. I remember being shocked that he was so light; he seemed, now, all hollow bone, like a huge bird. But I did not dwell on it; I would deal with it later. When I had him on his feet, swaying and fussing in his too-large pajamas, I bent and literally jammed his feet into his slippers. Then I pulled him down the stairs so fast that we both nearly tumbled to the bottom.

"What are you doing?" he kept demanding, in a sick child's whine. "Where are we going? What is the matter with you?"

We were halfway down the path to the pond when we saw them. I stopped abruptly, and he did, too. He stopped struggling with me and slowly, very slowly, his arms came down to his sides. Then he lifted them slightly, as if he might be about to stretch lightly after sleep.

The two swans were waddling awkwardly up the path toward us. Behind them, Lazarus capered, barking and barking, keeping his distance. Behind him, Dennis ran and fell and got up and ran again, laughing. Laughing. The swan in front was smaller than the one behind, obviously newly grown, and so white that she shone in the pale sun. There seemed to me no doubt that it was a pen. She was frightened and angry, and she kept stopping and turning around and darting her beautiful, sinuous neck at the larger swan and at Lazarus, and once or twice lifted her wings into the busking position. They glistened as if they had been dipped in liquid crystal. But the big swan behind her would hiss and grunt and thrust at her with his beak, and she would start forward again. Charles. There could be no doubt, either, that the big, dingy cob was

Charles, and that he was bringing his new pen to see my father. I sat down on the path and began to cry.

My father stood still until Charles had prodded and flapped and hissed the young pen to a position directly in front of him. Both swans stopped then, and Charles stationed himself behind the pen so that she could not bolt, and simply settled himself into his great, battered wings, tucked up a black foot, and looked up at my father. The pen settled herself, too, though she kept darting her head around, and her wings stayed in constant slight motion, like voile blowing in a spring wind.

Slowly, slowly, my father sank down on his heels into the crouch that I knew from a thousand days of my childhood, the one that he could maintain for hours. He looked at the swans, and then he said, in the voice I had not heard for a long time, my father's voice, "You old fool. Where the hell have you been?"

CHAPTER FIFTEEN

EASTER WAS AS LATE THAT year as I can remember, and it came in on the wings of a great nor'easter that seemed to say to the Vineyard, after we had basked gratefully in a string of perfect spring days, "Gotcha!"

Afterward, the old men at Alley's said that there had not been such a spring storm since most of them could remember, though a few of the very oldest claimed they had seen worse. I didn't see how there could be worse.

We had known it was coming, and I, as well as most of the up islanders who could drive, had stocked up on tinned food and sterno and wood and propane and candles.

"Will you be okay?" said Pat Norton, whom I had run into at the A&P in Vineyard Haven. "You're sure to lose power down there."

"I've got all the stuff for both camps," I said. "And Daddy has tightened some shingles, and I left him and Dennis trying to decide whether to board the windows. Dennis wants to do it, but Daddy is afraid he can't keep an eye on the damned swans if they do. I think I know who's going to win that one. There's not a one of us who can stand up against those swans."

"I'm so glad he's better," she said. "All I was hearing at Alley's for a while was how much everybody missed Tim Bell. It seemed to me you just plain had more than you could handle, but I didn't want to pry—"

I hugged her impulsively, and she smiled shyly, though she flinched away from the hug. I laughed.

"I keep forgetting I'm not in the South," I said. "Yes. He *is* better. Oh, Pat. What on earth would we have done without you?"

She shook her head impatiently, but then she said, "Stay, Molly. We've gotten sort of used to you. All us Ponders have."

I drove home in the stiffening wind, feeling as if I had been given the keys to up island.

The storm hit in earnest early in the blackness of Easter morning, and by dawn the glade had indeed lost power. I had cooked a ham the day before and made a drunken, lopsided coconut cake from scratch, and bought potato salad from Back Alley's deli counter, and I put it all out on the back porch to keep. The wet cold that came back with the storm would keep it better than the dead refrigerator. At ten A.M. I heard a crash that meant the telephone pole that served the glade was down, and shortly after that Dennis, swathed from head to heels in oilskins, knocked on the door and shouted above the roar of the wind and rain that he wanted to bring Luz down to our camp.

"It's warmer down here," he yelled. "I can't keep her warm up there; the fire won't reach into her bedroom, and for some reason the living room confuses her, and she cries for Bella."

His concern was real, although it was hard to

gauge the meaning of it. His relationship with Luz was complex, but it seemed comfortable to both. Whatever it was, I knew it was born, as he had been, of Bella Ponder, and that she was with him still, every day. He did not often speak of her, but she lived in the camp with him as surely as Luz did. She lived in my camp, too. Bella was vigorous and palpable in the glade.

My father put on his foul-weather gear and went out into the gale with Dennis, pausing to look under the porch, where the swans were huddled in their straw bower, fussy and miserable. Charles had one great wing fanned over Persephone, who had her head and neck tucked almost completely into her own shining feathers. The straw was wet, but the wind did not reach in so badly. Together, Daddy and Dennis brought Luzia, completely wrapped in blankets and oilskin, back in a fireman's hold. I have no idea how Dennis managed it; I could not bear to look. Both men were drenched when they came in, but Luzia was snug and dry, and so enchanted to be back in the little camp she remembered that she forgot to fuss constantly for the swans. I put her on the sofa and covered her and built up the fire, then sent Dennis and my father up for showers in the remaining hot water, and dry clothes. They were my father's, and they hung loose on both men. It did not matter. I was absurdly glad to have them here. I had planned to take Easter dinner up to Dennis's, but this . . . this was better.

The storm raged all afternoon. We could hear occasionally the crashes of trees going down in the woods, but it was impossible to see through the solid curtain of howling silver rain. When I did look out, the air was full of flying green as the wind stripped the new leaves from the oaks and hickories and hurled them aloft. The pounding of the waves over on the Bight and the Sound was audible, even through the wind, when the door was opened. We didn't do that often, needless to say. For some reason, I was never worried. It simply never occurred to me that we might lose our roof, or suffer a direct hit from a tree.

At two in the afternoon I served the ham and potato salad before the fire, and we had cake and coffee made in the spatterware pot over the flames. I brought out a bottle of Napoleon brandy my father had brought from Atlanta and we opened it. We had made a considerable dent in it when there was a great, furious flapping at the door and my father rushed to jerk it open and Charles and Persy literally blew into the room, wet and truculent and aggrieved. After a skittering skirmish with Lazarus, my father herded them into a pile of old blankets behind the sofa, and there they settled, fussily, to wait out the storm. My father put barley and water there for them, and occasionally went and crouched down and talked softly to them, and from time to time we all heard the great, liquid splatting that meant swan excrement.

After the first splat, I simply closed my ears to it.

"Relax," Dennis grinned. "Pat will surely know what gets swan shit out of chintz."

By late afternoon the wind was beginning to drop, as it often did when darkness fell during a nor'easter, and though we all knew it would pick up again with the coming of the next day's light, we stirred and smiled at one another, and I passed the brandy again, and threw a log on the fire. Dennis had put Pachelbel on his little battery-powered cassette recorder, and he and my father sat at the crooked table in the corner playing chess and sipping cognac. Luzia snored softly on the sofa, murmuring every now and then in Portuguese. Lazarus slept on the hearth rug, groaning deliciously, one ear cocked toward his feathered adversaries behind the sofa. They had not fussed or rustled or splatted for some time now.

I sat in the wing chair drawn up to the fire, nearly gone into sleep and cognac. I thought that I could sit there, just so, forever.

A log burned in two, then collapsed in a shower of sparks, and Lazarus twitched; behind the sofa a swan grunted crossly. The smell of pent-up swan was beginning to curl ripely into the warm room. I did not care about that, either. I sat up and stretched, and walked to the front door to look out at the storm. It seemed to catch its great breath for a moment before shouting on.

"It you're going into the kitchen, bring us back some of that Chunky Monkey," Dennis said lazily from the chess table. "I packed it in dry ice, but it's going to melt if we don't eat it."

I was suddenly pierced through with such a blade of pure knowing that I literally doubled over with it. Then I straightened up and began to laugh, softly.

Right now, I thought, just for this minute right now, we are a family. A six-foot Southern Betrayed Wife and her widowed father and a senile old Portuguese lesbian and a one-legged schoolteacher and a mongrel dog and two aberrant swans—we are a family. That is what we have made together. For just this moment, we are as real as any family anywhere in the world. Maybe one of us is dying. Maybe more than one. Or maybe not. Maybe one or more of us will fly away. Or maybe not. It doesn't matter. Right now, we are us and we are here.

Still smiling, I went to the hat rack and took my

mother's black hat from it and opened the front door. The wind howled hungrily. I looked at my father, and he looked back at me for a long time, then nodded slightly and smiled.

"What the hell are you doing?" Dennis Ponder said.

"Throwing my hat in the ring," I said back.

I opened the door and walked to the edge of the porch and stopped.

"It's not forever, Mama," I said aloud. "Just for right now. It was never really mine, anyway."

And I gave the hat to the wind, which took it and whirled it away over the lashing trees, toward Gay Head, all the way up island.

Low Country

For Gervais, Curry, Richard,
and Hart Hagerty,
the next keepers of the Ace

Nature's first green is gold
Her hardest hue to hold.
Her early leaf's a flower
But only so an hour
Then leaf subsides to leaf.
So Eden sank to grief,
So dawn goes down to day.
Nothing gold can stay.

—ROBERT FROST

Author's Note

There is no Peacock's Island on St. Helena's Sound, or anywhere else, that I know of, but perhaps there might have been, and if there had, I think it would be a lot like this one. There are no actual people like the ones in this book, but perhaps if there had been, they might have lived on Peacock's Island. There is no Gullah settlement called Dayclear, and indeed, the very name is my invention; the accepted Gullah word for dawn is "Dayclean," though I have seen "Dayclear" in one or two places. There *are* wild ponies, or marsh tackies, still on some of the Sea Islands, and there are resort developments on almost all of them, many of them called plantations, but Peacock Island Plantation is my own hybrid. There is, thank God, an Ace Basin, and it contains all the wildlife mentioned in this book and more, except a twenty-foot alligator named Leviathan and a one-hundred-and-twenty-five-year-old panther—and after all, in the Lowcountry, who knows?

My thanks and love to Barbara and Duke Hagerty, who shared their friendship, their library, their house and home, and their passion for Edisto Island and the Ace Basin; to Sandra Player, whose miraculous teenage years provided Caro Venable with a provenance of her own; and to Dr. Alex Sanders, president of the College of Charleston, who once again gave me words, flesh and blood for this book. He will know which ones.

My gratitude and admiration to the creators of two wonderful books,* whose pages I have borrowed liberally and literally.

And, as always, to Larry, Ginger, Heyward, and Martha, the home team.

Anne Rivers Siddons
Atlanta, Georgia
May 1998

"Ain't You Got a Right to the Tree of Life?"—The People of Johns Island, South Carolina—Their Faces, Their Words and Their Songs, revised and expanded edition, recorded and edited by Guy and Candie Caraway and published by Brown Thrasher Books, University of Georgia Press, 1989; *When Roots Die—Endangered Traditions of the Sea Islands* by Patricia Jones Jackson, published by the University of Georgia Press, 1987.

Low Country

1

I *think I'll go over to the island for a few days,"*
I said to my husband at breakfast, and then,
when he did not respond, I said, "The light's
beautiful. It can't last. I hate to waste it. We won't
get this pure gold again until this time next year."

Clay smiled, but he did not put down his
newspaper, and he did not speak. The smile made
my stomach dip and rise again, as it has for the
past twenty-five years. Clay's smile is wonderful,
slow and unstinting and a bit crooked, and gains
much of its power from the surrounding austerity
of his sharp, thin face. Over the years I have seen
it disarm a legion of people, from two-year-olds
in mid-tantrum to Arab sheiks in same. Even
though I knew that this smile was little more than
a twitch, and with no more perception behind it,
I felt my own mouth smiling back. I wondered, as
I often do, how he could do that, smile as though

you had absolutely delighted him when he had not heard a word you said.

"There is a rabid armadillo approaching you from behind," I said. "It's so close I can see the froth. It's not a pretty sight."

"I heard you," he said. "You want to go over to the island because the light's good. It can't last."

I waited, but he did not speak again, or raise his eyes.

Finally I said, "So? Is that okay with you?"

This time he did look up.

"Why do you ask? You don't need my permission to go over to the island. When did I ever stop you?"

His voice was level and reasonable; it is seldom anything else. I knew that he did not like me to go over to the island alone, though, for a number of reasons that we had discussed and one that we had not, yet.

The island is wild and largely undeveloped now, except for a tiny settlement on its southwestern tip, and there are wild animals living on it that are hostile to humans, and sometimes dangerous. It is home to a formidable colony of alligators, some more than twelve feet long, and a handful of wild boar that make up in ferocity what they lack in numbers. Rattlesnakes and water moccasins are a given. Even the band of sullen wild ponies that have lived there on the grassy hummocks between the creeks and inlets since time out of mind are not the amiable toys they seem. A small child from the settlement was badly kicked only last year, when he got too close to a mare nursing her foal. Clay knows that I have been handling myself easily and well on the island since I was a child, but he mistrusts what he calls my impetuosity more than he trusts my long experience and exemplary safety record.

Then there is the settlement itself, Dayclear. That beautiful word is Gullah, part of the strange and lyrical amalgam of West African and Colonial English once spoken by the handful of Gullah blacks still living in pockets of the South Carolina Lowcountry. They are the descendants of the slaves brought here by the first white settlers of these archipelagos and marshes, and some of the elders still speak the old patois among themselves. When I was a child I knew some of it myself, a few words taught me by various Gullah nurses and cooks, a few snatches of songs sung by gardeners and handymen on my grandfather's place. I know that Dayclear means "dawn." I have always loved the word, and I have always been aware of the settlement, even if I did not often visit it when I was growing up and have no occasion to do so now. I do know that it is made up now largely of the old, with a preponderance of frail old women, and that some of them must be the kin of those workers of my childhood, if not the actual people themselves. I know that there are virtually no young men and women living there, since the young leave the island as soon as they are physically able to do so, to seek whatever fortunes they might find elsewhere. There is nothing for them in Dayclear. There are children, small ones, left behind with the old women by daughters and granddaughters who have taken flight, and there are sometimes silent, empty-faced young men about, who have come home because they are in trouble and have, temporarily, nowhere else to go, but they do not stay long.

I have not been to the settlement for many years, as my route across the island lies in the dry, hummocky heart of it, and the house to which I go is at the opposite end, looking northwest toward the shore of Edisto. But when I think of it, I feel nothing but a kind of mindless, nostalgic sense of safety and benevolence. Dayclear has never given me anything but nurturing and love.

Clay fears it, though. He has never said so, but I know that he does. I can tell; I always know when Clay is afraid, because he so seldom is, and of almost nothing.

"There's nothing there that can hurt me; nobody who would," I have said to him. "They're just poor old women and babies and children."

"You don't know who's back in there," he said. "You don't see who comes and goes. Anybody could come across. There are places you could wade across. Anybody could drop anchor in the Inland Waterway and come ashore. You think everybody in that little place doesn't know when you're at the house, and that you're by yourself? I don't like it when you go, Caro. But you know that."

I did know, and do. But he does not forbid me to go to the island. For one thing, Clay is not a forbidder; he would find it distasteful, unseemly, to forbid his wife anything, the operative word being distasteful. Clay is a fastidious man, both physically and emotionally.

For another thing, I own part of the island. And if there is anything Clay respects, it is the right of eminent domain.

But the main reason he does not want me on the island alone is that he is afraid that I will drink there. I do drink sometimes, though by no means often, but when I do I tend to do it rather excessively. When I am with him, at this house or the club or the town house in Charleston, he feels that he can at least control the consequences of my drinking, if not the act itself. The consequences are not heinous, I don't think; I do not stumble and fall, or weep, or grow belligerent. But I do tend to hug necks and kiss cheeks, and sometimes to sit on laps, and sometimes to dance and sing, and I imagine that to Clay these are worse than staggering or tears. They might imply, to some who don't know us, that I do not receive enough affection at home. And they tend to dismay visiting Arab sheiks. So Clay, while he says nothing to me then or later and never has, stays close enough to initiate damage control when he thinks it is necessary. Perhaps if we talked about it, I could tell him that when I am slightly drunk I feel so much better than I normally do, that I am happy, exuberant, giddy, and wish to share the largesse with whomever is close. But we do not talk about it. To name a demon is to make it yours. Clay does not wish to own this particular demon, and I do not wish, yet, to give it up. So we do not speak of my drinking, though the time may come when we have to do so. Or maybe not. I do fairly well with it, as long as I have the island for refuge.

This is something Clay does not understand, and will not unless I tell him: that the island is the one place where I do not want to drink, or need to. I know that I could probably ease his mind considerably about my time over there if I told him so, but again, that would mean naming the demon, and we both know that we do not want its disruptive presence in our lives. It would be like having to acknowledge and live with an erratic, malicious relative who was apt to break the china, fart in public, insult our guests, change the very fabric and structure of our graceful lives.

So Clay goes on hating and dreading my trips

to the island but refusing to discuss them, and I go on going. It is a devilish seesaw, but it provides a sort of balance.

I looked away from him and out the French windows to the lawn and the seawall, and the beach and sea beyond. When Clay first began to develop Peacock's Island as a resort and permanent home community, he decided that we must certainly live there if anyone else could be hoped to, and so he chose the best lot on the island and had this house built for us. It *is* beautiful; even now, when I cannot look at the ocean without darkness and sickness starting in my stomach, I have to admit that it is a lovely house and an even lovelier situation, a perfect marriage of shore and sea. It was the first of the famous Peacock Island Plantation houses to be built, the model for that rambling, unobtrusive, graceful style of architecture that has become rather standard for beach and marsh houses in the various Lowcountry resort developments now. The architect who began it all is credited with our house, but it was Clay, all those years ago, who leaned over his shoulder for long hours at the drafting table, seeing in his mind's eye what the future homes of Peacock Island Plantation should be, and prodding until Dudley found the proper architectural metaphor for his vision. They dot the Lowcountry like beautiful fungi now, lying close along the shoreline under the twisted old live oaks and among the dark, cool thickets fringing the marshes on the landward sides of the barrier islands. They vary, of course; there is room for individual taste and interpretation, but no house is built in Peacock Island Plantation that does not meet the company's rigid design codes and so there is nothing intrusive here, nothing raw or ragged or incongruous, like you might see in other, newer and less carefully provenanced developments. Clay was adamant about that when he was young and new to the business and stood to lose a lot of money with his lofty design standards, and he has never loosened or amended them in this or any other of his projects. He likes to say that his family has loved and lived the Peacock's Island life ever since its beginning. And so we have, or at least lived it, for the past twenty years, when he moved us here from the cheerful suburb full of new ranch houses and young professional families where we started out, in Columbia.

Our son, Carter, was only a year old when we came to the island. Kylie was born here. They were children of the sea and beach and marshes; it was, to them, a known world, taken entirely for granted. It was, to me, like living permanently on a kind of extended vacation. I was born in Greenville and grew up in a succession of small South Carolina towns, all long hours from the coast, and came to the Lowcountry only during the summers, to visit my Aubrey grandparents. I still feel that way about living here. Sometimes I wake up before dawn, when it is too early to see that peculiar nacreous gray morning light that the beach and sea send backward to the land, when the wind is down and the surf is so sluggish that you cannot hear it past the dune line, and I think, Have I overslept? I didn't hear the garbage trucks. I'm going to be late for school. . . .

My lucky children, I have often thought, to gauge the rhythm of their days by surf and wind and the dawn chorus of a hundred different shorebirds, not ever to have known anything else. It seems exotic to me, foreign somehow. I used to say this to them, when they were very small, to try to explain this strange, suspended feeling that sometimes woke me in the earliest hours of the day, but I could never do so, at least not to Carter.

"That's dumb," he would say. "I don't see how you can still feel that way when you've been living here so long. This is better than garbage trucks and traffic any day. This is better than anything."

Carter, my pragmatist, so like Clay. To this day, I do not think anything out of his earliest childhood stalks him in the dark.

Ah, but Kylie . . . Kylie always knew. How, I don't know, but she did. She would ask endlessly for the story: "Tell about what you heard in the morning when you were little, Mama. Tell about the garbage trucks and the lawn mowers and the carpool horns . . ."

My small towns did not have noise ordinances like the island does; I realized early on that to Kylie, my childhood morning cacophony of manmade hubbub was as exotic as this profound, mystical sea-silence still is to me.

"Why do you want to hear that?" I would say. "This is much nicer. This is nature pure and simple; very few people are lucky enough just to hear natural sounds when they wake up."

But she was unpersuaded.

"Will you take me to see the garbagemen sometimes?" she would say, over and over. "Will you take me where I can hear a carpool horn?"

Kylie and Carter went to the island country day school, and were picked up at the head of our lane by a smart, quiet little school bus painted in the muted Peacock's Island tan and green.

Finally I gave in: "All right," I said. "Okay. We'll go spend a weekend in Columbia sometime soon, and you can see the garbagemen and hear the carpool horns."

We never did that, though. Somehow, we just never did. . . .

The sea at the horizon line was banked solid with angry purple clouds this morning, as it often is in autumn, but as I sat staring at it, the clouds fissured and broke and a spear of cold, silvery sunlight streaked through, stabbing down at the sea and lighting the tossing gray to the strange, stormy pewter of November. At the same moment the ocean wind freshened, lifting the fine, dun-colored sand from the tops of the primary dunes and swirling it spectrally into the air, rattling the drying palm fronds at the far edge of the lawn where the boardwalk down through the dunes to the sea began, stirring the moss on the live oaks that sheltered the house. It seemed for a moment that everything was in swirling, shimmering motion: air, sea, land, swimming in diffused light, drowning in silver. I looked away, back to the breakfast table and then up at Clay. On such a day, I knew, my stomach would roil queasily with the shifting light and wind, and my heart would beat queerly and thickly with it, until the wind dropped at sunset and the benevolent golden light of sunset spilled in from the west.

It was days like these that I most needed to be over on the island.

I speak of it as if it were a different island; we all do, though it is not, really. Technically, the island is the back third of Peacock's Island, the westward third, the marsh third. It is separated from the larger bulk of Peacock's Island proper by a tidal estuary that is full only twice a day; during the other times you could wade through the ankle-deep muck in the empty, corrugated rivulet that cuts the island like a snake, though no one wants to. The mud is deep, and stinks of ancient livings and dyings. You can better cross it, as I do, on a sturdy if raffish wooden bridge just wide and stout enough to hold a truck or a Jeep; the island is never truly cut off from the larger bulk of Peacock's.

It might as well be, though. It is another place entirely, eons older, wilder by millennia. I don't think it ever had a name, since it is of course a part of the larger mass. In my lifetime, in my time here, it has always been known simply as "the island," just as the larger, more hospitable two-thirds of it has been known as Peacock's Island, usually shortened to Peacock's. I think the inept old pirate for whom it is named would have agreed with the practice. If legend is true, he had no truck with the marsh-bound back third of the island, either, except to leave some of his hapless live captives there staked out for the alligators and the wild pigs and the savage, swarming insects and to dispose of the dead ones in the black, silent tidal creeks and rivers for the nour-ishment of who knows what. It is shifting, unquiet land, and it is no wonder to me that the unhappy victims of Jonathan Peacock are said to be unquiet, too, stumping about and murmuring querulously in the close, still nights. The Gullahs of Dayclear are said to be as familiar with them as they are with the terrible duppies and other assorted haunts who came with them in their chains to these shores, and on the whole, perhaps, prefer them. An unhappy ghost can be cajoled, soothed, propitiated, but there is no reasoning with a duppy.

Clay was still looking at me, studying my face as calmly and gravely as he had been studying the *Wall Street Journal*. Waiting, I knew.

"I'm almost through with the studies for the new painting," I said. "I've got everything but the light on the Inland Waterway at sunset. It's different from anywhere else; it's deeper there, and the water moves a lot more. That changes the light entirely. I really want to get that. I think a night or two would do it. I'll take the camcorder and see if I can get enough of the change from sunset to full night so I can finish it back here, if you need me. Is there something special?"

At first, when I started to spend time over on the island by myself, I used as an excuse the creation of a series of paintings of the marshes in all seasons and at all times of day. It was believable, if barely; I had not, then, painted in twenty years, but I did a lot of it once, and I have two solid years of training in fine arts at Converse. I was good then, good enough so that when I quit school in my junior year to marry Clay Venable, several of my instructors begged me to wait, begged me to get my degree first and then go somewhere specialized, like the Art Institute of Chicago, where two of them had taught, for further serious study. But I did not, and after Carter was born, I did not paint anymore. I never seemed to miss it, not consciously, and yet, when I pulled it out to excuse my flights to the island and began to actually dabble once more in oils and watercolors and pastels, it felt right and easy, supremely satisfying. After a while I was spending a great deal of time there trying to catch the fey, flickering faces and moods of the marshes and estuaries; it became important to me to do it as well as I could, to give the island its full due. After a longer while, even I could tell that the work I was doing was good, and getting better. Now, when I went to the island, it was not only that I was leaving Peacock's, I was going to something that was important to me on many levels.

Clay knew that, even if he did not approve. I was good enough so that the handful of small galleries on Peacock's and a few on some of the larger islands, and even one in Charleston, carried my work. He could not argue that it was self-indulgence alone that drew me back and back to the island. And to be fair, I knew that he was proud of me.

He had another weapon in his arsenal, though, and I knew now, without his saying so, that he was about to employ it. About five years ago he had asked me, almost casually, if I would involve myself with the young families who came to the Plantation to work for the company, to act as a sort of chatelaine-hostess-troubleshooter-confidante to them, especially the young women, most of whom were wives.

"You know," he said, "give dinner parties for them when they get here so they can get to know the others. Show them around, put them in the hands of the right real estate people so they won't end up spending money they can't afford for decent housing. Tell them about doctors and dentists and schools and play groups, and such. Maybe take the wives over to Charleston once or twice a month, show them the best shops and galleries and the right hair places, take them to lunch at the Yacht Club or somewhere flossy and fun. Just listen to them. It's not an easy adjustment for some of them. Some of them have never been closer to the ocean than a couple of weeks in the summers. I'm aware that it can get sort of cliquey and ingrown here; especially if they're slated to stay here for a long time. You could be a godsend to them."

Clay's company now encompasses properties as far away as Puerto Rico and the Virgin Islands; each project has a different management group, and he draws them from businesses and business schools all over the United States, but a preponderance of the young men and their wives come from the Northeast, from Wharton and Harvard Business Schools and others like them. No matter what property they are slated for, they all come here first. Basic corporate training in the Peacock

Island Plantation way of life starts here, and the average stay for a young family is two years. Some of them end up spending three, five, and more years. To a man and woman, they know little when they get here but the theory of business. It remains for Clay and the other Peacock executives to put a Peacock shine on them. It is often a hard and daunting process; it has not been all that unusual, in the past, for young marriages to be strained and sometimes broken, for destructive habits to take hold: too much liquor, too many recreational drugs, too much time spent in the attractive company of others than one's own husband or wife. The active one of the couple, usually the husband, spends long hours away from home, living and breathing the Peacock party line, leaving the young wife adrift on a languid island in a warm sea, cut off from home and family, alone with small children and only the company of other corporate wives, who have wrestled out their own places here and are not eager to take in the newcomer and her brood, lest she be the spouse of the very one who will oust their own husbands from their hard-won places in Clay's court. Clay argued, when he put his proposition to me, that he could not afford to take the time to arbitrate this sort of thing, and that if left unattended, it could come to wreck the famous Peacock morale. I thought the whole thing tiresome, heartbreaking, and entirely thankless, but I could see that he was right. Somebody needed to take hold of the newly arrived young. I just did not think it should be me.

But Clay did, and I could hardly refuse. I had not yet found refuge in my painting when he asked, and even I could see that if I did not find something outside myself to occupy me, I was going to be in serious trouble. I have always known that he asked more for my benefit than for the cadet corps of the Peacock Island Plantation.

I knew now with absolute certainty that he was about to produce a new crop of the needy young. He had that look. "Don't tell me," I said. "Let me guess. A new crop of lambs is incoming as we speak."

I smiled as I said it, though. He was smiling again, and I would give a lot to keep hold of that smile. After all, I had agreed to this role, and I do what we call the mother-superior bit rather well. The young women who are my charges all seem just young enough so that I don't threaten them with competition, and I have both the advantage of knowing the territory and the cachet of being the supreme honcho's wife. And I never drink when I'm on a mother-superior mission. I know that Clay doesn't worry about that. I don't do the children, though. Peggy Carmichael, the warm, big-lapped, grandmotherly woman who has been Clay's director of housekeeping since the beginning, does that. It works out pretty well, all told.

"Yep," Clay said, draining his coffee cup and leaning back. There was a sheepish cast to his smile now, which is the second most appealing smile that he has. The first, hands down, is his let's-go-to-bed smile. I am fairly sure that no one else but me sees that one.

"So? I didn't know you had anything new on the books."

"I don't, strictly," he said. "There's something on the horizon, a marsh property a ways from here that's looking real good, but I wasn't going to start staffing for it yet. But these three coming in are all special, top of their classes at Wharton and anxious to get started somewhere, and I was afraid if I didn't nail them down somebody else would get them. And some serious money looks like it might open up sooner than I thought. So I'm bringing them and their families on down. Just two couples and a divorced woman. I'm going to need you for this. Your light will hold a few more nights, I think. Will you, Caro?"

"So when are they coming?"

"They'll be here early this afternoon. I'm putting them up in the guest house until we can get two of the villas ready. Don't worry, they won't be staying here."

"Tonight! Oh, Clay! I can't get a dinner party ready by tonight; Estelle's got the afternoon off, and there's some kind of Thanksgiving pageant or something at school; all the others will be there with their kids. . . ."

"No, no. I thought this time we might just take them over to Charleston. They'll have time to freshen up and rest some, and we can show them a little of the island on the way. Maybe you could call the Yacht Club and see if they can get us in about eight. It's a pretty impressive place, and I hear one of the wives is not at all happy about leaving Darien and New York. Thinks she's coming down here to live among the savages. It won't hurt to throw some vintage Charleston at her. Let her know she can get to civilization in less than an hour."

"Ah, yes, the Holy City," I said, getting up to call the Carolina Yacht Club and make reservations. Clay has belonged for years now; and I still don't know how he managed it. Few outsiders made it into those hallowed halls on Charleston Harbor at the time he joined. I know that he never tires of taking newcomers there, just as I quail inwardly every time I know that I am going. Clay does not understand why I feel tentative at the Yacht Club.

"After all, this was your grandfather's town," he said. "And your great-great-great's, for that matter. You've got a more valid claim on it than half the people who live here."

I rarely answer him. It is a long way from

McClellanville, where my grandfather lived for most of his life, to Charleston and the Carolina Yacht Club, and the twain seldom meet. They never did for my grandfather, or my great-great-great, either, truth be known, but Clay has forgotten this, if he ever really knew it.

"Oh, wait a minute," he called after me, and I stopped and looked back.

"There may be a problem. This woman who's coming. She's probably the best of this lot, but I don't know if it's a good idea to take her to the Yacht Club. . . ."

"Why on earth? She's your guest. She doesn't have to have an escort of her own," I said.

"She's black," Clay said. "It might be a little uncomfortable for her."

"Uncomfortable is not precisely the term I would have used," I said, and went to the telephone and called Carolina's for reservations for a party of seven at eight o'clock that evening.

When Clay went upstairs to shower, I took my garden shears and a basket and went out into the yard to cut flowers for the guest house. Though it was nearly Thanksgiving, I still had some sweet, sturdy old roses in the beds behind the house, and it had been so warm that a few of the big, ruffled Sasanqua camellias had bloomed. They always do in our soft, wet autumns and winters; glowing like daystars in the grays and duns and silvers of this winter coast, then freezing and blackening to mush in the vicious little icy snaps that follow in January. We are subtropical here, and the Atlantic runs shallow and warm off our tan beaches. We have flowers long after the rest of the South has yielded up theirs to the cold. And there are vast greenhouses and acres of experimental gardens in the sheltered heart of the island, which serve the Plantation's floral needs as well as supplying its ecologically correct plantings and landscaping. I could have my pick of largesse from any of those. But I like to work in my backyard garden, and it feels right to take flowers from my own house to welcome Clay's young newcomers. And he likes telling them that I brought them my own flowers. So I usually do this when we have incomings. Augmented with the ubiquitous pansies that the landscaping people blanket the public spaces with in fall and winter, I would have enough for lush bouquets in all the rooms. I would take them down later so they would be fresh.

The guest house was bought to accommodate our personal guests at Cotton Blossom, the name Clay gave our house when it was built. But we have not had many guests, not for some years, and as the guest house is at some distance from us, it works well for temporary housing for company newcomers.

Cotton Blossom . . . the name sets my teeth

on edge, and I refuse to use it, or even to use the house stationery that Clay had made up for us. It sounds phony and overblown to me, a parody of every bad ol' Suthren joke I have ever heard. The rest of the homes in Peacock Island Plantation do not have names, that I know of, and even the named areas—streets, subdivisions, parks—wear the names of indigenous birds or flora. But Cotton Blossom was the name of the mean little cotton plantation my great-great-great-grandfather Aubrey built over on neighboring Edisto, where he raised substandard Sea Island cotton, and Clay thought to keep the name in the family, so to speak. Great-great-great-grandfather Aubrey is my only valid link to Charleston, and a tenuous one it was and is. . . . Grandpa's town house was small and cramped and well below the salt, and his presence in the Holy City seems to have left no more permanent impression than his passing. The Aubrey town house is a garage off King Street now. Clay does not find it necessary to point out the garage to prospective investors and residents of Peacock's, as he does the crumbling ruins of Cotton Blossom over on Edisto, which look, in their vine-and-moss-shrouded decay, far more romantic than the house ever looked in the days of its ascendancy.

"Caroline's people go way back in the Lowcountry," he is fond of saying, and I don't contradict him, because I suppose, literally speaking, they do, or at least Great-great-great-grandfather Aubrey's scanty tribe did. It's just that they didn't linger. My stake in Charleston and its environs is shallow indeed.

Clay respects my refusal to use the house's name, as he does most of my actions and decisions. He even smiles when I say that "Cotton Blossom" sounds like it ought to be wallowing down the Mississippi River, steam whistles squalling, pickaninnies dancing on the dock as it rounds the bluff. But he uses it himself, just the same, and in his soft, deep voice, it somehow manages to sound as dignified as he thinks it is. As I said, he is serious about keeping the few legitimate old Lowcountry names we have in the family. Not even our children escaped; Kylie was baptized Elizabeth Kyle Venable, after that same great-great-great-grandfather, John Kyle Aubrey.

"It's pretentious, that's all," I said, when she was born, trying to dissuade him. "Nobody in our family was close to the old skinflint, or even remembered him, that I ever heard of. If you want to honor my family, what's wrong with my mother's name? Or my grandmother's?"

"Olive?" he said mildly, looking at me over the small half-glasses he had just begun to wear. "Lutie Beulie? At least they'll know who she is in Charleston. They'll know what the name means."

And I gave in, because even then I was too

besotted with love and delight toward my daughter to argue about her name. In my deepest heart I knew who she was. I always did.

I put my flowers into the big, flat sweet-grass basket that I keep in the potting shed for the purpose and started back to the house. I love that basket; I love all the beautiful, intricate, sturdy baskets that the Gullah women braid from the dried sweet grass that flourishes in the marshes of the Lowcountry and sell for formidable sums wherever tourists gather. For once, I think, the tourists get fair value. The baskets are usually works of art and last, with care, for generations. The one I use for flowers we bought for Kylie to keep her toys in when she was a toddler. Carter has a larger one, a hamper, really, in his room, where his dirty clothes have more or less landed ever since he was five. It is traditional with Clay and me to give new families sets of the baskets at Christmastime, and they have always been received with what seems to me honest delight.

A flicker of red from the front of the house caught my eye as I came up the shallow steps to the veranda. It was a long way away, perhaps at the edge of the dunes, perhaps even down on the beach itself, and I felt my heart drop and pause and then start its old low, slow, cold thumping. I knew it was ridiculous, and I also knew that I was going to have to go down to the edge of the front lawn and see what it was. The sick coldness would last all day if I did not. I put the basket of flowers down on a wicker table on the veranda and went around the side of the house and across the front lawn, kept velvety and green all year by the Plantation groundskeepers, and around the tabby apron to the oval pool, and up to the little gray cypress landing that led to the steps and boardwalk to the beach. Only then did I lift my eyes to the water.

The sea was still gunmetal gray out at the horizon line, but the cloud rift that had lit the horizon earlier had drifted westward so that the beach shimmered in a wash of pale lemon light and running cloud-shadow. Strange, strange . . . somehow, even when the temperature is as mild as it usually is in November here, almost blood warm, like the water, the shifting dunes and flat beach and heaving sea seem cold to me, cold to the bone, cold to death. There is the damp, of course; the humidity of the Lowcountry is as much an element as its tepid water and low, sweet sky. The air of the Sea Islands is like a cloud against your skin in all its seasons. But it is more than that: taken in the aggregate, all that flickering, tossing, shivering, whispering pewter and silver seem to chill me to the core, and it always did, even at those infrequent times I came to a Lowcountry beach in autumn as a child. It is in this season, and in the winter that will follow, that I feel queerest, the most alien, here; there should be dark, pointed firs against the sky, not rattling, brown-tipped palms. Naked branches, wet black tree trunks, the bare bones of the earth, instead of the canopy of living green of the live oaks, the eternal fecund darkness of the sea pines. I looked at the sea and was cold in my heart.

The red turned out to be an open beach umbrella, bucking against the steady, moaning sea wind. I looked beyond it into the surf line, knowing what I would see, and did: swimmers, plunging in the lace-white edging of the breaking waves. Now that I saw them, I listened for and heard their voices: Canadians. Snowbirds. We get them every fall and winter, and we laugh and shiver when they swim determinedly every day but the very worst ones, and march up and down the empty, howling beach as if dead set on getting their winter vacation money's worth. If they ever hear the laughter and see the shivers they apparently do not care. I have seen one or two of them plowing mulishly into the ocean when one of our rare, soft, wet snows was falling. Don't laugh, Clay says. Without them the Inn and the villas and the restaurants would almost close down off season. I don't laugh. I have always liked and admired them, those tough, foolish migrants. Good sense was never a fault of mine, either.

My heart picked up its dragging pace and my breath came seeping back, and I took my flowers into the kitchen and arranged them in

some of the pottery vases that I collect and keep
for flowers, and left them by the door onto the
veranda, and went up to take my own shower. I
heard Clay moving around overhead in his
study and knew that he would be bent over the
architect's drafting table that he keeps there,
the working drawings for the newest Peacock
Plantation project, whatever it might be, permanently map-tacked in place there. Clay has
a design staff second to none when it comes
to attractive, ecologically sensitive Lowcountry
architecture and interiors, but nothing comes off
their boards that does not go directly onto his,
and this morning time in his study is sacrosanct
to everyone on his staff. Later he would tend to
the endless rounds of meetings and conferences
that made up his afternoons, and might go on
until very late at night, to dinners and conferences and cigars and brandies in restaurants and
drawing rooms from Savannah up to Myrtle
Beach, according to where the fat new money
was. But in the mornings he stayed at home and
put his hands directly on his empire. It probably
drove his people wild, but it had made the Peacock Island Plantation properties a name that
rivaled that of Charles Fraser's Sea Pines Plantation Company in its halcyon earlier days. I
smiled, thinking of him there; he would be fully
dressed for his day, in one of his winter-weight
tropical suits or perhaps a gray seersucker. Clay

almost never wore slacks and a jacket, and I saw him without a tie usually only in bed.

I went up the central stairs, a freestanding iron staircase made for Clay by an old black ironmonger on James Island when the house was built, and whose designs now brought hundreds of thousands of dollars, and paused at the landing. The house is open on both the seaward and the landward sides, so that standing on the landing is like standing suspended in a great cage of glass. It always makes me dizzy, as if nothing lies between me and the close-pressing darkness of the old oaks and the shrouding oleanders in back, and the great, sucking, light-breathing, always-waiting sea in front. I shook my head and went quickly up to the second floor, where the bedrooms were. They are open to the sea, too, the best ones, but you can close it away with heavy curtains if you choose, and the others, at the back of the house, overlook the dark-canopied backyard and feel to me like sheltering caves. I have moved my daytime retreat there, in the back corner, away from the beach and sea, though I still sleep in the big master suite hung in the air over the lawn and sea, with Clay. But when he is away I sleep on the daybed in my den.

Instead of turning to the right, toward our bedroom and mine and Clay's dens, as I almost always did, I turned left and walked down the hall toward the children's rooms. I think I had known all day that I was going to do so. I did not hesitate, and I did not think. I walked past Carter's closed door—closed because he had left it in such a disgraceful state when he left in September for his first year at graduate school at Yale that I had refused to go into it, and told Estelle not to touch it but to let him come back and find it just as he had left it—and stopped at the big ocean-facing room on the end, its door also closed. Kylie's room.

Unlike Carter, Kylie was neat to a fault; she hated it if anyone disturbed the strict order of her things, and had insisted from her earliest child-hood that no one enter her closed room when she was not in it. I had always respected that; I felt somewhat the same way about my things, though long years of sharing a room with Clay had loos-ened my scruples about order a bit. He is not untidy, only abstracted. I think he does not notice either order or disorder. I could still hear small Kylie, frustrated nearly to tears in her attempt to explain why she did not want me to come into her room when she was not in it: "But it's *mine*! It's not yours! You have a room of your own. Why do you need to go in mine?"

"What are you hiding in there, a pack of wolves?" I said. "Kevin Costner, maybe?"

She had fallen in love with the movie *Dances with Wolves*, and was so besotted with wolves that she was planning to be a wildlife veterinarian when she grew up, and work with the wild wolf packs of the Far West. It was a mature and considered ambition, and I would not have been at all surprised if she made it happen.

"I'm not hiding anything," she said, looking seriously at me, and I knew that she was not. Kylie hid nothing, ever. She was as open as air, as clear as water. Then she saw that I was teasing her, and she began to giggle, the silvery, silly giggle that, I am told, is very like mine, and then she laughed, the deep, froggy belly laugh that is mine also. In a moment we were both laughing, laughing until the tears rolled down our so-alike small, brown faces, laughing and laughing until Clay came in to see what was so funny, and said, grinning himself, "Ladies and gentlemen, for your enjoyment tonight . . . Venable and Venable! Let's give them a great big hand!"

And we rolled over on our backs on the floor of her room, Kylie and I, in helpless laughter and simple joy, because it was true. We were Venable and Venable. We simply delighted each other. There was nothing in either of us that did not understand and admire the other. Even when she was a baby, there was nothing childish, nothing condescending, nothing mother-to-child about it. We were companions on every level, confidantes, comrades, friends, lovers in the deepest and most nonsexual sense of the word. My daughter and I had fallen in love and delight with each other at the moment of her birth, and it was often all I could do to keep Clay and Carter from coming off second best. Because they are so ludicrously alike, and because Clay's mind is almost absurdly full of riches and Carter is a sunny, confident young man with a full and empowering sense of himself, I do not think that either of them has suffered. Rather, they, like most other people in our orbit, simply enjoyed and often laughed at Venable and Venable.

I opened Kylie's door and went into her room. At first the great surf of brightness off the noon beach blinded me, and I stood blinking, my hand shading my eyes. Then they adjusted and I looked around and saw it plain, this place that was, of all her places, most distinctly hers.

It was not a frilly room and never had been. Like me, Kylie was born with a need for space and order and a dislike of cluttering frills and fuss. She had always been a small, wiry child, almost simian in her build, narrow-hipped and broad-shouldered, slightly long of arm and short of leg, never tall, always thin to the bone. Ruffles would have been as ludicrous on and around her as on me. She was, instead, sleeked down for action; pared to sinew and long, slender muscle; meant for sun and sand and wind and water, and that was what her room reflected. I do not think she ever drew her curtains, even at night. Kylie fell asleep with her face turned to the moon and

the comets and the wheeling constellations, seeing when she woke in the night the dance of
phosphorus on the warm, thick, black summer
ocean, or sometimes the lightning of storms over
the horizon that looked, she said, like naval battles far out to sea. Waking to the cool pearl of
dawn on tidal slicks, to the pink and silver foil of
a newly warming spring ocean, perhaps to the
Radio City Music Hall dance of porpoises in the
silky summer shallows. Kylie went as far as any
human I have ever known, when she was small,
toward simply using up the sea.

Her walls were painted the milky green of the
sea on a cloudy day, and on them hung her posters
of animals and birds and sea creatures and the big,
luminous painting of Richard Hagerty's that was
the official Spoleto Festival poster one year, of
Hurricane Hugo striding big-footed and terrible
down on a crouching Charleston. I had not
wanted to buy it for her because I had thought it
would come to haunt her, but she was adamant.

"Yeah, but see, Hugo didn't win," she said.
"Big as a thousand houses, big as a booger, and
he still didn't win."

And I had laughed and bought it for her,
because I wanted her to remember that: the
boogers don't always win.

On the low bookshelves were the models she
had made of animal skeletons, from kits I had
ordered for her from marine biological laborato-

ries and supply houses, and three or four real skeletons we had found over on the island when she went with me to the house there: the papery carapace of an eight-foot rattler; a wild boar's skull with great, bleached, Jurassic tusks; the elegant, polished small skull of a raccoon. Estelle would not dust these herself but made Kylie do it. Clay was distinctly not amused by the skeletons, and even Carter only said, "Yuck. You're weird, Kylie." But I knew. It is important to know what the inside of things looks like. Otherwise, almost anything can fool you.

Her books were there, in a military order known only to Kylie. The old ones that I had loved: *Wind in the Willows* ("Mother! Listen! 'There is *nothing*—absolutely nothing—half so much worth doing as simply messing about on boats.' Oh, he knew, Ratty knew, didn't he?"); the *Waterbabies*; the Nancy Drew series; the Bobbsey Twins; the Lawrenceville Stories. For some reason they fascinated her. *Black Beauty*. *Silver Birch*. *Midnight Moon*. And alongside them, the handbooks and textbooks and charts and maps of the Carolina Lowcountry marshes and islands that we got for her from the Corps of Engineers and various coastal conservation and natural resources organizations.

On her desk, a small voodoo drum that Estelle's Gullah grandmother, who adored Kylie, had given her; we never knew where it had come from originally, but Estelle seemed to think it was the real thing. And the big osprey we had found newly dead on the bank of the tidal creek that cut through the undulating green marsh over on the island one summer day, still perfect except for the forever mysterious fact of its death. Clay had taken it to a taxidermist for her, and the great bird, wings spread, had kept yellow-eyed watch over Kylie and her room ever since. Of all her things, I think she loved that bird the best.

And that was all. Except for her neat, beige-spread bed and the matching armchairs, nothing else of her showed. Her clothes were shut away in the closet; she almost never left anything lying out. Her outgrown toys were in a hamper in her closet. The room did not look lonely, though. The space and order spoke of Kylie as clearly as strewn possessions would have of another child.

I walked over to the French doors that opened onto her balcony and leaned against them and looked back into the room. Something caught my eye, the edge of something blue, almost hidden under the dust ruffle of her bed. I leaned over and picked it up. A T-shirt, a small one, faded, that read PEACOCK ISLAND PLANTATION SUMMER RECREATION PROGRAM. You saw shirts like it all over the island; they were issued to children who joined the summer program, mostly the children of guests who wanted to enjoy the island's adult pursuits while their children went about their own, supervised activities. I remembered that Kylie liked the shirts but hated the program and absolutely refused to join, even when her father pointed out that it would be a real treat for the visiting little boys and girls to meet the daughter of the owner of the Plantation.

"Big deal," Kylie said. "You think I want to go on a nature walk with some kid who's gon' yell his head off if we see a snake?"

We did not make her attend the program. It would indeed have been ludicrous. Kylie was dealing calmly with bull alligators and rattlesnakes when the offspring of the Plantation visitors were shying at horseshoe crabs. She deigned to wear the T-shirts, though.

"That way the kids will all think I go," she said reasonably to Clay, and that was that.

I held the shirt to my face and sniffed. It smelled fresh and particular, like summer and sun and salt and Kylie herself, not at all like dust. But it should have smelled of dust; it must have been there, just under the fringe of the dust ruffle, for a long time. A little over five years; Kylie had been dead that long. I had not been this far into her room since the day we closed it, not long after her funeral, after Estelle, tears running silently down her long brown face, had cleaned it for the last time and closed the door. Sometimes I opened her door and looked in, and I knew that Clay did, too, but I did not think that anyone came all the way into it. I would ask Estelle. She must have simply missed the little T-shirt the last day that she cleaned.

I looked out at the ocean then. Kylie had died in sight of her room, in sight of our house, when her small Sunfish with the red sail had flipped in heavy surf after an August thunderstorm and the stout little boom had hit her a stunning blow to the temple, and she had gone down and not come up again, at least not until long after. None of the children she was with had seen it happen, or none would ever admit to seeing it, but then they were only ten or so, as she was, and all had been forbidden to take their boats into that stormy water, as she had been. They had been playing in a neighbor's yard after a birthday party, only three houses up the beach, and had slipped off and taken their little Sunfishes out while the adults were having their own lunch on the patio, behind heavy plantings. I was off the island that day, at the dentist in Charleston. I never blamed Marjorie Bell or her housekeeper; Kylie had never disobeyed us before in regard to the Sunfish, nor had the other children disobeyed their parents. Island children have water safety drilled into their heads almost before they can toddle. We will never know what started it all, what child dared the others, who first leaped to the dare. Kylie, in all likelihood. It doesn't matter. The children were so traumatized by it that more than one of them gave away their Sunfish, or let their parents sell them, and one family moved away from the island.

I have always wondered if she looked up just before the boom hit and saw the dazzle of summer light on her window, saw the roof and trees of home.

I wondered now what she would be wearing if she had lived, what I would be picking up from her floor. What color it would be, what size. What its smell would be, the smell of Kylie Venable at nearly sixteen.

I used to have the fancy that I wore Kylie inside me, just under my skin, that I was a suit that fit exactly the being who was my child, and that she was the structure that filled out the skin that was me. Since that day there has been a terrible, frail lightness, a cold hollowness, a sort of whistling chill inside me where Kylie used to be. It makes me feel terribly vulnerable, as if a high wind could simply whirl me away. As if there is not enough substance inside me to anchor me to earth. Usually the pain of her loss is dulled enough now so that it is more a profound heaviness, a leaden darkness, a wearable miasma that is as much a part of me as the joy of her used to be. But sometimes that first agony comes spiking back, as it did now. I sank to the floor, the T-shirt still pressed to my face, feeling the killing fire flare and spring and rage, feeling the great shriek, the scream of outrage and anguish, start in my throat, feeling the scalding tears gather and press at my eyes. I opened my mouth to let it out, but nothing happened, nothing came. It never did. I screamed silently into her T-shirt, my face contorted, my throat corded and choked with the need for her, but no sound would come. I could not cry for my child. I never had, not even when they came to tell me, not even when I watched her go down into the earth of the Lowcountry, riding in a fine carriage of mahogany and bronze.

I felt a hand on my shoulder and heard Clay's voice.

"Caro, don't. You promised you wouldn't. Come on with me now, and take a shower and get dressed, and we'll have some coffee on the veranda before we go. I'll take you by the guest house; we'll put the flowers around together. They're beautiful, by the way. Those old roses, they really have lasted, haven't they?"

I did not move to get up, and after a moment I felt his hands under my elbows, and he lifted me up.

"You need to work, baby," he said. "That's the thing that will help; that's what's helped me most. Real work. This is your job now, helping with the new families, you need to come and do your job."

I looked at him then.

"She was my job," I said.

But I did not say it aloud.

2

When I was sixteen, the son of the local undertaker in the little town where we lived asked me out on a date, and my stepfather promptly called the chief of police, who was in Rotary with him, and had the chief dispatch a deputy to follow us everywhere we went. My friend Lottie Funderburke, who is a painter and lives on the island (but *not*, she is quick to point out, in the Plantation) thinks this is the funniest thing she has ever heard. She may be right. It was not, however, very funny then, at least not to me. The deputy was a gangling, slouching eighteen-year-old named Honey Cato, low of hairline and waist and thick of shoulder and head, and he had been whistling and making stunningly suggestive and stupid remarks to me since we moved to Moncks Corner, when I was twelve. I had told my mother and stepfather about it, but my stepfather said only, "If you didn't run around with your behind hanging out of those shorts, he wouldn't do it. A lady doesn't get herself whistled at on the street."

I didn't mention Honey to him again. In the first place, I didn't intend to give up my short shorts. Every other teenager in Moncks Corner rolled her shorts as high as they would go, and I had a horror, then, of being different. In the second place, my stepfather never would have understood about Honey Cato or boys—I purposely do not use the word "men"—like him. Honey would have whistled and made his crude remarks to Helen Keller, or a nun. It was his duty as a South Carolina good ol' boy. My stepfather was from Ohio. The difference was measured in far more than miles.

"So what exactly did your stepfather have against undertakers?" Lottie said when I first told her. "I would think an undertaker made more money than a lot of people in Monkey House, or wherever it was you lived. And you could say it's a profession. Of sorts."

"Well, you know. An undertaker," I said vaguely. "And then there was always this rumor that Sonny's father ran some kind of illegal operation out of the funeral home. Running liquor or something; I never did know what. Whatever it was, my stepfather didn't think it suited the daughter of the town lawyer. Even if he did get his law degree mail order."

"Where was your mother on this?" Lottie said.

"Well, she usually sided with him. She'd worked too hard to land him, see; she wasn't going to screw that up by sticking up for me. And I guess I was pretty hard to handle at that age. Mainly, she didn't think dating the undertaker's son suited a future Miss South Carolina."

"Oh, Christ, that's right, somebody said you'd been in the Miss South Carolina contest. I thought at the time they had to be lying. Not that you aren't right presentable, when you're all cleaned up, but you don't have a dimple to your name, and you'd look like a first-class 'ho' with blond hair. I wouldn't have thought you'd had a chance."

"I didn't. Especially after I dropped my baton."

"Don't tell me. You twirled a flaming baton to 'Age of Aquarius.'"

"Yep. Only it was 'Yellow Submarine.' I dropped the sucker before the first five bars were over."

"God, Caro, couldn't you have sung the National Anthem or something?"

"Well, I did a tap dance while I was twirling. I never could sing. It didn't matter what you did, if your boobs stuck out and you could walk in high heels. I had pretty good boobs then."

"That's the most un-Lowcountry thing I ever heard," Lottie howled happily.

"I keep telling you, I'm not from the Low-country," I said. "I'm a million miles removed from the Lowcountry. I'm no more a Lowcountry native than you are. Everybody just thinks I am because Clay has made a religion of it. It's almost as strange to me right now as it was the first time I laid eyes on it. I get invited to parties South of Broad about as often as you do. It's Clay who goes to those."

Lottie is originally from West Virginia and is what Clay calls good old country stock. What he means is white trash. Hillbilly. She is nearly six feet tall, walks like she is plowing a mule, has shoulders as wide as a linebacker's and dishwater-blond hair chopped impatiently so that it will not hang in her eyes. Her skin is permanently the red-brown of old cordovan shoes, from the sun. Her voice is nasal and flat, her eyes are the faded blue of old denim, and her hands are the size and shape of coal scuttles. She is also an artist of stunning originality and talent. Her enormous, flaming primitive oils hang in galleries and museums all up and down the East Coast. Her strange, soaring iron sculptures are in collections all over America. She gets upwards of fifteen thousand dollars for her small paintings and I don't even know how much for the larger ones. She works so slowly that she rarely does more than three or four pieces a year, will not accept commissions, and still lives in the ramshackle former filling station that she moved into thirty years ago, on an undistinguished two-lane blacktop road that threads the middle of the island. My grandfather, who was intrigued with her gift and her grit, rented it to her some years before he deeded the island to Clay and stipulated that she be allowed to live there as long as she liked. Clay thinks that she was more to my grandfather than tenant, though she was only twenty when she first came to the island, and he may be right. Lottie sleeps with whomever she pleases and does not try to conceal the fact, though with no one from the Plantation, that I know of. Her gentlemen callers all seem to be from off-island, to judge from the tags on their automobiles. She built her studio herself, from random ends of lumber, and it looks like a chicken house on the outside and is glorious inside with light and space. When I asked her, when we first met, why she chose Peacock's Island, she said, "The light," and I knew what she meant. I soon found that I usually did, about everything. She is my best friend. Clay cannot stand her, nor she him. Both of them have finally worked around to a point where they simply do not discuss the other anymore.

But there are other ways of showing enmity, and Lottie's disgusted snorts and Clay's still, cold silences get their messages across. I know he thinks she is sluttish, slovenly, an eyesore in Eden, and worst of all in his primer of sins, lazy. He is probably right on all counts. She thinks he is cold, calculating, far fonder of money than me, and worst of all in her primer, a despoiler of the wild. I never thought of Clay as any of those things, not the Clay I met and fell in love with and married. But so many of the things I never thought have come about, and so many that I did think have failed to do so, that I sometimes trust my own judgment last after anyone else's. It's easier to think Lottie is wrong about Clay, though I have to admit that she has seldom been about other things.

But we all have our blind spots, don't we? Oh, yes, we do. And I figure Clay is hers. Just as he is mine.

Lord, the day I first met him! He will never seem more beautiful, more whole, more hypnotically charming than he did on the day his friend Hayes Howland brought him over to the island to meet my grandfather. Poor Clay; he would hate that if I told him, hate that in my mind, he reached his ascendancy before I even knew him well. But I never have told him, and I never will.

It was in July, just at dusk. It had been a strange, unsettled day of running cloud shadow; little winds that started up and doubled back upon themselves and then died; sudden warm, hard spatters of rain that left the earth and air steaming and shimmering. Later we would surely have a storm. I was visiting from Columbia, where we had just moved, and had brought my watercolors and easel with me and was sitting on the dock at the end of the long, dilapidated wooden walkway that led from the marsh house to the tidal creek, where my grandfather kept his Boston Whaler and his canoe, trying to catch the spectral light. I was between my freshman and sophomore years at Converse, just tasting my gift. The dazzle to the west, where the sun hung red, preparing to flame and die behind the long sweep of emerald marsh, was overwhelming; I could not look into it without shading my eyes.

I heard them before I saw them, heard the slow putt-putt of an outboard lost somewhere in the rose-gold dazzle, and turned to look toward it, squinting. The boat came out of the light, its engine silent, and loomed up almost at the dock where I sat. It bumped the rubber fender and wallowed to rest. Hayes got out first; I knew him slightly, from other visits he had made to my grandfather during my own summer stays, but I stared anyway. He was resplendent in a white linen suit, with the light gilding his red head, and looked far better in both than he usually did. Hayes is substantial and sometimes engaging, but he is not handsome.

"Hi, Caro," he said. "I've brought y'all a visitor."

"Hi, Hayes," I said back. "That's nice."

A tall young man got out behind him. He

wore white linen also, but you noticed the man and not the suit, instead of just the opposite, as with Hayes; it might have been his everyday garb, it seemed so right and easy on his long body. A white linen suit in an Edwardian cut, and white buck shoes. He had a great, flowing blue satin tie. It should have looked foppish but did not. The light made an old-gold helmet of his hair and slanted into his eyes so that they flamed out of his narrow, tanned face, an impossible, firestruck blue. He smiled and the spindrift light glanced on white teeth. He had a flower in his buttonhole, a small, tight, old-fashioned pink sweetheart rose, and in his long, brown hands he held a bouquet of them.

"This is Clay Venable," Hayes said. "We roomed together a couple of years at Virginia. He's been a fool over the Lowcountry since the first time I brought him home with me, and I've finally talked him into moving to Charleston. He wanted to see some real, unspoiled marshland and I thought of your granddaddy's place right off the bat. I guess you can't get much more unspoiled than Peacock's. This is Caroline Aubrey, Clay. Mr. Aubrey's granddaughter. Did I tell you she was an *artiste* as well as a beauty?"

"Miss Aubrey," Clay Venable said, holding the bouquet out to me. "I thought you might like these. We've been at a fancy garden party in Charleston and I stole them off a bush on the way out. Better take them before my hostess comes after me in a motorboat."

"Her gardener, you mean," Hayes said lazily. "In a cigarette boat. We've been at Marguerite MacMillan's, Caro. I thought if Clay was going to be a Lowcountry boy he might as well start out in the virtual holy of holies. Little did I know he'd be filching roses out of her garden before the afternoon was over. Can't take him anywhere."

I put out my hands and took the roses, but I did not speak. I could not seem to look away from this tall, radiant being clothed in white and molten rose-gold light. I remember thinking that his voice did not really sound Southern; it was deep and soft and slow, but somehow crisp. There was something else about him that did not seem native, either, though I could not have said what it was then, and still cannot. Clay was born on a farm in Indiana, but by that time he had so submerged himself into the fabric of the Lowcountry that there were few traces of the rural Indiana scholarship boy left, and of course by now there are none at all. Clay is more a denizen of this coast now than someone generations born to it.

"You gon' ask us in, Caro?" Hayes said, and my face flamed at the amusement in his voice.

"Yes. Please come on up to the house. Grand-daddy's having his sundowner. He'll love some company. He's always saying he'll never make a drinker out of me. Well, not that he'd really want to, of course . . . thank you," I said, remembering the roses, and caught my platform heel in a crack of the dock, and lurched to one knee. The roses sailed over the weathered cypress railing and disappeared into the sea of reeds and black water.

There was a small silence, and then Clay Venable said, "A simple 'no thank you' would have sufficed."

I froze in mortification, and then the amusement under his words penetrated my fog of misery, and I began to laugh. He laughed, too, and helped me to my feet, and Hayes laughed, and after that it was all right. By the time he had been introduced to my grandfather and the bourbon had been poured, and we sat on the screened porch looking out over the silvering marsh, Clay Venable was as much one of us as Hayes or any of the other young men from Charleston and the islands that my grandfather was accustomed to greeting when he encountered them hunting or fishing or canoeing on the wild tidal creeks and inlets of Peacock's Island. It was common knowledge that the island belonged to my grandfather, but it was also common knowledge that he did not mind the occasional sporting visitor, so long as they did not disturb the pristine tranquillity of the marsh and woods. Indeed, he had known most of them since they were small boys and came to Peacock's with their fathers.

Dark fell, the sudden thick, furry blackness of the Lowcountry marshes, unpricked by any lights at all except the kerosene lantern that sat on a table on the porch and the citronella candles I had lit. The house had electricity, but my grandfather disliked it, and often went days without lighting an electric lamp. He had no such qualms about other appliances, and happily used his small, battered refrigerator and the old stove and even the jerry-rigged washer and dryer that sat on the other end of the porch. But he loved lamplight, and it is what I use mostly when I am at the house even to this day. I find that it calls him back to me as little else does.

I don't remember much of what we talked about: Hayes's job at one of the ubiquitous law firms on Broad Street, I think, and how restless he felt there, closed away from the beaches and marshes and rivers and creeks where so many Charleston boys spent great chunks of their boyhood. My studies at Converse, and the painting that I was doing on the island that summer. The herd of wild ponies that had chomped and stomped its stolid way around the back part of the island since I could remember. The monster bull gator my grandfather had seen the day before, and the panther that he swore he had heard scream in the deep blacknesses of several past nights. The drought that was decimating the coast that summer and how badly my grandfather's year-round property in McClellanville was suffering from it. I did not think he was unduly upset about the drought in McClellanville; since my grandmother had died several years before, he had spent more and more of his time at the marsh house, and left it now largely to look after his banking business in Charleston, or to make a run to a hardware or grocery store. He had even, the winter before, put in a big cast-iron stove in the bedroom where he slept, so that, with the huge stone fireplace in the living area, the house was habitable through the brief, icy spasms of the Lowcountry winter.

"Don't you get lonesome out here?" I asked him once.

"No," he had said in honest surprise. "Why would I? Everywhere you look something alive is slapping the water or shiverin' the bushes. And when you run out of the live ones, there's plenty of not-so-live ones, let me tell you. Many's the night I've passed in the company of somebody who left these parts a hundred, two hundred years ago."

I knew that he was teasing me, but only with the top part of my mind. The old, bottom part nodded sagely: Yes. I can see that that's so. I have always felt that there were many levels of beings on Peacock's Island, many more souls than currently wear flesh. It is not, on the main, a bad feeling at all.

Finally, that night, we got around to Clay Venable. I knew that my grandfather was as curious about him as I was, but his natural, grave good manners decreed that he make Clay feel at home before asking him to share much of himself.

"I don't think you're native to these parts, but you seem to have taken to them right well," he said mildly to Clay after a while. They were on their second or third leisurely bourbons, and off in the trees the katydids and marsh peepers had started their evening chorus. Overhead the huge, swollen stars flowered in the hot night.

"No, I come from hill country, in Indiana, around Bloomington. I'd never seen the ocean till I got to Virginia and came home with Hayes. My folks were red-dirt farmers, poor as church mice. After that . . . well, I guess I was sunk. It was like I was born in the wrong place and only just found the right one when I got down here. There's never been any other part of the world I wanted to see, not after I saw this. I went back to Indiana after I graduated and worked at an insurance agency until I could save enough to pay off my student loans and get a little ahead. Then I headed down here like an arrow from a bow. I don't know yet what I'll be doing, but I'll be doing it here. I do know that."

It was 1972, and a looming recession threatened hundreds of thousands of workers across
the country. Small businesses were closing; larger
ones were cutting back or at the very least freezing their hiring. Around Charleston, the strictures
of an energy crisis and unavailable gasoline
slowed the flood of tourist dollars to a trickle. It
was a disaster of a year, all told, and yet Clay
Venable sat on my grandfather's porch and spoke
calmly of a limitless future in the Lowcountry
that was an assured fact, a done deal. I believed
him absolutely, even before Hayes Howland
laughed ruefully and said, "Lest you think he's
blowing smoke rings, at least three guys at Marguerite MacMillan's as much as offered him jobs
tonight. I don't know what it is he's got, but
whatever, this old boy's gon' do all right for himself down here."

My grandfather laughed. It was a friendly
sound, a laugh offered by one equal to another.

"What would you do if you had your
druthers, Clay?" he said.

Clay did not hesitate.

"I'd take all this"—and he gestured around
him at the marsh and the night—"and I'd make
sure that nothing ever changed the basic . . . nature
of it, the sense of it, like it is now . . . and I'd make
it available to a few very special people who
would see it for what it is, and love it for that, and
want to live here. And no one else, ever."

Hayes snorted, and my grandfather said, "You mean . . . a subdivision, or something? Develop it?"

His voice was still mild and interested, but I knew how he felt about the marshes and the islands of the Lowcountry. My heart sank. I might have known Clay Venable was too perfect; there had to be something wrong. . . .

"What I have in mind is about as far from a subdivision development as it's possible to get," Clay said, looking intently at my grandfather. In the lamplight his blue eyes burned. "In my . . . place . . . the land and the water and the wildlife would come first, people second. Not a house, not a hedge, not a fireplug would go up that did not blend so perfectly into the wild that you had to look twice to see it. Not an alligator would be relocated; not a raccoon or a deer would be run out. I would never forget who was here first. And I would have no one in my place who did not feel the same way."

We were silent for a moment.

"Never heard of a place like that," my grandfather said finally.

"There's never been one," Clay Venable said. "But there will be, and it will be mine, and it will be somewhere on this coast. I know that."

"Take more money than God's got," my grandfather said.

"I can get the money," Clay said. "If I can get

the right piece of land, I can get the money."

"Don't you have it backwards?" My grandfather chuckled. "How you gon' get a chunk of prime oceanfront or marshland without any money? Not much of that left. And another thing . . . any empty land I can think of around here hasn't got mainland access. Not an automobile bridge between here and Hilton Head. How you gon' find this wild land with a bridge already built?"

"Because I've got a master plan," Clay Venable said. "It's as detailed and complete as it's humanly possible to make it. I've been working on it for three years, ever since I got out of college. Since before then, really; since the second or third time I came down here with Hayes. I've gotten two or three of the best young architects on the East Coast to work on it, strictly gratis, and city planners and environmental specialists and lawyers, and I've gotten the Sierra Club people and the Coastal Conservancy folks to put in their two cents' worth, and the U.S. Corps of Engineers. None of them would take a penny. It will work. It's a beautiful plan. It's a beautiful concept. It's ready to go. I am absolutely sure that if the right people see it, the land and the bridge and then the money will follow. I *know* that. I don't mind working at . . . whatever . . . for a few years until I can get it going."

My grandfather took a long swig of bourbon and rattled the ice in his glass.

"Where is this plan?" he said.

"In a bank vault back in Charleston. And there's a copy at my bank at home in Bloomington."

"Who's seen it?"

"Nobody yet. Except the guys who've worked on it, of course, and they're sworn to secrecy. They'll be partners, so I don't worry about them letting it out. Outside of them, nobody."

"I'll say," Hayes said. "Not only have I not seen it, I haven't heard the first word about it. Jesus, Clay . . . I had no idea! Why didn't you tell me, show it to me? I can help you with it. . . ."

"It's not time yet. When it's time, I will. I wasn't hiding it from you, Hayes."

"I'd like to see a thing like that," my grandfather said, as if to no one in particular. "I reckon that would be something to see."

"I could bring it out tomorrow or one day soon," Clay Venable said, and smiled, a swift, transforming smile that I had not seen before. My breath stopped.

"Why don't you do that?" my grandfather said.

"Me, too?" Hayes said.

"Not yet. But soon. I promise," Clay said.

"Well, I like that! I take you to the party of

the year at the numero uno hostess's house in Charleston, and introduce you to the movers and shakers, most of whom are falling all over themselves to offer you jobs, and you won't let me see your . . . village Eden," Hayes groused. I thought that he was only partly kidding.

"You'll see it before anybody in Charleston," Clay said, giving Hayes the smile. Hayes nodded, apparently satisfied.

"Would you like to see it, Miss Aubrey?" Clay said to me.

I jumped. He had not really looked at me since we had settled ourselves on the porch. His attention had been bent upon my grandfather.

"Very much," I said, and my unused voice cracked, and I cleared my throat. "I would very much like to see it. If you can do all that and still keep the land . . . untouched, as you say . . . it would be something to see indeed."

I realized that I sounded adversarial, and started to amend my words, and then did not. I did not think what he proposed was possible, and I did not want to see his master plan and find that, after all, it was an ordinary subdivision that would clump on stucco feet through the rich, fragile coastal land and leave little of it intact.

"Then maybe tomorrow?"

"Tomorrow would be fine," my grandfather said. "You boys come out about midafternoon and I'll take you out in the Whaler. Let Clay run

Alligator Alley and see if he still wants to save the gators."

"I'm a working man myself," Hayes said, "but I know Clay would enjoy Alligator Alley. What a great idea, Mr. Aubrey. That's just what you all should do. Only why not take the canoe? See 'em better that way."

He came at three the next afternoon in the same outboard they had brought yesterday. I recognized it now as the one Shem Cutler, over on the tip of Edisto, sometimes rented out to hunters or crabbers. I was not waiting for him on the dock—I would have died first—but I was watching from the porch of the house. It is set on stilts, a former hunting shack grown large and rambling over the years, and you can see a long way from it. He was not nearly as proficient as Hayes with the boat. I could see that he was coming in too fast, and he hit the dock with a resounding smack, bounced off it, and had to balance himself with an oar when the resulting watery circles rocked him crazily. I smiled to myself. Ever since he had spoken about his impossibly idyllic Low-country community I had felt vaguely and sullenly resentful of him, the dazzle of his initial appearance safely dissipated. This place, this island, belonged to us, my grandfather and me, and the small settlement of Gullah Negroes over in Dayclear, at the other end of the island, and the ponies and the gators and the ghosts and all the other beings, quick and dead, who had their roots here. Who was this man, this upstart, land-bound Yankee, to come down here and tell us that he was going to transform it?

I was obscurely pleased to see, as he walked carefully down the listing boardwalk toward the house, that in the full afternoon light he did not look golden at all, not impossibly slim and tipped with flame. His hair was merely brown, the silver-brown of a mouse's fur, almost the same shade as his face and hands, and he was more skinny than slender. I could see, too, now that he wore an ordinary work shirt with the sleeves rolled up and not a suit of radiant white linen, that the tan stopped at his wrists, as a farmer's did, and that his legs, in a pair of faded cut-off jeans, were the greenish-white of a fish's belly.

"The mosquitoes are going to eat him alive before we've left the dock," I said with satisfaction to my grandfather, who stood beside me, and was surprised at myself. Where was this venom coming from? I had been ready to follow him to hell or Bloomington when I first met him.

"Young feller got under your skin, has he?" My grandfather grinned, and I had to grin back. It had long been a joke between us that as soon as a young man showed substantial interest in me, my own evaporated like dew in the sun. A fair number of them had, over the years; I had my mother's vivid darkness and my unremembered father's fine-bladed features, and knew that they all added up, somehow, to more than they should have. I was not particularly vain of my looks, Miss South Carolina notwithstanding; good looks had not, after all, gotten my mother very much except a young husband who left us when I was four and another who was, to me, as remote as a photograph. In my experience, a man who came in the front door was that much closer to the back one. I solved that by leaving first. I could see that I was doing it again. My grandfather was right. Clay Venable had gotten further under my hide in a shorter time than anyone ever had.

Just the same I was glad that he had proved to be an ordinary, skinny, milk-pale Yankee after all. I had nothing to fear from him. And then he raised his head and saw us on the porch and smiled, and the ordinariness vanished like smoke in the wind, like a disguise that he had cast off. My heart flopped, fishlike, in my chest.

"Shit," I whispered.

My grandfather laughed aloud.

Peacock's Island is a small barrier island in St. Helena's Sound, fitting like a loose stopper in the bottleneck formed by Edisto and Otter Islands to the north, Harbor and Hunting Islands to the south, and the shallow bay created by the conflu-

ence of the Ashepoo, Combahee, and Edisto
Rivers to the west. It lies in a great, 350,000-acre
wilderness called the Ace Basin, an estuarine
ecosystem so rich in layers upon layers of life, so
fertile and green and secret, so very old, so totally
set apart from the world of men and machines—
and yet so close among them—that there is literally no other place remotely like it on earth.
Other areas in the Lowcountry that were once
this pristine have irrevocably gone over to man
now, and cannot be reclaimed, but a combination
of private and public agencies have set their teeth
and shoulders to safeguard the Ace, and now
protect sizable swatches of it.

The bottom 91,000 acres of the Ace Basin are
tidal marsh and barrier islands, scalloped by
dunes older than time itself and thick with unique
maritime forests of live oaks, loblolly and slash
pines, palmettos, magnolia, and cedar. It is possible, on Peacock's and the other barrier islands of
the Lowcountry, to encounter, in a day's walk or
canoe trip: bald eagles, ospreys, wood storks, an
amazing variety of ducks and herons, wading
birds and shorebirds and songbirds. My grandfather said that someone had counted sixty-nine
bird species in the great arc of the Ace. You can
also see—or rather, perhaps, see tracks of—
another eighty-three species of reptiles and
amphibians, including a fearsome array of watersnakes and the big, thick, brutish rattlers of the

Lowcountry, and, of course, the ever-present ranks of alligators. I have seen, during my summers there, whitetail deer, bobcats, foxes, rabbits, otters, raccoons, wild pigs, possums, and some fleeting things that I will never be able to name. The ponies are an aberration; no one is quite sure where they came from, but my grandfather thinks they are offspring of the tough little marsh tackies that used to dot the interior of Hilton Head and the larger Sea Islands, themselves offspring, perhaps, of the ponies brought by the English planters to work the lowland fields. He believes that the first of the Gullah settlers over in Dayclear brought the sire and dam of this herd with them, and since no one is sure when that was, the provenance of the ponies is as misty and unsubstantial as the marshes themselves. The Gullahs can only tell you that the ponies have been there "always."

The panther that my grandfather swore he heard in the nights should not, by rights, have been on the island at all, since no one has seen or heard of a panther in the Ace Basin since time out of mind. I certainly never saw one. But I believe there was one in my grandfather's time, for in that vast, succoring basin, one-third light, one-third water, and only one-third substantial earth, life in all its abundance has evolved all but unseen for millions of years, infused twice a day by the great salt breath of the tides, and that panther was as surely a child of the Southern moon as the blue crabs and the dolphins and the eagles and the men who came so late to it. I believe that. I do.

It was out into all this that we took Clay Venable, my grandfather Aubrey and I, on a July afternoon in 1972, and none of us came back unchanged. You often don't, in the Lowcountry.

Alligator Alley is a straight stretch of Wappinaw Creek, one of the secret black-water creeks and inlets that cut the island like watersnakes. From my grandfather's dock you could reach it, in the Whaler, in a few minutes. In the canoe, however, it took about a half hour, and we passed that in near silence, broken only by the slapping of hands on mosquito-bitten flesh. They were mostly Clay Venable's hands, and his flesh. I had slathered myself with Cutter's before I left the house, and my grandfather, for some reason, never seemed to be bitten. Finally, after watching Clay endure the ordeal in silence, I relented, and reached into my pocket and brought out the tube of repellent, and passed it up to him. I sat in the rear of the big canoe, and my grandfather in front. Clay was our middleman.

He took the ointment from me and turned and gave me a level, serious look from the pale blue eyes.

"I forgot I had it," I found myself saying

defensively, and felt myself flush red. I would be all right, I thought, as long as I did not get the full bore of those eyes.

Clay still did not speak, but I noticed that his head was always in slight motion, turning this way and that, as he looked at everything we passed. An osprey took off from a nest on a dead bald cypress at the edge of the creek and Clay tracked it. An anhinga dropped from a low-lying limb of a live oak when we turned from a broader stretch of creek into Alligator Alley and he noted it. He marked and measured a turtle sunning on a reed-grown bank; the flash of a whitetail far off in a lightly forested hummock; the brilliant green explosions of cinnamon and resurrection ferns; the vast, rippling green seas of cordgrass and the great, primeval towers of the bald cypresses, dwarfing all else. I had the notion that he was somehow photographing all of it, so that he would never lose it, but could replay it at will on the screen of his mind whenever he chose.

I learned later that this was not far from true. Something within him, some sort of infinite receptacle, must fix, store, catalogue, file away. It was my first experience of his disconcerting, now-legendary intensity. When he brought it into play, it precluded whimsy, idleness, pensiveness, even the sort of comfortable, unfocused dreaminess in which I and most other people pass a good deal of our time. He can suspend this thing, whatever it is, when he wants and needs to, and often does, but I know by now that it costs him something; that the effort is to drift on the moment, not to focus and record it, as it is with most of us. That, of course, accounted for the impact of those extraordinary eyes, and the force of the smile was the sheer relief and exuberance you felt when he freed you of it. The smile was his gift to you. All this I saw in one great leap that afternoon, from watching the back of Clay Venable's head. The knowledge did not sit comfortably on my heart.

The banks rise higher along Alligator Alley, as flat on top as manmade dams, overgrown with reeds and slicked with mud. Over them, far away, you can see the tops of the upland forests, but in the near and middle distance there is nothing but reeds and sky and creekbanks. Stumps and broken logs punctuate the reeds and grasses on the banks and in the edge of the black water, and more stumps protrude from the water at intervals. It looks for all the world as if heavy logging had gone on along this creek. It is not a particularly beautiful or interesting stretch of water, and the sun beats relentlessly onto the tops of heads and shoulders, and if you are in a canoe, your shoulder muscles have, by now, started to sting from the paddling. In the canoe, you sit very low in the dark water. The landscape is completely bounded by the rough, looming sunblasted creekbanks.

I waited.

To me, it is always like those drawings you used to see as a child, the one where you are supposed to find the animals in the intricately drawn mass of a forest. At first you see nothing, and then they begin to appear: a lion here, a leopard there, the ruffle of a bird's wing in a tree, the smirking face of a lamb in the tall grass. That is how the alligators come. At first you see nothing but reeds and grass and broken stumps, and then you see, as if by magic, the great, terrible, knobbed head of a gator, and then the whole gator, and then another, and then another. Afterward, you can never understand why you did not see them at once.

So the alligators of Alligator Alley came. I heard Clay's breath draw in slightly as the first gator appeared on the bank above us, as if in a developing photograph. After that he was silent, but his head tracked them as they materialized, one after another. Eventually, there were eighteen or twenty of them in sight. I can never be sure I have counted them correctly.

I have seen them every summer now since I was seven or eight, and they never fail to stop my breath and chill my heart. I know all the comforting folk wisdom about them: that they cannot bite under water, that they seldom attack humans except in self-defense, that they do not go after things larger than themselves. Certainly not a boat. I know that if you sit quietly in your craft, or stand quietly, they will disregard you, and that they have poor peripheral vision, so that if you stay to their sides you are presumably safe. Still they make the hair on my nape and arms rise and something deep within me goes into an ancient and feral crouch. They are simply such sinister, implacable things, knobbed and armored like dragons out of nightmares, seemingly formed of mud and stone and obsidian and malachite, the color of stagnant water, the color of muddy death. And as for their reputed harmlessness, every Lowcountry native has a story about the cat, the dog, the small child snatched from the bank by those incredible scalloped jaws. I have seen myself, on the island, the nubs of an occasional hand or foot said to have been taken by a gator. And down on Hilton Head, in the big, developed resort plantations, the shelf life of poodles and shih tzus is not long at all, not in the prized lagoon homesites.

My grandfather taught me early to be absolutely silent when we passed the alligators, and so I always am. They are not always in precisely the same place, but they do seem always to be in a cluster, and so it does not take long to pass them. These today did not move much, except to lift their huge heads lazily as we drifted past, and once or twice I heard the dry swish as a thick tail stirred in the reeds. They are usually on the bank this time of day, in the summer, taking the sun now that some of the heat has gone out of it; earlier, they would have been in the water, only their knobbed yellow-rimmed eyes showing, so that they seemed to be submerged logs, or the knots of limbs and roots. Then you cannot see their size, but when they are on the bank, of course, you can. These were big ones, mostly. I'd say they ran from about ten feet to thirteen or fourteen. One or two smaller ones, adolescent children, lay curled close to their mothers, blending into the grayish mud. If there were very small ones they would be out of sight near the nests. Even with their fearsome bulk, they are misleadingly innocent when they bask lazily like this. They look as if they could not move except ponderously, dragging that scaled hugeness on short, bent legs. But they can move like lightning, can be down a bank and into the water in an eye flicker. I have seen that. I usually hold my breath until we are past them.

We almost were when one of the submerged logs in the water began to move, to glide lazily after the canoe. I drew in my breath and did not let it out again. My grandfather looked back at Clay and me and shook his head almost imperceptibly. I knew that he meant us to be still and silent. The alligator did not lift its head, but the eyes followed us, closing on the canoe, and my grandfather kept up his steady, leisurely paddling. I followed suit, but my shoulder muscles cried out to dig in, to paddle faster, to stroke with all my might. I did not look to the right or left, except once, and then I could see the gator's head almost abreast of me in the rear of the canoe. I looked back slightly farther. Just under the sun-dappled surface of the water I could see its body. It seemed, in the shifting green-blackness, to go on forever. It was like looking down into a bright summer sea and seeing, under its glittering sur-face, the long, dark, death's shape of a sub-marine, ghosting silently beside you. I shut my eyes and paddled.

After what seemed an eternity my grand-father said, in his normal voice, "I heard there was a big one around this year. Shem Cutler saw him early one morning, taking a raccoon. Said he looked like a damned dinosaur. Shem reckoned he might be eighteen or twenty feet. I hear they've been losing pigs and a hound or two over at Day-clear, too. I wouldn't be surprised if it ain't old Levi."

"Levi?" I croaked, finally looking back. The gator had apparently lost interest in us and turned toward the bank. He did not come out of the water, though. In another stroke or two we were past the convocation of gators.

"The Gullahs tell about a giant alligator that's always been around these parts, bigger than any of the others by a country mile. They say you can hear him bellowing in the nights as far as Edisto. Every time a piglet or a dog or a chicken goes missing, they say that it's Levi. Nobody much sees him and they say you can't catch him. Gators do live to be right old, but if the tales are true, this old boy would be near about two hundred years old. *If* that was Levi, you kids have got something to tell your grandchildren. Figuratively speaking, of course."

And he grinned at Clay and me. I felt the red flood into my face again.

"Can all that be true?" Clay said with great interest.

"Naw, I don't reckon so," my grandfather said. "Be something for Ripley if it was. All the same, the old tales don't die out. And that was one big mother of a gator. You just don't ever know, in the Lowcountry."

I felt something on the back of my neck that was like a cold little wind under the heavy sun.

"Who named him Levi?" I said.

"I've always heard that one of the first preachers at the little pray house in Dayclear did, after he was supposed to have gone off with three children in one year. It's short for Leviathan."

I felt the little wind again, stronger this time.

"God, that's marvelous," Clay breathed. "That's just marvelous."

He looked back, his face rapt and blinded. I thought at first he was looking at me, but then I saw that he was looking past me to the big gator as it lay submerged, just off the receding bank behind us. My skin prickled.

"Marvelous isn't exactly the term I would have used," I said.

But, "I reckon that's just what it is, Clay," my grandfather said, and I felt obscurely rebuffed.

We got back to the dock just as the sun was disappearing in a conflagration of rose red across the forest on the mainland to the west. The water of the creek was dappled red and gold, and the sweet, damp thickness that twilight brought seemed to drop down over us like a shawl. I have always felt that you wear the air of the Lowcountry somehow. It is not thin like other air.

Clay thanked my grandfather seriously and politely for the afternoon, but he made no move to go. He did not even look at his borrowed boat, bobbing in the settling wake our own had made. He simply stood there, tall in the falling darkness, his mouse-fur hair in his eyes, the angry splotches made by the mosquitoes glowing on his arms and legs. I knew they must itch fiercely by now, but he made no move to scratch them. A new squadron came in from the marshes, level and low, and sang around our heads. I shook mine angrily. Mosquitoes make me childish and stupid.

My grandfather swatted the back of his neck and I looked at him in surprise. I did not think mosquitoes bit him. He did not look at me.

"Let's get on in the house before they take us off clear over to Edisto," he said. "Clay, you need to put something on those bites, and then I think you ought to have some supper with us and forget about going back till the morning. We've got a guest room, such as it is, and I got a mess of crabs this morning. Cleaned 'em before you came. Some beer on ice, too. You don't want to try to feel your way back over to Edisto in the dark. Levi might get you if Shem doesn't."

I waited for Clay to demur, to say that he wouldn't think of putting us out, but he did not.

"I'd really like that," he said. "There's an awful lot I want to ask you about the island. Both of you," he said, looking at me as if remembering I was there.

"Granddaddy's the historian," I said shortly, and went to take a shower and anoint my own bites. I was annoyed with Clay Venable; he had said hardly a word to me all day. I would, I thought, have supper with them and then excuse myself and go to bed. Let them sit on the porch and gab the night away. . . .

But I pulled out a new pair of flowered bell bottoms and a pale pink T-shirt that I knew would look dramatic against my tan, and sprayed on some of the Ma Griffe my stepfather had given me for Christmas. I knew that my mother had told him what to get, but still, I liked the cologne. It smelled both sweet and tart, like summer itself. I twisted my heavy hair up off my neck and pinned it on the top of my head. The day's humidity had turned it to wiry frizz, and if I had let it fall loose it would have stood out like an afro. For not the first time, I considered ironing it and then shook my head angrily at myself and simply twisted it up and skewered it with hairpins. I did put on some lipstick, though, something I almost never did on the island.

"You look pretty," my grandfather said when I came out onto the porch. He and Clay were sitting in the old wooden rocking chairs, their feet up on the rail, drinking beers. Clay smiled at me.

"You really do," he said. "Like a Spanish painting, with your hair up. Velázquez or somebody. One of the infantas."

"You like art?" I said. "As well as alligators?"

"I like lots of things," he said, "art among them. I had four years of art appreciation at Virginia. They do pretty well by you. Your grandfather tells me you're a real artist, though. I'd like to see some of your work."

"Maybe sometime," I said, and then, because it sounded so ungracious, "If you still want to, I'll show you some of the things I've been doing this summer before you go in the morning."

We feasted on boiled blue crabs, then sat while thick, utter darkness fell down suddenly, like a cast net, and the stars appeared, hot and huge and silver, and fireflies pricked the darkness. They talked of the island, Clay and my grandfather, or rather my grandfather did, mostly. He talked of many things, slowly and casually, anecdotally, spinning his stories out judiciously like a tribal bard. He talked some more about Levi and about the skeleton of the osprey someone had found on Hunting Island, with the skeleton of the great fish still caught in its claws.

"They never let go," he said. "That fish was so big it pulled that old osprey right under, and he still wouldn't let go. Drowned him."

"God," Clay breathed, as if he was hearing stories of the Holy Grail, and my own eyes pricked with tears. I could not have said why.

He talked of the pirates who had dodged in and out of the Sea Islands, and of Captain John Peacock and his ignominious career, and of the great rice and indigo and Sea Island cotton plantations that flourished on the islands from Georgetown to Daufuskie Island, and of the plantation society and economy that had shaped a slow, graceful, symmetrical, and totally doomed way of life. He talked about the Gullahs and how they came over the Middle Passage from Gold Coast West Africa in chains to work the fertile lowland fields, specially catalogue-ordered by the American planters, from Senegal, Angola, Gambia, and Sierra Leone for the agricultural skills and the strong sense of family and community that helped ensure that they would not try to run away and leave their people. He told of the strange, rich old songs he had heard in the pray houses of the islands, and of the shouts that are songs, and of the dancing of ring plays and the knitting of circular nets and the weaving of sweet-grass baskets and the cooking of fish, yams, and okra; of the tales of trickster rabbits, vain crows, and sly foxes, and the darker, more terrible things that preyed in the nights on the unwary: the duppy and the plateye and their prowling succubus kin. He told of the language that was unique on earth, and sounded in the ear like music.

"Do you know any of it?" Clay asked, and my grandfather closed his eyes and sang softly, in his rusty tenor: "'*A wohkoh, mu mohne; kambei ya le; li leei tohmbe. Ha sa wuli nggo, sihan; hpangga li lee.*'"

I had never heard him sing or speak Gullah before and simply stared.

"What does it mean?" Clay Venable said.

"It means, 'Come quickly, let us struggle; the grave is not yet finished; his heart is not yet perfectly cool. Sudden death has sharp ears.'"

We said nothing. The words curled out into the night and rose and vanished.

"It's a funeral song, probably for a warrior," my grandfather said. "They were maybe the most important of the tribal songs, because the West

African people had such reverence for their dead, for their ancestors."

"Where did you learn that?" I said.

"My daddy used to bring me over here hunting with him when I was little," my grandfather said. "He had a friend, Ol' Scrape Jackson, who was a hunting guide for the rich Yankee who owned this place. Scrape used to sing that. He taught it to me and told me what it meant. I don't know why I've remembered it all these years."

"It's beautiful," I said softly.

"It is that," my grandfather said.

"Your people didn't always own the island, then?" Clay asked.

"God, no." My grandfather laughed. "Rich Yankee industrialist who had a plantation over on Edisto bought it off one of the old planter families down on their luck back around 1900, for a hunting lodge. Lucius Bullock, owned some steel mills, if my memory serves. My daddy and Scrape Jackson were his guides, and then his son's, and when I was old enough and my daddy died, I took over for the son. Jimmy, that was. It was good work, seasonal, as they say, and Jimmy paid me good to do my guidin' and to look in on the property once or twice a month when it wasn't hunting season. There's not much about this island I didn't end up knowing. You could have knocked me over with a feather when old Lucius died and left the island to me, the whole damned shooting match. Of course, it's not a big island, and there wasn't then and isn't now much access to it, but still, a whole island . . . Well, anyhow, Jimmy didn't want it and he wasn't about to turn it over to the government, so I guess I was as good as anybody. It liked to have driven my wife crazy. We had a nice little place in McClellanville and I did pretty good doing some general contracting over there, and I guess she thought I'd come on home and settle down when he died. After I got it, she wouldn't spend another single night over here. This girl is the one who's kept me company all these summers. Weren't for her, it would be mighty lonesome."

Clay said nothing, and then he laughed softly.

"What?" my grandfather said.

"It's a fabulous story," Clay said. "It just goes to show you that a cat may still look at a king. It gives me great hope."

"Glad it does," my grandfather said genially, and then, "Well, I'm going on to bed. You young people set awhile. I think there might be a few shooting stars tonight. Not like the big August hoohaw, but they're something to see out over the marsh. I think there might be a bottle of that fancy white wine Miss Caro likes in the fridge, too."

It was then that I knew that he had planned all along for Clay Venable to stay over. I knew that Clay knew, too. I did not know whether to sit still and pretend innocence, or simply get up and go to bed, taking my mortification along with me. I sat still.

"If you're embarrassed, don't be," Clay said finally, out of the darkness. "If he hadn't asked me to stay I would have just stood there until he did. I wasn't going home without getting to know what makes you tick."

Somehow that broke the back of my lingering reserve. We sat in the soft darkness until very late, talking desultorily of things so ordinary that I cannot remember now what they were, finally finishing the wine, still not going in. I had lit a couple of citronella flares, so that we heard the hum of the mosquitoes but they did not come in close, and in the flickering flare light I could see the planes of his narrow face, and the flash of his teeth as he talked. At some point in the evening, aided no doubt by the wine, it seemed simply and suddenly to me that I had known the geography of that face all my life, known always the music of the voice. When the stars began to fall we stopped talking.

The last one had sunk into darkness and gone back to black, and we still had not spoken for some minutes, when we heard the scream. It rose out of the far darkness, high and infinitely terrible, rose and rose to a crescendo of grief and fury and something as wild and old and free as the earth, broke into a tremolo of despair and anguish, and then sobbed away. The very air throbbed with it long after it was gone. All the little sounds of the night had stopped. I sat stone still, my heart hammering in my throat, tears of fright and something else entirely welling up in my eyes. My fingers gripped the arms of my chair as if they alone might save me. Beside me Clay, in his chair, did not move either, did not breathe.

"My God," I whispered finally. "My God."

"Not an alligator, was it?" he said.

"Oh, no. No. No alligator on earth ever sounded like that," I said. I had begun to tremble.

Then he said, "I know what it was. That was your grandfather's panther. That's what he's been hearing."

"Lord Jesus," I said, and it was a prayer. "Then it was true."

"Everything out here is, I think," Clay said, and got up out of his chair and came over and put his hands on my shoulders, and kissed me.

And that was that.

3

When I came downstairs, showered and more or less together, Clay was sitting at the round table on the back veranda making notes on the omnipresent clipboard that goes everywhere with him, and Estelle was pouring coffee for him out of the little French chocolate pot that he likes to use for his coffee. Estelle and I have both tried to persuade him that in this climate pottery or china would be more suitable, but he bought the little silver pot on our honeymoon, in Cuernavaca, and admires it inordinately. The fact that someone has to polish it after every use does not bother him in the least.

"What do we have Estelle for?" he will say when I fuss about the pot.

"Not for polishing your coffeepot every morning of her life," I say. "I've been doing it for years, if you must know."

"I do know. And I thank you," he says. "The pot makes me happy and it makes me happy that you polish it for me."

And so I do it, because I will not ask Estelle to, and it is, after all, a small thing. He does not ask much foolishness of me. There is not much foolishness in Clay.

I knew that he had chosen the back veranda because I simply could not have looked at the sea this morning. He loves the marsh vistas, and always has, but it is the open ocean that calls to him. I sometimes think that the sheer, intense orderliness of his soul finds a kind of release in that ultimate, untamable disorder. He can sit and look at the sea for hours, though he rarely sits and looks at anything anymore for hours but whatever is on his drawing board or his clipboard. He is restless during enforced inactivity; cocktail parties are torture for him, though he goes to and gives enormous numbers of them and does the walk-through perfectly. Clay never did drink much and is impatient with the slight silliness, the looseness, that ensues after an hour or so at the best of them. He chews ice fiercely and eats enormous quantities of hors d'oeuvres, waiting to be released. When we have drinks before dinner, either at home or at a restaurant, he can go through an entire basket of bread, waiting for everyone else to finish their drinks. He sometimes waits a long time. There seems to me to be quite a lot of drinking in the Plantation. Despite the munching, I am fairly sure he has not put on an ounce since we married. I never see him weigh himself, but the contours of his long, angular body do not seem to have changed.

Estelle poured out a second cup of coffee and plonked a plate of sticky buns down in front of me. They were still warm from the oven. The rich cinnamon rose to my nose and I sniffed appreciatively, though my stomach heaved at the thought of food.

"They smell wonderful, Estelle, but I think I'll just have coffee," I said. "Will you put some aside for me? I'll eat them with my tea this afternoon."

"You eat them now," she ordered. "You looks like the hind axle of hard times. You been up in that room, haven't you?"

I looked over at Clay, and she said, "Mr. Clay didn't tell me. I seen the door still open. And I know that look on yo' face. You ain't got no call to be broodin' in that room, Miss Caro. It don't do nothin' but stir you up. She ain't in there. She in a better place than this, and happy as a little lark. You try to rejoice in that an' leave her po' things be."

I bent my head over my coffee so she would not see the unsheddable tears gather. Estelle's faith is earth-simple and granite-hard. Not for the first time I felt a profound ache of pure envy. I had ceased negotiations with God on the day that my daughter died. I felt no anger at Him, only a dreary and cell-deep certainty that whether He was there or not, that door had slammed shut for me. There was a kind of peace in it.

We drank our coffee in silence. I was grateful for it. Clay knows that I cannot abide hovering when I am feeling out of sorts. Even if I could, I don't think it is in him to hover. He deals with his deepest feelings by snapping them firmly into the steel grid inside him and going back to work. The night that Kylie died, he stayed at his board all night, working furiously, while I slept in a thick swamp of barbiturates. The master plan for Calista Key Plantation, on the south coast of Puerto Rico, was conceived almost in its entirety that night. It is thought by most critics to be by far Clay's most innovative and attractive property. I have never been there. He does not go often, either. Neither of us can forget what terrible fuel fed the fire it was born in.

Finally he lifted his head and said, "You ready? I went ahead and put the flowers in the car."

And we went out into the misted morning to get the guest house ready for the new nestlings.

The Heron Marsh section of the Plantation is, except for the seaside neighborhood, the oldest. It was Clay's thought to offer to the first venturesome investors and home buyers the choice waterfront lots on the ocean and the marsh tidal creek that separates Peacock's from "the island." In between, he devised lovely neighborhoods of single-family and cluster homes bordering man-made lakes, lagoons, and a golf course, each with its own pool and tennis court. So, theoretically, everyone who lives in the Plantation has his own bit of waterfront. But it is the great dazzling vistas of sea and marsh that are the prizes, and they were gone almost in the first year of the Plantation's existence. I have always loved the Heron Marsh homes. They sit so deep in lush ocean forest that they are all but hidden from the road, and the contrast of coming out of that dark cave of green into the light that seems to pour like sour honey off the wide marshes is stunning. All the Heron Marsh homes have long back lawns and gardens that slope gently down to the reeded marsh's edge, and the deep, swift tidal creek that is the belt on the island's midsection is studded with docks at which cheeky outboards and slim sailboats bob. From this part of the creek you can reach the harbor and open ocean in a five-minute sail. The water is almost unfailingly calm and shining; even our fierce summer storms can't reach their clawing fingers here. I remember that I wanted to build on Heron Marsh when I first saw it, because it looks straight over into "my" part of the island, the secret green heart where I spent so many summer weeks with my grandfather. But Clay was in love with the ocean even then. It does not bear thinking that we might still have Kylie if we had come here, and I try hard not to. I really do. I have always known that there was simply no blame to be assigned, except perhaps to my child herself. Certainly not to Clay. I sensed even in the depths of my very earliest grief that that way lay the death of our marriage.

The house Clay uses as a guest house is the largest of twelve on the marsh. It was built for a very rich family from Spartanburg who had eight children and innumerable grandchildren, and so it sprawls octopuslike among its azaleas and oleanders and great ferns and overhanging live oaks, harboring a staggering number of smallish bedrooms, each with its own bath. There is an enormous family room and a kitchen and dining room that can accommodate an emerging nation, a wraparound veranda that steps down one step to a huge pool, and two Har-Tru tennis courts at the fringe of the water. It is made of our tradition-hallowed tabby, a mixture of sand and crushed oyster shell that dates back who knows how many hundreds of years in the Lowcountry. I always loved the thick, pitted surface of tabby; it looks as if it could stand for millennia, and may well do so. The tabby and the now-matured plantings are, to me, the only things that save the guest house from a rather daunting institutionality, which may be why the rich Spartanburgers sold it after the first year, though local legend says that it is because an alligator came out of the creek and ate the wife's Yorkie and was going for the youngest child as dessert before the screams from the children drove the sensible beast back into the water.

I always try to cram as many big, loose, rowdy bouquets as I can into the bedrooms and common areas, to soften the look of an upscale Elks Hall. Today the back of my Cherokee was almost full of them.

Clay helped me take the pails and vases into the kitchen and did not make a move to leave, but I knew that he was at least an hour past his customary time for going to his office, so I said, "Why don't you go on and catch up? I'll finish this up and then I think I'll walk over to Lottie's. She's starting a humongous new thing of the lighthouse that I want to see. I'll probably have some lunch with her, too. What time are your chickens coming in?"

"The two couples should be in about two. I think the woman . . . you know, the black woman . . . is getting in an hour or so later. Hayes is going over to Charleston to pick her up; the others are renting a car. Did I tell you that she's got a child with her?"

"Oh, Clay, no, you didn't. How old a child? She's surely going to need a sitter, isn't she? Or do you think she'll even want to go out and leave it? What is it, by the way?"

"A boy. I think she said he was five or six. Yeah, I guess she'll want a sitter. Can you leave them with sitters at five? I don't remember . . ."

"Just," I said. "But she may not want to. I'll pick up a few things for a light supper for her and the little boy in case she wants to stay here and bring them over after lunch. I want to put some breakfast things in the fridge for everybody, anyway. Lord, I hope I can get somebody at this late date. There's an awful lot going on around the island this time of year. . . ."

"Don't you bother with that; I'll get somebody in human resources to do it. There's a list over there. It's what they're for."

"No, I'll do it this time. I know how I'd feel if I was coming to a new place with a small child. If all else fails maybe I can heavily bribe Estelle to do it. She was saying the other day she missed having her grandchildren at home now that Emily has moved to the mainland."

He kissed me on the forehead.

"You okay now?"

"Yes. I'm sorry about that."

"Don't ever be sorry. Just don't do that to yourself. That's all I ask. Estelle's right. It doesn't . . . get us anywhere."

"I know."

He got into the Cherokee and drove away, and I filled vases and pitchers and set my riotous roses around, watching the stark rooms catch flame with them, and then I went out back and sat for a time on the low wall that bordered the veranda, looking west into the dull-pewter noonday dazzle toward "my" part of the island. From the dark line of the distant woods a pair of great, gawky birds rose into the air and lumbered away into the sun. Wood storks, I thought. They had been homing into the Ace Basin for some years from their historical habitats in Florida, because extensive development there has left them no home. Now, in all of the Carolina Lowcountry, they come only to the Ace. These, I thought, had been fishing one of the small freshwater ponds on the island and might be headed back to one of their rookeries. My grandfather had said, just before he died, that he thought there were perhaps three of them.

He had died seven years earlier, suddenly, because, as Kylie said seriously when we told her, "His heart attacked him." He died on the porch of the marsh house, his empty coffee cup overturned beside him, sprawled half out of one of the old green-painted rockers. He had not been dead long; I had gone over because he had not answered the telephone that morning when I made the daily eight A.M. call that was as much to hear his voice as to check on him. His heart had been ailing slightly for so long that we no longer really worried about him. When I found him, and touched his face, it was not entirely cooled and his hand was still flexible.

"Don't go," I whispered, tears starting down my face, but of course he had. All things considered, as Clay pointed out later, it was the place and the way he would have chosen, and after all, who of us could ask for more than that?

"'I know,'" I quoted at him, trying to smile, "'but I am not resigned.'" Clay was my husband and my love, but my grandfather had been the armature of my life. For a time after that, I felt tremulous, too tall on the earth, vulnerable to all the winds that blew. I think I feel so secure on the island now because it seems to me that part of him is still there.

We married in 1974, almost two years after we met. I think if I had not accepted Clay's proposal my grandfather would have seen to it with a shotgun. There was never a time, even after the Plantation was in full development over on the shore and Peacock's Island was alive with homeowners and guests, that he did not admire Clay. He probably loved him, but in his world men did not speak of that, and so he never said. I know that he loved me, and Carter, and most of all Kylie, for he said so once or twice, shyly and gruffly, usually after a shot or two of Wild Turkey. The only time I ever saw him in a suit was at our wedding, in the Presbyterian church in Columbia that my mother and stepfather attended. That he wore the suit surely spoke of love; that he came at all to Columbia, a city he loathed, to attend a wedding grandiosely funded by a man he loathed equally but silently, spoke more of it. He never mentioned his own son to me, the father I did not remember, and somehow I never asked him. I know that my father died well before I met Clay Venable, of the familial coronary disease that later killed my grandfather, in a small town in southern Colorado, but no one thought to tell me much more than that. My mother would not speak of him, either. By the time I felt that I should pursue the other half of my biology, if only for the appearance of things, it hardly seemed worth the effort. Shortly before she died, my mother gave me some letters from him to her that she had saved for many years, but I have not yet read them. My main men, as the kids say, are both here on this island. My grandfather's ashes are now a part of the ancient salt blood of the Ace; I scattered them from the dock on a still gray morning in early spring, when the marshes were just greening up.

On the day that we married he deeded the entire island over to Clay.

"It's really yours," he said to me, "but I didn't want you to have to worry about taxes and all that stuff. Clay will take the kind of care of it I would, or you would. I've seen the plan for the development over on the ocean, and I got to say it looks good to me. No sense thinking we could keep this island to ourselves much longer, and I'd rather Clay looked after opening it up than anybody I know of. He's going to keep what he calls the spirit of it, and that's all I care about. I ain't a fool; I put a line or two in the agreement that says if he's ever stupid enough to run off with his secretary, or if he kicks the bucket before you do, it reverts to you. But if that doesn't suit you, he and I will redo the agreement."

"No, it's perfect," I said, weeping into his neck with love for him and the magnificence of his wedding gift to us. "I don't want to change a thing."

But I found that ultimately, I did. I found that for a long time after he died I simply could not cross the flimsy little bridge from Peacock's to the island without getting a great, cold lump in my throat, and I could not bring myself to stay in the marsh house very long, or go with Clay in the Whaler out into the heart of the marshes. I could not go over to the little settlement of Dayclear without crying silently, and the sight of the obdurate, mud-encrusted little marsh ponies bolting noisily over a hummock moved me to sobs. The void my grandfather left on the island whistled in my heart, the emptiness filled and choked me.

After a time Clay grew impatient with me.

"What good does it do for us to own it if you never want to go over there again?" he said one night, as I moved silently around the kitchen getting dinner. We had tried again with the island, taking the two children over for an afternoon, and once again I had stayed behind, huddled silently on the sunny dock. "What would make it all right for you?"

And without thinking at all, without even realizing I spoke, I said, "I want the island. I want that part of it. I want it to be mine, in my name. I don't know why, but I do. It's like . . . he'll come back, then."

He hugged me silently, and two days later he came back from a trip into Charleston and said, "Now it *is* yours. I had it transferred to you. Come on by the office and I'll have Linda witness your signature. You now own fifteen thousand acres of swamp, a herd of mangy ponies, and a town full of Gullahs."

"Oh, no," I said in horror. "I don't own Dayclear! I don't want it; that's awful! You can't own a town! He never owned Dayclear; he's told me a thousand times that he thought old Mr. what's-his-name deeded those houses over there to the Gullahs way before he left him the island."

"Well, there's not a scrap of paper anywhere to that effect that I could find," Clay said, "but it may be true. Trying to get clear title would be a nightmare, but then I don't guess you're planning to sell it, are you?"

"Of course not," I said, running into his

arms. "Thank you, darling! I know it shouldn't matter, but somehow I just . . . needed it. And you've still got by far the biggest part, the part you really wanted, don't you?"

"Of course. If you're happy, I'm happy. Now, you think you can go back over there without crying on the dock?"

"Yes," I said, and from that day, I could.

I went back over the next day, by myself, and it was as if my grandfather had never left it, was simply off somewhere in the canoe, and I could move as easily about the house as I ever had. I drifted through it, straightening up, sweeping, dusting, making mental notes of everything that needed repairing and brightening, and then I went back out to the Cherokee and drove over to Dayclear.

I had not gone to the village often without my grandfather. He was scrupulous about according the villagers their privacy, and I, spawn of the sixties and seventies, had the Southern liberal's horror of appearing condescending to anyone with skin darker than my own. But I knew most of the old men and women living there, because I ran into them when I went with my grandfather to the scrubby little mom-and-pop store at the bridge or to the tiny post office. I knew which house Scrape Jackson had lived in, and that his son, elderly himself now, and ill with diabetes, still lived there, with his old wife and a rotating assortment of small grandchildren. Toby Jackson was usually to be found sitting out in front of the little unpainted house in an old armchair, covered with a paisley shawl that looked as if it might have once graced the shoulders of a fine lady or a grand piano on Tradd Street, weaving sweet-grass baskets and watching his chickens forage in the dusty yard. He was there that morning, and I stopped the car and got out and went over to him.

"It's Toby, isn't it?" I said, smiling foolishly and wishing I had my grandfather's natural ease with the Gullahs.

He nodded his head slowly. I noticed that his eyes were filmed, as if with cataracts, and realized that he probably could not see me well, if at all.

"Yes'm," he said.

"Toby, I'm Caroline Aubrey. Mr. Gerald's granddaughter. We've met, but you probably don't remember. I knew your daddy, though. . . ."

"I remember," Toby said.

"Well, I guess you know Granddaddy died not too long ago. . . ."

I paused, and he nodded.

". . . and I just wanted to let you know . . . let all of you know over here, I mean, that nothing's changed, and nothing's going to. This part of the island is mine, across the bridge over here, and I'm not sure what you all's arrangement about the property here is, but I didn't want anybody to worry that anyone would, you know, bother you about it or anything. It belongs to you all, just like it always did. It always will."

He did not speak but only nodded slowly. After a while I said, "Well, that's all I wanted to say. It's nice to see you again, Toby."

I had started back to the Cherokee, cheeks burning, when he called after me, "Miss Caroline?"

I turned. "Yes?"

"Thank you for telling us. I guess we been kind of wondering ever since Mr. Gerald passed. Couldn't none of us prove we owns our houses, I don't think, but they's been ours for a long time."

My heart smote me.

"Somebody should have come right away and talked to you. I'm so sorry."

He smiled for the first time. He had a large gold tooth in front, and his smile looked festive and sweet.

"We figured you git around to it sooner or later. You his granddaughter, after all. We all thought a sight of Mr. Gerald. We sure did."

I sang in the Cherokee all the way back over the bridge to Peacock's.

After that, I was at the marsh house at least twice a week. After school and in the summers, Kylie and sometimes Carter came with me, though, like Clay, Carter gravitated eastward to the ocean like an iron filing to a magnet. It was

Kylie who became my eventual companion on the
marshes. They sang to her as they never did to
Clay and Carter. She was especially enchanted
with the ponies. One, a cobby, dun-colored mare
of astonishing stupidity and passing equine sweetness, took to following her around, doglike, for
the lumps of sugar Kylie kept in her pockets.

"You'll ruin her teeth," I used to say, and we
would laugh, because the mare's long yellow
teeth seemed impervious to everything from
sugar to dynamite. We named her Pianissimo, for
obvious reasons. I still see her sometimes, though
never again so close as when Kylie came with me
to the island.

At nine-thirty that evening I sat at a round table
in the quiet patio room of Carolina's, listening to
the conversation between Clay and his new
cadets and sipping on my third glass of Merlot.
Ordinarily I do not drink at these shakedown
cruises, as Hayes Howland calls them, but
tonight's was going so badly that by the time our
appetizers came I could not bear the slogging
tedium and the Herculean effort of trying to
draw the young wives of the anointed into the
conversation, and when Hayes, who had joined
us, ordered a bottle of Merlot and put it down on
the table between us, I simply gave up and drank
each glass he poured for me. Clay was still toying
with his first glass of wine when we waited for

dessert, and the young men were sipping matter-of-factly and moderately, as if they did not realize they were drinking wine at all, hanging on to Clay's words, but the two young women were not drinking at all, and simply would not be either assimilated or consoled. After an hour of trying himself, Hayes had raised an eyebrow at me and murmured, *"À votre sante,"* and settled silently into the wine, and I had given up and leaned back and joined him. Clay passed me a level look or two, but when I lifted my shoulders in an almost imperceptible shrug and raised my glass to him, he did not look again. I knew that I had broken my end of the bargain—to engage and draw out the women while he began spinning their husbands into the cocoon of the company—but I was bone-tired and annoyed with them all, and wished suddenly for nothing so much as to be safely in the marsh house on the island and not required to speak another word until tomorrow. The morning in Kylie's room had bled me more deeply than I had thought. And my afternoon encounter with the young black woman Clay had hired had made me both angry and bored, a combination unbeatable for sheer enervation.

I had stayed too long at Lottie's studio, and by the time I got back to the house I barely had time to run out again to the little supermarket in the Plantation's chic, lushly planted little mall for provisions for the guest house. When I got back to the Heron Marsh house it seemed as empty as when I had left it, and the kitchen was in its same pristine state, so I put my grocery bags down on the counter and was unloading them when a cool voice said, "I beg your pardon?"

I looked around as guiltily as if I had been caught rifling the silverware. A tall young black woman stood in the door to the hallway. She wore a severely cut ivory linen pantsuit and simple gold jewelry, and was utterly beautiful; her skin was the color of coffee with a great deal of sweet cream in it, and her face looked like something on the wall of a highland African cave, newly come to light after millenna. She was not smiling. Her delicate brows were lifted high over almond eyes.

"I'm sorry," I said, smiling. "I didn't know anyone was here. Your plane must have been right on time."

"Are you the baby-sitter?" she said.

I laughed.

"No. I'm Caroline Venable, Clay's wife. I wasn't sure what you would want to do about dinner, whether or not you'd want to leave your little boy with a sitter, so I brought some things over for supper in case you wanted to stay in tonight. I know how it is the day you get in from a long trip. . . ."

"Mark is fine with sitters," she said levelly.

"Mr. Howland said the company had them available. I'm sorry, I thought you must be someone he sent. He's gone to the office to see about it. . . ."

"Well, I'm afraid we weren't able to do much on this short notice. This time of year is crammed full of things for the children. But my housekeeper said she'd be delighted to sit. She's wonderful with children; she practically raised mine, and she has a raft of grandchildren herself. . . ."

"That will be fine," the woman said, and then, putting her slim hand out, "I'm Sophia Bridges. I'll be doing research and development for the new property eventually, but right now I suppose there'll be indoctrination and that sort of thing. It's kind of you to bring these things for us, Mrs. Venable, but I mustn't keep you. I've got Mark down for a nap, so I'm going to use the time to get unpacked before we leave for dinner. What time could your housekeeper be here?"

Her hand was chilly in mine, and firm, but it did not linger. The slim fingers disengaged hurriedly.

"Please call me Caro; everyone does," I said. "I hope I'll be seeing a lot more of you, and of course I want to meet Mark. Estelle can be here around five, I should think. We'll probably leave for Charleston about a quarter of six. It takes an hour or so to drive it. We'll be taking two cars over, so I'll pick you up, or perhaps Clay will.

Somebody, at any rate. You needn't change, what you have on is lovely. . . ."

But I was talking to her slender back as she turned and went back down the hall toward the bedroom, where her son presumably slept a cool and orderly sleep.

"You're welcome," I said under my breath to her back, and only then wondered if there was a Mr. Bridges, and if so, where he might be.

There probably never was one, I thought nastily. He's probably a test tube somewhere in a fertility lab. I can't imagine any living man getting close to her long enough to accomplish conception.

I picked up my keys and started out of the kitchen, then stopped as I heard her voice behind me. I looked back. She stood in the door, poised like a royal coursing hound, perhaps a saluki.

"Your housekeeper . . . is she African American?" she said.

"Why . . . yes. She is," I said in surprise.

"Then I'm sorry, but I think I'll stay here with Mark this evening. He's never had a woman of color for a baby-sitter. I don't want him to get the idea that African-American women are subservient or take servants' roles. He's never seen that. I realize that may be a little problem down here, but Mr. Howland . . . Hayes . . . thought we could get around it. I'm going to want white sitters for Mark."

I drew a deep breath and let it out slowly.

Then want shall be your master, I thought, but aloud I said only, "Well, it could be a problem. So many of the black women on the island, or within commuting distance over on Edisto or St. Helena's aren't trained for much else, and the baby-sitting and housekeeping jobs they have are very important to them. They do them wonderfully well, and they know how much we appreciate and depend on them. We'll see what we can do, of course, but African-American women in white homes is simply a fact of Lowcountry life. I think your son is going to see a lot of it no matter who sits for him. Maybe when you see the reality of it you'll feel differently. These are warm, wonderful, skilled women; they are more partners than servants. . . ."

"I have made my own reality for Mark," she said without smiling. "It has cost me a great deal to keep it intact. Thank you, though. I'm sure the company's human resources people will get to work on it for me."

And she turned and went back down the hall with the stride of a big cat. All she lacked, I thought, was a great, switching tail. Obviously Ol' Massa's wife wasn't required to deal out her largesse here. Ol' Missus slunk back to her car and jerked it into gear and screeched back off across the island.

When Hayes Howland and I had decanted

our two passengers and gone back outside to wait for Clay, he said, "I presume you've met Mrs. Bridges and the crown prince?"

"I have indeed," I said. "They've gone into voluntary exile until a pale enough courtier for the prince can be found."

"Uh-oh," Hayes said, grinning his gap-toothed grin. "I'm afraid I dropped the ball, too. I could only think of that Filipino waiter at the Island Club, and that didn't suit, either. Maybe an American Indian? I hear the new teller at Palmetto State is half-Seminole. Maybe she's got a sister."

I have never really managed to like Hayes as much as I thought I would when I first met him, or as much as Clay wishes I did, but he can be bitingly funny. Tonight we burst into laughter, and could only stop when Clay pulled up in the Jaguar with the second of the two new couples in tow and raised his eyebrows at us and said, "Want to share the joke? We could use a laugh; the drawbridge was up for twenty-five minutes and I never could see why."

"Nothing worth repeating," I said, and took his arm, and we went inside, the seven of us, to begin the interminable business of assimilating four disparate strangers into the Plantation family.

We had stopped first for drinks at the town house Clay keeps in Charleston. Hayes had had his family's cook go over and open and air it, and set out the cocktail and appetizer things. Mattie sometimes does that for us when I cannot get over ahead of time, and often stays to serve drinks and pass around almonds and benné seed biscuits. Clay likes that. Mattie has a sure, unobtrusive dignity I cannot muster. Many guests think she is our employee, and neither Clay nor Hayes disabuses them.

The town house is on Eliott Street, a short, shady cobbled alley off Bay Street lined with dollhouse Charleston single houses. Clay bought the house years ago, when it became obvious that Plantation business was going to keep him in Charleston a great deal of the time. I know that even if it hadn't, he would have found an excuse to own a Charleston house. He has never stopped loving Charleston, as much, I think, for what it will not give him as for what it will. Clay has made a great deal of money, but there is a small core of old Charleston that does not care about that and will not admit him into its inmost bosom no matter what civic endeavor he underwrites. He will never, for instance, belong to the St. Cecelia Society, for the simple reason that membership is inherited, and he has come to ridicule it, but he never gave up on the notion that Kylie might come out there.

"You could cultivate Charleston," he said.

"You've probably still got kin around here you don't know you have."

"You remind me of Groucho Marx when he said he wouldn't belong to any club that would have him as a member," I said once. "You scorn it, but you want your daughter to make her damned debut there. What kind of message do you think that gives Kylie?"

"That there are some things worth having that aren't easy to get," he said. "That real quality is rare."

"And that exclusion by policy is the Amurrican way," I said. "I'm no more going to 'cultivate' Charleston than I'm going to let her go to St. Margaret's. She doesn't live over there, Clay. I'm not going to have her in a car for two hours every day of her life just so she can go to a silly dance. Country Day is as good a school as there is in the Lowcountry. You've seen to that. What's it going to say to these newcomers you hire if your child goes to school in Charleston while theirs are expected to go on the island?"

"That rank hath its privileges," he said, but he did not push it, and of course, as it turned out, it did not come up.

But Clay still loves Charleston with the single-minded passion of a man for a lost first love, and when Hayes found out that the little house was being put up for sale by the old couple who were moving to the carriage house of a child's home, he called Clay immediately. This was just before the first of the wealthy Northerners discovered Charleston and began buying up historic properties at prices the natives could not afford; Hayes, though never much of a lawyer in many respects, has the native's nose for real estate and knew that such properties would soon triple and quadruple in value. It was still early days in the Plantation, but Clay got the money together and bought the house sight unseen, as much for its street address as for its attractiveness or livability. It lies in the heart of the hallowed area "South of Broad," which in Charleston means more than the words might imply, and fortunately it is a prettily proportioned house that had been well cared for, needing only cosmetic attention. I have to admit that I am charmed by the little house and its walled garden, too, though I do not spend much time there. It never seems quite real to me, never seems to be our house at all, and when Clay refers to it as our pied-à-terre, as he often does, I can only look at him.

Charleston is as lovely in this soft, misted pre-Christmas dusk as it ever is, with gas carriage lights lit in the old district and warm lamplight shining from the shuttered windows of the old pastel houses and fingers of mist curling off the harbor up through the live oaks on the Battery and down the little side streets South of Broad. We walked the short distance over the glistening cobbles to Carolina's down on the waterfront. The streets were full of people walking slowly, looking into shop windows, laughing, talking. There are never many cars on the streets at night in the old district, though parking is at a premium, and walking is a good way to get your initial feeling for the city. I watched the two young couples as we walked. The men were so absorbed in Clay and his words that they might have been walking in downtown Scranton. They would have, after tonight, no feeling for Charleston at all. They followed him like ducklings, having imprinted upon him instantly and totally.

I have seen this before many times with the young who come to work at the Peacock Island Company. Just out of the pure ether of their Ivy League business or liberal arts schools, heads pounding with abstractions, newly adrift in a world so alien to the one they have just left that it might be in another geological epoch, they find Clay to be hyper-real, the Word made flesh, the only solidarity in a great mist of strangeness. He plies them like a Pied Piper. Nobody does it better than Clay.

Almost everyone does it better than me. The young women who clicked along on their sensible heels beside me in the soft, wet night, stumbling every now and then on a cobblestone, knew very well they were sacrificial lambs in an alien land, knew that they were here almost on suffer-

ance, to be petted and cajoled while their husbands were courted; knew that sooner rather
than later they would be on their own in this
wilderness, while their men received the keys to
the kingdom. They had a keen, if terrible, sense of
Charleston; I thought they might never alter it. I
felt an unwilling stab of sympathy. I suppose all
the new company wives go through something
like this unwanted epiphany, but some seem to
relish it, and others at least to try to put a gallant
face on it. These two did neither. Sally Bowdon-
Kirkland looked straight ahead, neither smiling
nor responding to anything Hayes or I said, simply gone away behind her long, narrow New
England features.

Barbara Costigan cried.

When we picked up her and her husband,
Buddy, at the guest house, her blue eyes were
swollen almost shut and her little porcine nose
was pink and raw. Allergies, she said; something
in the air down here that they didn't have at
home in Old Greenwich. But I know the stigmata
of tears when I see them. Later, on the way to
Charleston, I would hear an occasional rattling
sniff from the backseat, where the young Costigans sat, and a murmur of concern from the
stolid Buddy. In the restaurant Barbara's slitted
eyes leaked almost continually.

"Wow," she said over and over. "I hope
you've got some good allergists down here."

"Oh, yes," I said. "Some of them, I think, from Connecticut."

She and Buddy were a pair: both square and short and tanklike, though I rather thought that Barbara's flesh was newly acquired. Her short-skirted silk dress fit her like the casing of a sausage and was obviously a size or two too small. It was also a delicate shell pink, which might have suited her fair skin and flaxen hair if the former had not been splotched vermilion and the latter sprayed into a helmet against our all-pervasive humidity. Buddy was blond, too, but a lighter shade, near-white. His skin was red. His smallish features sat in the middle of a large face as if someone had drawn them on a balloon, and radiated self-confidence and benignity. I'd have thought him the archetype of the young German burgher but for the last name. Clay had said that his IQ was off the charts. They looked, all told, like a little couple on the top of a wedding cake. I winced, thinking of the twin sunburns they would sport from April to October.

The Bowdon-Kirklands were of a piece, too, though I thought that it was a spiritual twinship instead of a physical one. She was tall and very thin, almost six feet in her Ferragamos, and he was perhaps a half-inch shorter, and wiry. Tennis, I thought, for her and golf for him. It was obvious both of them were sports people. Their smooth tans spoke of good private grass courts and deep-water sailing and golf somewhere like the Maidstone Club, where both had been members since birth. Both were lank-haired, long-featured, and awesomely collected. Both were polite. Both were as distant as Uranus. He spoke pleasantly in a New England honk but seldom to me. She spoke hardly at all. There was no sign of tears in her slightly protuberant gray eyes. I imagined that she probably wept only when her favorite hunter had to be put down, and then a good grade of English toilet water, the kind with a number instead of a name.

Peter Kirkland had been first in his class at Wharton. Sally, I remembered, had done something at a museum in Boston.

I tried at first.

"Do you have children?" I asked the young Costigans on the way over.

A great sniff from Barbara, a hearty "Yes, we do, a daughter," from Buddy, followed by more whispering and sniffling. I wondered what was wrong there. Postpartum depression, perhaps? A child somehow flawed?

"She's only a month old," Buddy said. "Our parents thought it would be better if she stayed behind with her granny and a nurse until we know where we'll be living. She's a little beauty; her name is Elizabeth Sloan, but she's already Sissy, just like her mama was. We miss her a lot, don't we, Barbs?"

A sob, disguised as a little cough.

No wonder, I thought. Dragging that poor child all the way down here and leaving her new baby behind. What could he have been thinking of?

Turning around, I said, "Well, there are wonderful things for children to do in the Plantation. The children's program is famous, and of course the weather is almost always nice, and the beach is perfect for small children almost all year round. Sissy will love it. Summer is paradise for kids."

"We'll be spending our summers on Fire Island," Barbara Costigan said in her little-girl whisper. "My parents have had a house in Point o' Woods forever. We always go there. I went there every summer of my life. I met Buddy there. The house was my grandparents'."

"Now, Barbs," Buddy said heartily. "I bring you down to one of the most famous beach resorts in the world and you go on about Fire Island. Just wait till you see the beach in the Plantation; you'll change your mind in a minute."

Barbara was silent. There would be, I knew, no mind-changing there, about beaches or anything else. I could almost see the fine, tensile steel filaments that bound her to her family back up North.

Still, she tried, too.

"Do you have children, Mrs. Venable?" she asked politely.

"My son is twenty-two," I said. "He's in graduate school."

It is what I always say, when I am asked.

"Well, that's nice. I always thought boys must be so much easier to raise," Barbara said, in the tone of one who thought no such thing. "You're lucky you never had to put up with the wiles and the flirtiness of a little girl. Even one as little as mine—ours. They're just shameless. Sissy has Buddy wrapped around her little finger, and my father—"

She made a small noise and fell silent, and I knew that Buddy had heard about Kylie and pinched or poked her.

Another sob. I sighed.

"She'll have a lot of company," I said cheerfully. "There are several new babies in the staff family this year, and it seems to me that most of them are girls."

"That's nice, isn't it, Barbs?" Buddy said. She did not reply. I felt real joy when we saw in the distance the spires of the bridge over the river into Charleston.

Toward the end of the evening, when neither young woman had spoken for long minutes and I was considering asking Hayes to order another bottle of Merlot, he suddenly roused himself from the contemplation of his wineglass and said, "You'll have to go and see Caro's paintings sometime, Sally, you being in the art game yourself.

She's really good. She shows all over the place: Charleston, the island, you name it."

Sally Bowdon-Kirkland turned her fine mare's face to me.

"You paint?" she said, as if she thought I might perhaps have an example of my work with me, and she would be required to examine it.

"A little. Nothing special. It was my major at school. Tell me about your museum work; I've been meaning to ask you. Are you a docent?"

"Actually, I own the museum," she said, smiling a little for the first time and revealing long teeth. I felt as if I should offer her a sugar cube.

"Well, goodness . . ."

"It's a very small museum, really. We show mainly American minimalists who worked after 1980. I'm hoping to make it one of the tops in its field, though; and I'm having some luck with acquisitions. Or rather . . . I did have. I turned it over to my cousin when we . . . knew we were coming here."

I thought, not for the first time, how hard the life of a Plantation corporate wife is. They are not permitted by policy to work for the company, and the families are required by policy to live where the husbands work. That limits career opportunities to primarily resort areas. There is not a real estate position left in the Lowcountry, I don't think. Commuting to Charleston is almost out of the question, in drive time. Some of the young marriages do not survive it; some wives with esoteric degrees and formidable skills find that, after all, they cannot live in such air. Those who do not leave adjust, I suppose, make their separate peaces, but it seems to me that there is a good bit of drinking around the club pool in the afternoons. I know that human resources is kept busy with references for counselors, of one sort or another. There is a list of them posted in the corporate office, alongside the baby-sitters.

"Well, it's no substitute, but some of our galleries are really good, and there are about a million museums in Charleston proper. I should think any of them would carpet your path with palm branches, if you'd like to keep busy," I said.

It was not the right thing to say.

"Keeping busy is really not my first priority," she said. "Finding a new American idiom to nurture is. My family has been instrumental in that for a long time. A distant kinswoman of ours founded one of the great American museums. It's in Boston. The Gardner. Perhaps you know it."

"Yes," I said. "I know it."

I did not think that Sally Bowdon-Kirkland would be one of the ones who made a separate peace. Looking at Peter Kirkland, oblivious, as he had been all evening, to anyone but Clay, I wondered if he would notice.

A moment later Barbara Costigan suddenly

jumped to her feet, clutching her napkin to her chest, and fled, knocking over her water glass. We watched, open-mouthed, as she floundered around the corner toward the ladies' room.

"Oh, no," Buddy said. "I'm sorry, folks. She's . . . it's been hard on her, leaving the baby. I think she's got all kinds of hormonal things going on. . . ."

I looked over at Sally Bowdon-Kirkland. She was studying her newly arrived crème brûlée judiciously. She looked up at me.

"Do you think you ought to . . . ?" I began.

She lifted her shoulders.

"We just met this evening. I'm sure she'd rather have you," she said.

I got up and went into the ladies' room. It seemed empty, but I could hear alternating sobbing and flushing coming from one of the stalls.

"Honey, it's Caro Venable," I said. "Please don't cry. Come on out and let's talk about it. There's nothing so bad that we can't fix it, I promise. . . ."

She sobbed steadily for a time, but gradually she stopped. There was another flush and then she came out, rubbing her eyes like a child and scrubbing at the front of her dress. It was stained almost to her chubby waist.

"I'm so sorry," she whispered. "They leak; almost every time it's time to feed the baby, they leak awfully, even though she's not here, and I . . .

I thought I had enough Kleenex in there but I don't. . . ."

I looked at her in the harsh fluorescent light and felt an actual pain in my heart. I also felt a sharp, cold pang of anger at her husband and Clay and the company. Poor, bereft, sodden, frightened little soul.

"I remember that," I said. "It's awful, isn't it? But it stops. Before you know it it will have stopped, and then you'll have your baby with you and everything will be better. This is a hard time. I know it is. Come on, let's get your face washed and some fresh lipstick on you, and I'll just drape my cardigan around you . . . like this . . . and nobody will ever know. We'll say you spilled your wine."

"She'll know." Barbara Costigan hiccupped. "She'll know I was sitting there leaking like a cow and crying like a fool. You can just bet she's never leaked anything in her life, or even cried . . ."

I knew that she meant Sally Bowdon-Kirkland, and did something I virtually never do. I ridiculed one corporate wife to another. I did not feel one iota of guilt about it, either.

"If she leaked anything, it would be ice water," I said. "Come on. You won't have to see much of her at all, once this night is over. Being friends with every woman down here is not in the company policy manual. You'll find your own, and so will your little girl. I did."

She managed a watery smile, and we got her fairly presentable again, swathed in my scarlet cashmere sweater, and went back to the table. Clay was holding up his hand for the check. All of a sudden I did not think I could bear the drive back to Peacock's Island in the company of this forlorn child and her little Prussian husband. I simply could not bear it. Riding with the Bowdon-Kirklands seemed even worse.

"I think I'll stay over at the town house," I said casually, not meeting Clay's eyes. "There are some things for the garden I want to pick up in the morning, and I want to bring the summer linens back with me and pack them in mothballs. Clay, you can get everybody in the Jaguar, can't you?"

He looked at me. I knew that he thought I was going to go back to the town house and drink alone. Or perhaps stay and drink wine with Hayes Howland; I did not know which he would think more unseemly. I realized, too, that I was on my way to being quite drunk. There was a shimmery distance in the air around me, and though I did not and hardly ever do stagger, still, I was walking carefully in my unaccustomed high heels and talking very properly. Poor Clay. Twice now tonight I had broken our bargain. If we talked about it, I could have told him that I did not want to drink, did not even feel like it. I simply did not want to be with these awful, doomed

children anymore. I did not want to be with anyone.

But we do not talk about it, and I did not tell
him.

"Suit yourself," he said neutrally. "Be careful
of your car, though. Lot of traffic tonight."

I knew that he realized that I was not sober.
For some reason, that made me angry.

"I'll drive her back to the town house and
walk on home," Hayes said. "The air will do me
good."

We stood on the cobbles outside Carolina's,
Hayes and I, and watched Clay drive away in the
Jaguar with the two captive couples. No one
spoke for a moment and then Hayes said, "You
want to go back in and have a nightcap? That
was pretty awful."

"No, I really don't. Thanks, though," I said
wearily. "I think I'll just go on back to the house
and turn in. You're right. It was awful. I feel very
bad about it. I really didn't do much to keep
things going."

"Wasn't your fault," Hayes said. "You tried.
We both did. There wasn't any way those two
were going to let you draw them out. You were
doomed before the night even started."

"Why?" I said, surprised.

"Christ, Caro, look at them," he said. "And
look at you. One of them looks like a fat little
brewer's wife in a too-tight Sunday dress and the

other one looks like Seabiscuit, and there you sit looking like . . . I don't know, a Persian princess or something in that red silk, with all that black hair down your back, and you twenty years older at least than either one of them, and a million times richer . . . What do you think?"

"I never thought about it that way, Hayes," I said honestly. "I really never did."

"Well, it's true. You're something special, Caro. Time you knew that, if you don't already. Clay ought to tell you."

"Well . . . thank you," I said.

The car came, and we got in and drove the short distance to the town house in silence.

"Would you give me a nightcap if I came in for a minute?" he said, not looking at me.

What is this? I thought. This is Hayes. I don't know what this means.

"Lucy would kill me," I said lightly, and then, "And I'm really tired. Why don't we make it one night soon when Clay and Lucy can join us?"

"You got it," he said affably, and saw me to the door. I shut it behind me, but then I went to the front bay window and watched as he walked away down Eliott Street toward Bedon's Alley, where he would cut over to Church Street and home. In the light of the corner streetlight he stopped and looked back at the window, and I stepped back involuntarily, as if he could see me. But, of course, he could not.

For an instant, it was as if I had never seen him, was seeing him now for the first time. Only then did I realize that, whenever I looked at Hayes Howland, I had been seeing the young man who had been Clay's friend when I first met him, the irrepressible roommate from the University of Virginia, broad of shoulder and flaming red of hair, freckled of snub face and irreverent of tongue, a kind of sprite, an elf, an Ariel of sorts.

But now I saw that Hayes was middle-aged. It was funny; I did not see that in Clay, nor really, even, in myself, when I looked into my mirror. But it was true of Hayes Howland. He seemed older by far than any of us, older than he should by rights be. I saw that the broad shoulders were a little stooped now, with the beginning of a roundness to the back, and the red hair dulled and streaked with iron gray and worn away on top so that it was almost like a monk's tonsure. It made his pale face seem longer, and the glossy mustache he cultivated, which made him look, as Clay once said, like he was eating a chipmunk, was thinner and gingery. Even from my window I could see that the freckles on his face had run together in places, and the ones on the top of his head, so that he seemed splotched with darkness here and there. His raincoat had a rip in the lining, and part of it hung down below the hem. That meant nothing; Hayes wore wonderful clothes, but they invariably looked as though he had slept in them. But somehow tonight, the draggled hem and the bleaching lamplight and the rounded shoulders all added up to something else. Hayes looked . . . defeated. Seedy. I thought of Willy Loman.

I went upstairs and undressed and crawled into one of the pretty rice beds in the master bedroom. The sheets smelled a little musty but were smooth and cool. I turned off the bedside lamp and lay in the darkness, thinking about Hayes. The thought came, unbidden and as whole and complete as an egg: What does he get out of all this? What's in it for him?

He had been with Clay now almost since college. Day by day, closer than any brother, he had cast his lot with Clay at the very beginning of the Peacock Island Plantation Company, leaving without apparent regret the job with the Charleston law firm and coming on board as Clay's legal adviser, assistant, and general factotum. Hayes did everything. He advised, he traveled for the company, he ran errands, he oversaw personnel, he haunted building sites and construction crews, he sat in on marketing and advertising meetings, he scouted universities and graduate schools for the kind of young man or woman Clay wanted, those with the invisible but unmistakable stamp of the company upon them. Most of all he was Clay's link to the Lowcountry.

There was not an old family or a cache of old money from Litchfield to Savannah that Hayes did not know, or his family did not. Hayes brought Charleston to Clay. In turn, Clay took Hayes with him on his trajectory straight into the sun.

And yet . . . and yet. Somehow it did not seem that Hayes was a terribly successful man, much less a contented one. I could not have said precisely what I meant by that. It was just that Hayes had a restlessness, a kind of chronic discontent that his general affability and foolishness sometimes did not hide. He was court jester and confidant, but sometimes he was moody and bitter, too, and then Clay wisely let him alone. The moods rarely lasted more than a day, but they were real.

For one thing, I don't think Hayes and Lucy ever had quite enough money. He had married Lucy Burton the year after Clay and I had married; they had known each other since infancy, and were out of the same tiny, dense gene pool. Lucy's parents, like Hayes's, were an old Lowcountry family, though, as Hayes himself said cheerfully, poor as a cracker's pisspot. Hayes did not marry money, but he did marry Charleston, and that, from what I could see, was what always mattered to him.

But I thought now that it must have been a struggle at times for them. Hayes was officially listed as number two man in the company after Clay, but he had no financial interest in it, for all the joint venture money he sniffed out for Clay, and I knew that his salary, while better than any other in the company, even the one Clay allowed himself, was not spectacular. Clay puts most of the Plantation's money back into the company. Hayes and Lucy must have stretched his salary very thin to maintain her family's beautiful old Federal house on Church Street and give the parties that they did, and educate two daughters in the bargain, much less keep them in Laura Ashleys. I could not think there was much at all left over.

Once, I remembered, I asked Clay when he was going to give Hayes some sort of property of his own, a partnership or something.

"I guess when the right one comes along," he said. "Though if you think about it, can you imagine Hayes running one of the Plantations?"

"Why not?" I said.

"Well, for one thing, it would probably mean leaving the Lowcountry, and he'd let you cut his throat before he'd do that. And then, frankly, I think he gets off on being my sidekick. Who else thinks he's as funny as I do? Who else would let him fool around and goof off as much as I do? Hayes is a born second banana, and I think on some level he knows it. He's never asked me to let him have a crack at anything else."

I thought about that conversation now, as the night stilled and quieted outside my drawn curtains. Something was missing; something did not equate. Hayes was more than he seemed, had to be more. . . .

But the thought eddied away on the spiral of thick wine-sleep that took me under, and when I woke, only short hours later, with a cottony mouth and the beginning of a dull headache, it was gone from my mind. I sat up abruptly, as if summoned by an alarm clock, slid out of bed, splashed my face and scrubbed my teeth, ferreted out some old jeans and a sweatshirt of Clay's from the bureau, and was in the Cherokee and on the road south within an hour.

By the time dawn broke, red as the apocalypse to the east, I was on the bridge from Peacock's over to the island, and by the time the sun touched the tops of the live oaks that leaned over the marsh house, I was fast asleep again in the small iron bed that had been my first in the Lowcountry.

4

The five rules of sleep according to Kylie Venable:

1. Don't draw the curtains. God can't look after you if He can't see you.
2. Face the door. You need to be able to see what's coming.
3. Pull your knees up to your chin. It'll get your feet first that way.
4. Keep your ears covered up. You won't hear it calling you.
5. Never let your hands hang over the side of the bed. There's no telling what might take hold of them.

She made those rules for herself when she was about five, after a series of screaming nightmares that dragged us out of sleep night after night, hearts hammering. We wrote them down for her and pinned them on her bulletin board. If she followed them scrupulously, she dropped right off to sleep. If she omitted one, or fell asleep before she could complete her ritual, she would have the dreams. We were never sure why it worked. A child psychologist who was visiting on the island later told us that it was the instructive power of ritual, and that Kylie had, in effect, healed herself.

"But should we just let it go?" I said. "I don't want her getting the feeling that there's nothing between her and danger but some kind of magic ritual she thinks up. On the other hand, I don't want her to think she can prevent all kinds of harm just by doing the same thing."

"If it ain't broke, don't fix it," the shrink said. "It was about time for the nightmares, and it's about time for them to go away. Kylie has a good sense of her own needs, I'd say."

And she did. The nightmares faded, and she was never so afraid of anything incorporeal again. Or if she was, I never knew it. And I think I would have. But all of her life, she put herself to sleep at night by following her Five Rules of Sleep, and I often do it, too, to this day. It does help. I don't know why, but it does.

On this morning, I lay still in the tiny room that had always been mine, that looked out through a great, twisted, moss-shawled live oak to the marsh proper and the creek, and for a moment I did not open my eyes. I knew that it must be late morning or even early afternoon, for I had the cleansed, heavy-wristed feeling that you get when you have finally had enough sleep, but there was no sense of the strong overhead sunlight that should have fallen on my lids. I opened my eyes and looked out my uncurtained window into a solid wall of white. Fog. The dawn conflagration had told it truly: red sky at morning, sailors take warning. It was odd, though. We usually get those heavy, solid, still fogs in winter and very early spring.

I rolled over and stretched luxuriously, feeling each separate vertebra pop, feeling the long muscles in my legs pull. I lay still, smelling the peculiar island smell of damp old percale and salt mud, listening. But I heard nothing; not the songs of the migratory birds who often lingered on their way farther south; not the busy daytime rustle of the small communal wildlife in the spartina and sweet grass; not the faraway tolling of the bell buoy off the tip of Edisto; not the low throb of engines on the inland waterway. Nothing. The fog had swallowed sound as it had sight. I knew if any noise did penetrate, it would sound queer and displaced, without resonance. Fog bounces sound about like a ventriloquist.

I knew that I would take no photographs until it lifted, and toyed with the idea of simply burrowing back into the old piled, limp pillows and going back to sleep. But I did not need sleep; I needed to be out on the island, to let it slip its green fingers into my mind and draw out the sad silliness of the night before. Watercolors. That was what this day called for. Watercolors of the intimate, ghostly body parts of the island as they emerged from the whiteness and were swallowed again: a live oak arm with its sleeve of fog-covered moss, a cypress knee, the bones of the dock, the red hull of my grandfather's canoe, bumping against the rubber tire fender. I thought of John Marin and his watercolor *Maine Islands*, so much more powerful and evocative for what it hid in the fog than what it showed. Yes. A day for vignettes and glimpses.

I got up and showered in the rusted stall in the bathroom, letting the brackish, sulfur-kissed water sluice every knob and crevice of my body. I was, I thought, one of the few people on earth who liked the paper-mill stink of the island's water. I kept big drums of spring water at the house, both for drinking and cooking and for washing my hair, as I knew Clay hated the smell of it after I washed it in island water. Like a chemistry experiment gone wrong, he said. But I liked it. Today I would be totally a creature of the island; I would smell of it and taste of it, as well as see and touch and hear it.

I put the jeans and sweatshirt back on and

made coffee and found a rock-hard bagel and zapped it in the microwave, then took my breakfast to the table before the long windows that faced the creek. I ate staring into the shifting wall of the fog. After breakfast I rooted out my watercolor block and the tin box of colors, filled a plastic two-liter cola bottle with water, and started out the sliding door onto the deck. Silence and wetness smacked me in the face. I stopped and closed my eyes and breathed it deeply into my lungs.

I heard the hoofbeats while I stood, eyes still closed. It did not frighten me; I knew that it was the ponies. They had undoubtedly seen my lights and smelled my bagel, and were hoping for a handout. The Park Service maintained them nominally, but the Gullahs in Dayclear fed them biscuits and corn bread and whatever they had at hand, and so had my grandfather, adding grain in the winters, and the ponies had grown particular. I heard the stamping of hooves and an occasional snort and whicker, and I knew they would be grouped about the bottom of the steps up to the deck, waiting to see whether they would dine or would be forced to bolt. No one on the island mistreated or shooed them, that I was aware of, but sometimes they made a great, eye-rolling, hysterical show of fright and persecution, and went lumbering off in a pod as if ringmasters with chains were after them. There seemed to be no pattern to it. My grandfather always said, when they spooked and scattered like that, that they were simply bored, but Clay maintains that their brains are somehow smaller than those of normal horses, or that their synapses do not meet, or some such arcane genetic glitchiness. He does not care for the ponies. They trample grass and gardens and keep the shallow banks of the creek slick and muddy. And they leave their excrement everywhere.

I inched my way down the steps, talking softly all the while so that they would know I was there. I finally saw them when I had almost reached the bottom step. A small puff of breeze, the little wind off the mainland that usually comes up in the afternoon, blew aside the curtain of fog, and there they stood, perhaps seven of them in a loose knot, staring patiently at the steps where they knew I would materialize.

I do not know what they looked like origi- nally, but they mostly look alike now, distin- guishing characteristics blunted and buffed away by generations of inbreeding and the years in the subtropical wild. Now they are almost all a kind of taupish dun color, shaggy of coat and tangled of mane, with fat, hanging bellies from the rich marsh grass and the largesse of the islanders, and splayed, untrimmed hooves. Their coats are caked with the dust of their mud wallows in hot weather, when the slick odorous black mire is an effective fly and mosquito deterrent, and long and tattered like beggars' coats in winter. Their heads are large in proportion to their stumpy legs, and there is usually some sort of rheumy effluvia stuck in the corners of their large, feminine brown eyes. They have long eyelashes, ridiculously like cocottes in a French farce, and pretty, curly mouths like a fairytale illustration of an Arabian stallion. They are a very long way from being handsome creatures, but there is a kind of tough, cocky competence to them, a chunky briskness, that pleases the eye. They have attitude. For some reason, the sight of them always makes me smile. When the group shifted and I saw emerging from its middle the little goblin shape of a colt, I laughed aloud. I had not seen a baby in the herd since I myself was small.

One of the adults ambled out of the herd and stretched a stubby neck out toward my hand, and I opened it so that the sugar cube was visible. Long yellow piano-key teeth closed over the sugar and raked it none too daintily into a black-lipped mouth. Pianissimo. Nissy. And then the colt came scampering out, too, and bobbed its head against her flank and looked around her shoulder at me with huge, black-lashed eyes, and I both heard and felt my breath come out in a little puff of wonder and delight.

"Oh, Nissy, you have a baby," I breathed. "How pretty he . . . she? . . . is. What shall we call it? Oh, wouldn't Kylie love this, though!"

I fished in my pocket for more sugar and Nissy came closer and so did the colt, stretching its miniature neck out like its mother, ever so slowly, its head actually trembling with shyness and curiosity, and finally, delicately, it took the cube from my palm and crunched it, then wheeled and galloped away on its long, still-slender legs. Nissy swung her big head around to watch it, but she did not follow. The colt disappeared back into the body of the expectant herd. I threw a handful of cubes down on the ground and stepped back. Solemnly, not jostling and pushing as dogs or children would have done, the marsh tackies lipped up the sugar cubes, crunched them reflectively, waited a while until no more were forthcoming, and then, as if one of them had given a signal, wheeled and scampered clumsily away in one of their mock-panic attacks, snorting and whickering. The fog swallowed them almost immediately, and in another moment swallowed the sound of them. I was left standing on the bottom step surrounded by swirling white, with nothing for company but the memory of them and another memory that bobbed to the surface of my mind like a cork, bobbled there tantalizingly for a moment, and then lay still and whole in my head.

Another day of such fog, long ago, almost the only time I remembered a fog like this one,

for we did not come to the island so often in
winter. There was too much going on on Peacock's for the children then. But for some reason
we were here, Kylie and I, in a chilly, silent white
fog like this one, she perhaps five or six, still tiny
in her yellow slicker, waiting for my grandfather
to finish whatever he was doing in his bedroom
and come and take us crabbing over on Wassimaw Creek. I would not have taken the boat out
in such weather, but he knew every inch of all
the island's waterways by heart, and knew that
almost no one else would have a boat out. It
was, he had said the night before, a fine day for
crabbing. So we waited, and Kylie chafed. I usually let her run free on the island, but not in fog
like this.

Kylie had no fear. You needed a little, sometimes.

The phone rang, and I went into the kitchen
to answer it and talked for quite a while to Clay,
who was leaving on a trip to New York and could
not find his cuff links. When I hung up, Kylie was
gone.

My grandfather came out then, and together we went out into the white nothingness,
groping our way down the steps and across the
grass to the edge of the marsh, which dropped a
half-foot or so down from the hummock on
which the grove and the house sat. Scarcely six
inches, but the difference in terrain was dra-

matic. On the high ground, the earth was firm and level. On the marsh, it was ephemeral, trembling, not quite solid underfoot. Not precisely watery, or outright bog, but . . . not solid. When you could not see, as we could not on this day, the feeling was eerie, unsettling, as if you stayed on the surface of the earth only by its capricious sufferance. We called and called for her, hearing our voices stop short against a wall of fog, hearing nothing in return but the dripping from the old live oaks and the slap of the creek against the distant pilings of the dock. For the first five minutes or so I was very angry with her. On the sixth the fear came. By the time we had groped our way to the edge of the hundred-foot plank walkway that wound across the marsh to the creek, I was weak-kneed and nearly sobbing with fear.

"She can't have gotten far," my grandfather said over and over. "She can't be in any real trouble. If she'd fallen or something, we'd hear it."

"You can't hear anything in this fog," I quavered. "You can't even hear the fog buoy. . . ."

"You'd hear if she fell into the water," he said sensibly. It did no good at all. I was halfway down the walkway when we did hear a noise. I stopped. It was the muffled thundering of the ponies coming up over the hummock from the opposite direction, behind the house on the high ground. Above it I could hear Kylie's laughter. In

the distorting fog, it seemed to come from everywhere around us and from far away, from nearby
and nowhere.

I was back on solid grass by the time the
ponies materialized out of the mist, running hard.
One of them was a good half-head in the lead. It
was Pianissimo, and Kylie was on her back, bent
low over the thick neck, hands woven into the
straggly mane, clinging like a yellow-clad monkey. Kylie, laughing as hard and joyously as I
have ever heard her laugh in her life.

While I stood there, speechless with relief and
anger, the pony set her stumpy legs and stopped
abruptly, and Kylie half slid, half fell off her back,
still laughing. By the time I reached her, Pianissimo had lumbered away, back into the fog with
the other ponies. I could hear them as they trotted
along the line of the hummock toward the distant
maritime forest that often sheltered them, but I
could no longer see them.

Kylie was properly chastened when my
grandfather and I finished with her, but she was
not repentant. She had, she said, seen the herd
off at the edge of the copse while I talked on the
phone and went to give them sugar, and they
were so friendly, especially Pianissimo, that she
just wanted to see if she could ride. Nissy, she
said, had stood like a statue while she climbed
onto her back, but then had taken off as if she
had heard a shot.

"I rode her all the way down the old deer path, Mama," she said. "She can run like the wind, for a fat little old pony. It was . . . it was neat. Just me and her and the fog . . . and you could hear the others behind us. It was like we were leading them on a charge."

"Didn't you hear us calling you?" I said.

"Yeah," she admitted. "I did."

"Kylie, you know you have to come when I call you. That's not negotiable. You agreed to that. How can I let you out of my sight if you don't keep your word about that?"

"I was, Mama," she said. "I was coming faster this way than if I was on my own two legs. Lots faster."

She was right, technically, but I was not prepared to argue the point. I cut our visit short and we forwent the crabbing expedition and went back home to Peacock's. She was disappointed, but she did not whine or cry. If Kylie deliberately disobeyed me, or did something she knew I would not have permitted, she took the consequences without a murmur. She simply fell in love with an idea, weighed the pleasure against the cost, did the deed with relish, and paid the price uncomplainingly. It was a very adult way to live a young life, all told. Except that the final price had been more than she could have imagined. More than I could have, too.

I stood still on this morning, in the fog, thinking of that day, hearing again the thudding of the hooves of the herd, seeing again the flash of my daughter's yellow slicker in the cottony nothingness. Fog and ponies and Kylie . . .

Before I went out with my watercolors I called Clay at his office. Shawna, the office's forty-year-old receptionist who has never married and thinks that she is married to Clay, said that he was out of the office until after lunch. She did not know where he had gone, but she had an idea it was into Charleston.

"I hope he's seeing a doctor finally, Mrs. Venable," she said in the honeyed twang that puts my teeth on edge. Shawna is originally from New Jersey. The Lowcountry got her about the same time Clay did. She sounds as if she is chewing cape jessamine.

"What on earth for?" I said, surprised and faintly alarmed.

She was silent a moment, and then she said, "Well, nothing, really, I guess. It's just that none of us think he's been himself lately. You know, he's just so distracted, and abrupt, and it's as though he doesn't really see you when you talk to him. . . . We just thought he ought to get a checkup. But of course if you haven't noticed anything, then there's nothing. . . ." She let her voice trail off. My own blindness and neglect were implicit in the dying syllables.

"I think he's just fine, Shawna," I said briskly.

"But thank you for worrying about him. If there's anything amiss, I'm sure he'll let us know. We had a pretty late night last night, with the new people coming in and all. . . ."

"Of course," she said. "He's just tired. I keep telling him he ought to let somebody else take over those dinner things for the new people, but you know how he is. . . ."

"Yes, I do," I said, and thanked her and hung up smartly.

Did I, though? Had Clay really been all those things—distant, abstracted, tired, unseeing—and I had not noticed? I thought back. He had been working very late in his home office for the past month or so, but he frequently did that when there was a new project in the wings. And he had been silent and gone away behind his *Wall Street Journal* or his clipboard in the mornings at breakfast, and to some extent at dinner, but when wasn't he? Clay was not gregarious, not loquacious, not a mealtime gossip. He never had been, especially not since the Plantation companies had taken off like they had in the past four or five years, with new properties coming on line in half a dozen states and the Caribbean. Not since Kylie.

Both of us had been, to some extent, gone away since then. I had been content to have it so. I could not have borne the weight of a hovering, demanding relationship in those first few precarious months and years. I did not think he could have, either. It was as if we had had an agreement: when the time is right, when the healing is further along, we will come all the way back to each other. We will know when. There is no hurry.

But there had been no agreement. I had just assumed he felt as I did. I shook my head and went on out into the day. I would call again after lunch, and tonight at dinner we would talk about it. Finally, we would talk. I could not abide the thought that he was unhappy and alone with it.

The fog lifted about noon, and the sun fell so heavily on the windless marsh and creek that I was soon hot and sweat-slicked, and shucked my jacket and tied it around my waist. With the fog gone, my morning's pursuit of fog-sculpted vignettes vanished, too, and the glare off the water began to give me a headache. I trudged back to the house and put on a T-shirt, exchanged the watercolors for my camera, made myself a peanut butter sandwich, and took everything out to the Boston Whaler that bobbed at the dock. We had not yet put it away for the winter; there had been no real winter on the island, and there probably would be none. I could remember days in January and February out on the water, with the sun burning face and forearms and only a chill edge to the wind to remind you that the soft Lowcountry winter had teeth and could bare them if it chose. But it rarely did. Only occasionally did we get a slicking of sleet or ice, and only once in my lifetime did snow fall on Peacock's and the island. But it had been a spectacular snow, drifting up to eight or nine inches and lingering for three or four days. Snow on palms and Spanish moss . . . everyone had taken photos of it, to send to family and friends off-island.

I took the boat down Alligator Alley to Wassimaw Creek and over to the inland waterway, to photograph the steel winter light there. But the sky was too milky for much contrast, and there was a softening in the distance that spoke of returning fog. So I cut the motor and threw out the little anchor and let the Whaler drift. I ate my sandwich and drank the Diet Coke I had brought along, and then I stretched out on the backseat and pulled the Atlanta Braves cap that belonged to everyone and no one over my eyes and drowsed. There must have been virtually no traffic on the waterway; I saw none, and heard none, for the entire time that I was there. But for much of that time I was fast asleep, and when I woke, the fog was just reaching its succubus's fingers out to pat my face, and the heat was gone from the day. A solid white bank lay over the Inland Waterway, and I knew that it would drift up the creeks and estuaries until it swallowed the entire island. I pulled up the anchor and started the engine and putted for home. I was not worried about the fog, but I was cold in just the T-shirt, and I had a neck ache from sleeping with my head tilted forward against the stern. I wanted hot coffee and a shower before I left for Peacock's. More than that, I wanted not to leave for Peacock's at all. The island had done its work while I slept, and I felt washed and lightened and eased. There would undoubtedly be some sort of additional welcome ceremonies for the new people this evening, and I simply did not feel like wasting this beneficence on them.

"Please let them all have previous engagements," I whispered to the whitened sky, though what engagements they might have there among the alien corn I could not imagine. But when I got back to the house the answering machine light was blinking, and I picked it up to hear Clay's voice telling me that he and Hayes had to go to Atlanta on the spur of the moment and that the human resources people were baby-sitting the newcomers tonight.

"So stay another day or so, if you want to," he said. "I don't know how long we'll be. There are some money people who made some time for us earlier than we thought. I'll call you either there or at home when I know where we're staying and when we'll be back. Or I'll let Shawna know. Take care."

He did not say, "I love you," as he sometimes

did. He was using his flat, intense, strictly business voice. He did not use it for endearments. I
would not have had it so. I thought that the
money people must be pretty important. My
heart lifted. I could stay on the island. Clay
would not miss me in this mood.

I had my shower and built a fire and put on a
tape of Erroll Garner's *Concert by the Sea*. It was
an old recording; it had been my grandfather's.
Oddly, he had loved the cool, improvisational
West Coast jazz of the late fifties and sixties, and
I had transferred a lot of his old records to tape
for him. I loved this one, too. Perfect fog music. I
made a pot of coffee and rooted around in the
bookcase among the yellowing, damp-warped
books and magazines for something I had not
read recently. I settled on *Kon-Tiki*, another
favorite of my grandfather's, and curled up on the
spavined sofa to lose myself at sea.

An hour or so must have passed when I heard
the ponies again. The fog-flattened sound of their
hooves pulled me back from the wastes of the
Pacific, and I shook my head for a moment, not
quite knowing where I was. Then I smiled and
got up and went out onto the deck to see if I
could spot Pianissimo and her colt again.

The fog was blowing, spinning fast in the circle of yellow light from the overhead porch light.
A brisk wind from off the ocean meant that it
would be clear later tonight, and there would be

a sky pricked full of icy stars. In the swirling skeins I caught glimpses of the herd, moving restlessly around the support posts of the house. It was not full dark, but it would be in fifteen or twenty more minutes.

I went back for sugar cubes and then walked slowly down the steps, clicking my tongue.

"You here, Nissy?" I called softly. "Want some sugar? Come on, bring that baby up here and let's have a look at him. Or her."

A dark shape came out of the fog: Nissy, sure enough, with the colt close on her flank. I stretched out my hand with the sugar cube, and that's when I saw the child.

She stood off at the edge of the pale orb of porch light, perhaps thirty feet away, still as a statue, staring at me. Her head and shoulders were fairly distinct, but from her waist down she was lost in fog. I got the impression of a small brown face and great dark eyes that fastened intently on me, and a headful of dark curls with fog droplets clinging to them. She wore a yellow rain slicker. She looked to be about five or six, maybe seven. A small seven. She made no noise at all, and she did not move.

I did not, either. I could not have. My heart began to thunder, pounding so hard that I could hear only it and my blood, roaring in my ears. If she had spoken, I could not have heard her. But she did not speak. My knees and thighs and wrists turned to water. It seemed to me that only the powerful heartbeat held me up, that I hung from it like a marionette.

Nissy whickered and stamped her hoof, and I held out my hand toward the child as slowly as if to a wild creature.

"Who are you?" I meant to say.

"Is it you?" came out of my mouth, a crippled whisper.

The child turned and bolted. The fog took her before she had gone four paces. I could hear her footsteps for a bit before they were lost in the cottony whiteness. I thought she ran back around the house and toward the dirt road leading into the hummock where the house stood.

I could not make my legs go after her. In the space of a minute, I was not sure she had been there at all. I felt sweat break out in huge, cold drops on my forehead and at my hairline, and sat down heavily on the bottom step. I sat there until the ponies moved away, and then there was nothing but fog and silence and the yellow pool of light from the porch. And still I sat there.

Presently I got up and went up the steps, as stiffly as if I were very old or had been badly beaten, and into the house. I went to the closet where the cleaning supplies were kept. From behind a cardboard grocery carton of toilet paper I took a bottle of Wild Turkey. There were three of them there; they had been there since my grandfather died. I would not have thought I even remembered them. But my fingers did, and my blood. I took the bottle and a glass and sat back down before the dying fire and began to drink. I drank, not moving from the couch, until I passed out. It was not the first time that had happened, but it had not happened many times, and never in this place. One of the last things I remember thinking was, I've broken all my covenants now.

The first waking moments of a bad hangover are a time when all things are possible. Reality is canceled; it does not yet prevail. There is only, for the first instant, a purity of being, an utter, bodiless awareness. The body will get its licks in almost instantly, of course: the dry, knife-edged throat and lips, the pounding sinuses, the first roilings of the abused and mutinous stomach. Hard on their heels will come the sickly, slithering feet of the great shame and fragmented memories of the night before, sliding in like dirty water under a shut door.

But that first moment: that is pure Zen. Nothing is closed to you. Nothing is past and nothing is ahead; everything is now.

When I woke on the sofa in front of the dead fire the next morning, there was only me and the child I had seen the night before. That was the great, ultimate reality of my life in this moment. It remained only to decide what to do about it.

I lay without moving, eyes still closed, letting sensation seep in bit by bit under the great, white knowledge that enclosed me: stiff, cold limbs, pounding head, killing thirst, a great pressure on my bladder, a great pressure waiting to crush my soul. I pushed them all back; they could and would wait. Until I opened my eyes, until I moved, the child from last night was the one real thing, the one true thing, in my universe.

I remember clearly thinking: Madness is waiting for me. I can choose it or not. If I choose the child, I choose the madness. If I don't, I can have my life back like it was. I don't have to decide until I open my eyes. But I will have to decide then.

I lay still, eyes closed, not moving, reaching out to her with my mind and my heart and all of my being. I heard the morning wind start up in the live oak that hung over the deck and the first grumpy twitter of the anonymous little songbirds that lived there. A part of my mind noted that it must be very early. The light felt pearly on my lids. Everything in me called to her. I did not move.

I heard the ponies then. They came chuffing and trotting over the hummock from behind the house; I could hear them clearly. Their hooves had depth and resonance. I knew that the fog had gone. I waited.

And I heard her. I heard her small feet thudding after the ponies, coming closer, coming from the east, the direction of the road. I heard her laugh. It was a giggle: silvery, delighted, unafraid. And I heard her voice. It was the pure, generic piping of childhood: it could have belonged to any child.

Any child at all.

"Here, baby," she called.

Choose, my heart said, and I chose. I opened my eyes. I got up and ran lightly across the floor and out onto the deck, tiptoeing, heart bursting, lips curving in a smile that was only a remembered shape on my mouth. If this was madness, I thought, then I embrace it, now and forever. Oh, if this is madness, let it never lift. . . .

I started down the steps and stopped. She was there, looking up at me as she had last night, still wearing the yellow slicker. She did not move.

She was not my child. She was no one's child I had ever seen. In the clear, opalescent light of early morning a stranger's child stood there, poised for flight, dark eyes wary but not frightened, feet and legs bare under the too-big slicker, taking my measure as handily as she took my heart and turned it to frozen lead. She did not speak again. From behind the house, I heard the ponies begin to move back toward the road.

A man came around the side of the house then. He was not tall, but he was stocky and heavy-shouldered, tanned almost black and with a great bush of wiry, gray-streaked black hair. He stopped and looked at me; his eyes were hers, the child's.

"I'm sorry, I didn't know anybody was here," he said. "My granddaughter was chasing the ponies and got away from me. I hope we didn't scare you."

I simply looked at him. It seemed to me, in that dead moment, that no one and nothing would ever scare me again.

5

I sat down abruptly on the steps and looked at him. My legs and arms and, when I looked down, my hands, were trembling, a shivering so fine that it was hardly visible, but profound for all that. I was as weak as if I had been ill for a long time. It struck me that I had spent a lot of time, all told, sitting on these steps. The thought might have made me smile another time. I could not have smiled now, with my trembling lips and numb face. It was all I could do to focus on him.

He came closer, frowning slightly.

"We did scare you. You're shaking all over," he said. His voice was rich and deep, plummy, almost a theatrical voice. There was a note in it that was somehow foreign, though he spoke with no discernible accent. There were deep grooves in the leathery brown face, between his heavy, gray-spiked eyebrows, running from his brown avian beak of a nose to his wide mouth, radiating from the corners of his eyes. A well-used face. His crown of wild hair would have brushed the collar of his blue work shirt if it had fallen straight, but it foamed and frizzed in the heavy fog-humidity into an exuberant afro. It made his head look too large even for the thick torso. I thought distract-edly of a portrait of the Minotaur I had seen in a book of Greek legends once. I thought also of an aging hippie. The work shirt was knotted at his waist and exposed a tangle of gray chest hair with a medallion of some sort on a chain buried in it, and there was a flower in the top buttonhole, a drooping camellia. His blue jeans were bleached nearly white and frayed at the hem, and his feet were bare. Unlike the rest of him, they were neat and small.

He was no one I had ever seen and bore little resemblance to anyone who ordinarily came to Peacock's and the island, and it occurred to me that perhaps I should be afraid of him, but I was not. I was sick, depleted, utterly numb, and vaguely angry at him. Or, at least, I knew that I would be angry, when I could feel much of any-thing. Mainly, I simply wanted him to be gone, him and his intruding granddaughter.

"You didn't scare me," I said dully. "I thought for a minute the little girl was someone else. But you should know that you're on private property. I own this house and land. And I'm not feeling very well, so if you wouldn't mind I really think—"

"I wanted to see the horses," the child said in a clear treble voice. "There is a baby, Grandpapa."

He did not move, but his face went bone white and then flushed a dark red. He drew in a great breath and let it out again on a long sigh. He turned his face to the child, and tears welled in his black eyes, and his face seemed almost to crumple.

"Tell me about the baby, Lita," he said very softly. He was still staring at her; he did not turn to me. I thought at first he must have had some sort of an attack, a stroke or something, but then I could see that he was flooded with strong emotion of some sort, almost to the point of open weeping. I opened my mouth to ask them to leave. Slowly, I shut it again. The thought of this massive, dark man weeping on my doorstep was somehow more than I could bear to even contemplate. I hoped that, if I were still and silent, he would regain his control and go away and take his changeling with him. Then I could sit in the pale lemon sunlight of a Lowcountry autumn and see if there was a way to go on with this day and this life.

The child did not speak again. He turned his head to me finally. His face was relatively composed now, though the tears had overflowed his eyes and ran down his face into the chasms on either side of his mouth.

"She has not spoken in a very long time," he said. "The doctors weren't sure that she ever would again. I hope you'll forgive the sloppy tears. It's a happy moment for me." His face *was* happy, incandescently so, almost foolishly so. It was the face of a large, giddy child, rapt and open. I had seen no faces like this on any man I had met before. Most men learn early to shield the force of their loves from strangers. A tongue of sympathy and interest curled in my heart in the midst of all the aridity, infinitely small and alien.

"She spoke this morning, too, before you came," I said. "I heard her. She said, 'Here, baby.' And last night I heard her. I think maybe those doctors didn't know what they were talking about."

He looked from me to the child. She looked solemnly back at him. She had a strange little face, very brown and sharply triangular, with a small pointed chin and enormous dark eyes. Under the cap of lustrous black curls, it looked almost medieval, the face of a Florentine child on a triptych.

"She was not here last night," he said to me, still looking at her. "She was asleep in our house. I put her to bed myself. You must have heard something else."

"I don't think so," I said, smiling at the child.

"It was you last night, wasn't it? With the horses, in the fog?"

She smiled a tiny, formal little smile, but she did not break her silence.

"Were you here last night, Estrellita?" her grandfather asked her, very seriously. "Did you slip away and come looking for the ponies?"

She looked at me, and then down at her bare dirty feet, and then up at him.

"*Sí, Abuelo,*" she whispered.

He did not say anything for a long time, only looked down at her. I saw that he was once again struggling to contain the tears, and turned my face away. I was very tired, and once more wished that they would go, whoever they were. I wanted no part of their epiphanies.

He turned to me then, briskly, and took the child's hand. "We'll be on our way," he said. "We didn't mean to bother you. She thinks the ponies hung the moon, but she's never run away after them before, and she's certainly never spoken of them. I'll see that she stays closer to home from now on."

They turned to go.

"Wait," I said. They turned back.

"Who are you?" I said. "Who is she? Where do you live? How did you get all the way out here? Why has she not spoken for so long?"

He laughed aloud, a raucous, unfettered sound. Across the copse in the thick pine woods a flock of crows answered him, making almost the same sound. The child laughed, too.

"My name is Lou," he said. "Lou Cassells. This is Estrellita Esteban, my granddaughter. We're living at the moment over in Dayclear, up at the other end of the island. I'm working around there, and she's spending the summer with me. She has not spoken since her mama died three years ago. That was back in Cuba, where our family comes from. Her mama died in their house in the mountains, in childbirth. There was no one with her but Estrellita. The new baby was born dead, and Estrellita's mother died after two days. Lita was still at their side when they found her. It was almost too late; she was badly dehydrated, and she had not had food for days. She did not speak after that until . . . now. That we know of, anyway."

"My God," I whispered. It was literally incomprehensible to me that there was still a place in the world, especially so close to my world, where women and babies died alone in childbirth and small children starved beside them, waiting for help that did not come. How could this be? An old pain, sharp and terrible, that I thought I had buried forever, tore at my heart. I put out my hand jerkily, as if it moved by itself, and touched the black curls, then dropped it at my side.

"How did that happen?" I said softly and

fiercely. "How in the world could you let that happen?"

His face closed. It looked like a Toltec mask, severe and blunt and empty.

"Her father was dead. Her mother stayed on at the farm in the mountains because the baby was so nearly due; she could not travel. There were no close neighbors. Everyone had gone. It is very poor back in those mountains. Most of Cuba is very poor. I could not prevent it. I have not been back to Cuba in almost forty years. I cannot go back. I would be arrested."

"I'm sorry," I said miserably. "I spoke out of turn. It must have been awful for you. Was her father your son?"

"Her mother was my daughter."

We were both silent then. I looked at him across a sea of troubles that for once were not my own. It looked uncrossable. I was ashamed.

"Please come into the house and have some coffee with me," I said. "And I think there's a jelly doughnut in the freezer. Maybe by that time the ponies will come back and we can see the baby."

I smiled at the child and she smiled back, a fuller smile this time.

"Her mother's name is Pianissimo," I said. "My daughter named her when she was about your age. It's because she has big yellow teeth like a piano."

The child laughed aloud, a liquid gurgle of pleasure, and her grandfather smiled. I did, too, surprising myself.

"If she comes back maybe you can help me think of a name for her baby," I said. "Meanwhile, let me show you my house. I used to come here to the island to visit my grandfather, too, and this is where he lived. My name is Caroline Venable, but you can call me Caro."

The little girl made the shape of my name with her lips, but silently, "Caro." The man stopped and stared at me, and then laughed again, with surprise and, I thought, pleasure. This was a man, obviously, to whom laughter and tears and who knew what else came naturally and were not reined in.

"Mrs. Venable," he said. "I've heard of you, but I thought you'd be . . . older, I guess. I knew we'd meet sooner or later, though. I'm working for your husband."

I stopped and looked back at him, surprised. He was definitely not the sort of man who usually came to the Plantation to work for Clay.

"You work for the company?" I said. "For Clay?"

"Not really," Lou Cassells said. "This is a one-time-only deal, I think. I'm doing some landscape consulting for him. For the project over at Dayclear."

I stared at him.

"It's named for the Gullah settlement up at the other end," he said, mistaking my silence for ignorance. "You know, where the little houses are, and the old people. That's to be the center of it, so that's what your husband is calling it for now. Clay, yes. Privately I call him Mengele. I'm hoping to charm you thoroughly enough so you won't tell him."

Still I did not speak.

"If that was out of line, I apologize," he said, his face changing. "More than one person has told me my tongue is going to get me into bad trouble. Again."

I held up my hand, shaking my head.

"No. I mean, no, I don't mind you calling him Mengele. Well, I do, I just . . . I wasn't aware that there was a property planned for Dayclear. It's way back on the river, in the middle of the marsh. . . . Why would anybody want to make a . . . project . . . of it? How could they, if they did?"

He shrugged. "I thought you would know about it. I hope I'm not the bearer of bad news for you. Actually, it will make a beautiful . . . ah, property, as you say. The river is deep and wide and navigable there. Good natural basin for a marina. It would be simple to dredge the rest. I don't know, I only work there. Mengele . . . Clay . . . hired me to do a landscape workup, see what would grow there, what plants to keep, what to take out, what to import. It's my specialty. I have a master's degree in subtropical botany from Cornell. Please don't bad-mouth me to your husband; this is miles above working as a disc jockey in a twenty-megahertz rock 'n' roll station out Wappoo Creek Road. That was my last job."

I turned and went on up the stairs. They followed me. The hangover bell jar of detachment and torpor descended again. I pushed the thought of the development at Dayclear outside it. I would deal with it later; there was, of course, some mistake. This man had his facts wrong. It would be easy for a casual employee to do that. He probably meant that Clay was using the settlement and the land around it as a model for a marsh property he was developing somewhere else. The vegetation would be virtually the same. I would straighten this out with Clay when he got back from Atlanta. There was simply no sense borrowing trouble. Sufficient unto the day the evil thereof. It was something I had learned, and learned well, in the long days after Kylie died. I was good at it.

I sat them down on the sofa before the fireplace and lit the half-burned logs, and they leaped into life. The fire felt good. With the clearing of the fog had come fresh, stinging cold air from the west. I thought that we were done, now, with the last soft, wet traces of the Lowcountry Indian summer.

The child sat quietly while I made coffee, but

then her curiosity got the best of her and she got up and began to roam around the house. She picked things up and examined them and set them down again, very gently, looking at me as for permission. Her grandfather said something to her in soft, rapid Spanish and she stopped and clasped her hands behind her, but I said, "No, let her look. There's nothing here she can hurt. It's all childproof. I did the very same thing, and so did my daughter. . . ."

He spoke again, and Estrellita went back to her solemn examining. He got up and came into the kitchen, where I was getting mugs down from the rack beside the stove and pouring milk, and leaned against the refrigerator.

"This is a good house," he said. "It feels lived and loved in, and it looks just like it should. It honors the marsh."

I smiled.

"That's a good way of putting it," I said. "I think it does, too. My grandfather would have liked to hear that."

"He's gone then."

"Yes. For several years now. But sometimes it seems to me that he's still here, in this house and in the marsh. . . ."

I fell silent, reddening. Now he would think that Mengele's wife was some sort of New Age fruitcake, though why I cared what he thought I could not have said.

"Yes, it's odd, isn't it?" he said. "Odd and good, how our dead stay with us sometimes, if we are very lucky. I often feel my daughter close, though I did not see her after she was very small, smaller even than this one here. I wish I could feel my wife, but she does not come. Ah, well. She never did want to leave Cuba. Why should she leave it now?"

I shot him a swift look. He was smiling gently, as if the memory of his wife was a warm, quiet one.

"She's gone, too?" I said.

"She died two years ago, in Havana. She had been raising Lita. One of my Miami relatives was able to arrange to get the child out for me. I don't know what would have happened to her otherwise. I'm very grateful."

He spoke so matter-of-factly of his unimaginable life that it put me at ease. Somehow I thought he had learned to do that so that his American friends, so unused to this sort of tragedy, would not be smitten with guilt and pity. It was a graceful thing to do. I liked him for it.

I handed him a cup of coffee.

"I'm not going to pry into your life, but I wish you'd tell me how you got to the South Carolina Lowcountry. That trip must be some kind of story."

"One day," he said, smiling so that the crinkles fanned out from his eyes. "One day I'll do that. But

I want to hear about you now. You already know a lot about me. Turnabout is fair play."

We sat down on the sofa in front of the fire. Lita had gone out onto the deck and was swinging on the low branch of the live oak that curved over it, shawled in silvery Spanish moss. I knew that it was sturdy enough for her slight weight. It had borne mine, and later Carter's, and Kylie's.

"It's awfully tame compared to yours," I said. "I'd bore you to sleep."

I did not want to talk about myself. In fact, now that I had invited them in and settled them down, I wanted, perversely, for them to be gone again. The hangover and the shame and the accompanying uneasy fatigue surged back full bore. I wanted simply to lie down on the sofa and go back to sleep.

He seemed to sense my hesitation.

"Another time we'll meet and swap stories, maybe," he said. "I think you're tired, and you said you weren't feeling well. We need to get back, anyway. I don't think my hosts know where we are."

He started to get up. A thought struck me.

"Wait a minute," I said. "Why do you call him Mengele? Clay?"

He grinned. It was white and wolfish, framed in the dark skin. It was also the grin of a havoc-minded, completely unrepentant small boy, and I had to smile back.

"Well, number one, I'm Jewish, and I have a very well-developed sense of both paranoia and history. When somebody threatens me, I automatically think of Josef Mengele. Number two, those amazing blue eyes. They look at you as though he's wondering what would happen if he connected your liver up to your kidneys, whether you'd piss bile or what. No other reason. He's been a perfect gentleman to me."

"But he threatens you. . . ."

"Not so much me. Just . . . oh, shit, I don't know. Maybe nobody. For all I know he raises Persian kittens and butterflies in his spare time. It's just that I've seen eyes like that in photographs from Nuremberg. Haven't you ever thought how . . . extraordinary they are?"

"They are that," I said. "But I never found them threatening. Intense, maybe."

A stronger surge of nausea flooded through me, and the fine trembling came back, and I leaned my head back and closed my eyes for a moment. When I opened them he was looking at me gravely and the smile was gone.

"This is none of my business," he said. "But I think you ought to let me put a drop of bourbon in that coffee. I know a hangover when I see one. You feel like death. It'll help, if you don't have any more."

I started to protest, and then simply did not. I felt too badly, and there was something disarming about this man. He did not intimidate me in any way, despite the piratical skin and hair and the big Chiclet teeth. I suddenly did not care what he knew about me.

"How'd you know bourbon was my drink?" I said dreamily.

"Well, for one thing, I smelled booze on you when we first met. For another, there's a half-empty bottle of it just under the coffee table. And for still another, it was my drink, too, and I'd know the smell of good bourbon anywhere, even if I haven't tasted it for eight long years. I've been where you are. It feels damned awful. A little hair of the dog is not a bad thing, if you stick to one. After that I think you ought to go home. It doesn't do to be by yourself with a bad hangover. Is there somebody there to look after you?"

I thought of my vast, beautiful, empty house in Peacock Island Plantation.

"That's a good idea," I said. "I'll do that. I think I'll skip the hair of the dog, though."

He was silent for a moment, and then he said softly, "I think you're lying, but I've been there and done that, too. Just promise me you'll go on home and we'll be on our way. Your daughter, is she in school? You want to be there when she gets home. . . ."

"My daughter is dead," I said, still wrapped in the peace of the bell jar. "She drowned five years ago. She would be fifteen now. I thought your granddaughter . . . for a minute, last night, she looked very like my daughter at that age. She used to chase the ponies, too."

"*Ay, Dios,*" he said softly after a long while. "I'm sorry. Lita must have been an awful shock for you. I'll see to it that she doesn't come again."

"No. She's a nice child. And the ponies are obviously helping her. Later, maybe, another day, you can bring her over and I'll tell you where to find the baby and her mother. I think I know where they're hanging out this fall. I can't stop living. I don't want to. She's welcome here."

He got to his feet and went to the door and called to Lita to come in, it was time to go.

"You are a very nice woman, Mrs. Caroline Venable," he said. "I'm sorry if we brought any pain at all into your enchanted hideaway here. I think that you didn't know about Dayclear, and I've shocked you badly, and as I say, I wish I could bite my tongue out, but I'm sure it would simply go on flapping. Your husband should have told you about it. You must talk with him about it now."

Anger flared from somewhere under the hangover. How dare this man, this perfect stranger, this hired employee of my husband's, this trespasser, tell me what I must and must not do, or what Clay should have? I recognized the anger for what it was: a mask for fear, but that did not lessen it. I sat up abruptly and glared at him.

"I find that arrogant beyond belief," I said coldly. "My . . . relationship with my husband is absolutely none of your affair. It never will be. And you are dead wrong about the new project. You've got your facts confused. There is no way Clay would start to develop this island without telling me first. There's no way I wouldn't know. For one thing, he doesn't own this part of the island, I do. All of it, except for the settlement itself. And I'd never in this world permit such a thing. He knows that."

He looked at me silently for a long time, a level look suddenly as cold as my own. All the small-boy charm was gone from the brown face. I could almost feel the impact of the opaque black eyes. Uneasiness crept in over the anger. I did not know this man. How could I have forgotten that?

"They'd like to know that over in Dayclear," he said finally. "They're really upset. They're sure they're going to lose their homes. It's all they talk about, the old ones. There's not anywhere else for most of them to go."

"They do know that," I retorted. "Right after Clay deeded this part of the island over to me I went over and told them. I told Jackson. He said he'd tell the others. Toby would do what he said. I told them they'd never have to worry about losing their homes. My God, I love this marsh as much as my grandfather did, and all of them knew how he felt about it. . . ."

"Well, perhaps you'll pardon them for being a little confused," he said. "They've got surveyors over there, and people in pink Izod and LaCoste shirts thunking around in their little deck shoes with no socks, making notes on clipboards, and every now and then Mengele himself pays a royal visit and chats everybody up, and his trusty side-kick Goebbels is over there every other day, and then I come poking around in their bushes and sticking tags on their live oaks . . . you can see why it might look to them like something's up. And for the record, I'm not mistaken. I've seen the master plan."

I felt my face whiten.

"You are definitely mistaken. I don't care what you think you've seen. And even if you weren't, Clay does not own Dayclear, nor do I. It belongs to them, the people who live there. My grandfather always said that it did. . . ."

"Actually, nobody knows who it belongs to," he said. "There's no way you could establish clear title to those homes. I imagine they'll be offered a handsome cash buyout. That's the way it's usually done."

"And how can you possibly know that?"

"A friend of mine told me. Someone who lives in Dayclear. Perhaps you know of him. Ezra Upchurch? I gather he's rather well known in the Lowcountry. . . ."

"Ezra Upchurch! Living in Dayclear? I

thought he was on John's Island," I said. "Of course I know of him. I know him, too. I used to play with him when we were both about eight, but then his mother came and got him and they moved. . . . What's he doing back in Dayclear? I wouldn't think things were lively enough for him over here."

"He thinks otherwise," Lou Cassells said, smiling a new, cold smile. "He's decided to come back to the humble village of his birth and stay a spell. Rediscover his roots, so to speak. As a matter of fact, I'm staying at his house, his and his old aunt's. He'll be happy to know that according to Mrs. Mengele, Dayclear is safe as a baby's butt in a cradle."

Ezra Upchurch. Bastard child of a mother who fled Dayclear at fifteen, leaving him behind with his young grandmother. Changeling child possessed of a quicksilver mind and a steely will, so gifted that he graduated from the county high school at sixteen and went on to Morehouse College in Atlanta on a full scholarship, and from there to Yale Divinity School and then Duke Law. Full scholarships all. Then he came back to the Lowcountry and began a rich, glinting career that included preaching at the smallest, most time-lost pray houses in the marshes and woods, taking the smallest and most impossible pro bono legal cases for the remaining Gullah Negroes, playing piano in a number of scabrous, deep-woods roadhouses where few white faces were ever seen, disc jockeying for black jazz stations up and down the coast, racing his Harley-Davidson, and lecturing at colleges and universities all over the country for astronomical fees, most of which went to support the various drives, funds, and marches that he organized to improve the lot of his people. He was almost magically successful at these; the media adored him, as did what he called "my little folks" everywhere. A great many white Lowcountry people, particularly the gentry and those who aspired to be, called him an agitator. His supporters called him a savior. No one called him humble. His fat, flashing ego preceded him, to paraphrase Cyrano de Bergerac, by a quarter of an hour. To hear him speak was an unforgettable experience. I never had, not in person, but I had heard him on television; the fine hairs on my arms had risen at his words and voice. Ezra Upchurch, in Dayclear.

What must I think about that?

I shook my head slightly. It had begun to throb.

"Well, since you know him so well, you go back and tell him that none of it's true and I'm not going to let anything happen to this part of the island. And that includes Dayclear. And let that be an end to it. I don't want to hear any more about this . . . silliness. Do you understand me?"

He nodded his head and tugged at a forelock

in an elaborate parody of a servant with his mistress.

"Yes, Miz Mengele," he drawled. "I understand, I sho' does. You have, by the way, read *Lady Chatterley's Lover*?"

I stared at him, speechless.

"Ah, so you have. Well, then, doesn't it give you the least little pang of fear, or whatever, to realize that you're out here all alone in the wilderness with your husband's greenskeeper? You know what came of that for Lady Chatterley."

I got up off the sofa and marched to the door and opened it and stood beside it, speechless with anger. Beyond the glass windows I could see that Estrellita's mouth was open in a little round O and her black eyes were huge. She stared in at us.

He turned and went out the door.

"Go on home, Mrs. Venable," he said, without looking back.

"Go to hell, Mr. Cassells," I said, my voice shaking.

After they had gone I stood for a long time, staring out over the marsh and the creek, across it to the distant line of trees that marked the river. All of a sudden I could see it: a jumble of masts and flying bridges and antennas soaring over the rippling green marsh grass, villas and homes clustering around manicured lagoons that did not yet exist, golf carts crawling like beetles over the green hummocks where now the ponies cropped.

The ponies . . .

I would, of course, go to Clay about it the instant he got home. Of course I would. But that would be a while yet; I knew that he could not possibly be home yet from Atlanta. Usually his money trips lasted several days. So there was no need to leave the island and go back to Peacock's. No need at all.

I got up and straightened up the coffee table and plumped up the sofa pillows and gathered the spilled magazines and newspapers from the floor where I had left them. I pulled the bottle of Wild Turkey out from under the sofa and carried all of it into the kitchen. I tossed the magazines and newspapers into the trash basket and set it beside the back door, ready to carry over to the big Dumpster on Peacock's.

And then I poured myself another small drink and took it out onto the deck, and sat down in the old twig rocker, and put my feet up on the railing, as my grandfather and I had done a number of times before.

There was all the time in the world.

6

This time it was Lottie who woke me.

I know that I did not have more than the one drink, but when you have drunk as much as I did the night before, and when you are as small as I am, it doesn't take much to drag you under again. It's as if the alcohol still in your system is like a banked but living fire; it only takes the touch of a match and it's off and roaring again. I fell asleep sometime around eleven in the morning, in the rocker, and only woke when the sun was slanting toward midafternoon, my head hung cripplingly over the back of the chair. I heard myself give a great, gargling snore as Lottie shook me awake.

I snorted and gaped and blinked, licking my lips. They were dry and chapped, and the sick-sweet taste of bourbon was strong on my tongue. She came into focus as I squinted at her, seeming in the painful dazzle of light off the creek to loom over me like a colossus. She was leaning against the railing, scowling at me and rolling my empty glass back and forth with her toe.

"What are you doing here?" I rasped.

"Better still, what are you?" she said. Her voice was the familiar twanging growl, but there was something in it I did not recognize, or rather, something not in it that I missed. None of the usual fudgy, tolerant warmth was there today. Her leathery face was closed and scowling. Her muscular arms were crossed over her chest.

"You look like Daddy Warbucks." I giggled, and then hiccupped loudly. "Oh, shit," I said. "I think I fell asleep. My neck is killing me."

"I think you passed out," Lottie said. "I hope it *is* killing you. What the hell do you think you're doing, out here by yourself dead drunk?"

"I am not dead drunk," I said with what dignity I could muster. It was not much. "I had one little drink sitting out here, and I fell asleep. I hardly got any sleep at all last night. . . ."

"No wonder," she said. "It must have taken you all night to drink half a bottle of bourbon. This is bad stuff, Caro. I thought you didn't keep booze out here."

"Well, '*scuse* me," I said indignantly, trying to sound righteously affronted. "How many times have I rooted you out at noon with a hangover that would stun an army mule?"

"That's me," she said. "That's what I do. I've been doing it since I was fifteen, and I never do it unless I mean to. It's fun and I like it and when I don't want to do it I don't. It's different with you, and you know it."

"And why is that?"

"Because there's something in you that won't stop until you're dead," she said matter-of-factly. "I've always known that. There's something in you that doesn't have any limits. And you can't let go of all that precious pain, or you won't. It's a shitty combination, and I'm not going to sit around and watch you self-destruct."

"So who asked you to?" I said, shame and anger stinging in my throat. "I don't remember asking you to be my own private temperance society. And as for my pain, as you call it, what do you know about my so-called pain? When have I ever mentioned it to you?"

"You don't," she said, shaking her head slowly. "We all know you're too brave to mention that you're in mortal pain almost every waking minute of your life. God, everybody who knows you tiptoes around scared to death they're going to slip and mention death or daughters. You don't know how many times I've wanted to just ask you if your daughter was still dead."

I felt the blood drain from my face.

"How dare you?" I whispered. "How dare you talk to me like that? I've never . . . I don't . . .

you talk like I *use* Kylie or something, like I . . . hug it to me, like I cherish it . . ."

"Don't you?" she said, and then shut her eyes. "I'm sorry. That was rotten. But I hate to see this, Caro. I always thought of this place as somewhere you could come that was safe, where you didn't feel hustled or threatened, or need to drink. I didn't worry about you when I knew you were out here. I don't want to have to start now."

"So don't," I said snippily. "How did you know I was out here, anyway? For that matter, how did you know I drank half a bottle of bourbon?"

"Didn't you?"

"Yes."

"Well, then. As for how I knew, a little bird told me."

I saw it clearly, with one of those swift, untutored leaps of connection that you make sometimes, for no reason at all.

"He told you, didn't he? That awful Cassells man . . . Lou, or whatever his name is. Okay, Lottie, so how do you know him? As if I had to ask."

She grinned. It was her old grin, full and gleeful and lewd.

"I know him just the way you think I do," she said. "And I'm damned glad I do. He's as good a lay and as good a man as I've met on this island in a coon's age, and as long as he wants to drop on over of an evening, I'll leave the light burning for him. He's not a bad art critic either, among his other more obvious talents. I purely love fucking a man who can talk about something afterward beside his orgasm. I thought you all would meet eventually, but I can't say I had anything like this morning in mind."

"He told you all about it, undoubtedly."

"Of course. He has no secrets from *moi*. He was worried about you, incidentally. He doesn't go around gossiping about the boss's wife just to be doing it."

"Oh, I'm sure not," I said nastily. "Did he happen to mention that he insulted me? And that he calls Clay Mengele?"

She gave a whoop of laughter and doubled over.

"Oh, God! How perfect! I'll never be able to look at him with a straight face again. . . ."

"God*damn* it, Lottie!"

She held up one hand, palm out, gasping for breath.

"Okay," she croaked. "All right. Truce. I'll lay off Men—Clay if you'll go take a shower and toss the booze and let me feed you lunch. When did you eat last? Never mind. Shem just brought a mess of crabs in. I'll boil if you'll crack."

And because it was Lottie, and because I felt shamed and diminished and out of control and frightened by that, I did as she said. I climbed, shaking, into the shower and let the reeking hot water wash the agues and wobbles out of my head and muscles, and she tossed the liquor. I heard her ferret out the remaining bottles of Wild Turkey, heard them clink into the trash sack, heard the back door slam and a bit later her car trunk, and knew that she would haul them out to a Dumpster someplace. I felt better after that, as if a loaded gun had been taken out of my house. She was right. I had fouled my own nest last night and today. I did not intend it to happen again.

A little later we sat at the scarred old picnic table out behind her gas-station studio, cracking open the hot boiled blue crabs and picking the sweet meat from the shells. My hands and face were sticky with crab juice, and I could feel my forehead and scalp stinging from the spurted juice of an errant lemon. I imagined that I smelled about as bad as I looked, but I felt much better. Fresh crabs and Lottie have that effect on me.

Somewhere during the late lunch we had arrived at a tacit agreement not to speak of my drinking again, or of Clay, and I felt lulled and warmed by the sheer, rank, earthen force that was Lottie. The hangover was all but gone. So was the residue of last night's eeriness, and the near-madness. I could even speak lightly of it, and found that I wanted to.

I told her about seeing the child in the fog, and about sitting there in the firelight, drinking and waiting, and about waking to the laughter, and then running down the steps to meet not a revenant Kylie, but a strange, near-mute Cuban child and her black-furred grandfather. I even laughed a little, at myself and my lunatic, fog-fed fancies.

She did not smile back. Her eyes were dark with pity and something near fear.

"You want to stick a little closer to the world for a while, Caro," she said seriously. "I feel like this is a dangerous time for you. I don't know why, but I do feel that. Maybe you ought to lay off the island for a spell."

"Well, I will, I think," I said. "It's so close to Thanksgiving now, and there're a bunch of new kids in, and Clay's going to want to do that ghastly Lowcountry Thanksgiving thing for them and all the others who don't go home, so I'm just about out of time. Besides that, I don't want to run into Mellors the gamekeeper again. He could ruin a place for you in a New York minute."

She leered at me.

"I see the sexual aspect of the man has not escaped you. It's pretty powerful, isn't it? For an old man and a grandpa, he flat reeks of it. I gather he pointed out the similarity of your—ah, situations, yours and his and Lady Chatterley and company. He laughed like a hyena when I mentioned it."

"It was your idea, was it? I might have

known he'd never think of it by himself. What, a little pillow talk or something?"

"Or something. I did tell him about you, for what it's worth. He was curious about Clay, about what sort of wife he would have, what sort of children. Don't worry, I didn't tell him about Kylie. That's for you to do or not, as the friendship progresses."

And she smiled at me again, a wolflike baring of her big teeth.

"There's no friendship to progress and there isn't going to be," I said. "He's arrogant and insufferable, and if it weren't for his granddaughter I swear I'd try to get Clay to fire him. She's crazy about the ponies, though. She talked for almost the first time since her mother died when she was with them. It's the saddest thing, Lottie. . . ."

"I know the story. You're right. It's awful. Well, I don't think you need to worry about him hanging around. He's pretty busy over in Day-clear, from what he says. He also said he has no intention of bothering you again, said for me to be sure to tell you that. He was only there today because the kid ran away. But you're cutting off your nose to spite your face. He'd make you a good friend. You don't have so many of those around here that another one wouldn't help. Come to think of it, he'd make you a good . . . whatever else, too. A tad of Lady Chatterley would do you a world of good, no doubt about it. And I sure don't mind sharing. There's enough there to go around."

"I'm going home if you're going to talk like that," I said, face and neck burning. The thought of those dark hands and arms, those heavy shoulders, that black hair . . . would it be coarse? Silky? How would it be?

I got up and ran water from the outdoor spigot over my sticky hands and hot wrists, letting my hair fall over my face so that she could not see the flush. I heard her chuckle. To divert her, I said, "You know what he said? He said Clay's going to put a property, a resort community, right smack in the marsh where the river and creek meet, where Dayclear is. He says Clay hired him as a consultant about subtropical plants and landscaping for it. I think he must be really crazy. You know that's my land. You know I'd never let anything like that happen on the island. And you know Clay knows that, too. Next time you see old Babalu or whatever you call him, you might enlighten him about that. I certainly didn't get very far trying."

When she did not respond I straightened up and looked around. She was looking at the ground, and her face was very still. Lottie's face is many things, but almost never that.

"Lottie," I said tentatively.

"I don't know anything about that," she said. "You ought to talk to Clay about that."

"Well, of course I will, but don't you think it's the craziest thing you ever heard?"

"I've heard lots of crazy things, Caro," Lottie said. "Somehow that's not the craziest."

"But, my God . . ."

"Ask Clay. I don't know. I try to know as little about what goes on in his mind as possible. You know me. Just a little ol' trailer tramp, only interested in fuckin' and drawin'. Speaking of which, I've got a painting drying up on me in the studio where I just walked out and left it when I heard you were on a private toot on your private island. I need to get back to it and you need to get on home."

"Lottie . . ."

"Home, Caro. Not the island. Home. Okay? I'm going to call you in an hour and see if you're there, and if you're not I'm going to call the sheriff to go out to the island and get you. Now go on. Git."

She turned and stomped back into the studio, leaving the litter of crab shells and paper napkins reeking in the sun. I got up, fuming at her high-handedness. Under it all there was a small, cold curl of fear, like a worm.

It was close to five when I got home. I knew that Estelle would be gone, but she had left the kitchen and downstairs sitting room lights burning against the darkness that comes early off the ocean this time of year. I was glad. The wind had picked up and I could hear the surf, usually flaccid and sullen, booming hollowly on the shore beyond the house, and the palms rattling fretfully. It is the time of day that I like least in winter, and I went into the house singing loudly simply because I hate to be answered by nothing but wind and sea.

"'Trailer for sale or rent, rooms to let fifty cents,'" I wailed in my frail soprano.

I would light a fire in my little upstairs sitting room, I thought, and take a supper tray up there, and find an old movie on TV, and drift off to sleep on my quilt-piled daybed, and when I woke it would be to the sound of Estelle singing gospel down in the kitchen and the smell of coffee. And then I would find out where Clay was staying and I would call him, and he would tell me when he was coming home, and the free fall of the past two days would stop, and the orderly quadrille of my life on Peacock's Island would resume again. I realized that I was missing Clay very much. I missed Carter, too. Maybe I would call him tonight. Except that I almost never caught him in, and for some reason that depressed me. Oh, well. He would be home for Thanksgiving, and that was less than a week away.

There was a note from Estelle on the counter. It was sitting under the steam iron. I walked over and looked at it.

"It have play out," the note said, and a fat

black arrow pointed to the iron. I felt a smile twitch at my mouth, and then banished it. Clay thought Estelle's notes to us were wonderfully funny, but I did not, and I usually threw them away before he saw them, lest he take them to the office and show them around. More than once Hayes Howland had quoted an Estellism at a party, and I resented it sharply. Illiteracy in any permutation is not amusing to me. I was about to pick this one up and throw it away when I noticed that another arrow directed me to turn the paper over. I did.

"Mr. Clay be home tonite," it said. "He coming by privet jet. Home by midnite."

I did smile then, both at "privet jet" and the fact that Clay would be home by midnight. I wondered whose private plane he might be taking. He was adamant that no such amenity be purchased for the company, except for a small twin-engine Cessna that was virtually a necessity for island-hopping among the company's properties. When he traveled he was scrupulous about flying coach, and he insisted that everyone else on company business do it, too. He even turned his frequent flyer mileage back to the company. Hayes ragged him incessantly about it.

The house seemed to settle in around me all at once, fitting like a sweet skin. The dark night stopped pressing against the windows and wrapped them tenderly. I lit the logs in the big sitting room so that the house would smell of apple wood and peeked into the oven. Estelle had left a pot roast there, ready to be heated. Clay's favorite. That and some of the Merlot he had brought back from Atlanta the last time he went, and the last of the key lime pie we had had the weekend before . . . or, no, I would make something for dessert. It would pass the time, and please Clay, and I suddenly wanted very much to be in my own kitchen, making something wonderful with my own hands. I looked into the refrigerator. Creme caramel; we had everything I needed. When I went upstairs to our bedroom, I was nearly dancing on the steps.

He was late coming. At one A.M., I gave up and went upstairs and turned on my little television and found a rerun of *Pillow Talk* and fell asleep before Doris Day even had time to get pertly angry with Rock Hudson. I don't know how much later it was when a sound from the kitchen woke me. I got up and ran my hands through my tousled hair and shrugged into the nicest negligee I had, and hurried downstairs. I was not afraid. I knew it would be Clay.

He did not hear me coming in my bare feet. He was sitting at the kitchen table with the platter of cold, uncarved pot roast and vegetables in front of him, hands in his lap beneath the table, staring into space. I had never seen him look so old, or so tired, or so . . . ill? I was afraid suddenly, so afraid that for a moment I could not get my breath to speak. I remembered Shawna's words the day before . . . or was it the day before that? . . . and that I had brushed them aside impatiently.

Then I said, "Honey?" and he looked up, and his face was Clay's again, with only the normal fatigue of a late night home from a business trip on it.

"Hi, sweetie," he said, and got up, and came over and hugged me. His face against mine was cold, but his arms were tight and hard around me, and he held me for a long time. I hugged back, eyes closed, my face pressed into his shoulder.

"You hopped a ride on a jet," I said, still close against the fabric of his coat.

"Yep. The guys we went to see were coming to Charleston anyway, and I talked them into staying over a day or two with us. Well, not with *us*. I put them in the guest house, now that the new kids are in their own places. It saved me a bad three hours in the Atlanta airport."

"Clever," I said, kissing the side of his face. I felt stubble there, and was surprised. He hardly ever allowed a trace of growth on his chin. He must have skipped shaving that morning. I had never known him to do that in all the years we had been married, and the anxiety came nagging back.

"Are you okay?" I said, leaning back to look at him. "You looked awfully beat up there for a minute, and Shawna was carrying on the other day about being worried about you. Your health, I mean. I blew her off; I thought she was just being Shawna. Should I have?"

He made a small, disgusted noise.

"You should have. She drives me nuts with that sweet-concern business. I'm thinking about assigning her to Hayes. He can't stand her. Yes, to answer your question, I'm okay. I just hate Atlanta. And I'm getting really sick of this money-raising business."

"Why don't you let somebody else take that over?" I said, picking up the platter and putting it into the microwave. "Surely Hayes could do it by himself by now; he goes with you every time you go."

"Most investors still want to see the honcho do his dog and pony show," he said, rubbing his eyes. "Makes 'em feel like they can jerk him around. Which of course they can. You want a glass of wine while that's heating?"

"No," I said, perhaps more forcefully than I meant to, and he shot an oblique look at me but said nothing more. He poured himself a glass and sat back down at the table.

"So tell me about the island," he said. "I assume you stayed over there? Shawna said you hadn't called in when I called the office."

"I was going to call her in the morning and find out where you were and all that," I said. "Yes, I did stay over. It was awfully foggy, but I got some nice watercolors started, and one morning of photographs. Oh, and I saw Nissy and she has a colt! Wouldn't . . . isn't that something? You remember, we've never known how old she is, so we thought maybe she was too old to have a baby, but apparently not. I'd love to know who the daddy is. Oh, and I met that new man of yours. That Lou Cassells person. He came over looking for his granddaughter. She'd run away after the ponies and ended up at the house."

"Cassells . . ." he said reflectively. "Oh. Yeah. The plant guy, the Cuban. His granddaughter was at the house?"

"Yes. Apparently she saw the ponies and had been chasing them around for a while, and sneaked out early yesterday morning and followed them over to our place. I'd been feeding them, so they're hanging around. She's a nice child, about five, I guess. There's a sad little story about her I'll tell you sometime, but right now you need to eat and then I need a snuggle, and there's just no telling where that could lead."

I smiled at him and he smiled back. I did not mention seeing the child the night before, in the fog, and wished that I had not mentioned Lou Cassells, and wondered why I had. That could have waited for morning. This was not the time for that. Perhaps there would not be a good time for it. Perhaps I would, after all, just let the whole thing lie. I did not want to tax my tired husband with that can of worms. It all seemed, suddenly, so absurd as to have been a fairy tale, something I had heard long ago.

The microwave dinged and I took out the roast and carved him a couple of slices and spooned the browned vegetables onto his plate. He took a big mouthful and smiled appreciatively around it.

"Estelle never forgets, does she?" he said.

"Never." I smiled back. "I don't, either. I made crème caramel. We can eat it in bed."

"Well, you hussy," he said, grinning a little. It was the grin I loved most. I had not seen it in some time. "Can't you even let a man get his nourishment first?"

"Be quick about it," I said.

An hour later we lay tangled together in the big bed in our "real" bedroom, the one that faced the sea. The drapes were closed against the darkness, and they muffled the sound of the waves. The palms still scratched and rattled, though, and banged against the wrought-iron railing of the balcony that lay beyond the French doors. I burrowed my ear deep into the hollow of Clay's naked shoulder and heard, instead of the palms, the roar of my own diminishing blood and the pulse of his. If I moved my head slightly I could taste the sweet salt sweat on his neck. I did that, tasted the essence of Clay after love, and hugged him hard with the other arm that was flung over his chest. He hugged back.

"Not bad for an old bag," he said drowsily into my hair. His breath tickled.

"Or for an old crock," I said. "The only trouble is, I know all your tricks. Why don't you get some new tricks to amaze and delight me?"

"And just where do you suggest I get them? Shawna? Some daughter of joy from the mean streets of Atlanta?"

"You could get a book," I said. "Or we could rent a video. I bet Hayes knows some good ones."

He laughed and shifted me slightly in his arms. We lay still for a while, I listening to the regular cadence of his breathing. I kept thinking that I would get up and bring the comforter and spread it over us, but I did not move, and before long I began to think that he had fallen asleep. But he had not.

"So what do you think of him? My new guy?" he said, when I was just thinking that I would disengage myself and get up. My stomach gave a small squeeze of anxiety. I did not want to speak of this. I was done with this.

"Oh, who cares?" I said. "Go to sleep. It's almost three."

"I'm not sleepy," he said into the dark. "No

kidding, what did you think of him? His credentials are good, but I don't know . . . there's something about him. I realized after I hired him that I really don't know anything about him."

For some reason, I felt a stab of perversely proprietary protectiveness toward Lou Cassells. I said, "He seemed fine. Like I said, he had his little granddaughter with him and he's certainly crazy about her. He's apparently had a pretty rough life; he just lost his wife, and his daughter . . . died . . . having a baby, back in Cuba. He takes care of the child now. You've got to admire that."

"I suppose," Clay said. "I just don't much like the idea of him hanging around the house over there, or knowing when you're there and when you're not. I'm going to have to make that clear, I think."

"No, don't. He wouldn't have been there if the little girl hadn't come there. He told Lottie he didn't plan to bother me."

"Lottie . . . oh, terrific. I guess he's shagging Lottie Funderburke like half of the rest of my staff, huh?"

"Well, you don't have any rules about that, do you? Let him be. He was . . . nice. And apparently he's highly educated. He was telling me a little about himself."

Clay lay in the darkness for a while, and then he said, "What else did you talk about?"

"Oh . . . nothing. Everything. About Dayclear. He's staying over there, and you know who with? Ezra Upchurch. Isn't that something? Ezra, back in Dayclear?"

"There goes the neighborhood," Clay said neutrally. "So . . . did he say what he was doing over there? Ezra, I mean? Him, too, for that matter. I thought he lived on John's Island. I thought they both did."

"He's visiting his old aunt, apparently. She's the only one he's got left, Lou said. Ezra, I mean. As for Lou, he's there because he knew Ezra somehow or other on John's Island and I guess this is a lot closer to his work. He didn't say."

"Lou, huh?"

"It's what he said his name was, Clay."

"He told me Luis."

"Well, what's the difference?"

"It's just . . . familiar, that's all. I don't like the idea of him being familiar with you. I want you to tell me if you see him over there again. As a matter of fact, it might be a good idea if you gave the island a rest for a while."

"Why, for pity's sake?" I could not keep the exasperation out of my voice. This was not at all like Clay. Not at all.

"Oh, for Christ's sake, Caro, because I said so, okay?" he snapped. "Is it a terrible great lot to ask, just for a little while?"

I raised myself up on one elbow and stared at him.

"I think you're jealous, and I think it's absolutely ridiculous," I said.

He raised himself up, too, and glared at me.

"Jealous of you and a . . . Cuban Jew gardener? Not hardly," he said, and there was something cold in his voice.

I was stung.

"Well, maybe you ought to be concerned, though not for the reason you think," I said, trying to match his coldness with my own. "He seems to know an awful lot about your business. He seems to think you're about to put a resort over there in Dayclear. In fact, he's awfully sure about that. If he's telling me about it, who knows who else he's telling? If you have to make anything clear to him, that's what you ought to clear up. It made my hair stand on end."

The cold sickness did not start until the silence had spun out so long that it was obvious that he was not going to answer me. Then it flooded me and took me deep under, so that I could not move or get my breath to speak. Over it, very gradually, came not anger, or fear, but a terrible desolation that was the sum of every bad thing I have ever known was waiting ahead for me. It was not anxiety or even terror; that presupposes a catastrophic event still ahead of you. This event was here. I knew as certainly as I knew it was I who sat here in the dark with Clay that what Luis Cassells had said was true, and that my husband lay beside me pregnant with a great betrayal.

Presently I said, wondering that my voice was not cracked and choked, leaking life, "So it's true. I thought he was a liar and a fool. I guess the fool was me."

And the liar was you, I did not say. But it lay between us.

After another long moment of silence, he sighed, a thin, tired sigh, and said, "There's a lot I have to tell you, Caro. None of it's good. I didn't want to do it yet, and I didn't think I had to, until after Christmas maybe. And I guess I thought there was just a chance that I wouldn't have to tell you at all. But Cassells has put the kibosh on that. Maybe it's just as well. I just wish it had been me and not him."

"I wish so, too, Clay," I said, feeling the pain inside so deep and viscous that it felt like blood pooled in my chest. "You just don't know how much I wish it had been. So. You're going to tell me now, right?"

"I . . . Caro, Christ, I'm so tired I think I could die from it. Couldn't we just . . . sleep? Get some sleep, and talk about it in the morning? It won't seem so bad then. It's not so bad, come to think of it. It's nothing that can't be fixed. But I'm so tired. . . ."

"I don't care," I said, and found that I didn't. "I don't care how tired you are, Clay. I hear it now, whatever it is, or I'm getting up from here and going back to the island and I don't know when I'm coming back. Or if. You can't just . . . Listen, you tell me. Sit up and tell me."

And so he did. He turned on the bedside lamp and pulled on a T-shirt and sat up in our bed, half turned away from me toward the hidden sea, and he told me that things were so bad financially with the company that unless he got an infusion of cash very quickly, he ultimately stood to lose it all. All of it. The scattered island properties, even Peacock Island Plantation, the flagship of the line, the mother church, the first and still best thing he had ever created. He would lose it all. Everything.

I could not understand. I could not comprehend what he was saying. My head felt as empty as if my brain had atrophied. I simply sat in the lamplight, still naked and not noticing at all, and looked at him. Or rather, at the side of his face.

Finally I said, "You mean . . . we wouldn't have a place to live? We wouldn't have any money?"

"Well, it's not that bad," he said dully. "We could keep this house, of course. We own it. I'd keep some company stock. We have a few other personal investments. Carter's almost through school. We could live. It's just . . . that all this wouldn't be mine anymore. Ours, rather. I . . . Caro, I can't let that happen. I can't. This is everything, all this . . . ." He gestured, his hand taking in the sweep of beach and sea and land that spread out from the epicenter that was our bed.

"Oh, Clay . . . is it really?" I said, feeling the pain flare up until I thought I would die from it. This will be mortal, I thought. Those five words are what will kill me now.

He turned and looked at me wordlessly. His face was flayed, burned, scoured. I did not know this face.

"After you, it is," he said, eyes closed. "After you and Carter, it's everything. There isn't anything else. Not for me, anyway."

I lay back against my pillows, knowing that in some vital, visceral way I would never sit up whole again.

"I need to know about it," I whispered. "I need to know."

A great, indrawn breath. Then he said, "Remember Jeremy? Jeremy Fowler, at Calista Key?"

I nodded. Who could forget Jeremy? The golden boy, the chosen one, the flaming comet that had come streaking out of Texas when he was only twenty-two, just out of the University of Texas Business School, shining with youth and charm and intelligence and energy and Texas oil money, begging Clay to hire him, to let him do anything for the company, let him tend bar at one of the plantation clubs, let him trim shrubbery, let him answer the telephone or sort the mail. I'll make you glad you did, Jeremy Fowler said, and his voice held all the promise of the new millennium in it.

Of course, Clay hired him. And Jeremy did what he said he would. Within a year he was second in command at one of Clay's oldest resort communities, an established mountain family resort in Tennessee. In two years he was back on Peacock's, heading up the elite forward planning team. A year later Clay sent him down to Puerto Rico, to head up the just-borning Calista Key Plantation. He was by far the youngest project manager Clay had ever had, and his trajectory took him and Calista straight into the Caribbean sun. The first two years' reports out of Puerto Rico were stunning. Advance sales were unprecedented. Jeremy didn't come back to the States often; he made it a point to be a hands-on manager. But when he did, with his fey, beautiful, haunted wife, Lila, he trailed a kind of glittering aura that was nearly palpable, and he received a hero's welcome.

"He . . . Calista's bankrupt, Caro," Clay said. "The figures that came in were . . . not true. There's hardly any occupancy. The project is way behind construction schedule; he hasn't paid any of his suppliers in months. Nobody's been working since summer. Whoever went down there from the home office got shown a great bustle of activity and dozers and workmen, but they were freelances he hired for the day. The photos he sent . . . Christ, I think they were the same few units, in the various stages of construction, with different paint and plantings. From what I hear, morale is so bad that half our kids down there are drunk most of the time, and the other half are on drugs. Seven marriages have broken up. Lila Fowler has left and gone back to her folks in Philadelphia. The construction engineer split for Arkansas last month. Hayes says Jeremy is living in a broken-down hotel in Humacao with a Puerto Rican woman, drinking like a fish. He says there are chickens walking around in the courtyard."

He stopped and scrubbed at his eyes with his hands, as if the chickens were the worst of it.

"How could that happen?" I said. "How could that be?"

"I don't blame Hayes," he said. "I should have gone down there myself. Hayes is new to this kind of stuff. He's never overseen a project before. Jeremy always did have Hayes in his back pocket. He's not the only one, either. Hayes had no reason to doubt the figures or what he saw with his own eyes. And I didn't butt in because I wanted . . . I thought it was time for Hayes to have something of his own. And I thought Jeremy could handle it. I didn't go down there on purpose. I didn't want to hover. . . ."

"Hayes," I said leadenly. "Of course. It would be Hayes, wouldn't it? I thought Hayes didn't have a project of his own. I thought he was a, quote, perfect second banana, unquote."

"He didn't want anybody to know until he got the hang of it," Clay said.

"Well," I said, "so we lose Calista Key. Why does that mean that everything else . . . what does that have to do with the island? With Dayclear?"

"Because," Clay said, "I've . . . we've . . . things have not been so good for resorts in the last few years, Caro. I've kept expanding because I didn't think I had any choice. I could pay the Alabama Gulf investors, for instance, with the money we made when we opened up Biloxi. And we paid the Biloxi guys when we opened up Georgia. And so on. But Calista . . . we owed a ton of money on that one. That one was a money pit from the beginning. There's not enough cash in all the others put together for me to pay off the Calista folks unless I sell Peacock's. And when that goes . . . it all will. Eventually, it all will. Or . . ."

He fell silent. I waited. Then I said, "Or you could open up a new property, right? Get some more joint venture money. But you don't have enough cash to buy one, so you'd have to use land you already had. Like the island. My friend Mr. Cassells says it's a natural, that site. The only thing is, Clay, it's not your land, is it? It's mine. Did you forget that?"

"No," he said in a low voice. "I didn't forget that."

"Clay, isn't all this a pyramid scam or something? Isn't all this illegal? Who knows about this?"

"Not strictly, no," he said. "It's done often, and done quite successfully, if you can keep all the balls in the air at once. I thought I could. There was nothing to make me think I couldn't. Nobody said anything; none of the company money people ever said a word. Hayes has always been a wizard at finding properties and investors. He's the one who just might save us now. And to answer your question . . . nobody knows about it, I don't think. Not outside the Plantation family, anyway. I mean . . . they know about Dayclear coming on line, but not the reason for it. Yet. I don't think too many of our people know about Calista . . . yet."

He lay back against the pillow and closed his eyes. He might have died, he was so still, so white, his face so emptied of everything that had ever meant Clay to me. I waited for my heart to twist with pain, but it did not. My heart felt as cold and hard as a cinder, dead for eons.

"Remember how my grandfather felt about that land?" I said finally, feeling as if I were going to collapse from the effort to talk. "Remember what he said about the Gullahs in Dayclear always having their homes, about the wild things, the birds, the fish, the things that bloom and grow there that don't anywhere else? Remember the panther? Would you really . . . could you really just doze all that down and put up a . . . a . . . what? A golf course? A lagoon community? A marina? What? Cluster housing, condos where the old houses are now?"

"It can be done well, Caro," he said in the new, dull voice. "You know it can. I've got studies, a master plan, that leaves so much of the land and marsh in place that it almost looks as if it hasn't been touched. There's plenty of wild habitat still provided for, over where your grandfather's house is. I wouldn't . . . we wouldn't disturb that. This looks like an award winner; the joint venture people are crazy about it. . . ."

"I gather that's what you were doing in Atlanta," I said. "Peddling it. Who is it this time, Clay? Texas money? Los Angeles? Arab?"

"Local Atlanta," he said. "Fellow Southerners who know land like this. A long track record, lots of experience, solvent as all get-out, plenty of cash. I'll tell you about them later. They'd respect that land, I think. They've been crazy to get down here for a long time, but nothing's really pleased them till they saw the marsh property. If it's got to be done, I'm glad Hayes knew these guys."

"Clay. Listen to me. I'm sorry about . . . everything. But that land . . . that land is mine, Clay! Weren't you even going to ask me? Couldn't you at least have leveled with me before . . . before it got this far? Don't I matter? Doesn't my grandfather? Were you *ever* going to talk to me?"

"I haven't been able to talk to you for a long time, Caro," he said. It was almost a whisper. I opened my mouth to protest, and then did not. It was true. He had tried. Maybe not about Dayclear, but about other things that were important to the two of us. I had not refused to discuss them, but I had not talked back. My very silence had been his answer.

"What were you going to tell the people in Dayclear?" I said. "What were you going to do about clear titles and all that stuff? Providing that I agreed, which I cannot imagine doing?"

"Well, we'd do a substantial cash buyout. It would be more than enough for them to relocate, and we'd do that for them, too; find them homes, or maybe build some for them off-island. They'd be better off financially than they've ever been in their lives. . . ."

"Except that they wouldn't have their homes. Can't you understand what that means? It seems to me you should, if you're about to lose yours. . . ."

"There are other things we can do. Hayes thinks we might leave the settlement as is, maybe make a sort of cultural attraction of it. You know, a preservation center for the Gullah culture, with the Dayclear people doing the things their people have always done, planting and harvesting rice and cotton, spinning, dyeing, growing vegetables, making sweet-grass baskets, telling the old stories and doing the old dances, teaching visitors the songs and legends. . . ."

"My God. A theme park. Gullah World. That's just extraordinary, Clay," I said fiercely. Anger was beginning to raise its snake's head. It felt good, like scalding hot coffee when you are frozen and exhausted.

"It's not like that. It could be done with great taste and dignity. Sophia Bridges . . . you know, the young black woman with the child . . . she has an undergraduate degree in cultural anthropology, and she did her thesis on the Gullahs. She's going to do a great deal more research down here. She thinks it's fascinating, and that it could be an important cultural asset to the whole region. . . ."

"Sophia Bridges wouldn't know a real Gullah if one tackled her and held her down and put her hair in cornrows! This is not an experiment, Clay! Those are real people over there! My God! And the ponies . . . what about the ponies? Are you going to open up a Wild West exhibit with them?"

"The ponies are ultimately the responsibility of the government," he said. "The Park Service. We've been talking with them for months about the ponies. They've given us at least six months to relocate them or to cull . . ."

"*Cull?*"

He looked away again.

"They're not healthy, Caro. They're so inbred

that their genetic weaknesses are going to kill them in another generation or two. They don't get enough food, or at least not the right kind. They've just about grazed out the available hummock grass on the island. You can't let them starve. They'll be much better off on one of the undeveloped islands, where the grass is strong and new."

"They're not starving, they're fat as pigs," I cried. "Clay, this is . . . I won't do this, Clay. Not to the people, and not to the ponies. I will not give you that land."

He did not speak. I watched him, my chest heaving with rage and anguish. Finally he nodded.

"Then, as you say, it's your island," he said.

There was another long silence, and then he said, "Caro, I have to sleep. I'll die if I don't sleep. You should, too. I'll talk to Hayes in the morning, tell him it's off. The Atlanta people are still here; we can wrap it up before noon. But right now I'm just plain done for."

He turned over and reached up and pulled the chain on the bedside lamp. The room swam back into its comforting darkness. I heard him settle into his pillow and give the small sign that meant he was poised at the edge of sleep. I felt my heart contract slightly with the first frisson of pity. He had never before said he was too tired to talk to me. This must have taken a terrible toll on him. I remembered how it had been with him when he was first learning the island, in the summer days after Hayes had brought him over from Charleston the first time. I remembered the sheer enchantment on his face, the wonder in his blue eyes. You wouldn't lose that, not entirely.

I lay still, staring at the drawn curtains. A faint line of pale, colorless light had appeared under them. Dawn. The dawn of a day I wished I might never see.

"Clay . . ." I said softly into the darkness.

"Yeah."

"Isn't there any other way? I mean, anything you could do so that the people at Dayclear and the . . . the ponies and all . . . could stay, wouldn't be disturbed? Put it somewhere else on the island, or scale it down, or something?"

After a long time he said, "We could try. If you'd agree to think about it, I'd agree to go back to the drawing board and see if we can't do better for the people and the horses. We have until spring before we have to give the earnest money back. That money would keep the Calista investors off my back for a long time. Maybe long enough. I think we could . . . Caro? If we could show you how much better it could be? If we could show you it would really benefit the people at Dayclear?"

"I . . . if you could really show me, I guess I could . . . think about it. I guess I could do that. But oh, Clay . . ."

"We'll talk about it in the morning, baby. I promise you we can make it work. I promise you it won't be anything you'd have to hate. . . ."

"Will you promise me something else?"

"Anything."

"Will you promise me not to talk about it anymore until after the holidays at least? I don't think I could stand it, Clay. I don't think I can talk endlessly about this thing, or hear about it. Let's just get through the holidays. It's going to be bad enough, looking at all those poor, silly little new people and knowing what you brought them down here for. . . ."

I should not have said it. No matter what, it was a gratuitously cruel comment, designed to hurt, and it did. I knew even before he answered that I had hurt him.

"That shouldn't be too hard," he said in the chill, neutral voice I fear most. "We don't talk about anything else."

I lay still, wrapped in my own pain, until I heard his breathing slacken into sleep. I meant to get up then, and go to try to sleep some more on my daybed, but before I could gather the energy I fell asleep, too, and when I woke, the sun was high and straight over the sea, and he was gone.

7

It's funny how a night's sleep can change the complexion of things. I couldn't have slept more than five hours, but when I finally got showered and dressed and in some sort of forward motion, the terrible night before had faded and bleached itself down to a kind of half-memory, half-dream that lacked the poisonous immediacy of the night itself. I knew it was something I had done myself, while I slept, in order simply to survive and go on; I had done it sometimes when the pain of Kylie got too overwhelming. It was a kind of interior litany that threaded my troubled sleep and bore me up when I waked: Well, it was awful; it was the worst thing in the world, but here it is the next day and we're still here. The sun is still shining, the birds are still singing. It isn't going to kill us, and what doesn't kill us can only make us stronger. There's still Clay and me, the fact of us. There's still that.

I was so proficient at it that it was buried deep in my subconscious now, and I knew only that a night had passed and a day had been born and we were still intact. As long as we were, we could work this out. He had said so, hadn't he? He had said they'd go back to the drawing board with ideas for Dayclear. He'd said we didn't need to speak of it again until spring. It would take at least that long to come up with a better plan. I didn't have to do anything at all about this until then. The light would have turned to pale, tender gold and the marshes would be greening up before I ever had to think of it.

I ran down the stairs two at a time, eager to be out in the crisp, clear light that flooded the back garden. I would have coffee there, and then cut the last of the roses and bring them in. Then I would go back over to the island. There was one more thing I had to do before I could pack the enormity of Dayclear away.

An hour later I stopped at the little unpainted cabin that had served the settlement as a general store and community center since I was a small child, to ask where Ezra Upchurch's house was. I knew that Janie and Esau Biggins, who had kept the store almost that long, would know. They had served the settlement's needs and wants and its deepest aches for forty years. And they were Gullahs, too, originally from Edisto. There was little about the people of Dayclear they did not know.

The vertical planks of the little house were blackened with age and weather, and several had rotted through. The roof was rusted tin and missing many squares. The listing porch held a long-defunct metal Nehi cooler that squatted stolidly in a corner, like an abandoned god. Usually someone sat on it, or a group played checkers or cards on its pitted surface, but the day was sharp, and I knew that everyone would be inside, clustered around the black iron stove that would surely, as my grandfather always said, burn the place down one day. A few chickens pecked and scratched in the swept dirt yard and under the porch. They were Domineckers; I had always admired their precise tweed dress and vaguely African demeanor. They seemed to me so much more exotic than the fat, complacent Rhode Island Reds, almost as picturesque as the beautiful, witless, pin-head guineas that sometimes foraged alongside them. These did not stop their noshing as I walked through them and up the steps.

Inside, the thick, rank semigloom smelled of smoke and licorice and the dusty peanuts in their shells in a big barrel by the counter, and something else darker and older: dried blood from the carcasses of the chickens that were slaughtered out back and sold. I felt a little uncomfortable, for I knew that mine would be the only white face, but I had been here before, many times, and I was known. I would be treated with courtesy because of my grandfather. He would have been treated with affection.

Janie was behind the counter this morning. She smiled her gold-toothed smile and nodded but did not speak. That was for me to do first, and I did.

"I'm looking for the house Ezra Upchurch is staying in, Janie," I said. "He's got someone staying with him, a Mr. Cassells, that I need to see."

"Ezra, he stayin' with his auntie down at the end of the row, but he ain't to home," she said equably. "Seem like he say he goin' to town today."

I did not know if "town" meant the village on Edisto or Charleston or what, but it did not matter, since it was Luis Cassells I wanted. I was glad that I would not have to say what I had to say to him in front of Ezra Upchurch. The great wind of Ezra's presence would, I knew, overwhelm me. This was going to be hard enough.

"That's okay. I'll just walk on down there and see if Mr. Cassells is there. Thanks a lot," I said.

"I'm here," a masculine voice said from somewhere in the gloom behind the stove, and I peered into it. Luis Cassells was sitting in a spavined old rocking chair in the shadows, drinking coffee and smoking a large black cigar. Both smelled good, rich and masculine. They reminded me of my grandfather. There was a cardboard box beside him on the floor, and I heard a scuffling and scratching from it. Walking back, I peered in. There were three small black and tan hound puppies there, curled around one another. Luis was scratching their heads with the hand that held the cigar. He smiled up at me, his teeth flashing white in the murk.

"Pull up a chair," he said. "I'll buy you a cup of coffee. Or maybe you'd prefer a puppy. Esau's trying to find homes for them. Their mama got run over on the bridge."

"I wish I could," I said. "If he can't place them, I'll put a notice in the office. Where's Lita this morning?"

"Ezra's auntie is teaching her how to wrap her hair. She's been after me for a week to let her. Says that way I won't have to comb it for days and days, and she won't have to cry. She has a point. Combing hair is not one of my long suits."

I smiled. Then I said, "Mr. Cassells . . ."

He raised an eyebrow at me and I felt myself blush, and was glad of the darkness.

"Luis," I said. "I came to apologize. I was pretty crappy to you yesterday. And . . . you were right about Dayclear. There are some plans to develop it. I didn't know about them. But that doesn't mean it's going to happen; I *do* own this part of the island, and if it seems to me that the property would harm the settlement in any way, it's not going to happen. Clay and I have an agreement about that. I thought you might pass the word along. Nothing at all is going to be done until spring, and then only with their blessing."

He studied me for a space of time.

"I see," he said. "Well, that's good to know. Why don't you come on back with me and tell them yourself?"

"Because they'll be more apt to believe it if it comes from you," I said, knowing it was true. "They're nice to me because of my grandfather, but I'm whitey all the same. We don't have a great history of truth-telling in these parts. But you're one of them. They'd trust you."

He laughed, the big, rolling laugh I remembered.

"You're right about that," he said. "Nobody would confuse me with whitey."

I blushed again, hard.

"I meant that you're Ezra's friend, staying in his house. That would be enough right there."

"I know what you meant," he said, still chuckling. "You're right. They've taken me and Lita in like family, God bless them. I think it's because I've traveled such a long road. These are people that know a thing or two about journeys."

"You said you'd tell me about that road one day," I said.

"I did, didn't I? Well, since you honored me with an apology . . . completely unnecessary, by the way . . . the least I can do is honor you with the absolutely fascinating, never-equaled story of my life. Capsule version. That is, if you'll quit hovering and sit down and drink coffee with me."

I sat. He held up a finger and Janie brought two more cups of strong black coffee, smiling her gold-toothed smile as she did. It tasted strong and fresh and bitter, odd but good on this stinging day. I told her so.

"I puts a big ol' lump of chic'ry in every pot," she said.

Luis drained his second cup, set it down, and said, "Okay. Here we go. I was born . . ." And he grinned his pirate's grin. "Don't worry; it's the abridged edition. I was born in Havana in 1939, or just outside it. My family was rich. My father was third in a line of doctors and gentlemen farmers, and we had what you all would call a country estate here. The finca, we called it. I was supposed to follow in the family tradition of medicine, but I hated everything about it, and by the time I was ready for college I knew that plants were going to be it for me. The old man was furious, but he had my younger brother already in the fold, so he paid for me to go to the university and start studying tropical botany. That was in 1957.

"I got married the same year. We do that in

Cuba, or did, especially in the wealthy old families. She was the daughter of a neighbor; just as rich as we were, and I'd known her since we were in diapers. Her name was Ana, and she was little and round and soft like a dumpling, with the most wonderful giggle. All she ever wanted was to be married and have children and live exactly like the women in her family had lived for generations. And we got a good start on it; our daughter, Anita, was born the next year, 1958. Anita, little Ana. God, she was a pretty little girl. She looked like a Christmas angel.

"The next year Batista packed it in, on New Year's Day, 1959, and the world we knew turned upside down. The revolution was supposed to be for all of us, but it was clear very soon that that didn't include the quote, aristocrats, unquote. I could see what was coming, but my family never could, and Ana's couldn't, either. And her folks did a real number on her; when I begged her to bring the baby and come out with me, she wouldn't do it. It was all going to blow over in a few months, she said. She would stay with her family on the estate and wait for me to get it all out of my system. Then we'd go on just as we'd planned. She wasn't a stupid girl, but she was totally of her time and class, and she couldn't imagine that anything could ever change, even after it did.

"So. I got out with a young uncle on a commercial fishing boat out of Miami, and I stayed with some relatives there. There are Cassells all over the place. These didn't have half the money my folks did, but they were realistic about Cuba under Castro. They knew I couldn't go back. They found a job for me in a little Cuban radio station and I sent home what I could. I never knew if any of it got there or not. I didn't hear from Ana and the baby for almost a year, and by then things were pretty bad for all of them, my folks included. There wasn't a prayer of Ana getting out while the baby was so small. She wouldn't, anyway. Her family was in terrible shape, trying to do farm work for one of the cooperatives and dying from it. She wouldn't leave them. I knew in my heart that I wasn't going to see them again, though I wouldn't admit it to myself.

"I went back to Cuba in April of 1961 with the invasion forces that the CIA trained in Florida and Guatemala. I was captured almost before I put a foot on the beach and spent a year and a half in prison down there. I try not to talk about that year and a half. They let me out just before Christmas of 1962, and I was going to go and find my family, but I was met at the gate by a friend of my family in Miami and taken straight to the harbor at midnight, and put in the hold of a sailing sloop that belonged to some rich German dude who knew my uncle. That was the last time I saw Cuba.

"In 1963 my uncle sent me to Cornell and I got a graduate degree in tropical botany. I finished in 1966, with about as much chance of making a living in my specialty as if it had been sword-swallowing. But I'd met some people and learned some things at Cornell, and those months in that prison made something of me I'd never been before. There was a guy in Miami then, a fantastic man named Jorge Mas Canosa, sort of the legendary king of the anti-Castro exiles. The word 'charisma' might have been invented just for him. He founded the anti-Communist Cuban American Foundation, headquartered in Miami. It was the daddy of all the anti-Communist movements. He modeled it after your American political action committees, and he raised a ton of money for the movement, and got out the exile vote for the Republicans year after year. He was the most alive human being I ever saw. I would have followed him into hell. In a way, I did.

"He couldn't use a botanist, but he could a radio-TV announcer. He got me into Radio and TV Marti, his propaganda voice, which was nothing if not controversial in those days, and I just ate it up. I did everything. I read the news and played the music and kept the station logs and sold airtime and even had my own slot singing once, when we ran out of money and he couldn't get anybody else. But then I started to drink, which was almost endemic in the exile community in those days, especially among the ones of us who'd been in the invasion and in prison. Big man stuff, you know. I was one of the ones who couldn't handle it. It didn't take me long to go the whole way down. I was born to be an alky. I make a better drunk than I do anything else, probably. I got so bad on the air that he didn't have any choice but to fire me. Even I knew that. So I drifted around, doing landscape work and whatever radio and TV I could get. I didn't hold on to any of it. I never remarried and I never stayed with any woman long enough to settle down. I was married to the bottle, and that's no joke. I've done essentially that from the late seventies until now, only I've done the last eight years of it sober. I met Ezra in Charleston when he was speaking there, and he had this afternoon jazz and talk program on a station out on Wappoo Creek Road, and he put me on with him, and we played music and nee-dled the conservatives and he let me help him with some of his organizing. I helped organize the sanitation workers on John's. It was as big a thrill as I've ever had. But mostly I just do the radio program and what landscaping and con-sulting I can pick up.

"Like I said, I never went back to Cuba. There wasn't anything to go back to, really. My parents tried to run a little shop in Havana, but of course they knew nothing about that. They checked out with sleeping pills and rum one night about the time I discovered booze over here. My wife's folks ended up on one of Fidel's biggest agricultural cooperatives, doing field labor until they dropped from it, and my wife worked in the fields, too. I only found this out later. She never would come out, not even when I found a fairly safe passage for her and Anita. Ana always thought things were about to change. Always did. Anita married a young man from the cooperative and went with him into the mountains to start a new agricultural colony there, but it failed after the first year. It's hard to tell anybody just how bad things are up in those hills. Everybody was checking out right and left, but she was nine months pregnant and spotting, and she didn't want to risk the baby. Her husband left with the others, saying he'd be back in a day or two with food and supplies, and after the baby came they'd go back to Havana and start over. I don't know if Anita had any sense or not, but she was Ana's child to the core, and she believed him. I don't know what happened to him. I guess she didn't, either. Dead, probably, from liquor or a fight, a lot of them died young. Anyway, he didn't come back and she went into a long and awful labor alone in their little shack, and the baby was born dead. She lay there bleeding to death with Lita beside her. I never even knew I had a grandchild until after they were all dead but her. She was not quite five. She wouldn't leave her mother and the baby. She just lay down beside them and waited. It was days before the Red Cross found her. They located my wife back in Havana and brought Lita to her, and that's where she's been until I could get her out, after Ana died. She wouldn't let me bring Lita out before that. Still waiting for things to get back to normal, she was. I have no picture of my daughter but the one made at her christening, and I cannot remember what my wife looked like, except for a picture I have that was made on our wedding day. Well, you know the rest of it; I told you yesterday. So. Does that earn me the right to hear the story of Caro Venable, from gestation up to now?"

"One day," I said, my eyes stinging with tears. "One day, maybe. My God, what a life. How could mine compete with that?"

"Are we having a competition? I tell you, Caro Venable, for all its comings and goings and ins and outs and so forth, the best thing I can say about my life up to now is that I beat booze and I have Lita. It doesn't seem very much for the amount of energy expended, does it?"

"If that's all you think a life like that adds up to, you've got a problem," I said.

"It was a selfish life," Luis said briefly. "When all's said and done, I did just what I wanted to. Anyway, I have a feeling things are about to change."

And he gave me such a showily exaggerated Latin leer that I could only laugh helplessly. If he had had a long, waxed mustache, he would have twirled it.

"I have to go home now," I said. "I've hung on breathlessly to your every word, but now, alas, my own duties call me."

"And are you impressed beyond words and moved almost to tears?"

"I'll think upon it and let you know," I said lightly, but inside I was both those things, and not ashamed of it, though I would never tell him so.

When he walked me to the car, he said, "Will you be staying out here? Lita is wild to see the ponies again."

"I've got to do Thanksgiving for about a million homeless lambs," I said, "but I'll try to come out after the weekend, and we'll track them down. How will I let you know?"

"I'll know," he said, bowing from the waist and kissing my hand. "I assure you, I'll know."

I shut the Jeep's door a little more smartly than was necessary, and he went back into the store. As he walked away, I could hear him laughing his hyena's laugh. I laughed, too. It felt good.

Two days before Thanksgiving, Jeremy Fowler walked down to the sea in Puerto Rico at four o'clock in the morning, sat down, and blew his brains out with a police .38 nobody knew he had.

By noon we had the news on Peacock's Island. By six o'clock that evening the company was in deep shock and full mourning.

Clay and Hayes flew down from Charleston that afternoon as soon as they could get a plane out. I went to the office and put a note on the front bulletin board and told a weeping Shawna to pass the word to everybody: our house was open for whomever wanted to come. There would be drinks and some supper, if anybody wanted it.

Almost everybody came. Most of those who had expected to go to their respective homes for Thanksgiving canceled their plans and drifted in, distraught and aimless. The two new couples had both left earlier in the week, but Sophia Bridges, who had not planned to go back to New York until Christmas, came. I was a little surprised at that. She had not known Jeremy, and knew few of the others; I had heard that she kept pretty much to herself and did not attend the formal and informal social occasions the company provides its employees. Shawna said, sniffling, that she seemed to prefer the company of her son to anybody else's, and that that was probably a good thing, since nobody could find a baby-sitter that suited. The child was in the company's modern day-care center when his mother was at work, but the rest of the time he was in her company. I wondered what she had done with him this evening. She had obviously come to our house in haste; her sleek black hair was disarrayed, and she still wore the slim jeans and sweatshirt she had obviously changed into when she got home that evening. Whoever she found for the boy would have to have been a last-minute solution.

I had asked Estelle to stay, and she had ordered groceries and made sandwiches and cheese straws and baked a ham while I went to the liquor store and picked up deli potato salad and a couple of carrot cakes from the little specialty pastry shop in the mall. Clay's youngsters picked at the food, but they lit into the liquor as if they were dying of thirst. By eight that evening more than a few of them were slurring their words, and some were weeping aloud. I didn't blame them. If it had not been the time and place that it was, I would have loved to have drunk bourbon and cried along with them. I had known Jeremy, too, and loved him, as they did. It had been impossible not to. I knew that the tears were not only for his death but for the sad, shocking trajectory of failure and waste that led up to it. The word flies fast in a close, ingrown company like Clay's. Everyone there knew about the collapse of Calista Key. Most knew that it would be a severe blow to the company, although few if any could have known just how severe. Under the grief and incredulity was fear. Fear of what the catastrophe might mean to both the company and to them personally, and a deeper and older fear: the fear of the golden, vital young when the first and the best of them falls.

I moved among them, patting shoulders and kissing cheeks and hugging whoever held out their arms. Some of them are only ten or so years younger than I am, but they have always seemed like my children to me, or rather, like young kin that I do not see often but still feel a vague responsibility for. With the exception of Sophia Bridges, I have known them all for some time, and many for years. It was as easy and natural for me to mop tears and exchange funny or bitter-sweet fragments of remembrance about Jeremy as if we had all been students together or denizens of the same small town. The only thing I could not seem to share with them was the tears. Mine lay, clotted and swollen, just at the base of my throat, and would not fall. I remember wondering if I could not cry for Jeremy Fowler, who on earth would I ever weep for again?

In a way I was glad it was just me on this first evening. In deep distress Clay goes still and silent, and sometimes seems cold and correct but little more. This is not true, of course; inside he suffers and bleeds like everyone else. I have often thought of Emily Dickinson's "After great pain, a formal feeling comes"—when I think of Clay in grief. It is his only armor, and I bless it for whatever ease it may afford him, but others, the young especially, need to be wept with and held. I could do that or, at least, the latter. Clay could have done neither. Later was when his iron and still-ness would serve them. And as for Hayes, it seemed to me that he could only gibe. This night was not the time for that.

By nine o'clock most of them had gone home to drink some more or drive the baby-sitters home, to sit up into the small, cold hours of the morning talking about it, to cry again, and finally to sleep. I poured myself a cup of coffee from the big silver urn and went over and sat down beside Sophia Bridges. She was sitting where she had been for most of the evening, alone on the white sofa beside the fireplace in the big living room that looks out to sea. I had forgotten to draw the curtains, and, following her gaze, could see the distant line of white lace that was the surf curling in on the dark beach. The fire had burned itself nearly out.

"I'm sorry I haven't had more time to spend with you," I said, sitting down on the arm of the sofa. "This has just about done us all in. Jeremy was something special. I wish you had known him."

She smiled up at me faintly. Her face under the untidy hair seemed younger this evening, and softer. I thought perhaps it was because I had never seen her smile before.

"Oh, but I did," she said. "I've heard nothing but Jeremy since I got here. By now I feel like I know him like I would know my brother. I think maybe it wasn't such a good idea to come tonight, but I thought it would be worse if I didn't. He was obviously a powerful icon. I didn't want to seem to diss him."

She smiled again, as if to show me that her use of the slang was intentional. Two smiles in one evening, back to back. Through the fatigue that suddenly swamped me, and the numb, dumb desire just to go to bed and sleep, I felt a small sting of sympathy for her. It is not easy in the best of circumstances to walk into the Peacock Island Plantation Company and be instantly accepted. How much harder it must be if you were black, alone, and known to be "the best of the lot." I knew that I had seen no one in conversation with her for any length of time all evening.

"It was just the right thing to do," I said. "They'll all appreciate it when they've got a little perspective on this. I know it's not so easy at first, getting your feet wet down here. It must seem like the other side of the moon from . . . where was it? New York?"

"New York; right," she said, stretching her long arms and rotating them in their sockets. Even in the sweatshirt she looked as elegant as a Modigliani.

"We've lived in the Village since . . . for a couple of years. On Bleecker Street. A fabulous little carriage house; I was so lucky to find it. There was a woman next door . . . a lovely Swedish woman; she got to be a real friend . . . who came in and stayed with Mark every day. I wouldn't have been able to finish my doctoral degree otherwise. I guess you can see why I was so hesitant about having an African-American woman stay with Mark. He's never had one. For a long time I didn't realize that he's actually afraid of people with dark skins. Now I see that I was not only foolish to insist on that, but I was doing him actual harm. I need to apologize to you about that little remark, Mrs. Venable, among other things. When I'm scared I get snotty."

"Call me Caro, please," I said, liking her, all of a sudden, very much indeed. I could see precisely why she pulled isolation around her and her son like a cloak. She probably had few peers. How many young black women could imagine being where Sophia Bridges was in her life? How many young white women could imagine the life itself?

"You have absolutely nothing to apologize to me for," I said. "As I said, there are a million things easier than walking into a tight little society that has existed quite nicely without you for a long time. They'll come to you eventually; I've seen it happen over and over again. Though not many of them came here with reputations like yours preceding them. That may be part of the problem. Clay thinks you're awfully special."

The easy smile vanished and the remote Ibo princess was back. I knew that there would be no easy victories with this one. But it was good to know, too, that there were chinks in her armor.

"I'm glad to have his high opinion," she said formally. "I've worked very hard for a long time to be special. It's what I have now in place of friends or a nice house in Connecticut or a husband. In the long run, I've always known that when you're black you'd better be special, because you can't count on the rest of it. It's something I want Mark to learn young. But you were right that first day; he has to live in the world he finds himself in. My baby-sitter tonight is an African-American woman, and he was doing fairly well when I left him. He'd almost stopped sniffling. She's as old as his grandmother, and she's lighter than me."

"Well, good," I said, unsure whether it was the right thing to say or not. Was that going to be her criteria? Black women might tend her son only if they were mulatto matrons? I wondered if she had ever seen the movie *Six Degrees of Separation.*

She made no move to leave, and declined coffee or a bite to eat or another glass of wine. So I hauled myself up by my mental bootstraps and said, "How is your work going? Clay said you had a degree in cultural anthropology; are you finding it useful here?"

"Yes, that was my master's," she said. "Up to now I've mainly been doing orientation, and you know of course that that's the same for everybody. I'm starting now to research the Gullah culture, though. I'm going into Charleston to the library next week. It should have something. I understand that there are several neighborhood units in this area, almost intact. It would be interesting to tie that in with the new development somehow; I think a lot of prospective homeowners would find that sort of ethnicity an attractive part of the whole picture. It would give such texture and resonance to the package. . . ."

I thought of the dilapidated little gray houses in Dayclear, warm with pine and kerosene lamplight against the winter twilight, and the sweet, liquid, and nearly incomprehensible music of the Gullah tongue that was still sometimes spoken over on the island, and about the immense dignity and beauty of the old faces I knew from there. They would be amazed to know that they could be considered texture and resonance. My liking for her faded. I realized that I would love nothing more than to take her out to the settlement and fling her into the middle of it and leave her floundering there among her theories and pretensions.

"Then you should really come with me someday soon to my part of the island, back on the marshes," I said. "I spent most of my summer vacations there, in my grandfather's house, and the house is still mine . . . ours. There's one of the oldest Gullah . . . ah, units in the Lowcountry near there, a little settlement called Dayclear. Why go to the library when you can go to the source?"

"Clay mentioned something about Dayclear," she said. "I didn't realize it was actually part of the island. That would be a real opportunity for me, Mrs. Venable . . . Caro. I could take my tape recorder and a camera, and I'd love for Mark to see something like that *in situ*. Could we take you up on it soon?"

"Oh, yes," I said, baring my teeth in a smarmy smile. "We can go early next week, if you like. I'm tied up with this Thanksgiving oyster roast thing, but maybe the Monday or Tuesday after that?"

"I'll put it down," she said. In another five minutes she was gone and Estelle and I put the kitchen to rudimentary rights, then I sent her home and went up to my little study and fell asleep almost before I hit the daybed.

It was nearly a week later before I got Sophia Bridges and her son, Mark, over to the island. Late on Thanksgiving evening our crisp weather gave way to a long spell of fog and murk, with

occasional fretful spatters of rain. Despite the
company's advertising brochures, our late fall
weather is seldom anything to cheer about; it is
the start of our tenacious fits of sulking humidity
that the Gulf exhales all across the deep South.
Lingering leaves and moss hang sodden and sticky
at eye level; doors swell and shoes go furry gray-
green in closets, for the temperature is not cool
enough for heat and too cool for air-conditioning.
The air is the color and consistency of veal stock.
If we are lucky, this climactic tantrum will run
itself out a couple of weeks before Christmas, and
those holidays will be bright and crisp and mild,
the stuff of rhapsodic letters home from vacation-
ing Canadians. Christmas is the true time of the
snowbird, the season of the blue-fleshed but determined ocean bather, but we had a few of them
even over our soggy Thanksgiving weekend. I
saw them from the living room windows and was
doubly grateful that Clay had canceled the
Thanksgiving oyster roast. The weather, coupled
with the painful knowledge that it was on a Peacock Island Plantation Company beach that
Jeremy Fowler had made his final exit, put paid to
any notion that a seaside revel could be enjoyed.
Instead, we had everybody back to our house and
used the oysters as on-the-half-shell appetizers,
and Estelle and her niece and I cooked four
turkeys and panfuls of corn bread and pecan
dressing and made enough gravy to float a cata-

maran. By the time the last of our guests drifted home, I was drooping and stupid from fatigue. Clay kissed me on the top of the head, sent Carter to take Estelle and Gwen home, and pointed me upstairs to bed.

"I owe you for these past four days," he said. "You've fed and succored my flock twice now. I'm going to start cleaning up. Carter can help me when he gets back. You sleep in tomorrow. Don't get up till you wake up."

"You're walking on your knees yourself," I said, and it was true. His narrow face was actually sunken with fatigue and strain, and his crystal-blue eyes were dull. I knew the trip to Puerto Rico had been terrible for him. Jeremy's shattered parents had come from Texas, savagely seeking somewhere to lay the blame for their pain, and word had come that Lila Fowler had collapsed back in Philadelphia and been hospitalized at a discreet and prodigiously expensive private institution that specialized in treatment for substance addiction. Lila, it turned out, had been eating Percodan like after-dinner mints and washing them down with 150-proof Mount Gay rum. Her parents were threatening legal action. On top of his very real grief for Jeremy and the specter of the company's collapse, I wondered how Clay could bear it all.

But he insisted.

"I couldn't sleep," he said. "I'd just toss and

turn. Let me do this. I need to talk over some things with Carter, anyway."

"Does he know . . . about the company?" I asked.

"Yes. I told him when I went to pick him up in Charleston. He took it better than I thought. In fact, it seems to be a challenge for him. He had some pretty good ideas right off the bat. He wants to stay here after this semester is over and help out, and I think I'll let him. He might as well get his feet wet now as later, and a real crisis is not the worst way to learn a business. Everything after it will look awfully good."

"Well . . . if you think so," I mumbled, hoping that there would be an after. "I'd like for him to go on and finish school, but it's nice that he wants to come home and help you show the flag. It'll be wonderful to have him around."

"Well, actually, he's going to be in Puerto Rico," Clay said. "There's a lot of mopping up to do, and I thought he could take care of some of that for Hayes and me. We've got our hands full here and in Atlanta."

"Have they . . . have the Atlanta people gone back?" I said, not wanting to talk about it but feeling that I must ask. It was, after all, his future. His and mine.

"Yep. They weren't very happy about us wanting to go back to the drawing board, but they want this project awfully bad. They're willing to give us a couple of months to come up with something else. Then we'll see where we are."

"Clay . . ." I said, going to him and laying my head against his shoulder, "thank you for that. Thank you for trying again. Thank you for . . . not making me the heavy in this, and for not making me deal with it quite yet. I'll do better about it a little later, I promise. I just . . . I can't . . ."

"I know," he said, sighing into my hair. "Go to bed."

And for the next three days, I slept, off and on, as though I had been drugged. When I finally did wake up enough to know that I was slept out, it was the following Sunday evening, and the rain was still falling. So it was not until the Wednesday after that that Sophia and Mark and I set out in the Cherokee to see the Gullahs of Dayclear, as Sophia had said, *in situ.*

It had faired off clean and crisp, but the ground was still waterlogged, and I knew the marshes would be a virtual soup. I wore the oldest jeans I had, and an ancient waxed cotton waterproof jacket, and the over-the-ankle L.L. Bean rubber boots that had been my winter marsh footwear for a decade. They were so salt-bleached and mud-caked that it was impossible to tell what color they had been. When I picked the two Bridgeses up at their smart little condominium in the harbor village, Sophia wore a linen safari suit almost the precise color of her skin and a smart felt Anzac hat. She was strung about with expensive leather cases holding cameras, a tape recorder, and a bottle of Evian. She looked, I thought, like Ava Gardner in *The Snows of Kilimanjaro*.

Her little boy looked like a miniature Michael Jackson.

"I'm not kidding," I told Lottie later. "He's so sort of carved and delicate and perfect that he doesn't seem alive, and he's paler than most white children; if it weren't for a slight crinkle to his hair, you'd think he was Norwegian or something. And his eyes are this strange ice gray. I'm sure his father is white. But the real thing that stops you is this incredible air of . . . I don't know, fragility. Otherworldliness. He reminded me of Colin in *The Secret Garden*. He looks like he might have been ill most of his life. And he's so shy it seems like outright fear. He stood behind his mother the entire day, almost, and he didn't speak a word until it was almost time to leave the island. And I saw him smile exactly once. I'd love to know what's going on there. If he's that frail, no wonder she guards him like a lioness. I keep looking for the right word for him, and I almost have it sometimes, but it gets away. . . ."

"Fey," Lottie said.

"Fey . . . yes. But, Lottie, that means . . ."

"Doomed. Soon to die. I know."

"Well, I didn't get that impression; I don't think he's sick. He just looks like he might have been. But yes, that's the word. . . ."

It was a long time before I could think of little Mark Bridges in any other terms but "fey."

He sat silently and correctly on the backseat of the Cherokee as I drove us over the bridge to the island, and got out at the house when his mother told him to, but he stuck just behind her, and his eyes, as he took in the old gray and silver live oak grove the house stood in, and the vast sweep of the lion-colored marsh, and the tangle of silent green that was the river forest beyond it, were wide and white-rimmed. I did not think he had often been in places like this. Nor, it was apparent, had Sophia.

"It's stunning," she said. "Primeval, really, isn't it? We've been to several beaches around New England, but there are no marshes there, and nothing as wild as this. Look, Mark, see that big white bird? I'll bet they have birds like that in Africa." Turning to me, she said, "We plan a photo safari to Kenya when Mark is a little older. This will be a good start for him."

But I did not think Mark Bridges would be ready for Kenya anytime soon. The marshes of Peacock's Island seemed to intimidate him thoroughly. He took hold of the edge of his mother's jacket and did not let go until we had gone into the house. Then he sat on the sofa that faced away from the glass window wall, sipping the apple juice his mother had brought in one of her assorted leather pouches, and did not look at the marsh.

Sophia did not prod him to be more adventurous, or try to explain his timidity, as many other mothers might have done, and I liked her for that. This kind of fear, I thought, could only be healed by the boy himself. He would find his own talisman against it, or not.

"The place where we're going isn't so wild, Mark," I said to him. "It's a regular little village, where people have lived for a long, long time. There are little houses, and a store, and a tiny little church they call a pray house. I don't think there are many children, but I know of one who might be around. She's about your age, and she's a little Cuban girl, from a country way down south in the ocean below Florida. She may not be there, though; she goes out with her grandfather a lot. He's a very special kind of gardener, and he works all over the island. But the old people there know some wonderful stories and songs. Maybe they'll sing some for you. And there's a little herd of ponies somewhere close by, and one of them has a baby. Maybe we'll see them."

Mark edged a little closer to his mother. Apparently ponies were not a part of his special reality.

"We had a rather bad little scene with a horse in Central Park," Sophia said matter-of-factly. "I'd rather Mark didn't experience horses again until later."

"Well, these are very small horses, and quite shy," I said. "But I doubt we'll see them. They don't hang around the village much. How about chickens? Is he okay with them? They're all over the place in Dayclear."

"He's seen them at the Central Park petting zoo," she said. "I think he'll be fine with them, if nobody talks about eating them. He gets upset when he thinks he's eating anything that was alive."

"Well, I hope we don't come across anybody wringing a hen's neck for the pot," I said more crisply than I intended. I was getting a bit weary of this pair and their strange, self-constructed universe.

"Surely they don't do that," Sophia said, clearly disapproving.

"Sophia," I said carefully, "this is a real Gullah settlement, one of the longest-standing that I know of. They are quite isolated. They still live much the way they did a hundred years ago. They sing the old songs that originally came from Africa, and do the old dances, and tell the old stories, and raise their food and prepare it much the same way as they always have. They are quite poor by our standards, but they are self-sufficient and they do very well with what they have, all told. Their lifestyle is not the sanitized one we live. They kill chickens and they trap rabbits and they eat them. If that's a problem for Mark—and I can see why it might be; that's not a criticism— then maybe we should do this another day when he's in school or something. You can let him experience it gradually and it will probably be okay."

She stared at me, as if to determine whether or not I was, indeed, implying criticism, and then shook her elegant head. Her hair today was sleeked back and tied with a leopard-printed chiffon scarf. The hat hung down her back from a cord.

"No. It's an authentic ethnic culture, and I don't want him to be afraid of that," she said. "We'll talk about it all, he and I, when we get home and make a little parable of it. We do that a lot."

We finished our coffee and Mark his apple juice, and went down the steps toward the Cherokee, to set off for Dayclear. Just as we reached the bottom one, a great grinding roar burst into the clearing, and a spuming cloud of fine black mud swept, tornadolike, down the sandy drive, and we heard, over the roaring, shouts and catcalls and huge, raucous laughter. A hurtling shape burst out of the mud spray and I saw what it was: a great black motorcycle with two men astride it. They were shouting and beating on the sides of the machine, and laughing, looking for all the world like demented gods on a terrible *deus ex machina*. They were singing, too; under the bellowing motor I made out the roared words to John Lee Hooker's *Boogie Chillen*: "'I was walking down Hastings Street/I saw a little place called Henry's Swing Club/ Decided I'd stop in there that night/And I got down . . .'"

We stood frozen on the steps. The motorcycle swept into the yard and past us, missing us by what seemed inches. It roared out of the yard, made a circle, and came burring down on us again. The two men called greetings and laughed loudly. I could not make them out for the fantail spray of wet black mud.

Mark Bridges made a high, strangled sound like the squeak of a rabbit caught in a snare and threw himself down on the steps and rolled into a ball. Sophia hurtled off the bottom step like a missile. She ran into the path of the motorcycle and stood there, fists balled, screaming with fury. I could not seem to move.

"Stop that, you sons of bitches!" she shrieked. "Can't you see you've scared my child to death? Stop it this second or I'll get the police on you!"

The motorcycle skidded to a stop. The silence rang like a brass gong. Sophia did not move. The two men dismounted and came toward her slowly. I recognized Luis Cassells first, mud-spattered and windblown, his big, dark face crestfallen. Then I saw that the other man was Ezra Upchurch. He was even more mud-slimed and wind-savaged, but one would have known that squat, tanklike build and the massive, overhanging brow and the perfect blue-black of his skin almost anywhere. Practically every man, woman, and child in America had seen it in newspapers and on television since the late seventies.

"Jesus, lady, I almost hit you," he said, and the beautiful, coffee-rich voice seemed as familiar as a neighbor's, because I had heard it so often over the air.

"You almost hit my son, too, you complete, capering asshole," Sophia spat, and I gasped, simply because the words were so at odds with her chilly elegance.

"What's the matter with you that you think you can come roaring in here on that thing and run children down? Mark is a sensitive child; it's going to take me *days* to get him calmed down! I'm of a good mind to report you to the authorities *and* to Clay Venable. If you aren't aware of it, this is his land you're trespassing on. I happen to work for him, and this lady happens to be his wife."

Ezra Upchurch looked down at the crouched ball on the steps that was Mark Bridges. I had sat down beside him and put my arms around him, and I could feel the profound trembling that shook him like an ague.

"I'm sorry," Ezra Upchurch said. "I didn't see the boy. I know whose land this is, ma'am. Hello, Caro. Haven't seen you since you were in training bras. Come a long way, I see. Ma'am, my name is Ezra Upchurch—"

"I know who you are," Sophia said. "It doesn't make you any less an asshole."

Luis Cassells laughed.

"She's got you pegged, Ezra," he said. "Caro, I apologize. This is my fault. Shem was crabbing under the bridge when you came over and when we stopped to talk to him he said he'd seen you come this way with a . . . real fine-looking young lady. He didn't say anything about the boy. We wouldn't have scared him for the world. We were just . . . having fun."

"Oh, God, Luis," I said, my heart still hammering. "You could have killed somebody. Mrs. Bridges is new with the company, and I was about to bring her over to Dayclear. She's doing . . . some research for Clay. But I think maybe we ought to get the little boy home. . . ."

Ezra Upchurch walked close to Sophia Bridges. His coal-black eyes, lost in ridges of pouched flesh and a network of fine wrinkles, lingered on her, taking in the exquisite carved face and the long, slender body and the safari outfit.

"I do apologize," he said. "Let me make it up to your boy . . ."

He started for the steps, where Mark had

begun to sob. He did not move to uncoil himself from the anguished ball. Through the silky fabric of his little Shetland sweater I could feel his heart going like a trip-hammer.

Sophia Bridges moved like a cat. In a split second she stood in front of her son on the bottom step.

"If you touch my son I'll scratch your eyes out," she said in the cold, pure voice I had first heard at the guest house. "That's before I call the police."

He stopped and studied her. Then he smiled. It was a lazy, insinuating, completely sexual smile. I felt its sheer wattage even though it was not directed at me.

"Unnnh . . . *uh*!" he drawled. "What we got here?"

The lapse into street black was as deliberate as a pinch or a leer. Sophia Bridges's face blanched with fury.

I stepped in then.

"Sophia, there are chocolate chip cookies and fresh milk in the fridge, and the coffee's still hot," I said. "Why don't you take Mark in and give him some, and I'll just say good-bye to these two . . . gentlemen. I agree with you, they were foolhardy, but I know they didn't mean any harm. Mr. Cassells here has a granddaughter that he dotes on; you know, the little Cuban girl I was telling Mark about. And Mr. Upchurch was born and grew up in Dayclear. If you can find it in your heart to forgive him, he can tell you almost anything you might want to know about it. You couldn't have a better tour guide. He knows things I never will."

She said nothing but lifted her child up and carried him bodily into the house. I would have thought his weight, frail as he was, would be too much for her slender arms, but she carried him easily. I could hear Mark still sobbing into her shoulder, but it seemed to me that the sobs were growing fainter. Sophia did not look back.

"I thought maybe the little boy might like a nice, slow ride on the cycle," Ezra Upchurch said, pitching it just loudly enough for Sophia and Mark to hear. "The kids in Dayclear love it."

"Over my dead body," she flung back over her shoulder.

But Mark lifted his strange, tear-drowned little face for a moment and looked at Ezra Upchurch, and then at the motorcycle, before lowering it again to his mother's shoulder. Ezra made the old peace sign with his fore and middle fingers and smiled broadly at the boy. That smile had bent tougher spines than Mark Bridges's. Just before he tucked his face back into its nest of expensive Armani khaki, I thought I caught the faintest ghost of an answering smile.

I stood looking at the two men.

"Good work, guys," I said. "Maybe she

won't call the police, but she's going to tell Clay, sure as gun's iron."

"Not Mengele! Oh, no," quavered Luis Cassells, and I glared at him.

"I'll take my chances," Ezra Upchurch said equably. "Look, I *am* sorry, Caro. I guess she's got a right to be pissed. What's the matter with that boy, anyway?"

"I don't know," I said. "I think maybe he's been sick. And he's a long way from home, and he probably misses his father. They're divorced. She's pretty protective of him."

"She's pretty, period," he said, grinning. "But that mama is way too much mama for me. Whoo-eee!"

Then he fell back into the perfect, Harvard-inflected English that was one of his hallmarks.

"I hope you'll persuade her to bring the boy on over to Dayclear," he said. "I'd like to make this up to both of them. If it's . . . ah, research I believe you said . . . that she's after, I'd be delighted to play cicerone for her. You, too. I'd like to catch up with you. I know what you've been doing since I saw you last, but not how you feel about it. Will you try to change her mind?"

"I will, but don't count on it," I said.

But to my surprise, Sophia Bridges decided to go on to Dayclear. When I got inside she was sitting with Mark at the kitchen counter drinking coffee while he finished his milk and cookies, and both of them were neatened and brushed and face-washed and composed again.

"Mark has decided he wants to go," she said. "So we will. We'll leave now. But I'm adamant that I don't want that motorcycle anywhere around. I must insist on that, Caro."

"I'm sure Ezra can hide it in the swamp or something," I said, amused and not a little annoyed at her peremptoriness.

She stared at me hard.

"He better do that," she said without smiling, and I sighed, and we left for Dayclear.

8

In fact, he had done just that. When we got to the general store, I saw the motorcycle deep in the tangle of scrub and kudzu out back, hardly showing at all. Only its crusted headlights were clearly visible. But I was looking for it, and had no trouble spotting it. I do not think that Sophia Bridges saw it. She had begun photographing when we reached the sand road that led in through the woods to the settlement, leaning out the window and imploring me to go slower. When we rounded the last curve and the general store was in sight she was intent on capturing a back view of an old man leading a spavined mule down the road. Both wore straw hats. Mark may have seen the cycle, though. I heard a soft gasp from the backseat that I somehow did not think was alarm, but whether he was intrigued by the motorcycle or the chapeau-clad mule and its owner I did not know.

As we approached the old man and the mule I put a hand lightly on Sophia's shoulder and said, "I wouldn't photograph them head- on. Not right now. They're very shy about strangers until they get to know them, and they don't like cameras. Later on, after he gets used to you, he'll probably pose for you all day."

She turned a glowing face to me.

"They don't by any chance think the camera steals their souls, do they?" she breathed reverently.

"Not since they got here from Africa a couple of hundred years ago," I said acidly. "It's just not considered polite. I think the soul thing was that tribe in New Guinea that had never seen a white man, anyway. Maybe you ought to leave the camera and tape recorder here the first time out."

She did not want to do that.

"I want to be very clear about what I'm doing," she said. "Really up front with them. I don't want to seem as if I'd just come to gawk."

But I thought that without the tools of her trade she felt uncertain, somewhat at sea, and perhaps afraid that the people of Dayclear would not perceive her authority and expertise at first.

"You're with me, and they know me a little," I said. "That's the only entree that's going to work, believe me. You better hope Ezra *is* around. That's the best way, by far. Next to being long-lost kin, to be known by a native to the village is the

most acceptable way to come into a Gullah community. Their sense of family is tremendous; we
don't have anything like it in our culture, not
really. The family structure, the ancestors, the
tribe . . . it's everything. Mark will be a real draw,
too, even if he doesn't want to say a word. They
won't care about that. Children are almost magical to the Gullahs. Back in Africa they were the
responsibility of everybody in the village. Hillary
Clinton's right about that."

In the end she left the camera and the
recorder in the car, but she was more ill at ease
than I had ever seen her when we walked into the
little general store. I could not imagine why.
Surely her fieldwork in cultural anthropology
had led her into stranger and more threatening
places than this. Mark lagged behind her, clutching the hem of her jacket.

Janie Biggins was at the store counter again
today. She wore, over a shapeless black cotton
dress that looked as if it might have been a maid's
uniform once and probably was, a man's heavy
wool cardigan missing its buttons. The little store
was chilly. There was no heat except for the iron
stove in the back, but that was glowing red
against the nip of the bright, cold day. Several old
men sat in chairs around it. They stopped their
talk when we came in and stared at us.

Janie Biggins did, too. There was no cheerful
welcome for me today. I knew that it was partly

because I had brought strangers with me into the fortress of Dayclear, but I thought, too, that they had all probably heard by now about Clay's plans for the settlement and the land surrounding it. I knew that they would wait, now, to see what I would do about that. I felt a twist of pure misery, and a stronger one of anger. I hated being in this position.

"Good morning, Janie," I said politely. "I've brought some friends of mine to visit Mr. Cassells. Do you happen to know where he is?"

She shook her head slowly, not looking directly at me.

"I seen him a while ago, but I don't know where he got to now. I sho' don't."

I knew that she did know, though. Janie knew where everybody in the settlement was most of the time.

"We saw Ezra over at my grandfather's place, too, and he asked us to come over and meet his auntie," I said. Sophia shot a look at me, but I did not return it.

Janie met my eyes and I knew I had found the key.

"Ezra, he down to Miss Tuesday's," she said. "I 'spec Mr. Cassells be there, too. They generally both there roun' lunchtime."

And this time she did smile, just a bit. Ezra Upchurch was a powerful totem.

I thanked her and we walked out of the store

and down the sandy road that led through Day-clear. The little houses—shacks, really, leaning badly and unpainted and tin-roofed—were none of them more than two or three rooms large, and many had only one. All sat up on stones or bricks or rotting wooden posts. There were broken-down chairs on the small front porches, and a few under the great live oaks in the neatly swept white-sand yards, but they were empty on this sharp day. The usual cacophony of chickens and the sleeping yellow and black dogs were absent, too. The dogs would be inside, in front of fires along with their masters. Perhaps the chickens were, too. Seeing the look of clinical interest and faint distaste on Sophia Bridges's face, I hoped that they were. Some of the panes of the windows that faced the road were missing and had been replaced with cardboard and newspaper, but the ones that remained were sparkling clean. I knew that many pairs of eyes watched our progress through them.

On the other side of the little road there were cleared fields and small garden patches, neatly put to bed now for the winter, where the villagers raised their own food and the produce they sold to the truck farmers around the Lowcountry. Fanciful scarecrows tilted in the bare fields, doing nothing at all to dismay the flocks of cheeky black crows, and smartly mended rail and wire fences enclosed each plot. We could see the little lean-tos that housed goats and pigs and a few cows and the prized mules, but their occupants were inside like their owners, out of the strong wind. In all of Dayclear, we saw no one during that walk, but I felt the eyes of everyone. I wondered what they made of the elegant Sophia Bridges and her pale princeling.

Janie had said that Ezra Upchurch's aunt's house was the last one in the row before the forest started again. It looked just like the others, except that there was a new paint job in progress; the dingy gray boards were turning a sharp blue-white. Ezra, I thought. From under the porch a pair of wicked yellow eyes regarded us.

"Look, Mark, it's a little pet goat," I said before he could see the malevolent gaze and be panicked again. I hoped it was indeed a small goat, and a pet. Whatever it was, it did not leave its shelter to investigate us, and Mark did not shy at it. During the entire time we had been here, he had been silently drinking in Dayclear with his gray eyes, and they were as large and lucent now as small frozen ponds.

The front door opened before I could knock, and Ezra Upchurch stood there. He was clean, and dressed in a tweed sports coat and gray flannel slacks, and looked in his shining, tailored blackness like the president for life of some ancient, affluent African state. Behind him, Luis Cassells stood, holding a tray of something so hot that it smoked. Both of them were grinning hugely, near-identical, feral white smiles.

"I would have bet the farm you wouldn't show," Ezra said, "but Auntie said you would. Said she saw it in the dishwater this morning. She sent me out to pick collards and dig yams, and I went without a murmur. Auntie's dishwater seldom fails her. Come in and meet her."

Ezra's Aunt Tuesday Upchurch was so tiny as to be almost a dwarf, bent nearly double with arthritis and nearly blind with cataracts. I wondered how she could see the dishwater or much of anything else through the fish-scale films on her eyes. But she trained them on me intently when Ezra introduced me and smiled. She had few teeth, and one of those was gold. I thought she must be ancient beyond imagining.

"You be Mist' Gerald's gran'girl, I 'spec," she said in her tiny, piping wheeze. "You has the look of him, yes. Who you bring to see me this cold day, child?"

I thought Ezra had probably told her about Sophia and Mark, but I presented them as formally and politely as was due her great age.

"This is Mrs. Sophia Bridges, who is working for my husband, and her son, Mark. They've just moved to Peacock's from New York, and wanted to see all there was to see in the Lowcountry. Thank you for letting us come, Mrs. Upchurch."

She cackled.

"Hush, girl, I know you come to see this bad Cuban hire and my big ol' nephew, but never you mind, you welcome in my house, and yo' company, too. Come here, girl, and let me look at you, and bring that boy here," she said, turning the silvery eyes on Sophia and Mark. They came forward, Sophia pushing Mark ahead of her. Mrs. Upchurch put out her withered little claw, and after a moment Sophia took it.

Mrs. Upchurch held Sophia's hand for a long time, looking silently into her face. Whether or not she saw I could not tell, but I had the impression that she was taking Sophia's full measure.

"I'm glad to meet you, Mrs. Upchurch," Sophia said in her cool, clipped New York voice, and the old woman cocked her head. Sophia made as if to withdraw her hand, but Mrs. Upchurch held it fast.

"What your maiden name, child?" she said finally.

Sophia was silent for so long that I thought she was not going to answer, but then she said pleasantly, "McKay. Sophia McKay."

The old woman nodded slowly, and then looked down at the boy. He stared back, a fledgling mesmerized by a snake.

"I'm glad you bring this boy to Dayclear," Mrs. Tuesday Upchurch said. "We don't see many younguns here anymore. This boy be welcome. You bring him back."

Still Mark stared.

Just then Estrellita bounded into the room, followed by her grandfather, who had also changed into a jacket and slacks, though not so natty or well-tailored as Ezra's. The child skidded up to me and threw her arms around my waist and hugged me hard. I went still. I had forgotten the feel of small arms just there.

"Caro, Caro, can we go see Nissy and her baby?" she cried. There was nothing hesitant or unused about her voice today. I looked at Luis, and he laughed.

"She hasn't stopped talking since that day," he said, ruffling the glossy black hair. "Either you or those horses are powerful magic. Not today, *cara*. Today is too cold for the ponies. We'll go soon; it'll warm up again, you'll see. Maybe Mrs. Venable will take us. Meanwhile, say hello to Mark Bridges. He and his mother have just moved down here from New York City, and I bet you anything he doesn't know any little Cuban girls yet."

Lita swung around to Mark. He edged back behind his mother. I could sympathize with him; on this strangest of days, in this strangest of places, surrounded by this eldritch old woman and the two big men, this small, dark dynamo must simply be one elemental force too many.

"Let Mark get his bearings," I said softly. "It's hard to come to such a new and different place all of a sudden, when you're still small yourself."

"I know," she said sympathetically, and I winced. She did know; she of all people knew. "You'll get used to it soon," she said kindly to Mark. "It doesn't take long at all. This place is *paradiso*."

"That means she thinks it's a wonderful place, Mark," Sophia said, and her son merely looked at her. Who was kidding who here?

Mrs. Upchurch had cooked collards in a big black pot on the rusty old iron cookstove and baked sweet potatoes—she called them yams—in the ashes of the banked fire. We ate them at a rickety, immaculate, oilcloth-covered table, and the greens, redolent of smoky ham, and the potatoes, their jackets still dusty with ash, were as good as anything I have ever tasted. We ate hot crackling corn bread with them and drank strong coffee made in a spatterware pot on the stove. Mark had a glass of milk that, Mrs. Upchurch said, had come fresh from the cow that morning. His eyes bulged at that, but he drank the milk, glancing at his mother for approval. She nodded, but I could tell she would far rather it had come fresh and dated from the supermarket. She herself only picked at the sweet potato and left the grease-shimmering greens and the fat crackling bread untouched. She drank a lot of coffee. Ezra and

Luis and I finished off two helpings of everything. I would have, even if I had not been hungry. Mrs. Upchurch nodded serenely, smiling a
little, as if she were falling asleep, in her rocking
chair by the stove, and did not seem to notice
that two of her guests did not seem enthusiastic
about her lunch. I would, I thought, speak to
Sophia Bridges about this in no uncertain
terms. She could not hope to accomplish anything in Dayclear if she did not observe the
rudimentary rules of etiquette.

After lunch I could tell Sophia was eager to be
gone, but Mrs. Upchurch had moved over to a
big armchair before the fire, and Ezra took his
place at her side in a straight chair. We were obviously expected to stay, at least through whatever
came next. Luis settled himself into a chair beside
mine and Lita crawled into his arms and
promptly fell asleep in the warm, dim room. Her
small head lolled back onto my arm. Across from
me, Sophia perched on a milking stool in her mil-
itant Armani, looking like a peacock in a henhouse, poised for flight. Mark, his eyes still huge
and translucent, stood straight and still at her
knee.

Ezra cleared his throat.

"Luis and I have a little business in Columbia, but before we go, Auntie thought you'd
like to hear a story. In a Gullah home"—and he
looked at Sophia and then at Mark—"the host

or hostess wouldn't think of letting a guest leave without a story. How about it, Mark? You know the story of Ber Rabbit in the peanut patch?"

I saw Sophia frown and thought, If she says a word about not wanting Mark to experience the stories told in black dialect, I'll snatch her bald-headed right here, but she fell silent. Her eyes were cast down, though.

Mark's shone. He nodded his head, staring up at Ezra.

"Well, then. Here we go. Auntie, you're on."

The old lady closed her eyes and began rocking, a gentle, hypnotic movement. Her lips curved in a beatific smile. She rocked and rocked. Then she said, "I gon' tell a short story."

"*Uh hummm. Tell 'em.*" Ezra Upchurch chanted. He was rocking, too, and the bright black eyes were closed.

"Tell about the rabbit and the . . . the man . . ."

"*Uh hummm! Ber Rabbit! Ber Rabbit!*"

"Now one day the man catch the rabbit in his peanut patch. Trap 'im in the peanut patch. And he say, 'Now, Ber Rabbit, you always sharp! You always got a lot of scheme! But now, you know what I gon' do with you? I gon' punish you! I gon' throw you in dat fire!'"

"*Yeah, the fire!*"

"Ber Rabbit, O Lord! I tell you what he do. He say, 'Old man, throw me in the fire!'

"And the man say, 'No, you too free!' Say, 'I ain't gon' do that! I tell you what I gon' do with you. I gon' throw you in that river!'"

"*Yeah! The river!*"

"Ber Rabbit say, 'I tell you what you do. You throw me in that river. Let me drown in there. Just throw me in the river. I want a dead anyhow.'"

"*Uh hummm!*"

"Man say, 'No-o-o. I ain't gon' throw you in there 'cause you too free! You too sharp!' And he say, 'I know! You know what I gon' do with you, Ber Rabbit?'

"Rabbit say, all unconcerned-like: 'What you gon' do? What you gon' do?'

"And the man, he carry 'im to the briarwood patch. And boy! That briarwood been about high as his head.

"Say, 'Ber Rabbit, I gon' throw you in that briarwood patch.'

"'OOOoooo Lord!' say Ber Rabbit. 'Pleassseee don't throw me in there! Dem briarwood stick me up!'"

"*Ummm hummm! Stick 'im up!*"

"And the man take Ber Rabbit, say, 'Oh, I got you now, Ber Rabbit!'

"'Ohhhhhh, don't throw me in there! I rather you kill me!'

"So he take the rabbit and throw 'im in the briarwood patch. The rabbit say, 'You fool you! This where I born and raise!'"

"Born and raise! Ummm hummm!"

They both fell silent. Mrs. Upchurch's head nodded down on her chest. I thought she slept but could not be sure. No one moved or spoke. I looked over at Sophia Bridges. Her face was closed and still, and she had pulled her body slightly backward, as if to remove herself as far as possible from the story and the storyteller. I looked at Mark. He was rapt, his mouth in a perfect O.

Ezra Upchurch was looking at him, too.

"Good story, huh, Mark? You'll have to come back soon. She knows all the old stories there are to know. All the old games, too. Lita knows some of them; she can teach them to you."

Sophia Bridges stirred and started to speak, but he broke in over her.

"Now, before we all go, I want to sing you my auntie's favorite song. She always sings it for visitors before they go, but she's a little tired, I see. She'll jerk a knot in me if I don't sing it for her, though."

And he stood, as easily as if he were alone in the room, shining like a basalt cliff in the gloom, and threw back his head, and began to sing. His voice rolled and caromed in the little room, as full and complex as deep winter water.

"Honey in the rock, got to feed God's children.

Honey in the rock, honey in the rock.
Honey in the rock, got to feed God's
*   children,*
Feed every child of God."

Luis Cassells came in with him:

"Oh, children, one of these mornings I was
*   walking long.*
I saw the grapes was a'hangin' down.
Lord, I took a bunch and I suck the juice,
It's the sweetest juice that I ever taste."

The deep male voices climbed in the frail afternoon light slanting through the little panes, filling the house up to the rafters, spilling out into the clear air.

"Satan mad and I so glad.
He missed the soul that he thought he had.
Oh, the devil so mad and I so glad,
He missed the soul he thought he had.
Honey in the rock, honey in the rock
Got to feed God's children now."

When they had finished there was no sound but the gentle bubbling snore from Mrs. Upchurch, and the song seemed to spin on and on. I felt my hands and feet tingle, and my face burn as if I were blushing. It had been inexpli-

cably, incredibly beautiful. Across from me
Sophia Bridges seemed as still and empty as someone in a coma. Mark looked from one adult to
another, as if waiting for whatever would come
next.

Mrs. Tuesday Upchurch shook herself and
came back to us. She hauled herself to her feet
and tottered over to Mark and Sophia. She put
her bleached, wrinkled old hand on the boy's
head and smiled down at him. He did not move.
She picked up Sophia's limp hand and peered up
into her remote face.

"You remember about Ber Rabbit, girl," she
said softly. "When you born and raised in the briarwood patch, the briars can't hurt you."

Then she turned and shuffled out of the
room, through a dusty old velvet curtain hanging
in a doorway, and was gone.

"Auntie needs to sleep now," Ezra said.
"How about I take you all on a little tour of Dayclear, let you meet some of the other old-timers?"

"We have to go. We've stayed much longer
than I intended," Sophia Bridges said abruptly.
What was it in her eyes? Not just distaste. Fear?
But how could that be?

She turned to me.

"Mark has a French lesson at four. We'll have
to hurry if we're going to make it."

I stood, holding out my hand to Ezra.

"Ezra, please thank your aunt for us," I said.

"It was a wonderful lunch, and we loved the story and the song. I hope—"

"No," said Mark Bridges clearly.

"What?"

His mother looked at him. We all did.

"No, I don't want to go home in the car. I want to go home on the motorcycle," he said. His voice was a papery whisper, like the wings of a dead wasp.

"Mark, for heaven's sake! I'm not about to let you get on that thing; it scared you to death this morning," Sophia said. "Get your things now."

"No. The motorcycle."

He did not have a tantrum. He did not cry or beg. He did not even speak again. He merely looked at his mother with all the force of those enormous, extraordinary eyes. They seemed to spill pure, liquid light out into the room.

"It'll easily carry three," Ezra said quietly. "I can wrap you both up in my sweaters and scarves. We can go real, real slow. It hardly makes any noise at all that way. It'll only take a few minutes, just a little longer than the car would."

Mark stared, unblinking, at his mother. His face was suddenly heartbreakingly beautiful. Why had I ever thought it strange?

She raised her hands and shoulders and dropped them helplessly.

"All right. Okay. But if you miss your French

lesson, you're going to pay for it yourself, out of your allowance," she said.

Without moving at all, his face shone like the young sun. Hers was cold and shuttered. Ezra Upchurch merely smiled, his big, genial wolf's smile, and left to get warm wraps. Sophia would not look at me. She did not again, that day.

Luis walked me up the road to the car, carrying the sleeping child in his arms. He put his head into the open window after I had shut the door.

"You going home now?" he said.

"Yes."

"Going to have a drink with Mengele?"

"He's out of town. Don't call him that. I asked you not to."

"Good," he said, as if he had not heard me. "You drink too much."

"How do you know how much I drink?"

"I know about you."

"How? Why?"

"Research. I always know my territory."

"You're a tough cookie, aren't you?" I said.

"No. If I was a tough cookie I'd be back in Miami practicing pro bono law."

"So why *are* you here?"

He did not answer. Suddenly, I thought I knew.

"You're one of them, aren't you? You're with Ezra; you're one of his activists, or whatever it is he calls them. That's why both of you are in Dayclear right now. You knew all about the project before you even came to work for Clay. I could have you fired, Luis Cassells. You're a mole."

He shifted the child in his arms and looked at me levelly.

"You going to?"

I shook my head slowly, suddenly so tired I could hardly hold it up.

"No."

"Why not? It's the only loyal thing to do, Caro. You know you're going to go along with him in the end. . . ."

"I don't know anything of the sort. I just said I'd think about it. They're going to redesign everything and get back to me. There's all kinds of time yet. . . ."

"There's never time," he said, and pulled his head out of the window, and carried his sleeping granddaughter back down the sandy road toward the house of Ezra Upchurch's aunt.

9

*E*ver since I was a small child I have had the fancy that, between Thanksgiving and New Year's Day, time somehow stops. I knew then and know now, of course, that each day wheels past at its appointed pace, but it has never seemed to me that it is real time that passed. That strange, glittering, suspended time seems swung between two realities: it belongs to no sober workaday chronology that I know. It is, in effect, the Washington, D.C., of the calendar year. And so it was with this holiday season. I walked lightly and carefully in that bubble of timelessness and thought neither behind me nor ahead, and was for the interval oddly happy.

I did not really forget what had happened to the company and more particularly and terrible to Jeremy Fowler, but I found that I could put it away for the nonce. And there was no forgetting the heavy sword that dangled over Dayclear and my island, but I did not have to remember it until after the holidays were over. This gift of suspended time was one of the sweetest and most unanticipated that I have ever received. I was as awed and delighted with it as a child with a wonderful, unexpected present. And for that period I behaved, I believe, more like a child than I have since I was one myself, or my children were. I was sometimes shamefully silly when Carter and Kylie were very young, but the silliness went, as did so much else, with my daughter, down into the sea. Now it was back. I indulged it gratefully. I would, I promised myself, shape up and buckle down to my real life on the second of January.

I dragged home an enormous Frasier fir tree from the island nursery and put it up in front of the glass windows in the big living room and spent an entire day decorating it with the cartons of ornaments and lights we had stored when I took to having smaller, more understated trees and putting them in the small library that overlooked the back garden. After Kylie I could not seem to bear the thought of those tender, annunciatory lights shining on that black sea. No one had ever mentioned it, but when Clay saw the tree, and when Carter came home from Puerto Rico and first spied it, their faces lit in a way that told me the loss of the big tree had been hurtful.

My heart smote me. Selfish; I had never even thought of that.

And since we had the tree up anyway, I had an open house and asked everybody we'd ever known in the Charleston area, or almost, and was surprised and gratified that almost all of them came. It was an old-fashioned party; I had eggnog and Charleston Light Dragoon Punch and benné seed cake and my grandmother's fruitcake, and Estelle made divinity and peanut candy, but there was little on my buffet that was sophisticated or clever. Looking over my food list, I saw that I was indeed having a children's party, and so I moved the time to four in the afternoon and invited the children of my guests, and a great many of them came, too.

The party was such a success that many people suggested we make it an annual occasion.

"Of course," I replied, and "Why not?"

Next year was so far outside my bubble of now that it need not even be reckoned with. In the meantime, the assorted children darting and shrieking around the tree and through the living room and out onto the lawn gave our house the air of a Lord & Taylor Christmas window, and that is how I chose to regard it. We had recordings of the traditional carols, and small presents for the children, and there was enough laughter and singing to fill the vast cave of the living room, for once, to its eaves. When dusk fell and the lights of the tree swam in their underwater radiance against the darkening sea and sky, only living children were reflected in my wall of windows. If a small shade joined them, I resolutely did not see.

I was truly moved to see how much Clay enjoyed the party. I did not realize until I saw him laughing with his guests and their children how quiet he had become, how far into himself he had drawn. I was accustomed to Clay's going away inside his own head when there was a new project on his drawing board, but only when he emerged into our Christmas world, blinking and smiling, did I see that there had been a quality of somberness, almost of mourning, in his abstraction. Of course there was Jeremy, and the great peril that hung over the company, but I knew this was more, and I knew what it was. But I did not have to deal with it for the time being. It was enough that I had Clay back. I was determined to keep him as long as I could.

So we became social butterflies, something I, at least, had never been. We went to every party we were asked to; there was hardly a reception or open house or cocktail or dinner party from Georgetown to Beaufort that we did not attend. Sometimes, if the drive was long, we stayed over, either with friends or at an inn. We had done that so seldom in our marriage that it was festive and somehow erotic to me to wake up beside my husband in a pretty eighteenth-century bedroom that was not mine, with breakfast made by someone else waiting for us when we chose to come down. We slept late, ate heartily of shrimp and grits and oysters in every imaginable style and creamed seafood in patty shells and crab cakes according to the receipts of a dozen Charleston grand-mothers, and we danced, and we even sang a lit-tle when someone played a piano in the late evenings or with the car radio, riding home on the black, deserted roads, with the cold Christ-mas moon silvering the marshes alongside us. I had not heard Clay sing since we were young marrieds; it simply did not seem to occur to him. He smiled often, now, and laughed outright more than he had in what seemed to me years. When-ever I glanced over at him, at a party or on one of the moon-flooded drives home, I caught him looking at me with something in his eyes that had not been there in a long time.

I never wanted those suspended days to end.

On impulse we spent Christmas in Key West, meeting Carter there when he came in from Puerto Rico, and it was an eccentric, sweet, indo-lent time. I had a heady, sweetheart-of-the-regiment feeling the entire three days, with the two tall blond men on either side of me every-where I went, and the hot sun beating down on my bare head and shoulders. It was strange and funky and so tropical as to be safe, for there was no shard of Christmases past to sting and cut me. For the past five years, Christmas Eve and Christmas Day had been dead times for me. But this one was raffish, excessive, and totally alive. I thought that this would be what we must do each year from now on, though the thought of future Christmases seemed entirely unreal to me.

In the week between Christmas and New Year's we went to a party at Hayes and Lucy's house on Church Street. It had been Hayes's notion to invite his oldest friends, those who had grown up with him and gone to Virginia with him and Clay, and so we were surrounded with many of the people I had first met even before Clay and I married, the handful of couples who had been my first real "crowd," and who had remained so until our children started to come and we moved away from one another. Almost everybody came, for everyone loves to visit Charleston, and Hayes had taken a block of rooms at a nearby inn and footed the bill as his Christmas present to his guests. If I wondered how on earth he could afford it, I did not wonder long. Hayes's finances belonged outside the bubble. Inside there was only room for the funny, lost young Hayes who had brought Clay to me on a hot summer day, out of a blinding glitter of dying sunlight.

Hayes and Lucy's house is one of the big old Charleston double houses, which means that it is two rooms wide instead of one, and very long. Its upstairs and downstairs piazzas were hung with garlands of smilax and holly, and tinsel and tiny white Christmas lights studded the crape myrtle trees and the lower branches of the live oaks that hung over the garden. It was a crisp night, too chilly to be outside, but we went out at midnight to sing carols, and the sound of our whiskey-sweet voices climbing into the night sky over the old vine-covered back garden walls of Church Street, and the clouds of frosty breath on which the songs floated, and the yellow flames of candle-light from neighboring windows all made that night as enchanted as if it had fallen in Avalon. I stood in a circle with these people who had been my first friends as a married woman, who had been young with me, our arms around one another's waists and shoulders, and thought that if I should have to die suddenly, I would not be sorry if it was on a night like this. It was a seduc-tive enough thought to frighten me, and I went back into the house and asked Hayes for another old-fashioned. Looking back, I see that I drank a lot in those days of the bubble, but it was not as it was in other times. I never seemed to get tipsy at all.

We stayed over with Hayes and Lucy that night, and made hilarious and silent love in their high-ceilinged old guest room, under an embroi-dered coverlet that had come, Lucy said, with one of her forebears from England in the time of the Lord Proprietors. I think, though, that she exaggerated; Clay and I gave the coverlet a rather muscular workout and it was still intact in all its silky shabbiness in the morning. We laughed a great deal that night, silently, with our hands over our mouths, for our bedroom was just down the hall from Hayes and Lucy's, and neither of us felt like listening to Hayes's sly insinuations at breakfast. It was very late when we finally lay still and sliding toward sleep, and Clay said, "I wish this night would never end."

I traced my finger along his bare chest. It was slick with cooling sweat.

"I do, too," I said, feeling tears prick my eyes and blinking them back. "Oh, I do, too."

In all that spangled and fragile country there was one place that I could not go, and that was to the house on the island. I did not even try. I was afraid, and knew it clearly, and knew what I feared: both that in the long, still nights I would hear the laughter and voice of my dead child, and that I would not. The mere thought of sitting alone all night in that darkened living room overlooking the creek—for I knew that I would not sleep—made me break out in a cold sweat at my hairline. One way or another, the island house was haunted for me now.

Oh, I could go in the daytime for a little while, and did once or twice, but soon I stopped even that. The winter dark came down too soon. The silence that I had so loved waited too breathlessly for sounds that could not come . . . or could, and bring madness with them. I knew this notion of mine was not rational. I would, I resolved, deal with it as I could with all the other things that bumped like sharks at the aquarium wall of my bubble, after the holidays. But I missed the island, and I found that I missed the ponies and Lita and even Luis Cassells in some unexplored way. So I filled the days that remained to me inside the bubble with activity, from first light to long after dark. I polished silver, washed windows, cleaned out long-neglected closets, took curtains and drapes to be cleaned, attacked the neglected winter garden with a vengeance. It pleased and soothed me, somehow, to feel with my fingers the lares and penates of my marriage and my life with Clay, to tend them, to put them away renewed and shining. I sang as I tended and counted my treasures.

One morning toward New Year's I was preparing to leave the nursery with a trunkful of new rose cuttings and ran into Luis Cassells. It was a raw day, with wisps of the morning's fog still curling among the ocean pines and clinging in heavy droplets to the moss, and he wore a hooded sweatshirt and thick-soled boots caked with the black mud of the marsh. He had two enormous sacks of fertilizer in his big arms, and he grinned around them when he saw me.

"Miz Mengele!" he yelled across the parking lot. "Happy holidays to you and yours!"

Heads turned toward me, and my face reddened. I could feel it. At the same time I felt the corners of my mouth tug upward, and a laugh start low in my throat. He was outrageous and incorrigible, and I had missed him.

"And to you and yours," I called back, and went over to the Peacock Plantation pickup truck, where he was storing the fertilizer. "Have you had a good Christmas?"

"You ask a Jew that?" He laughed. "Oh, hell, what chance does a poor lone Jew have down here? We had an old-fashioned Dayclear Christmas, and that, my lady, is some kind of Christmas indeed. A combination of Southern Baptist and Kwanza and Hanukkah, with a little Anglican and Disneyland thrown in. We cooked and ate for three days, and went to a Christmas Eve watch service and shouted and sang until dawn, and Ezra cooked a wild turkey somebody shot illegally and gave him, and Auntie Tuesday made hoppin' John and cooked seven thousand pounds of yams, and I made black beans and rice to go with it, and Sophia ordered bagels and lox from the H&H deli in New York for Christmas breakfast, and Lita and Mark threw up three times apiece on Christmas Day. It was totally satisfactory."

I lifted my eyebrows.

"Sophia and Mark?"

He grinned; with only his face showing under the tight-drawn hood, I thought that he looked like a werewolf.

"Well, nobody else asked her for Christmas. Ezra thought it was the only neighborly thing to do."

"Oh, Lord," I said, aghast. "I thought surely she'd be going back to New York for the holidays. I should have checked; it's sort of my job to see that all the office crowd has somewhere to go for holidays. I just got busy, and then we went to Key West . . . I'll call her this morning and apologize."

"I wouldn't bother," he said. "Looked to me like she had a great time. Oh, she showed up in some kind of suede jumpsuit thing and high-heeled boots that cost more than Auntie's house, and she still isn't used to brushing a chicken off wherever she wants to sit down, but she's learning. She's learning. She makes careful notes on everything that happens in her little leather Day-Timer, and she's about to run everybody crazy with that tape recorder and camera, and she still talks about 'the Gullah experience' and 'the oral tradition' and a pile of shit nobody can understand, but she's Ezra's guest and they're getting used to her, and nobody gets ruffled up about her much anymore. And they love the little boy. He used to cry whenever somebody touched him, and it took him four or five visits to start talking, but he's jabbering a blue streak now. Lita has taken him under her wing. In another month they'll both be little Gullah younguns."

"Four or five visits . . . she goes over there often then," I said. Somehow I simply could not see it, remote, elegant Sophia Bridges spending her days in the hardscrabble clutter and the warm, smoky funk of Dayclear.

"She's come almost every day," Luis said. "She's taking her assignment from Mengele very seriously, whatever it is. She says only that she's studying the culture under his auspices and with his blessings. I don't ask her anymore what she aims to do with her newfound knowledge, or what he does. You'll notice I'm not asking you, either."

"I really don't know," I said, feeling the walls of the bubble quiver perilously. "And I'm not going to ask Clay. You know what I told you, about them coming up with a better plan . . . for everything. I'm sure Sophia's research is part of that, but beyond that I just—"

"—don't know," he finished for me. "Ah, yes. Well. Come and have a cup of coffee with me and tell me what you do know. I promise not to ask you anything else about the island except why you haven't been over there lately. We've been looking for you almost every day. Lita is driving me crazy about the ponies, but I'm not going to take her to see them without you along, and besides, I haven't seen them or their calling cards for a while."

I hesitated, but then I went with him to the chic little coffee shop on the traffic circle nearby. We took our cups to a corner table and he pulled the hood off his big head and was the Luis Cassells I knew again, half mythic creature and half lowland gorilla. His hours in the winter sun had kept him walnut brown, and his teeth flashed piratically in the dimness of the little shop. I saw a face I knew at a table across the room and sighed. Shawna would be in Clay's office within the hour, smiling archly and twittering about seeing me having a little coffee date with the hired help. I did not care if Clay knew, but I hated the smirk on Shawna's proprietary face and hoped devoutly that Hayes was not around when she told Clay.

"So why haven't we seen you?" he said matter-of-factly. "What's the matter?"

"Why does something have to be the matter?" I said, annoyed. "I've just been busy. Christmas is always a zoo down here, and then we went to Key West over Christmas Eve and Day, and there have been a bunch of parties in Charleston. . . ."

"Ah, I forgot. Miz Mengele is a social lioness. Of course. The Charleston parties."

His grin widened evilly. I could not remember if I had told him how I hated parties or not, but I knew that he knew somehow that I did.

"It's the only time of the year I go to them," I said defensively, and then laughed aloud. "Though why I'm explaining myself to you I do not know."

"Why, indeed?" he said, and then his smile faded. "What *is* wrong, Caro?" he said, and the softness in his voice startled me so that I told him.

"And you're afraid you'll hear your daughter in the night? Or see her?" he said, when I fell silent.

"I'm more afraid that I won't, I think," I said helplessly, at a loss as to how to make him understand and wishing I had not spoken of it. "Or that I will, and that she'll just . . . fade away then. That would be worse than not seeing her, but either of them just seem like more than . . . I could bear right now. I know it's stupid. I know I need to get myself over this."

"It's not stupid. But you do need to get yourself over it. Not only does it hurt you in more ways than I think you know, it dishonors your child. She should not be the agent of your fear. She would not want to drive you from the place you and she loved so."

"I know," I whispered, feeling tears but knowing dully that they would not, could not, fall.

"I feel responsible," he said presently. "It was Lita, after all, when she came that night after the ponies. I know that you thought . . ."

"I did, for a minute, and finding that I was wrong was one of the worst moments that I have ever had in my life," I said. "But that was scarcely your fault, or Lita's. And it's not that I'm afraid of my child. Oh God, of course not. If I thought she could truly come to me there I would go and never leave. I guess I'm afraid . . . of the long nights alone. I'm afraid of being afraid. Franklin Roosevelt would not be proud of me."

"Perhaps you should go and spend a night there and see that it does not happen," he said soberly. I was grateful to him beyond words that he did not laugh at me, or try to tell me that I was really being silly and hysterical. I knew that I was.

"I would be glad to stay with you," he said. "I would not even speak if you didn't want me to. I'd just be there. Do you think that would help? Or maybe your husband . . ."

"No," I said. I did not tell him that I would rather die than tell Clay I was afraid that our daughter would come to me in the night on the island and even more afraid that she would not. It would be a knife in his heart. Worse.

He nodded as though he knew.

"I think . . . that I'll have to do it by myself," I said. "And I will. Maybe in the spring, when it's light longer and everything's green again . . . I don't know. The thing is, Luis, I think that I can't stay there all night awake, waiting . . . and not drink. And somehow to drink over there is abhorrent to me. I hated it that time I did it. It feels as if it might finish me off somehow, just kill me. And . . . I don't know. Poison the island somehow."

I took a deep breath and looked up at him. I had never even admitted that to myself, and there it lay, out on the little marble-topped table between us, pulsing like a beating heart.

"It's a first step, Caro," he said, and covered my hand briefly with his own. It was enormous, and so callused that it felt like a leather glove that had dried in the sun. It was very warm.

"If you're going to start that twelve-step business with me, I'm going home," I said, annoyed that I had told him and near panic that I had actually named the beast. And not to Clay, but to Luis Cassells.

"No. It's not time for that. It may never be," he said. "I agree with you. The island house is no place for you to drink. And I also think you're probably right about doing it by yourself. Let me think on it."

"It's not your problem, Luis," I said, gathering up my purse and keys. "I didn't mean to burden you with it."

"You are no burden, Caro," he said, and he was not smiling. "I have burdens, but you are not one of them. I have an idea, though; why don't you come and spend a whole day there, and I'll bring Lita and perhaps we'll find the ponies, and maybe Ezra would come and bring Sophia and Mark, and we could just sort of . . . have a day at your place. Live a day in Caro's world. You've had one at ours, after all. It would be wonderful fun for the children, and who knows? It might start to give you back your island. . . ."

"Maybe," I said slowly, thinking of it. The sun on the greening marsh, and the quiet lap of the water against the dock, and the ponies, and the lazy banter and laughing, and maybe a picnic lunch . . .

The shadows that had lain thick over the house and the island in my mind lifted a bit.

"Maybe I will."

"Name a day."

"Well . . . after the holidays. Maybe a little later, when the marsh starts to green up?"

"You don't want to let it go too long," Luis said.

And as it turned out, I did not.

Two days before New Year's Eve Clay came home to dinner and said, "How would you like to spend New Year's in Old San Juan?"

I looked up from ladling the Portuguese kale soup that he loves on winter nights.

"Puerto Rico?" I said.

He read my face.

"It's a long way from Calista. And it's beautiful. A lot like Key West, in the oldest parts. Or vice versa, I guess. I thought you like Key West so much . . ."

"Oh, Clay . . ."

I did not know how to tell him that, for me, the very earth of Puerto Rico would always be stained now with Jeremy Fowler's blood.

I did not have to. He sighed.

"I know. I don't want to go, either. I swore I never would again. But Carter has a buyer, I think, and he won't talk to anybody but me. It's not going to do the company much good; the payments are spread out too far. But it'll get the investors off us for a while, and it's the only offer we're apt to get. The main man is spending the holidays in San Juan on his yacht, doncha know, and he insists that we do this right now or not at all. I think it's another case of jerk-the-CEO, but right now I'm not in any position to argue. I thought you just might want to come. You're apt to be lonesome here by yourself. I mean, you're not painting much anymore, are you? I didn't think you'd been over to . . . the other house for a while."

"No, I . . . well, maybe I will start again," I said, not wanting to get into my reasons for avoiding the island. "The weather's wonderful. And I need to give the house a good cleaning. . . ."

"Take Estelle for that, for God's sake," he said, lapsing into his pre-Christmas abstracted irritablility. "You don't need to be humping out houses yourself."

"I think it might be just what I do need," I said stubbornly. There was no reason on earth to quarrel with Clay about who cleaned the island house. I could simply do it myself and not tell him, if I wanted to. The fact was that I felt the walls of the bubble beginning to erode badly, and it frightened and angered me. Had it been so much to ask, this period of giddy peace?

"Suit yourself," Clay said coolly, and went upstairs to his office. Thus it was that when he left for Puerto Rico two days later, the kisses we gave each other were cheek kisses only, and glancing ones at that. I hated it but did not know how to get the past three weeks' intimacy back, and he gave no sign that he wanted to.

When he was gone, I sat down in my shining, empty house and suddenly could not bear it. I dug out my battered Day-Timer and consulted it, and then dialed the number I had written down for the little nameless store in Dayclear.

Janie answered.

"Sto'."

"Janie, it's Caro Venable. Could you get a message to Mr. Cassells for me, do you think?"

"Reckon so. They outside playin' football right now."

When he came to the phone, I said, "Don't you ever work?"

"Ah, if only I could," he said lugubriously. "But instead I must hang around this store waiting for you to call. I'm weeks behind. Mengele will gas me. Or connect my ear to my fat *Cubano* butt."

I laughed; I could not help it. The fragile sorcery of Christmas came drifting back.

"Do you think you could take your fat *Cubano* butt over to my house today? I'm going to be around, and we're not apt to get a better day to show Lita the ponies. If I can find them."

"My butt is yours," he said. "As a matter of fact, I think the ponies are around your place somewhere. Ezra was out on the creek yesterday and saw them hanging around under your porch."

"Lord, I hope they're not chewing on the supports again," I said. "They aren't pressure treated, and I've found enough teeth marks on them so that one day they're going to gnaw through them like beavers. Granddaddy said it was the salt that soaked into the wood that they like."

"I think it's more apt to be the six tons of windfall apples I've been lugging over there every week, at Lady Lita's direction," he said.

"You've built a pony trap under my porch," I said, grinning into the telephone.

"*Sí, senora,*" he said in a dreadful Latino whine.

"I'll be over directly," I said. "I'll bring a picnic lunch. You bring whatever you want to drink for the two of you."

When I got out of the Cherokee there was no one in sight, and I stopped still and looked up at the weathered gray house on its stilts, dreaming in its shroud of silvery moss and the mild sun. It was a warm, sweet morning, so much like the spring that was still six weeks away, that I could almost hear the little liquid sucking sound that the wet earth sometimes makes in spring, as the dormant roots come alive again and drink in the standing rain. Out on the creek the water danced and sparkled, and the sky over it was the pale washed blue that March brings. The sun was already warm on my forearms and the top of my head, and I took off the hat that I had worn. I waited. Nothing happened, nothing broke the silence except the distant cacophony of the returning ducks and waterbirds in the big freshwater pond across the river and the tiny rustlings of small things that should, by right, still be sleeping in the mud. Well, I thought, what did you expect to hear? But I knew.

Anxiety crawled out of the pit of my stomach and closed around my heart. I shook my head and walked briskly up the steps to the house. I would not have this. Not on this most beneficent of days. Not here. Not now.

There were baskets and grocery bags piled at

the door, and a small sack of the tiny, gnarled Yates apples that lay everywhere in the long grass of the island, the last spawn of centuries-old orchards. I knew they would be as sweet as smoke and honey, but that you were quite apt to meet half a worm if you bit into one. Pony bait, I was sure. So Luis and Lita were already here. But where? I saw no vehicle, and there was no sign at all of the herd.

And then there was. The familiar, half-spectral sound of their hoofbeats in soft, wet earth came bursting down the road that led into the hummock. My breath stopped. Then the herd itself swept into view, still looking like clumsily made toys. They were not galloping, as they sometimes did, but trotting phlegmatically along in a messy knot. At the rear, I saw the awkward sprite's shape of Nissy's colt, capering on longer legs, and then Nissy herself. Lita was on her back, sturdy little legs clamped around Nissy's fat, shaggy stomach, hands intertwined in the scabrous mane. Beside them, Luis Cassells trotted, breathing hard but keeping up. I put my hands to my mouth, my heart pounding. I had seen this before, in another, distant lifetime. I did not know if I could handle it again.

Nissy set her splayed hooves in an abrupt, skidding stop and Lita slid off her back, crowing with joy. She ran straight to me and threw her arms around me and buried her head in my stomach.

"*Ay*, Caro! The *jaca*, she let me *montar* . . ."

"English, Lita," Luis said, puffing and laughing. "*Ingles, por favor.*"

Lita threw her head back and looked up at me.

"Nissy let me ride her! It's the first time! Abuelo . . . Grandfather said I could surprise you. Are you surprised, Caro?"

I reached down slowly, almost reluctantly, and touched the damp curls on top of her head. It was all right. They were springy and a bit wiry, not like Kylie's at all. I ruffled them.

"I *am* surprised," I said. "You must be a witch. I didn't think the old lady would let anybody near her."

Not again, my heart said.

Luis pulled sugar cubes out of the pockets of his blue jeans and offered one to the nervously pawing Nissy. She looked at him, the whites of her eyes showing so that she looked wall-eyed and stupid, and then took it delicately. The colt came skittering up and nosed at Luis's hand, and gobbled his sugar so fast that he choked a bit, and coughed, and tossed his big goblin's head. We all laughed. He would grow up to be an ordinary, homely little marsh tacky like the rest of his herd, but right now he was an enchanting mixture of grace and caricature.

"He really does need a name," I said.

"He has one," Lita said shyly. "That is, if you like it. I call him Yambi. It means 'yam' in the Vai language. Ezra told me. He eats all the yams we bring him. Auntie Tuesday lets Abuelo take the leftover ones and put them under your porch, and they're always gone when he comes back. I know it's him that eats them. Abuelo found one that had little tiny teeth bites in it."

"Yambi it is then," I said. "Hello, Yambi. Are you an honorary Gullah like Lita?"

The colt cocked his head at us, saw that no more sugar was forthcoming, wheeled, and fled away on his still-delicate hooves. In a moment the entire herd had one of its feigned panic attacks and went thundering back down the road toward the line of the woods.

Lita's small face screwed up with dismay, and Luis said, "They'll be back after a while. You wait and see. They'll come back for lunch. There's not a marsh tacky alive that can resist the smell of . . . what, Caro?"

"Ham sandwiches. Egg salad. Tuna fish on hoagy rolls. Potato salad I made myself. Estelle's fruitcake. Chocolate chip cookies. Oh, and taco chips."

"Taco chips," Luis said triumphantly. "Marsh tackies never get enough taco chips. They'll be back begging and pleading."

We stowed the groceries and my picnic basket and Auntie Tuesday's big plastic jug of lemonade, and went back out into the sun. As if by previous agreement, though there had been none, we drifted across the wet grass to the edge of the marsh and stood looking across it toward the creek. The grasses waved in the soft, fish-smelling breeze like the sea that lay beyond, and I saw for the first time the faintest tinge of gold-green, just at the tips, so that they looked as if they were haloed. That suffusion of new green meant the coming of the spring in the Lowcountry.

Please, no, something inside me whispered. It is not time for the spring yet. It's much too early for the green-up. It's merely an aberration. We have weeks of winter yet.

And we did; I knew that. This haze of green *was* an aberration; it happened sometimes on the marshes, when there had been a lot of rain and almost no cold. I was still safe there in the bubble of winter.

The weight of the sun on us was palpable, and the smell of salt and clean mud and the billions of things growing and dying deep in the black silt was mesmerizing. Small white clouds that looked like washing hung out, sailed across the tender blue sky. Songbirds set up their choruses in the small knots of myrtles and scrub trees on the little hummocks that dotted the sea of grass. We stepped onto the creaking wooden boardwalk over the marsh and strolled out toward the water that glittered in the noon sun like crumpled foil. No one spoke. Sun and sleepiness lay heavy on my eyelids.

We sat silently for quite a long time on the little dock, swinging our legs over the edge toward the water. The Whaler and the canoe had been put away in their cradles under the house, but I had forgotten the salt-faded old oilcloth cushions, and we laid them on the uneven old boards and stretched out on them in the sun. I closed my eyes under its red weight. I could hear the water slapping hollowly against the pilings below and smiled slightly. It was the sound of all my summers in this place.

Beside me, Luis said quietly, "How is it for you? Is it all right?"

"Yes," I said, not opening my eyes. "So far it's all right. It seems that so long as the sun is out, it's okay."

"Then we shall stop the sun," he said in the tone of Moses commanding the Red Sea to part, and I smiled again. Pretty soon the slapping water faded, and I think that I slept for a while.

A great splashing and shrill shouts from Lita woke me. She and Luis were standing at the very edge of the dock, looking back toward the shore. I scrambled to my feet, sweating and confused, and staggered over to join them.

Dolphins. A school of them, huge and rubbery and silvery, so close that you could see their silly, cunning smiles and hear the wet, breathy little noises of their blowholes. They were churning straight for the marshy banks of the creek, silvery thrashing ahead of them. And then, incredibly, they drove a roiling school of small fish into the reeds and floundered, slapping and blowing, out of the water and onto the bank after them. Each of the six or seven huge dolphins managed to eat a fair number of the fish before they half rolled, half flapped themselves back into the water. They frisked for a moment, flashing tails and fins, and then were gone.

I began to laugh.

"My grandfather told me about them," I said. "I never believed him. He said there was a . . . what? A group, a pod . . . of salt river dolphins that actually drive the fish on shore and go after them and eat them. He said they only exist from about Seabrook down to Hunting Island, and that they taught themselves to do that ages ago, and it's almost a genetic thing with them by now. But only with this particular group. Any visiting schools have got to do it the old-fashioned way. They work for it."

"Ah, *Dios*, how perfect," Luis said softly. "They know so much better than we do how to use their world, and they do not need to either destroy it or leave it. They're very smart fish, dolphins. Do you know that some of the old Gullahs call them horsemen?"

"Horsemen? Why?"

"I'm not sure I understand. It's a tale one of the old men told around the stove at the store one night. I think it's because the fishermen used to know a trick: they'd go out to where they knew the dolphins liked to hang out, and they'd bang on the sides of the boat underwater, slow, heavy bangs, and for some reason that attracted the dolphins, and they'd come swimming toward the boat, driving the fish before them. So there was fish for everybody then: the fishermen and the dolphins alike. I made out that they call them horsemen partly because they work for men like intelligent horses do. The 'men' part I think has to do with certain . . . ah, bodily parts that apparently are quite like . . ."

"I get you," I said, feeling myself redden.

He leered.

Lita came running back from the bank, flushed with excitement.

"I touched one!" she cried. "I just reached right out and touched him on his head, and he let me! It was like touching wet rubber!"

"They're pretty tame," I said. "The ones around here, anyway. You know, sometimes they sleep right off this dock, just sort of drift suspended in the water and sleep all night."

"How do you know they sleep?" Lita said. "Maybe they're just fooling. I do that sometimes."

"You can hear them snore," I said. "No kidding, I'm serious. I've heard them snoring in the nights in summer, when the windows are open, so loud that you can't sleep. It's a funny, snorty, bubbling sound, but it's definitely snoring. When eight or ten of them are doing it, you can kiss your slumbers good-bye."

"I don't believe you," Luis said, obviously wanting to.

"Scout's honor. My grandfather said they'd been doing it since he was a young boy out here. If you don't believe me, you just come spend the night sometime and listen yourself—"

I stopped, reddening again.

"I'll do that," he said.

"Isn't it lunchtime?" Lita said from the end of the dock, where she was watching in case the dolphins came back.

"Can you wait a little longer?" Luis said. "We're having company for lunch."

"Who, Abuelo?"

"It's a surprise."

"Not much of one," I said, as the menacing growl of the Harley-Davidson curled into the still air. It grew rapidly until it and the machine burst into the clearing at the same time. I saw that three people rode astride, one sandwiched between the other two.

"It's Mark!" Lita shrieked in an excess of joy. "It's Mark the nark and Ezra Shmezra!"

"And Sophia, of course," Luis said dryly, giving her a long look.

"Yeah. Her, too. Okay. I know. I'll be polite."

I lifted my eyebrows at Luis over her head.

"Competition," he mouthed silently, and I laughed.

"It starts young."

"Does it ever. Of course, she is one fine-looking lady, you must admit."

"Yeah," I said. "I guess I must, at that."

"Just not my type." He grinned. "I like 'em down and dirty."

I bridled, and then looked down at myself. I was all black mud up to the knees of my blue jeans, and my rubber Bean shoes were caked with it. My T-shirt was spattered with marsh water. My hair hung around my face and stuck to it with noonday sweat, and I could feel twigs and bits of moss caught in it. In disgust I twisted it up off my neck and secured it with the rubber band I carry with me always, for just such a purpose.

"That's pretty," Luis said. "You look sort of Spanish like that."

"Like one of Velázquez's *majas*?"

"Yeah. Like that. I'll bet you've been told that before."

"Only once," I said.

Mark and Lita rushed to meet each other, shrieking in the ear-piercing treble of small children everywhere; I had almost forgotten it. They rushed off together down to the edge of the creek, where, from her extravagant gestures, I gathered that Lita was telling him about the dolphins. Ezra and Sophia came down the little rise to the edge of the boardwalk. He wore blue jeans and a red T-shirt and looked, Luis said in my ear, like a brick shithouse. Sophia, to my surprise, wore skintight, faded blue jeans spattered with black mud and a large, flapping man's blue work shirt with an elbow out and filthy, wet sneakers. She still managed to look like an Ibo princess, though. Just a slightly grimy one. She was carrying the smart Louis Vuitton tote that I never saw her without, and I saw the outline of the ubiquitous camera and tape recorder inside it, as well as several small, plastic-wrapped bundles and a long, pale brown baguette.

"Brothers and sisters," boomed Ezra. "Let us break bread. Since we brought it, that is."

"We did, too. Caro brought enough for an army," Luis said, clapping Ezra on his massive shoulder. In the sun that poured straight down, Ezra Upchurch shone almost blue. It was a beautiful color, rich and virile and somehow royal. I thought that he would match Sophia Bridges in elegance any day, as long as he stood in sunlight.

"Caro," Sophia said coolly. She looked levelly at me. Her face was calm and courteous, but closed.

"Sophia," I said back.

We lapsed into silence, and the men stood

quietly, too, watching us. What is the matter with
everybody? I thought in irritation, but still I did
not speak, and still we regarded each other,
Sophia Bridges and I.

What are you doing here? her long almond
eyes said to me as clearly as if she had spoken.
You are not a part of this company. You belong
on the other side of that bridge. You belong with
Clay Venable. Where do you stand in this?

I might ask you the same thing, my eyes said
back to her. So do you belong with Clay Venable.
So do you belong on the other side . . . of the
bridge and the fence. Where do you stand in this?

We were silent for another moment, and
then, just as Ezra drew a breath to speak, we
burst into simultaneous laughter, and the day slid
smoothly into afternoon, wrapped in sunlight
and the sweet false spring. Only then did I
remember that it was New Year's Eve.

We ate lunch late, and we ate for a long time.
I didn't remember being so hungry for weeks,
months. We ate most of my sandwiches and a
great deal of Estelle's fruitcake and divinity, and
we finished off the silky truffle pâté with corni-
chons and the baguette Sophia brought.

"Where did you get this gorgeous stuff?" I
said, licking a smear of truffle off my fingers. You
could probably get pâtés in Charleston, but I
knew that the closest Peacock's Island had to
them was liverwurst.

"She ordered it from this little bistro she knows, around the corner from her house in the Village," Ezra said, drawing out "beee-stro." "She sent to Charleston for the baguette. You could have fooled me. All this time I thought I was eating French bread."

Despite his disreputable clothes and shuck-and-jive demeanor, I knew that he was no stranger to truffle pâté and baguettes. Ezra had a town house in Washington, D.C., that I had heard was as spare and elegant as he himself was massive and shambling. Lottie had told me in amusement that *Architectural Digest* had been after him for years to let them do a spread on it, but he always told them that the hens were laying good and he didn't want to disturb them, or other of the down-home nonsense that so charmed the national media.

"I happen to know that you have a charge account at Zabar's," Sophia retorted. She was lying with her back against the railing of my porch, as indolent in the slanting sun as a jungle cat. After our explosion of mutual laughter, things between us had been comfortable, if not intimate. I enjoyed the comfort, knowing that intimacy with me or many other people was probably beyond this beautiful, tight-drawn creature. I saw her smile fully and often only at Mark—and once or twice at Ezra.

"Wouldn't *that* be something," I murmured

to Luis, when they had gone to the Harley to stow the plastic pitcher and the disposable champagne glasses they had had, Ezra told us, to go to the Edisto Wal-Mart for.

"A veritable mating of titans." He grinned. "But I wouldn't count on it. I'd just as soon woo a totem pole as Miz Sophia Bridges, and Ezra has at least six women in every port. I don't know how he's standing his enforced celibacy down here."

"Maybe he isn't," I said.

"Yeah, I think he is. He doesn't cross the bridge to Peacock's that I know of, and he's around Dayclear practically all the time."

"What does he do?"

"Hangs out, mostly. Talks to the old folks. Visits. Listens to the tales. Tells some of them around the stove. He's preached once or twice. You forget he's a preacher sometimes, but you should hear him in the pray house. It's something to make your hair stand up. And he's with Sophia and Mark a lot. He's showing them all sorts of stuff, and she's writing it down in the goddamned little book of hers, or poking that recorder in his face. And Mark is just drinking it in. That kid has bloomed like kudzu. I don't think he had any idea he was black. Now I think he wishes he was as black as Ezra."

"That's a switch for her," I said. "I think all their friends in New York were white as a field of lilies. I'm surprised she allows the exposure."

"Yeah, I am, too. There's something going on there, but I don't know what it is. Sometimes she gets the oddest look on her face, and sometimes she just . . . turns her head. Or walks away. But she's always back the next day. If I didn't know her for the little Mengele-ite she is, I'd think her interest was more than anthropological. But leopards like that don't usually change their spots."

The sun slanted lower, and was so beneficent on our faces and arms that no one moved off the deck for another hour or so. The children, worn out, napped on the living room sofas. We four talked, but it was not the sort of talk that demands or receives intense attention. It was as drifting and desultory as the talk between the oldest of friends, only we weren't that. I put it down to the cockeyed magic of this strange, displaced spring day that had fallen into our midwinter.

Presently, into a lull, I said, "Why do you come back here, Ezra?"

He did not answer for so long that I thought perhaps I had offended him, and looked over at him. But his big face was calm, and his eyes were fastened off on the creek, where the glitter was turning from hot white to gold.

"I think . . . to remember who I am," he said. "And to remember who they are. I don't think we're going to have all this"—and his big arm made a sweeping motion that took in everything my eyes could see and all that they couldn't— "very much longer."

I said nothing. Neither did Sophia Bridges. We carefully did not look at each other. I felt a bolt of complicity leap from my mind to hers, though. Shame and unease followed it. No fair. My bubble time was not up yet.

"Nothing seems to have changed in Dayclear in a hundred years," Luis said sleepily. "It's like Brigadoon."

"I wish it were," Ezra said. "The fact is, a lot has changed just since I was here last, and lots more since I left to go to college. The old ways are going. The old stories are being forgotten, and the old dances, and the old ways of making things . . . baskets, circle nets. None of the young folks come back often enough to learn the shouts or hear the histories and mythologies of their own families. In another generation, nobody is going to understand the language, much less speak it, and no kids are going to play 'Shoo, turkey, shoo,' or sing 'Sally 'round the sunshine.' Nobody's scared of the hags and the plateyes anymore. We'll even have lost our ghosts, and that's when you know you're a poor, sorry-assed people."

I felt rather than saw Luis Cassells's eyes on me. I would not look up.

"And you're here to try to preserve the old

ways? To see that they go on?" I said. I realized that I sounded like an elementary school teacher talking to her class, but I wanted to get off the ghost business quickly.

"Oh, no," he said, and laughed richly. "I leave all those fine endeavors to Miz Bridges here. She a cultural anthropologist atter all." He gave it the rural black pronunciation. Sophia's mouth tightened.

"No, I'm just here to . . . bear witness, I guess. Oh, I do what I can. When I preach I talk about the real world, of course, because they live in it, after all, but I always end with one of the old songs, and I use the rhythms of the old shouts. For one thing, I love them. They come right up out of my gut. For another, no preacher is going to survive in these little communities who doesn't tap into those deepest feelings.

"It's not that all the old ways are gone," he went on. "I could take you all right now and walk you not three miles from here and show you a graveyard that's completely surrounded with woods, just buried in them. Some of the graves are new, too. They're hidden in the woods so the poor spirits of the dead can't get out and get lost and roam away. And you'd be apt to find an alarm clock on lots of those graves, an old rusty drugstore windup job, with its hands stopped at the moment of the deceased's death. And pictures, photos, in fancy frames. Family shots, mainly, but always what the dead loved most. I know of one fine picture of a mule in that grave-yard.

"All the old Dayclear names are there. Some of mine are. My mama and grandmama are there. So is my uncle, Auntie Tuesday's husband. Peters. Miller. Cato. Bullock." He paused a moment and looked intently at Sophia, who was digging for the tape recorder, to catch the schol-arly words.

"Mackey," he said.

She put the recorder down and turned her head away. But before she did, I thought I caught the glisten of tears in her dark eyes, and then wondered if I had, after all. It did not seem possi-ble.

The silence that followed was no longer com-fortable. He seemed to realize that he had broken a spell.

"And I painted my front door blue, in D.C.," he said in a bantering tone. "Everybody admires it as a creative touch. They don't believe me when I tell 'em it wards off evil spirits. But I haven't had a plateye since I moved in."

We laughed, but we could not get the sleek skin of the moment back. I looked around rest-lessly. The heat was going out of the afternoon, and the sun was nearly level with the tops of the trees far across the marsh, on the verge of the inland waterway. The sky was turning gold.

The old anxiety came stealing back, rising in my throat, marching up my vertebrae one by one, like stair steps.

"I need to get back," I said. "This has been . . . wonderful. I can't tell you. But I've got . . . stuff I need to do."

"Me, too," Sophia said briskly. "Mark and I have been invited to a little New Year's Eve party with some of his kindergarten friends' parents. Let me go get those children on the road."

"Can I persuade either of you to stay and listen to me preach at the New Year's Eve watch service tonight?" Ezra said. "I can promise you more shouting and singing than you ever heard. I am amazing when I get going. You could get a whole chapter out of this thing, Sophie Lou."

"I really can't. Thanks, though," she said crisply. She got up and went into the living room to wake the children. In the darkening gold of sunset, she looked suddenly very small and thin. What was it he had said, to drive her away from us like this?

He looked after her, and then at Luis.

"Losin' my fabled touch," he said, and grinned, but there was no warmth in it.

He settled Sophia and Mark on the Harley and eased off down the driveway, slowly now, to take them back to Dayclear, where Sophia's car was. Luis and I sat on the steps, watching the night come in from the west. It was not coming fast, but it made me want to leap to my feet, to run for my car, to be away and gone. Lita slept on in Luis's arms. He looked down at her, and then at me.

"I left the truck a half-mile or so down the road where we saw the ponies," he said. "If you need to go, maybe you could drop us off there. I think I've lost the princess for the night."

"I will in a minute," I said. I sat, listening to the night wind that was ruffling the water far out, to the sleepy twitters of the birds as they settled down off in the hummocks. To the soughing of the great oaks over our heads. To the tiny scratchings and rustlings that meant the small night creatures were waking up, to hunt or be hunted. There was nothing untoward, nothing I had not heard a thousand times before out here. And still I listened. . . .

"Let her go, Caro," Luis said softly. "Just . . . let her go."

I turned my face to him, feeling the color drain out of it.

"You mean . . . just forget her? Just . . . throw her out?"

He shook his head.

"Of course not. You won't forget her. How could you? I mean . . . stop calling her back with your need and your hunger and your pain. It's too big a burden for one little ghost to carry. Send her off with your love and pride and all the things

you laughed at and all the tears you cried together. You won't lose her. It's like the old saying,
'Hold a bird lightly in the palm of your hand and
it will always come back to you.' And maybe
then there'll be some room inside you for . . .
other things. Other people."

I started to protest that there were other
people in my heart, many of them, but then did
not. There was a great grief rising in me, like a
storm.

"How will I live without her?" I whispered.

"I'll tell you. It's a game I know. It works for
me. Just close your eyes and think of what you'd
be willing to die for, and then—live for it. It's very
simple, really."

I just looked at him.

"The only rule of this game is that whatever
you choose has to be alive," he said very gently.

I dropped my eyes. The heaviness of tears
was near to overflowing.

"Go on," he said. "Try it. Close your eyes.
Say to yourself, 'What would I die for?' and grab
the very first thing that comes into your mind. No
thinking about it. The very first thing."

I closed my eyes. Behind them, red and white
lights arced and pinwheeled.

"What would I die for?" I said soundlessly
to myself, and saw, not Clay's face, not even
that of my lost child, or Carter's . . . but today.
The day just past. The island, the dock, the low

sun on the water, the dolphins, the ponies
pounding down the sandy road, a small child
who was not my child clinging in joy to one of
the stumpy necks. My house on its stilts, its
head in the moss and live oak branches. The
island. My island.

I looked back at him.

"Yes," he said, and now he was smiling.

"Well, let's get you going," he said, struggling
to his feet with the sweet, limp weight of the
sleeping child in his arms.

"No. I'm going to stay," I said.

He studied me gravely.

"Are you sure? There's lots of time for that.
Today was . . . a very full day for you."

"I'm sure. You said it yourself, not long ago.
There's no more time. Now is it, for me."

He stood quietly in the dusk for a moment,
and then he shifted the child to one shoulder. She
mumbled sleepily, but did not really wake. I
leaned over and kissed her swiftly on the top of
her head.

Luis Cassells put out his hand and touched
my hair, very lightly.

"Don't drink, Caro," he said.

He turned and went down the steps with his
granddaughter, and in a moment was lost to my
sight in the darkness under the trees.

Presently, I heard the distant motor of the
Peacock Island Company pickup catch, and then

it faded, and the great quiet came down again.

And I did not drink. I sat sleepless before my fire all through the night, and I saw the dawn of New Year's Day born red behind the live oaks, but I did not drink.

10

It was a curious time, the first hours of that new year. I should have been bone-tired, but I was not. I felt, instead, light and hollow and empty, but in no hurry to seek whatever it was that would fill me. I was content to sit on the dock in the little wind off the ocean, warm and heavy with the fragrance of things blooming far to the South. I felt that I was waiting there for something to come, but I did not know what, and was not particularly threatened by its prospect, not even curious. I was just . . . waiting.

Quite clearly my heart told me that it would not be my child who came, not again to this place, and somehow that was all right. I still had her at the core of my being. The morning was still new. Whatever was coming, it would emerge.

It was Hayes Howland who came. I was surprised by that. I had not seen Hayes at the island

house since the days just before Clay and I married. But here he was, in his growling little
Porsche, dressed in his customary disheveled but
well-tailored khakis and apparently-slept-in cardigan sweater. He picked his way through the wet,
mossy grass as if to spare the Gucci loafers, but
they were already beyond salvation. He wore sunglasses and had his hands thrust in his pockets,
and grinned up at me, the old Hayes grin.

"I thought you might be out here," he said.
"Got a hair of the dog for a sinner?"

"Nope. Got coffee, though," I said. "Come
on up. Did you sin egregiously last night?"

"I did. I sinned so grotesquely that I may not
be able to put my head back into the Carolina
Yacht Club again until the millennium. But if I
can't, at least sixty other people can't, and I don't
think the club can stand the loss of revenue."

He took off the glasses, and I saw that his
eyes were indeed reddened and pouched, with
bluish shadows in the thin, scored skin underneath. Like most redheaded men, Hayes was
aging early. The punishing Lowcountry sun was
not kind to him. There were splotches and
raised patches on his face and forearms that
would need medical attention before long, I
thought. The little white circles of scar that
mean treated skin cancers are a hallmark of the
Lowcountry male.

"Who all was there?"

I did not much care, but this was obviously a social call, since he showed no signs of having business to transact or news to relate. He leaned against the deck railing, his eyes shielded against the glitter of the sun off the creek, and drank the coffee I brought, and looked around, sighing appreciatively.

"Oh, the usual crowd. You know. This is really something out here, isn't it? I can see why you run away from home so much. It's a pity more people don't realize how beautiful the marshes are. They only want oceanfront."

"Well, let's hope they never learn," I said, annoyed by his remark about running away from home. "You know I don't run away out here, Hayes. Clay knows where I am. He's out here with me when he can be. And I'm really serious about this painting, whether or not you think it's worthwhile."

He lifted a propitiatory hand.

"Badly put. I know you're serious. You ought to be; you're really good. I was just admiring your view. It could make people change their minds about the ocean."

"Yes, well," I said shortly. I was not going to be baited into a discussion of the Dayclear project. My bubble time was not up yet. Technically I had until tomorrow. And when I talked of it, it would be with Clay, not Hayes Howland.

"So, did you see the New Year in all by yourself?" he said, dimpling at me. I thought I knew where he was going with this.

"I did. Absolutely nobody but me and a gator or two. Best company I've had in ages."

"Not what I hear," he said in a schoolboy singsong that made my jaw clench.

"And just what do you hear, sweetie pie?" I said, grinning narrowly at him.

"I hear that you're getting boned up on sub-tropical landscaping, if you'll pardon my pun."

"You didn't have to explain it, Hayes," I said, rage running through me like cold fire. "I get the allusion. And where on earth did you hear a thing like that? The only person I can think of who would know is our friend Lottie. You been calling on Lottie, Hayes?"

He flushed, the ugly, dull brick color of the redhead. Hayes disliked Lottie Funderburke even more than Clay, so much so that I often wondered if he'd made a move on her and been rebuffed. Lottie would not have had Hayes on her property. He kept the grin in place, though.

"Okay, truce," he said. "I was out of line. I didn't come to pick on you."

"No? Then why did you come?"

"I came to give you a message," he said. "And to put a proposition to you."

I looked at him wearily.

"Hayes, if this has anything to do with . . . you know, the new project, I don't want to hear anything about it now, and when I do, I will hear it from Clay. He said it was going to be spring at least before we were ready to talk again."

He studied me for a moment, and then set his coffee cup down with a thump.

"Well, things have escalated," he said crisply, and I knew that our pleasantries were over and the skin of my bubble had burst. I wanted to howl with desolation and betrayal.

"Whatever it is, I want to hear it from Clay."

"Clay is somewhere so deep in the wilds of Puerto Rico that they don't have phones," Hayes said. "And it can't wait. If it could, do you think I'd be here? Do you think this is my idea of a terrific New Year's Day? I'm missing four Bowl games and a brunch."

I sat staring at him. He returned the stare for a long moment, and then he dropped his eyes. Two hectic red patches of color bloomed on his cheeks.

"Okay. Here's the deal. The government is washing its hands of the horses. They had a ranger out here in December to try to make some kind of assessment about their condition, and he couldn't get close enough to the herd to even see them, except for an old mare and a colt. The mare kicked him. They're not going to maintain them anymore; not that they've been doing much for the past five years or so. I don't know what they're eating, but it can't be much of anything.

The guy said the hummocks are pretty much grazed out. Caro, they're going to starve if you don't let the company step in and do something about them."

I was having a hard time keeping the glee I felt at hearing that Nissy had kicked the ranger off my face. I straightened my twitching mouth and regarded Hayes with as much intelligence and interest as I could muster.

"What is it that the company wants to do, Hayes?" I said.

"Well, it all fits in with the proposition," he said. "If I promised you that we weren't going to try to round them up and . . . cull them . . . would you listen?"

"I'll listen to anything except the idea of anybody shooting them. I promise you I'll shoot the first person I see near them with a gun."

He shook his head impatiently.

"No. There are a couple of options. One, we could round them up and capture them and sell them to some sort of wildlife preserve outfit, seeing as they're bona fide marsh tackies. There'd be some interest in them. Two, we could sell them to people for their kids, or whatever. Then there's three. They can stay here and be maintained in comfort, some might even say luxury . . ."

"If."

"Right. If. If you'd be willing to entertain the

new proposal for the Dayclear project that we've come up with."

I sagged down slowly onto the top step of the deck and looked out over the sunny marsh to the creek. Over it a line of ungainly, prehistoric shapes lumbered against the sun. The wood storks, out fishing in the mild morning.

"Tell me about Dayclear, Hayes," I said dully. He sat down beside me.

"I'm going to leave it to Clay to tell you the whole thing," he said. "The nuts and bolts. He knows how to talk about densities and site usage and such better than I do. But what I want you to know especially is that, with this new plan, the settlement is virtually untouched. It stays just like it has been for . . . oh, a hundred years, I guess. The bulk of the project's . . . amenities will be downriver about two miles, nearer the waterway. We've ditched the idea of having the harbor there completely. All that, and the housing and the tennis complex will be sheltered with berms and heavy new planting. The Gullahs won't see anything when they look out their windows but what they've always seen. And the golf course will be a nine-holer, and it will be near the bridge, so it's isolated from the settlement, too. There'll be a quarter-mile of untouched woods around it."

"Wonderful. No idiot in a full Cleveland yelling fore and driving a Titleist right into the middle of your supper or your prayer service."

He frowned.

"It's a hell of a lot better from your stand-point than it was the first time, Caro," he said. "And that's just the beginning. We can divert the creek a little just where it swings close by your house and deepen the new tributary, so that boat traffic in and out to the ocean won't come by your dock. You shouldn't see a thing from here. You'll scarcely hear it. This place and the settle-ment will be completely isolated and set apart with plantings and earthworks."

"And the ponies? Do they get a berm of their own?"

He took a deep breath.

"What we're proposing is this. Not only will we preserve Dayclear itself, but we'll restore it. We've got some wonderful stuff from Sophia Bridges and there's a lot more coming; we'd re-create a Gullah settlement of a hundred years ago, with authentic clothing and housing and the old crafts, and young men and women plowing and harvesting and making baskets and circle nets and growing a little specimen cotton and indigo and rice, and the old folks telling stories and singing songs, and the children playing the old games. We'd have a sort of educational complex, with a little rustic building for films and dioramas, and a little crafts and artifacts museum, and shops, and docents to take people on tours, and special seasonal activities. Sophia has some great stuff about Christmas and New Year's services, and songs and shouts and such. A regular story program for kids, with a Gullah bard to tell the old ghost stories. A petting zoo. Maybe a simple little café, with ethnic specialties like yams and hoppin' John and crabs . . ."

He stopped and looked at me expectantly. When I did not speak, he went on.

"We'd buy out the village and pay each family a handsome annual salary to stay and take part in all this. We'd provide the clothes and the tools and craft materials, and of course we'd offer insurance and health coverage, maybe get them on some kind of regular medical and dental services from the county. Oh, and we'd electrify the houses that didn't have it . . . Sophia says some of them don't . . . and keep the houses and outbuildings in good shape, and see that everybody has plumbing and heating and television. . . . It's more than they could aspire to in their lives, Caro, and the best part is, they won't have to move and they won't have to scrabble for a living anymore. How can they lose?"

I looked at him. Black spots wheeled before my eyes.

"The ponies . . ." I whispered.

"We'd like to make a kind of wild, natural island out in the river where the two creeks run into it, dredge it there and build it up and landscape it and put some picturesque little lean-tos on it for shelter, and keep it planted in grass, and put the ponies there. They'd be fed grain and hay on a regular basis, and we'd have a vet look them over periodically, and if they tame up a little, maybe even curry them once in a while."

"You think they'll go for condos?" I said. My ears were buzzing. "I think they're more the time-share types myself."

He ignored that.

"We thought we might have a kind of monthly pony swim, from the new island over to Dayclear and back. Like they do when they bring the wild horses in from Chincoteague and Assateague, on the Outer Banks. They're a big favorite with families. That way the ponies would be healthier and better cared for than they've ever been in their lives, and they'd be a real asset, instead of parasites."

"I thought Clay was kidding," I managed to whisper through lips that felt blanched and swollen. "I thought he was teasing me. He laughed when I called it Gullah World. . . . It's a theme park, Hayes. How can you even think of it?"

"I can think of it because it's what your husband thought it would take to get you to agree to this, Caro," he said. There were mottled white spots on his clamped jaws now. "I can think of it because it's the only way either of us can see to save that goddamned flea-bitten settlement and those goddamned mangy horses, and Clay says we do that or we forget it. I wonder if you know what would happen to all of us if we forgot it, Caro?"

"Clay's told me about all that. . . ."

"I wonder if he's told you just how bad it could be? But the important thing is that South-Ward loves it, and we took an awful chance by insisting on revising the first plan. They didn't even want to listen to any changes at first. If you knew what Clay and I and everybody else has gone through to work this thing out for you . . ."

My hand flew to my mouth.

"SouthWard! My God, Hayes!" I cried.

"They're going to save your ass, Caro," he said. "All our asses, plus some black ones and some hairy horse ones. Nobody else would even listen. Clay and I have been all over the country with this. Nobody else even gave us an appointment."

SouthWard . . .

Once, when Clay and I had been newly married and the children had not yet come, we took a driving trip through the lower Southeast, so that Clay could show me other resort communities and tell me how his vision for the Peacock Island Plantation Company properties differed from anything yet in existence. We saw some well-done properties and some merely rather ordinary, and a few that I thought were ghastly in concept and execution. Of these, one or two were unique to me in their sheer bizarreness of taste.

One of these was in the mountains of North Georgia and was called Hillbilly Hollow. I would like to think that the name was someone's idea of tongue-in-cheek, but after we had driven through it, I abandoned that idea. Hillbilly Hollow was a caricature of every bad joke anyone had ever heard about the Appalachian mountains and the people thereof. By the time we left it I did not know whether to laugh hysterically or simply cry.

At the gate was a security guardpost gotten up like a miniature log cabin. Artificial chickens, pigs, and dogs dotted the little backyard. On the leaning front porch a guard sat in a rocking chair, dressed in tattered overalls and with a torn felt hat pulled down over one eye, holding a shotgun in his lap. A rustically lettered sign on a piece of knotty pine said, STATE YO' BIZNESS POLITE-LIKE. This particular guard wore wraparound yellow sunglasses and was reading *Rolling Stone*, but the effect was hardly diluted.

Inside the gates was a sales office in the same cabin style, but much larger, dripping with calico and gingham and more rustic sayings burned on pine. A woman in a calico dress and apron, with breasts like, as Clay said in wonder later, the bumper of a 1953 Studebaker, gave us literature about the different styles of resort homes and rentals available, and the amenities enjoyed by

the future residents and visitors to Hillbilly Hollow. They included a general store for vittles, a
brush-shrouded "still house for wines and
likkers," a large, supervised playground and
activities cabin for little billies, a lake with pad-
dleboats and motor rentals for when you needed
to make a fast water getaway, a miniature golf
course for when the city cousins came to visit, a
shuffleboard and hoss shoe complex, Ping-Pong
and bowling facilities, and an RV campground
and mobile-home theme park with hillbilly
rides and attractions for the rugrats. A senior citizens cabin community was planned for "when
grandmaw and grandpaw need a place to hang
their hats," and a shooting range and gallery
were under construction, so that "Bills and Billies
could keep their shootin' eyes sharp against the
revenooers." A smaller sign in the office said that
if you required tennis or handball or regular golf
or equestrian facilities, Atlanta was ninety miles
south thataway.

The Studebaker lady told us that Hillbilly
Hollow was already at ninety percent occupancy,
and the waiting list stretched into the next year.

"You folks better get your names in the hat
right quick," she said, smiling broadly.

Hillbilly Hollow was the first resort property
to be developed by SouthWard of Atlanta.

Over the years, SouthWard prospered, and
no one could quite figure out why. All of its

properties were themed, and none of them with much more innate taste than Hillbilly Hollow. Soon they covered the inland southeast like kudzu, and became a joke to the developers and residents of newer, more restrained and upscale communities and a near-bottomless source of income to their shameless and canny young developers. They were cheap to build, cheap to buy or rent into, and cheap to maintain for the simple reason that SouthWard did very little of that. After about ten years stories and news reports began to seep out about equipment breakdowns, failed inspections, sewage and gas leaks, pollution of nearby streams and rivers, and lawsuits against the company by residents and neighbors alike. SouthWard invariably settled. There was always a new theme community sprouting somewhere else to pay the freight. SouthWard was flush and fat.

They had never managed to get a toehold on the Southeastern coast, though. Waterfront land was at a premium by the time they looked seaward. Almost all of it was either under development, about to be, or privately owned. In the few instances that they saw a window of opportunity, local consortiums shut them out before they could even make an offer. They had almost resigned themselves to looking to the Texas coast for colonization, which did not suit nearly as well, since Texas itself often seemed to be a theme park and was therefore less receptive to their novelties.

Until now.

Hayes had the grace to redden.

"This is altogether different, Caro," he said. "For one thing, we're maintaining design control. For another, they realize they can't come into this market with anything like their others; Charleston and Lowcountry people would laugh them out of business in a month. This is going to be a new direction for them, a move into serious, substantial resort development, with all the responsible environmental concerns met, the whole ball of wax. Dayclear would give them the kind of dignity they want to project now. . . ."

He stopped. I did not think even he believed his words. I did not reply. I was trying very hard not to see it: fishnets and plastic crabs and black people dressed in aprons and head kerchiefs and faded overalls, plowing marsh tackies and picking cotton and singing. An RV village where the dense Florida maritime forest, untouched for eons, stood now. Miniature golf on the secret green hummocks.

But Hayes gave it a valiant try.

"If you saw the site plan and the density studies and the environmental proposals, saw that they were mainly Clay's and his strictest to date, and you had our promise in writing about the settlement and the ponies, would you be willing to take the proposal about Dayclear to the folks there? Just run it past them, see how the wind blows from that quarter? We thought they'd rather hear it from you than one of us. You're known to them, and they know how you feel about the island."

"Hayes," I said slowly, around the nausea and incredulity, "in the first place, what makes you think SouthWard would honor Clay's plans for two seconds after they owned the property? And in the second place . . . who is 'we'? You and who thought they'd rather hear it from me? Does Clay know you've told me all this?"

He puffed out his cheeks and blew a gust of air, like a man who must now do something distasteful to him. He looked away toward the dazzling creek, and then back to me, his hands in his pockets.

"There's something else I came to tell you. I don't want you to get upset, because it's all right now, I promise. But . . ."

"But what? God, Hayes, what?"

"Clay's in the hospital in San Juan. He had some kind of collapse or something last night; Carter called me early this morning. He wanted me to tell you. But Clay's okay now . . ."

He raised his hands toward me as I scrambled to my feet. I could feel the blood running out of my face and hands.

"No, listen, Caro, he really is. Carter's taking

him back to the hotel right about now. They just kept him overnight as a precaution. He's coming home in the morning. Carter says the doctor thinks it was exhaustion and stress plus maybe a 'mild heat stroke; apparently he was out all day on a boat, and then spent the late afternoon tramping around the Calista property with that guy who was looking to buy it. In the end the guy nixed the deal. Carter said he offered so low that they told him to eat shit and hit the road. It must have been the last straw for Clay. A decent sale could have changed things. There wasn't anything wrong with Clay's heart, though, or anything like that. They did find a duodenal ulcer, though. He's been asking for that for months; the strain of the business with Calista, and then the enormous stress of trying to get this Dayclear thing up and going . . . he hasn't been eating right, and the hours he's keeping are criminal. He's traveling way too much, too. Well, you know all that. Maybe now he'll cut back some and let me take some of the load. I've been trying to do it for a long time, but you know Clay. . . ."

I sank down on the top step, weak and trembling. Clay had always seemed to me simply . . . invulnerable. Put together from sinew and steel and powered with an inexhaustible energy, driven smoothly on the current of his extraordinary intensity. Clay in the hospital? Clay with an ulcer? What did this say about me?

"Why didn't someone call me?" I whispered.

"What could you have done? By the time Carter heard from the doctor, Clay was almost ready to leave the hospital. Neither he nor Carter wanted to scare you, and Clay'll be home before you could get down there. They called me because they didn't want that motormouth Shawna to get hold of it somehow and blab it to you. Carter says to tell you that if you really want to do something, pick Clay up at the airport in Charleston tomorrow and take him somewhere nice and relaxing for lunch, and then make him go home and rest for the rest of the day. I told him I'd tell you. And when I couldn't raise you at the house, I knew I'd find you here."

"Did Clay ask you to tell me all this, Hayes?" I said, my voice trembling. "Does he want me to take this proposal over to Dayclear?"

Hayes looked at me soberly, and then shook his head.

"No. He doesn't know I've told you about our needing to move things up, and he didn't ask me to ask you to go over there with it. I took that on myself. It might have been the wrong thing to do, and he'll probably be pissed as hell at me, but I just couldn't dump anything more on him right now. And this has got, repeat *got*, to be done and done soon. You can tell him I told you if you want to. You know better than any of us what he can take and what he can't."

"I wonder if I do?" I said so softly that I did not know if he heard me or not. Oh, my poor Clay . . .

"You really do love him, don't you?" Hayes said. "Your face looked like you were seeing ghosts."

"I was," I said drearily. "Yes, Hayes, I really do love him. I always did. Did you ever doubt it?"

"Then . . . are you going to tell him I told you?"

"I don't know. I just don't know. I'll have to wait and see how he is when I pick him up tomorrow. I'm not going to have him collapsing in the airport or something. You'll just have to trust my judgment on that. Eventually I will tell him, of course."

"Eventually I hope you will, or I will," he said. "It's just that right now he needs for things to let up a little. It's a damned shame that the project has got to go forward right away; I wish we did have those three months he promised you. I just thought you might be willing to take some of the load off him by talking to them over at Dayclear."

"You always did know which of my buttons to push," I said to him, and he smiled a little.

"I guess I did," he said. "You don't try to hide them, do you? Well, will you do that at least? Will you go over there and give them the proposition? If that hurdle could be behind him when he gets back, it would be a bigger help than you know."

"Hayes, I . . . yes. Okay. I'll do that. I may or may not tell Clay you came to me with this, but I'll go over there and tell them what you propose for the property. I may tell them I hate it, but I'll wait till they've heard the whole thing before I do that."

"When will you go?"

I shook my head.

"Don't push me on this. I'll get to it. I want to think it out first. You know I'm never going to find it acceptable. But it should be up to them, and I'll leave it like that."

"Fair enough," he said, turning to get into the Porsche and go back to his brunch and his Bowl games. "Don't leave it too long, though, Caro. It wouldn't do Clay any good at all to lose this offer. Not at all."

"You let me be the judge of what's good for Clay, Hayes," I said, but he had started the big, soft engine and did not hear me. I stood on the porch watching the Porsche race off through the trees, leaving a rooster tail of black mud-mist behind it, thinking it looked like blackness and misery and meanness on four wheels and very glad indeed that it was leaving my part of the island.

When I picked Clay up at the airport in Charleston late the next morning, he looked like a man returning from a funeral, and I hugged him hard and we went to lunch at a crab shack on Edisto and had crab cakes and beer, and then I drove us home and bullied him into taking a nap, and he slept far into that night, and I did not tell him what Hayes had come to ask of me.

Time enough for that.

11

I didn't tell him for over a week. For the first part of that time I was afraid that he was seriously ill. For the middle part of it he slept. During the last of it he was gone again. By the time I got to him, almost everyone on Peacock's Island knew what my decision was but my husband.

By that time, everything had changed.

I got him to the doctor the day after he got in. He did not even argue vigorously; he was too subdued for that, and his stomach was hurting him rather a lot. He did not tell me this, but he did voluntarily ask for an antacid. I had never known him to take one before. When he went to get water to wash it down, I called Charlie Porter in Charleston and he worked us in late that afternoon.

Charlie had been at Virginia with Clay and Hayes, and they had remained friends as well as doctor and patients. He had a lucrative practice in the new medical complex over on Calhoun, and he and Hayes played tennis a couple of times a week, or sailed from the Yacht Club. Clay saw him less often, but regularly, usually when he was in Charleston overnight. Charlie and Happy sometimes had him to dinner at their house on Tradd, or he and Charlie went to the club. Charlie was tall, thin, bald, and laid-back to the point of seeming asleep much of the time you were talking to him. But he wasn't.

"What you need most is a solid month at one of your own resorts," he said at the end of the day, when he had come with Clay back to the town house on Eliott and was having a drink with us. He stood in front of the fireplace, where I had lit the little fatwood fire that was kept laid there, his hands in his pockets, rocking back and forth.

"I don't feel tired," Clay said restlessly. "I never did. I just got too hot and got dizzy for a minute. You never got too hot?"

"I never move that fast," Charlie said affably, and took a swallow of his scotch. "I don't care how you feel. You don't know how you feel. That's your problem. You've been running flat out on empty for a long time. You need some rest and I'm not kidding about that. What do you think an ulcer means? What do you think passing out in the middle of a parking lot means? I know about that; Hayes told me. Carter told him. You're lucky there's not any permanent damage. Your heart and your blood pressure are basically okay, though I'd like to get the pressure down some. But there are other indicators and you've got all of them. God knows what your blood work will show. What are you eating? *Are* you eating? You say you're not sleeping very well. . . ."

"I never slept a lot. . . ." Clay said, not looking at him.

"You slept more than two or three hours a night or you'd be dead," Charlie said.

"Can you do anything with him, Stretch?" he said, looking over at me. He has called me that ever since we met. I come about to Charlie's shoulder when we stand together.

"Nothing short of drugging him," I said lightly, to mask the concern I felt. I was glad to hear that Clay's heart was not faulty, but I did not like the sound of the passing out or the insomnia. Not at all. I could not remember a time when Clay had not simply functioned physically like a well-made machine.

"Then that's what we'll do," Charlie said.

And that's what we did. Charlie wrote a prescription for Halcion and Zantac, and I went to the big Eckard's on Calhoun and had them filled. On the way home I looked at the dense little city unrolling outside my windows. It was still balmy and there were people on all the narrow streets in the historic district and around Colonial Lake, strolling or jogging or riding bicycles or in-line skating. The twilight was clear and green, the kind of late winter light that speaks of coming spring and blooming things, and indeed, the big camellia bushes in the gardens of most of the old houses were full to bursting, and whenever I got in and out of the car I caught the breath of the Confederate jasmine that is January's gift to the Lowcountry. I was caught and pinned with a sudden, overwhelming sense of sheer community, of the presence all around me of my fellow species. It was a benevolent presence, and I did not feel it as a weight but as a lifting.

Could I live here? I thought, turning off Meeting Street onto Tradd. Lights were coming on in the streetside windows. Through the sheer blinds and curtains that people in the shoulder-to-shoulder district South of Broad affect, I could see beautiful rooms swimming with lamp and firelight reflected off polished old wood, and the gleam of silver and china, and the dark chiaroscuro of gilt-framed ancestors on paneled walls.

If the worst happened, like Clay says it might, and we could not live on Peacock's anymore, could I come and live in the little house on Eliott, and be a part of this?

I could if I still had the island, I thought. But then the image came, of masts and antennas and aerials and putting greens and golf carts, and of the silent pewter creek "redirected" so as to fool me into thinking that there was no water traffic outside my windows. A lump formed in my throat, and when Clay asked if I wanted to stay over at the town house, I said no, that I thought we should go home. I did not think that anything but the dark marshes would cleanse my mind of the pictures there.

When we got home I gave him one of the Halcions and he went to bed in our big bedroom. He was sleeping quietly when I came to bed a couple of hours later. But when I woke up, he was asleep on the little daybed in my sitting room across the hall.

"I got up to get some water and just wandered in there and fell asleep," he said. But the next morning I awoke and found him there again.

"Okay. Tell me," I said, when he woke, cramped and stunned, to find me sitting in the wing chair beside him.

"I . . . Caro, do you dream about Kylie?" he said, and my heart stopped and then jolted forward again. Clay had not spoken of Kylie since before Thanksgiving when he had found me in her room.

"Sometimes," I said after a while. "I didn't know you did, though."

"I never have," he said, and his face was slack

and grayish in the early morning light, and his voice empty. "But for the past two nights I've dreamed about her, and they're . . . not good dreams. It has something to do with the ocean. It seems louder than it has, or something . . . it keeps getting into my sleep. I always liked that sound before, but now . . . Listen, would you care if I slept in here for a while? Just until I get caught up and back to the office?"

He had promised Charlie that he would take a long weekend off. I had thought it was a wonderful idea, but now I was not so sure. Maybe, in this new vulnerability of his, the structure and discipline of the office would serve him better than this utterly alien, unformed time. Then I thought, My poor lost Kylie. First I bind her with my own need, and then her father, whom we thought had let her go a long time ago, calls her back with his delayed grief, or whatever this is. I had assumed that he had dealt with his own pain in silence, but perhaps he had merely buried it, and it had found a weakness in the wall only now and broken through. Old sorrow and an obscure anger welled; I can't even handle my own need for her, I thought. Don't ask me to shoulder yours.

"Of course I wouldn't mind," I said. "It's probably a good idea. Didn't Charlie say that Halcion sometimes caused increased dreaming?"

Clay sighed and rubbed his eyes, and turned over.

"I guess he did. I think I'll nap just a little longer. Don't wait breakfast on me."

He slept for most of three days and nights. Sometimes I came and sat beside him and simply looked at him. In the dim light his Christmas tan looked bleached, and his sun-streaked hair was simply a lightless brown, dull, rough. He looked thinner and smaller under the light duvet I had put over him, and his face was naked and some-how blurred, hollow at the cheekbones and tem-ples. He looked at once much younger and quite old. I remembered how he had seemed to me the second time I saw him, when he had come alone to the island in Shem Cutler's boat, and I had seen that he was not golden and radiant after all, or limned in light, but merely a too-pale, too-thin outlander with no magic to him. Until he had smiled.

I wished he would wake up now and smile, but he did not. He simply slept, and slept, and slept, and I watched him as I had my children.

"Let him," Charlie said on the third day, when I called him, alarmed. "It's what he needs. It's what I hoped he'd do."

"He looks dead, Charlie."

"Who looks good when they sleep, Caro? Except you, of course. Find yourself something to do and let him sleep. He'll wake up when he's ready, and you'll see a big change in him."

And so, on the afternoon of the third day, I

got into the Cherokee and went at last to Dayclear, to do, finally, what I had promised Hayes I
would do.

In the days after Kylie, I became skilled at living
on the very top level of my mind. Part of this process consisted of a conscious, ongoing dialogue
with myself about the things I saw in the world
around me. I was aware that I was doing it; I even
came to call the process my little class trips, as in,
"Oh, look, class, there's the first robin of spring,"
or "Class, notice particularly how pretty Mrs.
Carmichael's tulips are this year." Even when the
nethermost core of me was screaming with pain
and loss, even when foreboding loomed in my
subconscious like an iceberg, I was able to take
my class trips and keep myself in the moment.
The amount of focus and single-mindedness it
required was astonishing. If I could have har-
nessed it I might have lit leaves and paper to fire
with the sheer force of my concentration. It is a
talent I have yet to find any real use for, beyond
the numbing of pain.

So even as I drove over the bridge onto the
island, passing over the rippling marshes and the
tranquil black water of the slough, I did not
think, as I might have, of what I would see here if
Dayclear became the epicenter of another Peacock Island Plantation property or, rather, what I
would not. And I did not see in my mind the face

of my depleted and diminished husband as he slept, or wonder what might become of him if I could not, after all, bring myself to deed the island back over to him. I only thought that if the mild weather continued we would have one of those rare, perfect, attenuated springs where everything reached its absolute optimum early and balanced there, shimmering with life and perfection, long after the savage young summer should have been born.

"A perfect spring for painting; I'll have to get back to it," I said chattily to myself.

But the other thoughts, the older, darker ones, were there. I felt them, bumping like sharks, down deep.

When I came into the settlement, it seemed that everyone in it was out renewing themselves in the sun. Old men sat on the porch and steps of the store, wrinkled old turtles' faces turned up to the light, drowsing or nodding among themselves. I knew that, barring a deadly cold snap, they would sit there now until late next fall. A ritual herd movement had taken place.

A few of the younger men and women were scratching in the bare garden plots across the road from the cabins, turning over the rich black soil, perhaps to ready it for planting—though that lay a month or so ahead—or perhaps just to see what they could see. Old women hung laundry on sagging lines behind the houses; in the soft, fresh little wind sheets and underwear and overalls billowed like sails, and would, I knew, smell fragrant beyond words when donned, sweet with salt and sun. A couple of old women sat in chairs set out in front of the houses, watching children toddling and stumbling after thin black dogs and chickens in swept-out dooryards. In a dooryard near the end of the line of cabins, old Toby Jackson, near-blind and smiling, looked into the sky. I wondered what he saw behind his useless lids. Perhaps he smiled because it was wonderful beyond the telling; wouldn't that itself be wonderful? His hands were busy with the coils of a sweet-grass basket, as they almost always were, and the grand paisley Legare Street shawl lay loosely on his shoulders, more decoration than protection on this soft day.

I went into the store and found Janie behind the counter, as usual. She had opened both the front and back doors, and light that did not reach the fusty old interior all winter flooded it, picking out the astounding clutter and shabbiness and dust. The iron stove was cold. All the old men were outside. Janie was propped, elbows on the counter, flipping through a book of lottery tickets. Out back I could hear garbage cans rattling. Esau, hastily tidying up for the spring that had come before he was ready for it.

"Hey, Caro," Janie said, flashing her gold-toothed smile. "It's God's day, ain't it?"

"It is indeed," I said, smiling back at her. "You fixing to win the lottery?"

"From yo' lips to God's ear," she said. "Shoot, why not? Lady over to John's Island won fifteen thousand dollars last month. Never had a pot to piss in before, neither."

"What did she do with it?"

"Got her boy to buy her a double wide over to Edisto. Gon' start a beauty parlor over there."

"Wonder why she didn't stay on John's?" I said.

"Oh, most of the folks around where she live is old. They either wears head rags or does hair wrappin'. Not much business in the old places."

"What about you, Janie? Would you stay here if you hit the jackpot?"

She looked at me out of the corner of her eye.

"You handin' out money today?"

"Well, I wish, but no, I was just curious."

She sighed.

"I don't know. That's God's truth. There ain' much over here. Never has been. But the spaces, they're easy on the eyes, you know. The marsh and the woods, they don't confuse the mind like the cities do. When I go over that bridge I always come home with my head achin' and my eyes wo' out from things and stuff. Look like I can't look at but one or two things at a time. I might feel different if I was younger, but I 'spec it's too late for me to move now. This old place, this is a good place for the old folks. We don't need much, but what we do need is right here."

I dropped my eyes. I had thought I might go from one villager to another, the ones I knew, anyway, and tell them what SouthWard proposed merely as part of an idle conversation on a spring day, but I saw that I could not do that. I could not say it but once.

"Is Ezra around?" I said. "I need to talk to him."

"He and Luis gone over to the old cemetery with Auntie Tuesday to clean up the family plots. They took the chirrun and that Sophie with 'em. She want to make pictures of the markers, she say. I don't know if Auntie gon' let her do that or not. Ain't too many white folks seen that grave-yard."

"Sophia's not white," I said in confusion.

"Yeah, she white. She might be black in her blood, but she white in her mind," Janie said. "Least she used to be. Look like she changin' some these days. Ol' Ezra, he talkin' his trash to her all the time now. Not many gals stand up to Ezra's trash."

I laughed, surprised at the acuity of her words. "White in her mind." It was just what Sophia Bridges was.

"You know when they'll be back?"

"I git 'em in here now if you really need 'em," she said, and turned and went out onto the rickety little back porch. I followed, protesting that I could wait.

But she had already taken up a weathered old wooden mallet, and with it she struck a mighty blow on a huge, age-blackened bronze bell that sat at the foot of the back steps. It was as big around as an oil tank, and rose above her waist. I thought it must be centuries old, and hand cast. It spoke with a great, ponderous boom that rolled away through the drowsing woods like summer thunder, echoing and echoing until I lost it among the farthest trees back to the west, fringing the inland waterway.

"My lord," I said reverently. "That's some bell."

"Sho' is. Used to be a quittin' bell on one of them big indigo plantations on Edisto. Called folks out of the fields five miles away."

"How did it get over here?"

"Esau's great-granddaddy took it when they 'mancipated him, instead of money or a mule. Took him three weeks to git it over here by oxcart. Said from then on he was gon' to be the only one to ring that bell, and while he was alive, he was. You listen now."

I did. From far away came the thin shriek of what I first took to be a hunting osprey, or perhaps even an eagle, but did not sound quite right for that.

"That's Ezra," Janie said. "He got him one of

them whistles ladies in the city carries to keep from gittin' jumped on at night. They be on in here terreckly."

And in ten minutes or so I saw them, trudging up the sandy white road that led away into the scrub and the forest. Mark and Lita capered in front, with Sophia just behind them. I could see the easy swing of her stride even though I could not make out her features yet. Then came Ezra's great bulk with the tiny figure of his aunt on his arm, and behind him, carrying what looked to be hoes and a rake, came Luis Cassells. I realized that I would know his great-shouldered slouch anywhere. Auntie's rangy yellow dog trotted at his heels.

When I had hugged the children and greeted everybody and they had settled Auntie Tuesday into a chair on the porch, Janie brought opened Mello Yellos and Mountain Dews for us, and we sat down on the porch steps. The old men nodded and smiled and dozed. No one spoke. Ezra and Luis looked at me keenly, but I simply could not get my tongue working. I wished I was anywhere on the face of the earth but here, about to propose this monstrous indignity to these dignified people.

Finally Ezra said, "I think you've got something to say to us, Caro."

And I sighed, and took a deep breath, and said, "I'm only here because I promised I would tell you this. I want you to know that it is not my idea. I still feel the way about this island that I always have. But I promised."

He nodded, not speaking. I could not read his eyes. Luis was not looking at me but out across the cleared field to the edge of the forest. Sophia Bridges looked at her feet. They were shod in muddy old tennis shoes and she wore filthy blue jeans and a sweatshirt whose message had long since faded. Her narrow, beautiful head was wrapped in a kerchief in the manner of the other women in Dayclear. She looked as near as Sophia could look, I thought, to belonging here.

Auntie Tuesday nodded her head and made a sort of hypnotic humming sound: "MMMMM hummmm, Mmmm hummmmmm . . ."

I realized she was singing to herself, but I could not tell what the song was.

And so I told them. About the dilemma Clay found himself in—though I could not have said why I did that—and about his and Hayes's long search for something that would save the company and the jobs of so many people, and finally about SouthWard. I did not think that the name would mean much to most of the villagers, but Ezra looked away from me, and Luis made a soft little sound of disgust, and I knew that they knew of it. I also knew, somehow, that they were not surprised to hear the name on my lips. I felt my face color, but I went on.

I told them everything Hayes had told me. I was very careful about that. I told them just what SouthWard proposed to build on this land, and also how they proposed to mitigate the project so as not to disturb the settlement or my house too much. I told them about the dredging and the rerouting of the creek, and about the berms and the greenbelts and the careful indigenous landscaping. I saw a few eyes go to Luis Cassells then. And finally I told them about the plans for the settlement, ending with the offers of health insurance and steady salaries and central heating and television and indoor plumbing for everybody, and about the catch-up tutoring for the children. Finally I fell silent. I was standing so that to look at them was to look into the sun, and I could not do it, and was glad. I pulled my sunglasses out of my pocket and put them on. In the dark green world the people of Dayclear stood silent and still, looking at me with polite, closed faces.

"You may want to talk about this among yourselves," I said finally. "You probably will. I don't think you have to decide one way or another right now, but I do think the company wants to move pretty quickly on it, so I guess I'll go on and let you talk. Maybe Ezra can come and tell me when you've made some decision. I'll let the . . . right people know. And I'll answer any questions you have right now, if I can."

I waited again. Nothing. Only still black faces, looking at me.

"Anybody?"

"I think everybody pretty much agrees that it's up to you, Caro. Not us," Ezra Upchurch said. His voice was as soft as the breath of a sleeping tiger, but it was still a tiger's breath.

"Oh, no," I said, distressed. "Of course it's not up to me. It's up to all of you; that's the whole point. I'm only relaying the message. It's entirely up to you all. . . ."

"Ain't us owns this island," a cracked old voice said. I did not know whose it was.

"I know that, but I'd never go against your wishes. You must know that. I promised my grandfather . . . I never would. . . . I only thought that this new thing might make things better for some of you. I know how hard it is to get good medical and dental care sometimes, and how much plumbing costs, and heating. . . ."

But I did not know those things and fell silent. I should not have come. I should not have let Hayes talk me into this. He had used my fallen husband to get me to do this; I saw that now. I took a deep breath and started to speak, but then Toby Jackson spoke. I had not seen him join the group on the porch. I supposed that his old wife must have guided him up the road.

"Miss Caro, is people gon' come over here and pay to look at us?" he said.

Something cold and rock-hard around my heart cracked and broke open. I almost stumbled with the release of it.

"No, they are not," I said as clearly as I could pitch my trembling voice. "They are not going to do that because I am not going to turn this land over to the Peacock Island Plantation Company. Not now and not ever. I'm sorry I even let them talk me into telling you about it, and we will not speak of it again unless you all bring it up."

I waited a while, my breath coming fast and shallow, to see what they would say. A few of them nodded, and one or two smiled a little at me, as they always did, but still no one spoke, and I wondered if I had made myself clear. I started to speak again, and then did not. I stood a minute longer.

"Thank you for your time," I said idiotically, and turned to go.

"Wait a minute," Sophia called after me. "If you'll give me a ride back it'll save Ezra a trip."

"Of course," I said automatically. My ears were ringing with the silence of the people of Dayclear.

She left to get her things together and call Mark from the backyard of the store, where he and Lita were chasing a platoon of squawking Domineckers.

Luis Cassells came down off the porch and fell into step beside me. He did not speak, either, until we had reached the Cherokee. I got in and he put his hand on the rim of the lowered window and looked in at me.

"How are you feeling about all this? It was a tough thing to do and a brave one," he said.

"It was a stupid thing to do," I said. "I never should even have mentioned it. It should not have come up. Luis, do you think they understand that I mean to keep the island? That they're okay; they're safe?"

"They understand everything," he said. "They're grateful to you, even if they aren't ready to show it yet. You don't have to worry about that. They've always known where your heart was, Caro. They just haven't been sure whether you would follow it."

"I've tried to do that," I said tremulously. I wanted to cry, to howl aloud. I had just doomed my husband's company.

I said as much to Luis Cassells.

"It was the right choice," he said.

"I just did in my husband's entire future," I said, trying to smile. "You'll excuse me if I can't feel too confident about my choice."

He shook his tangled dark head. "Your decision about Dayclear isn't the agent of your husband's future's tailspin, Caro, much as people might like you to think it is. And it's not the only one for him. He could have others that don't cost so much. You could, too . . ."

"No," I said. "Not Clay. For him, I think the company has been the only one."

"Then you don't know anything, *carita*," he said, and pulled his head out of my window and went back down the hill. It was not until Sophia and Mark were in the car and we were headed back down the road toward the bridge that I realized he had said not *Carita* but *querida*.

The Spanish for "dear."

We were across the bridge and back on Peacock's before we spoke. Sophia sat in the front seat beside me, her feet propped up on the Cherokee's dashboard, her head thrown far back against the seat. The sinews in her long feet stood out as she wedged them for support, and her eyes were closed. She still wore the headwrap. Her feet were dirty; somehow I liked that. In the backseat, Mark's sleepy grizzling had subsided into the real thing.

Finally I said, "I know you'll have to tell Clay about this, but I wish you'd wait until after I do, okay? He's not in good shape. It didn't go well in Puerto Rico."

"I'm not going to tell him," she said, eyes still closed.

"Sophia . . . where are you on all this?"

She opened her eyes and looked over at me.

"I don't know. I just . . . don't know. You going to turn me in to headquarters, Caro?"

I laughed.

"For what? Disloyalty? I'm really the one to do that, aren't I?"

"'Then there's a pair of us! Don't tell! they'd advertise—you know!'" she said, and her voice had a rich hill of laughter in it.

"When I first read that, in junior high, I thought it might have been written for me," I said, laughing at her laughter. "It was just the way I felt. 'I'm Nobody! Who are you? . . .'"

"'Are you—Nobody—too?' God, if you thought that was you, just imagine who I thought it was. A little black girl in Brooklyn Heights with a rich mama and daddy who raised her white . . . I didn't fit in anywhere. They left it up to me to decide which world I would live in. As it turned out, neither one wanted me very much."

"And which did you?" I asked. It seemed suddenly that I could ask her anything. We had been through a great deal together, Sophia Bridges and I, whether we had perceived it like that or not. We had both lived for a time with one foot in a near-alternate universe.

"Oh, white," she said. "You get lots more stuff white, and you get it easier and faster. I couldn't really pass myself; I know I don't look white. Just real classy black. But I rammed my way into the white world at school. And I married white. You probably guessed that. You can also probably guess it didn't last long. After the novelty wears off, white really wants white."

"Are you bitter about that?" She did not sound so, particularly. Not now.

"I was, certainly. When I got down here I was bitter about almost everything that smacked of either really, really white or really, really black. I can just imagine the message I was giving Mark."

"Why *did* you come? The Lowcountry . . . under the surface, it's about the blackest place I know," I said. "You surely must have had a world of choices about a career and where you would live."

"I had plenty," she said matter-of-factly. "The thing is . . . my people come from here, Caro. I didn't know that; I had no idea where our family originated. If my parents did, they never said. I think, in their minds, they just sort of invented themselves and me. But when I started in cultural anthropology one of the first courses I had involved the Gullahs of the Southeastern Lowcountry. I felt an immediate . . . I don't know, a connection, I guess you'd say . . . and I started sort of surreptitiously researching names. I know my father's family's was McKay. Eventually I found what looked like a link to some Mackeys on Edisto. Peacock's was mentioned. All this time I was either pretending none of it existed or that I was merely doing fascinating research. I never told Chris . . . my husband . . . what I was studying. He loved telling his little liberal white law partners that his wife was a cultural anthropologist. I don't think he would have loved telling them she was a Gullah Negro whose ancestors came over in the hold of a slave ship from Angola. Come to that, I had a fine time pretending mine didn't, either. Christ, I don't know where I thought they came from. Certainly not on the *Mayflower*."

She looked over at me obliquely.

"You could special-order us, did you know that? I didn't. But you could. A lot of the Charleston and Edisto planters did. Our people were known to be good agriculturists, and we were so ancestor and family besotted that we weren't likely to run away and leave our families over here. Made to order to the rice and cotton fields, wouldn't you say? You could specify how many of us, and what sex and what age, even what height and weight. I wouldn't have made a good field worker, but I would have done well as a house nigger. Skinny; not a big eater. Presentable enough for the front rooms. Light enough so if the massa knocked me up the kid could probably pass . . ."

I made a soft sound of pain, and she shook her head impatiently.

"I'm not trying to lay a guilt trip on you," she said. "I know you're one of the good ones. It's just that . . . it's my first experience with blackness. I don't know how I feel about it yet. I don't know what it's going to mean to Mark. I don't know where the next step will take me, or what it will be. I don't know if I can make being black work; I was white too long. And I don't know if white will ever work for me again. I don't even know what's important in the long run, in the big picture. Except that I know that is, over there." She gestured back toward the island. "I know that somehow that's awfully important. I know that it . . . needs to stay whole, over there, whether or not I ever set foot there again."

"So, are you a double agent or what?" I grinned.

"Or what, I guess," she said peacefully. "I don't seem to be in any hurry to make lifetime decisions. I don't feel like I have to, right now. It's been a great month or so, just *being* . . . just teasing along on the moment."

"Ezra's good company," I said.

"Ezra's a pain in the ass." She smiled. "But he's sure a whole piece of cloth, isn't he? I never met anybody like him. He's more things in one skin than I thought was possible."

"Maybe that's what we're all meant to be," I said.

"Maybe. Who knows? I guess it will emerge. For now I'm going to just let it carry me. You know, Caro, I guess I was waiting to hear what's going to happen to Dayclear, waiting to see . . .

what Clay will do. If he goes ahead with it, I know now that I'll have to resign. If not . . . well, I'm not likely to get another job that lets me write my own ticket in my specialty and pays me like Clay does. It's the kind of job that makes a reputation early, and that means big bucks. I want Mark to have the kind of education I did. He's no more apt to want to live in Dayclear than I do, even if his ancestors' names are on those gravestones, but he needs to be able to walk back and forth between worlds as easily as he crosses a street in Manhattan. Or as easily as you go back to . . . wherever it is you go back to."

"I haven't been back to my hometown in twenty-five years," I said. "But I see your point. There's nothing stopping me if I wanted to. I always meant to; my daughter, Kylie, always wanted to go so she could hear the garbage trucks in the morning. To her, that was about as exotic as you can get."

She put her hand over mine briefly. It was cold and rough with the dried mud of her ancestors' resting place. I rather hoped some of it stayed under the perfect ovals of her nails.

"You've never mentioned her name," she said.

"It's hard to talk about her," I said. "I'm trying to learn to make her a normal part of my life now. I think maybe I've enshrined her too long."

"I cannot even imagine what would happen

to me without Mark," she said. "I cannot imagine who or what I would be. I don't see how you've gone on."

"Well, I have other people I love, other things," I said. "All of us do. It's hard to see that at first, but . . . we do."

And then I remembered that, so far as I knew, she did not, and muttered, "Sorry. I assume a lot."

"Oh, I have them, too," she said. "Even if most of them are dead. I just found them. It's a powerful feeling."

"Maybe not all of them are dead," I said, thinking of Ezra's black eyes on her.

"Maybe not," she said. "Maybe not."

We were silent again until I pulled up in front of her condo in the harbor village. Despite the balmy weather, it was still winter, and the darkness had swept in suddenly and completely from the west. There were a number of big white yachts in the harbor, their portholes radiant with the lights of cocktails and dinners being celebrated, and the flagstone walkway around the harbor was full of tanned, sun-bleached people strolling to the shops and restaurants, or from one boat to another. In the old live oaks the tiny white lights that always reminded me of Christmas twinkled in the skeins of silvery moss. Soft rock music drifted from somewhere. It was festive and rich and quite lovely, and about as real as cotton candy. I knew suddenly that if I ever saw this over on the island I would have to leave. That day. That moment.

We made a date for lunch the next week—I was not going to let this accessible new Sophia go—and I drove slowly back to the house. It was dark except for the light I had left in the kitchen. As I pulled into the driveway, I saw a man come out of the back door and down the steps. Before I could even feel uneasy, I saw that it was Hayes Howland and felt a sharp sting of resentment instead. I did not want Hayes going in and out of my house when I was not there. I supposed, with weary resentment, that I would have to start locking my doors after all. It was ironic to think that when I finally capitulated to that, it would be Hayes I was locking out, and not the occasional random robber or rapist.

I met him at the back steps.

"Are you stealing the silver?" I said, trying for lightness.

"Looking for Clay. I haven't been able to raise anybody on the phone all afternoon, and I got uneasy. I saw Charlie at lunch, and he said Clay was not in such hot shape. You weren't locked, so I went on in. He's asleep upstairs. I didn't want to wake him."

"Good of you," I said waspishly. "He's been sleeping a lot. Charlie says he needs it. He also says he'll be just fine once he gets enough rest, so

I'm letting him do it. I expect he'll be back at the office in a day or two. Can it wait, whatever you wanted with him?"

"Oh, yeah. I was just being a mother hen. But now that I'm here . . . Caro, have you had a chance to do what we agreed on? About Day-clear?"

I knew in that instant that that was why he had come. Not to check on Clay, but to see if I had been to Dayclear yet, to put the company's proposal to the village. I don't know why it made me so angry. From the beginning I had known that he was in a hurry for an answer.

"I've just come from there," I said, looking straight at him in the darkness. I could scarcely see his face, only the gleam of his pale blue eyes.

"I told them exactly what you told me. And essentially they told me it was up to me since I owned the island, and I told them that it wasn't going to happen. And it's not. I'm sorry, Hayes. I know that puts you all in a bind. But you redid the plans once. Surely there's an avenue you haven't explored yet. In any event, I cannot let it happen, and I won't."

He stood silently, looking at me, and then down at his feet.

"I'm sorry to hear that, Caro," he said. "Clay will be, too."

"I know. Let me tell him, Hayes. I want him to hear it from me."

He shrugged. I could just make out the gesture.

"Better do it soon," he said, and padded away over the carpet of wet live oak leaves to the Porsche that crouched in the dark like a big cat.

I watched him out of sight, and then walked around the house and through the front yard, over the dunes and down to the beach. I had not known I was going to do that, but this time there was no heaviness, no darkness, no prickle of panic. I merely felt still and empty and very tired. I slipped off my sneakers and padded across the silky, snake-cold sand to the firmer, icy salt-slicked sand at the fringe of the surf and sat down on the trunk of the fallen palm tree that had been Carter's fort and Kylie's balance bar.

There was no moon, but the stars were huge and cold and near, and the sea itself seemed to breathe off a kind of radiance, like smoke. It made a long, infinitely gentle susurration: Hushhhhh. Hushhhhh. There was almost no surf at all; what there was was white lace against the blackness of the beach. There was no other sound, and no one at all on the beach. I knew that if I looked behind me I would see the lights of all the other houses that fringed our stretch of shore, see their windows lit for dinner and the coming evening. But I did not look back. I looked far out into the whispering sea, and I looked up into the sky.

"I wonder what you would make of all this?"

I said to my daughter in the sky, or in the water, or wherever it was that held her. I felt her very near. "I wonder what you would do about the island if it were your decision to make."

But of course I knew the answer to that; she would make the decision that I had made. She was me and I was her. There had never been any question of that. It struck me then that it was time. It was, finally, time.

"I'm going to let you go," I said aloud. "I don't know how to do it, but I'm going to do it tonight. You need to be your own person now. If you were still with me, I'd be doing this about now . . . trying to learn to let you be yourself. So this is it, kid. You'll have to help me. I don't know what I need to do next."

I wriggled off the log and stretched out against it, leaning my head back, letting it take my weight. The damp cold of the sand seeped through the seat of my blue jeans, but it seemed a point of connection to the earth, not an uncomfortable intrusion. I closed my eyes and willed myself to think of nothing at all except her. I tried to empty my mind even of the image of her, and let just her essence, the warm, secret displacement of air and space that was Kylie in my soul, fill me.

It was a mystery, what happened then. I think everyone gets perhaps one to a lifetime. I know that I made it in my mind, but I know, too, that it was more than that, and I will always know that, no matter who tries to dissuade me. No one will, because I will never tell anyone. Not even Clay. This was my mystery, mine and Kylie's. I lay still on that empty beach with her filling me, and behind my eyes there began to appear golden prickles of light, like the ones that always come when you hold your eyes shut hard. And then one of the pinpricks began to grow larger and larger and brighter and brighter, so that it pressed hard against my lids, and I opened them to ease the pressure and the light drifted out of me and into the air, very slowly, and up into the sky. I watched it as it grew smaller and smaller, and finally I lost it among the winter stars.

I closed my eyes again and waited. And then I saw behind my eyelids that very slowly, infinitely slowly, it disengaged itself from the body of stars and grew larger and more golden, and began to drift down again, down and down until it hovered in front of my face and bumped at my cheeks and lips with a cool sort of frisson, like the feeling a lit sparkler makes against your skin. A kiss, a nibble. I opened my eyes and it came in. I closed them. I felt it linger there just behind my lids, warm and cool at the same time, and then it slid down and down and came to rest in my chest, in what felt to be the absolute center of me. And there it stayed, until I finally opened my eyes for good and all and said, "Yes. Okay. You're safe and so am I. Thank you, darling. Go to sleep now."

And I believe that she did. And I believe that she sleeps there now and always, and will never again have to answer some sad, silly, frantic summons from me or anyone else. Wherever else she is I do not know, but I believe that the very living core, the essential flame of her, is inside me. I believe that.

When I finally got up off the beach and went inside my house, it was to find my husband still asleep on my daybed, his face looking, finally, cool and smoothed and full again. I kissed him on the forehead, and he stirred and mumbled, and then fell back into his long sleep.

"I just wanted to tell you that I have her home, and I think you can go back to your own bed," I whispered.

In the morning when I woke, I found a note on my bedside table that said, "Feel terrific for some reason & have gone into the office. Call me later. Thanks for hanging in there."

I lay there looking at the new morning on the face of the sea and thinking that if I was lucky there was time for coffee before I called him and blew his world to bits.

12

But I did not do that, after all, because when I finally had had enough coffee to jump-start my courage and called him at his office, it was to learn, from a Shawna whose smirk was almost visible over the wire, that he was gone again.

"Just ran out the door," she said happily. "Got a call about an hour ago from Atlanta and he and Hayes were out of here like scalded tomcats. He said for me to tell you when you called, and that he'd be away three or four days. The bigwigs are flying them to Texas to see some kind of Wild West theme park thing out there. Reckon we're all going to be wearing ten-gallon hats. Oh, and he said to tell you he was just fine, felt great, and to call Charlie and tell him. That's his doctor, isn't it? I could do that for you. I wouldn't mind talking to that doctor myself. I heard about Puerto Rico.

Somebody needs to tell him just what's going on, and I know Clay isn't going to do it. . . ."

"Thank you so much, Shawna," I said through clenched teeth. It dawned on me that my head was pounding badly and my nose was stuffed up. Sinus infections are spring's first gift to me, and if I was in for one, the last thing I needed was to listen to Shawna chirp her love and ownership of my husband to me at ten o'clock in the morning.

"I'll call Charlie myself," I said. "We went over last week and saw him; he knows all he needs to know about Clay's condition. He's been our doctor for a long time. He was in our wedding. He would want to talk to Clay or me."

I heard her affronted little snort and realized that I had been cruel, and did not care. Shawna set herself up for rebuffs like a tenpin, over and over again. I wondered if she thought that if I were out of the picture Clay would sweep her into his arms? Look at her one afternoon, walk slowly to her, pull the pins out of her hair, and remove her glasses and whisper, "My God. I never realized."

Fat chance.

The sinus infection settled in by noon. I knew that I had done it to myself, sitting in the damp wind on the wet beach last night, and did not care at all. The infections make me sick and so dizzy that it is hard to walk, and the pressure in my

eyes and cheeks feels like intense sleepiness. My
face swells and my eyes close, and I am good for
nothing but to burrow into bed and sleep. I know
that they last approximately three full days and
nights; if I take antibiotics, perhaps two and a
half. When the fourth day dawns I am invariably
as clear-headed and full of energy as I ever was,
and so I have learned to give in to them, cancel
whatever I can, and crawl into bed with hot tea
and magazines.

And that is what I did. Estelle knows the drill
now; she does not hover, but she keeps a carafe of
hot tea beside my bed, and leaves soup and sandwiches for me, and goes on about her business. If
Clay is at home he checks on me occasionally, but
I really do prefer to be left alone, and it pleases
me when one of the attacks happens to fall during one of his business trips. I don't feel so much
that I am wasting time.

I will wonder the rest of my life what would
have happened if I had not been at home in bed
for the next three days. Or what would not have.

On the morning of the fourth day I awoke
and the room did not spin and my eyes did not
feel poached and my face was not swollen to the
size of a cantaloupe, and I was ravenous. I showered and washed my hair and pulled on jeans and
a T-shirt—for outside it was still warm and sweet
with sun—and went downstairs. Estelle, smiling,
made me sausage and cheese grits, and gave me a

list of the calls that had come in while I was out of pocket. None were from Clay. One was from Shawna: Clay and Hayes were going on west with the SouthWard people, to see a gold rush theme park in northern California. Perhaps they would be in by Thursday. He would let Shawna know where he could be reached. They were on the move almost constantly; I probably couldn't reach him.

"I have my finger on him for you though, Caro," Shawna chirped. I made a rude noise at the answering machine and finished my coffee and thought about the soft golden week spinning out ahead of me. The light on the marshes would be wonderful: ineffable and radiant. I jumped up and rooted out my paints and camera and threw some clothes into my duffel and fairly flew to the island.

I was set up on the end of the dock, drowning in the gilt glitter off the water and the marshes, breathing in the clean old salt breath of the island, feeling the sun pouring like pale new clover honey over my arms and face, when I heard the shouts from the house. I knew without turning around that it was Luis Cassells, and that something was badly wrong.

By the time I had pounded halfway down the dock, he came around the corner of the house, stumbling and running, and in his arms he carried Lita. Her face was buried in his neck and she did not move. My heart swooped into my stomach and back up, and I stumbled and nearly fell. "Dear Lord, goddamn it, you take care of this little girl," I whispered as I ran.

I met him at the steps up to the dock. He thrust her into my arms and I took her automatically and held her close. She scrubbed her face into my shoulder. I watched him as he stood there, head hanging, chest heaving for breath enough to speak. While I stood I was going over the sick-child checklist in my mind, as I had done a thousand times; I did it automatically. Breathing shallow but clear, skin cool, grip strong. She was obviously conscious and I had seen no blood. Her arms were so tight around me that I could hardly get my own breath. I waited.

He lifted his head and looked at me, and his face was white under the tan and mottled red over his cheeks. His eyes were opaque black and blazing with something: fear and anguish, I thought, and fury.

"Take her to Auntie, over in Dayclear," he rasped. "Tell her to keep her warm. Then get Janie to ring the bell; Ezra and Esau are fishing down at the bridge. When they come, tell Ezra to bring a truck and meet me here, and to bring whoever else is around who can lift. And then go back and stay with Lita . . ."

"What is it, Luis?"

"It's the horses," he said sickly. "The mare

and the colt. We found them about a half-mile down the creek. We were bringing apples for them. They've been poisoned, and I think it was the apples; there are half-digested apples all over the place. Tell Ezra that, too. I'm going to wait here for them. I'll need something to carry some of the apples in, and a tarp or something to cover the pile under the house. Don't go near those apples, and don't let anybody from Dayclear but Ezra and the men come back here. Especially no children."

"I'll call a vet, and the rangers," I said. Lord God, please. Not Nissy and the baby. I was afraid to ask.

"*Not the rangers!* I mean that, Caro. Just get Ezra and tell him what I said. We'll take the colt to the vet in the truck, it's faster."

"Nissy . . ." I whispered in dread.

"We can't help her, Caro. But the colt is still alive, I think. It would be good if somebody could walk the creek and see if any of the other horses are . . . sick. There's no way to know how many of the apples were eaten. . . ."

"Who could do such a thing?" I said through stiff white lips; I had felt them blanch.

"Who, indeed?" he spat. "But I'll tell you who thinks she did. Lita does. She thinks she did it with her apples. She hasn't said one word since. I'm so afraid for her. My God . . . go on now. Get her out of here. Auntie has some kind of tea that she uses for sleep; tell her to give Lita some of that. . . ."

"Luis . . ."

"GO, CARO!"

I helped him ease the limp child into the Cherokee and ran up for my keys and ran back down. Clashing the Jeep into gear, I said to him, "Did she see?"

"She found them," he said, and closed his eyes. Then he gave the car fender a smack and said, *"Vamanos,"* and turned and went under my house to find the tarp that stayed there, over the whaler. I screeched out of the yard and headed as fast as I dared for Dayclear and Ezra's Auntie Tuesday. Lita lay with her head in my lap, eyes closed, perfectly still. Her face was as white and empty as that of a dead child. There were no tear tracks on her bleached cheeks.

When I reached the store I held the horn down with the flat of my hand. Janie came out, muttering darkly, saw me and the child in my lap, and put both hands to her mouth.

"Ring the bell," I called, and she turned and ran. In a second I heard it speak with its great dark voice, like eternity. The sound seemed to roll on forever.

"Send Ezra and Esau down to Auntie's," I said. "Luis needs them over at my place. Oh, God, I never thought . . . Is Auntie at home, do you know?"

"She to home," Janie said. "I seen her this morning, and she say comp'ny comin' and she got to brew some tea. I give her some lemons an' sugar for it. . . . What the matter with the baby, Caro?"

"Somebody poisoned the horses," I quavered. I was finding it hard to speak past the dread that lay cold and knotted in my throat. Under it was a red anger of a magnitude I had never known. But I knew that I could not let it out yet.

"This baby didn't get none of it, did she?" Janie cried.

"No. But she found the horses. The mother is dead. Luis needs Ezra and Esau to bring a truck; he wants to take the colt to the vet in it. And he needs some people to walk the creek and see if any other horses got into the apples."

"I tell 'em when they come. An' I go walk that creek myself," she said. "You get that baby on down to Auntie. I reckon she know what to do; she knowed you was coming, didn't she? Go on now . . ."

"Thank you, Janie," I said, and screeched off down the lane. Far off down the hidden creek I thought I heard the faint, stuttering drone of a faulty outboard engine.

Auntie Tuesday stood in her doorway. She looked from me to the child with her milky old eyes and shook her head.

"*MMMMM, MMMMM,*" she said sadly. "Badness walkin' right up here in the world today, sho is. Bring that baby on in here. I 'spec we can find somethin' make her feel better."

I lifted Lita and brought her up the steps. She still did not remove her face from my shoulder, and she still did not speak. Occasionally she shuddered, a deep, racking tremor that ran all through her, but that was all. I started to put her down on the little cot in the corner, where Auntie slept, but she shook her head at me.

"Set down in that rockin' chair and rock her," she said. "I done built up the fire. You jus' get settled comfortable and rock her now. Keep on a'rockin' her. I got somethin' on the stove do her some good. . . ."

"She's not sick or hurt," I said over Lita's head. "She saw something terrible and she thinks it's her fault. She's stopped talking again. But it's not physical. . . ."

"I knowed it wasn't her body," Auntie said. "Look like it worse when it git the soul. Well, we do what we can. We do what we can. The Lord give us things from the earth help the soul as well as the body, and He tell those of us what'll listen how to use 'em. It the tackies, ain't it?"

"How did you know?" I could only whisper it.

"Seen 'em last night. Seen 'em in the fire. Knew somethin' dark was after them. If it's a happy thing coming I sees it in water. Here, see will she take this."

She brought a chipped cup of something steaming hot from the old stove in the corner of the dark little room. I took it, not questioning for an instant the wisdom of giving a child the arcane brew of whatever this strange old woman found in the woods. I held the cup to Lita's lips.

"Take a sip for me, baby," I said.

But she turned her head away.

"Give her to me," Auntie said. "I been gittin' that tea down chirrun's craws for lots of years now."

She indicated that I should get up and let her sit down in the rocker and put the child in her lap.

"Auntie, she's too heavy for you," I said. "I'm afraid she'll break one of your little old bones."

"Ain't no child gon' hurt me," she said, and I got up with Lita, and she settled herself stiffly into the rocker and held out her arms, and I put the child into them. Lita's face found the thin old shoulder and burrowed there. Her legs dangled almost to the floor, but Auntie held her firmly. She put her face down to the top of Lita's head and whispered something into her hair, and began to rock. Presently I heard her begin to sing softly, in a thin reedy old monotone:

"Fix me, Jesus, fix me right,
Fix me so I can stand.

Fix my feet on a solid rock,
Fix me so I can stand.
My tongue tired and I can't speak plain,
Fix me so I can stand,
Fix my feet on a solid rock,
Fix me so I can stand . . ."

She sang it over and over, more a faraway, atonal chant than a song, and presently the dim little room seemed to shimmer with it, and the flickering light from the lit stove rose up to meet it, and song and fire and woman and child seemed to sway in the room until my eyes grew heavy and I nodded. Whenever I forced them open I saw that she still sat, cradling the child, rocking, rocking. The last time I looked I saw Lita lift her head from Auntie's shoulder and sigh deeply, and relax against her into sleep.

"Thank you," I whispered, sliding into sleep myself, but I could not have said who it was I thanked.

When I woke it was after noon; I could tell from the square of pale sunlight that was creeping across the cabin's linoleum floor, from the open doorway. The sweet smell of high sun on pine and salt from the estuary blew into the room. Another smell, rich and green and savory, came from a big black iron kettle on the stove. Janie Biggins was stirring it and smiling over at me. Her gold tooth flashed in the sunlight from the doorway.

"That smells good," I said. "What are you doing here, Janie?"

And then I remembered, and whipped my head around toward the rocker. It was empty. I made an inadvertent sound of fear.

"She all right," Janie said. "She gon' be fine. She sleepin' hard. Auntie and I put her to bed in the spare room. She sleep a long time, I 'spec. Need to. Auntie say when she wake up maybe she talk some."

"Oh, God, I hope so. She . . . There was a long time when she didn't talk at all, before she came here. Luis didn't know if she ever would again. I was so afraid that she'd lost it again. . . ."

"Auntie sing her a healin' song. It a good one. I've seed it bring the tongue back to folks what had been struck and ain't talk for months. 'Sides, Auntie seen her talkin' in the well water. She gon' be all right. Her mama gon' take care of her."

"Her mama's dead, Janie. She's only got her grandfather. . . ."

"Auntie seed her mama in the water, too," she said, and I could tell that for her, that ended the matter. I did not pursue it.

I got up and straightened my rumpled clothes and went into the tiny, shedlike room off the cabin's main one. A big, beautiful old rice bed stood against the far wall, the room's only furniture, looking like a great mahogany yacht in a tiny harbor. I wondered where Auntie might have come by it; it would have been at home on Legare Street. It gleamed with care and polish. Lita lay curled in the middle of it, covered with an exquisite ivory quilt so old that it was yellowed and brittle. Her fist was doubled under her chin, and her face was smooth and calm and flushed with sleep. I listened; her breath came slow and deep and even. For now, she seemed all right. For now . . .

"Where's Auntie?" I said.

"She down to the cemetery. She grow some things down there that help this child. Plant 'em there so the ancestors bless 'em. We gon' put 'em in this here soup when she git back, and they perk her up right good. You, too. You looks like the hind axle of hard times."

"I feel like it. It was so awful about the ponies. Has anybody heard from Luis and Ezra yet? I hate to think of that poor old mare just lying there in the sun. . . ."

My eyes filled up and I fell silent. It seemed too cruel for the mind to encompass.

"She ain't lie there," Janie said. "Esau and two, three of the others took Esau's tractor and some log chains and move her to the woods over behind the creek, back of our cemetery. There a big hole there, go way down in the ground. Been there a long time; don't nobody know who dug it. Our good old animals goes there. It deep and cool and real quiet. Esau drops pine branches over them."

I put my face into my hands.

Sleep well, dear old Nissy, I said in my mind. Down there in the deep, cool, quiet ground with all the other good animals, under your green blanket.

"Here, you take some of this now," Janie said, handing me a bowl of the soup. I took it and sipped; it was wonderful, silky and thin and tasting of green things and sea salt.

"What is it? You could make a fortune in any restaurant in Charleston with this," I said.

"Fiddlehead soup. Found the first fiddleheads yestiddy, out in the woods. They real early this year. Auntie say they has power, but I just thinks they taste good."

They did. Gradually the cold, hard knot of grief and the red lick of submerged anger deep inside me loosened and cooled. I went and stood on the doorstep of the cabin, looking off across the bare garden plots to the edge of the marsh and the creek. The sky was a tender, washed blue and in it specks wheeled and dove. Ospreys. I wondered if they were nesting already in the dead cypresses along the distant river. If so, we could kiss this terrible winter good-bye. The ospreys never miscalculated.

Behind me I heard a thin little voice: "Caro? Caro . . ."

I turned and ran for the bedroom. Janie stood in the doorway, smiling.

"Somebody wake an' talkin'," she said.

I sat down on the bed and smiled at Lita. She was half sitting, tangled in the quilt and frowning with sleep and confusion. Her wiry curls spilled over her forehead and cheeks, and she had the imprint of a quilted square on one of them. Her skin was lightly pearled with perspiration. She reached her arms up for me even before her eyes were fully opened, and I gathered her against me.

"You had a nice long nap, didn't you?" I said into her hair. It did not feel at all like Kylie's, or I don't think I could have done it.

"Are you hungry?"

"I don't know. Where's Abuelo? Caro, I had the most awful dream. . . ."

I sat her up and brushed the hair off her face and looked into it.

"I'm afraid it wasn't a dream, sweetie pie," I said. "You found the horses, and they were real sick, and it made you very sad. Your grandfather and Ezra have gone to take Yambi to the doctor so he can be well again. They'll be back before long, and they can tell you about it."

Please let it be so, I said to the distant God who took children and horses.

"They didn't take Nissy with them, did they?" she said in a tiny voice. I saw that she was screwing her face up with the effort not to cry.

"No, baby. They didn't. Nissy was too sick, and she died. We didn't see any of the other horses sick, though, so maybe they didn't eat the apples. . . ."

Her breath drew in, and I winced.

"You need to know that it was not your apples that made them sick, Lita," I said. "Somebody came and put something bad in the apples after you left them there. We know you would never hurt the horses. They know that, too. It was some bad people, and we'll find out who it was, don't you worry about that."

She was silent for a while, breathing deeply. Then she looked up at me. Her eyes were entirely ringed with white, remembering.

"Her teeth were sticking out all yellow," she said. "And there was flies in her eyes. I knew she was dead then. There was flies in my mama's eyes, too."

I pulled her back hard against me, my own eyes shut tight against the pain. I would have given anything on earth if I could have scrubbed the memories out of her head.

"You're a brave girl," I said. "It was a bad thing to see, but she isn't suffering now. Esau took her and put her with all the other good animals from Dayclear who have . . . died. They're all together."

She sighed deeply and relaxed against me a little.

"Yambi stayed with her," she murmured against my shoulder. "That was the right thing to do, wasn't it? He wouldn't leave his mama."

"That was just the right thing to do," I said, seeing in my mind the image of a small child huddled in a wrecked mountain hut, her shivering flesh pressed to the cold flesh of her mother. I did not think I was going to be able to bear this.

Suddenly she gave a great sob, and then pressed her fists against her mouth. Her whole body shook with the effort not to cry.

"It's all right," I said, beginning to rock her. "It's good to cry. It's the right thing to do. It's a way of honoring Nissy. She would be pleased with your tears."

And then they came, a great, wild storm of them, so hard and primitive and somehow ancient that I was, for a little while, frightened for her. She wept and howled, and sometimes lapsed into a phrase or two of anguished Spanish, and then howled again. I could almost hear this sound rolling out over a jungle somewhere, as old as time itself and as implacable. These were not a child's tears.

Presently she began to subside into simple sobs and, after a long while, sniffles. When she finally pulled herself away from me and looked up, her eyes were swollen nearly shut, and her face was congested with red anguish. But her breathing was slow again, and deep.

"I think I'm hungry," she said.

Auntie was back by now, and she brought in a bowl of the soup, presumably bearing its cargo of herbs, and a piece of hot cornbread. She sat down on the bed beside Lita and began to feed the soup to her by the spoonful, crooning wordlessly. I stood and stretched and looked down. The front of my shirt was soaking wet with Lita's tears.

"You go in that drawer in the front room an' git one of them ol' undershirts," she said. "Th'ow that shirt of your'n in the wash pot. Don't do to sit around in it. That's poison there."

I looked at her.

"It's what come out of her," she said, smiling. "The song and the tea drawed it. Look like it got most of it, too, but you don't want it soakin' into you. I bile it with lye soap when I does my wash and Ezra bring it to you."

"Oh, Auntie, I don't care about the shirt," I said. "I'm just so glad she's better, and so grateful to you. . . . What was in that tea? What was in the soup?"

"This 'n' that. Little feverfew, some gold-enseal, some seamuckle, jimsey, little life everlasting. You couldn't make it, chile. It's all in the words you says over it. I make some up before you go and you can give it to her if she git bad again, though."

"I don't think she'll be with me," I said. "I think she'll be staying with her grandfather, unless he's really late getting back. I'll be glad to stay with her until he comes, though."

"I give you some anyway," she said.

Lita fell asleep again, and we three women sat in chairs that Janie dragged out into the dooryard, talking idly of nothing much, taking the sun. It was slanting low when the noise of an old truck came down the road, followed by the angry burr of Ezra's Harley.

I met them up at the store. Luis's face was drawn and grim.

"Lita?" he said.

"Sleeping. She's been awake, and talked, and cried most of it out, I think. And she ate a good lunch. I doubt that she'll forget it, Luis, but I think she'll heal from it. Auntie . . . Auntie has been beyond wonderful."

"I don't think you've been so bad yourself, Caro," he said, relief making the tight muscles around his mouth sag into a tired smile. "You know, it was you she cried out for before she stopped talking."

"Oh, Luis . . ." I said softly.

I can't take the weight of this, I thought.

"It's okay," he said, understanding. "It's more than enough that you were here today."

I found some beer in the cooler and opened it for him and Ezra and Esau, who had come wearily into the store behind him. They all took deep swallows, but no one spoke.

Finally I said, "The colt?"

"The colt is alive," Ezra said, and his voice was hard and remote. I had not heard this voice before. His eyes were distant, too. I could not imagine what they saw.

"The vet thinks he'll make it. He didn't eat many of the apples, apparently."

"He likes sweet potatoes better," I said, and felt the tears sting again.

"Well, that saved him then, because those apples were full of it, whatever it is," Ezra said. "The vet isn't sure, but he's got a friend with his own lab who's running tox tests right now. He thinks probably botulism toxin. Nothing else is really powerful enough to down a grown horse so fast. He thinks that they ate the apples last night early. It would have been put in by injection. He found the holes in some of the apples."

"My God, you don't think it was a doctor!" I cried. Somehow the thought was horrifying beyond words.

"No, no. You can get the stuff; plastic surgeons use it, and other kinds of doctors, too. It's around. There's probably a real good black market for it, if you know where to go. And you can get hypodermics at any drugstore. I don't think whoever did it got the stuff himself, but I think somebody he knew did. We'll know more when the test comes in late tonight. If it's botulism toxin,

I think I know where to start looking for the source."

"Where?"

"Better you just don't ask," he said. "I've got some friends in not very high places."

We were quiet again for a bit.

"Do you think any of the rest of the herd got into the apples?" I asked.

"Doesn't look like it right now," Luis said. "Simon Miller and his boys from Greenville rode and walked every inch of the creek and the bottoms where they usually are. They didn't see anything. And there were an awful lot of apples left. It looked to me like the pile we took day before yesterday was mostly still there. They're in a croker sack in the back of the truck. I'm going to drop them in the incinerator at the dump on Edisto when I go tonight."

"When you go?"

"Walk me down to Auntie's," he said. "I need to see Lita. We'll talk on the way."

We walked side by side down the rutted sandy road. The swift darkness was rolling in from the Inland Waterway, and the shadows of the Spanish moss laid long fingers across the road. The air was cooling rapidly. Luis walked with his hands in his pockets, his stride heavy and slow. I cradled my elbows in my hands against the chill. The old white Fruit of the Loom men's undershirt was decent and clean, but it was worn thin.

"I'm taking her over to Edisto," he said finally, not looking at me. "Ezra has a friend over there who's not using his trailer. He left the key with Ezra. I can't stay here with her, Caro. Everywhere she looked she'd remember . . . And who knows what's going to come next? I can't take the chance. I'm quitting your husband's company, too, as soon as I can give notice in the morning. I'm not going to make myself a sitting target; she's the one who's vulnerable."

I stopped dead in my tracks, looking at him.

"Dear God, surely you don't think that Clay . . ."

"Of course not. But I think that somebody acting in his name, if not with his knowledge or permission, stuck those needles in those apples. We'll probably never find out who, but I don't really care. I can't afford to take chances with her. You can see that, can't you?"

"But . . . we . . . you were winning! I've already told you I'm not going to turn over this land; there's no more fight to fight. . . ."

He looked at me in disbelief.

"Winning what? The right to eat apples with botulism toxin in them? If that's a victory, I can't afford it, Caro."

I could not argue with that. Desolation settled over me. The night turned vast and cold. There were stars, the same ones I had seen over Kylie's ocean four nights before, but I could not see their light now. It did not seem to reach the earth.

"I'll miss both of you," I said as matter-of-factly as I could. My voice shook.

He took a great breath as if to speak in return, but then did not. Presently he said, "You could come by and see us sometime on your way to Charleston. It's not far off the highway. Lita would love that. I'll be around; I'm not going to look for anything for a while, till I know she's going to be all right. Maybe when we know about the colt. After that I'll find something and get her into preschool. Ezra knows a woman with a good little one near the trailer park."

"Well, of course," I said, thinking of it: this great, exuberant force of a man, with his wild darkness and his big shoulders, pent up in a double-wide in a trailer park. The living flame that was Lita battering at those enclosing walls . . .

I knew that I would not visit him on Edisto.

"So when will you go?"

"In the morning, I think. Or later tomorrow. If the colt comes along like the vet thinks he will, I'd like to take her by to see for herself. I think Esau and Janie will take him when he's well enough to leave; he'll be used to people then, and the vet doesn't think the herd will take him in after he's been away so long. They'll smell us on him. The Bigginses have a pen behind the store. I can bring Lita over in the summer and she can learn to ride him. You could come, too. . . ."

The plans sounded positive, full of hope, but his voice was merely defeated.

"Luis . . ." I began, unsure what I would say but willing almost to say anything that would bring life back into that voice.

"Don't, Caro," he said, his head down so that I could not see his face. "You can't straddle two camps, and it's not possible for you to choose one. You've lost too much already. I would not permit it if you could."

I was silent. What were we speaking of, or rather, not speaking of, here?

"Abuelo! Grandpapa!" a small voice shrieked, a voice with relief and joy behind it, and we looked up to see Lita tearing out of the cabin door toward us, her arms outstretched, her face wreathed in smiles. He opened his arms and took two great strides forward, and she ran into them and was enclosed.

After that I painted. I painted for almost two straight days and nights, faster and more intensely than I have ever painted before, virtually scouring color onto the paper and then, when it tore, abandoning my watercolors and pulling out my old oils and the moldy canvases I found stacked in the utility closet and slashing at them with palette knife and stiff drypoint brushes. I put on my grandfather's old tapes of Beethoven and Mahler, great, crashing, apocalyptic music, and I built up the fire, and when I got so tired and hungry that I dropped the knife, I opened cans of Vienna sausage and tuna fish and ate them with soda crackers and rat cheese and washed them down with Diet Cokes and fell asleep on the sofa before the fire, and dreamed more paintings.

It was almost like automatic writing, I thought, watching as if from a distance the work unrolling from my fingers onto the canvases. It was not that I was unaware of what I did; indeed, I felt an almost preternatural control, an awesome kind of focus, that I have never felt before. It was simply that I did not quite know where my subject matter was coming from. I did not go out into the marshes and sketch or photograph and return to work, as was my habit. I did not leave the living room of the house. What I painted was the island: the marshes and the river and the creeks and the ham-mocks, and the secret groves of live oaks and the shrouding moss, but it was not an island I knew. It seemed to be an island out of another time, seen through other eyes. I painted stormy skies and nets flying like clouds, and dark people in fierce colors with their heads thrown back and their arms outstretched, shouts and songs stretching the cords of their shining throats. I painted fires in black woods and not quite human creatures out of an African night a millennium before. I painted baptisms in blood-dark rivers and burials in firelit woods. I painted wild horses, running, running. Running free.

When I finished painting, as suddenly as I had begun, morning was well along on the third day after Luis and Lita found the horses, and I was as cool and dry and depleted as if I had given birth. And perhaps I had.

I took a shower and cooked myself a real breakfast and took the paintings out onto the deck and propped them in the white sunlight and studied them. They were crude and hastily done and primitive past anything I had never even seen in my mind, and they had a power that almost frightened me. I could not even imagine where they had come from. Well, that was not entirely true; I knew or could sense that they sprang from the bottomless well of red anger I had discovered at the poisoning of the horses, and the fear I had felt for Lita and the colt and the island . . . and for Clay. But the images themselves . . . it was as if they had passed through me from somewhere else, not had their genesis in my mind. I poked around inside myself, prodding carefully, to see if that all-generating rage still lived there. I felt none at all. Just the emptiness.

As if they had been waiting until I finished my work, Ezra and Lottie Funderburke drove up in Lottie's little Subaru truck. I greeted them calmly, almost peacefully. I had not known that they knew each other, but it did not surprise me. Two such forces of nature on a small island: of course they would meet. Incuriously, I looked at each to see if the nature of the relationship was apparent, but it was not. They could be lovers or mortal enemies during a truce. The only thing I thought that they could not be was casual acquaintances.

"Coffee, for God's sake," Lottie said, stumping up onto the deck, and then, "Jesus, God, Caro! Are these yours?"

"I think so. Nobody else here but us chickens," I said. "You want coffee, too, Ezra?"

"Please. Whhhoooee, look at that stuff! You been hag-rode in the night, Caro?"

"I honestly don't know," I said, and padded inside, barefoot, to put on the coffee.

When I came back out with the coffee tray and some stale doughnuts, Lottie was sitting on the deck floor with her back against the railing studying the paintings. Ezra stood looking out at the morning dance of the light on the creek.

"Whatever got ahold of you, you treat it good, you hear?" Lottie said. "This stuff is dynamite. I don't know if you'll do much with them around Charleston or in the village center. Likely scare the bejesus out of the culturines and the retired admirals. I know some odd little galleries around that would love to hang them, though. I'll put some up in the studio, too. The kind of people who'll buy them stop by my place pretty often. You think you've got any more of that in you, or did you paint it all out?"

"I just can't tell yet," I said. "It's like somebody else that I don't know did it. I'm not going to show it or sell it, though. Not now. Maybe when I can tell whether or not it's a real direction, or just a twitch . . ."

"More an explosion, I'd say," Ezra said, grinning. "You get any madder than that and you gon' blow a hole in that canvas."

"I don't feel mad now," I said. "I know I was the other day, but I can't seem to find it again."

"I don't wonder," he said. "It's all in there."

He gestured at the paintings.

"So, what about the colt?" I said. "What about Lita . . . and Luis? Have you gotten the toxicology reports yet?"

"The colt is up and running around and eating," he said. "I'm going to take him over to Janie and Esau's in the morning. He's already let the vet slip a snaffle on him. Lita is talking a blue streak and pestering Luis to bring her back over here. He doesn't feel like he can do that right now. He's got her in preschool half a day. The other half he stays with her. He's looking for somebody over there to stay with her after school; he's got to get some work pretty soon. Meanwhile, mornings, he's doing some legwork for me around the Low-country. The vet was right; it was botulism toxin. I know a guy who knows a guy knows a guy who might be able to find out where it was bought. We do that, we know who bought it. Luis is visiting old . . . contacts of mine. Be a good thing to know, that."

"Is it . . . Could he be in any kind of danger?"

"Not much, I don't think. Not till he gets closer to home base on it, anyway. Luis knows how to take care of himself. He's in less danger than he would be if he stayed on this island. I agree with him about that."

"Have you been to the police?" I said. "Surely if illegal poison was used . . ."

"No. Somehow I can't imagine the authorities getting real upset over a dead marsh tacky. The rest is speculation. I think it's island business. I think the island ought to see about it."

"I just can't believe this," I said. "Who on this island would hurt Luis? Who would hurt that child? I know you think somebody in Clay's organization is behind this, but I think you're just plain wrong. That's . . . that's James Bond stuff. I don't know anybody in the company who's even capable of thinking like that."

"Don't you?"

I dropped my eyes.

"No. I don't."

But I did. I don't know how I knew, but I did know.

"Well, listen, Caro, I hope you can scrape some of that mad back up, because I think you might need it," Lottie said. "I have a message for you from that nitwit in your husband's office, Shiny, or whatever her name is. She called me saying she couldn't raise you either at the house or over here. Your phone's off the hook. Said to tell you Clay was coming in this morning; he's probably at the office now. I assume you're going to want to share the little tidbit about the horses with him, aren't you?"

"Maybe he knows," I said. I did not want to have to tell Clay about the horses. I did not want, now, to have the conversation that we should have had almost a week ago. I just wanted to go to sleep, and then to get up and paint some more.

"I doubt it," Lottie said. "Old motormouth would have blabbed it if he did. She practically told me what color his jockstrap was before I hung up on her."

"I'll go over there after lunch," I said. "I really need to get some sleep now. I think I've painted through two nights."

Ezra looked at me.

"I think you ought to go now, Caro," he said.

I looked back at him. Somehow I did not want to ask him why.

They finished their coffee and left. Just before he got into the passenger side of Lottie's truck, Ezra turned and looked up at me.

"The paintings are terrific, Caro," he said.

"You really got under our black hides. I didn't think you had it in you."

I didn't, either, I said to myself, watching the truck lurch down the rutted road under the live oaks. And then I went to dress and go back to Peacock's Island and speak to my husband of things that would, I thought, wound us forever.

The anger came back when I crossed the bridge onto Peacock's Island. It sprang up like a living flame when I saw the first Mercedes station wagon leaving the nursery, laden with mature bedding plants that would have cost a family in Dayclear a month's food money. It licked higher at the sight of two groups of square, tanned women in little golf skirts and T-shirts and sun visors, piloting their private golf carts across the road from the harborside villas to the golf club. It spurted into my nose and throat like lava as I threaded my way around the lushly planted traffic circle that led into the main street of the tiny village center and saw the green-uniformed Peacock's Island ground crew tearing out great clumps of blooming pansies and setting in their places flat after flat of rioting impatiens and mature ferns. Instant tropical paradise; why had I always thought it beautiful? My hot eyes wanted the tangled, littered coolness of the dank marshes and the forest; wanted, instead of this studied, expensive order, wildness and the vast amplitude of water and sky. By the time I pulled into the parking lot at the company's headquarters, I was shimmering all over with rage.

"Well, goodness, Caro, where you been? We been lookin' all over the place for you. Your wandering boy is back and rarin' to see you, and here we thought you'd run off with the hired help or something. . . ."

Shawna was often familiar with me, when she thought she could get away with it, but she would not have dared go so far if she had not had an audience. It seemed to me that three-fourths of Clay's female office staff lingered in the front office where her desk sat, finding this and that to do while they waited for me to come. Lottie was wrong, I knew; the office staff knew about the horses even if Clay did not. They must have known I would be furious.

"Shawna," I said, smiling savagely at her, "eat a shit sandwich."

I did not hear the gasps and the murmurs begin until I had reached Clay's door, opened it, and gone in.

". . . completely lost her mind," I heard Shawna squawk as I slammed the door shut behind me.

Clay was standing at the window wall that overlooked the little enclosed courtyard behind his office. It had been planned to look like an old Charleston garden, sheltered with tabby and old brick walls and lushly planted with vines and shrubs and brilliant oleanders and cape jessamine and camellias. The camellias were out now, hanging from the great bushes like ripe, perfect fruit. The twisted trunk of the massive live oak that grew in the center of the garden was brilliant green with resurrection ferns. The little wrought-iron table against the back wall held the remains of a coffee and pastry breakfast for three or four people. I did not wonder who had shared it with Clay. I did not care. I knew before he turned to face me that I was going to say something that would change us both, would divide time. I could scarcely breathe around the anger.

He swung around. He needed a shave and looked a little faded, as he always did when he was very tired, but there was nothing of the past holiday's joy or the pain of Puerto Rico on it. Just the habitual remoteness that the office called out in him, and a cool impatience. I knew that he hated slammed doors. I could not imagine that anyone had ever slammed this one before. He wore one of his immaculate gray tropical worsted suits and a fresh shirt. On the lapel of his coat was a gold pin shaped like a ten-gallon hat. It said, REMEMBER THE ALAMO.

I had never seen even a Rotary button on Clay's person before. I stared. For some reason this object made me want to rip it off his coat, rip the coat off him, shake him, scream.

He looked down at the button and then back at me and made a small, fastidious face.

"The SouthWard brass came back with us," he said. "They've gone over to the island with Hayes. I guess I can take this thing off now. How are you, Caro?"

He did not call me "baby," as he sometimes did. The smell of anger must be coming off me like smoke.

"I am not really very good right now, Clay," I said, and was appalled to hear that my voice shook so that I could hardly get my words out. Where was all this rage coming from? This was Clay. . . . "While you were gone somebody poisoned the horses. The ones on the island. The mare—you know, Nissy, Kylie's mare—died. Her colt just barely lived. We don't know about the rest of the herd. It was botulism toxin. The vet is sure of that. Ezra thinks he's going to be able to find out who bought the stuff, or stole it. Then we'll know who . . . authorized it. You may know already, of course."

He sat down slowly in his chair and put his hands flat on his desk, and leaned forward, staring at me. The color went out of his face.

"What are you saying?"

I just looked at him.

"Do you mean to tell me that you think that I . . . that I . . . authorized somebody to kill those horses? Is that what you think? Have you lost your mind? I would never on this earth . . . I didn't know. God, Caro. *God . . .*"

He looked sick. It did not dampen the fire of my fury at all. The horrified face over that awful, silly Alamo pin made me angrier than I have ever been in my life. What right had he to mourn that old horse, if indeed that was what he was feeling, when what he planned for its island was so much worse than anything I could even imagine. . . .

"Don't be a fool, Clay. Of course I know that you did not authorize it. I don't think you had to authorize it. Do you remember, when we saw *Becket*, in Charleston? And Henry the Second said, 'Will no one rid me of this meddlesome priest?' and looked around at all his . . . his henchmen? He didn't say, 'Somebody go kill Thomas Becket'; he didn't have to. They all knew what he meant. And pretty soon a couple of them got up and kind of slid out of the room and you knew . . . Who said it here, Clay? Somebody did. Somebody poisoned those horses in the name of this company. If you didn't know about it, you ought to be able to figure out who did. I could give you a pretty good guess right now. He's back over there right now with that bunch of snake-oil salesmen you plan to sell my island to. Okay, I came to tell you what I decided about that. Listen up. There's not going to be any sale. There's not going to be any golf course, or marina, or shopping center, or Gullah World over there. I'm not giving it to you. And—"

He got to his feet and came around the desk.

"Caro, let's go home. We can talk about this at home. You're upset·about the horses; God, I don't blame you. We'll straighten it out, I promise. I could use some rest, too. We'll have lunch out on the patio and then we'll—"

I took a deep breath. I don't want to say this, I thought, but I did say it. I only knew as I did that I meant it. At least for now, I meant every word of it. It almost broke my heart.

"I'm staying over at the island, Clay," I said. "I can't go . . . home . . . now. I don't know when I can again. It just feels all of a sudden like I don't belong here and never did. But the island . . . at least that's mine. My place. Maybe in a little while I'll feel differently, but right now . . ."

"No," he said.

I stopped and looked at him. There was something strange and terrible in his voice. He had turned to the window again. I could see that his neck and shoulders were held as rigidly as a statue's.

"No," he said again. "It's not your place. It never was, Caro. It's still in my name. Technically, I can do whatever I want with it."

I could not understand what he was saying.

"But I . . . I signed that thing," I said. "You know, the transfer of title. Remember, you brought it home and I signed it, and you said that all that was left was for you to file it at the county courthouse. . . ."

My voice trailed off. He did not turn.

"You didn't file it, did you?" I said.

"I thought I did. Or at least I thought it had been filed," he said. "I gave it to Hayes to do; he's the company lawyer, after all. He said he'd take care of it. But . . . he didn't. I didn't know that, Caro. All those years I thought it was yours, too. He only told me when the business about Calista came up and it looked like we were going under. He said . . . he said that something just told him not to file that thing, to hang on to that land for me. He said he knew he should have told me, but he didn't think it would ever come up, and that no harm would be done by you thinking it was yours. And it wouldn't have . . . if things had been different in Puerto Rico . . ."

My head swam as badly as I remembered it doing when I was first pregnant with Carter and could hardly take an unassisted step for three months. I sat down abruptly in Clay's visitor's chair. He still did not turn from the window.

"You should have told me," I said.

"Yes. I should have. But by the time I knew, it looked as if we really might be able to come up with something you . . . could live with . . . and I could tell you then. I still thought so until this trip. Even with SouthWard in the saddle, I thought my . . . vision for it could prevail. You always liked my vision for the Lowcountry land, Caro. Your grandfather understood it, and liked it. . . ."

"My grandfather would die of shame if he knew about any of this," I said. "He would die. And your children. How do you think Kylie would feel about this? My God, I'm almost glad . . ."

I did not finish, but I saw the words hit home. He flinched slightly, but said nothing. Finally I got up and walked back to the door. I hoped dully that he would not turn around. I did not think I could bear to see the Alamo pin again. I did not think I could bear to see his face.

"Will you give it to me now?" I said, stopping at the door. I was amazed to hear that my voice was merely conversational.

"I . . . no. Caro, I can't. Don't you see? This will save us. This will save everything we've ever worked for, save everything I've ever built here, everything I've ever wanted for this land. . . . Don't you see that? Don't you see that it's for your future, too? Can't you see that most of it won't even touch you over at your precious house?"

"I'll ask you again. Will you deed it back to me?"

"I can't do that," he said. It was a whisper, a terrible sound. "I can't just . . . not have anything.

Not after having it all. Not after all this time. Not after what I've made here . . ."

"It was never yours," I said. "You were a guest here from the first time you set foot on this island. I asked you here. I let you come. My grandfather let you come because of me. It's a fine thing you're doing to repay us, Clay."

I went back out through the reception area. Neither Shawna nor any of the other women were there. The phones were ringing shrilly. I left them shrieking their frustration and went out into the sun. After the cool dimness of the office, it was blinding. Behind me, very faintly, I heard him calling me: "Caro! Caro!"

I don't remember thinking much at all while I drove back to the island except, I don't know how to be anything but Clay Venable's wife and Carter and Kylie's mother. That leaves one out of three. I wonder if it's enough.

Enough for what, I could not have said.

I drove over to Dayclear and asked Janie to find Ezra Upchurch for me. She looked into my face and said nothing, just went out back and rang the big indigo bell. I sat out front and waited for him, and she did not join me. It was high noon; no one was about. I supposed that most of the people of Dayclear were having their lunches and perhaps their naps. A few, I knew, would be looking at the beginning soaps. Their stories, as they called them. For a moment I ached with the simple, one-celled wish to be one of them.

Ezra came from behind the settlement, grease on his hands and shirt. He still carried a wrench. I knew that something mechanical in Dayclear had to be fixed every day. I wondered what the settlement would do when Ezra concluded his business here and went back to Washington, or wherever his next crusade took him. I found that I could not imagine this stark, sunny little street without him.

He dropped down into the chair next to me.

"He told you about the deed," he said. It was not a question.

I did not ask him how he knew. He told me, though.

"A deed's a matter of public record," he said. "I went and looked it up at the courthouse when I first knew what was going on over here. You always check your facts before you start a fight. I always knew that you really thought it was yours, though; I never thought you were just blowing smoke at us, to save your husband's fanny. Nobody over here did. Most of them knew your grandfather. They knew you were his girl."

"So . . . even when I was over here spouting off about nobody ever having to worry about anything again you all knew . . . Clay still owned it?"

"Yeah. But we knew how you felt. We still hoped you could change his mind about it. I take it that's not the case, huh?"

"I don't think it is, Ezra," I said. I was so tired that I thought I would fall out of the chair and simply lie on the sun-warmed earth of the Bigginses' storeyard until it swallowed me into the damp coolness under its surface.

"Okay," Ezra said. "Now we ruin his ass."

13

When Ezra Upchurch set out to ruin an ass, he didn't waste any time. By afternoon of the next day he had a press conference of national proportions set up for high noon two days later. Because he was Ezra Upchurch, the national media listened when his people in Washington called to announce it. Because he was Ezra Upchurch, most of them planned to attend. *The Today Show* was in North Carolina filming a series on black church bombings and would send a crew. All three major evening news shows scheduled reporters. Virtually all the national news magazines and many of the dailies would at least have stringers and photographers present. They would all meet at the bridge from Peacock's over to the island. Ezra would meet them there with the residents of Dayclear, five or six other Gullah communities in the Lowcountry, and representatives of every significant environmental group that could mount a presence. They would march from Dayclear to the bridge, singing and holding hands as they had done, many of them, so many years before, in Selma.

Even in my fugue state of a pathetic grief, I knew that it would be irresistible. No matter if Clay could have managed to prevail over the natural tastelessness of SouthWard and create something approaching environmental genius for the island, he would be dead meat now in the eyes of the nation, a despoiler of priceless wetlands and a fragile, ancient culture. It might not matter at all to SouthWard, but it would, indeed, be the emotional ruin of Clay Venable.

Oh, Clay, I thought in such pure sorrow that it surprised me, when Sophia Bridges told me Ezra's plans. What did you think would happen? Did you think the Sierra Club would give you a lifetime achievement award?

While I was still sitting in the chair in front of the Bigginses's store the afternoon I confronted Clay, spent and silent, Auntie Tuesday came out of her cabin, toddled down the street on Janie's arm, and brought me a giant pickle jar full of her tea.

"You take you some of this when you gits home," she said, peering into my face. "Take you another cup befo' you goes to bed. You sleep through without no hag-ridin'. You gon' need yo' sleep for a while. I fix you some fiddlehead broth tomorrow and send it over. This time I put some St. John in it. You gon' need yo' courage, too."

"Auntie," I said tiredly, "please don't ever tell me whether you saw all that in fire or water."

"Didn't see nothin' this time," she said. "Ezra been talkin' all along about callin' in those news folks did he have to. I knowed from the look of you when I seen you out my window that he gon' have to now. That gon' be hard on you. Likely gon' split you right in two. This he'p. It really will."

I hugged her when I left with my pickle jar, holding her hard. She was almost a head shorter than I and so frail that I could feel her tiny bird's ribs, but there was a strength in her that I could feel in my own hollowed and watery bones. I wished that I could simply move in with her and be cosseted, as she had cosseted Lita. But I knew that there was no place for me now in Dayclear. I was not the enemy. They all knew that. But I was married to him. I could not blame them if they wondered which loyalty would finally prevail.

So I drove slowly back to my island house and before the grief that hung like heavy, rotted fruit over my head could fall, I heated the tea and drank a cup. I could not handle much more right now than drowsiness, sleep. The knowledge of the betrayal needed time to work its way deep into the fibers of my mind and heart so that I knew its whole scope, its essential truth. Until that could happen, I knew that I would spend my time veering wildly from despair to denial, and back again. I had done it with Kylie. I would do it, too, now, with whatever might be left of my marriage. Better to drowse. Better still to sleep.

And I did. The smoky, slightly bitter tea eased the ache in my heart and the snarl in my head just enough so that I could read, and I stretched out on the sofa and lit my fire and pulled out the crumbling, yellowed old copy of *The Jungle Book* that had been Kylie's favorite. The exotic, firelit world of Mowgli and Baloo and Bagheera and Shere Khan swallowed me totally. I fell asleep before the fire and dreamed, not of my own threatened river and forest, but of a gold-green jungle where animals spoke and a child lived in a profound and sustaining harmony with them. When I awoke, it was almost ten the next morning, and I was cold and stiff and hungry, and the razor-sharp new pain was infinitesimally dulled.

It seemed to me that I should make a plan, a blueprint for living a new way, a map for getting through the next days in a new and diminished territory. So I showered and washed my hair and put on clean jeans and shirt and sat down on the deck with coffee and a fossilized bagel. I brought a legal pad and a pen with me for the outlining of my new life, but nothing came to me. Nothing at

all. I could not think of a life without this island
and this house, and I could not imagine one without Clay. It was a strange, suspended time, that
morning. I both had a husband and did not; both
had a home and did not. I would think, Well, we
can live very well over here if we lose the Peacock's house, and then think, But who is we? Or
I would think, This is absurd; Clay will no more
let me lose this place than he would let me go
naked, or starve, and then realize that he was prepared to put the machinery of that loss into
motion whenever he wished, and so far as I knew,
would do it without delay. I felt nearly crazy,
actually near insanity. I did not know how even
to think of Clay in any terms but the ones in
which I had always thought of him: my husband;
the man I had always loved; the man I would
grow old with; would, with luck, come to the end
of my days with.

And yet, for all practical purposes, he had
ended that life yesterday. Or had it been I? I did
not know even the most basic truth of all this,
and so I sat in the soft sun of late January and
waited for what would come next.

It was Sophia Bridges, on Ezra's motorcycle.
She came roaring into the clearing and slewed
smartly to a stop, dismounting in one single fluid
motion of her long, elegant legs and unpacking a
small sweet-grass basket from the saddlebag. I
stared at her. She might as well have ridden up on

a Komodo dragon. Even in my strange, suspended state, I realized how profoundly Sophia had changed on this island. There was little of the chilly, distant woman I had met in the kitchen of the guest house before Thanksgiving. She seemed almost totally a creation of this wild island now.

"I brought you some of Auntie's magic soup," she said, dropping down beside me in the rickety chair that had been my grandfather's. "And I wanted to see how you are. You took a bad knock yesterday, Ezra says."

A Southern woman is raised from birth to say when someone asks how she is, "Oh, fine, thank you for asking." I remembered saying it even when the enormity of Kylie's death was still new, and remembered the strange looks it evoked from the asker.

But now I simply said, "I think I'm in bad trouble, but I don't know how I feel yet. It's like being shot or something, and it hasn't started hurting yet but you know it will any minute. I don't even know how to describe it. But thanks for asking."

She grinned wryly at that last, and stretched out her legs in the old faded jeans that were her island uniform.

"I think I know. I remember when Chris told me he was leaving me. It seemed like there ought to be some kind of book that would tell me how to feel and what to do about it. You just don't know who or what you are anymore, do you?"

"I guess that's it," I said. "Mainly, I just can't believe that what's happened . . . really happened. I just can't believe it."

"I know. In my case, I didn't know who I was anyway, so in the end it wasn't so much different from the way I usually felt. But it must be awful for you. You never much doubted who you were, did you?"

"I guess I never much doubted *what* I was. I think there must be a difference that I'm just learning about. So much for teaching old dogs new tricks."

"Well, I guess the main thing is not to do anything sudden," she said. "Nothing's cast in stone, is it? I mean, you haven't decided really to leave or anything, have you? Things change so fast, Caro. They really do. That's one thing I've finally learned. Things change."

"I guess I haven't decided anything," I said. "But, Sophia . . . I don't think I can live with . . . what will happen over here. I don't think I can be around for that."

"Then where would you go?"

I just looked at her. I had not gotten that far. She was right. Where would I go? The town house? And risk running into Hayes Howland or Lucy every time I put my head out my front door? See the line of green on the horizon that was the fringe of Peacock's Island every time I walked on the Battery? No. Not the town house.

"I never got around to residential options," I said.

"Neither did I, but one presented itself, anyway, and one will for you," she said. "Maybe the first thing we both needed to learn was just to let go and let life do it."

"Well," I said, feeling absurd laughter start deep in my stomach, "life has done gone and done it."

And we sat in the sun and laughed and laughed, like schoolgirls giddy with new spring and limitless possibility.

Presently she said, "I came to tell you what Ezra plans to do. He wanted to come tell you himself, he's so proud of it all, and he was just sure that the jewel in the crown would be to have you march with them to meet the media. It's the old Upchurch touch, doncha know. The piquant, poignant little coup de grace. When I got through telling him how many kinds of assholes he was he saw the wisdom of letting me come alone to tell you. It's a good plan and I think it could work, but I can also see how it would just finish you off if you thought you had to be part of it. My advice to you is to go somewhere off-island . . . like maybe Jamaica or the U.S. Virgins, or Bhutan . . . until this is over. It's going to hurt some folks you care about before it does any good, and whether it will stop the project or not is anybody's guess.

Mine would be that it might stop Clay but it probably won't even make a dent in SouthWard's hide. But Ezra's good, I'll give him that. He's done more with less to work with than this. It's just that he is essentially a butthead and will never understand why you don't want to see Clay pounded through the ground."

"Do you understand?" I said.

"Of course I do, Caro," she said softly. "I've loved a man. You don't stop just because they've done a big awful. It may change the *way* you feel about them, but it doesn't necessarily lessen it."

I rubbed my eyes hard and said, "You better tell me what Ezra's got cooking," and she did.

When she was done, I said on a long breath, "My God. How could he do that in less than twenty-four hours?"

"His Washington staff did most of it," she said, and it was only then that I remembered that Ezra Upchurch did not always wear overalls without a shirt and work under the punishing Lowcountry sun with a hoe or a wrench, or even a mule team.

"You ought to know, too, that I've resigned and that I'm going to be marching," she said soberly.

"What . . . did Clay say?" I said.

"I don't know. He'd gone to Charleston. I left a letter."

"What will you do next?"

She shrugged and smiled. It was a peaceful smile.

"It will emerge," she said.

"I feel like I've fallen down the rabbit hole," I said, smiling back at her bleakly.

"Yeah. I meant it when I said you ought to get out of here for a few days. Get some perspective. I don't see how you can, this close."

But I found that I could not do that. I could see perfectly well the wisdom of her advice, but I could not seem to leave the island house. I did not feel anxious or afraid, and I was not terribly aware of anything beyond the dull, disbelieving grief I felt whenever I thought of Clay, but I still could not wander far from the house. So I cleaned. I put on all the West Coast jazz I could find—somehow symphonic music threatened my precarious hold on peace and baroque music seemed as if it would break my heart—and waded into cleaning my grandfather's house.

I had not thought it really dirty, only cluttered with the residue of many years of island living, most of which I was loath to discard, since it had belonged to my grandfather. But with my microscopic new focus I saw years, decades, of the kind of dull, mucky patina that humidity and steady salt winds leave. I scrubbed and mopped and scoured and swept and vacuumed and changed ancient, sticky shelf paper and threw out jars of rock-hard garlic salt and clumped herbs and

spices, and disinfected and polished and even did
a little touch-up painting. I slept and started over
the next day. When I was finally done, when I
could find nothing else to rout out or touch up or
scrub and my nails were broken to the quick and
my muscles ached down to the bone and my body
smelled of days-old sweat, I stopped and took a
long shower and looked around me. The house
shone. There was nothing more here that I could
do. And the telephone had not rung.

I realized only then that for three days I had
been waiting for Clay to call and say it was all a
mistake.

I sat in the sunset of the night before Ezra's
great march and felt the first sly, promissory fin-
gerings of a great grief and a greater rage, and
called Janie Biggins and found out where Luis
and Lita Cassells were staying on Edisto. And
then I got into the Cherokee and drove through
the translucent, fast-falling dusk until I was there.
If anyone had asked me why, the best I could
have done would be to say, I need to be with people who know who I am.

The Creekview Court had no view of Milton
Creek, which I assumed to be the nearest body
of water off Edisto Oak Lane. But it did have a
view of the island supermarket on one end and
a nice panorama of woods and marsh on the
other. I don't know what I had thought a trailer

park would be like; the only image that came
readily to mind at the words was the pitiful,
flattened wreckage left behind by the South's
frequent, vicious, trailer-eating tornadoes. But
the Creekview was as neat and pretty as any
small village whose inhabitants had considerable pride of place, and looked to me to be
about as permanent as most. It was apparently a
mature park; the plantings and trees were sizable and beginning to green up, and there were
towering camellia bushes blooming fervently
around many of them. Instead of rusted alu-
minum camp chairs and rump-sprung junkers,
there were gaily painted wooden outdoor furniture and big umbrellas and well-tended sedans
and midsize sports utility vehicles, and a good
number of bikes and skates spoke of children.
In the luminous green afterglow from the sunset, lights in windows were cheerful and wel-
coming, and joggers and walkers and in-line
skaters thronged the clean streets. A thin white
paring of a new moon rode high in the sky,
waiting to bloom. It reminded me of a village
scene painted by a minor Dutch artist of the
eighteenth century, naive and idealized. For a
long moment I paused at a cross street and simply drank it in. I would have given anything, at
that moment, to belong to a place like this, my
arena small and landlocked, my house as mov-
able as a turtle's shell in case of calamity.

The small side street where Luis and Lita were staying had only four trailers, and since one of them had a huge, muddy black Harley- David-son in front of it, I found it with no trouble. But I grimaced; I had not wanted to contend with Ezra Upchurch on this night. Only Lita. Only Luis.

I might have driven on past it, in fact, if at that moment Luis and Lita had not come around the side of the trailer from the back and spotted me. Lita had a big plastic bowl in her hands, which she tossed into the air when she saw me, and left to plop to earth while she streaked, squealing, toward the Cherokee. Luis held a cell phone to his ear, and when he saw me he smiled and said some-thing rapidly into it and shoved it into his pocket and trotted behind her toward my car. So, feeling as shy as a teenager calling at a boys' dormitory, I got out of the Jeep and went toward them across the tiny lawn.

Lita hit me around the knees and almost knocked me over, gurgling with laughter, and Luis caught her by the back of her T-shirt and restrained her while he put a big arm around my shoulders and drew me close in an exuberant hug.

"*Ay, querida,* but you are a sight for sore eyes," he yelled. "And an answer to a prayer. And whatever else a brighter mind than mine could come up with. Come in. We've got real pizza from the real pizza place in the village. None of that frozen stuff for the likes of us."

He walked me into the trailer, and I looked around, Lita hanging from my hand and chattering so fast in Spanish that she sounded like an Alvin and the Chipmunks recording. The inside was much more spacious than I would have thought, and sparsely furnished, but with obviously new furniture and some taste. A huge television set had pride of place, with a tomato-colored recliner and a rocking chair drawn up to it, and on a big red-plaid sofa there was a litter of books and toys and crayon drawings. On the small pine dining table was a welter of maps and charts and books and a half-empty bottle of red wine: Luis's territory, obviously. The real pizza box sat on a shining Formica counter, smelling so good that I felt water gather in my mouth.

"We almost ate it before we went to feed the raccoons, but Lita wanted to wait," Luis said. "She knew something I didn't, obviously."

"Told you she'd come," Lita said, rolling her bright almond eyes at her grandfather. "Told you."

"So you did. Fourteen million times," he said. "She's wanted to call you for at least three days. She was afraid you wouldn't be able to find us. But I thought you might need a little time to yourself. . . ."

Of course, Ezra would have told him about

the deed to the island, and the march, all of it.

"Where's Ezra?" I said. "I saw his machine outside."

"He swapped it for my truck for the night," Luis said, grinning. "He's got stuff to haul for the big doings tomorrow, and I've always wanted to get that hawg off by myself."

"And have you?"

"Yep. Lita and I went to the beach this afternoon. It was great. Just like *Easy Rider*. So. Not that you need a reason, and I hope it's purely because you've missed us, but I suspect there's more to this than a social call. Can we do something for you?"

His words were light, but his voice was gentle and his face concerned, and I felt a prickle of weak tears in my eyes, and turned away.

"Not really," I said. "I just was . . . at loose ends, sort of, and I guess . . . I think I might have been a little lonesome out there in the marsh. I'm awfully used to seeing this monkey face around by now."

And I gave Lita's hand a squeeze. She squeezed back, hard.

"A bad time for you, Caro, and that's no joke," Luis said soberly. "A huge betrayal. A huge loss. A true evil. I would have given a lot to be able to prevent it."

"It wasn't really deliberate, Luis," I said, surprising myself. "I know Clay feels bad about it, too. I think . . . he just can't see any other way right now."

"Then he's a worse fool than I thought he was. But I wasn't talking about Clay. I know the poor stupid bastard's hurting. Look what he stands to lose . . . No, I meant our friend Hayes. Goebbels. Iago. He who smiles and smiles, and is a villain. Of course Mengele should have told you the minute he found out about that deed, and fired Iago's ass, and taken you over there with him to watch him personally fire that sucker. But his head's so fucked up by all those years of playing God that he really thinks he created the heavens and the earth, and now he's got to save his holy empire or he won't get to be God anymore. He might have come around, given time, but ol' Iago did him out of any leeway he had. He's no fool, Iago. He always knew who would inherit the earth."

"Who?"

"SouthWard. You start screwing around with the wilderness and SouthWard is two steps behind you, sure as gun's iron. I've always known that. Those folks over in Dayclear have always known that. We know that at best we're guests on that land. Nobody owns it but the gators and the crabs and the coons."

"And the panther," Lita piped. "Don't forget the panther, Abuelo!"

I look at Luis in surprise.

"We heard him, Lita and I. We heard him early in the morning, right before we found the mare and her baby. I'd heard *of* him, of course, but this time I heard that sucker. Lita did, too. You don't forget that. She's right. I reckon that's who owns this island. Pity Mengele forgot that."

I turned my head away, thinking of the night we had heard the panther, Clay and I. It had been the beginning of it all, of everything.

"Clay heard him, too, once," I said. It was almost a whisper. I thought my throat would burst with pain.

"He forgets fast then," Luis said. "That cat ought to put his snout right down Mengele's britches and roar. Look, Caro, let me put a proposition to you. Not that kind, though don't I wish. It's this. I just got a call from . . . a person in Columbia, somebody I've been looking for but wasn't sure existed. If he's willing to do what he says he will, we've got this botulism business nailed. Name of seller, name of buyer, dates, places, the whole nine yards. It could lift that march tomorrow right up into the stratosphere. It could put the blame right where it ought to be, too . . . and that ought to get ol' Clay baby off the hook a little with the media. But I'm going to have to leave right now and go meet him; he won't talk over the telephone, and he won't talk at all unless he sees the color of my cash first. I've been racking my brains trying to think of somebody to stay with Lita; I don't want her over on the island until this is all over, and I don't know anybody over here who could come on such short notice. Lottie will come get her first thing in the morning and take her to her studio; she's keeping Mark Bridges, too, until the crowd's dispersed, but Lottie's . . . tied up tonight. I'd get Auntie, but she, by God, wants to march and I think she should. So . . . do you think you could possibly baby-sit for me, just till Lottie gets here in the morning? I'll probably be going straight to the bridge from Columbia. I wouldn't ask you except that I don't like thinking of you over there by yourself in that house, just sitting there and waiting for us to barbecue Clay right under your nose. In fact, I think you ought to be off the island completely till tomorrow night. Somebody in that pack of press jackals is bound to get wind of where you are and come beating on your door. I was going to tell Lottie to go get you in the morning and take you over to her studio till the dust settles, anyway. Could you stay here, do you think? It's a lot to ask of you, I know, to help us sink your husband. . . ."

He looked intently into my face and then looked away.

"It was a shitty idea," he said. "I'm sorry, Caro. Please forget I even mentioned it. I'm as bad as Ezra, trying to get you to march with us. . . . Fuck."

"No," I heard myself say. "I'd love to stay with Lita. You need to do this. Do it for the folks at Dayclear and the ponies; do it for Nissy and Yambi. You're right. If it was Hayes, God help him, then everybody ought to know it was. Apparently I don't know my husband as well as I thought I did, but I do know that he would never on this earth harm those horses, or let anybody do it for him. Do it for me if you can't do it for Clay. Please, Luis."

He took a deep breath and nodded. He turned to Lita.

"Will you stay with Caro and not give her any grief about going to bed, and not pester her for more than three stories?"

"I promise," Lita said. "She can have my bed and I'll sleep on the sofa, like you do. I'll be as quiet as a mouse. You said fuck, Abuelo."

"I did, and I should know better. I owe the jar a nickel. Go cut you and Caro a piece of pizza while she walks me out to the Harley. Look, Lita, I'm going to wear Uncle Ezra's helmet and leather jacket; will I look like James Dean, do you think?"

"Who's that?"

"Ay," he said, rolling his eyes. "I am too old for this. But I can't wait to straddle that hawg and eat that asphalt up. Think of it, Caro, a breath-held crowd waiting at the bridge, and I come thundering in on that thing with the proof of the pudding in my pocket . . . What more could a man ask?"

"Brains enough to be careful?" I ventured. "I don't like the sound of this clandestine stuff, Luis. If your guy knows that kind of stuff, he's a criminal himself. Are you meeting him in a safe place?"

"Deep in the sewers of Columbia at midnight," he said. "No, really. I'm meeting him at the VFW hut in the middle of the parking lot, with a fais-do-do going on inside. He's going to wear a red carnation in his navel and I'm going to carry a rose in my teeth. The worst danger is that he'll try to kiss me, and I can always claim sexual harassment."

"Then hit the road, fool," I said as we walked out into the night. Dark had fallen and the thin curl of moon had swollen and leaned closer. Someone nearby had planted Confederate jasmine; the sweet, tender smell almost took my breath. Even this far inland, the kiss of salt lay on the wet little night wind.

He pulled on the helmet and shrugged into the jacket. He should have looked ludicrous beyond words, but he did not; he looked enormous and rock-solid and somehow both boyish and dangerous, going off on this extravagant quest to save something not his own. But then, had that not been almost his whole life?

"Do you remember, you told me once to find

what I would die for and then live for it?" I said. "What is it you would die for, Luis? What is it you live for? What is it you ride this silly thing to Columbia at night for?"

He was not smiling when he looked at me.

"For the quaint, old-fashioned notion that people ought to be able to live wherever the fuck they choose," he said. "I ought to be able to go back to Cuba if I want to. That little girl in there at least ought to have a choice. The people in Dayclear should, too. You, too, for that matter. A great deal of this business is so that you can live on that island of yours if you want to. Didn't you know that?"

"I guess I didn't, really," I said, around the cold salt lump in my throat.

He reached out and touched my hair.

"I don't know what will happen with you," he said. "I do know that things change. I think things may change for you. I don't know what that means yet. But when I get back we will talk about it. Can we do that, Caro? Can we talk about that?"

"Yes," I whispered.

He stood still with his hand on my head, and then he leaned over and kissed me very chastely and softly on the forehead.

"Sleep well with my little girl," he said. "And I, I will ride like the wind until my great steed Rosinante brings me back to you."

"Get out of here." I laughed, choking on it.

He swung himself into the seat of the Harley and stomped down on the gas pedal. It roared into life, throbbing and bucking to get away, to ride out into the vast black night, to spit out the wind. He wiggled his eyebrows up and down like Groucho Marx, jerked back his thumb in the old WWII pilot's salute, and gunned the Harley. It leaped forward, roaring, and I watched it as he leaned into the turn at the bottom of the street, raised a hand, and was gone.

When I got back into the trailer, the pizza was waiting, smoking hot, on two flowered Melamine plates, and *The Lion King* was beginning on the TV screen.

"I always work the VCR," Lita said, settling herself into the rocking chair with her plate of pizza. "It makes Abuelo say fuck, and then he has to put a nickel in the jar. It's half-full now."

"I'll bet it is," I said, beginning to laugh. And that is what we had for our supper, Estrellita Esteban and I: pepperoni pizza from the real pizza place, with no anchovies, and laughter, and a golden lion cub growing through pain and despair into lordliness.

Lottie came so early the next morning that I was still in Luis's old seersucker robe, putting on coffee, and Lita was still asleep. She had had a restless night, muttering and whimpering, and I had heard her from the sofa bed in the little living room and gone in to her, and finally, when I could neither fully wake her nor quiet her, crawled in beside her. She had subsided then, but had rolled against me and clung there, and I was tired and sweaty when the first graying of the dark outside the high little windows came. I got up carefully, so as not to wake her, and found the robe hanging behind the bathroom door and put it on over my underwear, and went into the kitchen. The robe smelled of Luis and somehow of peat moss, an intimate, earthy smell. I drew it close around me in the morning chill.

When I had peered out to see who was banging so peremptorily on the trailer door and let Lottie in, she grinned, in spite of what was obviously one of her more advanced hangovers.

"Looks better on you than it does on me," she said, indicating the robe. I felt myself color, and she said, "Oh, for God's sake. I know he isn't here. He called me on his way out of town last night and told me you were staying, and to come over and get you all going early so you wouldn't run into reporters at the bridge. They're sure to know your car, and they know about Lita. He doesn't want them near either of you. You ought to know, too, that he and I are what they customarily call just good friends now."

"God, Lottie, I don't care . . ."

"Just so you know."

I gave her coffee while I went to wake Lita. She was fussy and petulant, and clung to me. I had never heard her whine before, but her manner this morning was that of a much younger child, and I automatically felt her forehead to see if she had a fever. She did not. Well, she was only a small child after all; she was entitled to a small regression now and then. I had never really seen her in any state but her customary cheeky, sunny one.

"Got up on the wrong side of the bed, did we?" I said, and she looked in fretful puzzlement at each side of her double bed.

"It's just an expression that means fussy," I said. "That's okay. I do it, too, sometimes. Let's get some breakfast in you. Lottie's here to take you over to her studio with Mark. You all are going to have a great time. You might not know it, but it's a real honor. She doesn't invite many people over there. She's a famous artist, you know."

She was unimpressed.

"Don't want to go," she said, scrubbing fitfully at her eyes with her fists. "Want to go with you. And I want to go with Abuelo and ride the hawg in the march. I want to go home, too."

"Well, you can't do all three at the same time," I said in the tone I remembered employing with Carter and Kylie when total unreason ruled. "You were all excited about going to Lottie's last night, to play with Mark. You can't come with me this morning, but we'll do something tomorrow maybe, or the next day. Where's home, Lita?"

I should not have had to ask, and felt a frisson of anger.

"Over there," she said sullenly, jerking her thumb back toward the road south. I knew that she meant the island. What would happen when Luis took her away from there, as he was bound to do sooner or later? Where would home be then?

"How about we go see Yambi tomorrow?" I said. "I hear he's been asking for you."

"Promise?"

"I'll do my best. It's up to your grandfather."

"He'll let me," she said, some of her sunniness returning. I thought that he would, too.

Lottie made appalling cinnamon toast while I got Lita into her miniature jeans and T-shirt and running shoes. When we were ready to go, Lottie said, "Why don't you pick out a few toys to take with you?" and Lita scampered off to gather her treasures.

Lottie turned to me.

"I heard about the island. The deed thing, I mean. I know somebody who does freelance hits, and in case you think I'm kidding, I'm not. He would probably do Clay and Hayes for the price of one. Are you going to get through this, Caro?

Why don't you come back with us today? It's not going to be pleasant, even over where you are. You're bound to hear some of it, and there's always the possibility that some of those assholes will track you down at the house. The patrician, betrayed, environmentalist wife . . . you're honey for the flies. Just for today? Luis and Ezra will keep them away from you after this, but they'll be tied up today. . . ."

"I can take care of myself," I said. "I think I could easily shoot any son of a bitch who comes over there with a camera. I wouldn't mind a bit. I don't need Ezra and Luis to fight my battles for me."

"Well, don't shoot anybody. Ain't none of them worth jail. Save the bullets for Hayes. Somebody ought to do it, sure enough. That poor old mare . . . What will you do today then?"

"I think I might be ready to paint. If I can do that, I won't hear anything from the bridge, and I won't think about it."

"Okay, sweetie," she said, hugging me. She felt solid and warm and smelled of bourbon. It was somehow comforting, and then I realized it was my grandfather's smell.

"I'm coming by after I take the children back to Dayclear tonight, though," she said. "I'm either going to spend the night with you or drag you back to my place. There are nights it's okay to be alone, but tonight is not one of them."

"We'll see," I said. The idea of Lottie's formidable presence on this looming night was oddly appealing. When it was over, something very basic to the fabric of my life would have changed. I knew that. I simply was not sure what.

It was still early when I pulled out onto 174 and drove south toward the bridge over to Peacock's. The sky was still pink behind the line of black pines to the east, and there was little traffic in the opposite direction. The islanders who worked in Charleston would just be leaving now. I thought that I would get home and take a long, hot, sulfurous shower and make myself some real coffee and dig out my camera and take the Whaler far up the creek. The eleven o'clock news last night had spoken of a powerful cold front working its way east through Alabama and Georgia, and predicted strong thunderstorms and high winds by the evening of the next day. I knew that meant a return, however briefly, of cold weather. We were not done with winter yet. This might be the last of the enchanted gold-green light on the marshes for several weeks. I remembered a poem Robert Frost had written about that first gilded green of spring. It ended, "Nothing gold can stay."

The line almost brought tears to my eyes as I drove. Why couldn't the gold stay? Was it too much to ask?

I crossed over to Peacock's Island and resolutely looked neither right nor left as I headed west, so that I would not have to see the company's offices or the artful stand of tropical plantings that led to the beach road and our house. I stepped on the gas when I got through the traffic circle; I had no wish to meet the first of the media gathered at the bridge over to the island. But when I approached it, it lay empty and dreaming in the first sun, only a couple of Gullah crabbers tossing their lines over into the black water. I lifted a hand and smiled, and they smiled back. I knew them but did not remember their names. I knew that they lived in Dayclear, though. I wondered how much longer they would be free to crab in this little estuary.

I flicked on the radio and found the station in Charleston that played baroque music in the early mornings. "Spring" from *The Four Seasons* uncurled into the Jeep, and I smiled. I turned off onto my dirt road and swept around the curve to the live oak hammock in a shower of glittering notes.

Clay's Jaguar was parked under the trees. Even as my lips framed the word "shit," my heart leaped like a gaffed mullet in my chest.

I stopped the Jeep a little way from the Jaguar and looked around. I saw no evidence that he was in the house; it was still dark, and no smoke came from the chimney. I did not see him on the hammock or out on the boardwalk to the dock, either. I sat still, trying to decide how I would think about this, how I would act when I saw him. I could not even imagine why he was here, on this of all days.

I decided on Dorothy Parker.

"What fresh hell is this?" I said aloud, in what I hoped was a coolly amused voice, as I got out of the Jeep.

No one answered me but an outraged squirrel in the live oak over my head.

I was almost up to the steps when I heard the faint putt-putt of the Whaler out on the creek. I went down to the edge of the boardwalk over the reeds and dark water and stood watching as it came out of the glitter of the morning sun and glided to rest against the dock. He got out and stood looking toward me. He was bathed in the dancing light, as he had been the first time I saw him, and he was as tall and flame-tipped and lithe as he had ever been then. This was not fair. I felt a great, simple, abject grief start in my chest.

"I want that back," I whispered aloud. "Oh, I want that back."

I went to meet him.

I was perhaps fifteen feet away from him before his face came clear out of the dazzle, and I gasped aloud and stopped. Clay had been crying. His long face was as red and congested as Carter's when he was a toddler and just coming out of a spell of weeping; his eyes were bloodshot and slitted, and the silver scum of dried tears glittered in the silvery stubble on his chin and cheeks. His hair had not been combed, and was wildly tangled from the wind on the Whaler.

I had never seen Clay cry. Not like this. I simply looked at him.

"I couldn't find you," he said, and his lips shook, and his voice broke.

"I wasn't here," I said stupidly.

He shook his head hard, and tears flew out into the warming air. His face contorted and he turned it away.

"I know. I know you were over at Cassells's trailer. I went over there, but the lights were out. . . ."

"He wasn't there, Clay," I said. "He went to Columbia. I was staying with Lita."

"I know. I didn't mean I thought you . . . I just . . . I just wanted to see your car, to know you were safe somewhere. I thought you'd have called by now. . . . I came over here to wait for you."

As if by agreement, we began to walk back toward the house. The boardwalk squeaked and swayed under our weight. We walked side by side, but we did not touch. None of this felt at all real. I might have been watching a movie of myself, walking along a boardwalk on a spring morning with a man who could not stop crying. A man I knew only slightly, from another time.

"How did . . . how did you know where I was?" I said, more to break the silence than anything. I simply could not get a sense that this was my husband.

"Ezra Upchurch came to see me last night," he said. "He told me. Among other things. Christ, if that wasn't a scene . . . it's two in the morning and Ezra Upchurch is knocking on the door yelling for me to open up. I'm surprised somebody didn't call the cops."

"Ezra?" I said stupidly. "I didn't know you knew Ezra."

"I guess he figured it was time he introduced himself," Clay said, and to my surprise began to laugh. It was not so far removed from tears, that laugh, but it was a laugh. I laughed, too. I could not imagine why.

At the beginning of the boardwalk my grandfather had built a pair of facing cypress benches, weathered now into a silky silver gray, and when we reached them he sagged onto one of them and I sat down on the other. We looked at each other across the boardwalk where we had met, all those years ago.

"Ah, God, Caro," he said presently. "So much shit. So much misery. So much . . . waste. I don't know what I was thinking. I really don't. Well, I *wasn't* thinking, of course . . . Listen, can we talk a little bit? Will you just listen to me without saying anything? I don't mean you should . . . change your mind about anything, but if you'd just listen . . ."

"Clay, I will always listen to you," I said. "When did I not?"

"Well, do you think . . . could you make some coffee? I couldn't find the cord to the pot. . . ."

"Come on," I said. "Let's go to the house."

All the way across the grass and up the steps my heart was hammering as if it would explode in my chest. What was this? What could this possibly mean?

I made the coffee while he took a shower. I saw that he had slept on the sofa under a welter of quilts. The fire was cold and sour, and I relit it. It was really too warm for it, but I wanted the intimate hiss and snicker of it, and the dancing light. The living room was still in darkness, from the sheltering oaks. I turned on the lamps and brought out a tray of coffee and some of the Little Debbies that were Esau and Janie Biggins's sole gesture toward breakfast food.

He came into the room in an old pair of madras shorts and a sweatshirt. His feet were bare and his hair was wet and standing straight up in spikes from the towel. The sweatshirt was a horror of Carter's that said, RUGBY PLAYERS EAT THEIR DEAD. I was sure that Clay had no idea it said anything at all. I felt wild, braying laughter behind the tears in my chest. I bit my lips and waited.

"All right," he said on a long, exhaled breath. "Listen. The press thing at the bridge . . . the march, you know . . . that's off. Ezra's Washington people have been calling all night. And the project, the development, you know, the Dayclear thing . . . that's off, too. I pulled out of it. I called the South-Ward guys at the guest house while Ezra was still at the house and told them to hit the road. He wouldn't leave until I'd given him the deed and he'd torn it up. Burned it, too. He's one tough cookie, Ezra Upchurch. And he still wouldn't leave until I'd called Hayes and fired him. That did it, though. After that we broke out the Glenfiddich and drank until about four, and then he left to get things straightened out with the press, and I went on over to Edisto, and then came back here. I hadn't been out on the water for fifteen minutes before you came."

He stopped and looked at me. I could not think of a single thing on earth to say to him.

"Why did you fire Hayes?" I said finally.

"Suspicion of equicide," my husband said, and began to laugh. I did, too. We sat in the growing light of this day I had dreaded and laughed and howled and wept and sobbed and laughed some more, and pounded our thighs with our fists, and when we finally subsided, Clay began to cry again.

I moved over to the sofa and sat down beside him and put my arm around his shoulder, very tentatively. I felt that I was trying to comfort a total stranger, someone I had met on an airplane

or something, who had become suddenly inconsolable. It was almost . . . unseemly.

"Did you really do those things, Clay?" I said
finally. "Did all that really happen?"

His face was buried in his hands, but he nodded.

I sat back and thought about that.

"Then . . . nothing is going to happen over
here. There isn't going to be anything built on
Dayclear?"

He nodded.

"Do you mean for now, or ever? You still
own it; will you change your mind somewhere
along the way? Will we go through this again?"

He raised his head and looked at me. It was
painful to look at him.

"Caro," he said, "Last night, when I finally
lay down to try to sleep, I thought Kylie was here.
I could have sworn on a stack of Bibles that I
heard her laughing, that I heard her walking outside; I'd know her step anywhere. I thought I
heard her . . . talking, but I couldn't hear what she
said. And when I got up to see, I heard . . . I heard
the panther. And I knew then that if I did anything to this island I would be haunted for the
rest of my life by it. I knew that it was theirs, not
mine, yours and theirs, and your grandfather's,
and the Dayclear folks . . . I knew that I never had
belonged here and never would, not the way all
of you did and do. They told me that, that pan-

ther and my dead baby. I know it's not possible, but that is what I heard. I started crying then. If I'm losing my mind . . . then so be it."

I felt joy and peace flood into my heart like an artesian well.

"If you're losing you mind, then I am, too," I said. "I've heard her here. I've talked to her. I've thought I saw her. And Luis and Lita heard the panther the morning . . . that Nissy died. I think . . . I think . . . that either that panther must be about one hundred and twenty-five years old or this island knows what we need to hear, and some-how . . . sees that we do. In any case, it doesn't matter. If you heard them, then maybe it can be your island, too."

He shook his head, no.

"But I'd like . . . I'd like to stay here on it with you, if you think you could let me do that. I thought you'd gone, Caro. I didn't think you would come back. I didn't think I could live with that."

I reached out and touched a tear track on his face. He covered my hand with his and pressed it into his bristled cheek.

"We'll lose everything, won't we?" I said, not pulling away. "If you don't do Dayclear? The company, the house . . . Is that why you're crying? Surely, Clay, there's something else you can do, some other way you can put your gift to work . . . and I don't care about the other stuff. I can live over here for the rest of my life. I was going to; I thought that was what I would do. I can sell my paintings. We could manage. . . ."

He shook his head and grinned, a small, watery grin.

"We'll do okay," he said. "I'll find somebody decent to sell the company to, somebody who'll be generous; there have been good offers along the way. The Peacock Island Plantation Company is not chopped liver. I have a ton of stock. We could keep the house if you wanted to, but somehow I don't think I could live there now, and I was sure you wouldn't want to. Carter may want to be a part of it, and we can work that out with the new owners. I don't give a shit about any of that stuff; it's history. I want to see if I can earn my right to be part of this over here. That will be enough to hold me a few thousand years. No, what got to me was . . . I guess the thought of Kylie, and how she would feel about what I had become, and then that poor goddamned horse, and the colt . . . Kylie loved those horses . . . and Hayes. Hayes was my friend, Caro. Hayes was my first friend in this place, almost my first friend period. . . ."

"Did he admit . . . that he had anything to do with the horses?"

"He didn't say he didn't. He just blustered and threatened and yelled; he really lost it when I told him there wasn't going to be any project.

Said I was ruining him. Said I had betrayed him, after everything he'd done for me. I remembered what you said about Becket . . . I think he did it, or had it done. God help him for that."

"There may be proof by now that he was behind it, Clay," I said. "That was why Luis went to Columbia. He has a contact there who's going to tell him, who can name names and places and all that. He was going to bring it back with him for the press conference. You should have it soon. . . ."

He turned his face away.

"I don't need it. I think I knew when you told me. Hayes . . . something has eaten Hayes up inside, like a worm. There's nothing left but rottenness. I don't know why I never saw it happening. He's going with SouthWard, by the way; it's been in the works for months. He hit me with that, too. He was to deliver the project and then go in as chief counsel and a managing partner. He'd have been out of Peacock's before the dust settled. The deal was that he'd be able to stay in Charleston, too; Hayes had it all figured out."

"Well, he'll have to refigure then. . . ."

"No, I think they'll still take him. Oh, he won't be chief anything, and he'll have to move to Atlanta, and that will kill him and Lucy, and he'll never make anywhere near the money he stood to make this way . . . but Hayes is good about finding venture capital. He ought to be able to smell out enough for SouthWard so that they'll keep him. I think, for Hayes, living in a suburb of Atlanta near a strip shopping mall and being a middle-level money cruncher for SouthWard will be worse than jail. Maybe there's some justice in the world after all. I'd like to think there's a little, after what I've done. . . ."

"But if you've pulled out of the Dayclear project, what harm *have* you done?" I said, reaching out to turn him around so that he faced me. His shoulder felt familiar again all of a sudden, muscle and bone that I knew.

He turned. His face shocked me. I felt my breath die in my chest.

"Ezra came for another reason," he whispered.

"Tell me," I said.

And that is when he took both my hands in his cold ones, and told me that Luis Cassells had spun the Harley off a long curve halfway between Edisto and Columbia near midnight the night before, and crashed into a tree, and died, the state patrol thought, on impact.

14

The storm the newscasts had promised us came a day early, screaming in from the west on a fast-running river of upper air. It hit about three o'clock that afternoon, out of a sky gone inky black and lurid with flickering lightning, and stalled out over the Lowcountry. It crouched there for twenty-four hours, alternately flooding the sea and marshes with torrential cold rains and scourging them with great, punishing winds. Sometimes there was the spatter of hail on the house's tin roof, and sometimes the light went queer and thick and green and Clay would stand me up and walk me hurriedly into the middle hall, where there were no windows, until the dull bellow high overhead passed and became ordinary rain again. Several tornadoes spun out of the low, flat clouds; I learned later that North Charleston had been nipped by one, and a couple of blocks were treeless and shingleless in Peacock Plantation, and the usual trailer park casualties had occurred. Much later Lottie told me that the trailer that Luis and Lita had borrowed was rocked off its foundation, though no real damage was done. It was as if the very air howled in grief and outrage for Luis Cassells.

I remember very little of the storm. For almost its day-and-night-long duration, I cried.

I began to cry at Clay's words that morning. I felt as though a lance had gone straight into a monstrous sac of pain deep within me and let it erupt. I cried great, shuddering sobs and moans that rose sometimes into real screams, and gasped for breath that would not come until my chest heaved and black specks danced before my eyes, and then sobbed again. I cried so much that I thought I would die of it; I did not think that the human heart and lungs could process that many tears, withstand that kind of savage, battering grief. When I stopped momentarily, gasping and rocking back and forth, I could feel a profound aching deep in the muscles of my stomach and under my ribs that felt mortal. I frightened myself badly with the velocity and duration of my grief and my inability to stop it, and I know that I frightened Clay. After an hour or so of rocking me in his arms on the sofa while the world outside blazed with lightning and boomed with thunder, and I wept, he picked me up and walked with me into the bedroom and laid me under the covers and crawled in beside me. For the rest of that roaring afternoon, he held me hard against him and I cried in my grandfather's old bed.

Sometimes, in a momentary lull, I would try to explain to him that it was not just for Luis Cassells that I cried, and I knew that that was true, although the thought of that lonely death on a dark country roadside would send me back into a fury of tears whenever it came, unbidden, into my mind.

"It's everything, Clay," I would hiccup. "It feels like it's just everything that ever happened to me. He was never . . . like that . . . to me. It's just . . . he gave me back Kylie, in a way. He showed me how to let her go so she could come back. And, Clay, he showed me how to stop the drinking; I haven't drunk anything since way before he . . ." And the tears would start again, endlessly, endlessly.

"I know," he would murmur against my hair. "I know. I know who you're crying for. You never did, did you? It's all right. Cry all you need to."

He didn't know, not really; I did cry for Kylie, of course, but through all of that vast storm of anguish I felt her, that fiery living kernel of her, within me, burning steadily. I cried, I think, for not having gotten her back sooner, and I cried for Nissy and her colt, and I cried for the awful, slinking thing that had ripped Clay away from me and had given me back this man who, even while I clung to him, was a stranger to me. I cried for the life that I had not even liked very much, perhaps, but that had been the one I knew. I cried for the fear that my foolishness had permitted the Gullahs of Dayclear. I cried for the gangling, vulnerable teenager who had grown to manhood waiting for me to really see him again. I cried for the man who had grown so nearly old waiting for the same thing. I even cried for Hayes Howland, for the young Hayes in tennis whites who had brought me my husband on a summer day.

All that I knew. Still, I could not stop.

Late in the afternoon the phone began to ring and people began to come to the house. Clay would leave me for a moment, to talk in low tones on the phone or to whisper hurriedly to whomever stood in the streaming doorway, but he always came back and got into bed with me again.

"Okay," he would say, pulling me against him. "Let 'er rip." And I did.

It was a strange state; in a way it was like the feverish fugue state in which I had painted that night before Ezra and Lottie had come. I seemed mired in the same fireshot old darkness, though I realized on some level that it was only the lightning outside, and the flickering of the fire in the little bedroom fireplace. I saw images and heard things with preternatural clarity: I heard Ezra's voice once, from the living room, talking about the funeral service for Luis, and I heard Sophia Bridges's cool clear voice saying, ". . . I'll take her, of course, but it isn't me she wants," and knew that she was speaking of Lita, and could not do anything at all about it. Lita . . . I found that I could not even think of Lita.

Later, in the full night, I heard Sophia again, telling Clay to give me a cup whenever I would take it, and knew that Auntie Tuesday had sent her magical tea, and actually smiled to myself before the tears started again. And I heard her telling him about Lita, about the horror that had taken her mother and baby brother and her journey to Luis, and about her silence. I gathered that she was silent again, once more at Auntie's house, and that the tea and the broth were not working, and that everyone was frightened for her. I was, too, but I could not make my muscles move me toward the edge of the bed.

"Ezra and I wanted to bring her over here, but Auntie says let Caro be. She says a lot of poison has got to come out before she can help Lita or anybody else. She says give her the broth and the tea until tomorrow and then we'll see. It's Caro's time now. Auntie will tend to Lita."

Presently she went away, back into the storm, and Clay came into the room with a tray of Auntie's steaming fiddlehead broth, and I took it from him and drank it down greedily. I knew that it would spin me down into sleep. I thought if I cried anymore I would surely die.

Sleep came then. A sleep unlike any other I have ever known. In it fires burned and drums beat and animals flickered through forests of a primary greenness I had never known, and children ran laughing and shrieking, and hot blue seas beat on yellow sand, and great, hectic flowers hung from vines like boa constrictors. I remember thinking, as you do in dreams, that this was Eden, and I must be very careful or I would be cast out of it. It was not a peaceful Eden, not sweet, not idyllic, but it was so ravenously alive and exuberant in its fecundity that I could almost feel the fabric of a still-wet new world forming itself around me.

I woke the next morning with tears still damp on my face, but this time they were tears of a fierce joy. I knew, without knowing how, that for a time I would not cry again.

I was alone in the tumbled bed. I stretched long and hard, feeling the soreness around my chest and diaphragm muscles from the storms of tears, and listened for the storm outside. It had slunk off in the night, leaving only a steady rain to patter on the roof. Even in my drowsing state I knew that it would be a cold rain. Spring had left us on the wings of the storm.

"Breakfast," Clay said, coming into the room

with a tray, and I sat up. He was in the ratty old terry cloth robe he kept out here, and there were damp comb tracks in his hair. He was freshly shaved, too, but his eyes were wary and darkly shadowed, and the muscles of his jaw were as slack as if they had been pounded. I doubted that he had slept at all.

He brought coffee and pastries that I recognized as Janie Biggins's cream cheese turnovers, and orange juice. And he brought a damp washcloth and a mirror and comb and a long-sleeved flannel nightgown smelling of mothballs.

"Good morning," I tried to say, but my voice was a painful husk in my sore throat.

"Don't talk," he said. "You'll bust something for good."

He handed me the hot washcloth and I scrubbed my face with it, then looked into the mirror and flinched. A wild-haired, slit-eyed, mottled-cheeked witch looked back at me. I combed the snarls out of my hair and tied it back with the shoelace he had found, and took a long, scorching swallow of the coffee.

"My God," I croaked. "That was . . . extraordinary. I'm sorry, Clay. I had no idea . . . I don't know what . . ."

"You're entitled," he said. "As long as you give me an hour's notice if you think you're going to do it again. I thought you were dying. I thought you were just going to . . . cry up your

insides and die. So did everybody else. Only
Ezra's aunt seemed to know what to do for you.
Is her name really Tuesday?"

"It really is. She's a conjure woman, they say.
A healer. And she *can* heal. I'd take anything she
gave me, even if it was green and smoking. She
sent the tea and the broth, didn't she?"

"Yeah. I was afraid to give it to you, but
Sophia said for me to."

"I thought I heard Sophia. I hope . . . I know
she resigned, Clay. I hope there's no hard feelings
between you. She's a good person. She's been a
good friend to me."

"Caro, I didn't even think about that. I don't
think she did, either. She told me some more about
Luis, and about the little girl. Did I know about
her? I can't remember if you told me. God
almighty, what is there left to happen to that
child? We need to see if we can do anything for
her. . . ."

"I'll have to go," I said, feeling a great, listless
white fatigue wash over me. "I'll have to go over
there. Sometimes she'll talk to me when she
won't to anybody else. I don't know if she can get
over this, though . . . but oh, Lord, Clay, I am just
so tired. . . ."

"I know. You're not going anywhere today.
Tomorrow, maybe. Carter's coming in tonight
and will be out to see you and talk to me some
about what happens next; he'll stay at the

house and make the office his headquarters for a while. I don't think I'm going back in there. He can run it. Everybody's jobs are okay for a while, until something happens. I'm going to give him carte blanche to fire Shawna's ass if she mouths off to him, though. Caro, I'm just amazed at that boy. He's breathing fire to get hold of this; he really thinks he might be able to work something out with the investors so we can keep some of the Plantation. I'm going to let him try. I'm going to sign the whole thing over to him. If it goes under the onus will be on me, not him, and if he can salvage anything, he'll be a legend before he's thirty. Why didn't I know he could do this?"

"Why didn't I?" I whispered with my cracked voice. "He's very like you at that age, isn't he? I think I knew that, but not really . . . I haven't been very interested in Carter for a long time. I don't know if I can make that up to him or not."

"He understands. He'd heard about Luis, by the way; apparently he's some kind of folk hero among the Gullahs and the grounds staff."

I nodded. They would make a song about him now, I knew, about the big Latin man who rode out on the motorcycle to save their village and died for it.

Oh, Luis, you idiot, I thought, the tears rising again. Why couldn't you just have lived for it?

I shook the tears away. I knew that they

would come back, but not yet, and perhaps never again in such a surf of anguish.

"Tell me about the funeral," I said, and Clay did.

They were going to bury Luis in the little old cemetery in the woods beyond Dayclear. There would be a graveside service only, and Ezra would preach it. I was invited to come, and Lottie Funderburke, but no other white people would be there. Clay was not invited.

"Well, I shouldn't be," he said. "I didn't know him. And yeah, they know by now that I'm not going ahead with the project, but I haven't given them much reason to trust me. I'm going to have to earn that, if I ever can. It wouldn't be right for me to be there. I wouldn't go if they asked me. But I want you to, if you're up to it. And Caro . . . afterward, you do whatever you need to do."

I looked at him.

"About what?"

"Anything. Anything at all."

For the rest of the afternoon, I slept again, off and on. The rain stopped and a cold wind blew the tattered clouds away, and a hard blue sky glittered like steel over the marsh. Clay built up the fire in the living room and we moved there on the sofa, and between my naps we talked. Not about much of import, and not for long, for the sleep would take me almost in mid-sentence, and I would go under. But we talked. It was a beginning.

Out of that afternoon came one thing that shines for me like a Christmas star. We decided that the entire island, "my" part of it, would become an irrevocable trust called the Elizabeth Kyle Venable Foundation, and that it would hold the land as it was, against any development, in perpetuity. It was Clay's idea. I did not doubt that it would happen. This was not the same man I had left in his office a few days back, calling angrily after me.

Early that evening Carter came. I was asleep on the sofa and could not seem to wake enough to do anything but smile at him and hold him as he bent over me. He looked so like the young Clay that it was almost laughable; the same messianic glint in his blue eyes, the same hunger as he looked out over the darkening marsh and creek.

"I hope you never lose the look in your eyes, but you can't have my island," I said sleepily to him.

"I don't want it, Ma," he said, kissing me on the forehead. "Gon' have my own island."

I slept again. When I woke it was to a cold, blowing blue morning, with the marsh grass rippling silver before the wind. The gold was gone. January was back, and Luis Cassells's funeral loomed like a great, dark rock.

* * *

I drove to Dayclear alone, and parked the car at the Bigginses's store. No one was there and it was locked. I knew that all of Dayclear would be at the cemetery except Auntie Tuesday. Sophia had called that morning and told me that Auntie was staying with Lita, and asked that I stop by on my way to the service.

I walked down the rutted road, Clay's down jacket pulled tight against the cutting wind. I dreaded this visit. Sophia had said that Lita was very bad and Auntie was worried, but she had not said in what way the child was damaged. I knew, though: the great, dead silence would be back. Of course it would. Lita had lost the one great, fine, solid thing she had left in the world.

"Has she asked for me?" I said to Sophia, dreading the burden of Lita's need, for I still felt frail and hollow and as transient as milkweed. But she had not.

"She hasn't spoken. She hasn't moved. And she hasn't slept. This is for two days now, Caro," Sophia said. "She lies in Auntie's bed all curled up like a fetus, and she just stares at the wall. Auntie says she doesn't think she's closed her eyes since Lottie brought her. She won't take the tea or the broth. She's like she's dead."

"What will happen to her?" I whispered in pain.

"I don't know. Auntie can't keep her forever;

this is wearing her out, and she's God knows how old. Ezra doesn't know of anybody in Cuba, but he's going to get his people to look around in Miami and see if there's anybody who can take her. I might sometime in the future; Mark's crazy about her, but I don't know yet what we're going to be doing after this, and if there's anything she doesn't need it's more uncertainty, more disloca-tion. I could wring Luis's neck if he hadn't already done it. Anybody responsible for a child has no business running off in the middle of the night on a motorcycle . . ."

I agreed with her, but I did not want to hear any such talk about Luis.

"Well, she has a hero for a grandfather. That's no small thing, is it?" I said crisply.

She laughed a little.

"No. I guess not. It's just that a dead hero isn't going to take care of her right now, is he?"

So I walked the few muddy yards to Auntie Tuesday's house in pain and dread of what I would find. I did not know if I could get through the funeral without the endless salt surf of the tears breaking over me again, much less take the weight of this mute, shattered child.

Auntie was in her rocking chair before the roaring stove. The little shack was dim and warm to stuffiness, but it felt good. Auntie smiled up at me but did not get up, and I saw that she was weary down to the very bird's bones of her. I wondered how long she could withstand the sucking tiredness before she simply crumpled before it like tissue. Ezra would have to get her some help when this funeral was over; bring in a nurse or a girl from another village, something. She was simply too frail to tend this stricken child.

"How you doin', chile?" she said, and I sat down opposite her on the old rump-sprung Morris chair.

"I'm better than I was, thanks to your tea and your soup," I said. "I was in awful shape, Auntie. I should have been over here helping you, but I was . . . I don't know. Almost crazy, or something. I think you saved my silly life."

"No, you find the way to do that by yo'self," she said. "I just hurry it along a little. You need to git them tears out; I've knowed that ever since yo' baby died. And Luis, mmm, mmmm. He's one of God's good ones. We gon' miss him, yes, we are. You done right to cry for him. I cried, too. We all did. I just wish his grandbaby could cry for him, but she in there like a little stone baby. Don't look like any of the old things gon' work for her now."

"You want me to go see if she'll talk to me?"

"Not till after the service," she said. "You needs to go to that. You needs to bear witness with the others. After that you come on back here and we'll see does she want to talk to you. The thing is, she think you done gone, too. I say you's coming this afternoon an' she just look at me. I know what she thinkin'. She don't even want to go see that colt. I know she thinks he dead, too. An' why wouldn't she? Everything and everybody she love done gone and left her. . . ."

I looked down into my lap. The tears were very near.

"Go on now. The cemetery's just through them wooden gates behind my house. You cain't see it from the road, but it there. The others are already down there, I reckon. Been workin' since early morning."

I followed her directions through the wet tangle of undergrowth behind her cabin. Sure enough, there were the old rail gates, weathered silver and half-collapsed. I went through them, and pushed through a thicket of vines, and the cemetery was there.

It was little more than a clearing in the woods, and I remembered that Ezra had said the woods around a Gullah cemetery were left thick so that the souls of the dead would not become confused and wander. Would Luis want to wander from here? I thought. He knew little else but wandering. . . .

The headstones were small and listed in the wet earth, and some were very old. I could not read most of them for the encroaching moss. Most had the dried carcasses of wreaths and faded plastic flowers around them, and many were hung with what seemed to be photographs and small household objects. Hadn't Ezra said that the Gullahs often adorned the graves of their loved dead with the things they had cherished in life? There was a bleached and unraveling rag doll on a small grave, and a rotting pair of boots that had once been fine on another, and most of them had framed photographs that had gone yellow and brown and indistinguishable in the Lowcountry humidity. Around the perimeters of the little cemetery the sheltering moss hung down to touch the ground, like curtains that had been drawn to enclose it. How cozy it was, this tiny village of the dead of Dayclear, I thought. Nothing could reach you here.

Almost the entire village stood around a new oblong in the black earth at the far side of the cemetery, near the hanging curtain of moss. Beside the hole a raw yellow pine coffin stood beside a mound of fresh earth. My knees felt as if they would buckle. I don't know what I had thought, but somehow not that I would really stand and look at the box that held the still body of my friend who had never in his life been voluntarily still. Everyone looked up as I came into the clearing, and most of them smiled. The silence was as thick as air. They had been waiting for me.

Sophia Bridges stood in the small crowd. She held her hand out to me, and I went and stood beside her. She put her arm around me. I let her take part of my weight; my knees seemed reluctant to stiffen. As the silence spun out, I made myself look at the grave and the coffin beside it. "Bear witness," Auntie Tuesday had said, and I would do that. I would not forget this place where we were going to leave Luis.

The hole in the earth had dark water in the bottom of it. A bucket sat beside it, and I thought that they had been trying to bail it out, but I knew that it was groundwater and that bailing was useless. The water was never far from the surface of life on this island. That was all right. Let the clean, dark old salt water take him. Better that than the arid earth of some perpetual care field in an anonymous city. I had wondered if Luis would have wanted to lie here, so far from the country that he had never, after all, gotten back to, and had thought that perhaps Ezra should have looked into a burial in Miami, among other Cubans, some of whom Luis was sure to have known. But this, this felt right.

I looked more closely. There were a few florists' wreaths around the grave, which had cost their senders more than the florist would ever know, but most of the flowers were cut from the first of the marsh's blooming things: jasmine, and camellias, and great, drooping fronds of willow that were always the first to green up. In the middle of the coffin lid was a clock banked in flowers, stopped at eleven fifty-two. How did they know? I thought, and then, of course: his watch.

The tears threatened. I turned my head. Then I looked back.

On a small sapling that leaned over the grave someone had hung photographs. I saw one of Lita, obviously taken at some school event, solemn and alien in a dark dress with a white collar and a little wreath of flowers in her wild hair. There was one of a smiling young couple in front of a great wedding-cake church: Luis and his bride on their wedding day. Oh, dear God . . . the last one was a photograph of Lita on Nissy, taken at my house on the marsh. I recognized the steps up to the deck. Luis's dark-furred hand held a rope that had been slipped around Nissy's neck, and she had pulled it taut, but was standing, still and mulish, with the grinning child on her back. Behind them, almost out of focus, I stood, smiling, the light from the creek silhouetting my flyaway hair. I remembered that day: it had been New Year's Eve, the day we had all spent at my house, the day of the night when I first stayed alone at the house after the great fear had begun, and did not drink. The day that Luis had told me about finding what you would die for, and then living for it . . .

I felt my knees give again, and Sophia tightened her hold around my waist. I knew that she had taken the photograph and that she had prob-

ably placed it there with Luis's other sparse treasures. I did not think, after all, that I could do
this.

As if at a signal, though I heard none, the
people began to hum quietly, and to sway back
and forth to the rhythm of the music. It had no
words, and the tune was atonal and sounded very
old in the cold, quiet glade. Outside the wall of
trees the wind moaned, but in here it did not stir
the bare branches. The people hummed and
hummed, and I closed my eyes and let the sound
take me where it would.

When I opened them again, the humming
was slowing, and then it stopped. Ezra Upchurch
came out of the small crowd and stood beside the
open grave. He wore overalls over a flannel shirt,
clean but worn thin and faded almost patternless.
He had a great, vivid camellia in his overall strap,
and he looked down at the coffin of his friend and
put his hand lightly on it. There were silver tear
tracks on his dark face. He took a great breath
and looked up at the crowd, and said, in a voice
that rang out over the clearing and into the
woods: "Our friend Luis felt that cycle leavin'
him, and he say, 'Uh-oh, Lord, I think I'm coming
home.' And the Lord say, 'I know you, Luis.
Come on home . . .'"

And I knew that I could not stay. Murmuring to Sophia, I turned and stumbled back out
of the clearing and through the vines until I

stood again in the muddy road. Tears flooded my face and soaked into the collar of Clay's jacket, and my chest heaved and bucked. The big grief was back, but there was something else, too. It was a simple, one-celled gratitude. I had wondered if it was the right thing, laying him to rest here so far from anyone and anything that he had known. And I saw now that it was. He would be a part of them forever now. They would make him so. They would make a song of him and for him. They would make a great tale of him and for him. He would belong to them in a way that many of their own never did, and their children would sing of him, and their children, and as long as Dayclear stood, Luis Cassells would be at home.

And Dayclear would stand.

Looks like we're stuck with you, I said to him in my head. Looks like you're stuck with us. You're ours now. Sleep tight, Luis.

And I went back down the road to Auntie Tuesday's house.

"It ain't over, is it?" she said. She had been nodding by the stove. Its red was fading to gray, and I stooped and opened the door and poked at it until it leaped into life again.

"No. I . . . I just couldn't be there anymore."

"That all right. We knows you come. He knows, too."

We sat in silence for a bit, and then I sighed

and said, "I'd better go see what I can do about Lita."

She nodded. "I tol' her you was on your way. She just turned her head. I 'spec it be all right now, though."

"Don't count on it, Auntie."

"Well, you know, I seed that it was."

I shook my head and got up and went into the bedroom where Lita was.

It was darkened, obviously in the hope that she would sleep, but she was not asleep. She lay very still, curled on her side, facing the door. Auntie had covered her with the same beautiful quilt she had laid over her after the mare had died, but it seemed to me that the little body under it was vastly diminished now, much smaller than the one I had seen here before. I could not make out her face, both because of the darkness and the tangle of hair that had fallen into it. But I could see the gleam of the whites of her eyes. They did not seem to blink.

I sat down on the bed beside her. She did not move. I reached out to touch her hair, and she flinched slightly, so I let my hand fall to the quilt.

"Hello, baby bug," I said. "Auntie told you I'd come, didn't she?"

She did not move.

"I know that you don't feel like talking right now, and that's okay," I said. "It's all right to be sad. I'm sad, too. Your abuelo was the most wonderful man, and we'll miss him terribly. But there are still a lot of people who love you, and we're all worried because you won't talk to us. Do you think you might just try a word or two?"

Nothing.

"Well, then, I'll just sit here with you for a while. I think Auntie's making us some supper. In a little while I'll go get it and bring it in on a tray, and we can have it together right here. Like a picnic. Would you like that?"

She did not speak, but she put one hand out and clamped it onto my wrist. The strength in it was almost frightening.

"You don't want me to go?" I said, looking into her face.

This time she shook her head, very slightly, no. No.

"Then I won't. Auntie will bring in our supper. Would you . . ." And I knew that it was something I must do. "Would you like me to stay here with you tonight?"

She nodded her head, still not speaking. Yes. Her fingers tightened on my wrist.

"If I stay, will you try to close your eyes and sleep a little bit? After our supper, I mean."

No. Her head shook back and forth, harder and harder. No. There was fear in her white-ringed eyes. Well, I could not blame her. The last time she had shut her eyes her grandfather had died.

But we could not sit here like this forever, her hand fastened in a death grip on my arm, her eyes staring, staring.

Then I had a thought.

"Would you like to go see Yambi? He's right up there behind Janie and Esau's store, and every time anybody goes by he says, 'Where's Lita? Where's Lita?' I bet he's lonesome, too. He lost his mommy, just like you lost your abuelo."

She stared into my face intently for what seemed a very long time. Then, very slowly, she pulled her arms out from under the quilt and held them out to me. I could literally see them quivering with fear, but she did it.

I reached out and took her into my arms and held her close to me for a while, feeling the rabbitlike tremor of her heart, and then got up and carried her out into the living room. Auntie looked up and smiled.

"MMMM hmmm," she said. "Yes*sir*."

"We're going to walk up and see Yambi," I said over Lita's head. She had buried it in my neck, and was clinging for dear life. "I think we might like a bite to eat when we get back."

"Got me some vegetable soup and corn bread," she said. "And got a warm yam here for that colt. Been savin' it. He like to eat me out of yams, but this one's special. Wait a minute, let me put somethin' round her."

She pulled herself up out of the chair and tottered stiffly over to a hook behind the back door and took a thick old maroon cardigan from it and wrapped it close around the child. I settled her deeper into the circle of my arms and went out of the house into the wind.

She weighed almost nothing, but I was still breathing hard when we reached the store, partly because of the fear that gripped my heart. What if she did not speak? What if she never did again? Who was there that could heal this child?

We did not see the colt at first, but I called softly, "Yambi, Yambi," and then he came, trotting around a little lean-to that Esau had obviously made to shelter him from the weather. His legs had grown longer, and his mane and tail were more luxuriant than the little stiff brushes I remembered, and he looked altogether better than I could have expected. The Bigginses or someone had been currying him; his coat was as sleek as I supposed a marsh tacky's ever got, and on his narrow little head was a soft rope snaffle. He stopped and looked at us.

"Look, Lita," I said. "He's waiting for you."

Against my shoulder, she shook her head. But then slowly she turned it, and she looked. I felt a tremor go through the little body.

I reached into my jacket pocket and pulled out the yam. It was still warm and ashy from its tenure in the coals of Auntie's stove.

"Why don't you give him this?" I said, and

she held her hand out very slowly, and I laid it in her palm.

She looked up at me, and then she held it out over the barbed wire fence.

The colt was still, his head cocked. We were not among the callers he was used to. On the other hand, we came bearing yams. I watched while he worked it out. The yam won.

He came trotting with his springy step up to the fence and put his black nose into Lita's palm and took the yam with his rubbery black lips. He gulped it with one great swallow, nosed at her hand, and then put his head over the fence and began to nose and sniff at her arm and neck and face and hair. I felt rather than saw the beginning of the smile on her face.

We stood there for a long time, the silent child and I, she smiling now, her eyes closed, as the colt nuzzled her face and neck with his wet black nose. Tears ran down my face in sheets, and I did not even realize it until much later, when my wet collar began to grow cold.

We must have stood there for ten or fifteen minutes when she turned her face back into my shoulder and gave a great sigh and said, so softly that I almost did not hear her, "It's time to go home now, Caro."

I stood very still, holding her. The colt began nosing at my arms and hands. I looked far into myself, feeling with my heart. Yes, she was still there, my daughter, the tiny, focused, radiant essence of her, burning steadily.

"Can we do this?" I whispered.

And as if she had said it, I knew that we could, knew that the point of flame that was Kylie Venable could warm both me and this cold child, and could do so forever. I put my chin down on the top of Lita's head.

"Yes," I said. "Yes, it is. So let's do it. There's somebody I want you to meet."

Anne Rivers Siddons's bestselling novels include *Sweetwater Creek*; *Islands*; *Nora, Nora*; *Low Country*; *Up Island*; *Fault Lines*; *Downtown*; *Hill Towns*; *Colony*; *Outer Banks*; *King's Oak*; *Peachtree Road*; *Homeplace*; *Fox's Earth*; *The House Next Door*; and *Heartbreak Hotel*. She is also the author of a work of nonfiction, *John Chancellor Makes Me Cry*. She and her husband, Heyward, split their time between their home in Charleston, South Carolina, and Brooklin, Maine. Visit her website at *www.anneriverssiddons.com*.